the arrange-
ment

A NOVEL BY

ELIA KAZAN

the arrange-ment

STEIN AND DAY/Publishers/New York

The Beanbag Song on page 288 is by Jerry Lester, Milton Delugg and
Willie Stein © 1950, 1951 by Frank Music Corp., 119 West 57th Street,
New York, New York 10019—All Rights Reserved Used by Permission

This work is fiction. The characters in this book are fictitious; any resem-
blance to real persons is wholly accidental and unintentional.

Published simultaneously in Canada by Saunders of Toronto, Ltd.
Manufactured in the United States of America
Stein and Day/*Publishers*/7 East 48 Street, New York, New York 10017

To the girl from Makrikoy

I STILL haven't figured out my accident.

I've gone over and over the events of that day, the day of the crash, with all the hindsight I've gained in the years since. I've gone over the events of the months leading up to the crash, the events that should account for it. But there is still a mystery.

The riddle is not that a man as successful as I was would try to kill himself. There were reasons why I might have. I had everything, as they say, but still there were reasons. The mystery is in the way it happened.

I don't believe in ghosts. But even today, when I'm a totally different man and live in a totally different way, when I ask myself exactly what happened, I next ask myself what hand and whose it was that reached in out of the absolute blue, jerked the wheel of my Triumph two-seater around, and, despite all my strength and all my will, held the course that plastered me against the side of a speeding trailer truck. It all happened in a short second or two, but that is what I distinctly remember.

Success ought to provide some protection against ghosts or the unconscious or whatever it was. That is the least you should be able to expect of success. Or of money. But they didn't, either one. I found myself helpless—I'll say it again—against the strength of that "hand" or whatever it was that wrenched the control of my Triumph TR 4 out of my grip, held it unswervingly on course, and finally packed it against the side of that trailer truck.

The events leading up to my accident don't tell the reasons. True, eleven months before, I had given up a girl to whom I was very attached. But I had righted myself during those months; in fact I was doing great. My wife Florence and I were the envy of every other married couple in Beverly Hills and Bradshaw Park. The Golden Couple! That nickname was awarded us during those very eleven months between the day I gave up Gwen and the day of my accident. Besides, most of the men I know have faced a similar painful choice at some time in their lives—made it and in time recovered, feeling deprived perhaps, but much sounder.

And I knew I had to give Gwen up. I knew the moment was on me, that moment when you can still walk away free and clear, without lasting injury to either side, and just before that other moment when somebody's going to get hurt. I had a pretty damned good idea of the danger I was running; in fact I had said to myself again and again, "Walk away, kid, before it's too late!"

I had asked myself the basic questions. I mean if you're with a woman twenty-one years as I had been with Florence, there is something of value there. And not to mince words, divorces are costly things. I didn't even really know this other girl, or to speak the truth, I knew one side of her very well: every little flesh pad and pocket.

But hell, I thought, I have too much to lose. I mean I was an established man, then; I was solvent, set for life. I owned this beautiful house in the Bradshaw Park section of Los Angeles, and I had there (this will seem absurd, I know) the goddamnedest lawn in that whole area, and some wonderful plantings that I had put in myself, and a really great record collection, including many rare 78's; two valuable Picasso original drawings; a deep freeze that held thirty-six cubic feet of food; and the three cars: Florence's Continental, my daughter Ellen's Karman Ghia, and the Triumph TR 4 which I was later to smash up. All that and a swimming pool. It was a lot to give up for a good lay, or even a great one! And when I looked at all that stuff and my family too, I thought what the hell am I getting into? Every man will know just what I mean, especially Europeans, who despite general impression are much less romantic than we are and really understand property.

I'd begun to behave like a damned fool with this girl, Gwen. At first I used to meet her two, maybe three times a week, without rippling the surface of my respectable existence. That was the way I wanted it. For instance I used to stop at this motel on my way in to the office, and get a room. Then some time during the business morning I'd call Gwen. She also worked (doing no one was quite sure what) at Williams and MacElroy, where I was part of the brass. I would tell her where and the number, say room 535. Then we'd both make up some excuse to get out for a couple of hours. Being a wheel, I had much more leeway in this than she did. Even if it was only for the lunch hour, in those days it was worth it to us. I'd go to the place first, fix the door with the folded "Don't Disturb" card so it would close but not latch, pull the shades down, undress, turn the lights off, and lie there and wait for her. When she came in, she'd lock the door and without saying a word undress, and—well, there's nothing to say about what went on then except there was very little conversation. That coming together in the dark of strangers was exciting to us. We cultivated that.

Then something that I couldn't control got into me. Men will know what I'm talking about; I mean that desperate thing that happens at forty-three, which I was, or forty-five or seven or nine. Anyway, before I realized what was going on, it was a different dance done to a different tune. No longer did I see her maybe a couple of times a week in a motel room. I got real careless, necked in the corners of bars where people inevitably saw us, or drove to the beach and lay out there with her. Of course it had to get back to Florence. I can't answer this question: did I subconsciously want it to get to her?

What was dangerous was not that I was seeing a girl so often. After all, I had always had someone. Just before Gwen, in fact when I met her, I had a select little string of creatures. The danger was—you've heard this before, too—I was falling in love with Gwen. And I had made up my mind, some years before, after an earlier such episode, never again to expose myself to that. I had learned—or so I thought—the importance of final indifference. But despite this, there it was, happening again.

For one thing I was beginning to be obsessive about Gwen, wondering where she was when she wasn't with me, and never daring to let her go for too long. Nature loathes a vacuum, and the thought of an unattached and unsatisfied Gwendolyn Hunt hitting the spots (with someone) in the Los Angeles jungle—well, it worried me.

Then there was another bad sign. It had to do with my work. I lost interest in it. Before I knew it, my professional standing and so my bank balance and therefore my peace of mind, all, were in danger.

Another danger sign. I soon got to where I couldn't do it to any girl but Gwen. And that wasn't only because she kept me well milked. I just didn't want to diversify. I knew I was in trouble then. I'd never before been faithful to anyone. That, I had found, was safest. But now!

I even found myself dissolving my harem. I had a drink or lunch with each of those good, good girls and told them I wasn't going to see them any more. Some of their reactions were not very flattering to me. The first one cried. That was o.k., I expected that. But the next one's eyes wandered almost immediately (we were at Romeo's) to every other man drinking his lunch there that day. Just the instinct of self-preservation at work, I suppose, but she didn't even wait for the espresso. Then there was the girl who immediately set out to borrow money, money she didn't have the vaguest intention of repaying.

Anyway I got rid of them all. The amazing thing about it was that I didn't take this step in response to any demand of Gwen's. I did it because I wanted to. For maybe the first time in my life, I was faithful to one single person, her—and Florence, of course.

For I did keep up with my wife, Florence, once, maybe twice a week. No, more like once. Anyway, she didn't at first sense that anything different had happened to me. I mean my ardor for her had wilted long before. I just wasn't there with it for her. But goddammit, once a week isn't bad, considering we'd been together twenty-one years and that we got married too young, especially me. Besides she was forty-three now, the same age I was, almost to the month, and that age is o.k. for a man, but her ass was well waffled, and there was a lot of crepe on her, and all the rest of that, flab, you know. And it worried her, poor kid. I caught her looking over her shoulder into the mirror one day, looking at the back of her legs. She knew what was happening. For instance her style in bathing suits changed. She began to wear swim suits with tiny little skirts, and she'd frown on the girls who came to our pool in those hairline bikinis. She began to find reasons to keep them away, not because of what they wore, of course, but because they were too noisy or they threw cigarette butts around on the grass, or because it was so nice to have quiet and privacy when you swam. But I knew what it was. Their legs were intact. So when I caught her look-ing in the mirror, I really felt for her. But what could I do—make nature fair or life just? We'd been married twenty-one slogging years, and there are no miracles.

So say I lost control a bit, and then a little more than a bit. Up to then I had always prided myself that it was I who controlled the events of my life and not vice versa. Florence and I had had, without talking it into the ground, a sort of understanding or arrangement, that just so long as I didn't make a fool of her with our friends or publicly humiliate her, she'd look the other way. Or maybe she really didn't know. I never was sure. Anyway, this arrangement was as much a part of our marriage and our household as the stove and the insurance, the hi-fi and our bank accounts, the lawn and our portfolio of stocks.

I really had a problem. I loved Florence. Which is not saying a damned thing, I know; everybody loves everybody now. What I'm trying to say is, our bond was close. We'd met when I was at col-lege, and ever since then she'd been my good magic. I was a mess when she met me, crouched down in my little burrow, my legs drawn up under me, ready to spring and snap, teeth bared and ready, eyes frantic. She was the first one who dared reach down to me. She coaxed and eased me up and out of my solitary hole. It took time, and I snapped at her gentle patrician hand a few times—more than a few times. But she persisted and finally managed it. Then she set about straightening me out of my crouch, or was it a cringe, the posture I'd been in all my life.

Florence had seen something in me no one else had. Just the way she looked at me—I remember the testimony of her eyes in my favor the first time she left those eyes open for me to look down into, the first time I really saw them unveiled, soft and warm in a face of English pink. I remember other things about her then, too: her hair, how it was combed, not set, not done, not arranged, just combed and brushed. She looked at me in those first days, and she didn't have to say, "Believe me—" or "I'm telling you the truth—" like most people have to. She just had to look at me and I knew she believed in my worth, whether anyone else did or not, and that she loved me, whether I did her or not, and that she was mine for-ever, whether I wanted her or not, no questions asked.

She pledged herself to my cause from the beginning. She made me believe that when I got straightened out of my cringe or crouch, I was going to be something. She made me believe what no one else ever had, that I had worth. It was her faith that transformed me. She was my magic, my talisman of success.

You owe a person like that something.

Also you're afraid to do without a person like that. Over the years I'd broken out and away from her more than a few times, yes, but never very far, and always with a return ticket in my pocket.

So I faced a choice. I asked myself what do I really feel. I tried to introspect, without the help of an analyst. I discovered that in my own miserable way I loved them both. I don't think any analyst would have let me discover that, would he? But I've never understood why a man couldn't or even shouldn't love two or three women at the same time. I mean really love them with all his heart. After all, which is better, a peach or a pear?

But it was too late for that kind of thinking. I had tried it once on Florence. Her reaction was biologic. She said that despite the fact that I claimed to be Greek, I must have Turkish blood in my veins, because in certain areas I just didn't think like a western man. When I said I thought like most western men I knew, but they wouldn't admit it, she just looked patient.

One day Gwen gave me her ultimatum. We had driven out to the beach together. It was our arrangement that on the beach side of Sepulveda Boulevard we drove with the top down, both of us perfectly visible, she sitting close to me and the hell with it. But on the Beverly Hills side of Sepulveda I'd put the top up, and from there on in she'd sit on her side of the car, right up against the door, and put on her dark glasses, and when we passed certain blocks and certain houses, she'd slide down out of sight.

Well, this day we were coming in from the beach, the sun pouring down through the smog, and she was sitting there with her yellow hair flying in the toxic breeze—God I really loved her hair, so fine, so silky. Being Greek, blondness is my fetish. I was given black hair, a little on the oily side, once very thick, then just beginning to thin, once very dark, then beginning to gray. Now it's gray and going.

At any rate, when I stopped to put the top up, she wouldn't. Anything. She wouldn't sit to her side; she wouldn't lie down on the seat when the time came for that, despite the fact that it was Saturday and everybody was out. She wouldn't even put on her dark glasses.

She just said she was sick of the whole arrangement and she wouldn't weasel any more, that we'd gone on long enough this way and I'd have to make up my mind.

So there I was in the middle. Not a new experience for me. I've always had "both" trouble, as I'll soon explain. I had gone along telling myself that I could stop any time, that it was only a matter of biological attraction. But it was not only that, not even primarily that. It was something else, and to describe that I've got to go back to eleven months before my crash and back still another year to the day I saw Gwendolyn Hunt for the first time.

It was in a presentation room at Williams and MacElroy, and I disliked her on sight.

As it happened, it was on the day of my coronation.

One of our larger accounts, Zephyr Cigarettes, was dying on the vine. The whole brand was in trouble. It was obvious that a complete new attack vis-à-vis the public was needed. But no one could agree what. It was a critical meeting for our side, the Williams and MacElroy advertising agency. No one had to spell it out. If those Zephyr fellows didn't get the help they needed from us, they'd get it somewhere else.

The account was such a fat one that Mr. Finnegan pulled me off everything else and put me on Zephyr. His instructions were simple: save the account.

Man, they were a miserable looking crew at that meeting, those fellows from Zephyr. Our boys looked even worse for trying to give off optimism. They all had gruel in their guts that morning. Skipping to the happy ending, it went something like this.

Eddie Anderson talking—I, Indispensable Eddie. Quote. "Well let me show you how it would work! Give me that pad, Benny, will you? Now look here." I was sketching. "We show, for instance, this fine old man, ruddy cheeks, hair gray but not too gray, get it, grandchildren in the background, or maybe they're his children, you're never quite sure which, and there's this real pretty woman in the middle ground, unidentified, mind you. Is that his ring she's wearing? She's not too young—like this, sort of. No, more mature breasted, maybe a young forty, and she's big-eyeing him like this, see, polite, yes, but you know, no frontier to sex these days. Give the impression that maybe he's still what we all hope for ourselves, you know? And the caption? Very simple: 'Your whole life long smoke the clean cigarette, Zephyr.' And we logo 'clean,' make the word look clean. Isn't that what everybody's worried about today? Even England! It's on everybody's mind. Note: I don't even mention the big bad word. But Zephyr, the *clean* cigarette. They'll get it. And it's an angle no one else has dared to take. Or here, again, look: like we show this doctor type, never say he's a doctor mind you, never label anything, but he's got that white coat on, and this same type looking at him, a lady, lecherous, but refined, you know? And he's a fine man. Now! Caption: Come on? Anybody? 'The people you respect smoke the clean cigarette, ZEPHYR!' See, we never mention doctor or anything. But it hits at what everybody's worried about, doesn't it? And we logo 'clean' like this, make it float, like it's riding the west wind. *Clean!* When we show Zephyr on the idiot box we always have the sound of this breeze through the willows, and maybe superimpose a fresh air shot—trees, country, clean white clouds. Very simple. Like any idea that's really right, it's been there all the time. It just took somebody to bend over and pick it up. Might have been any one of you. It happened to be me."

Well, the room fell down. They were speechless, all that Zephyr brass! There was no doubt what the future course of their cigarette was to be. Clean! It didn't need a vote! They were all sitting there and giving me those clean smiles, I mean sincere, because the stock options they had in their inside pockets began to feel warm again. They were all giving me those rare, rare smiles.

All except this one girl in the corner, the one I disliked on sight. I didn't know who she was then. She was smiling at me too, but her smile was not sympathetic. In fact, it was like a pail of cold water thrown in my face by a total stranger.

I just stared at her. And as I thought "Who the hell is that?" she dropped her eyes.

The waiter came in with the drinks. I had timed that perfectly, and the celebration was on. A second waiter came in with a tray of those little gourmet items to nibble on. And, oh boy, they went for those, not only because every client is a free-loader in his heart, but because the pressure was off. They were throwing all the sand bags over the side, and that big balloon, optimism, was soaring. So I rushed everybody over to LaRue's for lunch. And that's the second time I took notice of Gwen.

I picked the menu myself, and it was good. After all, Mr. Finnegan had said, "Save the account at any cost," and Mr. Finnegan is boss. Those fellows were plowing up the table, and drinking like it was prohibition eve. Finally the president of the company himself got up, and in the silence which naturally opened up for anything this man said, we could all hear: "How do you do it, Eddie? You get sex into everything." I smiled on cue. He said, "You're Greek, aren't you?" "Yes," I said. "I knew it was something," he said, shaking his head in amazement. Everybody laughed, and that put the cap on the thing. They were scrambling all over each other to get on that "clean" bandwagon.

That's when I began to really notice this girl. Not only was she ignoring the main subject of the meeting, me, not only was she giving out with that same sour little smile, when she gave out with anything, but she went too far. She turned her back on our celebration, talked a bit to some people at a neighboring table, clearly not about Zephyr or "clean" or me, and then without a word of explanation or apology, she up and left.

She sat in on the next big product meeting we had on Zephyr, again in the same corner, her head down, making notes, or doodling, just as before, while I was speaking. When I got through and was being agreed with all around, she lifted up for a minute and looked at me again with that smile. "Who the hell is that?" I said to the fellow sitting next to me, indicating her. I didn't care if she could hear me. "She's from Mr. Finnegan's office," he whispered.

In the weeks that followed, while we were gunning up the new Zephyr campaign, we all had plenty of opportunity to become acquainted with her. She was always there at the presentations, but no one succeeded in making her acquaintance. Of course this made us all even more curious. Everyone asked everyone the same questions about her identity. But no one knew. She even began to show up at the Review Board meetings (the Review Board was our Supreme Court, our top body, and I was a member). But Mr. Finnegan, who presided at these meetings (and only at these meetings), did not introduce her or explain her. He was reputed to have said once to someone, "She has a built-in shit detector!" But that's all. I'm sure he preferred her to be a mystery around the shop.

Actually Mr. Finnegan had several times before employed such a character on his personal staff. One of his theories was that it was important to have one very, very negative person around, one person who will always say the worst possible thing in any given situation. It was part of his operational philosophy to face the negative before it hits you on the goddam head, that it's better if someone working for you razzes your campaign before the public does. Then you have a chance to do something about it.

Anyway Miss Hunt (there was many a play on that name) was turning up at more and more meetings, sitting in her corner, never commenting but never missing a move. And pretty soon there was this undercrackling all around her in the office. She was always either doodling or making notes, no one was sure which, and people began to try to see what was in her notebook and, failing this, to notice when she put pen to paper as if that might give them a clue to what her function was. Well, it didn't take them long to come to a decision. Very soon Gwendolyn Hunt was known to the office population as Finnegan's Fink. People treated any room she was in as if it was bugged straight through to the boss's throne.

I think she annoyed me more than she did the others, because in those days I lived on enthusiasm or, to nail it down, approval. I just had to have it. I dried up if I didn't. That's how Florence first thawed me out. Flattery? Let's call it faith. But this Gwen, every time someone else was impressed, she looked like she was scoffing. I mean who the hell was she to scoff at me, I thought, beginning to burn; I was one of the most successful men in the world at my trade. And even if there is a lot of BS in my profession, it's an open question if goods would move without us, not the mass of stuff this country has to move to keep the gross product figure up where it has to be.

And goddam it, I was good at my job. I could walk into a room full of wrangling men, or into one of those big glass boxes known as sponsors' booths, sort of a snake cage with everyone writhing and taking bites out of each other's hides, and I'd just walk in and all the snakes would curl up pretty as you please, lay their little pointy heads down on their coils, and that was it. Hell, it got to be a superstition around our store. People used to say: all they have to do is see that little Eddie Anderson bastard walk in.

But Miss Hunt was not in the least impressed by Indispensable Eddie. I got fed up with her. One particular day she'd sat through an entire meeting I'd brought from chaos to harmony, and as I got up (I always pretended to have another pressing engagement; my father had taught me that successful men are always in a hurry) and walked out, receiving the tribute of everyone's smiles, I got a smile from her too, but it wasn't admiring. What made me furious was a sudden realization that for some perverse reason I was beginning to make that lemon smile part of my conscience. I was really concerned about her reaction. I'd begun to turn to her automatically, to see what she thought. And every time I did—pow! like those comic strips, that pail of cold water.

This day I followed her, found her going down the hall, ambling since everyone else was hurrying, walking to her own music, moving among the others as if she didn't see them, like a young lion, a superior being who asks no understanding from anyone, neither sympathy nor friendship, nothing of what every other human animal must have to make it through from one day to the next.

I came up to her, caught her arm, and swung her around. She didn't seem surprised; on the contrary, she behaved as if she had long expected me to accost her.

"What the hell are you always smiling?" I said.

"Always smiling?" She paused. "When?" Her voice was surprisingly soft.

"At the meetings. You always sit there like—like now—you're smiling. What's that?"

"I suppose I'm amused at something. Do you mind?"

"Yes, when it's me. You seem to be scoffing."

"Well, don't mind. It's really just the way my face is made."

And she walked away. But there remained on my hands the feel of her arm, so lithe and so firm. And on my sight the image of her neck and shoulders, all a delicate lemony tint. A fragrance was left in the air, a promise of what was to come. And when it did, when in time I did uncover her, I found she was made just as I'd imagined, all of white meat. Her flesh everywhere, between her thighs in particular, was covered with skin like India silk. There wasn't a part of her that wasn't perfect and delicate and fair.

From that day on I was aware of her always. I found myself showing off to her at the meetings with clients, showing off sometimes so that I was more effective than ever and other times in such a way that I jeopardized accounts. But always with an awareness that my final judge was that compact girl with the denying smile who sat in a corner and took notes, or pretended to.

I asked her once, "Who are you taking notes for?"

She smiled and said, "I'm writing a book so that none of all this will be lost. Would you like a copy?"

One day when she'd gone to the washroom, I sneaked a look in her little pad. There was a drawing of my hand—I think it was mine —a rather hazy drawing except for the thumb, which was shown in great detail. And alongside the drawing of my thumb was a drawing of a penis, pendant, of good length. Well, what the hell, I suppose girls have fantasies just as men do.

The big question around the office was why she was tolerated, why she hadn't been fired since she was so openly cynical about everything we were doing. Well, I was watching her pretty closely now and beginning to get an idea of what Mr. Finnegan saw in her. I had underestimated Gwen, as had everyone else.

At first I couldn't figure out whether she was very intelligent or downright stupid, or whether it made any difference. Clearly she didn't have a formal education. And that stood out, because the joint was full of Vassar and Radcliffe. These other girls, you never knew what they themselves finally thought about anything, even after you'd hit them with a couple of doubles. I mean they gave out with opinions, but whose were they?

Gwen, I found out in time, never talked beyond her own personal knowledge. She wasn't handing down the dicta of Max Lerner or that fellow Podhoretz or Alfred Kazin or *Time* magazine. She talked from her own experience and from what she'd figured out herself. Everything she said, she really knew something about. She'd lived with him or worked with him, fought with him or suffered him, or she wouldn't say anything about him. She'd had it rubbed into her, or been bored to death by it, or been hit on the head with it, or had it rammed up into her—or she'd have nothing to say on the subject. She spoke her own truth and that was all.

Clearly, too, she'd waded chin deep through the sewer. Yet there were days when she glistened with the dew of innocence. And when she finally came on with me, she was irresistible.

It started at an office party. There is more bull written about office parties. For its entire course this one was as dull as all the others. Gwen and I spent hours just sitting in a corner of Mr. Finnegan's office drinking and talking. I began to get the idea that she wanted him to see her drinking with me. If this was so, Mr. Finnegan was too cool a cat to show any reaction, or maybe even to care. When he went home, most of the others did too. In time, Gwen and I were left alone. The porter came around to tell us that he was closing up. I looked at Gwen and she said, "Why don't we have just one more?" So I said to the man not to bother us, that I had my key and would double lock the door from the outside when I left, and for him to double lock it now and leave. I gave him a fin.

I discovered that I had forgotten what a hungry young girl was like. I'm talking about a girl who was really interested in devouring me, and whom I wanted to devour. I guess I'd allowed even my infidelities to get down to a routine. The routine of the respectable wife and the equally respectable harem of girls, lovers in name only, none of them genuinely awake to the possibilities of the thing. The point with Gwen was not that she was more ready or more aggressive or more demonstrative. She was simply genuinely interested in mixing it up. She did a wonderful thing. She *un*routined it. You knew you were going to get it, but you didn't know how or when. And you never knew that there wasn't more. You wanted her as much after as before. She, too, just seemed to keep quivering and coming, her insides grasping and ungrasping, in those sets of spasms. Well, after a while, I thought I was through. But in a matter of minutes, at the age of forty-three, I was mounting her again, fully erect and desiring her more than ever.

I'd forgotten it was possible. I didn't care what happened. We had our clothes off and the next day was Christmas Eve and everything seemed in chaos and I didn't even think what I would tell Florence. (I told her that I had fallen asleep, drunk, on my office sofa, and found myself there at dawn. Florence laughed and kissed me.)

And when I thought I'd had it all, we were in another office, in another position, violating all the sacred Poobah places, like the Afghan sofa of the faggoty head of the art department, or the window bench in the treasurer's office which was in plain view of the whole towering city if there was anyone still up to see, or on Mr. Finnegan's own leather settee just under the official photograph of his wife and three daughters.

Gwen had it all. It wasn't only her sexual responsiveness, her delicate balance of frailty and passion, her lemon skin, her fragrant but not heavily scented pubic hair, the delicate petals of her inner

lips, her eyes flashing, then begging, then looking at me with gratitude, the all-in-all feeling that she had been waiting for this, just
this, me. Whatever it was—scent, taste, feel, pressure, need, devouring appetite, a subtle playfulness, a delicacy of touch, a desperate
series of sounds and facial expressions that were so naked, and suggested danger ahead—she had it all.

At dawn when I took her to her apartment I still wanted more,
and I asked her if I could come up. She said no, I'd better go home.
I said immediately that someone else was up there, right? She said
true. "But," she said, "I will send him away and won't see him again
if that's what you want me to do."

I said, "That's what I want you to do." I knew I was crossing
some kind of line right there. She asked me again, "Do you really
want me to send him away?"

And I said, "Yes."

She looked at me a long time, as if she was asking herself some
questions about me. Then she got up out of my car and left.

I called her the next day and on Christmas too and on the following day, Sunday, and the story from her switchboard was the same.
"Out." I began to wonder where she was. I thought about it in some
marginal way all through that holiday. We had a wonderful Christmas, actually, Florence, my daughter Ellen, and I. We gave and received many beautiful presents.

Monday morning I saw Gwen the moment I came into the office. I
tried to talk to her but there were several other people within ear-
shot, or in adjoining rooms. And she wouldn't say anything except
"Don't!" when I tried to touch her. But that afternoon I got an
envelope from her. It contained a key.

I went there right from work. Monday night was Florence's night
for civil rights. She never pressed me to go to these meetings. I used
to kid her that she preferred going alone, so she could feast her eyes
on all those beautiful young Negro men. She'd laugh at this, a little
nervously because it was true. Not that Florence would ever do anything. But she several times did dream about them. Florence was
never embarrassed to tell me her dreams (of course she had cleared
them with her analyst, Dr. Leibman, first). If the dreams were un-
flattering to me, or if they suggested that there was trouble coming,
she'd urge me once more to go and have a talk with Dr. Leibman
myself.

This was one thing that Florence and Gwen had in common. They spoke of their dreams as though they were as real as life. For instance they'd both say, "I had a dream last night and you were very mean to me." And then they'd look at me reproachfully, as if they expected me to give some accounting for my bad behavior.

That was their only similarity. Florence's whole aim in life, at that time, was to get me to accept her theory (actually Dr. Leibman's theory) of limited objectives. She said that adulthood lay in the acceptance of limited objectives in life, that though as a boy you dream of being a great man, if you keep on with this after a point it is unrealistic and inevitably leads to severe disappointment and lowered self-esteem, then to self-reproach and to self-disgust, and so to self-hatred, and finally to suicide of one kind or another. Florence used to say to me, "Now, dear, it is clear by now, isn't it, that you're not going to be Tolstoi? So you're not going to be Tolstoi, so what?"

I couldn't accept that. I still thought I'd straighten myself out some day, take a new course, find a new vein of talent, and astound the world. Florence would say, "Well, you *should* feel that way. But you shouldn't base the solid facts of your life on that feeling, should you?"

"What do you mean by that?" I'd say, resenting hell out of her.

"I mean," she'd say, "that as a woman and your wife, I'm awfully glad that you have the job you have at Williams and MacElroy, that you're so good at it we can afford a nice home and the help to keep it up, and that I can buy the best books and, when the Broadway shows come to the Biltmore, sit in the best seats, and that Ellen can go to Radcliffe and feel free to give consideration to other assets in her husband-to-be than whether or not he has a substantial bank account."

Gwen was different. I'd bring up the advertising business and my problems with it, and she'd say, "It's just a way of paying the bills, isn't it?" She'd dismiss it. Then we'd get on to my life, my victories, my defeats, my hopes for myself, the hopes I'd found, to my surprise, I'd given up on. Some things exist only because they're talked about. I had stopped talking about what I used to hope for myself, because those dreams, in the context of the life I lived, seemed absurd. For instance I actually did have a thing about Tolstoi, his yearning for simplicity and that act of his, cutting himself a walking stick and just walking out on everything. I thought about that many times. Actually I don't even know if it happened. What's the difference? It was real to me, his philosophy of simplicity. Of course I could see that that way of living was unthinkable in a society as complex and mechanized as ours. But Gwen had no closed doors in her mind, no forbidden rooms. You could say anything to her, no matter how silly. She didn't seem to realize that I'd already run my race.

So I talked about what I used to hope for myself, and for the first time in years and years with a sense that the book on me had not been closed.

Now, at the client conferences and promotion presentations, I began to see another side to this girl. You had to look fast, but I did detect another ingredient mixed in with that famous sour smile. For instance, she'd be sitting there and I'd be brilliant, really thinking faster than anyone else, bamboozling everyone and at the same time making people who had just been excoriating each other suddenly delighted to be in the same bed. Having accomplished this, I'd find myself turning to her for the final accolade (I just couldn't break myself of that habit). Sure enough she'd be on me, but immediately drop her head and make out she was doodling. If I looked fast, I was able to see what no one else did: a flash of some kind of anxiety or worry, or simply concern. For me! I couldn't label it or describe it. No one else saw it. All the other people saw that she was doodling instead of awarding me the applause I deserved, and that she was now sitting there, not paying the least respect to the justified hostility pushed at her by every person in that room.

One day somebody somewhere gave a signal, and the hounds were loose. Gwen was marked for extermination. There started in that office an extraordinary campaign of snubbing, ostracism, and insult. It could have been grade school for some of the tactics. I mean it got right down to filling her pocketbook with water, and once with piss. Notes of an extremely impertinent nature were left on her desk, along with the most insulting drawings, sometimes pornographic, with Gwen cast in the leading feminine role. Groups would break up when she came along, the Ladies' Room would empty. Caricatures of her were everywhere, the product of our excellent art department. A photograph of her was used as target in the office dart game. The pack wanted the blood of Finnegan's Fink.

Well, they'd picked themselves a scrap. Gwen had never learned to back up. In fact a fight exhilarated her. And since they were trying to cow her, she suddenly became quite vocal about how she felt about everything. She began going to many more meetings, walking in with a jauntiness that was perfectly calculated to outrage her antagonists. Because they had branded her "tramp," she gave them that in spades. She took fewer and fewer pains to keep her clothing well-ordered. Soon no man could keep his mind on the job when she was in the room, for looking at the thigh exposed below her hem.

Then she took out after her chief tormenter. One day I caught her flirting with this man. I knew she was up to something, and by God she soon had him going around like a dog with the hots smelling the bitch on the other side of the wall and unable to get at her. Then she gave him just a little, attention and company I mean, and he came on hard for more. She went out with him, then again, and soon she had this man reversing his whole previous stand. Now he was covering for her, explaining and justifying her. She also had him believing that he was getting closer and closer to what he was craving. Finally, she told me later, there came what he thought was going to be the big night. The man took her to Romeo's, which is the classic spot for dinner before. Everything was going beautifully, as he saw it, until she struck up a chance acquaintance with a young man at a neighboring table, no more than an exchange of words it was. But sometime between the Gorgonzola and the Zabaglione, she excused herself, she had to repair her face she said. She never came back. The man at the neighboring table disappeared too.

That was it. The big guns of morality were rolled into position. The holy war was on. The office sisterhood started a whispering campaign that had her sleeping with everyone in the place. A letter invoking the cause of office morale was put on Mr. Finnegan's desk. It was mutiny.

Mr. Finnegan finally did speak to her, Gwen told me. The result, knowing Gwen, was predictable. The next day, she farted at a meeting, and when somebody looked her way, she smiled in acknowledgement and waved the air. At an important presentation, she put her hand in the lap of a vice president—another one, not me—as she leaned forward to make a point. (She was taking part now; her silent days were over.) The poor man didn't know what to do.

She invented new ways to defy prudery. She'd stare noticeably at the point where men's trousers come together. Most girls do this—not stare, of course, but they are curious—and do their best to conceal it. But Gwen brandished a false curiosity. She began to fondle her tits in public, just as men often adjust their balls. She seemed impelled to outrage the righteous wherever and however she could. It was her way of waging their war.

She began to win it too. They couldn't get her to quit, or holler cop. After a couple of weeks of this, you could feel the whole office population slowly give up. Gwen had them beat. If she was going to quit, she was going to quit in her own time, for her own reasons.

Of course that day came. I didn't see the blow-up, but I heard about it and in detail. It happened at a campaign presentation before a client with a very lucrative account. So when the story got to Mr. Finnegan, and it did like a flash, there was nothing for him to do but fire her. Gwen must have known that was inevitable, so she spoke her mind, in the calmest of voices, in front of the client. She said what she thought of the claims they were making for the product, what she thought of advertising in general, what she thought of the men at Williams and MacElroy and what she thought of the women, which was worse, and then what she thought of the whole civilization which could produce, afford, and depend on so general a fraud. All this articulated in the quietest voice and in the most refined accent, a Bryn Mawrese she'd picked up somewhere and with which she had several times amused me. All the while she was smiling and smoking, and even holding a match for someone else who was preparing to smoke.

I was out of the office that morning on something to do with Zephyr and didn't get back till well after lunch. She was gone by then, all her stuff with her. I called her place, but she was out, or not answering the phone. So I stayed at the office, with everyone watching me. Of course it had gotten around that we were seeing each other. I believe that some of the people there half expected me to quit with her. Or to run right out and find her. But when a couple of people tried to bring the episode up with me, I behaved as she would have; I gave them nothing.

There was another reason, I'm embarrassed to say, why I played it cool. Maybe, I thought, this crisis is a godsend. Increasingly, I had had the sense that our affair was getting out of my control.

I did call the Shelbourne apartments, where she lived, and talk to the girl at the board, whom I had gotten to know. She said that Gwen had given notice, in fact paid her bill, and where she was going was New York, and where she was now was picking up her air ticket. For the Midnight, she said. She'd listened in when Gwen made the reservation.

So then this voice inside me began again. "Let her go. Later, get her New York number, and bawl her out, say you called and called and she didn't pick up the phone, and that was a hell of a way to leave."

I had a date to meet Florence and our friends the Bennetts at the Brown Derby that evening, and afterwards we were going to the Biltmore to see "Camelot" with the original Broadway cast. Now, I thought, this gives me a perfect excuse for Gwen. I was with Florence and the Bennetts, and I just couldn't get away. I couldn't even get to the phone. By tomorrow morning, she'd be in New York City. Time and distance would do the rest.

I have to admit that what they had been saying about her in the office had gotten to me. Gwen, they said, had been making it with a couple of other fellows, one right in the office, Otto the logo man. I know that wasn't true. But doubt is the most corrosive thing in sex. While I saw Gwen often during the day, I hadn't been able to see her at night except on Monday, Florence's night for civil rights. What the hell, I thought. Whose hands am I putting my life into?

When I walked into the restaurant, I knew this was the night and that the crisis would turn on a very simple thing: a phone call, if I made it or if I didn't. And it would have been all over that night, except for the Bennetts.

They drove me nuts.

Dale Bennett is a screen writer and was, at that time, one of my best friends. He is a tall, thin, gray man who looks like a provincial governor of a British Caribbean colony who has been in the sun too long and has taken to rum. He once won an Academy Award, and sooner or later someone always gave him a job despite the fact that his stuff for the last ten years had been old fashioned even for Hollywood. At the same time he is dead certain that his stuff is great, and rails against critics and producers who are taken in by the New Wave, out-of-focus photography, reverse printing, and jump cutting. These men, he says, prize form over content. He being "content." Bennett talked about "my writing" and about "prose rhythms." But whatever pleasure he derived from artistic composition could not compare with the pleasure he got from making his deals. That's where the excitement was for him. The process of writing the script, which followed, had to be an anti-climax.

So the talk at the Derby that night had to do with deals. True, it started with a long bit about which wine to order, and so to the bargains the Bennetts had picked up, a dozen-odd cases, in the chateau country of France in the course of their last visit, how much money he had saved by getting not quite the best years, but, as he well knew, just as good. Then the conversation got down to his favorite subject: his deferments and residuals. It went from this to some rulings that Internal Revenue had made especially in favor of his case, and then on by easy transitions (I was getting bleary) to the special tax lawyers he had engaged—yes, they were expensive, but after all, deductible, and saved many times their fees—and so to the insurance they had advised him to take out with Lloyds of London (my eyes were beginning to see double) which was to guarantee his estate that the deferments and residuals would come in over the years, as they were scheduled to. "Columbia could go bankrupt, you know, it's possible."

Bennett chuckled and went on and on, right through the rôti of beef and the raw spinach salad with bacon crumbles. He was now set for life he said (later I picked up the check and I wasn't set for life); he had secured his artistic freedom. From now on he could write exactly what he wanted to—that is, as soon as he had cleaned up the two pictures remaining on his old Paramount commitment, and then there was that picture at Metro that he was trying to get out of, but it might still be fun because the lunches at the Metro commissary were once again, as they had been in L.B.'s great days, the best in town.

Then he started on me, how I didn't know how to run the financial side of my life. And Florence encouraged him by telling him every stock she owned and every bond we held, asking him, as if he was Billy Rose or somebody, whether we had put our money in the right places. Old Bennett, he really knew the market; he had no false modesty. He also knew a big scene, like the one he was about to play, would only gain by postponement, so he cleared his throat and ordered a special dessert for four, a pot au crème. Then he cleared his throat again and made sure that everyone was attentive. ("Are you expecting someone, Eddie?" "No, why?" "You keep looking towards the door." "Sorry.") With that he launched into how absurdly misjudged all our investments were.

At that instant I went mad or blind or, anyway, completely out of control. I saw everyone in that restaurant as naked. Steam-room naked! First and especially Bennett with his concave chest and his convex belly, his extraordinary pot which started, a perfect biologic surprise, just below his rib cage and then swelled majestically, like that of a papier-mâché African idol in one of those Tarzan films, the white god of a tribe of benighted movie niggers. And his wife, too, was revealed, sitting there with her enormous pouter chest and no breasts, and her poor withered nipples. They had had one child by Caesarian section and I could see the scar quivering like a neon light from her belly button down to her massive "V" mound and its Amazonian foliage. There naked was my wife, with her flab problems, poor dear. And the waiter too, that phony refugee bastard who was always telling us what the gossip was at the next table, so *had* to be telling *them* what *we* were saying at ours. Then the whole restaurantful was revealed, suddenly without the protection of their clothing, all sitting there in corn-fed majesty. With the exception of a nubile chick at the table opposite. She was naked too, but on her it looked good. (Bennett was talking all this time, but my mind was flying!) She was with a young screen writer who was kept on at Warners, so the gossip had it, only because he was such a good tennis player. Jack Warner liked to play tennis with him Sundays. No one would really trust him with a script, but he had to make the long ride to Burbank every day and pretend. So he kept himself from going nuts by screwing, matinees every day. This squab he had with him now, Christ she was prima. You could see the marks on her as she sat there naked, you could see where her body had been clamped to and kneaded and scuffed up. I looked at this pair sitting thigh to thigh, just waiting for the meal to be over so they could get at it again, thinking, "Gwen is prettier, the hell with this, Gwen is prettier, Gwen is prettier!" All that time, in the distance, I could hear Bennett, selling hell out of me, so he thought, and for sure selling the hell out of Florence on engaging the same business manager and the same investment counselor he had: two different men getting two different salaries, but worth it, he was saying (I could barely hear him now over the distance growing between us), "absolutely worth it because with them on your team, you can have your mind really free for creative work, Eddie."

All this time I was looking at this nubile chick, and thinking of Gwen, and getting a hard on, and soon I stopped listening to Bennett altogether. She was looking at her boy friend, now, just the way Gwen looked at me when she wanted it. She wasn't talking, but I could hear her, just as that tennis player could hear her. "Let's get out of here," she was saying. "Come on, let's go." He heard and called for their check. And suddenly I got up. I didn't say to myself, "Get up," I just did. I was up, and saying "Excuse me" to the whole naked bloody Derby, and walking.

Florence later told me that was the first time she had a glimpse of the disaster ahead, the first time I seemed out of control.

My mobility a little impaired by my condition, I hobbled to the phone booth and dialed her number. I knew, as I heard Gwen's phone ring at the other end, that I had crossed the line.

2

Now to speak of "boths."

I had two jobs in those days. My bread and butter was Williams and MacElroy. My other work kept me living.

What I did was write for magazines. I called them "justice pieces." I'm not now putting them down; some of them were deadly to the mark, and murderous. I guess after all the advertising custard I had to let my true feelings out some way.

Lincoln Steffens, with his obligation to justice, had been my ideal all through college. All my adult life I had to look for frauds, social or human, uncover them, and help destroy them. I had these justice pieces in magazines like *Harper's, The Atlantic,* and once *Partisan Review*. But mostly I worked for a really rich outfit which gave me a drawing account. Since I'd get into hock with myself from time to time (there are the most surprising expenses in California), I'd also get into hock with them. They were decent people and along with my drawing account often gave me other favorable considerations, like travel expenses and money for research assistance.

These magazine pieces gave me my self-respect. I used to accept the fact that, just like the rest of mankind, I had to lie, little white lies, gentle weaseling lies, sparing-other-people's-feelings lies, avoiding-unnecessary-conflict lies, wishful-thinking lies, lies that were really just fantasizing, and part of my artistic inner life—well, whatever, I've always had a lot of trouble telling the unadorned truth. But I used to say to myself there was one place where I never lied, and that was in the pieces I wrote for the magazines.

It was pretty nice, this "both" arrangement. Williams and Mac-Elroy paid my running bills: the house, the mortgage, the upkeep, the maid, the lawn, the gardener, the insurance, the garages, the utilities, the appliance servicing, the premiums and the monthly payments on our annuity, my wife's clothes and her goddam psychoanalyst, Dr. Leibman, my daughter Ellen's clothes and her gyp-size tuition at Radcliffe, and a little psychoanalytical consultation that Florence would from time to time talk her into ("Just go and have a chat with Dr. Leibman, you'll find him absolutely human"). And finally all the simple things like food and liquor. In other words, everything.

Which meant I could be damned choosy about what articles I wrote and how I wrote them. The pieces didn't even have to pay, except they did and pretty well, too. And it was really nice having that drawing account always there and ready. But since W. and Mac-Eee paid for everything including vacations, everything else I did was for the good of my soul. You'd be surprised how many people manage their lives that way. I read somewhere that the poet Wallace Stevens worked or works (is he still alive?) as a top executive for a Hartford, Conn., insurance company.

So, in a way, I was two people. Well, not just two. Actually, my table of nomenclature was quite complicated. I was eldest son to a man named Seraphim Topouzoglou, who was born in Anatolia and brought to this country by his elder brother, Stavros Topouzoglou, the first of our tribe to cross the Atlantic. Stavros landed on Ellis Island in 1899, and the first thing he did was change his name to Joe Arness. A few years later, when he brought over my father, his younger brother Seraphim, he made him take the name of Arness. The boys didn't have to be geniuses to realize that you cannot be successful in business with the name Seraphim—not in America. So my father changed his name to Sam—Sammy to the buyers who patronized this lively and obliging little Greek—Sam Arness, Oriental Rugs and Carpets.

There is always a little betrayal in the stomach of a man who has abandoned his family name. So when Sam Arness had his first child, a son, he tried to make up for what he'd done by baptizing the boy Evangelos. That's me. In college my report cards said Evangelos Arness. The boys at school quickly shortened it to Eddie. (And was I relieved!) When I got married, the name on the license was Edward Arness. After the war, when I got into advertising—but quick! I had to catch up—the agency people all felt that there was something just the least bit fishy about Arness, especially for the very WASP accounts towards which I seemed to be headed. So Arness got changed to Anderson. (Mr. Finnegan's idea. I was his favorite, so he personally straightened out my name problem. I was flattered.) When it came to my magazine writing, I went back to Arness, but I still couldn't go for the Evangelos, and I thought Eddie too common. So Florence had an idea. Evans. My pen name became Evans Arness. Conclusion: in one job I was Eddie Anderson, in the other, Evans Arness; my wife called me "Ev," my mother called me "E," my father called me "Evangeleh!" when he didn't call me "Shakespeare."

Is it any wonder that the drama of my life has something to do with which face to put on in the morning? But no sweat, because until I met Gwen, all my identities were going along great, firing their sixteen-inch guns and hitting target center often as not.

That's the set-up I was putting in danger when I went to the phone in the Brown Derby that night and called Gwen.

When I told her I was coming over, she didn't say do and she didn't say don't. What seems like coldness in Gwen is—well, it's coldness, all right. But, I thought as I walked back to our table at the Derby, don't most of these people here pretend more warmth than they feel? And pretend they're more sure of what they want than they are? When Gwen is pulled two ways, I thought, or when she really doesn't know what she feels, which is the way most of us are most of the time, she simply says nothing. Not a solution to the problem of human relations, but better than the syrup the rest of us pour all over each other every time we make contact.

Back at our table I did some of my finest broken field running. I said there was a crisis at the office, put on that big sincere show, acted harassed and overwhelmed, a martyr to the cause of Williams and MacElroy. Then I shoved their three tickets across the table and told them, "Go ahead, I'll meet you at the Biltmore Theatre just as soon as I've got everything back on the track (track! what track?). Sign for me, Florence. Goodbye."

I didn't care if anyone believed me or not. Dale Bennett looked pretty suspicious and huffy, his mouth full of *pot au crème chocolat*. Florence told me later that he had every right to be p.o.'d, considering I had pressed him (I had pressed him! When did I ever press him?) to advise us about our investments, and just as he was getting warmed up to it, off I stalk like I'm in for the day from outer space and heading right back.

Anyway, I escaped. That's all that mattered to me right then. I was out of there, off and running. I put the top down again (I had had to put it up to protect Florence's hair-do). What a relief it was to drive along absolutely alone, with the top down and all that cool carbon monoxide ruffling my hair. I was at Gwen's in a record ten minutes.

To my surprise she was warm and welcoming. Usually I feel impelled to do it to her right away every time we come together, I suppose to reassure both me and her that everything is still o.k. But she was so loving that we just sat there and talked. She told me she had made up her mind. When I protested she really talked to me like a *mentsch*. She said, "Eddie, you've got your life arranged in a certain way. If you go past this point on this night it will smash everything all to hell. And you're not a man for that. So let's let it go, what do you say? It's been fine and I've enjoyed you and you me."

She was giving it what's been called the full masculine treatment. In other words she said to me just what I had said to myself a few hours before.

But for some reason I felt I had to put on an act, and I began to BS and play deprived. I guess maybe I'd been pretending so much for so long that I didn't know what I felt any more. For instance, did I truly, truly want her not to go? I said it with all kinds of conviction, all right, but would I miss her in a month? Or even in a week? Or was I just talking the way I thought a sincere man should behave in this situation, the way I wanted everyone, including myself, to think I was? I really didn't know any more.

She suddenly looked at her little traveling clock and said, "Oh!" and jumped up. She was on the Midnight and hadn't begun to pack. I lay on her bed and watched her. And I began to break up. I felt my life was going. I was lying there and letting my life of feeling go. I couldn't seem to do anything except watch it go.

She saw the way I was and got on the bed, and began to love me, telling me that she loved me, but it was time to stop. "You'll thank me six months from now," she said, and, "Eddie, Eddie, don't Eddie, don't."

After a while I was in her and saying what I meant, after so many months of being careful and not saying what I felt. I had never be-

32

fore told Gwen I loved her; I just hadn't used that word, because I calculated it gave her some kind of edge on me that I didn't want anyone to have (what edge?). Or because it would weaken my position (what position?). With all the circusing we'd done, I'd never used the big word. Nor had she, I realized, both of us determined, I suppose, to keep one last bit uncommitted. But now I did. Again and again. I was also saying, "You're the only thing in the world I really care about, don't you know that?" And there, suddenly, being on top of her, and in her, I struck her with all my might, my open palm across her face, not in anger, but to make her believe what I was saying, or was I making myself believe it?

When I hit her, something broke down inside her; something gave up, and she began to cling to me. She was crying, too, and behaving for the first time since I'd known her without that final bit of reserve. I'm a Mediterranean, true, but I'm self-trained not to give in to excessive emotionalism. I broke myself of crying when I was a kid. But I cried that night, and I gave her an awful belting. After which she forgot her traveling clock and the Midnight.

We lay there, together and quiet. She had her thoughts and I had mine. Looking back, I can remember what I thought, but it's embarrassing to me, even now, to recall it. I was such a goddam snob in those days. Because what I was asking myself as we lay there, our arms around each other, was, "How can you really go for this girl this way? How can you risk so much for this person?" I thought myself much superior to her. And so, just a few minutes after all that heat, I marveled that I had ever been so frantic about her. For in my heart I guess I really did agree with what people in the office had been saying about her. I thought of her as soiled. That's a good Greek middle-class word. I'm embarrassed to recall this now. After all, I had run some pretty fancy patterns myself.

Intellectually I felt myself far superior to her, in fact too good for her! For she was an uneducated girl, and didn't know how to pronounce certain words. Even spiritually I considered myself of finer stuff, because I was an idealist and a liberal from way back, anti-Communist now, of course, but still very progressive, and I had a position, philosophically, a lover of humanity, profoundly optimistic, while Gwen was just owl shit, really, habitually defensive and chronically disruptive (I was a builder I thought, she a destroyer) and never not suspicious—Gwen, scornful of everything, and just

33

versus, generally versus. All in all a sort of monster disguised as 108 pounds of beautiful young woman.

What bewildered me was that a few minutes before I had truly felt I didn't want to live without this girl. How could I need this kind of person that much? What was happening to me?

In a couple of hours I was home safe, going my normal two-timing way, lying comfortably on my side of the bed, Florence on hers, listening to her bawl me out for never making it to the Biltmore. I apologized to her just to shut her up so I could sleep. The love making and all that excessive emotion had exhausted me. But Florence went on, all about "Camelot" and the art of Alan J. Lerner vs. the art of T. H. White, who had written the original book which Florence had read and, I gathered, preferred. Poor thing, I thought, poor thing, as I fell asleep. And the last thing I heard her say was, "Ev? Are you asleep?" which I didn't answer because I was.

I kidded myself, the next morning as I drove to work, about my excursion into emotionalism. It had accomplished, I said, this much: now Gwen was officially my mistress. I would have to organize a way of life for her. But as for the future, who knew? Also: be careful!

She was my mistress. I couldn't believe that she'd hold me to anything more than that, though I had said a great deal more, using words like "always" and "forever," words that I had so carefully avoided all my adult life, even with Florence. With every girl I'd ever known, I'd always made a point that everything in life is temporary. I'd always kept the back door unlatched so I could make a get-away if things got too sticky at home or elsewhere. To be absolutely precise, I had always kept five hundred dollars in a sealed envelope, locked in a drawer of my bureau, so I would always have the wherewithal at hand if I suddenly wanted to disappear. I had a fetish about freedom.

So now it was a matter of making some kind of practical arrangement for Gwen, one that would satisfy her without compromising my final freedom. I had to face the fact that I had said to her: "You are my woman and I don't want to live without you." Hell, the whole truth is that in the heat of that occasion, I had said a great deal more. "You lost control here," I said to myself as I turned my Triumph into the office parking lot. "You even said to her, 'I want you to be my wife some day,' which you don't. You don't have the least intention."

And I didn't, not the vaguest! Because my God! I liked Florence. In fact I loved her, and the arrangement we had worked very well. Besides, there was just too much at stake financially. I'd just better watch out when I get worked up that way, I thought. Some day somebody might believe me. That's why emotion is such a dangerous thing. I thought I had conquered all that!

I met Gwen for lunch. She was very demure, very poised. So calm, sweet, and composed, it took me by surprise. And made me wary for a moment. But then we got talking, and she said some things to me that I must have been hungry to hear.

She said she did love me. But she despised what I did. My profession. She said it was despicable work. She just couldn't stand by any longer and watch me do it. She loved me too much to watch me behaving like those other people at Williams and MacElroy. For I was not really like those people, she said. I mustn't spend my life lying about somebody's products. And working for men I despised. Didn't I despise them?

"Yes," I said. And the fact is that right then I did. I allowed myself to feel the hatred and scorn I had choked down for years.

As Gwen talked, my dead pride awoke. Where had it been? It felt good. And she had done this, with her words. I looked at her and felt surprise and admiration and even gratitude.

It was then I told her about my other life: which magazines, the kind of articles, how much they meant to me. Well, she didn't read those particular magazines, she said. She looked at me very strangely and said she marveled how, through all our intimacy, I had successfully kept from her any knowledge of something that meant as much to me as this apparently did. (I had told her that it was the one area of my life where I lived completely honestly.) How come, she wondered, she hadn't even had an inkling? I told her that I wrote my magazine pieces under another pseudonym, the name by which she knew me, Eddie Anderson, being already a pseudonym of course. I told her about Evans Arness, and Evangelos Topouzoglou, and all the rest of it. But she wasn't listening. She was looking at me, again marveling that I had been able to keep a whole other life, another name or two as well, completely secret.

I acted rather pleased about it all. I explained that Anatolian

Greeks, like all other minorities of long history, tend to be secretive. In my case this was compounded by the basic law of Big Trading: namely, never reveal more than you absolutely have to in order to transact the business at hand. Play poker in everything!

I told her that I had just accepted an assignment from the magazine with which I had a drawing account to write a long piece on a new figure coming onto the national scene. The target's name was Chet Collier, and I was supposed to kill him, if possible without his realizing it. This was my specialty. I would make friends with a subject, win his confidence, make him reveal himself. Then I'd write my piece. Weeks later, the man, to his complete surprise, would find my attack on him in print. And there wasn't a damned thing he could do about it, because every quote was accurate; he had checked them all himself. I'd seen to that!

With the Chet Collier assignment came two large manila folders of staff-prepared research. But since I insisted on researching every subject myself, there was also a budget item for a research assistant and travel allowance for two. I always insisted on this, the travel. It was part of my deal with Williams and MacElroy. There have been times in my life when I felt the only way I could survive Los Angeles and my personal situation was by extricating myself geographically for a breather. This way I had a defensible excuse for suddenly pulling up stakes and leaving the whole complex. Florence sometimes insisted on coming with me, especially if the trip was to New York (shopping, the theater, culture). So there was often a subtle, underground tussle to see if I could arrange things so that I could go alone. Now, without arousing Florence's suspicion, I had to contrive to hole myself up in a New York hotel with my research assistant, Miss Gwendolyn Hunt.

I told Florence that I was going to move right in with Mr. Collier, his place was near Weston, Connecticut, and since he was a supermale type, I'd be spending a lot of time in drinking and rough talk. The presence of a woman would inhibit this. Florence went for my reasoning. Then I had to deceive her another way. Her natural assumption was that I was going by plane. I wanted to go by train, have two days and three nights with Gwen in a stateroom on the Super Chief and the Broadway Limited. So I had to make these reservations myself, and have my secretary (to whom Florence talked daily) make plane reservations which I would cash in later.

It all worked out. Gwen and I had two days and three nights of the most continuous intimacy possible, all under the benign stewardship of a fine old Negro to whom I gave twenty dollars at the beginning of the trip rather than at the end. He saw to it that we never lacked for anything, never had to do for ourselves, in fact never had to move. We were thus able to devote ourselves, for those days and nights, to research into each other, especially into each other's sleeping habits, for we hadn't up till that time spent an entire night together. Actually we raised the shades only twice through the whole trip, and both times it was dark, a night of sixty hours duration.

I remember the first time we raised the shades. The train had stopped, and we woke tangled in each other, feeling marvelous, and decided, after some discussion, that we'd risk breaking the spell. So we raised the shades and we were somewhere in Colorado. The grave old men of the line were walking up and down checking axles and supervising the loading of Rocky Mountain Brook Trout, the very fish, it turned out, that we had for breakfast the next morning. The other time we raised the shades, we had just left Erie, Pennsylvania.

In New York we moved into the Algonquin. There was a suite waiting for Mr. Evans Arness, here on another writing assignment, the exact nature of which no one knew. Even the elevator starter, who knew absolutely everything, didn't know this. However, the room service waiters did report to him that Mr. Arness was working very hard, and that his secretary, who had the small single adjoining, spent the night with him. This, of course, got around. But not far, since it was nothing out of the ordinary, in fact had happened before with Mr. Arness and other secretaries. It was natural that a man of Mr. Arness's importance would require complete servicing.

We spent the first few days in the Algonquin digesting the research. The Republican Party, it seemed, was combing the country for hopefuls in whom they could actually hope. Chet Collier was the hope of the Elephants of Western Connecticut. I read and reread all his public utterances, the second time with a pencil at the margin for quotes. I couldn't believe there was anyone who'd hope for anything from a mind like this one. But, after all, there had been Goldwater. So I began to believe that someone had actually said what I was reading. Then I began to feel that I might have some fun with this one. Certainly the editors of the magazine knew what they were doing when they chose me. Not that they ever suggested an attitude or an approach to me; they didn't have to. They knew that my response to Mr. Collier would be the response of a hawk to a squab.

As we drove out I told Gwen about Chet Collier. He'd gone to the same college I had. I'd been one of the mutts, but Chet was a three-letter man, had in fact, made all-New England in something, and had been tapped—I remember that June day—for the Senior honorary society. He'd also been a Deke, and Delta Kappa Epsilon was the class house on that campus. I had been a dishwasher at the Zeta Psi house, in the days before dishwashing machines. My clothes smelled of dishwater for four straight years. So I was still, for those reasons and others, full of unexercised revenge.

As soon as I saw Chet, it was evident he hadn't changed. He didn't have a single self-doubt. Towards others he felt the kindly tolerance of the man who does not question his own superiority. He had nothing to fear, never felt truly challenged, and was, therefore, never unreceptive to anyone. Physically, he was in the pink, always looked as if he had just walked off a squash court. He drank to excess, but I don't think he ever paid the price of a single hangover. He made the best martinis I have ever tasted, or not tasted—they were that dry. He drove an English two-seater (as I did), preferred English cars and said so in all his speeches. Furthermore, he said that the reason they were better was that they were made better, and the reason they were made better was that the English still had some tradition of craftsmanship, and the reason for that was that the unions were less powerful there (not at all true, of course), and that they were not dominated by gangsters as were ours (nonsense). Furthermore, he said, the English had a basic and enduring religious tradition. How this made for better cars I don't know. Chet himself played golf every Sunday morning.

He called America the spoiled child of the world. He spoke of tightening our belts. At the same time he weighed 200-odd himself, though I had to admit that most of it was above the waist. He talked a lot about the last war, said that that was the one time his country had a unified spiritual idea. He never let up about his war record, and illustrated the points of his speeches with little symbolic scenes from his combat experiences. He said that life was essentially savage, man essentially predatory, naturally ruthless, and that modern society had disguised all this but not at all changed it. He said that a man should—at regular intervals—risk his life, and he meant literally, just so he could get back in touch with the way things really are. He had red hair, thinning, and a red beard, not thinning. He kept adjusting from one side of his trousers to the other as we spoke, even though Gwen was right behind me, with her sharp little eyes missing nothing, her sharp little pencil making notes of everything, including that.

You had to see him to believe him. I thought they had discontinued that model. He aerated all that romantic hogwash with the greatest air of good feeling and patience with the blindness of the rest of us.

His favorite target had to be the liberal intellectual. He immediately tagged me one. I imagine he was disappointed I was not Jewish, because he asked me at the beginning, and then again a few hours later, having forgotten, if I was. I called his attention to this and asked if it was important to him. At that he burst into uninhibited laughter, said to Gwen that I was subtle, wasn't I? Why didn't I just ask him if he was anti-Semitic? Then he began talking to Gwen right past me. He asked her what in the world she was doing with a creep like me. He suddenly turned the force of a lot of charm on her. It was immediately very flattering, and certainly found its mark. But if he thought he could fluster her, he soon found out different. She was just as cool as he was direct and pressing. After he had kept on a bit with this talking past me to her, it began to get under my skin. He was quick to spot this, so from time to time he'd revert, talking to her as if I wasn't there. I must say the son of a bitch was enjoying himself.

Actually the interview was only a matter of my trying to see how far into political and moral fantasy I could drive him. I had this knack of getting lively copy by rubbing a target the wrong way and prying where I shouldn't. Usually people you interview are so anxious for you to write favorably about them that in a very short time you can make them say just about anything. You give them just a little friendship; then ask all the impertinent questions you can think up, then watch them duck and waver, find ways to agree and ingratiate, poor buggers. Soon they're barely hanging on, hoping you'll think they're not too bad, and not too different from the rest of the world.

But not Chet Collier. He loved to differ—compulsively. Even when I pretended to agree on something, he found a point of difference as quickly as he could. After about a half an hour or so of this,

Gwen, suddenly and unexpectedly, asked him, "Mr. Collier, don't you care at all what we think of you?"

"Not at all," he said, and laughed without inhibition. Naturally I looked for a nervous edge to his laughter, but there was none. I remember Gwen was laughing too, and he was speaking to her, again past me: "I knew what to expect when I said I'd see him. I don't want him to write favorably about me—it would cost me a lot of votes." And more of that not very funny crap. Finally he said to Gwen, "Come on, let's go get some sun and see how the animals are doing." And he took her by the elbow and led her out. I followed.

About this time I detected a contrary twinge in my feelings for this creature. I have never had a spontaneous laugh, and always wished I did. I choked down this feeling—envy? even admiration—as quickly as I could. It wasn't right; I shouldn't admire this man in any way.

We walked around his acreage. There was a Ford Farmall tractor parked not far from his front door next to our U-drive. There was no lawn, just field grass. And mud. Collier had on some kind of boots, I my city shoes. Gwen was shod strictly Italian, with the thinnest possible soles. He sent someone into the house to get her a pair of galoshes and lifted her into them himself. They were too big, and she looked very cute. He offered me no such courtesy.

The trees we were walking under were very old. So were the house and the outbuildings. It had been rather chilly inside—he kept it that way in the fashion of English country gentlemen—very cool indeed from my point of view. I wondered if Southern California had thinned my blood. At any rate, the sun was welcome. The domestic animals were all out enjoying it. Gwen made a note that he had eight cats and six dogs of different breeds, high bred as well as mongrel. The place was crawling with these animals, all walking around among each other, feeding various ways, quarreling as was natural, fornicating, reproducing and nursing. There were puppies and there were kittens. The scene was Brueghel. The animals were as at home as the humans.

Collier led us around the back of the house to some cages where he kept wild animals. There was a weasel which he had just caught in a Have-a-Heart trap. We watched him transfer the animal to larger quarters. There was a bob-cat with a bad foot which he had rescued from the trap of a neighboring farmer, a jaguar kitten that a friend had sent him from Caracas, and a large bedraggled hawk that looked well past its prime (Collier said it was) and was content, I thought, not to be any longer at liberty (Collier winked at Gwen and said I was projecting).

Again I have to admit I caught myself envying him. I had always wanted lots of animals around, but Florence had pointed out, quite correctly, that our lives would be restricted by them. "I mean," she used to say, "suppose we want to take a trip suddenly? What would we do with them?" What did Collier do with them when he took his trips? I supposed they just stayed there and ate each other. I was about to ask him, when I noticed that he had taken off his lumber jacket (the sun had gone behind some clouds and the temperature had dropped abruptly) and was putting it around Gwen's shoulders. The son of a bitch was making a run for my girl!

Well, by this time I was ready to kill him. But that was only the beginning.

He got onto subjects that he knew would outrage me. And make me write pure murder about him.

First he started on the Jews. He said he found that most American Jews were ashamed of it. What did I think?

I said I didn't agree.

He said Jews considered those girls of their tribe the prettiest who looked most Christian. What did I think of that?

Nonsense, I said. By now he was interviewing me.

He said Jews always married girls who looked the least Jewish, preferring those with pretty little turned up noses, and if they didn't have noses like that, their fathers would rush them to get a nose bob and, while they were at it, an electrolysis of the upper lip to get rid of their mustaches. What did I think of that?

Pure prejudice, I said.

He said he approved of the Black Muslims. Did I?

I said no, I didn't.

He said that he couldn't see how the mass of Negroes managed to be so patient. That if he had been a Negro, he would have turned to murder long ago, wouldn't I?

No, I said.

He said the only way they'd get respect from Whitey was with their fists; they had to literally fight for it, with guns if necessary. Did I agree with that?

Not at all, I said.

He said that he didn't believe in all that non-violent twitter because the only way history moves is through blood-letting—look at our history—and didn't I at least agree with that?

I said I certainly didn't. He was really enjoying himself, the bastard.

Well, he said, did I really think that all that hymn singing, those preacher-politicians, and those long herd walks were really doing any good?

I said, most certainly yes.

He burst into laughter and said I deserved what I was going to get, and that he'd ask me one more question: did I really and truly want the Negro to have absolute equality in this country, to examine my conscience and tell him, did I truly want that?

I said I didn't know what he meant. Of course I did.

He turned to Gwen and said to her, "Come on, I'll show you something," and walked her off. Which gave me a chance to pull myself together and tell myself to be patient, I'd get him later—with my typewriter.

He showed us his two racing cars, a Porsche Spyder and an old Maserati, beautifully kept up. By now he was talking only to Gwen.

"How come you're speaking only to my researcher and not to me?" I said.

"Well, you're not interested in racing cars, are you?"

I said no, I wasn't, but neither was she.

"Yes," he said, "but she's interested in me."

We all laughed. What the hell was I laughing at?

A bit later he got out his Australian bull whip, and did some target practice, making an old oil can jump around. (He must have known I'd make a fool of him on that bull whip bit.) And then his pistol, did I want to do some shooting? I said no, I didn't approve of guns.

He turned to Gwen and said, "Oh, our friend doesn't approve of guns." He was doing everything possible to bait me.

So I just tuned him out. I began to write the piece in my mind. That gave me comfort. The son of a bitch was a fraud, and I was going to pull that big damp stone off from over him and let the light of day hit him. He was able to live the way he lived for one reason only: his father had left him a bundle. Disguised under all that romantic roostering was the soul of a coupon-clipper. He'd never earned one cent himself. For all that farm life he was parading before us, he was a bourgeois slob, just as bad on his end as those Hollywood Cadillac Communists were on the other.

I came to. He and Gwen were both looking at me. When he noticed I was paying attention again, he said to Gwen, "Miss Gwen, don't you think they might at least have sent an unprejudiced and fair-minded individual to interview me?"

Gwen said I was fair-minded. Why was I surprised that she had defended me? They were standing there, side by side. I saw her look at him a certain way, and I realized she liked him.

I guess it was his candor. And some kind of male exuberance. His step had bounce, and his stance was fearless. He faced men combatively, and women as if they were his natural quarry. At one point he admitted that he was a womanizer and said, "Put that down for him, Miss Gwen, an admitted adulterer, a man who lives in the corrupt new suburbs and doesn't go to work but spends his days talking, farming, drinking, reading, and pursuing his neighbors' women. Oh I forgot politics," he winked at me, "and I don't lie to myself. And oh," he said, "I'll give you another one. Write this down for him, Miss Gwen, my favorite author is Kipling. How's that?" he turned to me. "Better than you could have made up, isn't it? Come on, I'll read for you."

And goddam if he didn't. He got out a book of Kipling's verse and kept us there drinking his bone dry martinis long past dark. He turned on only one light, so we couldn't do anything except listen to him reading that stuff rhythmically, in an old-fashioned sing-song style, beautiful in its way it was, but who reads that stuff any more—and in that way? He even read "Boots."

Then somebody brought in tea and a nut cake he claimed he had baked himself that morning, in anticipation of my visit, he said, just to surprise me, and to give me, if I liked the cake, at least one good thing I could say about him. "Just for relief," he said, "from the rest of that bilge, one friendly homely note?"

I ate my cake and didn't answer. I wondered: was he putting reverse English on the whole interview, was he trying to be so far out that I'd think him in?

We all had a lot to drink. He began to talk about chaos, his favorite theme. He really rolled out on that, the importance of recognizing the element of chaos in life and how important it was to look that one in the eye as early as possible and be prepared to meet what was going to happen, prepared for hatred and conflict and confusion and no-happy-ending and no-victory-for-the-just. He said we all spoil our children by protecting them too much. He said we should encourage them to have fist fights early on, because that way they would be ready for what was ahead. Then he took out after our schools. Especially the progressive private schools, with their emphasis on adjustment. He was drunk by then, and the room was pretty dark, and he roared, "Anybody who's adjusted to the way this country is today is an idiot, and a man who tries to train his children to adjust to what's around them would do better to slit their throats." His voice was going up and down in a sort of chant. He was getting out of control. He moved over and sat next to Gwen on the sofa, barely recognizing my presence. I believe he could have made love to her with me right there and maybe would have tried, except that he couldn't tell what Gwen felt. She certainly didn't move away (I knew she wouldn't give him that), but she was looking at him in that cool way, measuring him for something, it wasn't clear what.

It was at this point that I said, "Gwen let's go," and he bellowed out, "No, you're going to spend the night here; we're just getting started."

I had had enough. "Come on, Gwen," I said, picking up her things.

Somehow we got out of there. I couldn't wait to attack him. I assumed Gwen and I would feast on his corpse.

But she liked him. I don't mean sexually, although the fact is that in women all feelings mix together—sex, intellectual judgment and all —in one big ragout. Whatever the components, she liked him. Was it because he came on with her?

She asked what it was I didn't like about him.

I said, "Everything. He's prejudiced and bigoted, a reactionary politically, socially, and philosophically, an arrogant super male with his goddam fornicating animals and penis symbols all over the place —whips, guns, racing cars—and that phony country gentleman air. And Kipling! That's where he belonged—in His Majesty's Khyber Rifles!"

I was yelling at her, but she looked at me with cool interest and said, "Yes, I see what you mean. I guess you're right. But I like him."

I said just because he came on with you, and her answer was, yes, that was enjoyable, she did enjoy that. Well, I was ready to lift off! I said hell the man is just a filthy ram, did you smell him? By now we were back at the Algonquin—and I got so worked up I took her in anger. When we were done, she said, "Well, thank you, Chet Collier," just as a joke, but I couldn't see where it was so funny.

We left for California the next day, this time by plane.

I was furious with her and didn't really know why. I was doubting something about myself that I had never before opened to doubt: my judgment, my basic point of view, my taste, my stance in the world.

I'd say Collier was a mass of prejudice (I was beginning to write the piece now), and Gwen would say that it was I who was prejudiced, that I had written my piece in advance, had never given the man a chance, had gone to interview him with every judgment made. I had pre-judged him, which is what prejudice is, isn't it, she said. And I roared.

Well, one afternoon I was going on about Collier's sexual self-advertising, how he was pushing his product all the time, strutting his *macho* and rattling his *cohones* (we'd just done it in Gwen's apartment, and were maybe getting up to the point of doing it again), when Gwen began to giggle and my male column collapsed.

"What the hell are you laughing about?" I said.

"You do the same damned thing."

"The hell I do."

She called my attention to the running commentary with which I often accompanied our love making. She said what the hell, it's just natural and sort of charming, most men do it, say something during the act, and in some way ask for compliments afterwards, just natural she said. With me, she said, it sometimes even reached the level of boasting.

I said, getting pretty teed off now, when the hell was I ever boasting?

"Well," she said, "like for instance you always ask, 'Are you coming again, my darling?' What do you call that if it's not boasting? Aren't you calling attention to how good you are? And that condescending baby voice you use on me. 'Are you coming again, my sweetheart,'" she imitated me.

Well, this made me really blow. I couldn't do it to her for a week after that, the bitch! A woman is not supposed to do that! A male ego is a fragile thing and has to be sustained, not put down. Gwen has been around enough to know that, I thought, so she must be doing it on purpose. That's it. She's attacking me for some reason.

One day I read her some of what I'd written and she acted bored, getting up once to open a window, another time to get an orange stick, which she began to use. So I finally quit. When I scolded her, she said she wasn't interested in Chet Collier, only in me. I said what the hell was wrong with me? She said my whole way of life. And I said, ready now to kill, what was wrong with my whole way of life?

She said I should for once in my life live what I talked. "Put your money," she said, "where your mouth is. For example," she said, "I'm pretty damned tired of your beefing about the middle class all the time. I don't even know what it is, those bourgeoisie you talk about, which is only a hangover from your left days or something. Who lives more middle class than you do, with your insurance, your cocktails at seven, your dinner at seven-thirty, and your respectable civil-rights-loving wife, and the same executive-type haircut your friends have and the same executive-type friends and the same suits they have, and the whole damned thing—your lawn, don't let me forget your lawn—and you go bitching and complaining about the middle class. You talk about the Cadillac Communists—isn't that what you are? I mean if you'd shut up and enjoy it, I could take you. I mean you're part of the general fraud; why pretend to be better? You sit here and draw yours twice a month, a big fat check it is too, from an industry whose only function is to sell people things they don't need, and you do it by lying about them, and you know it, and you think just because you subscribe to a couple of those magazines like the *Nation* it makes everything all right. You constantly bitch about the establishment—what the hell is the establishment except you? I mean why don't you just be a slob like everyone else and enjoy it, you'd have a hell of a lot better time. That's my advice!"

"What else?" I said, ready to murder, egging her on. "What else?"

"Everything," she said, "we're all phonies but you're a safe phony, so why don't you be nice to your fellow phonies? They're no worse than you, only different. They buy their neckties in the same place, mix their drinks the same way, turn in their cars once a year like you do, and all have their little piece of tail they're doing on the side just like you do me. And they lie to her about maybe someday marrying her, and they don't mean it, any more than you did when you said all that crap to me that night. They just play the game, and you play the game."

I blew up. "If you don't like it, what the hell are you doing here?"

"Because I'm no different and no better," she said. "How could I be? I'm dependent on you phonies for my living. And you, at least you personally—"

"Are just a little better than the others?"

"I wasn't going to say that. Not better, only *you like me* a little more. You're anxious or something, so you cling to me a little more."

She leaned forward to touch my cheek. "And you are sort of sweet . . ."

I brushed her away and said, "Never mind that. Finish what you were going to say."

"No," she said, "now you're sore at me. And I don't want you to be sore at me. You're not so bad, despite the fact that you've been conning me all along. It's only that since you're not really different than the rest of us, I can't stand that lard of your being so superior to everyone."

"I don't think I'm so goddam superior . . ."

"Well then tell me what the hell is wrong about Collier being so healthy and physical? Take a look at your middle. I mean I don't say anything about it, but sometimes when you're propped over me on your elbows and knees, you hang down like, in puckers and flab and rolls, and I don't stop and say I find you disagreeable physically. Because you're the way men are in the cities and offices. What's wrong with Collier's health? I like looking at him, and to tell you the truth, I liked it when he put his hand on me."

"When did he do that?" I said quickly. I hadn't seen him do that.

"Every time you weren't looking."

"What the hell did you let him do that for?"

"Because I wanted to see what it was like. And he kissed me, too."

"When?"

"When you went to the bathroom that time, he came over and he kissed me."

"And you let him?"

"Yes."

"Why didn't you tell me?"

"Because I didn't want to! Am I supposed to? I knew you'd feel you had to be real masculine and defend me or God knows what, and he would probably have had to beat your brains out. Besides all it was to me was . . ." She seemed to hesitate.

"What?"

"No, I'll tell you the truth, it was rather nice."

"Did he put his tongue in your mouth?"

"No, he knows his moves."

"What moves?"

"You know what moves. He just put his two lips on mine. He was very gentle, he just touched the tip of my tongue with the tip of his tongue."

"What moves you talking about?"

That girl had certain ways of talking that were right out of the gutter.

"You know what moves," she said, "the right moves at the right time."

"And what does that mean?"

"You know what that means. It means he's been around, been there and back, and knows how to set a pace, and what moves to make when, without too much early foot, you prig, by which I mean he knows better than to come on too fast, but to judge the company he's in and what the traffic will bear, you prig, and not get stirred up faster than he was stirring me up, which he *was* right then, damn right well was, straight up, you prig, you know what moves, so why act so superior, and don't make me tell them unless you're looking to get hurt. Because I'd just as soon, you liar. You talked one story to me when I was packing to get on the Midnight that night and another story since; no mention of all you said to me that night! No mention since. Silence! O.K. I'll take it that way. Because you're the best I've got right now. But don't put me on trial. Who the hell do you think I am? Your wife? I haven't given you the right to put me down. So he wanted to do me, so what? At least he didn't hand me a lot of those I love you lies. If you want to know the truth, I wouldn't at all mind trying him out. I don't have any obligation to you. Where are we, in the last century? I just might; you keep that up and I just might!"

I had left.

It was either leaving or murdering her.

I couldn't figure out what got into her so suddenly. It started out to be a perfectly normal discussion. I guess, like me, she'd stored up resentment and anger and pretended everything was all right till BOOM!

Well, after dinner that night, Florence and I were sitting around watching one of those CBS White Papers when Irene, the maid, came in and told me that there was someone from the office on the telephone.

I got up and went towards the phone. Then I suddenly stopped. I figured it was Gwen. I sat down for a moment. Irene was waiting, and I told her to say I'd be right there. Then I went to the bar and poured myself a Dewars just to gain time. I said to myself: stop. Think. A woman who resents you and despises you that much, who needs that. I took half my Dewars.

There was another consideration, not a very noble one, but I have to admit it crossed my mind. My allowance on the magazine's budget for a research assistant had given out a week ago. If Gwen was to be paid this week, and from this week on, it would have to come out of my pocket. I had a hunch if I told her this, and stopped paying her, she'd pull up and go back to New York. In other words . . . in other words . . .

In other words what the hell did that have to do with it? I finished my drink. I hated her one way. I was out of my head crazy about her another way. I'd never really desired anyone as much. Nor had I ever resented anyone as much. Nor, I thought, been so bewildered. I certainly couldn't take any more of that scorn. I went to the phone.

Gwen sounded soft and subdued. Oh my God!

She said she was sorry. She sounded as if she had been drinking. I didn't say anything, punishing her.

She said, "Eddie . . . Eddie . . . are you there?"

"Yes," I said.

"You're all I have, Eddie."

Out of the blue.

"How come?" I said.

"Because nobody else can stand me, daddy." Then she said, "I can understand where you wouldn't want to have anything more to do with me."

I didn't say anything.

"Well I was thinking maybe it would be an idea if I divided myself in two, you know, like if I was your assistant, like your secretary part of the time, typing what you tell me to type, and researching what you tell me to research. No comments, no discussions, no judgments. Just like I was working for another man. Then there'd be our time together. Do you think something like that would work, Eddie?"

I said nothing.

"Eddie, are you still there? You're all I have, Eddie."

"I doubt that."

"That stuff I said, will you forget it? I know you can't say anything now because you're home. And I'll get the hell off the phone. Shall I come over when you said tomorrow, Eddie?"

"Yes," I said. And hung up.

I had never heard her that way. I didn't know she had it in her.

When I came into the other room, Florence looked up. "I wish the office wouldn't bother you at night," she said.

3

THEY say you can't compartmentalize life. But for a time the arrangement Gwen suggested really did work.

Then Florence began to notice something.

One night we were expecting the Soloffs for after-dinner bridge. We were just getting through our food. The record player was on the last of the stack we put on for each meal. Florence kept clearing her throat all through the brown betty, so I knew she had something to say to me. But I wasn't in any hurry to hear. I'd been to the beach with Gwen that afternoon, and I needed a nap, if only for ten minutes, before the game started. I'm a miserable bridge player at my very best; my mind wanders. Florence is damned good. That's why I occasionally used to play. It gave her a chance to be damned good.

But that night she had something to say to me before the Soloffs arrived. Over the Drambuie and the mints it finally came out.

"Sugar," she said, "you've begun to talk to yourself."

"I've always talked to myself."

"Yes, I suppose we all do. But I don't think you realize how bad it's gotten."

"Oh, Florence, let me live, will you?" I was rather relieved this was all she had on her mind.

"Did you know your lips keep twitching?"

I was spending my days in violent debate with myself, but I didn't know it showed. "Ellen's noticed it, too," she added. "Nothing unusual has happened at the office, has it?"

"No, I don't think so."

"Well, something's got you for sure. Did Dr. Massey say anything to you?"

"About what?" Massey was our dentist.

"I went in for my checkup today, and he told me he had seen further evidence in your mouth that you'd been grinding your teeth. Didn't he say anything about that the last time you saw him?"

"Maybe. Now that you remind me."

"He said that was pretty common today. The age of disbelief and all. But I thought our life was so remarkably free of tensions that—"

"It is, it is," I interrupted hastily.

"Evans," she said in her calm voice, "I didn't finish my sentence."

"Well, I know what you were going to say." That crack always made her furious.

"Don't you see how presumptuous that is, dear?" she said, being very patient.

"I think the Soloffs are driving in," I said.

"Evans, it's eight-twenty, and the Soloffs are not due till eight-thirty, so you can't get out of it that way."

Ten minutes is a long time, I thought. "Florence, how would you like another—"

"You are constantly cutting me off in the middle of a sentence," she said, cutting me off in the middle of a sentence. "I don't mind when we're alone, but when we have guests, particularly people like the Soloffs who notice everything and are terrible gossips . . ."

"What the hell do we have them here for, if they're such terrible gossips?"

"Because they play excellent bridge, and you just did it again."

"What?"

"Cut me off in the middle of a sentence. And it goes on all night."

"You mean when I sleep I cut—"

"Your teeth grind, and you talk to yourself. Sort of a civil war you're fighting, Dr. Leibman said it was. The other night, you said in your sleep, 'I hate her.' You don't hate me, do you, Evans?"

"Of course not."

"Well then, who is it you do hate?"

"How should I know?"

"Who should know if you don't?"

"The Japanese sandman."

"Last night, you lay there for hours, just staring at the ceiling, with your lips moving. What were you doing?"

"Thinking. Anything wrong with that?"

"Of course not, but sometimes, honestly, I can actually hear you grinding your teeth," she laughed. "And once you sort of pounded your fist. That was the time I jumped clear out of bed." This seemed to amuse her no end.

"Florence, I'm not doing it on purpose."

"But why all of a sudden do you grind your teeth, have nightmares, and talk to yourself all day long?"

"Florence, what's all this leading up to?"

"You know what it's leading up to. I do wish you would, Evans. Ev!"

"I can't stand Dr. Leibman."

"Just try it for a while. Dr. Leibman could help you, Ev."

"Fuck Dr. Leibman."

"I have no intention of doing that. Ev! Really, dear, really. Oh damn, here are the Soloffs." This time it was.

Florence went to the mirror for her last-minute checkup. "Anyway, I do wish you'd try to control your lips tonight. The Soloffs might think you're sending me signals." She laughed. She had the laugh of a little girl, a darling laugh. "I mean, if you must talk to yourself all through the bridge game, that's your privilege, I suppose . . ."

"You're goddam right that's my privilege. And furthermore, it's the only way I can get through an evening with the Soufflé." That was my pet name for Mrs. Soloff, a large, puffy woman.

That made Florence laugh. "Shhh!" she said. "There's the bell. Just try not to let it show quite so much. And some day, monster, do tell me what's going on. And whom you hate. I must say I prefer that to your loving someone. Just so long as it isn't me. Are you sure it isn't me you hate?"

"Sure."

"Then come on," she said, indicating a place on her cheek. I kissed where she pointed. In came the Soloffs and caught us in the act.

"Ah, we interrupt," said the Soufflé. Mr. Soloff never spoke except to bid. He was a libel lawyer for a large motion picture company, a very cautious man. The Soufflé, though, did all the talking necessary for both.

"Yes," said Florence, "you certainly do interrupt." Then she sort of kissed them both, and we sat down to those five long rubbers.

The Soloffs won the first. We went down some eight hundred points. I played miserably, worse than usual. But I did control my lip movements. We stopped for a moment and stretched. The Soufflé had to take a leak, and Mr. Soloff used the phone quickly. Florence had a chance to whisper to me, "Sugar, if you're going to play that badly, maybe you'd *better* talk to yourself."

She bid four spades, first hand, second rubber. I jumped to six. Florence almost went the whole hog, but, because of a general distrust of my bridge, didn't. By the rules, she should have. I certainly had the strength. "Thank you very much, partner," she said when I laid down. I did the ritual of crossing behind her and looking at her cards, and said, "Very nice, partner," which relieved me of further responsibility for that hand. Then I ran upstairs and dialed Gwen's number. She was not at home. Or wasn't answering. I went downstairs and to the bar.

"Where the hell is that bitch?" I asked myself. Then I said to myself, "You're talking to yourself." Then I said to myself, "The hell with it—I'm going to talk to myself all night tonight. I'll choke to death if I don't talk to myself. Everything I say to anyone else is strictly parenthetical."

("Can the dummy get anyone a drink? No?")

Well, *I'm* going to have one! Better make it a single, though, Eddie. There. That helps. Why the hell did Massey mention about my teeth grinding to Florence? Where's his professional discretion? Everyone's teeth grind today.

("Grand slam! Very good, partner. Oh, sorry. Mr. Soo, of course, you're absolutely right, bid six, one over. Right.")

Your mother too! But you know, Evans, Eddie, Evangelos, whatever your name is, it's true what she said. You are losing control of yourself. Like this afternoon? Hell, that wasn't my doing; that was Gwen's idea. The girl controls things like that. But to do it on the beach, in the middle of the afternoon! What have I got, some kind of compulsion to break the law? Or do I want to get caught? Williams and MacElroy Vice-President Given Prison Term For Indecent Exposure. Mr. Finnegan would love that! Well, it wasn't quite that bad. The nearest people were fifty feet away. At least. Anyway, it was her fault. She covered our bottom halves with a towel. Go tell that to the judge. Your honor, our bottom halves were covered completely with a Chorpenning towel, deluxe grade; we handle their account. Why do I keep imagining myself arrested? And on trial? And besides, the nearest people were a good seventy-five feet away, lying on their backs, faces turned up to the sun, and their eyes absolutely closed. No doubt thinking how much they'd give to be young again. Not that I am. But she makes me feel young. Like a wild kid she is, and like a wild kid she makes me feel.

("Oh, sorry. I bid . . . I bid . . . I'll say one No.")

I've really got three, but if I say three, I'll have to play the thing. This way Florence will probably bid another suit and be so grateful for my support she won't notice me going upstairs again. So she says don't get sand up. But those were her last words. Only gasps from then on, oh my God, with the sun and the sea and the breeze and her face shining and her hair flying . . .

("Well, partner, no, I think I'm going to let you play it. Three hearts? I'll say four.")

How can you blame me, how can you ever blame me with that silky hair blowing, and her nose just a little red from the sun, and her eyes wild with breaking the moral law, and she herself breaking to bits there under me.

("Why, you're welcome, partner. I thought you'd like them apples.")

Dear silly-dilly Florence. You'd think by this time she'd suspect that my sole aim in the ancient art of bridge is to always be dummy.

("Well, partner, I'd say I was leaving you in pretty good shape. Now, can I get anybody anything on the way back from the little boys' room? A drink, Mrs. Soof? No? O.K.")

Someday I'm going to come out with Soufflé, and that, chum, will be the end of these particular games. But there's always another card lover waiting in the woodwork. I never used to puff running up these stairs. The strange thing is that ever since the day she told me off, I've wanted her only more. Has anyone yet studied the connection between hatred and sex? Well, I wish somebody would and let me know how it turns out. Now she better be in. She told me to phone her later. No answer. Goddam her, where is she? The movies, no doubt, I hope. Stop worrying about it. Better get downstairs. That's what I like, when she loses control, when she's helpless, her insides working every damn which way, that tight little ass pumping, and those fragrant terminal quivers. I thought she'd never stop. I tell you it's holy. Not to be questioned. . . . And when she let out with that moaning, that song of love, right there on the beach. What? No one could hear that! With the sound of the surf and all! But really, what am I trying to do, get arrested? And faint, did she faint after? She lay there like she was faint. Ohh, I'm sure enough out of control. Like at that party the other night. Insanity!

("Good work, partner!"
"Wasn't that beautifully played, Mrs. Soof?")

Well, say so, you bitch! But really, Eddie, you better be careful! Meet me upstairs in the bathroom in five minutes! For chrissake! And *that* was your idea. Then on the tile floor yet. With Florence downstairs talking about moral rearmament. I've forgotten whether she's for it or against it. I mean something is out of control somewhere. No wonder you're grinding your teeth.

("Well, I know I gave you good support, but as Mrs. Soof says, you did play it astutely.")

Mrs. Soufflé and her ass-tutely—that would be a sight to behold! Hell, it's my deal. Well, I'm going to say Bye no matter what I have. And where does she get off with that prejudice shit?

("Ooops! Misdeal—sorry, all! Cards getting sticky, I guess.")

I may lie everywhere else, but not when I write a serious piece for a serious journal. Eddie lies, but not Evans. Name me one person who's done more to expose fraud in public life. Well, I can. But not many. Or done it as well. I write exquisite literary murder.

("I bye. Sorry, partner.")

And I'm not like these people here. No? Then what the hell are you playing cards with them all the time for? Not all the time, twice a month. Can I help it if Florence . . . ? Fuck Florence. You fuck Florence.

("Sorry. Can't help you partner. Bye.")

Oh mother, now I'm going to have to play a hand. Teeth grinding. Lips twitching, nightmares. I'm afraid to go to sleep at night. That bitch sure got to me. Maybe I'll just take her off salary. Who's kidding? I'm paying that bitch out of my own pocket—and for what? To insult me? So I'll just stop shelling out one of these days, and she'll get the message. When the shoe pinches, throw the shoe away.

("Sorry, Mrs. Soof. I didn't realize you could see my cards.")

Gwen's nothing anyway. What did she ever accomplish? Nothing. That's why she has to put down anything anyone else accomplishes. It's so easy to sneer. This is the age of the critics. Eunuchs in a harem. Thank you, Brendan Behan. Now there was a man! What would he do in your situation? Leave 'em both. Well, I'm enjoying the best of both. Though maybe enjoying isn't the word. I'm walking a tightrope, Mancini. Yes, give me a man who can make something, I mean, DO! I'd rather be a first class mechanic than the editor-in-chief of the *New York Review of Books*. That bitch. I wonder where she is tonight. I am crazy about her. Gone. Out of control. Yeh, yeh! Well, enjoy it as long as you can, and then one day walk away. That'll teach her who to attack. I'm a bourgeois slob am I? Well, screw you, Sister Kate. Will the real Miss Gwendolyn Hunt stand up and answer this question? What can you do, aside, I mean, from putting people down? I'll answer that. Boff.

("Oooops! Sorry Mrs. Soof. Of course, I'll wait till you play next time before I drop my feeble card. Thank you.")

Your mother too. Boff! She hasn't even got an education. P.S. 69. Then a B.A. from Copulation College, followed by a postgraduate degree sweated out drop by drop from Semen Seminary. Boff! Where does she come off criticizing me?

("Well, I'm sorry Mrs. Soloff. I'm certainly not conveying signals to Florence with my lips. That's just my nervous tic. Haven't you noticed how I keep jumping up and down to go to the bathroom? I'm really awfully sorry, but you've got this all wrong. Really. No, it's nothing serious, but . . . no need to apologize. Thank you.")

Jesus! Am I going to hear about this from Florence!

That's the way the game went. Finally, about eleven-fifteen, when I was dummy again, I got Gwen on the phone, and she sounded all right, faithful and all. Of course, that's when they're not. But she really did sound loving. And she told me where she had gone (a New Wave movie) and with whom (a faggoty hairdresser who tells her all the movie star gossip). And it all sounded plausible, if maybe a little too sincere. You just never know. So I told her to come over tomorrow; I had some work for her to do. And she said o.k., she would, goodnight darling, I love you. I told her I loved her too.

We beat the Soloffs out of some twenty dollars. Florence said, just before she put out the lights, that we were really a pretty good team, and that I could be real good if I'd only concentrate. Again my mind had been somewhere else all evening, she said, but except for that one incident, I had controlled my lips better.

Exhausted by the exhilaration of the contest, Florence slept. But I lay awake and thought about my friend Pat Henderson. Pat, the office joke, hadn't been able to bring himself to break off from his wife. His girl friend worked in the art department, and everyone had advised her to forget about Pat, give him up. Then one day when Pat was in New York for a big client confrontation, he sat down in his room at the Commodore and wrote them both letters.

And he put each letter in the other envelope. That was Pat's hand from outer space.

I was thinking of Pat when I fell asleep.

Next thing I knew I was the man in charge of the dike which was holding back the flood. A huge pile-up, it was, of whatever I could rush to meet the mounting tide of water—planks, old doors, dining room tables and other furniture, some of it oddly familiar, along with all the debris of the deluge—uprooted trees, and the bloated bodies, intertwined, of domestic animals and of people, some of whom I thought I recognized, but had to pass by (I couldn't help them; I was in too much danger myself), and whole houses, askelter, among them the one I used to live in as a kid—the whole piled-up structure rickety to the point where it rose and fell with the heaving weight of water which it couldn't hold back any longer. I could see the waters bursting through here and there, and I'd run to stop a break, barely holding off the imminent collapse, when farther along I'd see another gushing to which I'd have to turn, whispering all kinds of false good news as I ran ("Stop talking to yourself!") and there frantically thrust not my Dutchboy finger, but my whole body's bulk into the rupture, again just managing to hold off the catastrophe, though not for long because there was too much water coming through all up and down the line, and I had nothing left to stop the breaks and didn't know whether to go this way or that ("Stop grinding your teeth!"); it was all going down, down, and down, and I was standing there beaten, in tears, the sounds of disaster on every side of me, and I knew that something more important than my life had been at stake, although I couldn't say in the dream what that was, except that when the dam collapsed, everything did, all hope with it, and I just did manage to throttle the sound that would have vented my shame, a sound that Florence certainly would have heard.

I was awake. I wanted to wake Florence, to tell her everything. Because I couldn't contain the situation any more. I just did catch myself. I had to get up out of bed and walk myself over to the far corner of the room and sit in the chair there. My hand had actually been on her shoulder to shake her. The sight of her face in the immaculate pink of sleep, so trusting and so peaceful, had aroused something that I could call by name, and that was self-disgust at what I was and what I was doing. My whole chicken life had been lived in a terrible straddle, never wholeheartedly for anything, not really with Florence, never really with anyone else. Again I was close to waking Florence. I had to hold myself down in that chair. There was something in me I could barely control, something trying to tear down the whole arrangement by which I lived my life. And I wasn't going to let it, goddam if I was! My body was covered with perspiration, but I wasn't ready for that yet. It was still on me, that impulse, like a dog at my throat, and I was breathing as if I'd just run a mile.

I must have fallen into a kind of sleep again, though there was no boundary of consciousness that I remember crossing. I heard voices like the cries from the streets of revolution. I was huddled in a hotel room, now, the door barricaded with whatever was in the room—anything handy, including some of the flood's debris—and I was waiting alone in the room for the terrible thing to happen, with no way to prevent it. I knew the palace guard had been killed, because the massed voices were coming down the avenue closer and closer, now almost on me. Again I knew that what was at stake was nothing as trivial as this girl or that; it was something about my whole goddam existence, something like the hopes that I had once had for myself, or the thing honor, the thing that's always threatened —honor or my dying self-respect, one of those words you never use now because it seems irrelevant to the way we live our days. Then, heard apart from the clamors of disruption being flung aloft like banners from the burning streets, there was one voice that was closer. Although I recognized it as that of my chief antagonist, it was also the friendliest voice of all. It spoke softly in mournful warning, giving me the news I dreaded, that the compartments could no longer be kept watertight and had burst, and what was coming was now hard on me. I could see the tides had reached where I was; the water was flooding under the door and beginning to fill the room. I was soaking wet, cold and trembling, and Florence was shaking me, trying to wake me, saying, "What are you doing over here, you silly thing, come back to bed, baby. Oh, Ev, dear, I wish you would just see him a few times; he could really help you, he really could, but never mind now, just come back to bed, you're so wet." And she led me back to where I slept the rest of the night without dreams.

When I woke next morning, Florence had already left the house.

I had my breakfast alone. I read the sports page. I drove to the office. There was nothing in the mail. I was my usual cheery, aggressive self. By noon I was back home.

Gwen and I were piecing together what I hoped would be my final draft of the Collier piece. I was getting angry at Gwen. I suspected she was subtly influencing me to go easier on Collier than I was disposed to. I asked her, in the most matter of fact tone, never lifting my eyes off the page I was working over, did she like the piece. Which wasn't a friendly act, because I knew I was forcing her to say something I wouldn't like.

She answered just as impersonally and just as coolly, "No, I don't agree with anything in it." We continued working in silence for a bit. We were both self-trained not to show reactions. But my face was burning. And when she looked at me, I could see she was frightened. She went to the door, closed it, came to me and kissed me, and said, "But I do love you."

What happened next I don't understand, except that you certainly can't call it love; it was more like its opposite. But whatever it was, I went for her, right there in my own study. It was an insane thing to do, because everyone was in the house—Ellen, the two servants, and the man fixing the TV aerial—everyone except Florence. But even if she had been in, it wouldn't have made any difference. And in the middle of it all I thought, am I trying to be found out, do I want to be discovered? Like my friend Pat, who wrote the right letter and put it in the wrong envelope? But all through, I didn't say a word or make a sound. I clasped her blindly, as if our intercourse was the one thing in the world I was sure of.

It happened that Gwen left her marks on my back, not at the shoulders, where she held me with cupped hands, but down at the sides, at my waist, towards the back, where she had held on like death with her nails. There were traces there, when we got through, bleeding a little.

We were both perspiring. Gwen quickly composed herself and resumed typing. But I was too bewildered by what had happened. I grabbed a robe, walked out of the room, out through the house and to the pool, and fell in. I soaked there for a while, the warm water relaxing me. Then I crawled up the side and fell asleep on my face just where I landed.

That is where Florence found me. She came up and saw me and

61

saw—or didn't see—the marks on my back. Barely disturbing my sleep, she went into the house, up the stairs and came on Gwen sitting at the typewriter in my study, using an emery board. Gwen was not aware, for a moment, that Florence was in the doorway, watching as she tested the filed-down nails on her upper arm. Not satisfied, she resumed filing, and it was then, she told me later, that she became aware of Florence. They exchanged pleasantries, and Florence went on down the hall to her room.

By the time I woke and went in for my Gibson, Gwen had left. Florence asked me, in a very offhand way, if I would indulge her in a prejudice. She said Gwen looked like a tramp to her, and she would rather appreciate it if she could do my work at the office. I played it equally offhand and said sure. Then she asked, "She's not working for you much longer, is she?" I said, "She's only on the Chet Collier piece." And I wondered how much Florence knew and what she was thinking. Because if she had seen the marks on my back and put them together with the evidence of the emery board, she should have made a hell of a row.

So I took no chances. I told her that, quite seriously, Gwen was not much of a researcher, and I was glad to say she would be through this coming weekend. Furthermore, if Florence didn't like to have her around the house, I'd see to it that she wasn't ever again. Florence seemed satisfied. Since it was only a few days more, she said, it didn't really matter.

I asked Florence to make me one of those superior Gibsons of hers, figuring if she did, it would be an absolutely reliable good sign. She made me a beauty. I'd squeaked through again.

It was obvious that my days with Gwen were numbered. But I wanted every minute of what time was left. So I was extremely careful. When we got to the beach, I took her much farther out, first to the stretch of sand north of Malibu, and then as far as Zuma, and finally above that to the Ventura coast.

All the dangers she and I were running, and particularly the recognition that our days together would soon be over, made us closer, even more in love. At the end of one long afternoon, a perfect afternoon when the sea was a lake, not the grumpy, dirty Pacific—clear and clean, not full of kelp and refuse—we were out there in the still water up to our waists, standing there, just holding hands, and Gwen looked at me with such love, and with such sadness, and she said, "Eddie, what's going to happen to us?" The water kept moving around us, moving and washing and stirring to remind us that nothing stands still, and nothing human endures, and that our lives are nothing, and that even the sea, in its own history, was not there once, and it too would in time be gone. And I said to her, "Gwen, I need you." And she looked at me so sweetly and said, "I know you do." She smiled at me, and I at her, and we both knew that I hadn't answered her question.

A person doesn't pay recognition to his immortal moments at the time they're happening. But we did that afternoon without knowing it. We took what turned out to be the official photographs. At the time it seemed mostly like a lot of horsing around. I had my Nikon with me, and I put it up on a rock, focused it on her, set the timing device, and than ran around and got into the picture with her. Those first pictures don't look like much, mostly just friends, no real hint of what was going on between us. But towards the end of the roll we did what I imagine many lovers have done when silly-happy. We wanted to immortalize ourselves. I don't know if it was she or I who said something; more likely we didn't need to, either of us. It was spontaneous for us to take off our bathing suits and pose that way together. Each time, I'd run around to make sure of the focus and the exposure and then run back and stand in with her. So we celebrated ourselves, that moment in time, that condition of feeling. Like a nation might issue a memorial stamp to celebrate an important event in its history. Then we did a few funny ones—at least we thought they were funny—my ogling her tits, things like that. She was awfully proud of her tits in those days. I don't think she feels that way now. Tits are temporary, like flowers; they change. I can't remember anyone except Gwen, and Gwen just at that time, who was perfectly proud of her tits. Everyone else I've ever known has thought something wrong. Too "A," too "D," too chesty, too pendulous, too wall-eyed, too cross-eyed, too much nipple, too cherry, always something. I mean the human ego!

Anyway, that afternoon we were in our glory, like two animals in an animal conspiracy against mankind. It never got any better between us after that day.

We had a tough time getting the films developed and printed. She finally got them done by a "member of the sorority," she said. I guess she meant the sorority of the girls who carry-on. This member was a professional photographer. You could tell because the final prints turned out so beautifully. Gwen wouldn't tell me her name. But she sure was good. I asked Gwen what she had thought of me, and she said, "She thought you were o.k. But she thought I looked wonderful." All the girls were envious of Gwen's figure in those days. That's what gave her that bounce when she walked. Gwen didn't need an analyst to build her self-esteem. All she needed was a mirror.

Anyway this carrying-on sorority sister bound up a set handsomely for each of us because, as she said to Gwen, a perfect moment is also a work of art. I kept my set in a drawer, the one that locked, the one where I kept my five hundred dollars get-away money. I guess everyone has such a drawer, one that locks. Everyone except Florence. It was against her code of honor to have secrets in a marriage, so she didn't need a drawer that locked. I know because I looked to see.

I had to have such a drawer. I am a student of my past. Nothing fascinates me as much as the course of my own life. I still have the photograph of the first girl I kissed, the first ad I wrote, and the speech I made at my graduation from the Albert "Zooboo" Leonard Junior High School, the speech called, "Columbus, the First American!" I have, by the ton, photographs, love letters, notes of assignation sacred and profane—all manner of shameful mementos that would have been an embarrassment and a shock to Florence. I kept these locked. Because the very essence of our arrangement was discretion. Don't hurt feelings, and don't upset the home. That above all!

Up until this business, I had handled it all very well. I had kept my whole rebel life locked safely away in that drawer. And I had the psychic equivalent, a compartment in my feelings which I could also lock the moment I entered the house. The compartment was labeled with a motto: "Indifference Saves!" That's the secret as I saw it then, final indifference. The first sign of my slipping was when I fired my harem. It meant that I wasn't indifferent about Gwen. That should have warned me. The next sign was when I went home and cleaned everything that didn't pertain to Gwen out of that drawer. I didn't throw anything away, of course; I tied it all in one big bundle, sealed it, glued it, scotch-taped it, and waxed where the strings crossed. And then I put it in the big metal closet behind Mr. Finnegan's office where I had the other private papers that I didn't want to keep around the house.

So the day I forgot to lock the drawer, the day that our maid, Irene, opened it, all she found was a few notes from Gwen, which gave away very little, and this beautifully printed and beautifully bound collection of beach art, which gave away everything.

I woke up with my head in a fog that morning. (When I was this way in my high school days, my father used to look at me and say "Hey, Shakespeare! Wake up!" Then he'd laugh, shake his head, and look around for a witness to his trouble, and if he found one, he'd point at me and say, "Hopeh-less Case!") From the moment I woke that morning I didn't know what I was supposed to be or do, where to go, what to try, and why pretend. I got up and no one else was up, so I wandered around, made coffee—it tasted bitter—walked around the yard, thought I'd cut the grass, thought I wouldn't, felt I was waiting for something, didn't know what, opened the Los Angeles *Times,* shut it, then just gave up. I sat myself downstairs in our formal parlor, a very dark room, very expensively furnished, sat there in my shorts and my oldest bathrobe, staring straight ahead of me for about an hour. Everything seemed tasteless and unreal, without "tam" as the Jews say, not worth getting up and moving for. Finally, in an effort to revive some sort of appetite, I went upstairs and looked at the official photographs. They made me feel better. So I thought I'd take a shower, and then look at them again. I put the pictures carefully in the drawer but didn't lock it since I was going to be looking at them again in a few minutes. Then I entered the stall and ran the hot water over me for about ten minutes, just standing there with my head bowed. Why do those photographs make me feel better, I wondered. Maybe because at least that is real for me. I may not be what I dreamed I'd be when I was a kid, but at least in that respect I exist. There's the evidence. I got out of the shower, and was singing, and Ellen, hearing me, came in. She looked so fresh and pretty, so goddam hopeful without hoping for anything in particular, just because it was that time of her life, that I decided to have breakfast with her. Which I did. Then we walked the flower paths back of the house. When we came to the pool, it looked like you could drink it, so I stripped to my shorts, she to her bra and panties, and we jumped in. That made me feel wonderful. So before I knew it, I was on my way to see Gwen, which I did often on my way to work, just to start the day right. After which I decided to take the face to Jerry the barber, and let him spoil it with attention and lotions. And as I sat in Jerry's big chair and felt the first hot towel hit me, I thought, my God, I forgot to lock that drawer.

Irene, the maid, must have had quite a moral struggle. She was a fine old girl, happy in the grip of the Abyssinian Baptist Church. Part of the deal with Irene was that somebody had to take her to that Church, way down on Central Avenue, and bring her back every Sunday morning, or else she wouldn't work Sundays. She had high ethical standards. But the most trying kind of moral dilemma is that between two moralities, in this case between honor (it was obviously a private drawer even if it wasn't locked right then; Irene had no business even opening it) and loyalty to her sex, with that number one corollary: keeping husbands on the straight and narrow. Irene must have hesitated about it quite a bit. I didn't know till later what made her decide to give the photographs to Florence. But she did. She was finally convinced it was the right thing to do. I've had a lot of trouble all of my life with people who were doing the right thing.

But Irene didn't know Florence. And mind you, Florence liked the woman. Irene was good at her job and absolutely honest, and maids were, and still must be, hard to find. And Irene was doing right, was on her side, solidly for the home and militantly against husbands who strayed (as her own had, permanently). None of this made a difference. Florence fired her that morning. Told her to pack up and get out, and sent her away in a taxi within the hour. Florence wouldn't have a maid in the house who pried.

After Irene had gone, Florence was left there with the pictures. I guess she must have looked at them hard and long. I rushed home at lunch on some pretext I cooked up. Florence met me at the door, told me that Irene had gone, and why. Then she looked at me. I knew I couldn't get out of this one.

Florence was around the house for a while. I didn't chase her down, because I couldn't think of a damned thing to say. In those photographs, there was no mistaking the look in our eyes, Gwen's and mine. You know that absolutely hostile look a cat gets when it's doing it to another cat? I mean some of those photographs weren't playful. And Florence had to think, just had to: how long since he looked at me that way? And she must have looked at my cock too, had to. In one of those photographs, Gwen was holding it. Now what the hell did I take that picture for? I must have been out of my loving mind.

I heard Florence's car drive away. Dr. Leibman, o.k., I figured. I felt sort of sick, and a little afraid.

So then started an afternoon of what they call agonizing reappraisal. But while I spent those hours doing all that spiritual self-examination, Florence was much more practical. She didn't bother with Dr. Leibman. Not till later. She went straight down to see her lawyer, Arthur Houghton. (Actually, Arthur was our lawyer. But when it came to a crisis, he became hers. He bet the winning horse.) They had a "preliminary discussion." Arthur told her reassuring news about some interesting precedents for divorce settlements. In the light of that discussion, immensely comforting to Florence, it became evident to her that she held a hell of a whip, and that by the time she was done with me, all I'd have left in the way of material possessions would be those same photographs of Gwen and myself, and those only because she didn't want them. Florence's father is the retired president of a New England college (the one I went to) and the senior member of a large WASP law firm which includes Arthur Houghton. Florence said later, in a burst of good humor and over-all confidence, that she had always resented the members of that WASP law firm for looking so much like each other and so little like me. But in the present circumstances, she suddenly found she even liked the way they looked. Anyway, she sure found out she was protected. And that gave her confidence. And accounted for the startling change in her attitude next time I saw her.

I didn't go back to the office that afternoon. I didn't call Gwen to tell her the news either. I just sat by the side of the pool and said to myself that perhaps the moment I'd been waiting for all these months was now here. Of course! No Italian, no Spaniard, certainly no Frenchman would give up his home, his life's savings, and his wife for a piece of tail. And no Greek, ancient or modern, would discommode himself in the least for any such trifle, no matter how succulent. The Greek would simply accept the fact that a man had to give up a lot of things in life to hold on to the main thing. Then I fell asleep.

I was enjoying my nap by the pool and no dreams, when I became aware of Florence standing over me. I purposely stayed half asleep, because I wasn't ready for a confrontation. But she had a drink in her hand, always a good sign, and it was my favorite, a bony

Gibson. She put it down on the little table next to the pool-side recliner. And she said softly, "Dinner will be in half an hour, darling, and I think the new maid's cooking is going to be just wonderful!" Then she walked away.

What the hell was going on? I'd expected her to be carrying a baseball bat, not a Gibson. Would Gwen have done that? Never. So I went to the house and made me another—a beaut, double stiff. Then I thought, since this may be my last dinner in this house, I'll get real dressed up. I went upstairs to the bedroom. There I saw the development.

We had a large sofa against the foot of the bed. Florence had fixed it to sleep on. She was just coming out when I came in, and I said in the tone of a child's protest, "Am I supposed to sleep on that?" She said, "Of course not, darling. I'm sleeping there."

Whatever had happened between her and Arthur Houghton and during her later visit to Dr. Leibman, the result was tonic. The meal that night turned into a kind of celebration.

We did fall into luck with the new cook. Florence had been clever enough to tell her to make her own favorite dishes. Well, this cook, another portly Negro matron, had just spent twenty years with a Jewish family. What she prepared that night was sauerbraten, potato pancakes, red cabbage, and applesauce. Oh my! With it we had a Burgundy which Florence selected and I opened and poured tenderly. Candles were lit. And the hi-fi played Strauss.

Ellen, who ate with us, must have known there was a crisis. But I think what gave her that puzzled look was how it was being played out. For Florence had class. She carried it off as if life has its ups and downs, and the downs have to be combated, not given in to. She was going to make life as pleasant as possible during this painful period.

I couldn't make out what Ellen thought, or felt. Her date arrived right in the middle of dessert, and Ellen, when she saw him, seemed very relieved. She came over to me, kissed me good night, and then looked at me rather strangely, as if she wanted to say something but couldn't just then. She ran out without kissing Florence. In the spirit of the evening, I tried to cover this. "I think she's having some kind of trouble with her boy friend," I said. But Florence hadn't noticed. She had eyes only for our trouble.

If nature and society ever turned out a woman without connivance, contrivance, or any psychological curves—a troubled woman, yes, but straight and true no matter how troubled—that woman was Florence. The only way you can finally judge a person is how they behave under stress, especially when they're hurt. That night, with the blood still flowing from the big wound she had suffered that morning, and the terrible knots of pain still in her stomach, Florence showed her class.

We were sitting in the parlor having Drambuie and green mints. She had lit my cigar, thin and long, and she was blowing her uninhaled cigarette smoke up to the ceiling, and there was silence for a while. Then quite deliberately she took my hand, and smiled at me with the simplest friendship. I suddenly felt much love for her. It seemed that her first impulse was to be understanding of my pain. And to give me time to collect myself. What she said was, "Why don't you go to bed now, darling, and get a good night's sleep? You must be exhausted. And I think you'll sleep much better tonight. I don't think you'll grind your teeth tonight, or talk to yourself, because now there's nothing to hide, is there? Go on. We'll talk tomorrow maybe, or maybe in a day or two. Go on."

And I decided to do just that. I was damned grateful for her concern and for her generosity. As I went up the stairs I thought: you still haven't called Gwen, you haven't talked to her since morning, and if you wait till tomorrow before you talk to her, well you know that bitch, it's just possible she won't be there by then. All she needed was the slightest hiatus, and all the outrageous and unfair and humiliating things about our arrangement would come home to her. She would be on the next plane east.

The hell with it, I thought. This is my life at stake. I'm not going to be rushed. I'm going to go my own way, in my own time, and let everyone else go their own way in their own time. In fact the first thing I'm going to do is take a bath. I had a shower before dinner, and now I'm going to take a long, long hot bath.

I loaded it with salts. Florence laid out a fresh pair of pajamas. I really took my time. When I finally came out, there was Florence sitting in the *chaise longue,* smoking a cigarette, uninhaled, and watching CBS Reports on our bedroom television. As soon as I came in, however, she pressed the remote control button and killed the program. And we were alone. Completely.

Then she spoke, ever so gently. "Quite frankly, darling, my impulse when I first saw you was to simply bash you one. I could have killed you. But it always helps to let just a little time pass and talk to a few people you trust . . ." She went on to tell me about what Arthur Houghton had said, and what Dr. Leibman had said. I heard some of it. But the reason I stopped really listening was that I saw she was treating me like a "sick" person, handling me gingerly, the way you do someone who's off his rocker or about to go and with whom you have to watch every step. She was right! I had been behaving like an insane person. When I tuned her back in, she was saying, "So I thought, it hurts, it hurts like hell, but it's Evans who has the problem, not me. And then so much was suddenly clearer to me, all your talking to yourself, and your poor old teeth grinding, oh dear! And I felt so sorry for you, because you're obviously not responsible for what you do any more, not really. I knew who it was you hated when you said in your sleep, 'I hate her!' That is the one thing that gives me the most hope. It is she, isn't it? I don't mean to quiz you" (she was handling me so gingerly); "I know you hate to be quizzed, but just answer that one question, and I won't ask another all night long."

I said, "Yes, it was her I meant when I said, 'I hate you.' "

"Of course," said Florence, "so I know something of what's happening inside you. There's your nightcap, darling, right by the bed. I know how hard it must be to be in bed with your old wife and quite possibly yearning for another woman. I've often thought that, when I've watched you lying on your back there" (I was on the bed by then), "looking up at the ceiling, your lips moving. You remember the night you were aroused. I knew it wasn't for me. Well . . . I don't think you should be quizzed and badgered tonight. Or tomorrow, either, or for a while maybe. I *know* what tremendous pressure you've been under. And finally, dear, not now, but finally you will have to make a decision. Because it's very simple isn't it, as simple as her or me? I know how hard it is for you to make a decision, but I'm afraid you will have to this time. For, after all, I have to make a life, if not with you, then with . . . some other kind of a life."

She took a long drag of her cigarette, looked diagonally up at the ceiling, blew out the smoke she had not inhaled, and said, "Darling, when it first hit me, you know, the photographs and all they implied" (she was tucking me in), "I was very, very angry. Are you comfortable? Yes. Good! But I'm not angry now."

She walked away and spoke from the bathroom. "I'm not angry, because you've had to bear it all alone, without anyone to help you, and no one to talk to about it. That's what Dr. Leibman called to my attention when I saw him this afternoon. So you see he's really not against you. He's really on your side. I can see now what he saw months and months ago. 'Think of him as sick,' he said. Oh, I know that word has bad connotations, none of which I mean. Think of it as a gentle word, expressing true concern on the part of your friends. It's even a loving word—just a little sick—you see how it can sound?"

She looked out around the edge of the bathroom door. She was undressing now, and smiled and said, "I want to help you." And then she pulled her head back. She had smiled her simplest, warmest, and most civilized smile. I wondered how could anyone be like that. I mean after having seen those pictures that very morning.

She continued from the bathroom: "One of the most damaging and deluding notions people have is that they can carnally love only one person at a time." She pushed her head around the corner of the bathroom door and she was naked now. The main light was off in the bathroom; only the tiny blush pink dressing lamp was on, and Florence looked—well, just as she would hope to look. And she went on, "People in our western Christian tradition profess to believe that you truly love only one person carnally at a time. Is it possible that your tradition, the more pagan tradition, is the more honest one? And that people in our society" (all this from the bathroom, a faucet running, turned off) "profess one way, and actually live another way?" She put her head out for a moment, then a little more, and as she stood there, waiting for my answer, I realized how long it had been since I had seen her naked, that I had rather avoided seeing her naked, perhaps out of some involuted loyalty to Gwen. She smiled at me confidently and disappeared from sight again. Her breasts—which I had not looked at for quite a while—were larger than Gwen's. And she was continuing from the bathroom: "For instance, I can't be with you now. And I don't think, despite your tradition and different background, you can with me. Oh, you've tried, but it hasn't been the real thing for quite a while, has it? I mean I've known you were elsewhere. You're too honest, darling, to successfully disguise anything as important as that."

Now she came back, dressed in a nightgown, one she knew I liked, no lace on it or any of that peek-a-boo nonsense, nothing fancy about the hems or trimmings, no please-untie-me straps or ribbons, just a woman in an envelope of beautiful light cloth, not too long, not too tight, walking in my direction. "I must tell you," she said, "that both Arthur Houghton and Dr. Leibman advised me most strongly, one from the legal point of view and the other from the medical and psychic point of view, that I should definitely not sleep in the same room with you tonight and preferably not in the same house. Nonsense, I said, he's a human being. And he's still my husband. I said 'for better or worse' once, and I meant it. But forgive me" (she had stopped at the sofa) "if tonight I simply can't come any closer."

She got into the bed she had made for herself on the sofa, and I lay on my back in our bed, and didn't say a word. Then I heard her weeping. Not loud, because Florence is tasteful in everything. But the pain came out as it had to.

"Florence," I said.

"Oh, it's nothing, darling," she said, "it's just that I was thinking what to do and I thought: well, I'll wait for him to make up his mind, to choose, no matter how long it takes. And then I thought, after all, I'm human, and after a while I may have to have some human warmth too. I can see from those photographs, despite their vulgarity, that you do have a close relationship with this tramp—excuse me, darling, I didn't mean to say that, but only that I'll wait as long as I can. I'll do my best. I will, I promise you that. By the way, how do you get photographs like that developed and printed?"

"She has a darkroom," I lied. I couldn't tell the truth, because Florence would worry about other people having seen the stuff.

"Who does?"

"Gwen."

There was a silence, and after a while I could hear her crying softly. I thought how difficult her code of fairness was in these circumstances, and how fine her effort was to live up to her code now. She cried a while, there alone on the sofa, and there was so much longing in the sound, so much hunger.

Well, it had to happen. She didn't mean a seduction, I'm sure. But that woman's need, and that goddam effort of hers to behave correctly as she would hope and expect herself to behave by her code of fairness and civilization and WASP tradition—that did get to me. I doubt that any man with a heart could lie there and not answer need as strong and pure as that. Those tears were her hope of life running out.

In the middle of it she said, "Evans, Evans, what's going to happen to us?" I said, "We're going to be all right, darling." And I meant it.

Later she said, "Evans, what do you want of me?" I said, "You, darling, I want you."

All that time I was passionate and aroused. Somebody should study the connection between sex and pity. It was the closest we had been in years. And afterwards, while I was thinking what a mess I was (directly after it was over I had begun to wonder what Gwen was doing; I hadn't called her all day), Florence, who had fallen asleep, revived, and as we lay there as we used to with her leg over mine and her head on my shoulder, she spoke lovingly: "You see, Evans, I know that finally you'll come to your senses. What we have together is just too much to give up. You must see that. All this has happened before to millions of couples." She kissed the side of my face and smiled. "So people have worked out a way to deal with a situation of this kind. That's what civilization is, darling, these tried and true forms. There is one for this situation we are in. I will continue to be your wife; I know there is now going to be an interval, but I have faith that it's going to be temporary. All I have to do is to take one look at those photographs, and I can see that she is an absolute tramp, darling, forgive me. I know that one day you will see, like by a flash of lightning, what everyone else can see now by just looking at her. I mean, she's not in your class, Evans, poor dear Evans, it's really so silly, all this, but if I don't see you through this, what will I ever see you through? Only try to let me know soon, won't you? Soon? So all right. Let's say we have an arrangement, all right. I never thought I could, but—only, Evans please, Evans." She fell asleep for an instant, then, "Please, Evans . . . Evans . . . what you truly want, see her if that's what you truly . . . Oh, I don't know what I'm saying. Don't see her is what I mean. Don't love her. Love me."

I said I didn't want to, that it was all over, that it was completely over.

She looked up at me, raising her head off my shoulder, and said, "You don't have to say that." And she smiled at me. "But it's nice to hear, and I hope it's true. Anyway, it was nice tonight? Wasn't it, Ev? Like the old days?"

"Yes," I said, "like the old days!"

She kissed me, smiling a little wickedly, as if now it was she who was stealing someone else's fellow. And then as happy as I'd seen her for a long, long time, she fell asleep, smiling like a bride.

4

F LORENCE had fallen into a fine sleep, but I lay there as if I'd been hit on the head. I was at the top of a psychic slalom, beginning to go down, but with no way of anticipating how fast and how irreversible the descent would become. I didn't yet know that there are no markers—and only very short distances—between what is called normal behavior and what is labeled mental illness. I've since come to believe that both these labels are useless. There are only human beings in various developing conditions, all continuations of what has been there all along unnoticed.

That night with Florence was my first experience with the true dilemma of "both." I'm not talking about an arrangement, the technique of keeping one woman in place while you temporarily carry on with another. What struck me as I lay and listened to Florence's even breathing was that both acts, the one with Gwen on my way to work that morning and the one with Florence, while coming hard upon each other, seemed perfectly natural and oddly equal. That shocked me. Not the fact that I had had sexual relations with two women on the same day—I had often done that and never felt a qualm. But I had made a genuinely loving connection with two different women, one right after the other, and I was not prepared by my training and tradition to believe that possible.

I couldn't lie there any longer with Florence's head on my shoulder and her leg over mine. Ever so gently I began to extricate myself. I didn't want more talk with Florence right then, so I was very careful not to wake her. She murmured a few times as I disentangled myself. Then she was again safely asleep, and I was out in the hall.

I wanted to go down and brew myself some coffee, but I heard Bartok. That meant that Ellen and her boy friend Roger were down there with the lights off. So I couldn't go down. I wonder how far they went. Bartok was coming to one of his half-assed climaxes. I wondered if they were, too. No. Florence had assured me just a couple of weeks ago that Ellen was intact.

Anyway, they were doing something, because I couldn't hear their voices. I sat on the steps. I didn't want to go back in the bedroom, and I couldn't go downstairs, so I sat there.

The human cock, I reflected, is the most honest part of man. I guess the human cunt is the same, though I'm considerably less sure of that. The cock I know more about. The great thing about it, the thing that makes it so completely moral, is that it doesn't pretend to any morality.

For instance, I thought, the cock would never use the words "ought to." And never the word "should." Right there, what a load to lose! All the Bird knows is "I want." Or, to be more exact, *"Now* I want." None of that forever-and-ever shit. Which has brought more people to early decay than any other sentiment. As well as to destructive acts against their fellow men and women. Most evil is done in the name of good.

I WANT!

Come to think of it, that phrase, "I want," expressed precisely the humanness I had lost. I simply didn't know what I wanted any more. I couldn't make a choice; I was swamped in unresolved boths. I was not doing anything for the simple reason that I wanted to. The simple, pure, direct, human, downright babyish "I want"—where had that gone?

Long lost. I sat there on the top of those steps and thought, long gone. I'd lost the knack. I'd killed the gift. I didn't know what I wanted any more. I felt only that I *must* do this and *should* do that, and I was *expected* to do such and such, and it was my *duty* to perform this-a-way and my *obligation* to see this thing through, and it was demanded of me to *fulfill*—always—what other people wanted of me. I didn't even know whether I wanted Gwen any more. I hadn't called her up, thought I should, had no expectation I would, thought it might be too late if I did, hoped it would, was anxious that it should not be, and so on.

The worst of it was a whole other set of imperatives that I had allowed myself to become subject to. These were the Expedients. Again not what I wanted, but what was useful at a certain time in any situation. "Expedient." The word written on the tomb of our generation. They did what was expedient.

Especially me.

But just plain, raw, meat-handed I WANT? What had happened to that? Long gone!

Those shoulds. They kill you, those shoulds.

Well, to go back to Peter. One-eye Dick is free of shoulds. And oughts. And all the troubles deriving therefrom. The Erect One has one eye on top of his head; he sights what he wants, takes aim, and charges straight for it. In the spirit of the great Teddy Roosevelt, he calls for all forces to get behind him and charge the hill. And the body, recognizing Tumescent Teddy's pure want, gets behind him and charges with all it's got.

Here's another thing I respect about the Joint. You can't quite make him get up and pretend. If he doesn't want to, you can beat him and scold him, but he won't go. El Conquistador will lie there and sulk. A soft-on is a reproach to its owner. It says, you're lying, kid. Later, when the false occasion has passed into history, the Member will sit up and look around, then stand up pretty as a tulip and say, like the comedian, "Wha' Hoppen??"

Not that the Root has to want a *lot*. But it has to genuinely want some. On the one hand he doesn't need, nor does he fall for, that no-one-but-you shit. His point of view on that subject might be expressed thus: Quote. You neurotic son of a bitch, why must you pretend or require that all desire be perfect, complete, and forever? Or the greatest? The girls made up that "forever" shit and that "greatest" shit and that "only-you" shit over the centuries to protect their fading years. You can't blame the girls for that. Their fading is fast. But why do you pretend? Close quote.

Now they say a stiff prick has no conscience. But let's face it. It's the honest part of us all, men. And the most democratic. It doesn't differentiate between rich and poor, and it draws no color line. Our brothers in our southern states profess to draw the color line everywhere. But Big Peter never went along with that color line, and there are millions of witnesses to that.

Old One-eye, like all pure things, tends to be naïve. And wherever you find something pure and naïve, you also find someone trying to corrupt it. So the Mindless One is often the unconscious tool (and victim) of the corrupt mind and spirit of the person to whom he is attached. Men try to use their better part in so many different ways they shouldn't. To put girls down, to put other men down, to show off, to bully, to compete, to make up for defeats in other arenas, to revenge themselves, to collect scalps, and one of the worst, to satisfy idle curiosity. God knows there are hundreds of variations of perversion. Like the very ethical, very famous public figure I know who could do it to his wife only when she was asleep. We take out so many of our sicknesses through our Little Friend. But you can't finally corrupt the Shiny-Headed One. He will come back, see something he wants, and just naturally go for it. What could finally be more innocent?

With Florence that night, Peckerstiff was more honest, more gallant, more kind, and more human than I was prepared to be. He felt for Florence, responded to her clear and urgent need. And where my mind was all messed up with conflicts and blocks, the Bird found his nest, didn't pretend he was going to stay there forever, but entered, dispensed his grace, and left to rest. Love and kindness are the finest mixture.

Downstairs the music had changed. I figured Ellen's intellectual boy friend had gone home. The instant he's out of the house, Ellen reverts. Out come my old jazz classics, and out comes Ellen herself.

I tiptoed down the stairs. I wanted to make damned sure that Roger had gone. I didn't feel like being patronized and disapproved of right then. I looked from the back of the dining room through the dark pantry and into the brightly lit kitchen. There was Ellen, dancing by herself, bump bump on one side, then bump bump on the other. I was dead certain she was alone, because she had an enormous piece of chocolate cake in her face. And she was enjoying it to beat hell. Neither the watusi nor the chocolate cake are images she presents to Roger.

I watched her from the dark, and suddenly she seemed to be aware that someone was there. She stopped, and peered, not seeing me, but attentive and still as a deer. Those were the days of the Brentwood rapes, twelve of them within three months, and the man still loose. All those rape jokes were making the circuit. Ellen looked scared. She walked towards me. Suddenly she screamed. I didn't move, perverse son of a bitch. Then she saw it was me, and said,

"Oh, Daddy," ran into my arms, and there was chocolate icing all over me. I saw she was crying, and had been, I suppose, as she did the frug and ate the chocolate cake. I said, "What did he do to you? I'll kill that son of a bitch."

"Who?" asked Ellen.

"The brain," I said.

She burst out laughing. I asked her what she was laughing at, and she said, "Because you hate him so."

"I don't hate him," I said. "I do have a certain dislike for him."

"Oh, Daddy, don't be so noble. I wouldn't like it if you weren't jealous."

Then I saw that Ellen had been drinking. I went over and had a taste, and it was vodka, straight, which is o.k., I suppose, but she was high as hell, high enough to mix Bavarian chocolate cake with vodka. The young have stomachs.

Suddenly she said, "Oh God, I can't go through this any more. I'm going to tell you."

"If it's about Roger," I said, "don't tell me."

She laughed again, this time the vodka definitely showing—eighteen years old she was—and she said, "It's not about Roger. It's about you." Then she said, "Don't be sore at me, Daddy. I can't stand it when you're sore at me."

I said, "Baby, why should there be anything you can't tell me?"

She said, "Wait till you hear what it is." She hoisted herself up on the kitchen counter, lay down on her side, her woman's hips, I noticed for the first time, raised higher than her chest. "Promise me you won't be sore at me."

"I won't," I said, "I really won't."

"You will be," she said, and proceeded to tell me. And I did get angry.

Irene, the maid, had come to her with the photographs of Gwen and me, and Ellen, of course, had told her to put them right back where she'd found them. But later Ellen had this impulse, and said, "Show them to my mother." Which Irene did.

"What the hell did you go and do that for?"

"Guess I was wrong," she said. "But you looked so goddam happy with that girl. And, Daddy, you always look so miserable with Mum. Even when you're smiling at each other. From the first time I ever had a thought about anything except my toys and candy and things like that, from the day that I thought of Mum and you as two separate people, I wondered why you stayed together."

"There are reasons," I said.

"There's only one reason," she said. "Me. I've seen you with Mum all my life, and I never saw you look at her that way. You'd put your arm around her and all that, especially when you knew I was looking. And I know you hold hands when you sleep. But I'm talking about the real thing, like those pictures. I was shocked first, I admit that, because a couple of them are downright obscene. But when I looked at them again, I saw how—gee, she's pretty, she really is. And I began to think, he's going to give that up some day soon on account of me. I didn't want to do anything to hurt Mum, much as I love you. But I'm sick of it, Daddy. Like I told Roger tonight, is this it, that marvelous thing we read about, that the poets tell us is so temporary that we mustn't lose a breath of it? Old Roger, he and I were squabbling tonight like an old married couple, and I said, goddam it, Roger, go away, just go away. We have all the disadvantages of marriage and none of the advantages. I got so angry with him that I threw his Bartok out the window. It's still out there, except he's so neat he probably picked it up before he drove off."

My curiosity took over: "Have you ever made love to Roger? Really, I mean?"

"No."

"Well, I'm sort of glad."

"It's not me. It's him. He won't."

"I mean I'm glad you're still . . ."

"Oh, Daddy, that's only something I tell Mummy. I've been with quite a few boys. I go to Radcliffe after all, haha. Daddy, did you really think that?"

"Does Roger know?"

"Roger! He's my going-steady fellow, I couldn't tell him. But I'm eighteen, Daddy, and sometimes—like the books say—I have very strong urges. Don't you know it! Anyway, the minute Roger got out of here, I put on all those old Dixieland 78's of yours. I'm careful of them, don't worry. I listened to them and thought, that's the way Daddy once was. So what happened, do you know, Daddy? I love those old 78's. Roger hates them. Only Miles Davis for him. He says the rest of that stuff is white."

"What does that mean?"

"The way white men like to think a Negro is—you know, sort of primitive and bestial. That annoyed me, too. I said, you mean to tell me you are not white? You creep! Get out of here. And I really went after him. You don't fight me and you don't love me. Except I didn't say love. So what's the point of it? Get out, I said, get out. Give me another sip of that vodka; come on, Daddy, it's late now, and a little more will just make me sleep. Thank you. A series of petty squabbles, when the whole world is out there waiting. And that's how I felt that day with Irene; I suddenly said, 'Show it to her. Smash it up!' Scared hell out of Irene. Then Mum had to fire her of course. But I'm going to send her money till she gets another job.

"Afterwards I was watching you two at dinner. I couldn't see where anything had happened. You were just like before. No signs of life. But I thought, Daddy's not that way; he's got life in him yet, like those 78's just a little, maybe, but some. That's why I came over and kissed you before I went to the movies. Then right in the middle of 'Wild Strawberries' I had this terrible thought. I remembered those photographs, and I thought, now *they* could have children."

Ellen was an adopted child. Florence and I had taken her on when it became clear we couldn't have our own. We did the usual tests with the best doctor, the tubes, the smears and specimens, the semen count, and all the rest of it, and he said looks bad but keep trying, you never can tell. So we did, but nothing happened. I guess it's Florence—well, I know it is. I once knocked up a TV actress, and once the wife of my best friend. Both had abortions. But I didn't tell that to Florence. I just went through that whole test rigamarole with her.

"You mad at me, Daddy?" I had been silent.

I didn't answer. I looked at Ellen. An adopted child starts out as if she's your own. One day she takes your thumb and puts her whole hand around it and you fall in love. You forget she's not yours. You're just gone! From then on it's what's good for the kid that decides everything you do. You forget Europe and Asia and Africa; you spend your summers in a place where the kid will have playmates. And, God, I did love Ellen, all through her babyhood, and her young girlhood, and her teens. But starting maybe when she was seventeen, she suddenly began to look like *not* our kid, like a stranger had gotten into our house by some mistake. And the terrible thing was that this made a difference. We looked just the same to her, Daddy and Mummy, but she looked different to me. That night as I looked at her, she looked older, and, I'm embarrassed to say, coarser than I had ever seen her.

"Anyway, what I want to say to you, Daddy, is don't do it any more for me. I don't want to be the reason you stay together."

Silence.

"Because," she went on, "when you think of the whole world for its possibilities, all that could be, Daddy, isn't it a shame?"

I didn't say a thing. Now she came off the counter and put her arms around me.

"Why don't you go with that girl? She makes you happy."

"Ellen," I said, "I don't think anyone really knows what's best for another person. And you really don't know a damned thing about your mother and me, not a damned thing."

She washed out the glass, so there wouldn't be any evidence.

"Ellen," I said, "I'm not angry at you."

She kissed me on the cheek and said, "O.K., Dad." But she sounded heartsick.

She left me alone in the kitchen. I had some Bavarian chocolate cake. Sweets comfort me.

I walked in and out of the rooms, and finally I went to the phone and dialed Gwen's number.

"Hello," I said.

"Eddie, did you have an accident?"

"No. Did I wake you?"

"Are you kidding? What time is it?"

"About four."

"Something happened?"

"Yeah, but I can't talk now."

"Something with Florence?"

"Yeah, I've got a problem."

"Oh."

"I can't see you for a few days. I'll phone you about it tomorrow. O.K.?"

"O.K."

"I'm going to hang up now."

She didn't speak.

"But I want to have a real talk with you tomorrow. I got a problem."

She didn't speak. I said goodbye and hung up.

There was always the danger, in that kind of call, that Florence might pick up the extension upstairs.

When I phoned Gwen from the office the next morning, the girl at the switchboard told me that she'd taken the plane to New York.

That afternoon, there was a telegram at the office: "Now you have no problem." Dateline New York. No signature.

I couldn't keep my mind on Zephyr cigarettes. I went up to my office, and Sylvia, my secretary, told me that Mrs. Anderson had called and said I'd find a note at home. That sounded a little ominous. But whatever it meant, I didn't feel like doing anything about it right then. I felt like sitting there. I made a sling shot out of a rubber band, straightened out a lot of paper clips, and began to shoot. I shot at the Zephyr ads; I shot quite a number at the pictures of myself with various celebrities, scoring heavily. I spared Florence and Ellen. I shot the real heavy clips at the autographed pictures of Mr. Finnegan. Then I turned and began to shoot out of the window at mankind in general. I didn't realize till she cleared her throat that Sylvia was watching.

"What is it, Sylvia?"

"Well . . . may I suggest that you take off the rest of the afternoon?"

"Why?"

"Well . . . Mrs. Anderson . . ."

"What did she say?"

"Well, nothing in particular, but she—"

"Now, Sylvia, let's not play games. You know she said a lot in particular that you're not telling me, isn't that so?"

"Oh, no, sir, only . . ."

"Get Mrs. Anderson on the phone for me."

"I can't—"

"You know where she is; get her on the phone, Sylvia."

"You can't speak to her right now, Mr. Anderson. She's in her car, on the road."

"In other words, you do know where she is."

"Mr. Anderson, if you think I like the position I'm in, between you and Mrs. Anderson, you are very mistaken—"

"I do think you like it, and I am not very much mistaken, and I will follow your advice and go home and read her note."

All the note said was, "I've gone to the Springs for a few days. Will be at the Bennetts." No love.

The new maid knew nothing, except the lady had said she'd be away for a few days, but would call her each day in the morning to tell her what to prepare for me that night. Tonight it was going to be one of my favorites: tamale pie.

Every once in a while there is a miracle in southern California. The day turns raw and wet like real weather. It reminds you of the East, and makes you feel something, all different things—nostalgia, sorrow, like working, like leaving town—but something! That miracle happened that day. There was a cool, wet wind blowing, and it reminded me of New England. It even blew leaves into our pool. I hadn't realized those trees shed.

The bad weather also made me feel mean, which is to say, human. It isn't really human or natural for us to feel optimistic all the time, or to pretend to be friendly all the time, or to like anybody most of the time, or to get along with our fellow humans. It's natural, I think, to be unfriendly and selfish and mean and ornery and involved only with our own problems. The most unnatural sound I know in the world is the voice of the telephone operator in the Beverly Hills Hotel. It is always friendly!

Olga Bennett's voice, when I finally got her, was excessively cheery. In the background, there were sounds of conviviality. Girls, happily without husbands, were having cocktails.

"What are you drinking?" I asked Florence when she got on.

"A Bloody Mary," she said.

"Made with husband's blood?"

"Evans, we're feeling very charitable and loving towards the whole human race. Even husbands!"

"What happened?" I asked.

"Just hold it a moment, dear, won't you, I'll take it on the extension." I heard some byplay and chatter, and Olga got back on and said, "Evans . . . she'll be right on," and then, "You better be good to Florence, do you hear?" From which it was clear that Florence had told her the whole story. At that moment Florence lifted the extension phone, and Olga said in this real cute voice, "I'm gettin' off! Love you both!" and hung up.

Before Florence could say a thing, I said, "What did Leibman say?" I knew who the villain was.

"Oh, you know," said Florence, "he never says anything. He sat there and looked at me and smiled, which was just wonderful because it put everything in proportion. But then he did ask, 'What do you have in mind exactly?' and by now I know that when he's elliptical he's trying to make me think. So I was silent a long time, and finally he said only this one thing—that we don't yet know what the solution is, but we can have considerable doubt that the kind of rapprochement we had last night is a genuine rapprochement. Do you understand, Evans?"

"And then he told you to go to the Springs?"

"No, that was my idea. Olga's been asking me, you know that, and when I woke up this morning, I was furious, not with you, with myself. And although Dr. Leibman didn't really say anything, I know him well enough by now to say confidently that he was furious with me, and just a little disgusted, maybe!"

"Too bad about him."

"Evans, if we do have a chance, it's for you to go to Dr. Leibman. Otherwise, I really don't think we have a chance."

I didn't answer that.

"Evans?"

"I'm here."

"That's not his idea, mind you. He doesn't need any more patients, nor does he make a practice of taking both wife and husband. It's my idea. Evans?"

"I'm here."

"I won't say I insist now, because I want you to finally go there only because you want to. But I will say this, that what happened between us last night represents no real change. It's time for us to do some very basic rethinking about our relationship. I think we could have a fine life together, but as Dr. Leibman said, I must never, never think I can't get along without you. Because that isn't so. I can. And rather than ever be humiliated that way again, Dr. Leibman said, we—"

"He seems to have done quite a lot of talking."

"Evans, there's really no point to sarcasm, and furthermore your hostility is—"

"Say listen, Florence, I thought I'd go away for a while, maybe a week, to New York, see my father and mother, and see Collier once more and . . ."

That was the first I'd heard of that. I hadn't planned to say that.

"I think that's a very good idea," said Florence. "You'd get away from us both that way and . . ."

"That's right," I said.

Don't model your sons after me.

"And you can have a chance to . . ."

"Think," I said helpfully.

"That's right. Evans, I've been doing a lot of thinking. On the way down here I almost had an accident. My mind was wandering, and suddenly there I was on the wrong side of Highway 94. That jolt was just what I needed. I remembered Dr. Leibman's words, 'You must never say to yourself you can't live without him.' "

Dr. Leibman was a presence in my life.

I suppose I was going to New York out of some sort of pique at him. Because I found it hard to go once I was alone in the house. Ellen had gone with Roger to the Bergman Festival at the Fine Arts again, and I had a tamale pie all to myself. Later I sat in the living room drinking. I had called up and made a reservation on the eleven o'clock plane, but I wavered a lot, drinking and wavering. Florence had this picture of herself, framed in silver, in which her eyes looked particularly fine—large, luminous, decent, and kind, full of pain and trouble she would not inflict on the rest of the world. I looked at this picture and at Florence, at her nose with its high bridge and its judicial austerity (I guess I never forgave her that her great-grandfather's brother had been on the Supreme Court). Then I examined her forehead—high, clean, clear of any hair; it was brushed straight back. Florence had no flirt in her. And I thought she had only turned so completely to Dr. Leibman because she couldn't to me.

I remembered all the things she had done for me, the support she had given me when I was just starting, the loyalty and patience she had squandered on my behalf, the awful things I had done to her, and how she had seen me through all of it, all of it, for twenty years. She deserves honesty, I thought, deserves to know where she stands, and what she can expect. In other words she deserves a husband.

Then I had a thought that surprised me. Dr. Leibman is absolutely right to tell her that she can get along without me, because she might just have to. I went over and kissed her photograph as you might an icon. The photograph, which was smiling, said, "What's that for?" and I said in my controlled-drunken voice, "Just because." Then I took an oath that I would act as her friend, and give her what a friend should—the truth. If I couldn't save myself, if I was too far gone, at least she could save herself. I packed a bag, called a taxi, and just barely made the eleven o'clock.

I was stoned when I got on the plane, and after one drink the stewardess wouldn't give me another. That had never happened to me before. It was a bumpy trip. During the worst of it, when the plane was tossing like a twenty-foot outboard off Montauk Point, I thought we were going to break apart, and I wouldn't have cared if we had.

The next morning I was operating out of the Algonquin again. I told the magazine people that the piece was turning out well, but that I had to see Chet Collier once more. They said fine, fine, which meant that they'd pick up the tab for the plane. That was now important to me. After that, I did nothing for the rest of the day except wander around the city looking for her. I had left home without anything to read, so I bought a book about the sexual customs of primitive civilizations, just to see, I suppose, if this would shed any light. I discovered that among the Papuans, when a man reaches forty-five, he can behave sexually as he pleases without censure. I suppose they figure he won't be around much longer, so forgive him any and all aberrations, tolerance being due a man who has lived that long. Thus fortified, I continued my search, now in Greenwich Village, in her favorite hangouts, and about midnight, looking into the windows of a coffee shop called The Figaro, I saw her, sitting with a group, but not part of them.

She finally saw me. She continued to sit there for a few moments, giving no sign, no longer looking towards me. Then I saw that she was excusing herself, complaining, from her pantomime, of being weary. I walked off down the street, so that I would be out of the line of vision, and there, presently, she joined me.

Her first words were, "I've missed you." I'd seen that as soon as I'd seen her.

She was living at the Chelsea temporarily, she started to explain, while looking for a permanent— Then she broke off. We were silent. There was nothing we cared to talk about.

We stood on the dark pavement of that side street, not looking at each other. A cab came along. I put her into it, got in myself, and said to the driver, "The Chelsea." Gwen gave no sign. We didn't speak on the way, didn't embrace, sat side by side, like two condemned people.

Her room was exceedingly small. We slammed into each other, overpowering every reluctance. We made sure we didn't have the time nor, later, the energy to think, not once through that long night.

When she finally fell asleep, I held the length of her body, head to thigh. I'd fall asleep, only to start awake and quickly reassure myself she was still there.

When I woke in the morning, she was up and dressed, and she said she had made up her mind to quit me. She didn't explain, and I didn't ask for explanation.

Clearly she was looking for a way to break off—not geographically or verbally, but in fact—to smash the thing within herself so it would be over forever.

I asked her—halfheartedly—why we couldn't continue as we had been.

She said, "If I were a strong girl, I could go on that way. But I'm not that strong any more."

By then I was fighting for days, for hours. I'd have told her anything to hold on to her for another week. I would have sold my soul for another month.

I told her I was going to see Collier, a final interview, to check certain points, and asked if she'd come along.

She said no.

I said she should, to finish what she had started.

She said it was pointless.

I said I knew we didn't see the man the same way, but the conflict of viewpoints, hers and mine, was stimulating to me; in fact, I had given a lot of thought to what she had said about Collier and me, and I had to say now that she had aroused certain doubts, serious ones, in me; in fact (I was fabricating frantically), I really wanted to see Collier not so much to find out about him as to find out about myself.

I called Collier then and there. He was too busy to see me until I dropped that Gwen was coming along.

"You see," I said to her, "he won't see me unless you're along."

She was silent at this, from which I gathered she had acquiesced.

I was determined that this meeting with Collier not be a repetition of the previous encounters, in which he had carried on and I had not said anything I really felt. I was determined to be fair and honorable and open with him—to impress Gwen.

As soon as we got there, I offered to let him read my entire draft. This I thought would be taken as a token of honesty. Collier asked me would I change anything if he objected to it.

I said of course not.

Then he said, "What's the point of my reading it?"

The rest of the afternoon he spent talking to Gwen. Apparently he had thought a lot about her. And somehow something more was involved. I guess it must have been his taste in revenge. Since I was going to destroy him in print, he would try to take my girl away from me.

Gwen, cool as always, unresponsive as if nothing was happening, sat quietly in a chair between us. She smoked and drank and seemed to be lost in thought. Something was going on, but you couldn't tell what. If she noticed that Collier was talking exclusively to her now, she gave no sign.

I persisted, despite the fact that the man ignored me. I asked him about some facts in my piece. He said I had them correct. Then about some judgments of mine. He said that it was all cheerleading, couldn't matter less.

I asked him what he meant by cheerleading.

He said I was speaking exclusively to people who agreed with me —the Ritualists, he called them. I was not changing anybody's opinions, nor was I really dealing in controversy. Merely leading cheers and boos. He said everything in my piece was predictable. That I was appealing to prejudices and fixed attitudes. He said that I had lost my ability to think, to even see clearly, that I had had my mind made up when I first came to see him. Even the research provided for me by the magazine had been chosen carefully to fit a certain viewpoint.

"I would like you to read me," he said, "just one sentence that will surprise your editor."

I got up. "Let's go, Gwen," I said.

She didn't move. Then she said, "I think I'll stay here." She turned to the man, and said, "May I?"

"Welcome," he said.

"Gwen," I repeated, "we're leaving."

"You heard what she said," said Collier, "she's staying here."

"She came with me, and she's going with me," I told him. "Gwen."

Collier burst into laughter. "Listen, bright eyes," he said, "did you ever hear of the civil rights of the individual, those that you're always writing about? Ask the lady what *she* wants."

Gwen got up and came to me.

"Go on, Eddie," she said, "I'm going to stay here."

I spun around and walked to the door, grabbing hat and coat and putting them on outside.

Halfway across the yard to the Hertz car, I lost control. I dropped my hat and coat, walked back into the house, went up to Collier, and went after him.

Collier could hardly believe his eyes. And then he gave a sigh, a profound sound of relief—I can remember it well—like an exhalation of gratefulness it was, thanksgiving. And then he went to work on me.

I'm 5′ 6″, but I'd done some boxing at college. I think if I had been in the ring with him and we'd had 16-ounce gloves on, I might have held him off for a round or two. But this man had been a Ranger. He took me apart in ways I didn't know existed. It happened so quickly I can't describe it. It was a little like being in an auto smashup, where the events are ticked off in tenths of seconds. It had nothing to do with the art of the Marquis of Queensberry, and just a little to do with slaughtering and sectioning beef. My mouth filled with blood, though he hadn't hit me there. He made a pudding of my eyes, and broke my nose. If Gwen hadn't interfered, it would have been worse. But she really went after him, biting, scratching, calling him every sort of name from her larder of gutter expletives, kicking him in the balls, plowing up his face with her nails and going after his eyes, and so finally forcing him to back off me, saying, "Don't you dare lay another hand on him, you son of a bitch; don't you touch him again, because I swear to God, I'll come here with a gun and kill you." Words you don't believe when a person says them unless you hear them and believe them.

Gwen got me to the car. I couldn't see for the blood in my eyes. I could just make Collier out walking alongside, half apologizing, half explaining for the tenth time that I had started it. I was barely conscious, the blood coming out of my mouth, nose, and the corners of my eyes. Then Gwen was bending over me, tucking her coat around me, and telling me to lie down—in the back seat I was—and to be still.

She drove me to the Chelsea, got me a doctor who gave me a shot to put me to sleep. When I woke, Gwen was in bed with me, holding me in her arms. It was the simplest and purest love she had ever shown me. I went back to sleep.

When I woke next, it was night again, and I was hungry. I went to the bathroom mirror and looked at my face. It was pretty bad, but not as bad as I thought it would be. She ordered dinner delivered from the Mexican place near the Chelsea, a big paella and two bottles of Chilean wine, well frosted. It was a hell of a meal, but there was no conversation.

When we'd finished, we sat where we were and listened to the wind blow the refuse around the parking lot at the back of the hotel. There was nowhere further for us to go.

The phone rang. She picked it up and said, "I'm not in now."

"Who was that?" I asked. She didn't answer. I knew who it was. I was through. It was over.

The next morning I was on the plane back to L.A.

The last thing she had said to me was, "I guess the truth is, Eddie, you can't get out of the thing you're in; you're too far gone."

I hadn't answered.

She said, "Be my friend now, Eddie; if that's the truth, say it to me. It wasn't my fault."

"Yes," I had said, "I'm too far gone."

She kissed me where my cheeks burned. And that was it.

I went from the airport straight to the offices of Williams and MacElroy and explained my face: I'd been mugged in New York. People shook their heads about New York. You couldn't live there any more, they said. This was before Watts.

I cleaned up the accumulated mail. There was a Zephyr crisis. I solved it. They were grateful.

I told Florence over the phone not to be shocked at the way I looked, that I had been mugged. She welcomed me, wined me, dined me, fed me my favorites, stacked my favorites on the hi-fi: Schubert's C Major Quartet, and Franck's Piano Quintet. I fell asleep in perfect peace, as the music played. It was amazing how my broken face straightened everything out.

I woke in the dead of night, and determined that whatever it was that had all my life run me from girl to girl, I would now control. I resented being at the mercy of whatever that was. If it was sex, which I doubted, I just didn't need it that much. I vowed to kill it. I determined to be a good husband.

The first thing I had to do was make Florence believe I really meant this. The quickest way to convince her, I immediately saw, was to follow her suggestion and have a couple of talks with Dr. Leibman. Which I did.

I must have passed the test, because he was able to recommend me to my wife. In his judgment I was genuinely determined now to make a go of it, be a good husband and an honest man.

What he didn't know and what it took me eleven months to find out was that I was indeed "too far gone," that, as the Turks say, too much had been written.

But I did my best.

It was eleven months until my accident. For those eleven months, I did try.

・ 5 ・

Now came the time of the fortress.

Florence and I built it together. Or, rather, she had already built
part of it, and invited me in, and we finished it together. We lived
in it for eleven months, and Florence made me accept it, even like it.
In its way, the fortress was perfect.

She started it the night I came home. The beating at the hands of
ex-Ranger Chet Collier was a professional job; it changed my face.
It wasn't so much that I didn't look well; I looked different. Especially my eyes. The openings were smaller, like those of an animal
peering out of a deep cave. And they had a pleading look.

Florence responded to this. She made me so comfortable that for
the first time in my life I appreciated having a home. I was forty-four
now, and you'd think that somewhere along the line I would have
appreciated having a home. I thought of my parents' home as a
place to get away from. And after the first year or so, I thought of
the places Florence and I lived in the same way. I couldn't wait to
get out every morning.

But now Florence made me actually enjoy a way of life I never
thought I could tolerate. "I don't deserve all this," I said. "It's not
a matter of deserving," she said. "We had a very narrow escape,
darling, and I'm so relieved you're back safe. We almost lost you."

A few days later, when I was beginning to feel like myself again,
she started in on her fortress ideal.

"It's true, dear," she said, "we set out to be something else. We
thought the job with the agency was going to be a means to something. Instead it seems to have turned out to be *it*. Doesn't it?"

93

I didn't say anything.

"So we're disappointed, right? We are. Let's admit it. I remember the day you were chosen class poet after four years when nobody but me knew you were alive. I remember you standing up in Woolsley Hall, in front of that whole damned college, and reading your poem. I didn't hear a word, because what I was looking at was your face, God love you. Everything was possible to you that day. And now it seems like some sort of grotesque joke. To use all that talent and all that training—how you worked!—to use all that to sell cigarettes. I know I'm embarrassing you to even say this. But now, just once, I'm going to say everything."

I must have looked like I expected to be hit, because she laughed and kissed me and said, "Darling, it's not going to be all that bad. First I want to ask you one question. Isn't that the way life is? Isn't it, Ev? Say?"

"I guess so."

"No one reaches their dream, baby; whoever has?"

"Nobody, I guess."

"It's o.k. with me if you're not delighted with everything every day. As long as you don't take it out on me. Don't make me the heavy."

"I didn't mean to do that."

"No, but sometimes you forget who I am, baby. I'm the girl who thought you were somebody when you thought you were nobody. Remember when you used to walk the campus from the Zete house to the post office and never lift your head, when you would cut across the street to avoid the chance that someone might not say hello? I'm the girl who made you raise your head and look at people; remember me? I'm the one who told you it didn't matter how you wore your tie, and the fact that you were foreign or thought you were, that didn't matter, and even your pimples, they'd go away, which they did, didn't they, baby? And most of all what your father thought of what you were doing or not doing, that didn't matter, because if you want to be angry at somebody, be a little angry at him. But don't you dare tag me as one of those Hollywood wives. If it weren't for you, I wouldn't be here. I didn't want to live in this Spanish Renaissance ranch house. I don't need the three cars. I don't even use the pool. I'm here, baby, because you're here.

"You want to quit this place?" she said. "Come on. Let's sell it.

Let's move. You miss the days when you had a cause to fight? Well, there's still a big one, but you won't do anything about civil rights. I've asked you again and again. But you won't. So don't. That's your business."

She calmed herself—it took an instant—and then she said, "Well, since we're here and it looks like that's the way it's going to be for the rest of our lives—which it does, doesn't it?—since that's so, then I'll tell you I'm glad that Williams and MacElroy think you're Indispensable Eddie. Because that pays the way so every once in a while you can afford to write a piece on Chet Collier. And Ev, you're going to feel a whole lot better about absolutely everything when your piece on Mr. Collier comes out and people start complimenting you on it. A lot of people have it a lot worse, my dear."

"I know that."

"But you keep forgetting it."

"I guess I do, yeah."

"First let's admit some defeat. Then let's stop looking to the world to solve our problems. Let's start looking inside ourselves. Let's pull back now and put a wall around ourselves, an impenetrable wall, a fortress, with walls so thick it will keep everything in our environment we detest outside. And inside, where we can control the way things are, let's have everything as nearly as possible the way we want life to be. That will be our fortress. I'm ready to live the rest of my life inside those walls, baby, because I love you. I do. Wait a minute. I want to show you something."

Florence had been reading a book by a man named Hesse. The story is called *Siddhartha*, it takes place in India. It's the story of the search of a handsome and favored young man for the things in life which have permanent value. It is also his search for harmony with the universe. And for peace. This young man, it developed, had a period when his dissolute side was controlling him rather than vice versa. I suppose that's why Florence thought it would be a good idea if we read that book together. In time and after a lot of inner pain and hardship, this Siddhartha brought the corrupt part of himself under control. He had a narrow escape though. He got involved with a beautiful courtesan, who almost did him in. But he rescued himself. At the end he was poor and alone, but he had won an ability to accept all the phenomena of the outer world, no matter how harsh and hostile, with equanimity, even with a feeling of love.

This philosophy of the author of this book, Hesse, seemed to be a negation of the ego as it's thought of today. It seemed to Florence and to me, as we read along, that it was a reach for a different kind of ego, not aggressive or competitive or acquisitive, but simple, unafraid, and accepting. And the self that developed would be in harmony with the universe, and even with the environment. It didn't feel compelled to beat anybody or to win anything. And, therefore, it was relaxed, accepting, and generally happy. This philosophy eschewed what was external and material and placed primary value on what was inner and spiritual. I'm sure I did not understand it too well then, and still don't. But I understood what Florence herself meant about us very well.

I found out that Florence, besides seeing Dr. Leibman three times every week, was also taking yoga lessons from a swami who lived in a "retreat" up the coast near Santa Barbara. I don't mean to make fun of this either, because those eleven months when we were both influenced by this man and his way of thinking and by the book, *Siddhartha,* were the most peaceful days of our life together.

Florence began to create, inside the walls of our fortress, a world of "real" things, the inner things that endure. She said there was nothing we could do about what was corrupt and dismaying outside our fortress. We lived in a certain place at a certain time, and we were dependent for our bread and butter on a certain industry, to which we had certain definite obligations.

But, she said, we must place around our house a kind of spiritual fence, and that fence would start at the street line. We actually planted a border of beautiful evergreens and rhododendrons on this line to mark the place where the outer world ended and our inner world began. Inside this hedge of evergreens was our domain. There we were to abandon our old selves and create new selves, with new dimensions, and a new structure made of a new fabric. Inside we would divorce ourselves from things of the flesh and the marketplace. Florence said that the struggle of all the great men was precisely this one. Jesus, Buddha, Tolstoi, Thoreau—all the great teachers worked to free themselves from the standards of their fellow men, the requirements of competition, and the terror of the predators of their own societies. No matter what shameful things they were involved in outside, they built an inner life that was so strong that nothing could shake it.

So I began on this with Florence, the first time we had ever worked on something together.

Since I was no longer seeing Gwen, I found myself with a lot of time on my hands. I ended each business day as early as I could and rushed home. There I would change my clothes, and get into something loose and soft. First it was a pair of old pants and a sport shirt. Later I went even further and put on a robe, short and lightweight. I soon came to a point where I resented any clothing which constricted me. I even changed my business clothes. I gave up belts and neckties, wore loose slacks, soft jackets, and shirts unbound at the neck.

Then Florence said, "Don't do anything because you are anxious or fearful. There is no cause inside the fortress for fear or anxiety. Do only what you love. Find all the things in the world you really care about, and give your time, and so your life, to them. In this way, spend as much of every day as you can in harmony with your innermost being." She asked me what had I always wanted to do that I had not done. She said now I should do those things, no matter what they were.

Well (this seemed odd), one of the things I wanted most in the world was to raise tomatoes. They were my favorite vegetable. I ate them like fruit. I'd never had time, however, to raise them myself. Several times I'd put them into the ground. But then I'd get involved somewhere with something, and so the borers would get to them, and the blight would leave little black circles with a hole in the center, and the fruit would rot on the ground. But now, nothing was more important to me, and I got results. I forked up a piece of ground in the backyard, just the other side of the swimming pool, where there was almost constant sun. And I put in ten tomato plants and four cherry tomato plants, with plenty of room between. I dug in bone meal and dehydrated cow manure. I bought a bundle of bamboo and constructed frames for the plants to grow on. I read up on the tomato blight, early and late, and bought the indicated powders—the Sevin powder, and 7% copper dust—and a long-throated duster to blow these pest killers onto the plants. I bought enough hose so I could water the plants twice daily because, as the book said, no one ever killed a tomato plant by drowning it. I enjoyed it all. There is nothing I love as much as the smell of a tomato leaf.

Then I decided to make a collection of every book I wanted to read for the rest of my life. It was great fun making the list, and I made it meticulously, considering every book carefully. I realized as I made it that it was already too late, that there were quite a number of books that I had always hoped to read that I would never get to read, and that if I hadn't decided when I did—well, it would have been quite possible that I never would have read most of the books on my list. Then I found out I could cover quite a few of my titles by buying the entire Modern Library. So I ordered it and built shelves for it myself. Then I bought the titles I had listed which were not in the Modern Library. There was really no hurry about this, but I wanted to have them all at hand so I'd be ready to start.

I discovered that I needed some kind of place where I could be by myself. So I decided to build a tiny room, a fort within the fortress; above the bathhouse this was, but facing away from the swimming pool and towards the plot of ground where the tomato plants were growing. It was there that I put the Modern Library and the other books (taking off all the dust jackets), and also some shelves for current magazines, and stacks for back issues. I put in a sofa as well as an armchair, so I could be comfortable in every conceivable position, and a couple of those extra bright little lamps, because my eyes were not as good as they once had been.

Here, too, I put in a stereo record player. One of Florence's limitations was that she could not listen to music. She said she liked it, but as soon as some quartet or opera was playing, she'd start to talk. Conversation was more important to her than Beethoven. I could lie and listen by the hour, dream as the music played, let my mind wander. I bought Beethoven's late quartets complete. I had had these on 78's when I was in college, but had never listened to them since. Never had the time! But now I did, and as I listened I remembered my college days and my home and my father and my mother in the old days, and my uncle Joe, Stavros was his real name, the man who brought the family to this country, and my brother Michael, and the things that had happened to me and him way back in grammar school, things I had forgotten. I spent whole afternoons that way. And my life seemed rich for the first time.

Each day I made entries in what you might call a spiritual diary. Immediately, I noticed my handwriting had improved! Without trying I was suddenly writing the 26 characters more evenly and more beautifully. For the first time I enjoyed the actual act of writing words. I would put down what I had reflected on and experienced that day. It's amazing how much happened that I never would have noticed before and how important everything that happened suddenly became. As I got to thinking, I wondered why I had become what I had become. I began to feel that now, finally, I was doing what I wanted to do with my life.

Often I fell asleep in that little room of my own. And too damned often, when I fell asleep, I would dream of Gwen. I couldn't yet control my dreams.

There was another thing that I could not control. I could not make love to Florence. I don't know why, I just couldn't. Maybe it was my time of life. Or maybe it was some physical thing. Well, no, I know better than that; it was psychological all right, but I didn't know what to do about it. No matter what Florence would do, I could not get an erection with her. A sort of one, yes, semi, but nothing useful. Florence was wonderful about this. We discussed it frankly. She said not to worry. That Dr. Leibman said I was shifting spiritual gears, that she understood and wanted nothing from me except what I could do with all my heart, that I had a ways to go to come back to her. But when I did, she'd be there waiting for me.

In every other way we were the closest we had ever been. I even went shopping with her, and she with me. If there was anything I hated in the old days, it was shopping. I used to send my secretary, Sylvia, out to buy my shirts, socks, and underwear. As for my suits, I found a tailor who used to make me two suits from a set of measurements and trick photographs, and they were always the same two suits: one dark blue for evening wear, one business brown.

But now Florence bought my clothes. We decided together that I looked best in gray, not blue or brown, with a spot of color perhaps in my necktie, but gray suits, gray suede shoes, and soft gray shirts. This allowed Florence to dress colorfully, but in such a way that she'd be in harmony with my grays. There would always be some bit of gray in her ensemble.

Now I became interested in the art of women's clothes. For the first time I really began to notice what women had on, whereas before I had only been interested in the location of the crucial zippers. I went shopping with Florence for all her clothes, and—as she said— I soon knew what she looked good in, what points she emphasized, and what points she minimized or even concealed. She really began to value my opinion of a dress. It was fun. I really thought so.

In time we began to be known among our friends as the "Golden Couple." It wasn't because we spent, each of us, five minutes every day under the sun lamp and in fact looked golden. People thought ours was the ideal marriage. Wives were holding me up to their husbands as the perfect husband. When the men, in petty pique, made snide remarks about my very loose past and so on, the women, by God!, defended me. They said apparently that had been necessary for me at one time, and furthermore it had in all likelihood been wildly exaggerated, out of jealousy, those things always are. "But," they'd say, "just look at him now!"

Of course we were constantly being asked out to dinner. We used to walk in, Florence first, and she'd stand there with her back to me, while I took off her coat and handed it to a maid. Then we'd go into the parlor, or, in the summer, into the garden and sit side by side on a sofa or garden bench. I'd tell the host or butler what we both wanted—it was always the same, but still I asked Florence each time—a Manhattan. Everyone knew we preferred to sit next to each other at dinner. So there was always this "Now we just have to break you two up for an hour or so, can you stand it?" And we'd fuss and demur, but end up sitting across from each other. She'd watch what I ate; I'd watch what she ate. We were both trying to cut down on calories. I carried a little silver box which held the sucaryl wafer for both of us. I was allowed one cigar a day. She carried it in her purse, so it would not get crushed in my pocket. She'd give it to me at the end of the meal.

We'd always excuse ourselves to go home just a little earlier than the other guests, the inference of course being that we could not stand to be physically separated one minute longer. I'd help Florence into the Lincoln Continental, and we'd be off, leaving behind us a great number of discontented wives.

If at home sexual intercourse was not bringing us together, other things did. We allowed each other one final drink, a nightcap, which we had together. Sometimes, if it was not too late, we'd enjoy a quiet game of double solitaire as we sipped our scotch and soda. Then we'd slowly mount the stairs, she to her dressing room and I to mine. There we took a long time undressing, each with our thoughts. And so in time we'd meet in the bedroom, face to face with the developing reality of our relationship. She had bought herself some sexy nightgowns, rather more elaborate than she used to wear, and some that she knew I liked, the real plain kind. But neither one nor the other worked. And by now we didn't expect anything. I no longer felt that any explanation was necessary or possible. Instead we would read; that is, I would read and she would listen. For a long time we were reading *Siddhartha,* and it was amazing how much more we got out of it the second time. But the real reason we were with that book so long—aside from the fact that it needed to have its meanings unearthed page by page, paragraph by paragraph—was that Florence would very soon fall asleep. Then I'd lie there a long time thinking, what's happening? What's happening?

Sometimes, then, I did think of Gwen. But I tried not to. Gradually I killed it. There was no point.

If it was no longer a physical union between Florence and me, I had to admit that for the first time it was possible for us to be friends. I did love Florence. She was my true friend. In fact, for the first time I got to know a different Florence from the girl I married, just as I was different from the boy she used to meet secretly on the top floor of her father's house. At least now, there was friendship.

It was a way of life.

Since we were invited out so often, we had to return the favors, and soon we were either eating out or having guests in every single night of the week—every night, that is, except one. One day of the week we fasted. I suppose it was the Eastern influence. I made it a little easier for myself by fasting from after an early lunch Monday till just before a late lunch Tuesday, exactly twenty-four hours. Florence missed three meals. It's amazing how I began to look forward to this day when I didn't eat. It was a triumph of a kind, I suppose.

Each detail served to bring us closer. For instance, there were regular times each day when I called her on the phone. First at about twenty minutes of eleven, just before she went to see Dr. Leibman. Then again at about four, when she had come back from her shopping and her yoga lesson or session or whatever you call it. She, in turn, always called me directly after my lunch to see if I had stayed on my diet. The boys at the office used to kid me about this, saying she was checking up on me.

Soon every detail of our lives was synchronized. Even down to our charities. We decided we should give one afternoon a week to volunteer hospital work. I used to take off from W. and MacEee every Wednesday after lunch (on the same day and at the same time I used to take off for Gwen! How much time I had, once I stopped seeing her). We'd drive out to the Veterans Mental Hospital near Sawtelle, on the way to the beach (that brought back memories too!). There we'd give what comfort we could to the committed, reading to them or just listening to their pathetic, distorted stories. Sometimes, I must say, I felt these poor distraught buggers made sense. Despite my gray ensembles and my air of affluence, I often had the feeling that it wasn't very far between the top and the bottom in our society. I guess in my guts I knew I had had a very narrow escape from something very much like this. Florence knew it too. So our visits, you might say, were ransom paid.

We decided to subscribe to certain magazines together. First, the *Nation*, in which we both enjoyed Harold Clurman's reviews so much. They were written in such a way that you could enjoy them even if you hadn't seen the plays, which, of course, we hadn't. But we found we agreed in principle with every one of Mr. Clurman's evaluations. Then there was *Esquire*, where Dwight Macdonald ripped all those phony pictures to pieces with such gusto. We made a list to be sure we saw everything he recommended. And finally the *New Republic*, where there was Robert Brustein, probably the most brilliant of them all. Clurman and Macdonald and Brustein were really all you needed. They were not only perceptive but witty and amusing. We used to just run to get into bed and read their reviews out loud to each other.

We sent for various catalogues. We ordered LP's together, and books, and we ordered all kinds of fascinating gadgets from the Hammacher Schlemmer catalogue, and outdoor clothes and fishing equipment from Abercrombie & Fitch. What sport it was when the stuff arrived! We'd always wait until the other got home, so we'd share the fun of opening the packages. We surprised each other on our birthdays and on Christmas. For my birthday present she bought me an entire camping outfit from Abercrombie & Fitch, every detail, including a portable toilet. We immediately planned a trip to Yosemite, but meantime I pitched the tent in the backyard, just behind the tomato plants, and laid out all the equipment. Sometimes I'd come home for a quick lunch and eat alone in my tent. Sometimes I'd just lie there and reflect.

We discovered, to our total surprise, that we both had wished for a long time that we could speak and read French better. So twice a week we began to use the lunch hour to have a French lesson together, the man coming to the house, which made it nicer. Florence would serve us lunch, something light like a Dover sole *meuniére,* and we all gabbed away in French as we ate—the best way to learn, I'm sure.

We found that we both read very slowly and wasted so much time. So we took one lesson a week in speed reading. I actually doubled the number of pages I could read in an hour, and Florence close to trebled hers. It was amazing how much more we could get done.

Physically I was in the best shape of my life—except for that one thing: my stomach was hard but Peter Pumpkin-eater wasn't. That was just psychological though and, we both firmly believed, temporary. All you had to do was look at me to see that physically I was A-1. On the Beverly Hills dinner circuit I was known as the man who looked younger every year. Florence got a lot of the credit for this, especially from the women. But the fact was that I did the Royal Canadian Air Force exercises for ten minutes every single morning. They're really all you need. I used to give copies of the booklet out to my friends, just a little gift out of the blue. But I doubt if many of them had the discipline to do the exercises every day.

We took this occasion to organize our finances together for the first time. I had always kept my holdings separate and secret from Florence, and she had kept hers secret and apart from me. I never did know how much money she had. But now, with this new harmony and that terrible importance lifted off material things, we became frank with each other about money and property and insurance and annuities and all the rest of it. In fact we had a meeting with our lawyers, and we were able, for the first time, to be absolutely plain about how much money she had and how much money I had. When we had carefully reviewed our whole financial situation, I signed a lot of my things over to her for tax reasons (I was later to regret this). I felt so keenly my inability to give her physical love that I wanted to give her everything else. I would have given her *all* my financial resources and property at one point, except it was explained to me that from the tax point of view this would not have been wise.

It began to appear that with both our possessions now amassed in one portfolio, and with the pleasant surprise I had as to the amount of her estate (she wasn't dead yet, but I guess "estate" is the word), we would be more or less set for the rest of our lives.

It appeared to both of us, in fact, that we had enough to justify a little splurging. So we bought an acre and a half of land, not in Palm Springs, where it would have been prohibitively expensive, but in Indio, only half an hour farther away. There we planned to get away from the winter rains and the L.A. smog, and get us some of that real skin-penetrating heat. We designed the place ourselves, sitting around in the evenings, sometimes under a sun lamp. We decided it would be tiny, just for two. We would construct it so well that it would last the rest of our lives. We decided to insulate it with the most advanced and most expensive insulation, so it would do for summer and winter. All so that no matter what happened in the world, we two would be all set with a *place*.

Florence had a very real fear of the Bomb. She would not be poohpoohed out of it. Indio seemed to her much safer than Los Angeles. But it wasn't as safe as she'd like, because there were some factories nearby—airplane parts and assembly—and there were some bigger ones coming, natural targets. In fact, the day we signed the deal for the acre and a half, we saw some big Delta jobs overhead at about seventy thousand. This disturbed hell out of her. So the very first thing we did was revise our plans so as to put a cellar under the house, and later she whitewashed its cinder-brick walls herself. We put some sealed jars of water and some fine canned goods in there. Florence figured we'd be good in that tiny cellar for about three weeks. Of course we had the portable toilet there, too.

All in all, this was one of the happiest times of both our lives.

Florence often said that it was the very happiest time of hers. That is why the events that followed were such a shock to her.

We did everything together. For instance, we had my eyes checked, and I got some Ben Franklins. Then we had her eyes checked, and she needed a new prescription. Neither of us liked to carry glasses; we hated bulges in our clothes. So we both got glasses for upstairs and a pair for downstairs and one for the car and one for the place in Indio.

We went and had physical examinations, deciding to make this a regular thing, too. I found that my spleen was enlarged, but that this was no cause for immediate concern. It only meant that I had to watch certain things in my diet. So Florence used to call up the morning before we went to dinner at a friend's and gently explain to the hostess what I could and what I could not eat. Florence's own examination showed that she would live forever. It seemed to me that her energy level was not as high as it used to be. She got tired easily. But all the man would say about this was that she was no longer twenty. The same doctor examined us both. There was no doubt in his mind that the fact that our marriage was so ideal had a lot to do with our superior and relaxed physical condition.

Actually, I had become so relaxed I used to fall asleep at movie theaters, and directly after dinner, even when the dinner was at a friend's house. Twice I actually fell asleep *at* the dinner table. Florence too had begun to fall asleep early and rather easily. It was a joke around our dinner circuit: the Golden Couple who were always so sleepy—from an excess of love making, it was supposed.

Not only had I become relaxed physically; I had become relaxed psychically. I stopped fighting, not only with Florence, but with anybody about anything. Even at the office I had taken on the posture of a benign Brahman whose vision was always focused far into the future, and who had no concern with mundane problems. I began to give the impression that I didn't really care which of two sharply contrasting selling programs was chosen by the client. I had stopped caring. Although there was still a lingering superstition that my presence at a client conference meant everything was going to be all right, there was some grumbling about me, too. In fact, Mr. Finnegan called me into his office one day and told me that the new advertising director for Zephyr cigarettes had complained about my dozing at two of their recent conferences, and considering the five-and-one-half-million-dollars billing that Williams and Mac-Elroy had with Zephyr, the least Zephyr felt it could ask of the account executive was that he stay awake.

So I tried. But I didn't think that in the eternal scheme of things it mattered. Now, looking back at it all, it seems to me there was something much more mischievous at play. I had buried part of me alive, and it was struggling down there, kicking and flailing around. But I was determined to conquer that demon. I did not ever again want to be out of my own control, not for a minute.

There were a couple of sour notes. There were three if you count the big one, my impotence, for that's what it finally came to be known as. After a few months of it, Florence and I had had to accept the fact that for whatever reasons—age, bad circulation, under-powered gonads, whatever—I had become sexually impotent before my time. It caused less of a fuss than you might imagine. What woman wouldn't rather have her man impotent than off with some-one else?

Then there was the airplane. Here's how that happened.

Every morning at exactly ten before eleven I used to lock my office door, spread newspaper on the floor, lie down to do my ten sit-ups, then turn around to do my twenty push-ups. Well, this morning, push-ing my head up and down, this ad caught my eye. It said, FLY—$5. Well, I stopped the exercises, read the rest of the ad, and rather than go to the meeting of the office pension plan committee, I drove out to the Valley and busted out five dollars worth. I'd flown ATS dur-ing the war, but after almost cracking up several times, I swore never to fly again except as a passenger on regularly scheduled airlines. But it all came back for that five dollars, the exhilaration of riding the air. I began to rent a plane three or four times a week. Then one day I did the only thing during the whole fortress period which I did not tell Florence. I made a down payment on a Cessna 172. I went up in it every chance I could make. I guess, looking back, I was keeping something alive that way. Because up in my plane I'd talk to myself and say things that I could never say or even think on earth. Oh yes, I had some insane moments in that airplane. I remember once I was talking to Gwen, cursing her, telling her that I knew what she was doing with Chet Collier (for I was sure she was with him now, the attraction had been too obvious). I would describe what they were doing, shout curses at the heavens against her. Then dive into a cloud, reviling her, and later crying, for I did long for her. But finally I'd turn for home, and by the time I touched down, I was completely in control of myself again. I loved that plane.

The last sour note was Florence's fault. I discovered gambling. When she figured out the new regime, Florence thought that I really ought to have one evening a week away from her and she away from me. She still did her civil rights meetings every Monday. But even after I met James Baldwin at a party and found him surprisingly friendly, I could not get interested, not honestly, in anyone else's troubles. I know it's disgusting, but that's the truth. So Monday, when Florence and some of the other wives went to the civil rights meetings, we boys had a poker game. And with the blessing of the women, because all losses were absorbed by us and all the winnings went to the NAACP.

I was a lousy poker player. A good player plays one hand out of three. Maybe. I had to play every hand. So I lost quite a lot of money, and this began to worry Florence. In fact, she suggested that perhaps instead of poker I might join the class in gourmet cooking which some of the other husbands were taking. But I drew the goddam line there. Finally Florence had to find comfort in the fact that though I lost quite a bit, my losses were the winnings of other men, and they went from them to a good cause. She asked Arthur Houghton, our lawyer, to find out if my losses were, therefore, deductible.

So the months passed. One week we'd discover a wonderful new ethnic restaurant for our nights out. The next week, maybe, we'd go see my tailor, Florence having decided that something a little softer in a drape would make me look more like the kind of person I was trying to become. We both started taking tennis lessons from a wonderful girl, a former champ that the Bennetts recommended to us. Florence felt much more comfortable with her than with a man. And we really splurged by buying ourselves all nine folio volumes of the Oxford maps of the world.

Gradually I stopped using the word "I" almost entirely. I'd say, "We went there," "we like this," "we see so and so," "we wear gray." That old self of mine, the one which had caused all the trouble, was fast disappearing. It was becoming blended with Florence, as it would, in time, we hoped, be blended with something even bigger than Florence—the universe. I looked for less and less from life in a material way. I parted my hair in the middle and let my sideburns grow longer, because Florence said I looked more spiritual that way. I made certain discreet purchases of prints and lithos of the modern masters and even some original paintings by young artists that no one had heard of but who, Florence was convinced (she was also taking a UCLA class in modern painting), would some day be important. Besides, she explained, these purchases were really investments, excellent ones. And they made for a more diversified portfolio. After all, who knew what was ahead.

On the day of our wedding anniversary, I took Florence to the best jeweler in Beverly Hills, the fellow across the street from the California Bank Building. Twenty-one years before, when we were married, I had refused to wear a wedding ring. Since we were short on funds then, all we could afford for Florence was a very narrow silver ring. Now that we could afford it and now that we felt the way we did, I bought us, on that day, our anniversary, two identical heavy gold bands. We wore them out of the store. Florence said it was the first time in twenty-one years that she had felt really married.

So the months passed, eleven of them. I was the most orderly and the most controlled I had ever been in my whole life. And when I thought about it, I thought I was happy.

And then one morning, when I was driving to work in my Triumph TR 4, and felt, as far as I can remember, perfectly adjusted and perfectly calm, suddenly, on Christ knows what impulse I . . . or was it a hand from out of the blue that turned the wheel of my baby black car and piled it into the side of that enormous trailer truck speeding in the opposite direction?

That was my accident. It changed my life.

6

THE first visitor I had at the hospital was not Florence. At the instant of the crash, Florence was riding California One north to Santa Barbara. It was her morning with the swami. An acey-deucy English novelist with golden hair met her, as she rolled onto the Retreat, and told her the news. Florence turned right around, but it was well past noon before she got to Cedars of Lebanon. The insurance fellow had been and gone by that time.

He got to me in Emergency and questioned me before my head cleared. I told him the simple truth, that a hand had come in from outer space and turned my little Triumph into the side of the speeding trailer truck. He tried to shake my story. But I assured him repeatedly that's what happened, and finally he left. I heard later that he went among my friends trying to find out if I had always been "eccentric and fanciful." I suppose that's where the story got started —the one which was soon all over our circuit—that there had been some brain damage. I never denied that story, incidentally. The fact is I have never been the same since my accident.

I told Florence I knew that a hand out of the blue makes sense only in a comic strip. "But goddammit, Florence," I said, "*I* didn't turn the wheel of that car into the trailer truck. I didn't have any reason to kill myself."

The nurse just then was pushing another big load into the vein of my arm. I remember thinking, "This is not affecting me at all. Why don't they use the real stuff?" That's all I remember, though, because that "nothing" load got to me and put me out for almost a day.

The next morning I did one of those sly things convalescents do. I woke, heard the doctor talking to Florence at the foot of the bed, but didn't open my eyes. He was telling her that while I had six broken ribs, a badly wrenched neck, and all manner of contusions and lacerations; none of these was serious. Nor, in all likelihood, was my resounding concussion. No doubt there had been some intracranial hemorrhaging. But, as far as he could tell, this was not profuse or extensive, and therefore it was probably not dangerous. That was when Florence dropped her voice and asked him if there had been any brain damage. He said he'd rather not be held to anything on that yet.

I passed the next week mostly asleep or pretending to be. Then they shipped me home in an ambulance. And there I embarked upon the happy life of a convalescent.

Convalescence!

I spent most of mine sitting in a deck chair by the side of our pool. I was still being beefed up with drugs and knew no pain. The weather was beautiful, and I enjoyed every minute of it. I watched the world not go by, but come to see me. My visitors came out of the back of the house, which was about a hundred and fifty feet from the pool and on a rise. They'd come down across the lawn, spend a severely restricted visit with me, pay their respects, and go. They'd put on a sort of cheerfulness; then they'd turn and go back up the slope with Florence. I could see by the way they walked and the way they kept looking back that they were very worried. I did look considerably worse than I felt. A bit of my scalp had been laid bare, and my head was in a cocoon of bandages. "Now I'm a swami, too," I said to Florence. She managed a laugh.

I was enjoying it all. I've always liked receiving presents, and I had lots, some from people I didn't know cared, and even from people I had always thought of as downright hostile. The notes were interesting. I'd analyze them for Florence. She said I was too cynical. And the choice of gifts! My brother Michael sent fruit to California; he was always an original, my brother Michael. My mother and father sent me a letter; that is, my mother sent me a letter, and my father put his trembly hand at the bottom. His handwriting had sure become shaky. I had a lot of time to reflect, and I remember I determined that the one accurate way of predicting a person's future was to examine his handwriting. You can—with very little expertise—see what's coming. Didn't you ever pick up an old letter from a friend, written just before he had a stroke or a heart attack and think to yourself, how could I possibly not have seen it coming? I remember I looked at my father's scrawl, and I had a premonition about him that soon turned out to be accurate.

Mike Weiner, my literary agent, came to see me. The reactions to the piece on Chet Collier had been "unprecedented," and the magazine had a "fabulous assignment" which they were holding for me, so better get better quick, Mike said.

Mr. Finnegan came by in his Rolls. He slipped me a little flask full of my favorite rum. He said don't worry, take your time, and all the rest of it. Then he went slowly and gravely up the slope, talking to Florence.

It was obvious that my visitors thought I had suffered brain damage. They looked at me with that extra kindness. When a person has been defeated in life, his fellow predators can afford to be kind. After all, the contest is over. They have survived and therefore won. So they indulge themselves in goodness. This sudden concern and generosity was a surprise, because no one had ever seemed to like me much before. But now it was being poured all over me, the milk of human kindness.

So I became suspicious. An invalid is prone to paranoia. I sat by the pool, watching them come and go, the curious disguised as the solicitous, putting on those solemn concerned masks full of Christian feeling as they came down the slope from the house, being ever so cheerful with me, then turning around and walking up the rise with Florence, heads bowed, in the gait of mourners. They really can't wait to write me off, I thought. When I heard that solid middle-class click of the doors of their upper-price-range cars, I knew that as soon as they were out of my driveway they'd be discussing me much more plainly. And I knew what they'd be talking about would be brain damage.

There was one memory that kept coming back to me, again and again, as I sat there on my deck chair looking into the perfect blue water of our pool.

I went to Nassau once for a holiday. I'm not much for snorkling. But I did lie on the surface of that absolutely clear water and watch the fish below through a glass. Nowhere is the nature of life clearer than under the surface of the sea. You can see it all there, through the glass, so simple, so undeniable—no romance there, no Christianity either. No fish loves his brother or pretends to. There were those herds of fish—I think they call them sheepsheads—with small, round, blunt-end teeth, adapted for grazing. They'd move along the bottom slowly just like a herd of sheep, heads down, feeding. They reminded me of the great grazing herds that I had seen in motion pictures of Africa. And just as in Africa, along the perimeters of the great herds of antelope and wildebeests and zebras, there were lions, so along the perimeters of these herds of fish were barracuda. Except that I never saw the barracuda strike. I heard that they eat four or five or twenty times their weight every day. But for the longest time I never saw a kill. One day I found out why. It happened too fast. I was lying on top of the water that day watching a herd of these grazing fish through my glass. One of them was having difficulty, just a wobble, a faltering fin, barely discernible. But everyone down there discerned it. I mean they didn't turn and look. Fish don't do that. But they did something I have never forgotten. The herd edged away, delicately but surely, from their brother fish who had this hint of a wobble. I guess none of them meant any particular harm. But they also knew damned well what was coming. If you can't see it, you can't describe it, the move the barracuda made. In a short second, that wobbly fish was across the cuda's jaws like an ear of corn. Then shake, snap, and crunch—the grazing fish was in two parts, and another barracuda had his share. The herd meantime was just a little way off, going about their grazing, heads down. Not one of them turned an eye. Things went on, business as usual.

My boss, Mr. Finnegan, came to see me for the second time. With him was the man who had stepped into my job when I had the accident. They said, you look good, Eddie, much better than last time. But I noticed that when I talked to one, the other was examining me very sharply. And vice versa. They were measuring my prospects. They had to figure out what their next move was going to be. I wasn't absolutely sure that day that Mr. Finnegan wished me a quick recovery. After all, he was human and in business. When someone's away from a big functioning organization like Williams and MacElroy, and everything seems to go along perfectly well without him, the question naturally comes up: why pay that salary? I couldn't help wondering if Mr. Finnegan was thinking that.

He was looking at me like an appraiser. For instance, when he told me quite casually, dropping that hot rock in my lap as he bent over a border of poolside hydrangeas, that my assistant was doing all right in my job, was that an accident? And when this fellow said, Don't hurry back, Eddie, just take your time, was I wrong to get suspicious? Was I becoming paranoid, or was I seeing things more clearly?

The odd part of it was that I didn't know if I wanted the job back. And so, I thought I'd have some fun. Instead of maintaining a cautious and discreet silence until I was sure whether I wanted to go back, I popped out with, "Boys, don't worry; I'm not coming back." Of course this caught them unawares. They just looked stunned for a minute and didn't speak. Were they shocked because I read their thoughts? Mr. Finnegan looked at my assistant accusingly, blaming him for the thoughts that he, Mr. Finnegan, had had.

Then I saw it hit Mr. Finnegan—the thought that if I didn't come back, he might be left with this jerk in a very important spot. And I saw it hit my assistant: can I really handle Eddie's job? Do I want it, the responsibility? Am I safer where I am?

They looked at each other and didn't say a thing. They didn't know what to say, since they couldn't say what they really thought. There was quite a silence. (I sat there enjoying it.) Finally Florence broke it. She had this measured, reasonable tone of voice with which she met all emergencies, and a little controlled laugh which meant that nothing could be too bad, as nothing ever is if you've had money all your life. She said, "Eddie, we're not going to hold you responsible for anything you say now. He's only joking, boys." I muttered something to the effect that I wasn't joking in the least. I was enjoying my new game too much to give it up that easily. But they all went off laughing in relief, yukking it up as they walked up the slope towards the house.

As soon as the Rolls was out of the driveway, Florence rushed back down and said to me in her most pleasant and controlled voice, "Eddie, please don't feel that you have to decide anything now. They need you in that company. That cigarette account relies on you. And, hell, Eddie, when you get well enough, take a look at that pile of bills on my desk . . . but don't think of that now. Now just relax, Eddie."

Well, I had found a pretty good game, and I played it a lot from

113

then on. Instead of carefully organizing my thinking and speaking as I always had, I just blurted things out naturally. I even let my mind express itself in those mad jumps it had made all my life, but which until now I had thwarted. I allowed myself to say what I felt on every subject. I found that I could not insult anyone. Everyone was amazingly patient with me. I would say to a visitor, for instance, that I really didn't want to see him. He'd smile and leave. The energy I would have wasted in pretending in the old days! My "brain damage" allowed me to express exactly what I thought of anything: my dislikes, my likes, my wishes.

The most dramatic discovery I made was about myself. I found that I had become so accustomed for so many years to censoring what I thought, and guarding what I said, that by now I often didn't know what I believed, only what was correct for me to think and expedient for me to say.

But now I just popped out with whatever came into my head, without attention to whose feelings I was hurting or whether I was embarrassing poor Florence (I generally was).

Soon I couldn't wait for more visitors to come. It was amazing how far I could go. The fact is that in my first crude ventures into the unexplored region of the spontaneous truth, I did go too far. I mean, to question the total integrity of Florence's best girl friends, one after the other, in some subtle or not so subtle way, and watch the poor bitches smile at me tolerantly, patiently, and then become even more friendly—what an experience!

All these benefits from just one little auto accident.

There I sat poolside, like a demented king, with my castle up a slight rise behind me. And down the hill came juice and tea and lunch and an occasional drink. And this stream of visitors, one after the other, coming down full of the milk of human kindness, and going back up dismayed and bewildered and full of pity. How could you get angry at a man who had suffered serious brain damage?

I guess I took advantage. But after a bleeding lifetime living in calculation, saying not what I felt but what was expedient to say, how could anyone blame me for enjoying myself this way? Most of my victims enjoyed it, too. They competed, I found out later, telling stories about my awful behavior. And there was no end to their thirst for forgiveness. "Brain damage," they'd whisper to each other as they drove off with their cheeks still burning from my latest rudeness. "Extensive brain damage."

Over all this bizarre drama hovered poor Florence, laughing nervously, wondering what horrible thing I was going to say next, or chattering with subdued hysteria to distract me or to distract my visitor at the moment of the harpoon's impact. Or cutting into one of my sentences just before its point, or trying to change the subject, to make it all seem like just kidding. Sometimes, in front of our guests, she'd say that I was a naughty, naughty boy, which characterization, of course, was highly accurate. I was an idiot child king, full of the sense of new power and naughty as could be.

Florence had her reward. Everyone complimented her on her patience. They didn't see how she took it. Later some of them would send her flowers.

But even Florence's patience began to show cracks. Once I caught her pointing to my head when she thought I wasn't looking. So the next time I put a good gaff into someone, I pointed to my head. It was then that Florence got the idea I was enjoying it all. She scolded me and said she wouldn't let her friends visit me any more if I insulted them. That was the afternoon she asked the doctor right in front of me whether there had been any brain damage. He picked up his cue and said he was now certain there hadn't been any.

But I wasn't ready to give up my new privileges. I challenged him and said what was it, then, that made my head tip over to one side all the time? Why hadn't the pain disappeared from my left temple? Was he sure that there was no hairline crack in the skull there? He brought out the latest X rays, which I waved aside. I was sure that there was something wrong, I said.

Then Florence made good her threat. She discouraged visitors. No one came to see me. So I entered the second stage of my convalescence.

It started the afternoon I drank the entire contents of Mr. Finnegan's flask. That's a lot of rum for a man who has been confined mostly to poached eggs on spinach. It hit me hard. And I fell asleep. And when I woke up I was a Nothing.

When I was a little boy, my daddy once brought me a toy I loved. It looked like a fierce little warrior. It carried a spear and a shield. It wore formidable boots. But it had no face. It had everything but a face. And when grownups asked me what it was, I used to say: "That's a Nothing!" And they'd laugh.

Well, suddenly I woke up and I was that. For a minute I was pretty bewildered. But then I remembered how, on the radio, I'd heard them go up to perfect strangers and find out all about them in a few minutes by just asking a series of questions. So I thought I'd try that.

"Sir, why do they call you a Nothing?"

"Because that's what I am."

"What do you do in life?"

"Nothing."

"Are you a businessman?"

"No."

"Then what are you?"

"Nothing."

"What do you love, sir?"

"Nothing."

"Not even yourself?"

"Especially not that!"

"What do you hate then?"

"Nothing."

"Are you a Greek?"

"I can't even speak the language."

"Are you an American?"

"Almost, but not quite."

"Are you a believer?"

"No."

"An unbeliever?"

"Of course not. I'm a Nothing."

"Why do you keep smiling all the time?"

"Do I?"

"Yes, you keep smiling at me; at least I think that's a smile. What is that? Where your face should be?"

"Nothing."

It was true. The Nothing just schlunked there with that "nothing" smile on his face. So the interviewer moved on through the crowd to find a more responsive subject.

I began to use a weapon children have: silence. I wouldn't answer questions or express wishes. I seemed to want nothing. I was neither hot nor cold, hungry nor sated, for nor against. It was a matter of indifference to me what I had for dinner. I didn't want guests, but didn't protest when they came. I no longer insulted anybody. I sat there silently, smiling vacantly, neither friendly nor hostile.

I wasn't doing all this consciously or as a technique of some kind. I was getting better, but what resulted from my successful convalescence was not a cure; it was a change. I discovered, with quite a shock, that what had started as fancy had come true. I was a Nothing. I asked myself, did I want to go back to Williams and MacElroy? Of course I didn't. Did I want any of the rest of my life? Florence? The house? The whole deal? Even my identity? Did I want to be who I was? Would I prefer to be someone else if that could be managed?

There was one daydream that I kept having. Well, "having" is not accurate. Actually, I would summon it up. It's a fantasy many men have in one form or another.

I'd be sitting there in my deck chair looking at the front page of the Los Angeles *Times*. There'd be nothing on it. Then I'd turn the pages, one by one. Nothing! Until on about page eighteen, I found a small but very important item. Eddie Anderson, a vice president of Williams and MacElroy, had disappeared from his Los Angeles home, leaving not a trace. The police had searched vigorously, but no one knew where Mr. Anderson was. Not even his wife. But I knew where he was. He had disappeared on purpose. He was alone in a city he had never been in before. Usually that city was Seattle. He knew no one there. No one knew him. He could walk the street all day, and no one would come up to him. Or talk to him. He lived in a tiny furnished room, very warm. Alone. For a long while he just didn't do anything. He had his five hundred get-away dollars, and that would last him a long time. He stayed in, kept his own hours, ate when and what he wanted, read, thought, wandered around. He had no commitments. No one expected anything of him. All was quiet. There were no phone calls from his office, because he had no office and no job. His old life had been washed completely off the blackboard, and when that blackboard dried, it was clean. No trace! Eddie Anderson had taken advantage of one of those rare opportunities in life—the chance to start all over again. He had done what other men dream about but never do.

"What are you crying about, Evans?"

Florence had come up.

"Nothing," said Nothing.

"Please, Evans, tell me."

"It's really nothing. I'm o.k."

"Is it that tramp, do you still think of her?"

"No, I haven't thought of her in a long time, Florence."

I hadn't. But I guess Florence put an idea in my head, because the next time I was in Seattle, Gwen was there too. She lived with me in a slightly larger room, very, very warm, with a three-quarter bed, and a two-burner range that had a tiny icebox under it, and just a few simple things around. This time I had a job, an outdoor job near Puget Sound (I had never seen Puget Sound); there was no smog. The wind blew, a clean wind, and I came home after work and got into bed with Gwen. Then later we had dinner, then got back into bed. Later at night I'd read. Hundreds of books. I read all those goddam Modern Library's I had collected in the fortress —how they got up to Seattle I don't know. In the morning I'd make coffee. Gwen would be gone—I don't know where—because I like to be alone in the morning; I like absolute silence and the newspaper. I was losing my Nothing look; my face was growing back, a new one. The worry marks were off it; the creases of anxiety had disappeared—there was nothing to worry about. How simple life was in Seattle!

So for about two weeks I lived in Seattle every chance I got. As far as poor Florence could see I was just sitting there in my deck chair, without will or appetite, not insulting anybody now, but not insultable either. I would smile like Buddha (Florence said) and keep my peace. Florence soon thought I was carrying the Buddha idea too far. Once she screamed at me, "Say something!"

Nothing said nothing.

It wasn't long before Florence wished that I was back insulting people. She brought some potential victims down to me, some beauts. But all I'd do is lie back, pretend to listen, and smile. Or sit there and nod and look at our flowers, but always with that nothing smile.

As an experiment Florence even brought in some people to pick a fight with me. They'd say something to outrage me. But Nothing would just smile and say, "That's o.k. with me." That was Nothing's favorite phrase, "O.K. with me." Sometimes I'd whistle some cool, nothing-type music. Remember "Big Noise from Winnetka," how it used to come out from between that singer's front teeth?

Finally Florence got desperate. I think the growing pile of bills finally drove her to action. Also the fact that I didn't seem to be getting either better or worse. I didn't seem to have the least desire to terminate my convalescence. So I guess Florence figured she'd terminate it for me. One day she brought our doctor in, and there was a carefully staged scene, very jolly. In among the jokes, the doctor declared that if I felt like resting a few more days, that was o.k. with him, but as far as he was concerned, speaking as a medical doctor, there was nothing wrong with me. He had the latest X rays with him, and he showed me that there was no evidence of that hairline crack I kept hoping for. So I was as good as new, haha! I could go back to the salt mines, haha! Nothing nodded and said, "O.K. by me." The Medical Scientist laughed, tried one more joke, got a nothing smile as reward, then went up the slope with Florence, both of them chatting vivaciously.

A few minutes later, as the second act of this carefully staged drama of resurrection, Florence came down the slope carrying a tray of Manhattans, a little dish of hazel nuts, some tuna fish whipped in mayonnaise with slivers of onion, and a little jar of caviar that she had saved since Christmas. We had our Manhattans together quietly, just like in the days of the fortress.

After the third cocktail she asked me gently, when was I going back to work? I said without thinking, in that way I had become accustomed to, I said, never. She had another sip and asked what did I mean by never? I said immediately, again not letting myself think, because if I thought I'd say some sort of half-lie, or moderate the truth, "I mean I'm not, ever." Then Florence said, impulsively, "Goddam her!" I said, "Who?" though I knew damned well who. Florence turned away to hide the tears in her eyes, and said, "That diseased, dirty tramp!" (There was no use pointing out that Gwen didn't have a social disease.) "Ever since that girl," she said, "you have not been yourself." There was no use reminding her of the eleven months of the fortress, when I was certainly not myself.

Because Florence was in such visible, awful pain, it was I who was patient. I told her the truth very gently, that all this had nothing to do with that girl, that I had just been thinking things over. Florence seemed to accept this; she certainly made every effort to. I'd never seen her look so composed and still so terrified. I wondered how my not going back to work could produce such terror in this person.

Her voice very controlled and very calm, she said, "Well, darling, then do tell me, if you are not going back to work, what *do* you intend to do?"

"Nothing," I blurted.

At which she laughed. I did a little, too. It was such a relief to clear the air. From her reaction, I had said something patently absurd. But then, for the first time in many long years, I tried what I never tried again, to convey the unconveyable. "Please," I begged her, "don't be frightened, but I must tell you I don't like my life. I don't like what I have done with it. I don't like what I am. I don't like the way I live. I don't like my home, darling—please, it's nothing against you, I lied. I feel I'm in a trap here, a trap that opened when I had my auto accident. Many times I've thought that wasn't entirely an accident. Maybe I was just trying to get out of the trap that way because I didn't know any other way to get out of it. I think that auto accident was a success. It gave me a breather, a little trip to another country, a few quick minutes to think for the first time in my life."

Then I stopped, because I could see in her eyes no understanding, even the fading of the desire to understand. Only terror! "Evans," she said, "let's be sensible, dear. Tell me, what *do* you want now?"

So I wouldn't have a chance to make up anything sensible, I popped out with, "I haven't the vaguest idea."

She laughed that cultivated laugh of hers. "Well, darling, that is not at all unusual. Dr. Leibman told me it happens to many men at your age. In fact it has a name: evolutionary melancholia, he said it was called. But I'm sure it's a sign of your basic mental and spiritual health. I wouldn't like it at all if you didn't face the basic questions, the real big ones, at some time of your life."

"The basic questions?" I asked.

"Yes," said Florence, "like what is it all about? And why do I feel disconnected from everything around me? What is truly important to me and what isn't? What do I really want? I've just been reading Camus' *The Myth of Sisyphus,* and I'm going to give you my marked copy."

I saw it was useless. She was trying the best she could. She was so

120

frightened. That I would leave her, I suppose? What the hell, I thought, whatever is going to happen will happen, so what the loving hell!

"O.K.," I said, "I guess you're right. I'm going to go back to work tomorrow."

"Darling," she said, "take the weekend, and go back on Monday."

So I said, "O.K. by me!" real nothing style, and she kissed me and I kissed her, and I had another cocktail, then another, and then another. Florence put on some music. It had to be some of the songs that Gwen and I used to play together. I lay there and remembered that time I was in Gwen's place and she was cooking spaghetti and she wore an apron and nothing else and she was at the stove and I came up behind her and the spaghetti didn't turn out al dente.

I hadn't thought of Gwen for a long time. Except in Seattle sometimes. But in the last few days the erotic side of me had begun to come back to life. Now when Florence came to lie on the sofa with me, I had to turn over on my stomach. There wasn't really room on the sofa for both of us. There would have been for Gwen and me, or for Florence and me twenty years before. The size of a sofa sure varies, I thought, and when it seems big and when it seems small is a pretty good measure of the situation. I put my head down on Florence's shoulder, and soon I was asleep.

When I awoke a few hours later, Florence was asleep. I looked at her face, no longer in the iron control in which she held it through her waking hours. It looked fragile and anxious. I felt so sorry for her, and for all struggling humanity trying to keep some sort of order and meaning and continuity in life, not succeeding, not ever succeeding, failing up till the moment of death. I bent over and kissed Florence as she slept, and she smiled with the radiance of a child. I made up my mind. I would try my best at Williams and MacElroy. Gwen was long gone! Seattle was silly! I was not a Nothing! I did owe Florence years and years of love and loyalty.

Monday I went back to the office. There were flowers on my desk, my favorite cigars—a box of fifty—and ice in the bucket. And there was a flow of visitors with good wishes. On my desk were the latest sales figures for Zephyr, which were not so good. The clean cigarette had problems. So, after the presents and the visits and the good wishes on the hush-a-phone, things very quickly got down to business. It was my cue to pull off another miracle. Something was seriously wrong. Zephyr was running next to last in its field. The parent company put out four brands of cigarettes: a straight, a filter, a menthol, and Zephyr—the clean cigarette which has everything. Of the parent company's four, two were leaders in their fields. A third was second. But a close second. Zephyr was next to last.

It was said of me later that I didn't have my heart in it when I came back. Not true. I tried as hard as ever. But I did the unforgivable. I told the truth. I sent the Zephyr crowd a report after a week (too quick, everyone said later, for a real study; I was telling the truth fast so it wouldn't be diluted with expediency). The point of my report was that my "clean" campaign had failed, and it was time to admit that the Zephyr concept had been surpassed. I advised them to give it up. For the first time in my life, I made an entirely negative report without a recommendation.

The unfortunate part of it from the agency's point of view was that my report was given to the Zephyr crowd before Mr. Finnegan or our system of checks and balances, namely the Review Board, had a chance to go over it. My relationship with the Zephyr people in the past had been so good that no one even thought to check on my dealings with them. Furthermore, I had never in all my years with Williams and MacElroy handed in a defeatist report. That's what shocked them now, they said, the defeatism of it. Nobody would ever forget or forgive my final line. "Gentlemen," I had said in conclusion, "we are working on a stiff."

Well, the repercussions from my bomb were picked up on every seismograph from Wilshire Boulevard to Madison Avenue. The story was out: Williams and MacElroy's hold on the Zephyr account was slipping. The Zephyr people were seen having lunch with top personnel from other agencies. They wanted to get some fresh views. Meantime, they said, they were giving my report the benefit of the most careful study. But the fact was that their thinking over my report was done in five seconds. And their reaction, among themselves, was expressed in two words: "Fuck him!"

They let a decent interval elapse, a week, and then they invited me to come over to their office. After the ritualistic swapping of jokes and gossip, their chief cleared his throat and said they had thought my report over especially carefully because they had such profound respect for my sagacity and so much appreciation for my candor, and it was time for candor certainly; look at the sales figures! Nevertheless, they had decided to continue the Zephyr brand.

They sat back and looked at me and waited. I knew it was my cue to say that the best man to promote something was certainly not the man who had no faith in its future. But by now I had a rock in my gut. I knew how serious the situation really was. So I ducked. I said I'd get back to them on it. And I hustled over to see Mr. Finnegan.

He knew all about everything and was furious with me. Williams and MacElroy was in danger of losing over five million per annum in billings. Mr. Finnegan called up Zephyr right there in front of me and said that the point of view of Williams and MacElroy was not, in this instance, the point of view of its account executive, in this instance, Mr. Eddie Anderson. Furthermore, Mr. Anderson was no longer the account executive for Zephyr. He, Finnegan, wanted an immediate meeting on their problems. They said fine, of course, of course and fine, but they had been developing some other ideas along some other lines with some other people. The fellow talking never finished that sentence. Mr. Finnegan jumped in like Superman and said that he had meant to tell them at the upcoming meeting, but what the hell he might as well say it right now, over the phone, that he was taking over the account himself, and would from now on give it his personal supervision and vision, too.

I listened to this catastrophe as if it was happening to someone somewhere else. Way off in the distance I could hear the earth buckle and the buildings crash. Suddenly I was Nothing again, and I could hear that cool nothing music or whistling or whatever it was. Even as Mr. Finnegan was on the phone, my mind wandered. I thought of this and that and the other, all pleasant but nothing to do with Zephyr cigarettes. They don't have them in Seattle.

"What are you smiling at?" asked Mr. Finnegan as he hung up.

"Nothing," said Nothing.

"There's really nothing to smile about," said Finnegan. He turned to press a button. Nothing got out of there!

How slowly things go up; how fast they come down! Although the Zephyr people sat down with Mr. Finnegan, it was too late. That memo of mine had killed the account. While they did try to be polite, they finally had to come out with it. In the light of changing conditions, they said, they had been worried about the inflexible way Williams and MacElroy had been handling Zephyr. While they had felt sympathetic concern for my illness (look at the presents they had sent me), nevertheless, they finally had to blame the mediocre performance of Zephyr and its collapse on the policies I had failed to adjust to the constantly changing market. In other words, there has to be a heavy in this world, and I was tagged. Even my position at Williams and MacElroy quickly became equivocal. No one was sure where I stood. The talk of "brain damage" started again.

It disturbed hell out of a lot of people that I was still on salary. The other thing that drove everyone nuts was my goddam high spirits. I seemed so relaxed about it all. Finally some of my peers asked Mr. Finnegan if it was really necessary for me to attend Review Board meetings. As a stockholder, I was a member of this Board, which passed on every policy move our company made. I had been, before my accident, one of its most honored members, perhaps the one with the most highly honed critical mind and the most caustic voice. Now I sat there and made jokes as if my mind was somewhere else. I must say Mr. Finnegan was very patient with me. But he finally suggested that it wasn't necessary for me to attend the meetings. From that moment, my days at Williams and MacElroy were numbered.

Florence said I was thirsting for failure. And she couldn't understand it, she just couldn't.

The day after Mr. Finnegan took over Zephyr, I showed my class by going over to the magazine's west coast office and having lunch with the fellows there. They were really glad to see me. And full of compliments on the Chet Collier piece. Of course he had threatened a law suit. And worse, they said laughing. If I ever met him, it might be a good idea if I had a friend or two with me. But that was to be expected from so fine a piece. Evans Arness had fortified his reputation as the leading dispenser of justice then at work with a pen.

Waiting for me was another portfolio, bulging with research and tear sheets. Once again the target was a political hopeful, this time right in California. The expectation was that I would start right in carving this guy, do like I did with Collier. I felt that Nothing feeling coming on, but I choked it down. I had promised Florence I'd try.

They noticed right away that I was not quite myself. Instead of that thoroughly-on-the-ball attention I used to pay, I just schlunked there, thumbing through the research in an absent-minded way while they tried to pump enthusiasm into me. I seemed not to be paying strict attention. Suddenly I said I'd like to meet the girl who had done the research.

Back at the office they brought her in, an eager-eyed kid, maybe twenty-three-four-five, very very admiring of me. She sat there looking at me, and I looked at her till she dropped her eyes. Gwen had sat in that chair, and I was thinking of her, Gwen, now long gone and deep with someone else, and he deep in her. I sat there, thumbing this kid's research and wondering if Gwen was o.k. and not listening to what was being said. I wondered if Gwen ever thought of me now; I could hear in the distance these people telling me about what they wanted, which was a replica of the other piece. I could hear phrases like "Boy what you'll do with this guy!" and "Remember Collier's cars . . . well this guy's got motor boats: Catamarans, wave skimmers, you name it."

I kept looking at the girl and thinking of Gwen. Suddenly there were tears in my eyes. I don't think anybody noticed, except the girl; maybe she did. I heard all the talk from a greater and greater distance. I was thinking how much verve Gwen had, how smartly turned out she'd be sitting there neat and compact right there in that office like she'd once been—I wished she were now—with her bony little knees cozy out of the hem of her skirt. And suddenly I heard Gwen's voice saying, "Research the guy yourself. Don't take anybody's word for anything," and I was saying to the assembled editors, "Fellows, I'd like to know I can start from scratch on this one—excuse me, Miss, I appreciate how hard you worked, but . . ." They all smiled, very relieved that that was all that was wrong, and said sure, sure, of course, naturally, fine, and all that lard. The girl said she had a lot more tear sheets and quotes at home, if I cared to see them.

Why not, I said.

She was originally out of New York, presently putting up in one of those one-and-a-half-rooms in a building called the Oasis. All over the table, the two chairs, and the studio bed there were piles of books place-marked with little slips of paper and magazines with other magazines thrust into them and legal pads and stenographic notebooks, pencils, pens, paper clips, and a stapler, I remember, actually in the bed. That girl had earned her salary! There really wasn't anywhere for us to work except on the bed. So we did. Normally it would have been a perfect set-up for me. The girl was a hero worshipper, had read everything I had ever written. She told me at great length what she liked, which was just about everything. I don't know how I got to give her her reward with all that stuff all over the bed, but I did.

It seemed like something we had done many times before. And I had. To Gwen. Love in the research debris. One moment I seemed ardent. Then I'd fade away like a sick radio. I pumped and I pumped, and I didn't come. The poor kid didn't know what the hell to make of it all. After a while I just stopped and lay there. We looked at each other, I still erect but nothing. Finally I said, "Excuse me." I got up. There was no point. It wasn't the intercourse of love or affection or even of sudden desire. It was a case of mistaken identity.

Going down the stairs, I whistled "Big Noise from Winnetka" through my front teeth. It surprised me that my longing for Gwen was still that strong, after all those months. And about the piece, I couldn't kid myself. Not only didn't I want to do it. I couldn't have done it, even if I had succeeded in pretending to myself that I wanted to. I was in a phase of disconnecting.

So I called the magazine and said that I wasn't interested in doing the story.

They were shocked. They protested that this left them in the lurch, that they had held the assignment open all these months for me.

I said that I had already done that piece, except the names were different. Use the other story, I said; just change the name Collier to Blanton, and change automobile to motor boat.

Stop kidding, they said, I just had to do it; no one could write it except me, and there was also a gentle reminder that I had drawn pretty heavily on my account with them. So I had to fall back on my illness. I protested—the crap was really flying both ways by then —that I still felt pretty weak, not like myself (I could hear that piteous note come into my voice), and that I had fits of nausea and dizziness. Hadn't they noticed how pale I looked under my tan?

They had to confess that I really didn't look too well. They made me promise not to go back to work again until I felt entirely better. I promised most solemnly.

I walked out of that phone booth. It was three-thirty in the afternoon, and I was a free man. As the song goes, I didn't know where I was going but I was going.

One thing for sure, my convalescence was over.

7

I WAS on the street. I didn't know exactly where. It was hot. Above me the sun was shining. There was one place in the cover of smog brighter than the rest. My eyes smarted. I could smell the industrial waste. I could taste it. There was something malignant in the air. I needed shelter. I thought of Florence's little cellar in Indio. That would be cool and safe. But it was too far to go. I didn't want to go there anyway.

In some cities you go into a bar and get a drink to comfort yourself against the cold. In Los Angeles you go into a bar to get out of the hot lard people live in and breathe.

The interior of the bar was very dark and very cool. It was a great relief. I finished my first vodka and tonic before my eyes adjusted to the point where I could see around me. Then I noticed men standing at the bar on both sides of me. What were they doing there in the middle of the business day? Each man was looking straight ahead of him, disconnected from his neighbor. They all looked to be respectable representatives of prospering companies. Had they quit their jobs, too?

I didn't want to go home. Like the other men at the bar, I seemed to want nothing more than to stand there and feel like a big explosive on a short fuse. If someone drops a flaring match into this place, I thought, it will blow up.

I went to the juke box and found Al Hirt. When "Java" came on, no one applauded my choice; no one objected.

The bar was decorated in Hawaiian-type decor. There were no Hawaiians in sight. I had another vodka, and left.

It was only four o'clock. If I went home now, I'd have to explain a lot of things to Florence.

Outside it was even hotter. My eyes began to water. I could taste the corrosive stuff in the air. I had to get out of it.

I passed by a motel. I went in. It was called The Palms. There were no palms in sight. The room was air-conditioned. I fell on the bed. The windows were closed. The ceiling was spotless, no sign of life, not a fly! The room had just been "bombed." I got up and turned on the TV. I got up and turned off the TV. I had noticed on my way in that The Palms had a pool. I walked around the back to where it was. It looked good, the coolest aquamarine. I knelt and dipped my finger. The water smelled heavily of PTH and chlorine. I went back to my room and washed my hands. The bowl had a strip across it vouching it had been sterilized for my protection. The towel smelled of disinfectants. So did the sheets when I lay face down on the bed. I turned the air-conditioner up to blow the smell away. It blew a blast right across my bed. I had been perspiring, and now suddenly I was dangerously chilled.

I got up and went back out to the street. A taxi came along. I hailed it and told the driver to take me to the airport where I kept my Cessna 172.

The mechanics were glad to see me. They hadn't heard I'd been taken off the Zephyr account. I was just the man who owned the Cessna. Through my convalescence, the one thing I had not been eccentric about was the schedule of payments on the Cessna. So when I asked them to roll it out, they did.

When I got up through the smog, I was at seven hundred feet and just crossing Santa Monica beach. I turned north. I could see all the acrid stuff on my right. Some of it had a yellowish cast. Sulphur.

Just north of the Malibu Colony, the stuff thinned. I nosed down and did Zuma Beach at two hundred feet. Then I decided to go up into the Canyons. The air was clear here. The sun was at an afternoon angle. The hills were dark on one side, brilliant on the other. I spotted a herd of deer, most of them still asleep. They feed by night and bed down in the brush by day. I buzzed them, and they were up and running. It was beautiful, because there were these deep shadows where the sun didn't reach and you couldn't see them running. Then they'd come up and over and down the sunlit slopes.

I turned south. Over downtown L.A. the smog looked like something antique, a gas laid down in World War I, which had killed everyone and never blown away. A few of the buildings came up through the stuff, including the tower where Williams and MacElroy had their west coast offices. I began to circle this tower at a speed close to stall. Around and around. Once again I began to wonder: was it a hand that had turned my car into the side of that trailer truck? Ridiculous! Then why did I keep saying that? Well, because whatever it was, it was involuntary. It was not me. I opened the door on my side, and leaned far out. I waited. The plane circled the tower. I said, "Whoever you are, the hand of my enemy or the hand of my friend, come on!"

Meantime they were all cussing me out over the VHF Comm. I paid no attention. I just wanted to find out if, given this perfect opportunity, the "hand" would show again, maybe jam the plane's elevators or give me a heist out; it wouldn't take much with me leaning way out that way.

Of course it was ridiculous. I circled and circled that tower, waiting for something to happen. I was shouting, "Evangeleh!" (that's the name my father calls me) "Evangeleh! Why do you want to destroy yourself? Evangeleh, say! Where have you betrayed yourself?" There was no answer. No sign, no heist, nothing!

I noticed a police helicopter up there next to me. They were waving me away, and yelling at me over the VHF Comm. I realized that with all that tumult up there, I wasn't going to get answers to my questions that day. Especially with me clamoring like an insane prophet in the corniest of biblical epics. It would come, when it did again, unexpectedly.

They were waiting for me at the strip. Officials had come out of the woodwork especially for me. They promised they'd do me a lot of dire things. I gave them my best nothing smile and got into a cab.

They were waiting for me at home, too—Florence and Dr. Leibman. There was that awful calm these people put on when there is a hysterical situation. They even stood up when they saw me. Dr. Leibman grinned at me and was charming; Florence was charming, and I was charming. But I knew and they knew what the order of the day was. I should have busted up the place right then and there! What the hell did they think I was? Some kind of nut? Just then some cops in civilian clothes appeared, walking up the drive from a real alert-looking radio car. When Florence spotted them, she rushed off saying, "Don't worry, dear, I'll take care of them." And there I was, alone with Leibman.

He gave me his best open-hearth-type smile. I countered with my choicest nothing smile. And we were all even. He said sit down, won't you have a drink, like it was his home. I said sure, what have you got, like it was his bar. He laughed. I could see the spaces between his small sharp teeth. So I whistled "Big Noise from Winnetka" through my teeth. He listened like it was a music appreciation course and he had to guess the composer. Then there was a solid pause.

He kept studying me. When I couldn't take it any more, I headed for the pool. Leibman was right on me though. "How am I going to get away from this guy?" I said out loud. I sat down. He sat down. He was apparently not a man for hints. He turned now and looked at me. He seemed to be waiting for me to speak.

I began to be definitely uncomfortable. Aside from everything else it was awful hot. I had begun to sweat. I took off my shirt. He still seemed to be waiting for me to say something. But I outwaited him.

"Florence said you wanted to talk to me," he lied. Then he grinned. I peeled off my pants, kicked off my loafers, and jumped in the water.

"Well," said Dr. Leibman when I surfaced, "there you are!"

"Are you still here?" I said.

"Yes. And waiting."

"Well, don't. Because I've got nothing to say."

"Say anything," he said smiling.

I had an even better view of the spaces between his teeth. He reminded me of someone.

"Start anywhere. For instance, what are your problems now?"

"The only problem I have right now is how to get rid of you."

And I submerged. When I came up, he was laughing and looked just like one of those little Jewish kids that used to play on our street. I couldn't take him seriously.

"Tell me what you're thinking right now," he said.

"Nothing."

"Nothing? It's impossible to think nothing."

I was holding on to the edge of the pool. He cozied his chair alongside.

Suddenly he said, "What? What?"

I hadn't said a word.

"What were you going to say just then?"

"I wish you'd blast off!" I said.

"Ah," he said, like he'd made a big discovery. "Now! So now tell me why your orientation towards me is so hostile, my friend. I'd like to hear about that."

I went for pool bottom. This guy's got me cornered, I thought. I can't stay down here very long, and he's up there waiting. They got me in the last hole left on earth, the one with the water in it.

I surfaced, and as I broke water, I shouted, "Florence!" I stayed there in the middle of the pool, shouting "Florence! Florence! Florence!" till she came running down the lawn and took the man away.

He was sure telling her, all the way up the hill and into the house. I stayed in the pool until I heard his car drive off. As I climbed out, Florence came down from the house.

"Well," I said, "what's his diagnosis?"

"Diagnosis!" she said, and began to laugh as if that was certainly a subtle word to use for so obvious a situation.

"How did you get rid of the cops?" I asked.

"I promised them you would not drive a car again!"

"*You* promised them!"

"Yes." She had a most absolute tone of voice when she expected opposition. "As for your exploits in the air, that is *verboten*. And not *my* doing, darling. The Civil Aeronautics people were on the phone with me before you ever got back here. They wanted to tell you that, pending a full inquiry, you were grounded. And that there would be other, more serious consequences."

I jumped back into the pool.

Usually I can't stay under water very long. But now I circled the bottom like the seals do. When I finally came up, I saw Florence walking up the hill towards the house. I watched her go, and I said to myself, "Why do you torture that woman? Leave her, for chrissake. Go to Seattle. She's probably wishing, in her secret heart, that you'd disappear. She could shed tears for a few days, and it would all be over." I couldn't stand the sight of Florence's pain. So I went down again. I liked the bottom of that pool better and better.

"Poor thing," I thought, "those bags under her eyes, they were pretty bad this morning." She had come to refer to them as "your bags," meaning I had put them there. I knew that every time she wiped them at night with Spread and Sparkle, or Wipe and Wonder, she blamed me. I can't say she wasn't right. If I was my wife, I'd have bags, too.

I swam around the bottom of the pool, slowly and easily, like a seal. I suddenly had great new powers for underwater swimming.

I remembered the time I went to New York to see Collier with Gwen. Just before I left, Florence told me she was going to have her face lifted while I was away.

"What do you want to do that for?" I asked.

"Do I look good to you now?"

"You look . . . well . . ."

"Like a wife. I know. Well, Evans, that's turned out to be slow death. I don't deserve to be ignored as a woman, night after night. So I'm going to do something about it. Even if you don't care how I look, I do."

When I got back she had indeed done it. They do it right behind the ears. Just a tuck or two. I told her she looked much better, which was true. But it didn't affect me as she hoped it would. And the new look didn't last. The *schmerz* soon enough hits you somewhere else. So now it was my bags under her eyes.

I came up for air again, and Florence was coming down the lawn towards me, wearing her lioness costume. Not visible, of course, but plainly there. She arranged herself firmly in one of the metal chairs and said, "Evans, I want to have a talk with you."

Whenever she spoke that particular sentence in that particular way, I felt like a servant about to be let out. She'd sit in a chair like now, blow the uninhaled smoke out of the side of her mouth, and I couldn't help thinking, I hope she'll give me a good reference.

Then I looked at her and realized how unfair I was being. Because the woman was frightened. She was talking to a husband who had just tried to kill himself again, this time in a plane. She was a decent person, scared stiff.

"I'm awfully sorry, Florence," I said.

"Oh, darling, it's not a matter of that; I just wish . . ."

She couldn't talk.

"What, dear?"

"I do wish you'd think of me, just once, as your friend. I'm not against you, Ev; all I want in the world is to help you."

"I know."

"Come up and sit here with me."

I did.

"Evans dear, you told me you don't want me, you don't want this house, you don't like the way we live. I haven't forgotten that conversation. But now, I want to ask you—and please think of me as your friend asking—what is it you *do* want?"

"I don't know."

"Do you want her?"

"Who?"

"Who!"

I didn't say anything. Silence, that's my strong point.

"Evans, I'm your friend. If that's what you truly want, you can have her, if that's what will really make you happy. Evans, don't be afraid of the truth."

"I really don't think that's it."

"Evans, I'm your friend."

I felt like jumping into the pool again. She must have sensed it, because she said, "Now don't go jumping into the pool again. You're such a darned kid."

So I sat there on dry land, out of my element of the moment, silent, forty-four and fucked up, not knowing what I wanted. I wondered, is this what it is, a breakdown? Because, sure enough, something central had broken down. I couldn't do or not do, go or not go; I could barely talk. I felt like going to the bottom of the pool, that's all. But it didn't feel bad, the breakdown, if that's what it was. I simply existed, without will, without desire or resistance, without even my own weight. I floated.

"Florence," I said.

"Yes, Evans."

"Nothing," I said.

It is said of the giraffe that he has no voice, that when his neck is in the lion's jaws, he can't protest his own murder.

"Why don't you talk to Dr. Leibman again?"

"I did—three times. At 50 per."

"He's a very sensible, decent, and understanding person, and he's a kind man, too."

"I want to talk to someone who is violent and destructive, ruthless and murderous."

I looked at her and smiled.

She smiled back at me, the smile of an angel. And again I thought, what am I doing torturing this woman? I should just disappear. Go to Seattle. Really! It's not necessary that the life of this perfectly decent person be intertwined with yours. Liberate her! Before you quietly murder her.

"I'd like to take a nap now," I said.

"I'll keep everyone away. Would you like a pillow down here, or a drink, or some juice, or anything, Ev, tell me."

"No, I'm just going to lie down and sleep awhile. I guess I'm tired. I don't want to talk any more."

I went to where she sat, kissed her cheek, and said, "I'm sorry the way I am. It's not your fault. Please don't think it has anything to do with you. You're a wonderful woman."

She made a sound like a gasp, hugged me with all her might, and kissed me, tried to, on the mouth. But I couldn't do that, I just couldn't. I did hug her, and said, "Thank you, thank you. There isn't a better girl in the world than you. All this is just me."

"You see, Evans, I don't walk away and leave a person. I'm not made that way. Go on, now, sleep."

She turned and went up the hill. She did look better.

I got up. I felt my belly. It was thickening. My father and my uncles, I remember, were proud of their bellies. A pot meant only one thing among oriental rug merchants: that they were successful, and depending upon the size of the protuberance, how successful. It was an index to their bank balances. Me? I was embarrassed by extra weight. I began to do push-ups. Then suddenly I fell out of one of them, fell flat on my stomach, and was almost immediately asleep.

I have a gift. I can always sleep. In the days when Florence and I cared enough to fight, in those first months, or maybe a year or two, we had some terrible quarrels which left her trembling with rage, all night sometimes. But they'd leave me asleep. There she'd be sitting up in bed, spoiling for another round, but there'd be nobody to fight. Once she got so furious she went downstairs to get a kitchen knife; she was going to kill me. But when she got back upstairs, I was asleep. And you can't do that to a man who's sleeping. Asleep we all look innocent, thank God. Especially when you're in the wrong, sleep is an invaluable ally.

They tried to wake me for dinner. But I wouldn't. I knew I couldn't cope with things awake.

So they moved me upstairs. I undressed as I walked and fell into that big, beautiful double bed, without pajamas, without washing my teeth.

I wanted a long cease-fire!

But it didn't work.

That was the night our marriage broke.

I don't know when, at what hour it happened. Sometime in the dark and unconscious middle of the night I woke. Florence was asleep alongside, breathing heavily. I could hear the house. I remember I could hear the sounds of the appliances turning on and turning off, those gentle sounds, freezing this, heating that, whirring and spinning, clicking, starting, stopping. They're nice peaceful sounds, all those faithful little motors, precision engineered to do their little jobs quietly while we sleep. I remember I was listening to them, and I must have fallen off, because all of a sudden I realized, I remember, I was making love to her, to Florence. And I could. Actually it was just beginning to go into her. And suddenly I woke. And she woke. We looked at each other. And without realizing how horrible it was, I did a horrible thing. I looked at her and recognized that it was Florence, my wife, and not Gwen, who it had been in my dream, and I pulled out. I rolled over, away from her—violently—and lay on my stomach.

She lay there looking at the ceiling. I could hardly breathe. For once I couldn't fall back asleep. It was the longest night of my life. The facts had asserted themselves!

The next morning there was no visible break in our routine. We both liked to read the news with our coffee; we both liked our papers unrumpled, so our custom was to have delivered to the door each morning two copies of the Los Angeles *Times*. We sat there, now as always, on opposite sides of the glass-top garden table, both in our robes, both safe for the moment behind newsprint.

Florence looked bled out. She was wearing her rose-colored negligee, which looks sweet on her when she's feeling well. But rose is a treacherous color, and this morning it dramatized her pallor.

We didn't say a word all through breakfast. I believe that Florence didn't trust herself to take a position or even have a clear strong reaction any longer without first talking to Dr. Leibman—which she was scheduled to do at 9:20 that morning. At 8:30 she went upstairs to dress. I sat there awhile. We were on the verge.

It was another glaring gray day. I went upstairs to get my dark glasses.

I was barefooted, so Florence didn't hear me. She was standing looking at herself over her shoulder in the pier glass, examining the backs of her upper legs. They had begun to waffle badly, the subcutaneous matter quilting up. I felt sort of guilty, as if, somewhere along the line, I should have been able to stop it or at least reassure her that it didn't make any difference. But I hadn't, because it did.

I tried, now, to get out without her noticing, but she saw me in the glass, and quickly adjusted her skirts as if I was a stranger. I started out, but she called me back.

"That party is tonight," she said.

"Oh, my God, what party?"

"If you'll think, you'll remember that the Bennetts are throwing a welcome-back party. For you. Do you remember now?"

"I guess so. I mean we'll go, huh?"

She didn't answer. Finally I turned and left.

I had mortally hurt a person.

I went back to the door of the bedroom. "Florence," I said, "I'm sorry." She was putting on lipstick.

"Evans," she said, "if you were really sorry, you'd do something about it. But you won't. So please don't expect me to believe you're sorry. I don't think you're in control any more of what you say or feel or do." She was out of the room.

I walked down to the pool. But I didn't feel safe there now. After all, how long could I stay at the bottom? I thought of going to a Turkish bath. I once stayed in the Luxor for three days. But I couldn't summon up the gumption to do that. So I took off all my clothes, lay on the diving board, and waited for it to happen. I was at anyone's mercy. All I could hope for now was a miracle. Perhaps some awful catastrophe would happen and rescue me! Maybe I'd be killed, or Florence would, or there'd be an earthquake or a war. I understood why a war is so attractive to people. It rescues them from their hopeless personal situations. In fact, it makes everything personal seem trivial. It's even better than a Turkish bath. It excuses everything and erases everything. Oh, I thought, if only there'd come a war to rescue me! If they'd only blow up an atom bomb by mistake! I could go sit in that cellar in Indio.

So I fell asleep.

When I woke, Florence was back from her session with Leibman, and sitting in the poolside armchair. It was scary the way she looked at me. Either murderous or suicidal, I couldn't tell which. The most terrifying part of it was that as soon as she saw me, she put on her very controlled smile. She was pleasant. Leibman really earns his money, I thought. He had done a most effective hurry patch job that morning. I admired him in spite of himself. How long would it last? Till she saw him again tomorrow at exactly 9:20. He kept her going from day to day; whatever he did lasted just 24 hours—planned obsolescence in the spiritual field.

"Aren't you going to the office?" she said, lightly, as if it didn't really matter to her.

"What?"

"I said, aren't you going to the office? It's nine-forty-five."

"What office?"

She turned and looked the other way. She was controlling something, because her whole body shook for an instant. I thought, stop playing games with her, tell her the deal, get it over with.

"No," I said. "I've quit."

"Well, that's news."

"Yes, it is."

"When did you decide that?"

"Just now, though it's been happening all along."

"So what are you going to do?"

"I don't know."

"Are you sure you know what you're doing?"

"Does anybody?"

"Evans, that's sheer shit! For chrissake! Yes, anybody does; people do!"

Then she controlled herself again. Clearly Dr. Leibman had told her to be calm under all provocation, to wait things out. Christ, I thought, if I were her analyst, I'd advise her to empty both barrels of a shotgun into me.

"Dear," she said, "have you told them? I mean . . ."

"No, but I'm going to . . . I've decided. I have quit."

"What?"

"Everything!"

"Me too?"

"I don't know. Maybe. Maybe everything. I'm not sure yet."

"What am I supposed to do now?"

"About what?"

"About my life. I've got to have a life."

I didn't say anything.

"You haven't thought about me, is that it?"

"I guess not, no."

"Sorry to bother you with such trifles, but—well—for instance, what am I supposed to think about what happened last night?"

"Last night?"

"I'll spell it out. Before your accident, I thought it was something physical: your circulation, or your gonads, or your nervous system. But now—well, it's there all right, isn't it? But it's not there for me. I mean, who did you think I was last night?"

I didn't answer.

"Silence. O.K. Well, I've had it. It's thirteen months now. I don't know what you expected. I guess you expected me to wait around while you found whatever it is you've been looking for. Or whoever."

"I haven't been with anyone else in that time, Florence."

"That's probably a lie, but if it's true, it's your problem. I'm not going to play your hand and mine, any more. You're a person who looks out only for himself. I'd better begin looking out for myself."

She walked up the slope and into the house.

8

I STAYED in my little fortress most of that afternoon. When it came up five o'clock, I had no choice. I had to go back into the big house. I found Florence drying her hair. Her party clothes were laid out, so I gathered she was going with me. Just to make sure, I asked, "What am I supposed to wear tonight?"

"Call Olga Bennett," she said, then, "Oh, balls, Evans! Stop acting like a baby. When I wear a short dress, you wear a blue suit. And since we've been called together to celebrate your recovery, why don't you make some effort to be on time?"

We didn't exactly chat our way over to the Bennetts. But Florence did make one request. "Considering the way you behaved during your convalescence, I think Olga and Dale fantastically generous to throw you any kind of party. But Dale considers you one of his close friends. If you've got a defender left in this community, it's him. I know that doesn't mean anything to you now. But Olga *is* my best friend. So I wish you wouldn't be insulting tonight. Do you think you might manage that? As a parting favor to me?"

"A parting favor?"

"Well, we're separated, aren't we? Let's get at least that much settled."

I didn't answer.

"Silence? O.K. Let's see how you like the game when it goes the other way."

End of conversation.

What a strange phrase that is, I was thinking—"close friend." I had known Dale Bennett for seventeen years, played tennis on his court countless Sundays, had dinner with him and his wife Olga at regular intervals. But were we really close friends?

We met right after the war, when Williams and MacElroy first opened a west coast office. I would have sworn then that I was in advertising only temporarily. I was very busy looking around for what might turn out to be my real career. For a couple of years I became interested in films, thought of becoming a screen writer. It looked easy—especially when you met the men who did it for a living.

It wasn't. During those two years, I sold exactly one original story. It was called *The Red Arrow,* and it came out of some of my war experiences in the Philippines. Dale Bennett, then a recent Academy Award winner, was assigned to make it into a screen play with me, which, everyone told me, was a great break, because it gave me a chance to learn my trade from the then number-one man in the field. I must have had a premonition though, because I held on to my advertising job and moonlit the script. Dale preferred working at night anyway.

He was some five years older, and immediately took a fatherly interest. I, in turn, paid him all deference, kneeled and knuckled. From the time I was a kid, I'd found that the best way with anyone I felt I had to please. Dale and I always agreed. I saw to that. When I didn't agree, I swallowed it. That was our working arrangement.

Five months of work and Dale's best efforts succeeded only in revealing the basic weaknesses of *The Red Arrow.* Finally Dale felt he had to recommend that the studio shelve the property. He observed, in his funeral oration, that I had a lot to learn about story construction. He did not encourage me to continue in the field. I said, as we cleaned out our desks in the Writers' Building, that my basic story had never been really sound. I could see that now, I lied. All of which left the failure mine, and made Dale feel warmly towards me. So our relationship began, a social habit like dogs running together. Actually I didn't agree with him on politics, prejudices, taste, what a nice day was. He even found Gwen unattractive when I introduced her to him.

As Dale got older, fashions in screen writing passed him by. In fact he had had trouble, the last few years, getting decent assignments. But very recently this had changed in his favor and for a very odd reason. The party he was throwing that night had little to do with celebrating my recovery. What Dale really wanted to celebrate publicly was a killing he had made in the stock market with a company organized to manufacture birth control pills. He had got in with a buy of ten thousand shares at, I think, two. A week ago when he had decided to throw the Welcome-Back-Eddie party, the stock was at seventy-six and going up, which gave him a paper profit of almost three quarters of a million dollars. The odd part of it was that, whereas everyone had come to think of Dale as an old-fashioned hack, when the news of his killing got around, Dale was once again, as he had been fifteen years before, one of the most sought after screen writers in the industry.

I was thinking, so I missed the Bennetts' turn-off. Florence called this to my attention with a minimum of sarcasm.

"What's the film tonight?" I asked.

"You don't have to make conversation," she said. "We're almost there."

"I'm not making conversation," I lied. "I'm curious."

"I doubt that. But if I knew, I couldn't tell you. It's a surprise, for you, Olga said."

End of conversation.

Nearly all Hollywood parties climax with the showing of a film, usually one that hasn't yet hit the theaters. The film saves the evening as the conversation crumbles. As soon as I walked into the Bennett home, the surprise was revealed. The film we were to see was *A Cry From the Steeple,* a *cause célèbre* before its release. Its director was the soft mountain of man I could see on the sofa, pontificating to the people around him.

Dale rushed up and greeted me ardently. "We've been waiting a long time for this, you and I." He took me over and introduced me to Gottfried Hoff. Dale and I had talked about Gottfried Hoff for over a decade, but I had never really met him. Close to, now, he reminded me of the beached hulk of a great ocean liner.

Dale and I had first become aware of Hoff a year or so after we quit on my story; Dale had taken me to a literary party, and there he was, drunk and sounding off that all Americans are cultural savages, which sounds twice as mean when said with a German accent. That night he was surrounded by lefty intellectuals, amen choristers to everything he said. I'd come back, not too long before, from the Pacific, where I'd seen a lot of fellows die in a war that one of his countrymen had started, so I resented him immediately. Dale, who had been in London in 1941, wanted to kill Hoff on the spot. He vowed we'd get him.

A mutual enemy is strong cement. More than anything else, our unfriendly interest in Hoff kept our relationship close over the years. When we drifted apart, I'd forget about Hoff until Dale would call up with a fresh bit of gossip about him. Dale never forgot him.

We started off by finding out all about Hoff's past. He had made some fine pictures in the Germany of the twenties and early thirties. Then, comfortably anticipating Hitler's take-over (that's how Dale described it), Hoff got himself to southern California. There he enjoyed the war years. (I was slogging from Hollandia to Biak to Tacloban to Luzon. Dale was ducking the V's, one and two.) Hoff made some films, but spent most of his energy going to parties and accepting tribute. His chief exercise was bowing from the waist. He also had the pick of the crop of sunkist girls. (I had the Asiatic crud, Dale the Piccadilly clap.) Hoff soon established himself as king of the satyrs. For many years it was considered statusy among the local ladies to have been had by Gottfried Hoff. His arrogance was his lure. At regular intervals over the years, Dale used to call me and tell me with absolute astonishment the details of Hoff's latest conquest. More often than not it was a very "nice" girl, a very prized girl. Hoff, it seemed, never missed. His unfailing success further sharpened our appetite for revenge.

Hoff, of course, had not gone back to Germany as had other artistic *émigrés*. "The son of a bitch's got it too good here," Dale once said to me. "A house on Pacific Palisades, a nisei couple, a wife who's a perfect servant, the kind you can't find any more, and all the tail he can handle. That kraut bastard won the war for a fact."

Now at Olga's party he was riding the obsession of his life, the injustices committed in this country against his talent, his work, his self. Clearly he had extremely high blood pressure. His face was doused with perspiration and very red. His wife, who wore what can only be described as a small black tent, sat next to him and mopped his forehead with a man's handkerchief. She did not speak, smile, or frown. Hoff was her total field of vision.

Dale leaned over the back of the sofa and took the empty out of Hoff's hand, replacing it with a full. He either didn't notice or chose to ignore a request from Mrs. Hoff's eyes that he not give her husband a fresh drink. Hoff was talking about the outrageous treatment he had received during the production of *A Cry From The Steeple*.

Anyone who read the columns knew all about that film. The story was what is known in the trade as an inspirational subject with (in Dale's words) "this Jesus-type leading man, Mexican but clean." Dale's brother wrote for *The Hollywood Reporter,* so Dale was able to give me, in regular installments, the goodies of Hoff's squabbles with his producer. The first time Hoff had shown his version of the completed film to his producer, he had brought to the projection room, as his guest, his pet monkey, explaining that he wanted to see what the animal's instinctive reaction to the film would be. Since the producer was notorious for bringing his wife to the first public showing of each of his films, notorious, too, for following her "instinct," he called it, he naturally resented Hoff's swipe. (Even Dale had to admire Hoff for this one.) Well, after the film had been run off, the producer took Hoff and his monkey aside and officially informed the maître that he was not at all satisfied with the way the film had been put together. Which was not only what Hoff expected, said Dale, but what he obviously wanted: another international scandal of culture, another chance to publicly scorn the U.S.A.

Hoff called a press conference the next day. Every representative of the foreign press was there and delighted. They would trumpet again how Hollywood was ruining the work of this unique genius. Hoff concluded the conference by saying that under the circumstances, he had no hope for the film and would never see it again.

How Dale had managed to make Hoff change his mind was Dale's secret. But there he was now, about to see his mutilated film for the first time.

"How did you ever manage it?" I whispered to Dale. (We were standing right behind the sofa where Hoff was holding court.)

"I did it for you," Dale answered in a normal voice. I remembered that Hoff was partly deaf. "All for you."

Actually Dale's interest was his own. You might think, now that he was rich and in demand again, he'd have everything he wanted, but not so. He desperately wanted the recognition of the "in" crowd. Of course he would not admit this, especially to himself. But he had read what *Cahiers du Cinema* and *Sight and Sound* said about his films. He knew there wasn't a chance that he'd ever get favorable recognition from them. So the next best thing was something he could get—revenge. Hoff was one of the chief darlings of the "in" crowd, and *A Cry From the Steeple* was, by all gossip, a disaster.

Dinner was announced. Mrs. Hoff began the labor of getting her husband to his feet.

"I've put you right next to him at dinner," said Dale. "Keep his glass full. When he sees what that producer has done with his film, he'll blow. I want the blast-off to be worthy of the preparation."

Then he took Hoff by one arm, and holding me by the other, walked us into the dining area.

I immediately noticed how many of the guests were in on the deal. As the meal progressed, they pretended sympathetic interest in Hoff's stories, the while making snide remarks just below his hearing. It became a game to see how close you could come to being detected. As for Mrs. Hoff, they behaved as if she wasn't there.

Florence had caught on to what was going on, and I could see she didn't like it one bit. But her polite efforts to change the subject, or put a pleasant cast over it all, simply didn't work. The guests would not be pulled off their fun.

I was sitting right next to the target, and I caught it all: the salivating of the sadists, what they said that he heard, what they said that he missed. Predators around a wounded animal. To my surprise I began to feel for the man, I suppose because he was the underdog. He was so conceited, so self-centered, he was absolutely unaware he was being set up for slaughter. And this, what was in effect his naïveté, also began to enlist me. In some totally unexpected way, he was innocent.

Dale was looking at Hoff's empty glass, then at me. I pretended not to see. Dale finally had to say, "Eddie, Mr. Hoff's glass is not full." As I obeyed, I felt ashamed and resentful. Mrs. Hoff was giving me the same pleading look she had given Dale earlier. But it was too late. I was filling the glass.

And my own. From that moment, I matched Hoff drink for drink.

I remembered the stories I had heard of Hoff's great drunks, how he would hole up in a hotel suite for a week with a case of booze, Mrs. Hoff sleeping across the threshold of the locked bedroom door so her husband could not get out without her knowing it. In this way he would manage what was apparently necessary for him periodically: to disappear from the face of the earth. Looking at him now, with his uneven complexion, his gross fleshiness, his baggy black suit, those fabled drunks struck me in a different light. They were the actions not of a proud but a shamed man. What made Hoff sweat was not arrogance as much as violent self-disgust, an emotion I now knew well. He was gulping his food like an animal who had stolen a carcass and had to defend it till he had it all down. When I didn't finish my venison, he asked me if he could. And he quickly did, perspiring all the time.

I suddenly had an impulse to wipe his perspiring forehead. Mrs. Hoff had been placed at the opposite end of the table from her husband, so he was without an attendant. I took out my pocket handkerchief and mopped the massive moist dome. Hoff acknowledged my service with a side-flung look that contained no thanks. He merely accepted the attention of a newly acquired slave. He was hard to take, Mr. Hoff.

I poured us both another.

Then, somewhere between the Brie and the baked Alaska, it happened. The bating of the man had become bolder and bolder, and suddenly I had had as much as I was going to take. "Oh, knock it off," I said.

The table conversation went on for an instant before people realized I had done something extraordinary. Then the whole room was silent. And I said again, this time directly at Dale, "What do you say, Dale, let's knock it off, kid."

Dale looked at me quite a while. "What was that, dear boy?" He'd called me "dear boy" for fifteen years, and I suppose I had always thought it patronizing, but I'd never said anything about it.

"What I said, Dale, was let's cut it out."

"Cut what out, dear boy?"

"You know damned well what," I said.

"No, I really don't. Be more specific, if you're able to be. Also think very carefully before you go on with this."

"I've been thinking about it for quite a while, and I'm asking you, since I'm the guest of honor and this pigsticking is being staged to entertain me, I'm asking you to turn the victim loose."

"I don't quite get what . . ."

"You get it. I want you to stop fattening this Berliner pig for the slaughter. You know damned well what you're doing."

146

"And what's that?"

"There's a word for it."

"And what's that word?"

"You know the word."

"No, I don't. I'd like you to say it."

"Well, it smells of sadism to me."

"Oh, it does?"

"That's right."

"And you don't like it."

"I don't like it one bit."

By now I regretted ever having started. After all, I didn't have the flimsiest friendship for Hoff. But once I started, I couldn't cop out. And why the hell should I? The hell with Dale, I thought, it's the truth. What's all this close friend routine anyway? I was now pretty drunk and said to myself, "You have no right to blame Dale. You had no business pretending to be his friend all those years. You're as responsible for all this as he is."

Dale Bennett turned to Hoff and, indicating me, said, "Gottfried, do you feel like a pig being prepared for slaughter?" At which the whole room laughed.

For the moment the tension was eased. Hoff, the rat, said, "My dear friend." (He was speaking to me.) "Don't be a child. What are you talking?" I thought the "dear friend" extravagant, and since he had often said publicly that all American men were children, I didn't particularly care for that designation.

So I said to myself, the hell with you, too, brother, and I determined to shut up and be a "nothing" the rest of the night, and maybe go home early.

Florence was the first to leave the table, followed by my agent, Mike Weiner, who had been sitting next to her.

I caught Bennett measuring me. I guess he was trying to figure where to gaff me first. As we got up from the table, he tossed off, "Speaking of sadism, dear boy, what have you been doing to Florence lately?"

"Why?" I said, real nothing.

"Because she looks terrible. I must tell you we like her a hell of a lot better than we do you, and, dear boy, now that you have officially recovered from your accident, I think you might give her an occasional thought."

We got separated in the crush going downstairs. The guests were being herded into the rumpus room, a big cellar fixed up Wild-West-saloon style, with a long bar at one end, and the entrance to the Ol' Crick—that is, the swimming pool—at the other. There were a lot of toys for adults in the room, including a stand of one-armed bandits, some old-fashioned flip-card movies featuring naked women of a bygone age, a row of pinball machines with all the little signs rewritten cleverly for local allusion, and a dart game with the head of Castro for a target. Painted on the barroom floor were the faces of the hosts' dearest friends. I was featured, an enormous Zephyr cigarette in my grip.

Some of the men immediately sat down at the barroom table and began the inevitable gin game. Among them was Hoff, who could hardly see by now. Even sober, he was a notorious pigeon.

Bennett followed me. When I sat down, he sat down next to me. "Now is the time," I said to myself, "for that famous silence of yours."

"Dear boy," said Bennett, "I can't help wondering why you're so worried about Hoff."

I noticed people moving closer. Quarrels, after all, are still our best entertainment. Dale began speaking partly for the benefit of his growing audience. "After all, he's nothing but a cultural Commie, with the psychology and manners of a storm trooper. He's been in this country since 1940, made a fortune by pissing all over us in his films; we've discussed all this a hundred times in perfect agreement, Eddie."

I held my mouth closed.

Dale was smiling. "What do you say?" Everybody was waiting for me to say something. Dale continued, "You gave me reason to believe you'd be absolutely delighted to see him finally getting his lumps."

I smiled my nothing smile, whistled my nothing tune.

"So what happened, Eddie?"

By now my silence was choking me to death. I'd gotten a taste, during my convalescence, of blurting everything out. I hadn't forgotten how good it felt.

At that moment, there was a wave of new entrances, the after-dinner crowd. Dale had to go greet them.

It's interesting who smells a fight coming first. Now gathered around me, waiting for Dale's return, was a la-de-da clothes designer, a man who had done a lot of Florence's clothes; you wouldn't think him bloodthirsty, but he was, ravenous. With him was his dykish wife, who doubled as his business manager, and she had that ringside look, too. There was one of the really big agents in town, a leader in the agents' take-over of the film business, a man with one of the greatest collections of French Impressionists in the world, but personally a hood. With him was his wife. Also with him was his girl friend. There was the disappointed and abandoned second wife of a very well-known producer. And there was the disappointed and abandoned third wife of the same producer. They were given to attending wrestling matches in each other's company, always in the front row, side by side. There was the aging ingénue star who still managed to play bobby soxers but was threatened with premature baldness, as anyone could see when she stood with a light behind her. At her side, as always, was her husband, the scion of the Willingham hotel empire, which his father, at his death, had left in perfect working order, so perfect that all the scion had to do all day was sit by the pool of his country club and make sure no Jews got in. Next to her was the queen, Emily Adams, the leading lady critic in town. She wore a heavy gold cross on her well-braced bosom. With her was her husband, a cretin. All these people had smelled a fight and moved in from nowhere like a circle of hyenas. Joining them were some of the kids, the latest squab come to town on the Greyhounds, and the wolves who had scouted them out and were presently showing and giving them the works. They just wanted excitement.

"I wish I felt free," said Emily Adams, "to tell you the names of some of the gals this man has hurt and hurt badly. If you knew some of the inside I know, you wouldn't permit yourself to be quite so sympathetic."

I was just about to say something to this bitch that would have busted up the evening and good, but I stopped myself in time, got to my feet, and from habit went looking for Florence.

She was sitting with a man I had never seen before. Florence was doing all the talking, her new admirer paying devout attention. I could see the route she was going.

Since Florence was occupied, I sat down next to our hostess and said, "Olga, hold my hand, will you? Your husband wants to pick a fight with me, and I really don't want to."

"Then go tell him you're sorry."

"For what?"

"Eddie, what's the matter with you? Have you lost your mind? You called Dale a sadist in front of the whole dinner table, and in his own house. Do you expect people to take that? Since your accident, you've gotten away with insulting everyone who came to see you, including many of Florence's best friends, saying any malicious and irresponsible thing that came into your head. We all made allowances because we were loyal to Florence. But Eddie, the accident is over. That's really why we threw this party, to draw a line. Anything you say from now on you have to mean. Put up or shut up. Because Florence forgives you everything doesn't mean the rest of us have to. If you and Dale weren't the oldest and best of friends, he'd have had you out in the backyard by now. I wouldn't respect Dale if, the next time you make one of your cracks, he didn't bop you, but good. I'm sick of *that* you. So is everyone else here. I'm sick of hearing you knock this town and knock these good people. You're in God's clover here, and if you think it's poison ivy, don't bitch about it; move!"

She started to walk away mad, then came back. "Eddie, Dale's the best friend you've got in this community. You better find your senses again." She took my hand and began to pull me over to where Dale was. I was going to apologize, too.

Apparently it hadn't required a pistol in her ribs to persuade Emily to go into the details of Hoff's sex life. Olga tried to get Dale's eye to make him aware that I had something to say to him.

"Oh, Emily," he was saying, "dear Emily, you're so refined. I'm sure that's why your column is such a success. But we're among friends tonight, so let's speak plainly. Mr. Hoff's taste is distinctly for the rounded heel, for the simple reason that's all he can now get. His latest, I understand, was something sorry named Gwen, I believe Hunter, and she had an opening the size of the subway entrance at Forty-second Street and Broadway. And quite as many people had used it. And the price, if I may stretch the parallel a bit further, was just a token. Olga, did you speak to me? And who's that with you?"

Olga was not so sure, now, that she wanted to bring us together.

Gwen, of course, had never met Hoff.

Dale got up and began to work his way through the crowd to me. I was waiting for him.

Just then a servant came down the stairs and said to Olga, "Mrs. Bennett, the film is ready upstairs." Normally it would have been another hour before Olga led her guests to the projection room. But she sized me up and sized Dale up, then she raised up on her toes, and belted out, "Show time! Movie time, everybody!"

There were groans from the gin players who had just begun to get into Hoff. But Olga got even more insistent. "Get up, get up, everybody!" She pulled me toward the stairs, calling back over her shoulder, "Dale, darling, will you bring Mr. Hoff along?"

My head was full of blood. It beat so hard it hurt.

Olga never let go my hand.

Everyone wanted the seats near Hoff. Dale put him down in the very front row, and everyone who could crowd around him did. The rest tried to find seats at the side where they could enjoy his reactions.

The lights went off.

It didn't take long for the sport to start. The under-title music was not what Hoff had caused to be written. "This is not my music," he mumbled. "What have they done to my music?" he said more urgently. "I cannot permit this." Everyone laughed. "This is schmaltz!" he said with a thickening German accent, "Yiddisher schmaltz!"

He was hard to take, Mr. Hoff.

"My vision didn't need this schmaltz!" he said with his knockwurst accent. Everyone was laughing now. The evening was going to be a success.

The film itself started. Of course it had been considerably rearranged. And provided with an opening narration that underscored the Biblical parallel. "Schtinks!" said Hoff. "Gabidge!" Then on the sound track came a genuflection to organized devotionalism, spoken in unctuous tones by a famous TV personality, whose voice no one could fail to recognize.

"I piss on that bastard," growled Hoff.

I must say I felt the same way.

But others didn't. Along with the laughter, there were some hisses. I could particularly hear Emily's, "Will you please keep quiet, Mr. Hoff, so those of us who want to can enjoy the picture?"

At this moment Hoff discovered that one of his favorite shots—an establishing long shot that covered 360 degrees of Mexican desert littered with cadavers, skeletons, skulls, and other symbols of death, the whole composed to represent the "Waste Land which is the culture of our time" (quote from Hoff to the foreign press)—this shot was cut.

"Where is my long shot?" bellowed the drunken genius. He addressed himself directly to the people assembled there. He was standing now, and pointing in the manner of an Ernst Toller hero. Again there was a hostile reaction. "Will you please shut up . . . sit down . . . shshsh!"

But Hoff wasn't about to. "What have you done with my long shot?" he bellowed at everyone. He had described this shot in detail to the foreign press. "Three hundred and sixty degrees, all back lit; how I did it is my secret." He had promised them that they'd see at least that much of his vision intact. Now, caterwauling pure pain, he rushed up the aisle and into the projection room, from where he could be heard accusing the projectionist of having jumped a reel.

"Dale, would you send that man home immediately," said Emily, the gold cross heaving on her pink bubs. "I like this picture, and I will not sit here and . . ."

Hoff rushed back into the room. "I will sue him!" he announced to everyone. "If there is still a law in this country, I will bring this filthy little tradesman to his knees." Some people thought he said the word "Jewish." I didn't hear it.

"Who is Hitler's victim talking about?" a man whispered to Olga.

"His producer, I believe," she whispered. Then she turned to me and said, "And you have sympathy for that man, Eddie?"

The Jesus type, Mexican but clean, had come on the screen now. It had been Hoff's intention to introduce his hero at a high moment when he is driving the money changers out of the temple (a Mexican provincial cathedral). Apparently the hero's tell-off speech had been completely rewritten by the producer. The gossip, as Dale had passed it on to me, had the producer commenting on Hoff's original, "Mr. Hoff seems to be saying that people are bad simply because they are rich. I don't think this idea will find general acceptance in America." He wasn't kidding either. "Furthermore," he had gone on, "I noticed that when Mr. Hoff and I were having our salary discussions, he squeezed for every cent. He even demanded a secretarial job for his wife, who still can't write her name in legible English. Publicly, Hoff scorns money, but in fact he is a formidable trader, with a very solid feel for a dollar."

Whatever the truth of this, the producer had the speech completely rewritten, and had directed the new version himself, "So that Jesus would come out more Christian," he had said, "and less of an out-and-out Commie."

When the rewritten scene came on, Hoff stood in the projection beam, flailing his arms around and screaming, "Drek! Take it off! This is not mine!"

It was at this point that Emily stood up, all her jelly atremble, and said, "Dale Bennett, either he goes or I go. Take your pick." Now other people began to talk back to Hoff. He was yelling at the projectionist, right through the wall, "Take this off! At once!" (Et vunce!) There was an avalanche of "Et vunce's," riding on hysterical laughter, and at the same time, some very angry talk.

"What are you laughing?" demanded Hoff now, directly at the audience. "What are you laughing, you pigs?" (You had to admire his guts.) At which everybody who was laughing laughed louder. A male voice yelled at Hoff, "I'm going to kill you, you Nazi bastard!" People were restraining Mike Weiner, my agent, because they knew if he got to Hoff he would indeed kill him.

Nothing fazed Hoff. The man was ridiculous, preposterous, shameful, despicable. Though I knew he was probably everything Mike Weiner wanted to kill him for, I still couldn't help being enlisted by his pain. "This is desecration!" he announced to everyone in the room. "Where is your humanity? They have killed a piece of my life, you murderers."

The mask of levity was dropped now. Hoff was facing a roomful of jeering people. And he did, I suppose, the only thing he could to stop the film. He picked up a letter opener from the magazine table, rushed up to the screen, and ripped it to bits.

Then he pushed his way up through the aisle of jeerers, waving his hands, accepting their insults as if they were tributes. Someone tripped him. He got up, and smiled, and made a deep bow of gratitude. You just had to like him a little for that. Then he was out of the house, his wife following, head down and silent, looking as if she had never expected anything better from Americans.

Amidst the hysterics and laughing, there was another reaction, quieter, more sober. "It's our fault," said an old Western star—a dignified old man he was—"for letting people like that make films for us." This analysis drew a chorus of approbation.

The lights in the room were turned on now. The projectionist came out, looked at the screen, talked to Olga about getting a bedsheet and putting it up with thumb tacks.

The people who had been laughing most, the good-natured majority, headed for the big bar downstairs. The haters stayed. The room was suddenly very quiet and very tense.

I felt at bay. I was all alone up front. Olga had left with the projectionist. I took a quick look around for Florence. She had disappeared. I looked for the man who had attached himself to her. I didn't see him. Everyone who was still in the room had gathered at the back. They were talking intently. I couldn't hear what was being said, but I got the idea.

I felt like an enemy spy in a foreign country. I also felt very very weary, like the time in the spring of forty-five, after fifty-two days on the Villa Verde trail in Northern Luzon, the campaign in which the Red Arrow division lost one thousand and eighty men, I found myself in a front-line emergency hospital, watching them take shrapnel out of a boy's leg, the metal bits dropping into a pan, ting, ting, ting, and over the Armed Forces Radio came V-E Day, the big announcement. It was over in Europe. But no one gave a shit. All anyone could think was "When do I get out of *here?*"

I could feel a migraine coming. I had also drunk too much, and that was beginning to hit me. I sat there, my head in my hands. I just wanted to be forgotten.

But Dale Bennett hadn't forgotten me.

"Eddie, what do you think?" he said.

"About what?"

"You were defending Hoff before. What do you think now?"

Dale wanted me to crawl.

I had a headache now, definitely.

"Come on, Eddie," Dale persisted. "What do you think?"

"I don't think Hoff's worse than any of the rest of us. I think it's all the same here."

Dale took it calmly. "What do you mean *here,* Eddie?"

"Just what I said."

"You mean here in America, or here in California, or here in the industry, or here in this room—where here?"

I got up and started out. "I'm going home," I said.

They came down on me like wild animals. It sounded like one long garbled sentence spoken by many people: he got just what he deserved, that moral leper . . . no wonder our town is in trouble when reprobates like that make our pictures . . . European decadence doesn't go here; that's why no one goes to the movies any more in this country . . . our industry is built on the home . . . men like that bastard glamorize infidelity . . . all those Berlin sex perversions and all that running wild our kids are doing—that's where they get their ideas . . . it's our own fault because we give them all our prizes . . . show those New York critics decadence and they cheer . . . what happens to the picture of just an ordinary decent American family . . . Bosley Crowther's ax is what happens to it . . . this is still a Christian nation, isn't it?

My head was throbbing like I was going to have a stroke.

It wasn't that I wanted to defend Hoff. I just didn't want to shame myself. They wanted me to crawl.

I didn't want to shake up my hurting head. I sat down in the middle of them, and I talked to them the gentlest way I knew how. I did it quietly, but I tried to tell the truth. Why not, I thought; I'm finished here anyway.

"*I* just don't think any of us in this room should heave the first rock," I said. "Because I've led a fucked-up life, right, but I've led some of that fucked-up life with some of the fucked-up girls in this room. Haven't I? Well, you remember, Betty?" I was speaking to a woman, the wife of a TV producer, everyone knew had been around; I was making no revelation to anyone. Even now, pushing forty, she was on some bachelors' calendars. "You know, Betty?"

Then I turned to one of the other women; she had been a slim thing when I knew her, but now she was built like a cop. I was going to recall some history to her, too, but then I said, "Well, let's stop with the names. I mean we all live by forgetting, so let's all take the fifth. I've been with an awful lot of you girls here; now you remember, don't you? We all played the same stands, so I can say who did and when and where and how often, and what the bedroom Nielsens were. I'm sorry I mentioned any names, Betty. But maybe we shouldn't put on this big moral show-show tonight. Or maybe we should; probably we have to pretend like we do—all of you girls with your husbands for instance—because if we had to look at ourselves every day the way we really are, who could take it? The only thing I'm saying is, I think we should be kind to the other grotesques like this Hoff. Because I don't think any of us are any better than him."

They were furious. But not one would speak, not even Emily. When I first came to California, Florence had stayed in the East, to get rid of our apartment and the furniture, and I had a chance to sample the stuff. I made the same route everyone else was making. And among the station stops we all hit was the one called Emily. She was just beginning to climb then, and she climbed the familiar way, but covered her tracks more cleverly than most. So now suddenly she wasn't talking either.

The picture saved them all. The projectionist had put up the sheet, and the adventures of Jesus *au sombrero* were rolling again. The Rurales were chasing him through the cactus, and El Jefe was a bastard named Pilotes for Pilate, get it? Suddenly everyone was very interested in the film.

The oddest reaction of all was Dale's. He just sat there, studying the face of his close friend. He kept his gaze leveled on me. I knew it was time to go. I got up and nodded at him.

He didn't give a sign.

So all this would have passed into history, too, except that as I was leaving the room, at the very door, Betty's husband—the Betty whose name I had mentioned like a damned fool—this man came after me. He was a TV producer, and right behind him was his agent, an Italian fellow who had once been a fighter, sort of. This agent didn't rank high in the cadre of the agency, but was carried for laughs, the joke being that he was head of the procuring division for visiting exhibitors. Well, this twosome got to me, and the producer grabbed me by the lapels, like they do on his television shows—a case of life imitating art it was. And he said, shaking me, that he hadn't at all liked what I had implied (implied?) about his wife Betty. So I apologized. But I must have smiled or maybe laughed when I did. Well, this got him. He refused to accept my apology. Besides, there was his agent right behind him, and this gives strength. He said my slur was a malicious lie, or my life was a magnificent slur, or something; I had stopped paying strict attention by then. He was storming, for the benefit of everybody in the room, how I had been allowed for much too long to get away with it. He went on and on. I couldn't figure why he felt he had to go through all those heroics; all he really needed to do was hit me a couple so his wife's honor, that old thing, would be publicly reconstituted. I was going to let him have a shot or two at me; what the hell, he was in the right. But he kept slapping me, and my head ached like one big tooth. So finally I closed my left hand and stuck it right in his nose. He sat backwards, plop, into the arms of his agent, who then put his client down gently and came for me. He did revenge Betty's honor, so notably, in fact, that she later rewarded him personally in the way she knew best.

All the time, the film was rolling. Now some people turned in their seats and watched the fight—if that's what it was, with me doing all the catching. They watched as if it was, for the time being at least, the more interesting of the two shows. They didn't try to stop it any more than they would have tried to stop a film. Because, after all, it wasn't happening to them. They weren't hurting. These people, I thought, are trained sideliners. Murder for them is a spectator sport.

But then, even as I was taking my shellacking, I saw that maybe some of them wanted to intervene. What stopped them was the severe way Dale Bennett was watching what was happening to me. He was presiding at a tribunal of justice.

The agent punching me didn't know who he was hitting or really why. He certainly didn't care about Betty's honor. And he had nothing against me. He was simply implementing what he took to be the general will. That was his profession; he was the agent for all of them. He was doing what they, for certain reasons of civilization, could not do themselves: the ten per cent dirty work.

I noticed the agent was beginning to puff badly. I got a spurt of strength, enough for one punch anyway, and I clouted him right in the Caesar salad. It may not have hurt him much, but it sure as hell surprised him, because he drew back for one big look, long enough to allow Mike Weiner, who was then coming down the stairs, to come to my rescue. And me to get out of the house. I never did find out what happened between Mike and the Italian guy. But the affair ended fitly: two agents fighting for their clients.

A ball hammer was beating in my head. I couldn't remember

where I had parked the car. I could think only of one thing: Dale's cold eyes holding back everyone in that room from their humanity. They had sat there, ready to acquiesce to my murder.

The cold damp air made me feel better. The hell with them all, I thought. They're not going to kill me, any of them, with their wishes, conscious or unconscious, or by their indifferences either. Because the only one who has the power to kill me, and is liable to kill me, is myself. And not in my Triumph or my Cessna either. In some invisible way, much more silent, but also much more lethal and much more terrible. Like my fourteen years silence with Dale. That's self-betrayal. That's self-murder. Denying myself! And last night, that with Florence, that's denying myself, too. That's self-murder.

I suddenly saw the whole incident in bed with Florence quite differently. I saw that when I turned on my stomach and denied the evidence that I was still alive, when I squashed that down, I was only doing what I had been doing for years: denying my own life's expression, saying that I must *not* feel such and such a way, and that I *must* feel such and such a way, when I clearly no longer did or could. And above all, saying this thing with Gwen or whoever should not be and therefore wasn't. Like the old Leadbelly song, I was denying my name, and so murdering myself in a way much more lethal and final than the accident. They picked me up out of that accident, living. But I had been squashing life out of me so long that another few months and I would have been dead for good. I'd really had a narrow escape.

I remembered now where I had left the car. But it wasn't there. I suppose Florence had gone home in it. I didn't know where to begin to get a cab, except by going back into the Bennett house and calling for one. So I thought, maybe it's a mile; I'll walk it. But I was pretty wobbly. The cops said later that when they found me, I was walking the center stripe on Crescent Drive, shaking my fist at something they couldn't see. They tried to question me, find out who I was, but I didn't know. They went through my pockets. I don't carry a wallet. When they asked me where I was going, I said I had to find a catastrophe that might save me. When they asked me where my home was, I said I didn't have any. I kept saying through it all, "I'm through, I'm through here!" Those cops certainly were patient with me. They said, almost apologetically, that all in all it might be better if they took me in to cool me off, and later somewhere for observation.

On the way to the station house in the patrol car, I slept. Later I was in a room with some other men, and I slept there, too. Then there was a man calling out, "Anderson? Is there an Edward Anderson here?" I gave myself away, they told me later, by saying, "No, he's not here." Florence said, "That's him."

When we got home, Florence woke me. She said that the very first thing I had to do was call my brother Michael in Westchester. He'd been trying to get me all night; it was urgent. By that time, she had him on the phone. Michael was just about to leave for the hospital. He told me that my father had pneumonia. They had caught it in time, he said, except at that age everything is serious. But he was full of miracle drugs, so don't worry. There was one other thing. My father's arteriosclerosis, he said, had progressed, and this, in turn, had increased his hallucinating. The last couple of days he had repeatedly asked for me, believing all the time that I was just outside in the hospital corridor. Several times he had addressed me as if I was there in the room with him. Once he had even asked Michael to leave, so he could talk to me privately. Apparently he had something he urgently wanted to tell me. Could I, asked Michael, who was very impressed with my position and activity, could I come East, maybe immediately, if it was at all convenient; it would be wonderful if I could. If I couldn't not to worry, because there was nothing seriously wrong, not immediately—and so on.

Well, there, I thought, I have my catastrophe. Not one I'd want, my God! But there it was.

I made a reservation on the first plane I could get on, the one leaving at noon. The sun was well up now. The smog seemed to have blown elsewhere. I walked down to the pool—my farewell visit it was to be, but I didn't know it. I took off my shirt, lay down on the diving board, and fell asleep.

· 9 ·

Not for long. Ellen was shaking me. I was aware of fright. Ellen's, then mine. My first thought: something has happened to Florence. "How bad is it?" I asked, still asleep.

Ellen shook me till I woke. She told me Sylvia, my secretary, was here. It was the day of the month when she got together with Florence to do our accounts.

"I didn't know whether to wake Mummy or not," Ellen said, "so I went to her door and opened it just a crack. She is making some very strange noises, Daddy."

I got upstairs as fast as I could. Florence was crying in her sleep. Great rips were coming from her, like those a knot in an oak plank makes as it's split and shredded. In the time that I'd known her, I'd never heard Florence cry like that. She was scrupulous not to burden other people with her pain.

Florence's father, a severe man, despised her mother, a sniveler. Florence, an only child, aspired to be what her father would like. Since she couldn't be a boy, she learned to win his praise by not mentioning the fox gnawing at her chest. She never knew the relief of a whimper. In my memory, whenever she felt she was about to break down, she would rush to get behind a door she could lock.

The sounds she was making began to wake her. She became aware that I was next to her, so she turned over and muffled her mouth with the pillow.

I took her in my arms and held her. She clenched her whole body, forcing herself to be quiet and lie still. I thought she was asleep again, but she wasn't.

160

"Ev?"

"Yes."

"What did I do wrong?"

"You didn't do anything wrong, baby; it's me, not you."

"What did I do wrong?" she insisted. "Because I love you with everything I have, and you don't seem to know it."

About to weep again, she turned her face down. After a moment, she continued.

"I drove a man home last night. If you asked me, I couldn't spell his name. When he touched me, I went dry. He got furious with me, said I'd been leading him on, only he didn't say it that way. Get me a Kleenex, Ev, will you? God, I hate to do this."

When I sat down next to her, she pulled me down, holding my arm so I couldn't move. "I'll wait for you, Ev," she whispered. "I'm not asking anything. I'm just telling you, I will never give you up."

An honest person lives in vulnerability. The rest of us don't care. Florence was putting herself at my mercy, telling me she couldn't possibly go with anyone else, refusing to threaten she might. The rest of us love those who love us, but Florence lives by principle. She stayed with me because of principle, and when she left me, finally, she left me because of principle.

Now she turned, faced me. "Only, Ev, help me just a little, will you?"

"I'll try," I lied. "Sylvia is downstairs," I said to deflect her.

"Oh God, that's right, I've got to get up, don't I?"

"Yes, I guess so." Then I said, "I could tell her to come back tomorrow."

"No, don't do that. How long have you before your plane?"

"I have to leave the house at eleven."

She sat up and looked at the clock. "Oh, lord, it's ten after nine. I've got to get up. I must be a mess."

"Don't worry about Sylvia; she can wait."

"There are a couple of things you simply must do before you . . . I better hurry."

She got out of bed and went into the bathroom. "Tell Sylvia I'll be right down."

When I came back up, Florence had put on a robe of rather magisterial cut. But it didn't help. She looked anxious and frightened. "Ev," she said, "now bear with me. I haven't bothered you

161

with the financial facts of our lives for about—well, however long it is—six months, have I? But I have to now. Sylvia and I have prepared a sort of statement for you to study. And I'm sorry, but it simply must be acted upon before you go . . ."

She had gone to the window, as she often did to see what kind of day it was, and what she saw there stopped her.

"Did Ellen hear me crying?" I didn't know what to answer. "She's down at the pool looking up at this part of the house."

"Yes, I think she did. But that's not bad, baby."

"Just today it's bad. I wish she . . . Ev? Will you help me this morning? I need a lot of support from you this—"

"Sure, baby, sure." I've got to get out of here, I thought.

"We have to hurry," she said. "You remember three days ago Ellen left to spend a weekend with the Becks in Balboa?"

"Oh, yeah," I lied. She's appealing to a man who isn't here any more, I thought.

"Yesterday morning it occurred to me she might want to come to your get-well party. So I called down there and got Jenny Beck on the phone. You know who she is."

"One of . . ." I didn't know.

"Right. One of Ellen's classmates at Radcliffe. Jenny blurted out that Ellen wasn't there and hadn't been there. Then she realized she might be giving something away, so she began to weasel and lie. I asked if I might speak to her mother. That poor woman had no choice except to tell the truth, which was that there hadn't even been a discussion of a possible visit."

"Where was Ellen?"

"She wouldn't tell me. When Roger brought her home—"

"You mean to say she was with Roger for three days?"

"No. I'm coming to that. She arrived just as I was leaving for the police station to bail you out, about five in the morning. I guess I was a little abrupt with her. But I have my nerves, too. Besides, I was perfectly within my rights to ask why she had lied to me and to insist on being told where she had been for three days, don't you think so?"

"I guess so, yes, sure."

"You know what Ellen said? That it was none of my goddam business where she'd been. Quote! And into the house she marched without so much as good night to the young man."

"What did he have to say?"

"He didn't know where she'd been either. He said he was fast asleep in bed when he got a call from her majesty, and she asked him—didn't ask, demanded—that he pick her up in front of the Mersey. The Mersey is not, as you may suppose, the name of a river in England. It's a rather disreputable discotheque down at the slum end of the Strip. Don't ask me how she got there. When this poor boy picked her up—"

"Why didn't she take a cab?"

"Well, I wondered that, too. So I did something I shouldn't have. When she rushed upstairs, she just threw her things on the hall table, and I looked in her bag. She had a grand total of thirty-four cents. And some Mexican pesos."

"Where had she been?"

"That's what I want you to find out."

"Oh."

"She won't talk to me. I've lost that girl, Ev. I've failed with her. And it's killing me. She's changed so fast. It's scary how far away she is some days. Sometimes when I walk into a room, she gets up and walks out. I mean it's not an accident, that, is it?"

"It might be," I lied.

"Every time she's home on vacation, I think now is my chance; this time I'll get to know her; I'll build that bridge back between us. Then the vacation passes like it was twenty minutes. Good morning, good night, pass the butter, and she's gone. And we've hardly talked."

"But Florence darling, you mustn't blame yourself; kids go through these stages. What did Leibman say?"

"Are you kidding me?"

"Not at all. Why would you think that?"

"He says we adopted her; now she has come to the point where she wants to adopt us. Which is not a bit of help, is it? Also he says don't be decisive; live through it."

"I think he's right there."

"Ev, that would just be giving up. We have to do something to keep her from drifting away any further. I think this is the moment to make an issue. I mean I know I've failed with her but . . ."

"You haven't failed, Florence."

"I can't give up, can I? It seems to me that if we let this pass—

well, now is the moment to get some things settled. I mean if I'm her parent, then I've got a right to know where she's been and, goddam it, who she's sleeping with if it's now come to that. And if you feel you can't do it, then I'll simply have to—"

"No, I'll talk to her."

"Try to help me out of this, please, Ev; it would kill me if I failed with that girl."

"I'll talk to her, Florence, and you mustn't be so hard on yourself."

"I'm trying to face the facts. Ev, kiss me, will you?"

I did. Her face was eroded with anxiety. I kissed her again.

"Don't ever leave me, Ev," she whispered. "I'm going to wait for you, Ev. I'm trying my best."

"I know you are, baby. I better get Ellen."

"I'm scared. Because we have to have this other meeting, and I hate to talk about money, and I know it upsets you, and it upsets me when you get a certain way. But I'm at the end of my string, too. I mean there's simply no more money, none in our joint checking account, and—well, I'll give it all to you in black and white. Sylvia and I have worked it out very carefully."

I started out.

"Hurry, won't you, Evans. All I want is the simple truth. That shouldn't take too long."

"Is Mummy all right?"

"Oh yes, it was just a bad dream."

"She sent you down to talk to me, didn't she?"

I bent over and kissed her on one eyelid.

When Ellen was a baby, I'd go into her bedroom to kiss her good night; I'd kiss one eye closed, then the other, she would say good night daddy, I'd say good night angel, then I'd tiptoe out of the room, close the door, and she was officially asleep.

When I did that now, she threw herself into my arms and said, "Oh, Daddy, I knew you'd be on my side."

"On your side?"

"Hasn't she just been telling you what happened last night?"

"Well, yes, a little."

"I'm not going to take any more of that."

"Of what, Angel?"

"There are certain things I may want to tell you, and there are certain things I may want to tell her, and there are certain things I may want to tell neither of you."

"Well, o.k., Angel, just calm down."

"I want you to do something for me, Daddy, will you?"

"Sure I will, what?"

"Well, there's something big I want you to do, but first will you go up to the house and get me a vodka? I'm afraid to go, because she might see me, and if she starts to talk to me the way she did last night, I may just—"

"What happened last night?"

"I'm not a criminal and she's not a judge and I have a right to—"

"She was just worried about you, Angel."

"I don't want to be put down that way any more. Please, Daddy, will you? The drink? Because I want to tell you something, and if I don't have a drink, I won't be able to."

I kissed her again and went up towards the house. Halfway up, I looked back. Ellen hadn't moved. Guinevere, she was, in a white dress, by the side of that perfect blue pool. A vision of the young person in America who has everything, an illustration for *Life* magazine. Yet now, at nineteen, there was a weight on her, as if her story had already been written, and what remained of her life was fated. What had gone wrong?

The first time I saw Ellen, she had come down off the domed ceiling of an Italian Renaissance church, an angel, with hair of curled gold and the most innocent face in heaven. That face is still there, though she has become the most directly aggressive woman I have ever seen. She can have any man she wants, and does, simply by presenting her innocence to him.

Ellen was the talisman of our marriage. After four years of touch and go, Florence and I decided a child might keep us from splitting. On the afternoon we picked up Ellen at the adoption office, on the ride home, we set about spoiling her. At nine months she had learned that all she had to do was threaten to cry, and she could have anything she wanted. By the time she was three, she was an angel with the power of an absolute dictator. We didn't realize how fast things were going till we noticed that some of our friends were reacting to her with less than our wholehearted admiration. Florence rushed her to Dr. Leibman. But Ellen couldn't stand anybody who wasn't completely approving. Whatever Dr. Leibman is, he is not that. He told Florence that the child had definite problems, and he couldn't do anything for her unless she came regularly for treatment. Ellen wouldn't.

I was aware that I'd spoiled hell out of the kid. But I didn't care. And Florence didn't care. Because the talisman had worked. We'd stayed together.

Sylvia and Florence jumped when I walked in—as if they'd been doing something against me.

"Well?" said Florence.

"We're just beginning to talk," I said.

They both looked at the Atmos clock. "You'd better hurry," said Sylvia. She was holding a bristle of papers.

I poured the vodka and went out the back. I can't solve all this now, I thought. I'm through here, my plane takes off in two hours, I'm going, I'm not going to be stopped.

Ellen swallowed half the vodka. "Daddy, sit down please," she said. "And don't hurry me; I need your help."

"I'm catching a plane this morning," I said.

I've abandoned ship, I thought; it's everyone for himself now.

"Don't hurry me, Daddy; you've got to help me. This is it."

"O.K., Angel." I sat down.

"I don't want to live here any more."

"What?"

"I'm going to move out of here for good."

"Why?"

"I want you to tell her that for me. I can't talk to her."

"Whoa, baby, whoa."

"I'm warning you, if you make me talk to her, I'm liable to say some things to her that she'll never forget for the rest of her life."

"She was just asking where you'd been for three—"

"Christ, Daddy, you haven't told her the truth for I don't know how long. How come you expect me to level with her?"

"Whoa, baby."

"I won't whoa. Every time I start talking to her, she acts like I was asking her *permission*. She says yes you can or no you can't, and I'm not about to ask anybody's permission. All I want to do is leave without a big fuss."

"It would kill her if you moved out of here."

"That's the way she's made *you* do what she wanted all these years. Well, I can cry, too; you want to hear me throw a fit?"

"Ellen, listen, she's awful shaky right now; everything has knocked hell out of her; I've knocked hell out of her."

"Then *you* stay here and look after her . . ."

"Just let some time pass; go back to Radcliffe, and—"

"I'm not going there."

"I thought you were catching a plane tomorrow."

"I'm going back East, but I'm not going to Radcliffe."

"Ellen, I'm putting this to you, I don't want you to do that to Florence, not right now. Do you hear me?"

She got up. "I hear you."

She walked away from me, and around the pool. At the other end she sat down.

"Angel, let's jump in the water for a minute; it'll be good for both of us."

"I can't."

"Why not?" I asked. "Oh, that."

"Not exactly. I had an abortion day before yesterday. That's where I was, Tiajuana. You expect me to tell her that?"

"Are you all right?"

"Sure. Nothing to it. Yesterday I was a little tired and sleepy, so I stayed there—they have these cribs, like—and I slept most of the day. You expect me to tell her that?"

"No. I expect you to tell me that."

"You would have made a big fuss."

"How do you know I wouldn't have suggested your having the kid? Whose was it?"

"Oh, he was in my Chaucer class."

"It wasn't Roger?"

She laughed. "Roger. He's just my going-steady boy friend."

"Ellen, if you're not going back to school, where do you intend to live?"

"It doesn't make any difference where. It's how."

"Well, how? Let's talk about it."

"No. You can't help me and she can't help me. I have to find out a lot of things for myself. I don't even know who I am. The only thing I know is I'm not the way you think I am. That's why I never liked you calling me angel."

"Why didn't you tell me?"

"Because that's the way you like to think of me. I'm not the way Mummy likes to think of me either. I hate Radcliffe. I don't have any interest in books or politics or science or civil rights or any of that stuff.

"But there's one thing Mummy isn't and there's one thing you aren't that I can be, and that's an honest person. I'm not going to tell a single lie, no matter how small. I'm going to invent a different way of life. I'm only going to bed with boys I'm crazy about, and I'll never go to bed with a man because I'm legally supposed to, or just to pass the time, or because it's easier than explaining why I don't want to. I'm not going to ask him to stay with me, either, when he really doesn't want to."

"But my dear inventor, people have thought of all that. I thought that way once."

"So then tell me, what happens? Why do you all pretend? Isn't it better to be whatever you are, no matter how crummy?"

"Ellen, you're exaggerating."

"I mean you, too. I first figured you and Mummy were staying together only because of me. Well, now I see I'm just a handy excuse. And where before I said to you, don't stay together on my account, now I say nothing to you, Daddy, nothing."

A fly landed on me. I hit it harder than necessary.

"Evans!" I heard. Florence was standing in the doorway. "You better come up now. There isn't much time."

"I'm on my way," I yelled back.

Florence waved at Ellen gaily. "Don't wear him out, Ellen; save a little for me." She laughed and went back into the house.

"Angel, when are you going back East?"

"This afternoon, as soon as I can."

"Well, I have to go too, my father's got pneumonia."

"Oh, I'm sorry."

"He's o.k. but he has these spells now, seems to be talking to me when I'm not there; keeps calling for me and well, anyway, what I wanted to suggest is that you come back on the same plane with me."

"When?"

"The noon United."

"O.K., if I can get on."

"Then we can talk some more." I started up towards the house.

"You'll do the dirty work for me—with her?"

"I'll try. She's going to ask me where you were the last three days. Well, in line with your new resolve, test number one: should I tell her the truth?"

"I made up my mind this was the last lie I was ever going to tell."

"And you'd rather have me tell it?"

"The only reason I have to tell it at all is because I live in this house with you and your wife. I'm sorry."

"O.K., I better go up. She has a lot of papers about my financial situation and so on. Well, I'll make up something."

"Good luck."

"By the way," I had started up, "if you're not going to Radcliffe, where are you going? Do you mind my asking?"

"I don't mind unless you try to stop me. I have this new boy, and his family has a place; they're away and . . ."

"We better get you a device right away . . ."

"A device! That's cute." She laughed.

"Well . . . Don't rely on a boy. A girl should protect herself."

"Daddy, I know. You're a pal."

"I have my own problems."

"You do. She's a wonderful woman, in some ways. She's all the virtues, isn't she? Still she's killing you. Daddy . . ."

Ellen jumped up and kissed me. "I'm sorry, Daddy, I hate to talk to you the way I did. It doesn't help, I know."

I turned and hurried up the hill.

What I have learned from years of experience with lying is that you tell as close to the precise truth as you can. That's the best technique, because the facts, as they are bound to emerge from questioning, investigation, and the passage of time, will most support that kind of falsehood.

"She went to Tiajuana," I said to Florence.

"Tiajuana! That filthy little town! What for?"

"Just to see a different side of the world, I guess."

"That it certainly is."

"And to think."

"Did she have to go there to think?"

"You know how kids are."

"Whom did she go with?"

"All alone."

"What did she do there, all by herself?"

"Walked around, but mostly lay in her hotel room and thought about her life."

"Thought what about her life?"

"Everything. You know. Kids!"

"If she wanted to think, there are so many nicer places she might have chosen. What conclusions did our student of life come to?"

"She didn't say."

"Do you see any reason in the world why she couldn't tell me all that?"

"Maybe you caught her at a bad time."

"It was a perfectly reasonable time. After all, she had lied to me—oh, let's forget it. We simply haven't the time. . . . Have you packed?"

"No. Nothing."

"How much time do you need for that?"

"Oh, about ten minutes."

"Ridiculous. Suppose we give you twenty. Do you think you can manage? I'll help you."

"Oh, sure."

"Well then, Sylvia, that gives us just about half an hour. Sit down, Evans. Let me have sheet number one, Sylvia."

Sylvia handed her a sheet of onion skin. Everything was in triplicate that morning. Florence put the thing in my hands.

"This is for you. You can keep it, of course. It lists your assets. Let me read these figures to you quickly. If you have any questions, please express them. There is first of all your account at the Bowery Savings Bank in New York. That of course stands exactly where it did when we left there, except for the accumulation of interest. The figure on the last line of your book now is $7,809.43. The next figure is your checking account, and your balance there is $17,122.92. Williams and MacElroy have not, through any of your troubles, even questioned continuing full payment of your salary. Mr. Finnegan must really like you. Now! You had in our safe deposit box—they are presently here in this manila envelope—three government bonds, Series "G," each with a maturation value of ten thousand dollars. And finally you have your stocks, which were purchased as speculation for the most part and, I thought, rather impulsively, without proper advice. They were intended to give some sort of balance to your dollar holdings. But they have not done well. Klondike Airlines, for instance, was an out-and-out disaster. I told you not to buy that. The idea of an airline whose total purpose was to scout the wilds of Canada for possible uranium deposits was on the face of it ridiculous. Well, leave the post mortems. You bought six hundred shares at 19. It is now 2 and no buyers. The rest of the stuff you have did fairly well, but not up to the market. At any rate, Sylvia and I estimate that your total portfolio of stocks is worth in the neighborhood of $15,900, and so the total value of your personal assets is—well, neither of us is too good at addition, but our figure is $67,132.35. Any questions?"

"We're rich," I said. It was much better than I had anticipated.

"Wait until we examine schedule three before you say that. Schedule two is next. This lists our joint property. Included are this house, which is now about two-thirds paid for, the shack in Indio which I thought was paid up but found there were two payments still to be made—one for the land and the other to the contractor—which I made and which appear as items on schedule three. There are the three cars, the hi-fi, books, records, *objets d'art,* and so on. You will see them all listed there. Here, take this, Evans. Take this paper, please, and look at it. Now. You will see, at the bottom, where it belongs, our joint checking account, from which I pay all the household and joint expenditures. It is at the moment as you can see—right there, Evans. See?—it is at rock bottom, $103.23.

"Now comes schedule three. Evans, I don't enjoy this any more than you do. I'm only doing it, in fact, because you won't. So if you don't mind . . ."

"What did I do wrong?"

"It's just the tolerant expression on your face. What are you so superior about? Excuse me, Sylvia. Now please take schedule three and look at it and do question anything. We are not accountants; we just did our best. Here."

She handed me the sheet.

"This is the point of this conference. It lists the money which I have paid out over the last six months from my personal checking account into our joint checking account. And so, it is in effect what you owe me. I advanced the monies which, by our basic understanding, *you* were to make available. I paid everything, because during your illness I didn't want to bother you with the facts of life. But now I need to be paid back. I have no more in my own checking account. If I wanted to buy a bobby pin this afternoon, I'd have to go into capital. And, Sylvia, we took a vow when we married never, never to go into capital. What I have is the bequest of my father, and we resolved to save it for emergencies, in case something happened, you know?"

Sylvia didn't know if she was supposed to comment on this.

Florence said, "Is that right, Evans?"

"Right."

"Thank you. Now let's go over schedule three, item by item. The first listing is $3,000 mortgage on this house. I paid that, which, of course, is exactly like saving money. The next item of $8,200 is the household expenses, like food, the very basic things of the past six months. I paid that. It seems high to you, I know. But I wish you'd try doing the shopping any month you like. The next item is my clothes. It is a little large, $4,753.50. Most of these bills, which are clipped together here—let's have them, Sylvia, thank you—you can examine the items at your leisure. Of course you won't, but if you did, you'd find that most of them are from before your accident, when everything was going beautifully. Since your accident I have cut way down, just as I have now on household expenses. By the way, there are itemized bills for every one of these items, in case you think we are just bedeviling you. Then there is the garage bill next, $385.86. I simply think those people are crooked. I mean—here, Sylvia, thank you—here is the itemized bill, I don't know why, for instance, the Continental should need a new muffler after less than eighteen months of use. But there it is; they didn't even ask. I think we should look for another garage. But I can't do that. And you didn't have the health to do it. And now that you are recovered, I suppose you won't have the time to do it. The next item covers bills for utilities over a six-month period, $1,142. That is also itemized and incontestable. After all, we have to have lights and gas, don't we? And telephone. We could give up one extension, the one to the pool; why don't we do that? Evans?"

"What?"

"I was suggesting giving up the telephone extension to the pool. What is your decision on that?"

"I don't . . . o.k., why not, yes, good idea."

"Now just try to stick with it; it won't be much longer, Evans, and it's all leading up to something I want you to do: namely, pay me back what I've paid out. So please, for your own peace of mind in the days to come, pay attention. The next three items are for Ellen: tuition, eighteen hundred—high in my opinion; clothes, twenty-two hundred—fair enough, at least in Beverly Hills; and monthly allowance of two hundred times six, which I urgently suggest we cut down to one twenty-five—it will have a good effect generally, and it will be something of a savings. Do you object?"

"No . . . well . . . yes . . . I think I do."

"All right, Sylvia, make a list—items for future discussion. Obviously, Evans, we haven't time to discuss anything in detail now, with you running off to a plane. All right, Sylvia?"

"Yes, Mrs. Anderson."

"The next item is a large one. I had no choice but to pay it— $6,268.49 to finish building the shack in Indio. McDonough assures me it's the last bill. It's high, of course, because of the cellar, which I added and wasn't on the original estimate. But McDonough promised . . . what is it?"

"Nothing," I said.

"Of course there is."

"No, no really!"

"I really would like to know why you were smirking in that superior way!"

"It's just that—you know how I feel—we're never going to use that cellar."

There was a burst of hysterical laughter from Florence.

"Read the papers!"

"I do," I said.

"I mean really read them. And if you don't mind, we'll discuss that some other time. Sylvia, add that to the list. Though, of course, the cellar is installed, thank goodness, and completely furnished. And stocked. So. Now . . . let's see. Where was I?"

"Maid and part-time gardener," I said. "Six months, $3,600."

"Right, and any time you want to eliminate the gardener, it's fine with me. I have never liked that man, so if you will do the work, or if you can manage to find time to look for and find someone cheaper, do it; it's up to you. The liquor bill I've cut way down. For instance, I've simply stopped buying anything but American wines. Anyway, there it is—it won't ever be that high again, I promise—$420.99. The next $200 is our dues at the Beverly Hills Tennis Club. I've decided to stop playing tennis and going there for lunch, so you'll never see that item again. The New York *Times,* the books, magazines—the *Nation,* the *New Republic,* the *New States-man, Harper's, Atlantic, Vogue*—well, those are things that keep us in touch with the living world, and they'd be the last items I'd cut down. But I'd like to hear what you think; the item is $340. The swimming pool service is outrageous at $480. I don't know what to do about those people. You do whatever you like. Turn the pool into a tomato garden; I don't use it any more myself. But Ellen loves it, so you and Ellen decide. Now these gardening mate-rials—bone meal, and dehydrated cow manure, and cypress chips, and seed, new plantings, and new tools—that is the one that gets me. That oriental son of a bitch, excuse me, seems to require a new set of tools every year. Forgive me, Sylvia, I know I'm disgraceful about him, but that man arouses all my latent chauvinism. Doesn't he yours? Oh dear! The next item, where is it? Oh! $600, for charities. Well, I've cut that way down and will more. The only cause I really feel like supporting today is civil rights. I will not cut out our contri-bution to that."

"Looks like someone ought to give us charity," I said.

"Right. Haha. Yesterday I put another two thousand dollars, the very last I had in my checking account, into our joint account, to take care of the simple running expenses of this household for the coming month. You owe me that, too. I'd be perfectly willing to try to lower that. I mean like steak just twice a month and stay with frozen vegetables. But Beverly Hills is expensive, and that's the fact of it. Then, look there—almost over, dear—look, there is $3,800, the final payment on the Indio site. That is final and you can't contest it, because it is, in my opinion, the realest asset we have. I've given up entirely the hope I had of acquiring the lot next door to protect us. As I told you I would, I have paid for every stick and stitch of furnishings in that place myself. It was a very large item, using up all my savings for ten years, all the interest on my capital, that is."

She took a breath, and looked at me with sudden anger.

"Here now," she said, "are the last two items. If you say one word to contest them, I'll scream. Dr. Leibman is the only reason we're now here in the same room, I assure you. I'll cut down on everything else, not on him. Maybe a day less a week. But you know what happens when I don't go to him every day."

"What would you do," I said, "if your husband wasn't earning that kind of money in the first place?"

She raised her arm in the air, and she made a gesture to suggest to me that she would slash her wrists.

"I'm sorry, Sylvia," she said.

"I'll see if I can get me a cup of coffee," said Sylvia.

"Do," said Florence. "Charlotte will help you."

Sylvia left.

"She's a wonderful secretary," said Florence. "I simply forgot she was in the room."

"What time is it?"

"You have another ten minutes. Where are you going? Evans!"

I had stood up. "I just want to make sure that Ellen is packing. She was going back to Radcliffe on the night plane. I talked her into going back on the same plane I'm taking."

"Oh, that's wonderful, Evans." She sounded so relieved.

"Yes," I said, "Ellen and I can continue our talk, and I'll write you."

"Well, you'll be back in a day or two or three, won't you?"

"Oh, yes sure . . . I just want to make sure she was able to get on the plane. . . ."

"Evans, just one more second, then we'll be finished with this dreadful sheet. I'll be very quick. Leibman. Fifty per session. Five times a week. Twenty-six weeks. Makes exactly $6,500. Then you went yourself that time, three times fifty, one hundred and fifty. Now grand total—see, there?—$44,222.78, money which I have paid out of my account into yours. Money which has actually been spent. That does not represent our actual standard of living. I mean the whole Indio shack adventure won't happen again. And I have just now decided, because of the expression on your face, that I will pay Dr. Leibman in the future out of my own money, out of capital, because I do consider that a daily emergency. Now run. But come back! Because I want to have a clear understanding with you. In fact, I'd like you to pay me back now, before you go. Sylvia brought the check books and the bonds, too, in case you need them. O.K., dear, that's all! Now run!"

I did run up the stairs. From all of it, two figures stuck in my mind. Assets more or less 67. To be paid to Florence about 44. That leaves me something over twenty, which should give me a chance to find my way without working, at least for a year. It wasn't quite as bad as I'd feared.

Upstairs, Ellen was packing. She ran up to me and pulled me into her room. "Daddy," she whispered, "what did you say?"

"I said you had gone to Tiajuana."

"To do what?"

"To think. You did think, didn't you?"

"Oh, Daddy, you're so clever. Well, I guess practice makes perfect?"

I was beginning to resent Ellen a little. "Did you get on the plane?"

"All set. You want me to pack for you?"

"No." I started out.

"O.K. Thank you. Come on, kiss. Kiss!" We kissed.

"Well, let's get at it," I said, as I ran down the stairs.

I noticed they were talking in low voices. Again I had the feeling that it was conspiratorial, somehow against me, or at least in a way I wouldn't like.

"What's up?" I said.

"I forgot something, Mr. Anderson," said Sylvia. "It's the federal income tax, two installments. And the California state."

"What do they come to?" asked Florence.

"The federal is two times six, that's twelve thousand. But there's another installment due next month."

"Well," said Florence.

"Just make the check out," I said. I'll be out of here in another twenty minutes, I thought. "Just make out the check."

"And . . ." said Sylvia, looking nervous.

"What else?" I said. "Just make the checks out, Sylvia."

"Well, there's the California state tax. . . ."

"Well, let's not embarrass the State of California!"

"And . . ."

"Come on, now, what else? You may never find me in this pay-everything mood again. Come on!"

Florence laughed.

"He's right, Sylvia, better get him while you can."

176

"Well, it's the accountant's bill, for last year. He called today and asked about it."

"Make out the check."

"It's twelve hundred and fifty . . ."

"Make out the check."

Florence said, "Evans, now just calm down and let the girl think."

"Total is?" I said. "Total is, Sylvia?"

"Now Evans," Florence laughed nervously.

"Where are my schedules one, two, and three?" I demanded.

"You're sitting on them, Mr. Anderson."

I got up and there they were, badly rumpled. "I just wanted to see how much money I've got in assets. Or had."

Sylvia had everything added up. "The grand total, schedule three and additions, is $58,422.40," she said.

"That is grand," I said, "but is it a total?"

"Yes," she said positively. "I think so."

"Are you sure? I don't want to neglect anybody. Oh, my God, what about the hospital, you dopes, and Dr. Arnstein? My God. . . !"

"Calm down, calm down," said Florence, "that's the little ray of sunshine. Most of it is in the Thank-God-for-Blue-Cross depart- ment. I mean there will be sizable bills; they haven't been finalized yet. Dr. Arnstein has been very patient and very helpful. He says we'll end up having to pay maybe around three thousand, but think what it might have been. Or don't! It sends a chill through me."

"And that's it?" I said.

"That's absolutely it."

"You sure? Sylvia! Are you sure?"

"Yes, sir. I'm sure."

"O.K.," I said, "if I may take charge for the moment. Here's what we do. You make out the checks and I will sign them. Is that clear? You brought the bonds, right?"

"Yes, Mr. Anderson."

"Well, I'm going to sign them away."

"Oh, Evans," Florence laughed weakly.

"Right here," said Sylvia.

"Thank you. And while I do that, you make out a note to my broker instructing him to sell everything including the Klondike. If I do that, will that cover everything? Let's see, that will leave me . . ." I was trying to figure out the schedules and then do the necessary subtraction. "That will leave . . ?" I said.

"That will leave . . ." said Sylvia.

"That will leave me?" I said.

"That will leave you," said Sylvia, "about . . ."

"About $9,000. Minus the next tax installment and whatever the hospital and Dr. Arnstein come to. I won't have to touch . . . well, anyway, I don't have to touch my savings account."

"Not till next month," said Sylvia. "The federal . . ."

"I was just going to say that. But by next month won't there be enough in from Williams and . . ."

Then I thought, "My God, I'm going to quit that job."

"What's the matter, dear?" said Florence.

"Just thinking ahead," I said.

"I know," said Florence. "I really think you should."

"Yeah," I said, "but not too much. . . ."

"We'll talk about all that," said Florence, "in a couple of days when you get back. Let's settle this first." She indicated the place on the back of the Series "G" bond where I had to endorse it. Which I did. Then she gave me the next bond.

"Hurry, Sylvia," said Florence, "he hasn't much time."

I signed another bond. Sylvia ripped the letter to my broker out of her portable, and laid it on the table in front of me. I signed the last bond. Sylvia began to do some figures. I put the three bonds in a neat pile and picked up the letter.

Sylvia said, "That will leave you, in your savings account and in your checking account, a grand total of $8,709.95. What will be due to the federal government and the State of California next month comes to $7,200, which leaves $1,509.95. The bill from the hospital and from Dr. Arnstein, when it arrives, will be about three thousand, he said—well, no one knows exactly. That's the whole story, Mr. Anderson."

"I'm in the red!" I said, exultantly signing the check.

"Yes," said Sylvia, "unless you have some money I don't know about."

"I wouldn't do that to you, Sylvia."

"Evans, don't look at the gloomy side of all this. I know how it must seem. You have been working here in California for sixteen years, and you have less now than when you came here. . . ."

"Don't worry about it, Florence."

"But I do."

"I feel o.k."

"I can see that you don't."

"But I do!"

"You don't! Now will you let me finish, please! Just consider. We own this house; it's two-thirds paid up, and that's worth a lot of money. We have the shack in Indio, and that's the very best investment we could possibly make. I could live there, if anything happened, the rest of my life. Any time you want to take me up on that, say so. We'll sell everything, go down and live off the income from my capital. Because, Evans, we haven't touched that. Think of that! It's all still there, worth at least as much as it was the day my father left it to me, despite what's happened to the purchasing power of the dollar. We'd just dig in there, the two of us, cut our expenses to the bone, read and think, and enjoy that wonderful sun."

It sounded like the fortress again. I stood up. "I've got to pack," I said.

"So run," said Florence. Suddenly she turned to Sylvia. "You sure everything is in order, Sylvia?"

"Yes, Mrs. Anderson."

Florence turned to me and said, "Oh, darling, thank you. Thank you. I know I get too anxious about money. But after what you told me—Sylvia, maybe you'd get me a glass of water?"

"Yes, Mrs. Anderson."

Sylvia left.

"I didn't want to say this in front of her. But you can't blame me for being anxious, can you? After your telling me the other day that you were quitting your job. But now that you see what's involved, you may think a little differently. I mean it involves a lot, that decision. Doesn't it? But, you know, Evans, I was never really worried about you, because I know, with your energy and your competitiveness, you couldn't remain idle long. It isn't your nature. I know that you'll make a big comeback soon; you'll come back bigger than ever."

"I have to pack."

"Do you mind if I come up and talk to you while you pack?"

"Florence, I've only got a very few minutes now."

179

"All right. After all, you'll be back in a few days. I'm sure your father is fine."

"What makes you say that?"

"He's just got to be, darling." She ran up to me and kissed me. "Thank you, Evans," she said, "for taking care of everything so quickly. I do feel much much better. I do. I know I exaggerate about money, worry too much about it. But really, money isn't only money. It's liberty," she said, "because when you haven't got it, you know, you have to do all kinds of dreadful things just to pay the bills. Evans? Are you listening?"

"I've got to pack," I said, starting up the stairs.

Just then Sylvia came from the pantry carrying a glass of water. "Mr. Anderson," she said.

"Did you forget something else? Make out the check!"

She laughed. "Oh, nothing like that. I just wanted to give you your messages." She ran to her dispatch case, and got a yellow sheet of paper.

"And, Evans," Florence was saying, "I just thought I'd call up Mr. Finnegan."

I was running up the stairs. When she said that, I stopped.

"And tell him what?" I felt murderous.

"Thank him for keeping you on that way he did, tell him that you're going to New York and why, and that you'll be back at the office in a few days. . . ."

"Please, don't call Mr. Finnegan," I said.

"All right, dear, all right." Florence was quite thwarted, though. "I was only . . ."

"Just don't!" I said. And ran up the rest of the stairs.

I threw off my clothes. I went through the pockets. I had about thirty-three dollars. Then I remembered the get away five hundred under the paper lining of my locked drawer. I got it out. Ten fifties. Right. I would have to pay for my airline ticket. That would leave me three hundred odd. Suppose . . . well suppose . . . what? God, how quick it happens! I was broke. No sort of. I was broke. For a moment I sat on the bed immobilized. I read the messages. There was a message from Mike Weiner, my agent. Call him. Urgent, it said. I did. I had to get some money coming in. Maybe the magazine had something in New York; that would at least pay for the plane trip, and if I didn't like it I wouldn't go through with it.

Well, the tumblers fell just right. They had a story they wanted me to do—a couple, in fact, but one in particular—in New York: a Puerto Rican politician named Rojas, Mike said, sounds interesting. I wasn't even listening. I didn't care, suddenly, what attitude they wanted me to take to the material.

"O.K.," I said to Mike, "they're on!" I'd get to New York on my own, give them my transportation bill there. "Please reserve me my usual at the Algonquin." They'd pay for my hotel, too, I thought, and hung up.

I looked at the time, dressed, packed, and had a double.

10

I HAVE a problem with liquor. It sobers me. So I try to stay away from it.

But this particular morning I needed a drink. As I was packing I experienced a totally illogical fear that something, at the last moment, was going to prevent my departure.

Florence was so relieved that I had assumed responsibility for Ellen, so pleased at my speed in signing checks, so delighted at the respect I'd shown Schedule Number Three, that she wanted to drive us to the airport herself. But I insisted on calling a cab. I knew damned well if she ever came that far, something would go wrong, and I wouldn't be able to make my getaway.

Absurd? Of course. A sober man wouldn't have such thoughts. So the moment the door of the taxi closed, I had a long pull on the pint I'd concealed in the folds of my canvas coat. That sobered me. At least you've made it this far, I thought; you're in a cab, we're out of the driveway, here's Sunset, and we've turned just as we should. So why are you worried?

At the ticket counter I felt the panic again. I didn't like the people checking onto our flight. They all looked like losers making last minute getaways. And there was something oblique about the behavior of the counter clerks. They seemed to think it was a joke to announce a delay. They said it would be a short one, mechanical difficulties, something about a compass. That sounded very fishy. I went to the men's room, rented a cubicle for a dime, and had another pull off my pint.

There was something reassuring, however, about the way they finally closed the door of the plane. I heard a big bar drop into a metal pocket, and a heavy click. Then they locked it from the inside. I felt some hope we'd make it.

They even turned off the cabin music.

But then we just sat there.

I noticed the plane was less than half full, considerably less. I wondered why. Was there something wrong with the plane that they weren't telling us? Ellen went up front to get some magazines, and I stole another drink.

Finally the accordion entrance passage was pulled back, and the plane with its load of survivors (for so they seemed) was at last cut off. At no particular signal, the plane began to roll. We were going to make a quick try at getting off the ground.

At the end of the runway, the refugee plane with its load of survivors stopped, turned, cleared its throats, and began its run. There came that desperate swooping rise which only the jets can pull off. We were looking down at the smoking city. A moment later we were over the water; there was the sea, still at its priestlike task of pure ablution, but having a tough time of it with all that multicolored industrial waste bleeding into it.

At last the pilot realized we were going in the wrong direction. The plane banked heavily, and turned its back on the Pacific. I sighted the Sierra Madres again. We were heading east. We'd made it. I had a drink, this time to celebrate.

Ellen seemed relieved, too. She had a determined little profile. Naturally, I thought, since she's determined to invent a whole new way of living. Not that I thought she'd succeed. But in this, like in everything, effort is all. You can choose which effort to make. Since this is so, it matters less that you will certainly fail.

It seemed obvious to me, since I had sobered, that what had been killing me was the order of my old life. The only time I had really been happy was when I was with the kind of woman my upbringing had taught me to avoid, a person I had never trusted and never could, unreliable in her temperament, unsettling in every attitude, selfish perfectly, vengeful instinctively, a lone miserable bitch who gloried in disruption and bloomed in venery. She had made me happy. The same order of married life à la mode had eviscerated me.

My head now cleared by drink, I determined to smash my life to pieces, so it could never be put together again. Not even by me!

The last time I saw Gwen was the last time my blood had pulse. Because even when she and I had done disgraceful things in public, foolish, adolescent acts, they bespoke something, not very gracefully or clearly, but they bespoke us. Of course we had behaved like goddam fools, but the goddam fool part of us was the living part of us. And the sensible part of us was the dead.

If I don't recognize my medicine, I thought, I don't deserve to live.

I began to think about Gwen—where she was, what she was doing and with whom. I knew you couldn't go back to the street where you had dropped something of value well over a year ago and expect to find it still on the sidewalk.

But I'm the man who goes to the railroad station without calling information, and expects the right train to be on the right track pointing in the right direction and waiting just for me. As for her being with someone else—everybody is with someone else. And who knows what's written, as the Turks say. (Allah. I hadn't consulted him recently.) Maybe my name was there inscribed for a second time. (*Inshallah!*) So plunge in. You're certain to lose. Don't worry. It will end up bad. Spin the dice. That train may just be there waiting and you'll ride a few stops. Who the hell has more?

Ellen reached across and took my hand. The motors had made that sudden frightening stepdown in power, and the plane, while still climbing, was doing so at a less confident angle.

It was all quiet, when I heard a familiar laugh. Chet Collier was on the plane. Now that the seat belt sign was off, he was the first one out of his seat and heading back.

I quickly raised the *Los Angeles Times* up over my face. He went by, still chuckling. It must have been a hell of a joke, one of his own, no doubt. He was still enjoying it as he went glad-mitting it through the gaggle of stewardesses and into the men's room.

I slowly put the paper down and sat there listening behind me. My heart pounded. I felt humiliated by my behavior. A man of forty-four hiding behind the *Los Angeles Times*. I'd received congratulations from every side for destroying that bastard. Why was the newspaper over my face?

I could hear Chet coming out of the cubicle. He was sharing the largesse of his humor with the girls hustling lunches in the galley.

184

The son of a bitch always behaved as if he'd just won the decathlon. Apparently my article hadn't even chipped his self-confidence.

Before he got to our row, I slid from the middle seat to the aisle seat and, as he went by, reached for the bag of his pants and pulled him to a stop. When he turned, I saw his face had gotten heavier with good living. He looked like a prize McIntosh.

"Well," he said, "my murderer."

"Apparently I missed the mark," I said. "You're looking damn well, I'm sorry to say."

"I'm glad I can't say the same for you. I heard you caused a car accident." His eye shifted to Ellen. "Are you traveling with this man?" he said to her.

Ellen said she was.

"Are you someone I can poach on?"

"I'm his daughter," she said. He made a little face at this, and she laughed. She liked him immediately, just as Gwen had.

"You know what I'm going to do?" he said to her. "I'm going to visit with you awhile."

"Well, what do you know!" was the best I could do.

"Excuse me," he said to me with a salaam. He slid by into the seat between Ellen and me. Then he buzzed the stewardess. "I'm going to order us a drink. This calls for a celebration."

"I'll get the drinks," I said.

"You don't have to buy my favor. That won't help." He turned to Ellen. "Did you read that shameful piece he wrote about me?"

"I don't even know who you are," Ellen said.

"You see. You didn't recognize me from his description. I'm Chet Collier."

"I thought that was an excellent piece," said Ellen, though I suspected it cost her an effort.

"It wasn't about me."

"Look," I said, "I'll admit when I came to see you I was prejudiced. But as I got to know you, every prejudice was confirmed."

He paid no attention to my nonsense. He was smiling at Ellen, cocking his head and measuring her. "You're very pretty," he declared. "I can hardly believe you're his daughter."

"I'm adopted," said Ellen.

"Another minute, I would have guessed it. Have you caught on to him yet?"

"Caught on to him? What do you mean?"

"Found him out?"

Ellen smiled. She didn't know what to say.

Chet patted her hand. "Don't answer that question," he said.

The stewardess was alongside. "Eunice," he said to her, "I want you to bring this lovely young lady the one drink in the world which will give her the most pleasure at this moment."

"What'll it be, Miss?" said the stewardess.

Ellen said, "I don't know, it's sort of early."

Chet was sitting, not standing, but he seemed to be bending down over her solicitously.

"You will have . . ." he said to her, as though he was giving the matter infinite thought, "the same thing I'm going to have, a feather of a drink, mild as milk. Eunice, bring us two double Dubonnet frappés on shaved ice, with just a dash of absinthe and . . ."

"Mr. Collier, we're trying to get lunch out."

"Now, Eunice, do what I told you, run along."

"Daddy," said Ellen, "what will you have?"

"Yes," said Chet, "don't forget him."

"I want a double Canadian Club," I told the girl. I didn't know what to do with this man. It was the same as last time, spitting at a rock.

Now he was studying me. "You've already had a couple," he announced.

"I did."

"More than a couple. My God, man, what's happened to you? You don't look at all well. Is it the accident or . . ." He turned back to Ellen. "Did you know your father and I once had a little physical encounter?"

"Who won?" said Ellen.

"My dear," said Chet. "It was shooting fish in a barrel. I've always been ashamed of what I did to your father on that occasion. Even though he came flailing at me in that ineffectual way, it wasn't necessary for me to break his nose and black his eyes." He turned to me. "Do you forgive me?"

"No," I said.

"I don't forgive you, either," he said, "for anything." He turned back to Ellen. "I'm glad you're here. My God, the fantasies I've had about your father! What I'd do to him if I met him. Now here he is. What could I possibly do to him without embarrassing myself? Look at him!" He shook his head in mock pity.

Ellen laughed.

"What are you laughing at, Ellen?" I asked.

"I really don't know," she said, surprised at my question. "He's funny."

"That's my way of meeting this situation," he said. Then he turned to me. "How are you going to meet this situation?"

"Wait for it to be over."

"But now that I've finally found you, I have no intention of depriving myself of your company. There's no other entertainment on the plane."

Just then we hit turbulence, and the pilot turned on the seat belt sign.

"Fasten your belts, everybody," said Chet.

The stewardess came back with the drinks.

"Ah!" he said, "how wonderful of you to rush these, Eunice."

"Mr. Collier," said Eunice, "you're such a BS artist."

"He is, he is," chirped Ellen.

"Eunice, I find the unvarnished truth too dull to endure. Here, see if you don't like this," he said to Ellen.

"It's good," she said.

"And how's yours, ferocious?"

"All right." How much of his crap are you going to take, I said to myself.

"Well, don't gulp it down that way, man. What's the matter with your father?" he said to Ellen. He turned to me. "You know, Gwen and I had many conversations about you. The subject make you nervous?"

"Not nervous."

"Good. You see, dear," he said, turning to Ellen again, "I had an interlude with a young lady, Gwen Hunt was her name—do you mind my bringing this up in front of—?"

"You're goddam right I mind. How much of this crap do you think I'm going to take?"

"I'll bite. How much of this crap *are* you going to take? You've had a year and a half to think over our last encounter. And there are certain similarities." He turned to Ellen. "You see, my dear, I had a love affair with this young lady who had also been an intimate of your father's . . ."

I reached up and pressed the button that would bring the stewardess.

"Now, now," said Chet, "that won't help. Nor is it really necessary. I'm not going to say anything that will splotch this child's picture of you, absurdly idealized though it is."

I could see that Ellen had finally caught on. And about time! She was looking at me anxiously, as if waiting for instruction.

The stewardess was alongside.

"Yes, Mr. Collier?"

"Ah, Eunice, Mr. Arness wants to know if there is a policeman on board." Eunice giggled. "Why do you laugh? They have them on subways. Shouldn't the rich get equal protection?"

"Miss, I'd like a refill," I said. I'd made up my mind to just get through it somehow.

"Oh no, you've had enough," said Collier. "He had a double, didn't he, Eunice?"

"Yes," she said, then to me, "We're only allowed to serve two drinks to a passenger."

"But I can have another," said Collier, "because I only had wine. Now, Eunice, pay careful attention. I'd like one part Dubonnet to five parts gin. There seems to be a change in the atmosphere here, and I want to be ready for whatever comes."

"I want a refill," I said. But Eunice had gone.

Collier turned to Ellen, who didn't find him amusing any more. "This young lady became my sweetheart, and in the course of our intimacies, she told me every detail of her go with your father, each and every lie he told her in the heat of courtship."

Ellen got up. "Excuse me," she said, slid out of her seat past Collier, and walked to the front of the plane.

"What the hell are you trying to do?" I asked.

"Why? What upset you?"

"What upset me!"

"I was a model of restraint. For all your pretty little adopted daughter knows, I rather like you. She has no idea what I really feel."

He wasn't playing a game with me now.

"You know I can't do anything except holler cop, you know that."

"Don't worry, I'm not going to hit you again. But that doesn't mean I've finished with you. You're going to have my teeth in your neck for the rest of your life. You shamed my name in front of a lot of people who don't know better and believed what you said about me." He shook his head slowly from side to side. "But that's the least of it," he said, "the least of it."

There was a sudden suffusion of pain over his face. "At one point I decided to sue you, but there's nothing I want from you except your running blood."

The stewardess came with his drink.

"If you want that drink now," he said, "I'll permit you to have it. I want to talk to you. About something else. Well?"

"I don't want it now."

He gulped half his drink. The disguise of impermeability had dropped, and I could see his real face. Something terrible was happening to it. The composition which had always held it together was suddenly falling apart. The intensity of his pain shocked me. He seemed to hate me more, though he also seemed, for the first time, close to me, not in friendship but in experience.

Now he was shaking his head again, slowly from side to side, never taking his eyes off me. "But that's not why I hate you, Eddie, not because of anything you wrote."

I found my bottle of Canadian Club and had a pull on it.

"There's one question I ask myself whenever I meet a German Jew." Collier said this very slowly. "A German Jew who lived through a concentration camp. And that is, how did he do it? His father, his mother, his sisters, his brothers, his cousins, his friends—they're fertilizer. But these—" he stopped and tasted the next word, "survivors, they're plump as corned beef. And doing great. How? Do you understand what I'm talking about?"

"No," I said. "What are you talking about?"

"The reason I hate you is that you're a murderer and you've survived. Understand now?"

"No."

"Because you almost did it, Eddie."

"Almost did what?"

"You almost killed her. And perhaps you did. There's no way to measure things like that."

"Oh, come on now, she had a history. I was the last of a line."

"But she didn't open herself to the others. She gave you a shot at her vitals. And you took it."

"Well, we all do that to each other."

"The hell we do! Look at me when I talk to you," he snapped. I did. "Some don't survive, but you *always* did. I know about you. You've left corpses all over the place. The field behind you is covered with bodies."

"Oh, come on . . ."

"The question is how did you survive?"

"Stop it!"

"And the answer is that you're not one of the prisoners, you're one of the guards. You're one of the people who survive by sacrificing the others. And end up prosperous, approved, happy—you know, dear father to dear daughter and all that shit—the whole respectable show."

"You don't know anything about me."

"I know everything about you. She told me every detail."

"Where is she now?"

"What do you want to know for, to finish her off?"

I didn't answer that. He spoke slowly and with labor. "She was a wreck when she came to me. She hardly ate, and when she did, she couldn't hold it down. She couldn't sleep, even after we'd made love. But when she did, she had nightmares. About you."

I was thinking of Florence, how I had sickened her sleep, inhabited her nightmares.

Chet was going on. "Night after night I lay alongside of that suffering person. She'd have these terrible spasms and shudders; suddenly she'd be shaking all over. And I'd hold her—that's all I could do for her; night after night, I held her while she talked to you. You understand now how I feel?"

I did.

"I'll bet you never lost a night's sleep over anyone in your life."

I didn't tell him how close he was to the truth.

"Do you have any idea what you did to her?"

"Come on, stop it!"

"Why should I? The survivors finally have to account for themselves. I told you to look at me when I talk to you. I'm going to tell you what you did to her. You convinced her, how I don't know, that she wasn't good enough for you. She accepted you as the big man,

190

the good man, the man of honor and integrity and education and position and standing, and she was nothing. Is that right? I told her she was worth a thousand half-brains like you, but—"

I started to get up. People had begun to notice us.

"Where are you going? Didn't you hear tell? There are no cops on the plane. Sit down. And tell me, do you think I'm wrong?"

I couldn't answer that. I thought he was right.

"You're not saying anything. Have you nothing to say in your defense?"

People were looking at us.

I slumped in my chair.

"I caught you, didn't I? The way you murder people doesn't show; you leave no marks. But I held your victim. I know what you are."

"But she left me," I said.

He noticed the people looking at us. He glared at them till they turned away. Then he was silent for a minute.

I was remembering Florence, the way she was when I held her that morning, the sound of the oak plank shredding and splitting in her breast.

"I want to tell you something else." His voice was moderated now. "She believed all the lies you told her, that you needed her—you told her that, didn't you? Come on, say."

"Yes, I did." I was trying to talk very quietly. People were listening now without turning their heads.

"And that you didn't want to be without her. Did you say that to her?"

"Yes."

"And that she'd brought you to life for the first time. Did you say that?"

"That's right," I whispered, trying to keep his voice down.

"Then can you blame her for believing that sooner or later you'd leave your wife? Can you? Say. Speak!"

He seemed on the verge of shouting.

"No," I said in a careful whisper. "I don't blame her."

"That's what she was waiting for. Did you know that?"

"Yes."

"You even told her that she was the only one who wanted for you what you wanted for yourself. Do you remember saying that to her? Do you?"

191

"Yes, I remember."

"That stayed in her mind."

"I imagine it did."

"Well, did you think that would not affect a woman who was in love with you. . . ."

"People are looking at us."

"I don't care. I want you to answer me. If you say all that to her, she must believe you mean it, and if she believes it—well—answer me!"

"I don't know what you're asking."

"Did you have any idea that she was still waiting for you? When she was with me?"

"No."

"Every time the phone rang, she'd look around like the current had passed through her; when telegrams were delivered . . . I couldn't look at her face the way she got when the boy at the door said 'Telegram!' You understand now how I feel?"

"Yes."

"You were in my bed every night, survivor!"

I had another drink.

"You do understand me now? I want to make sure."

"Yes."

"But that's only a small part of why I hate you."

I wanted to leave again. I realized now that I could have taken another seat. But I obliged myself to sit there and take it. Despite my fear and loathing of this man, I knew he was telling the truth. Not about Gwen maybe, not about Florence perhaps, but about me.

He looked at me intently.

"There are days when I could take you in my hands like yesterday's chicken and pick your bones. The next time," he said, "use a pistol. It's humane."

Then maybe all that Canadian Club finally got to me, or what he'd been saying about Gwen's nightmares and my own memories of Florence. Maybe all that reached me and added up, because I suddenly said, not to him, but to him as Gwen's caretaker and even as Florence's caretaker—I was that drunk—"I'm sorry," I said, "forgive me."

"I never will," he answered. "I'll be satisfied when you're dead."

He was finished now, or so I thought, because he turned front.

We sat there side by side. There was nowhere for either of us to go.

Finally he turned. "I want to ask you something." He seemed anxious; apparently it was a difficult question for him to get out. "You must have thought about me some. Do you think it's possible for me to love anybody?"

"Now I do, yes."

"You're wrong," he said. "Now I can't. Not now. But back then, starting the night of the day she put you on the plane and then came out to my place, then and for three months I could; I actually did. I discovered the thing."

He looked at me, but obliquely now. Not as before. "You saw how I lived. I had myself perfectly organized. I thought women weren't worth what they cost. Who needs them? You know what they are—a nuisance, an everlasting fuss, an unnecessary complication, a whole set of transparent tricks, a concoction of intrigue. But this girl, she never said a false word. She wasn't out to trap me, and she wasn't even out to please me. She's the only girl I've ever been with I didn't wish would disappear the second after I came. You understand that?"

He was whispering now. "And for the first time in my life, you son of a bitch, I considered—considered, hell—I begged her to marry me." He looked at me again, sort of crosswise, suspiciously, as if he'd given me something I could one day use against him.

"Then why didn't you marry her?" I said.

"I just told you. Every day I'd fill up with hope; every night I'd see it was hopeless. I couldn't marry your leavings. So I left her."

He seemed to be considering whether he could or could not trust me. He must have decided he could.

"That's not the truth," he said, "what I told you. I didn't leave her. She left me. I got fed up with her fits and nightmares, with being in bed with you every night. So one day, on an impulse, I said the hell with it all, called up an old girl friend, one I'd had a lot of fun with, and asked her if she wanted to go down to the Mill Reef Club in Antigua. I thought I'd just have fun, like I used to have. The water is beautiful there. But it didn't work. I didn't have any fun; I thought about Gwen all the time, wrote her every day, finally sent the other girl back, tried it alone a couple of days, gave that up, decided to break the trip off, rushed home, and when I got there, she had gone. Disappeared."

"She does that."

"Well, I couldn't figure it out, at the time. I thought maybe she'd found out I was with someone else. But it didn't turn out to be that. Hell, she disappeared for nearly a year."

He looked at me again in that curious way, then slowly reached into his pocket and pulled out a notebook and a pencil. He scribbled some numbers and letters on a page. Then ripped it loose and handed it to me.

I read: 166 West 12th St. Watkins 2-3479.

"Why are you giving me this?" I asked.

"That's where she is."

"Yes, but why . . . ?"

"I want you to find the rest out for yourself. You planned to see her, didn't you?"

"Yes, I had planned to."

"Go see what you've done."

He got up, apparently having decided not to say anything more. He was in the aisle, then decided to come back. He leaned over the back of the empty in front of me.

"She's with someone else," he said.

"I figured."

"It's not what you figure at all. She's with my brother Charles."

"Are they married?"

"I guess I'm sort of warning you. Because the way your brain works, you're certain to misjudge him, and that could be dangerous. He is an innocent, Charles, hasn't quite grown up, but—well, you'll see."

"They're not married?"

"I'll tell you how I found out she was back in New York. I got a call from my sister, a woman to whom I generally don't speak—she's with that UN crowd of pink niggers. She said, 'Guess what? Charles brought this girl home, for chrissake, to meet mother. He wanted mother's approval. He's going to marry this girl.' Well, my sister, she's been around; she can read Gwen's biography right on her face. And of course she knows what Charles is; he still believes what the Sisters taught him. 'The Slaughter of the Innocents!' my sister said.

"But I didn't agree with her," Chet went on. "I thought about it and came to the conclusion that maybe Charles is just what Gwen needs now. Not you. Not me. A guy like Charles. The miraculous part of that girl is that with all that's happened to her, with all those ins and outs, she still has something that makes men take her to see their mothers. She has that Mexican gift, you know, renewing her virginity, like they do down there. Because you remember how it was when she started coming, she'd say, 'There!' like with surprise, 'there!' like it had never happened to her before. With most women it soon becomes nothing. But this girl—she washes the blackboard and it's clean. I don't think anybody could touch her now."

He looked at me, trying to read my face.

"What have you got in mind?" he said.

"Well," I said, "I'm glad she's got somebody who's good for her."

"You're a liar," he said. "You always were. You always will be."

He passed Ellen going up the aisle. He said something to her that I couldn't hear. She smiled and looked at me.

I picked up the *Los Angeles Times* and put it up in front of my face.

11

Ellen had to help me into the
terminal building. She regarded the fact that her father was by now
a rather wobbly drunk as a simple practical problem, which she
quickly solved by planting me in a chair and tying my coat belt to a
post. "Now you just stay put," she said, and went for our luggage.

I have come to the conclusion, against the opinion of all the
experts, that kids are not very sensitive. I've seen them playing happily in the rubble of their homes. I've seen them forget their parents
a week after they die. Kids don't feel obliged to mourn, so they
don't. In relation to disaster they are more selfish and so more
honest than adults.

When Ellen came back, I was asleep. She untied me, hugged me,
and helped me follow the porter to the cab. Nobody felt disgraced.
That was when I began to like Ellen as she was and not love her as
my "angel."

On the taxi ride in, she asked me questions about Gwen. I suppose she was working out the details of her whole new way of life,
so deviant behavior by a woman intrigued her.

The Algonquin had my suite ready. But they hadn't been able to
find a room for Ellen. I asked could they put a cot in the sitting room
for her. They must have thought she was my girl friend, because they
moved the cot in all right, but nobody came to make it up.

In the closet I noticed the rate card. The charge for that suite was
thirty-five dollars per day. Good thing I'd decided to write the Rojas
story. On my own, I'd have been broke in a week. Only company
men can afford modern living.

No sooner had I tipped the bellboy than the phone rang. New

York is swift. It was a photographer named Manny Stern. He was in the bar, he said, and had caught a glimpse of me on my way to the check-in desk. Could he come up? I said no. He said my piece on Collier was the talk of New York. I said, no, he couldn't come up. He said he'd been assigned to the Rojas piece, and wasn't that wonderful? I said, yes, I was glad he was assigned to the Rojas piece, but no, he couldn't come up. In fact, he said, he had already been working on the Rojas piece for two weeks and had some sensational photographs. I said I wanted very much to see them, but not tonight. At this he gave up hinting and insisted he'd bring me a bottle of whatever it was I was drinking and we'd have a nightcap; what was I drinking? I said Canadian Club, but no, no, no. He said, I get it, you got a girl with you! Yes, I said, my daughter, and I didn't want her to see the human ordure to be found in New York City. He laughed and said I couldn't insult him; he didn't know what ordure meant, but if it meant shit he'd been called much worse. I'd run out of answers, so I hung up.

My original plan had been to rush out to Stamford General and see my father. But it was almost ten-thirty, and I was in no condition. So I called my brother Michael. He sounded surprised that I was in New York.

"I know how busy you are," he said deferentially, "so I appreciate your coming."

He really pissed me off. "What made you think I wouldn't come to see my own father?" He had no answer. But I had. What makes Michael think anything he thinks? His wife, Gloria. His wife Gloria and I were the family feud. We were so unfriendly we even talked to each other, that is, we made no effort to conceal our hostility. But Michael is an angel of kindness. Either that or he's a coward who doesn't dare acknowledge conflict, so always acts as if everybody loves everybody. Or there is the third possibility that he thinks if people see him being patient with his wife, they'll be patient with her, too.

I suspected Gloria was on the extension, so I said, "Gloria? Are you there?"

She answered in her contralto, "Hello, Eddie." I told them I felt awful tired, and would come out first thing in the morning.

"Make it about noon," said Gloria. "That's a better time."

"Come any time," said Michael.

"Noon's better, Michael," she said.

"How are you, Gloria?" I said.

"Oh, she's wonderful!" said Michael.

"I know that," I said, "but how's her health?"

"Why?" said Gloria.

"I'm just inquiring about your health," I said.

"My health is all right," she said. "See you tomorrow, around noon, right?"

I was going to say something disruptive, but just then there was a loud knock on my door, and Michael heard it on the other end of the line and, after apologizing for keeping me so long, hung up. Gloria didn't hang up till after I had.

I opened the door. In came a fifth of Canadian Club, followed by Manny Stern.

"I brought you a bottle of Canadian Club."

"Thank you, goodbye."

"That's a hell of a greeting," said Manny. "We're going to have one drink anyway."

"O.K., one drink, but that's it."

"Big deal. One lousy drink."

"Order some ice," I said. "This is my daughter, Ellen. I'm going to the bathroom. . . ."

As I shut the door, Manny was already on the phone with room service. Manny is the complete contemporary man, born with a phone in his hand. What are mechanical devices for the rest of us are parts of his body for him. He's got a tape recorder somewhere on him that he can turn on without anybody knowing it. You never know when he's recording. And besides the Leica M3 and the Nikon F which always hang from his neck, he has a Minox, so small he can palm it. With this he takes pictures of what you don't want pictures taken of. He's always turning up with scandalous tapes and sensational photographs which he recorded and snapped unbeknownst. There is nothing forbidden this man hasn't perpetrated, nowhere his lens, his tape, or his fingers haven't been. He steals—not money or jewelry, but letters, notes, bits of evidence, a lipstick a wife left in the wrong husband's apartment, and so on. And he's everywhere. On a field trip you have to shake him out of your pants in the morning, like you do scorpions in North Africa.

He is also the most adaptable man I've ever seen. Well, his name tells it all. In New York he is known as Manny Stern, which is his name. But he discovered that in postwar Europe, his identity was a handicap. So he dyed his hair a rich blond, had a slight nose bob, and for Europe changed his name to Manfred von Stern. It worked. He found he was welcome and could function professionally in Germany, Russia, and all sorts of places where the Jew isn't welcome. The "von" enabled him to double his rate.

Manny's adaptability is further illustrated by his extraordinary gift for languages. For instance, this New York Jew, if he doesn't say too much and keeps his dye job fresh, passes in Berlin as a Pole, in France as an Alsatian, in England as a South African, in Rio as an Argentinian of German descent, and in Greece as a distant relative, illegitimate and therefore not recognized, of Queen Mother Frederika. He is not only welcome everywhere the jet set goes, but sought after. The women particularly like him. One reason is that he is gently, but effectively, hermaphroditic. He never presses, but he is ready to service either sex when it's to his advantage. This makes him privy to many sources of information that he might not otherwise be able to milk. So he is always up and in—I mean up on the latest gossip, and in on the latest modes, manners, dances, and groupings. He is an advance courier of custom in all fields of human behavior. Also one of the great pimps. He is forever tucking impossible combinations into bed together; in fact, that is his hobby.

The final reason why all the girls have Manny's phone number in their address books with an asterisk in front of it is that he always has marijuana with him and horse not far behind. If given a little advance notice, he can not only get anything, but also get anything into anywhere. Fathers and husbands may forbid the stuff in their homes. But adventurous daughters and bored wives know that they have only to call on Manny or Manfred, depending upon which side of the Atlantic they're on, and in he comes with the pot, weed, shit, or horse. Whatever!

I shouldn't be leaving this son of a bitch alone with Ellen, I thought.

When I went back into the sitting room, the floor was completely covered with photographs. Ellen was down on all fours giving them the O.O.

"Pick them up," I said to Stern.

"All right, why are you getting so damned excited?"

There was a knock on the door. The ice.

"Give me a quarter," said Stern.

"I only have a half dollar."

"Give me that."

I looked at the photographs. I couldn't help it.

"That's your whole story, right there," said Manfred von Stern, as he overtipped the bellboy with a flourish.

"I don't start working on that story till tomorrow."

"Who's asking you to? My God, Eddie, what's the matter with you? You're section eight, all right, just like I heard."

"What did you hear?"

"Did you see this one?" he said, pointing with his toed foot. He was fixing our drinks. "There's your man really off the record."

"Who's that with him?"

"I heard he had a girl stashed away. So you know, Manny hears, Manny finds out. There she is, if you want to use her. You'd be a damned fool if you don't, which you're not, I know." He handed me a drink.

"Look at these," he continued. "He thought he was posing for *Fortune*—you know, that corporation-president, blue-suit art. What he didn't know was that I had an 18-millimeter on. Look at his nose! That fore-shortening makes him look like a spic Durante."

"I don't want to see these pictures."

"So why are you looking? I got three-quarters of your work done for you, but don't look at them. Ellen, you want a drink?"

"Can I, Daddy?"

"No."

"Geezus, Eddie, what a creep you turned out. I heard you had a nervous breakdown. I had a dozen, but I didn't change. You turned creep. Here!" He gave Ellen a drink.

"Pick them up, Manny. I don't want your angle on this. Maybe I'll like the guy."

"Ah, he's on the take like every other politician. He's even got this little place he's building with invisible money, the pennies, haha, of his constituents. I'm going to fly down there, Ponce, on the other side of the island from San Juan, and photograph this little villa by the sea; he's got it in his brother's name, natch. I'll have that picture for you, too, don't worry. This will be your greatest, Eddie . . ."

Manny's drink had made me feel better. "Tonight is your chance," he was going on. "His favorite daughter is getting married, and he's throwing this affair. Everybody he owns and everybody he owes will be there, not to mention his wife, his father and mother, and her father and mother, and his mistress and her father and mother and all three brothers. So with the relatives, the rum, and the rumba, you never know what might not pop."

"I'm not in the mood for drama tonight."

"I'm-not-in-the-mood-for-drama-tonight—geezus what a creep! This is your only chance to observe this guy without his knowing who you are. Anything you want taped, touch your ear; anything you want me to put the Minox on, wink your eye. I'll say you're my assistant, see? They expect me anyway. I already gave them a bunch of stills, the flattering ones. They figure they're going to get the wedding covered free. Which they are. But at the same time, Manny'll be getting us a lot of stuff they don't know anything about. Look, just look at this one. Did you ever see anything like it? Did you? I had to wait over an hour on the roof across from his apartment till he was ready to go to bed. Still in good taste, right?"

He was chortling at his own cunning.

"You know the one thing nobody's got the guts to attack is a Puerto Rican. God knows the niggers get away with murder. They kill people right and left, and the papers report the color of their shoes, but not the color of their faces. But the PR's, they're the real untouchables. It takes guts like you got to do this job. And you can learn more tonight than you could learn in a month of interviews after this guy knows who you are."

I went for another drink.

"Isn't this the best way," he demanded, "when he doesn't know who you are? Am I wrong?"

"You're not wrong."

Just before I left, I took Ellen into the bedroom and tried to talk her into coming with us. She said no, she was going to stay in.

"And do what?"

"I'll call my friend."

Now for chrissake, I thought, don't go getting yourself knocked up again! But how do you say that to your daughter?

"Why don't you stay in and rest tonight, Angel, just not see anyone? Then first thing in the morning, I'll get you outfitted."

Ellen burst out laughing.

"Outfitted!" she said. "Sounds like we're going to Abercrombie & Fitch. Do they sell those things at Abercrombie & Fitch?"

The shindig was in Spanish Harlem. Mr. and Mrs. Alberto Rojas had rented a large ballroom and were playing host to some three hundred. Everything was extremely proper and orderly, downright formal. There was an orchestra playing, and with a little encouragement it could have put out some good sound. But only some twelve-year-olds were dancing. Everyone of substance was sitting around the perimeter in family clusters.

"What's everybody sitting around that way for?" I asked Manny.

He explained they were waiting for the bride and groom to start things off. Then he took me over to meet the Rojas family.

I liked Rojas immediately. He seemed like an energetic, life-loving politician, as corrupt as the next guy, but no more so. I went for him so completely I told him who I was. "Damn fool!" hissed Manfred, who had introduced me as his assistant.

Now the bride and groom had taken the floor, so other couples began to get up. Rojas ordered me a drink, which I didn't really need. We made plans to start talking the following night. In fact, he said, if I would come to his house, he would get his wife to make me Turkey *Molé.* Rojas introduced me to her. She nodded and smiled, but seemed abstracted. After another minute Rojas left me with her. He walked about twenty feet down his side of the perimeter to a group of people around a very pretty girl. I recognized her from Stern's photograph as Rojas' mistress. Massed around her were her father, mother, two uncles, and three brothers. Rojas bowed to them, then took the girl to the floor and opened his arms. She stepped into them, and they began to dance. His style was old-fashioned but ardent.

Stern picked up one of Rojas' other daughters, danced with her as close to Rojas and his mistress as he could get, and began to use his palmed Minox. He caught me watching and gave me a quick wink. I looked at Mrs. Rojas out of the edge of my eye. She was watching her husband dancing with this girl, and there was such an air of sadness and yearning on her face that I knew the news had reached her. Now she leaned forward to steal a look at the girl's family. They, coincidentally, were at that very instant stealing a look at her to see how she was taking it. When their eyes met, they smiled at each other, as if Rojas and the girl were the newly married couple and they were the in-laws. They nodded approval at each other, saying in gesture, they do make a lovely couple. There are all kinds of arrangements, I thought.

Mrs. Rojas dropped her eyes to her hands. Her fingers were short, her nails long. She had them cut very sharp and coated with a heavy red lacquer that was beginning to peel. She picked at them as I watched her. She was a plump, short, Puerto Rican matron, about thirty-eight or forty. Like all these women whose entire exercise consists of walking from the bedroom to the bathroom to the kitchen and back, she was a well-filled skin. Especially her buttocks, they were big buns, and her thighs were so thick that when she crossed her legs, her skirt hiked up and you could see where she'd stopped shaving. Now she noticed me noticing her, and she pulled at her skirt. But there wasn't enough material there, so she uncrossed her legs and crossed her ankles, and left it at that. I tried smiling at her, but got nothing back. Now I was intrigued. Order-professed, chaos-concealed was the subject that intrigued me most in the world.

"Nice party," I said.

"You like? I'm glad. Have you met the bride?"

"No. But she's very pretty."

"Yes, she's suddenly pretty," she said looking out at the dancers. I saw she was watching her husband and his mistress dancing, not the bride and groom.

"I want to talk to you," I said.

"Me? What for?"

"Well, I have to write about your husband, and naturally I must know what his wife thinks of him—of his work, that is."

"You going to write good about him?"

"Well, I think so. I just met him now, so I don't know."

"You'll see. He's a fine man."

"I see he's a good dancer."

"Yes," she said looking at the floor. Then she became aware that I was watching, and she stole a look at my face. But I had my mask up, and she didn't see that I knew anything.

"I imagine you are, too."

"I am too what?"

"A good dancer."

"Before I had my children maybe . . ."

"I heard you used to go dancing together a great deal when he was courting you." I hadn't heard any such thing, of course.

"Yes, yes, true. . . ."

"How many have you?"

"How many have I what?"

"Children."

"Six. I had eight, but two die."

"That takes a lot out of a woman. I mean it's a full time job."

"What else would I do with my time? Listen, mister, you don't have to sit here and talk to me."

"I know I don't have to. I want to."

"But why? I'm just an old married woman. You like I get you someone to dance with? Lots of young girls."

"I'd like it if I could dance with you."

"With me? You crazy?! Why you want to dance with me?"

"Why do people dance at all?"

"You know why, why you ask why?"

I smiled at her. But she didn't smile back.

She said, "Mister, I know you want something, but you don't say what you want."

I figured I better speak out. "Well," I said, "I've written a lot about politicians, and especially those on the way up. I can see that your husband has many things. He's handsome, and people trust him right away. They follow him just because he is a man you follow. But many times I've seen them start nice, like your husband is nice, and a few years later they're just as big crooks as the others. Especially since I see your husband enjoys his power. I mean he enjoys that people follow him. What I had on my mind, that I wasn't saying, was that if I was that woman, you, I'd be scared a little. Are you? At what's ahead for you and your family?"

She hadn't expected me to speak that frankly.

"Yes," she said, "I am scared."

"I can understand that, but . . ." Then I said to myself, shut up now, and let her talk.

"But I trust Alberto, you see, because he is a good man. At bottom he is for the people. And he's a good husband." She looked back at the floor. Then she turned and saw me looking at her, smiled at me like you would at a friend, and said, "You really like to dance?"

I jumped up. "Yes, I really would."

"*Andale burro!*" she said and began the process of getting her feet back into her pointed shoes, which were too small for her.

"I've had a drink or two," I said, "so if I said anything wrong, please . . ."

"No, you were right . . . I'm frightened. Please don't say so when you write."

We didn't do too badly. I wobbled a bit at first. But the little Puerto Rican matron inspired me. It was so important to her that she do well on the floor that I made a greater effort than I otherwise would have, and did some of the best social dancing I'd done in years. Even Rojas nodded appreciatively to us. And Stern was sufficiently impressed to take his camera off Rojas and his mistress and take one shot of us.

The set came to an end. I'd become aware of her scented perspiration, so I took her out on a small balcony which overlooked 116th Street to cool her off.

I really had drunk too much, because I then did a damn fool thing. I said, "Do you think we made him jealous?"

She looked at me, and now she knew I had caught on. "No," she said.

"Oh God," I said, "I'm sorry."

"I only wonder," she said, not looking at me, "is it so clear everyone can see what it is?"

"No, I don't think so," I lied.

"Are you telling me the truth?" she said. "Or like before?"

"No, I'm a writer, and I see what other people don't see—I hope."

"Are all writers liars like you?" she said. And when my face fell, she laughed and smiled at me with some affection. "I can tell you what I think," she said. "I think everybody sees what you see, maybe more."

"Well," I said, "I don't know about that."

"I tell you something else. The men, naturally, they understand and expect. It's the way they are. But the women, they're worse. They pretend it's a sin, and make those noises, tst-tst-tst-tst and so on, but they all wish it was them there with him." She indicated the dance floor. "That Ramera," she said, "that *puta*." Then she went off into a whole gulp of Spanish and ended with "What I'm saying is, that whore, she's been waiting two years for this chance. But

I knew what was coming, because my father had someone and then another one. And I saw my mother, when he didn't use her any more, how she got fat, too. Don't look at me."

"I'm sorry," I said.

"I was jealous of my father and those girls, but I also admired him, because he was *macho*. So it is the world; isn't it the world? The woman lasts short time. The man has to show his *macho*. But Alberto is a goddam good man. Even with her, or whoever, he never let anyone hurt me the rest of my life."

I felt a wave of admiration for her. No, it wasn't admiration at all, goddammit; it's patronizing to admire someone in that much trouble. I just felt for her. And I thought, goddam if I'm going to make it worse for her by what I write.

We were standing there on the balcony overlooking 116th Street, cooling off, each with our thoughts. Mine were: it is one thing to write literature and another thing to be a goddam hack journalist like you are, kid. Because in literature you commemorate people's experience, their living, and their pain; you celebrate their humanity. But what you've been doing, Evangeleh ("Evangeleh," the name my father used to call me, my old name and my right name), is to destroy people for the entertainment of your readers and for the swelling of your bank account. In case you don't realize it, that is the real *puta*, kid, and all those other words she used, it's whoring in plain English.

She'd been thinking, too. "What scare me, like you say, what I'm worried is he doesn't take what he wants. He gives them what they want. Like that *puta* there. He could get much prettier. But she chase him, and I'm pregnant with the last one, and she chase, so one day, hell, he give in. But I understand in politics that would be bad. Like you say he could be just like the others, do anything for the vote. Instead of saying this is the way I want it. Am I right? Maybe you put that in your story, it will make him understand."

"I want to show you something," I said. I led her back to where we'd been sitting, picked up Stern's portfolio of photographs from under the table, and took her to the corner of the hall at the opposite end from the music. I put the portfolio on an old banquet table and opened it. One by one I showed her the pictures, the worst of them. She didn't say a word. At the same time I instructed her as to my technique. I told her that my first step was to make friends and get people to trust me. Then maybe they'd invite me to have *Molé Poblano* or whatever, and they'd tell me everything. I'd write down what they'd later wish they hadn't told me. And I was going to use the pictures she was looking at to illustrate the story about her husband.

She kept her head down all through this, looking at Manny's stuff, not saying a word. But I could see her chest heaving. Then she began to tear up the photographs. She was one hell of a girl!

The set was over, and the dancers began to leave the floor. Some of them noticed what was happening at the far end of the room. Stern had missed his portfolio, and was looking around. Now he saw me standing by while this woman ripped his precious stills to scraps. He gave a cry that was pure New York, and came running! He grabbed Mrs. Rojas and tried to pull her off. But she bit his arm, then gave him a shove which landed him right on his epicene ass.

Rojas, who had also run up, did succeed in pulling his wife off the portfolio of stills. Meantime Stern was up and after me, yelling, "What the hell you let her do that for? You insane or something?"

"Let her?" I said. "I gave them to her." I grabbed a still, a jumbo, and began to rip it up.

Meantime, Rojas' mistress had come up and found, among the scattered photographs, one she particularly liked. "This is beautiful!" she said. "Alberto," she cried in a high fluted voice, "Alberto, can I have this one?"

This hit the limit of Mrs. Rojas' patience. She pulled loose from her husband, who had relaxed his grip, and went after the girl. *"Callejera!"* she screamed. *"Puta!"*

She went for the girl's eyes and face with her short stubby fingers and her long sharp nails. She ploughed that young girl's face up, so that whatever happened to her the rest of her life, she'd never forget that evening.

At this, the young girl's massive mother, with a jungle cry of her own, lit into Mrs. Rojas. And two to one, they were rocking and rolling all over the place, nails flying and hair-dos collapsing. Mr. Rojas, of course, had to come to his wife's aid. The mistress's brothers, all three of them, jumped Rojas. He was very *macho,* as Mrs. Rojas had said, and he gave as good as he got.

The parish priest intervened, but soon wished he hadn't. Into the melee came Mr. Rojas' old father, aged seventy-odd but tough as an old tree. Coming at a run was Rojas' bodyguard, a murderous little fellow who knew his trade and proceeded to do what he had to. The management came running from several sides. A member of the orchestra, the horn player—he must have been high on something—he got into it. Someone had sent for the police, two of whom had been standing in the street-level entrance. They were up now, and that made it official.

I was watching, with the greatest satisfaction, this marvelous, disgraceful scene, the chaos so much more honest than the order before.

Stern was screaming in my ear, "I'll sue you, I'll sue you!" Then yelling, "Police! Help! Police!" But suddenly he must have realized that what was taking place was a better story than any he had photographed, and after all, what the hell, he had his negatives at home. So out came his Minox, and he began to photograph the exploits of Alberto Rojas among his constituents.

It was then that I did my last act in the magazine world. I grabbed Manfred von Stern's miniature camera where it was tied by a long woven metal chain to a place in his clothing, and I jerked it loose. Then, twirling it around my head three, four, five, six times at the end of its chain, I smashed it and its total precious contents against the nearest post. That was the end of Evans Arness. He went to join Eddie Anderson.

At this demise, I was taken with a fit of laughter. The fact that Stern was at my throat shaking me and trying to punch me seemed nothing but terribly funny. I felt light and free and released from all earthly responsibilities.

"You are insane," screamed Stern. "Do you hear that! I'm going to put you in jail, you insane man."

"Go ahead!" I yelled back. The thought of being put in jail only brought a promise of further exhilaration.

"What are you laughing at, you maniac or something?" yelled poor old Manny. I suddenly grabbed him and hugged him with drunken affection. But he took it as an attack, pushed me off, yelled, "Police!" and then jumped me. I was too weak from laughing to do myself much good. But someone must have pulled him off me, because next thing, I was looking for Rojas, Stern still following, still promising he was going to put me away.

Rojas had succeeded in pulling his wife off his mistress, and was holding her with some difficulty, because she wanted more blood from that girl's face. That's the end of that arrangement, I thought. By then the melee was so general and so noisy that the only sound you could distinguish as separate came from the police whistling for reinforcements. I thanked Mr. and Mrs. Rojas, who couldn't hear or care less, for their hospitality. I told them that I wasn't going to write the piece, so I wouldn't be coming to their house for *Molé Poblano*. Stern was in my ear, making this final word with the Rojases difficult, so I took a larger pitcher of rum punch and emptied it, limes and all, over his dye job. And while he was spluttering and spitting, I shoved him into the heart of the dogfight, where he was soon lost to sight in the general stew of Rojas' mistress, Rojas' mistress's brothers, mother and father, her uncles, the parish priest, the turned-on horn player, Rojas' bodyguard, the police, the management, and every manner of fun-loving young mover.

As I went down the stairs, police reinforcements were arriving. I slipped into the bar next door. They had no Canadian Club, but I had some of their best rum. I stood at the end of the bar near the street window and there got to see a hysterical Manfred von Stern in the middle of the main street of Spanish Harlem, summoning a cab. When he rolled off, the episode had become ancient history. I knew he'd be at the office first thing in the morning, and I thought maybe I better call first and quit before I'm fired. But that seemed like a boring point of honor, so I relaxed.

When the orchestra began to play again upstairs, I walked out into the street. It was one of those exhilarating, drizzly evenings that you get all winter long in Paris and London but only occasionally in New York and never in California. I walked along and I thought, Well, you've finally got it like you want it: chaos. I now had no job, no source of income, no reason to be considered reliable. Looking at it from an opposite point of view, Florence's for instance, I was so clearly undependable that I was no longer a meal ticket. Either and both ways, I was free.

And broke. They won't give me the money I paid out for my airplane ticket, I thought. And they certainly won't pay my hotel bill.

I looked into my pocket to see how much money was there. I had a big three hundred dollars. Not too bad. I certainly felt richer than I had that morning. I only had sixty-seven thousand dollars then. I felt so bullish, in fact, that when I passed a little flower store, just then closing for the night, I went in and bought a corsage of rosebuds, and gave the guy an extra buck to take them to Mrs. Rojas himself with a message of admiration to be spoken by him in Spanish.

Now, since there was no reason to do anything, there was no reason not to do anything. I was too drunk and too happy to think of values and consequences. I only wanted to deal with impulses and desires. I desired to go downtown and see Gwen. Was it reasonable? Would I be welcomed? Would she be alone? Or even there? I did not entertain these questions, because the answers would not affect my decision to walk from 116th Street on the east side to 12th Street on the west side, where she lived. "I have been making, gentlemen," I said out loud, "certain experiments in appearance and reality, in profession versus performance. Now I want to consult an expert in social anomaly and general fraud who lives on 12th Street. So, as Mrs. Rojas would say, *'Andale burro!'* "

I was on top of my drunk now, going with it, not fighting it. I opened my tie, loosened my coat. I took my hat and put it on the head of another drunk, who was asleep on the sidewalk in front of a liquor store. Whether he was protesting its being locked or waiting for it to open in the morning, I couldn't tell. Then I went into the last store still open on the street and bought a cigar for eighty-five cents.

Here's what happened between One hundred and sixteenth Street and Lexington Avenue and Ninety-sixth Street and Fifth. I decided not to please anyone but myself in the future. I decided I had done my bit for others. I had made my sacrifices to society, my fellow man, the common good, and my immediate family. I decided, in fact, that I had spent much too much of my life in the service of others, convincing them, winning them, deceiving them (for their own good), selling the products they made, selling the ideas they wanted sold. And, getting closer to home, supporting others in the way they, not I, wanted to live. I'd even allowed myself to be shot at by a lot of anonymous Japanese fellows for the sake of "our way of life." So now I plumped down for the sanctity of selfishness. From now on I'd be a nice, quiet, selfish failure, a self-sufficient, antisocial prick, an irresponsible, slippery, evasive, noncommunicative horse cock. And if they didn't like it, *andale burro.*

I crossed Fifth and Ninety-sixth, and headed into the park.

After all, I thought, Florence is set for life. In the second place,

210

she has dear Dr. Leibman, dear as hell at fifty per, but she has the fifty per, so forget her. And Ellen is delightfully indifferent to any problem other than her own, so she's so brimming with mental health. My father and mother? Where did I get the idea that I was everyone's custodian? I loved them and the hell with them. What's so sacred about parents? I'd just have to learn to live like the animals live, side by side, but not responsible. In general, I would do nothing because I ought to, or should. Ought to! Should! *Andale burro!*

To be concrete, I didn't need houses, gardens, swimming pools, an office, a secretary, a hush-a-phone, three cars, and a million records and books. I didn't need any more clothes. The way I felt that night, I didn't even need food to eat. It was clear to me I could sustain myself on the damp air and the night sights. My body seemed lighter, thinner, more resilient, and generally invincible.

At the tennis courts, in the darkest part of the park, I did thirty push-ups.

Facing me were the battlements of Central Park West—the Imperial, the Beresford, the Dakota, the Majestic—a profile of towers and machicolations. Most of the lights were out. The massive middle class had made it through another day. Congratulations, all! Now safely put away for the night in their arrangements of locked boxes on those piled-up shelves, they slept the sleep of kings. Everything was in order. Or at least it would so appear. No one flung himself out of a tower window while I was looking, or off an east terrace. They were all up there, as their way of life demanded, being kept safe, clean, and out of trouble till morning. When the sun came over the Carlyle, and the bedside clocks turned on WMCA, they'd all jump up, refreshed and ready to continue at their jobs, meet their obligations, fulfill their responsibilities, and lead the world for still another day.

Goodbye all!

Andale burro.

In front of the Majestic I thought of Florence. She was probably just waking now after her first hour of "good" sleep, and taking two Nembutals to dope her into her second sleep, not as good as the first natural sleep, but still. And I said, Goodbye, baby.

In front of Ethical Culture I recalled our fine days together, as a person might after a wife or a husband has died. I recalled when and where we met, and as I passed the West Side Y I recalled the first time we made love, on the shore of a lake it was, and the croakers in full song. And I said goodbye, little baby! Then as I passed the National City Bank, the bank which murdered my father in twenty-nine, I said goodbye to all those good old days. In front of the old Garden, I didn't resent anyone any more, because you only resent a prison, and I was out!

At Forty-seventh Street and Eighth Avenue, I went in out of the beautiful drizzle and had me another drink. I was just wet enough to need it, just chilled enough to enjoy it. It was a miserable bar, full of impoverished quarrelsome actors and prospering quarrelsome stagehands. They were bickering and teasing and arguing. And I listened to the bickering, the teasing, and the arguments, and I felt warmed by all that sourness. Where had I wandered so far from home? Nobody was pleasant in that bar, nobody gracious, nobody sweet-tempered, nobody compliant, nobody altruistic. What had I given up all this wonderful sourness for?

In front of Penn Station, which was being wrecked that year, I touched my toes twenty-three times in commemoration of the old building which was coming down like my old structure was coming down. *Andale burro!*

I had another drink in the Port Said on Twenty-eighth Street. I knew if I was sober I'd never do what I was going to do. Without that good sustained drinking, I definitely would not be going down to Twelfth Street to haul my old girl's ass off the block of ice which had kept it sterile and intact for a year and a half (intact?). Without the particular help of this last drink, I might turn the other way and soon be sensibly asleep in my own little box in the Algonquin.

I had the slip of paper Chet had given me. When I came to her place, I rang her bell. No answer. I made a note of the apartment number, 3F. F for front. (My brain was really working!) I went out front and my eyes went up the building. Her apartment windows were dark, her shades up. I decided to wait. I crossed the street and sat down on a hydrant. New York has no place to sit down. I stood up. I had been about to fall asleep. Then I sat down again, and, securing my balance, fell asleep.

I have second sight when I'm asleep. I suddenly woke and saw Gwen coming down the street, and with her was a very bulky young man. I jumped to my feet and stood at attention. I got up so abruptly that for a moment I thought they must have seen me. But they hadn't. They turned into the hallway of Gwen's house and stood there talking very gravely. Sometimes they seemed to be looking right at me. But, of course, I was in the dark and they couldn't see me.

The classical conversation was going on, the one to decide whether the man is going to go upstairs with the girl or is going to go home. They had not yet reached the stage, apparently, where the man comes up as a matter of course. I recognized that this fellow was inexperienced, because an experienced fellow would have gone right up. "Don't ever ask, friend," I said out loud, "just go on up. They have to follow."

Obviously she wasn't gone on this guy, because if she was, being Gwen, she would have pulled him upstairs. Most girls give in because it is easier, because they don't like to disappoint, because they have nothing better to do, because the man persists, because the expression on his face is so needy, and it doesn't mean all that much to them anyway. But Gwen never gives in. She decides, like a boy, to go for it. "Then," I added out loud, "her strength is as the strength of ten."

This time there was no traffic, and they heard the drunk across the street talking to himself. But paid no mind. The lummox, a two-hundred pounder, at least, bigger than his brother Chet (if he was who I thought he was) seemed to think that reason would gain the hill. He stood there, jawing at her, with his engineer-type eyeglasses and his correct frown. Gwen was like it didn't matter much to her one way or the other.

"I don't think she likes you, fellow!" I said out loud. I know they heard that, because they turned and looked for a minute at the drunk across the street. Then Gwen took Charles' hand—I guess she was just sick of the gab—and led him through the door and up the stairs. "Now look what you've gone and done!" I said to myself.

But actually I felt exhilarated. Not by what she had done, but by what she had not done. She had not admitted him as a matter of course.

"And now, you son of a bitch, go back to your box in the

213

Algonquin and read *Siddhartha* or some other paperback that stresses the glories of the inner life."

The lights went out in the apartment above. First in the room with two windows (must be the living room, I thought) and then in the room with a single window (must be the bedroom; my brain is really working!). I stepped forward to see more clearly what might be happening up there, and a *Daily News* delivery truck almost made its own news.

"Be careful; they'll hit you if they can," I said to myself.

When the truck moved out of the way, I saw the shade in the bedroom being pulled down. That's that, I thought, go home!

I was punchy, so I backed away till my heels hit, then I sat down. There was a telephone booth there, so I sat on the curb, or was it in the gutter, and I leaned back against the booth. And there I was, stockholder and vice president of Williams and MacElroy, the man with the equity—if only through marriage—in a luxurious Los Angeles home plus swimming pool, the male half of the renowned Golden Couple, sitting in the gutter contemplating how short a distance it finally is between the top and the bottom. In this act of contemplation, the great man fell asleep.

Again, my eighth sense woke me. The lights in the apartment were just being turned off. Then the shade in the bedroom was raised and the window lifted to its full height. I didn't remember Gwen being such a fresh air bug. "He probably needs it for energy," I said. "A hulk like that must use a lot of oxygen puffing and grunting and shoving." Thank God I'd kept my weight down. A hulk like that must sweat a lot, I thought.

I was getting pretty ridiculous, so I decided to go home. I got up. It was raining now, not drizzling. I went into the telephone kiosk and leaned against the wall, looking at the building opposite. Then I noticed a cop coming down the street. And me in a phone booth! I couldn't remember a single New York number to dial. So I took out the slip of paper and a dime and I dialed Gwen's number. I'd wanted to, anyway, I guess. I could hear the phone ring in the apartment. And just as the cop came opposite me, the shade in the single window was pulled down, and the light went on behind. Gwen answered the phone. She said, "Hello, hello." There was a long pause.

"Who is it?" she said.

The cop had passed, which is what I was waiting for. But I didn't hang up. I said out loud or to myself—I could no longer differentiate—I said, "What a beautiful voice she has!"

That she heard and must have figured me for one of those nuts who call people in the middle of the night to breathe at them, because she quickly hung up. But in those few words, it had all come back to me—her voice, it was the same beautiful voice, so girlish. It was my girl's girlish voice.

Now I felt ashamed of the ridiculous and sophomoric way I was behaving, so I decided again to go home. I straightened myself out and was about to go out the door of the telephone booth, looking at the window one last time. Some of the shade, perhaps five inches or so, was below the level of the raised window, and it swayed in the bedroom breeze. There was life back in there. I wondered, did he take his glasses off?

I'll break it up, I thought, dialing her number. I'll interrupt the action. And maybe after, he won't be able to get it up again.

I ought to have been put away that night.

No one answered. But I kept ringing. I realized with considerable satisfaction that I must indeed be interrupting something. When she finally picked the phone up, her voice did sound different. I made a noise in the phone which sounded like, "We have that number for you now, Mr. Anderson." What an inept phony, I thought—a secretary, a male one yet, this time of night. No, it's the headwaiter at the Little Club, I thought. Oh! I didn't really care so long as I stopped those obscene goings-on.

"Hello, Gwen?" I said, as casually and as pleasantly as I could manage. "Hello, Gwen, this is Eddie!"

From the time I was a kid, I'd always announced my name on the phone as if it were an event. Despite that, there was now a long pause.

"Am I interrupting something?" I asked.

"No," she said, "that's o.k."

Now the shade went down and the light went on behind.

"How have you been?" she said.

"Oh, fine, fine."

"Where are you?"

"Here in New York. In a sort of restaurant. The Little Club. I've come East to do a story."

"Oh," she said.

Oh what, I thought, oh what, baby?

"I'm sorry, it's sort of late to call," I said, "but I did call you on and off and you were always out."

"I was, yes, and it is, yes, late. Why don't you call me tomorrow?"

Oh, you do want to talk to me, I thought! O.K., that's all I wanted to know.

"I'll call you tomorrow," I said.

"O.K., tomorrow."

You don't want to talk to me in front of him, right? I thought.

"You don't mind my calling you?" I said.

Let's see what she'll say to that.

"No, why should I?"

Par for the course. One of her "No, why?" evasions.

"Because," I said, "I have something urgent to ask you . . ."

Good! Ask for urgent help! That always gets them!

There was some murmuring off mike, as they say. Then apparently Charles got out of bed and went into the other room. Because, when she talked again, she sounded like she was less on guard. Well, I thought, if she's on guard, that means she must be feeling something that she doesn't want him to know about.

"All right, now," she said. "How have you been?"

Need her help again, I said to myself; ask for her help again.

"Oh, I don't know," I said. "You know me, I never know how I am till months later. Unless somebody tells me."

"Oh, stop acting like a baby, Eddie, you know how you are, how are you?"

That made me laugh. Gwen was sounding less girlish and more like Gwen. Then I noticed the living room. The shades had not been lowered, and I saw Charles there. He was in his underwear, top and bottom, standing a little back from the window. He was proportioned like a large carpet, rolled up, that is. My God, I thought, does he go to bed with her in his underwear?

"Eddie?"

"What?"

"You were silent. I thought you were gone."

"I was wondering, did I wake you; sorry if I did."

"Well, I had fallen off."

Charles reappeared at the window, holding a beer by the can.

216

"Well, then, I'm really sorry," I said. "Go back to sleep. I just needed some help."

"Oh."

"In a delicate matter."

"Is she knocked up?"

Was she jealous? Charles was drinking his beer. Better get you another one, kid, I thought; this may go on awhile. I put in a nickel.

"Eddie?"

"Yeah."

"You keep disappearing."

"No, I'm here. You know. Memories. Sorry. It's about my daughter, Ellen, and it's not what you said. You remember Ellen?"

"I remember Ellen."

"Well, she's a big girl now."

She didn't say anything. I could see that Charles was saying something to her from the other room, something that I couldn't hear across the street. But what I did hear, despite the fact that she must have had the mouthpiece covered with her hand, was that famous two-timer's refrain, "He's just an old friend." Now he was saying something else, and I thought, get yourself another beer, square ass, because "just an old friend" may be on this line for quite a while yet.

"Eddie," said Gwen, "I think I better go now. It's getting sort of late."

"Well, o.k.," I said, "I'll tell you all about it when I see you."

"When is that going to be?" she said.

My God, I thought, that's a strange arrangement up there!

"Well, what would be a good time for you?" I said.

"It would have to be rather late in the afternoon."

"Morning's no good for me, either. So Ellen will just have to wait a day."

"Is she sick or something?" she said. "I mean, why me?"

It was getting what the English call sticky.

"I'll tell you tomorrow afternoon. What time?"

"Six," she said. "Good night."

"Wait, wait," I said.

"Eddie," she said, "it's just occurred to me you're drunk."

I saw that Charles was doing something mighty strange in the other room, a sort of pantomime, like a kitten playing by itself. He was making like a T-formation quarterback, taking the ball from center, falling back into the pocket, spotting a receiver, and getting the ball off downfield.

"Eddie!"

"What—oh, excuse me—some sort of brawl is going on outside the booth; can you hear it? This joint is full of football players. Was there a big game played in the city today?"

"I don't know," she said, "I don't like football. By the way, Eddie, where did you get my number?"

"I met Chet Collier in the airplane. He gave it to me."

"So you also know where I live."

"116 West 12th. It says here."

"Then I'll see you tomorrow." And she hung up, turned off the light, and raised the shade. I stayed there awhile watching Charles. He made his first down, sent his fullback through the line once, then on the second down went for the long bomb, found a receiver, and hit him. Touchdown. Charles had won.

I walked to the corner and hailed a cab. At the Algonquin, there were three messages for me. All the same: Mr. Manny Stern had called.

Upstairs, Ellen was not there. But I found a note. "Your friend, Mr. Collier," it said, "called, and since you were out, he said I would do. He's showing me *his* New York." Then there was another bit in a different hand: "We may be out pretty late. But I'll take care of her. Yours faithfully, Chet."

It was then three o'clock, going on four.

I was too tired to speculate.

12

I WAS up on a wall, hung by a cleat in the middle of my back, securely suspended, but upside down, with my works in hopeless disarray. I had been a disappointment from the beginning. To whom? There was no one in the long rectangular room. But the wall opposite was filled, as it had always been filled, with an enormous eye! And arched over the eye was a familiar brow, stiff with disapproval. Something was expected of me that I was not fulfilling. But what could I do, wrong side up and helpless to change my position? And that glaring eye threw my mechanism off even further. Relent, I begged, stop looking at me that way! Give me a chance. But the eye was right. I was defective in some essential respect, and I couldn't do anything about it.

I was about to sob again. That's what I used to do when I was a kid, and it hadn't done me any good then. The eye had not softened. And now, hiding under the sheet, my blanket pulled up over my head—what good was that? My advice: shut up and take it. That's the way it is for you. Live through it.

So I did. And in time I felt the heat of that eye cool, and I knew I was in a bed, and that bed was in the Algonquin Hotel, and I was cold. Despite the bedclothes up over my head, I shook with chills. I also had a walloping headache and nausea in gulps. But I was safe. I was not a malfunctioning clock, and I was not helplessly cleated to a wall. The nightmare was over.

What the hell was going on?

The first time I had that nightmare was during the influenza epidemic. I had a high fever for a week. Each night during that week, as soon as my mother turned off the lights and left my room, I would cover my head with the bedclothes and wait. But no matter how far down under I got, that nightmare would find me. It came every night, and every night it left me terrified and sobbing in a way I could not explain. Then, the epidemic over, the fever down, I slept without fear. But the next time I was sick with fever, it came back. Once again I was cleated to a wall, upside down and malfunctioning, the object of terrible but deserved disapprobation.

I grew up, went to college, to the war and back, settled the score with my father, went my way, not his, and never had that nightmare again.

Till now. What the hell was going on?

My stomach gulped again. I knew I better get to the bathroom fast.

After I throw up I always study the mirror. I figure it is the nearest I'll come to seeing my face the way it will look when I'm dead. Understandable curiosity. I looked a long time at the piece of gray sculpture I'd spend my whole life working on. The head in the mirror still pleaded for consideration, still said, "Relent. Don't judge me unkindly. Give me a chance."

"To hell with all that," I said out loud. I made my face look fierce and strode through the curtains between the two rooms.

Ellen had come home. On the floor beside the sofa where she slept was a note, printed in a big hand. "Don't wake me. Ever. Love. Ellen. P.S. Your friend is not your friend. Beware."

Out the window it was still dark. Five before six. The streets were enjoying their last silence. One thing I did recognize in that dream: the eye. I knew the hypostatic light that burned there. My father's glare had been the climate of my boyhood.

I'll go see the old man *now,* I thought; the hell with Gloria and her come-at-noon! I began to dress.

I remembered the clock, too. It was the clock on the wall of our dining room. It was long and coffin-shaped, and it was indeed fastened to the wall with a big cleat. I often had had to climb up on a chair, under instruction from my father, lift the old discombobulated thing off its cleat and, carrying it ever so gently, put it in the back of whatever car we had at the time so it could be taken to the clock hospital. It was in everlasting need of repair. As I would take the clock down off its cleat, the resonating tubes in its body would glance off each other and sound their chimes. But they never seemed to work as part of the clock's functioning. Sometimes, when no one was home, I'd climb up on one of the dining room chairs, tap them, and listen to their tones. But the best efforts of the clock hospital couldn't make them sound when and how they should. That old clock was willful, and that's not a virtue in a machine.

My father was devoted to that clock, but he didn't trust it. Whenever the time was really important to him, he'd call Information. In those naïve days, the Westchester telephone people would give out the time free. They've come to their senses now; they charge a dime. I think my father would have paid the dime. He liked the time exact. Then, knowing what the clock didn't know, he'd get up on one of the dining room chairs himself and correct the minute hand, all the while saying unkind things to the clock in his Anatolian argot.

He never allowed anyone else to wind it or correct it. Sometimes I did it on the sly. I'd call Information and get the exact time, and then I'd climb up and correct the minute hand before my father got home. Once Michael, who was just a kid and meant no harm, informed on me. I remember how my father arched his brows till they were tense, and how he glared at me and made it plain that I was not to touch the clock ever again. He was trying to find out just how defective it was, and how could he do that if I fussed with it? So I never did again. My old man's word was the law of God in those days.

At Grand Central, the train was on the lower level, waiting for me. I bought a ticket to Stamford and off we clogged—125th Street, Mount Vernon, Columbus Avenue, Pelham, New Rochelle—the path worn smooth by my father and a million million commuters. And going over that old ground, it came back to me, the life I'd lived with that man.

Well, it wasn't exactly a life; I didn't see him much more than an hour a day. Mornings I simply stayed in my room on the third floor till I heard him get into the cab waiting to take him to the station. I'd run down the stairs, swallow my breakfast, and run all the way to school. I was often late, but it was worth it just to avoid exposing myself to my old man in the morning.

There was no way to avoid seeing him at night. In fact the climax of the day—my mother's, Michael's, mine—was the arrival of my father in the evening. As the moment approached when he would walk in the front door, all three of us grew more and more tense.

221

There were two factors which would determine his mood, what sort of morning he'd had with the buyers at his store—Sam Arness, Oriental Rugs and Carpets—and what sort of afternoon he'd had with the bookies at Aqueduct or Belmont. You could tell as soon as he walked in the front door. If he had had a good day, he'd bring fruit. He loved peaches and pears and ripe apricots, plums and every kind of melon. But above all he loved those white seedless grapes, especially those little sweet ones.

The first thing he did after he got home was to call the members of his circle of bridge players and arrange that night's game. Only after that was done would he sit in the armchair at the head of the dining room table and proceed with our evening. He'd pour himself an *oozou,* fog it with water, and call for "a little something," his *Mezeh,* the appetizers. My mother had them ready, too, on pain of terrible displeasure. She ran them out to him: sardines perhaps, pistachios always, fat-cheeked Greek olives, soft as plums, and some of the sour, salty, hard cheese which they make in that part of the Turkish highlands from which my father came, the cheese named after the province, *Caesari Payneer.*

Then, having taken just enough edge off his appetite, he would turn his attention to me. He had poured himself a second *oozou* by now, and the hypostatic light in his eyes burned bright. Turning it directly on me, he would stiffen his brows, look at me appraisingly, and ask, "What did you do today, my boy?"

I've never forgotten the hell that question raised with me. In a matter of seconds my lips would dry. They'd cling together. When I finally forced them open to speak, some sort of stickum which had formed between them would snap.

I'd say, "Nothing."

"Nothing?" he'd say, measuring me with that terrible eye, and sending me tumbling into total malfunction. "Nothing?" Then he'd wait for me to explain, cracking his pistachios. When I didn't because I couldn't, he'd say, "What kind salesman you going to be, my boy?" He'd say the word salesman as if it was three words: sale is man. It was rough! I knew he was supposed to be kidding, but it wasn't kidding to me. The main thing I remember about my father is that he was disappointed in me.

He'd continue his joking, fixing me with that eye, a god in malevolence as well as in power, his eyebrows hard as scimitars, and he'd demand, "How much money did you make today?"

Now what kind of goddam question was that to ask a kid just starting high school? He'd glare at me so it was impossible for me to answer, my lips were so dry. But he'd drink his *oozou,* nibble pieces of that crusty goat cheese, and wait. "Putter, putter," he'd say, referring I suppose to the evidence of my nerves.

"How much money?" I'd finally say.

"Yes," he'd say, "money, you've heard of it. How much?"

"None."

"So what's going to happen?" cracking his pistachios.

"When?" I said, trying to laugh because it had to be a joke; he'd played more or less the same joke on me the night before.

"When? In my old age! I hope somebody will support me. But who?"

"I will!" I said, with a flash of desperate energy and courage. "I will support you in your old age; don't worry, Pop!"

"Will you, my boy?" he'd say. "Will you?" And then he'd lean forward and take my whole cheek between the knuckles of his second and third fingers, and he'd squeeze so hard that he'd leave a red brand on the pink. Then he'd take an even tighter hold, and shake my whole head till it slopped around inside, I smiling still, so it would all stay a joke.

"Good!" he'd say. "Good! So now, my boy, explain me why when I tell you take typing, you don't take typing? I tell you take shorthand, no one here mentions the word shorthand? Shakespeare, yes, but shorthand, nothing! Shakespeare going to support me my old age? I see all kinds books here" (my mother had come in with the dinner). "Thomna, I say I see all kinds books here, but no shorthand books. I tell you thousand time, Thomna, put boy commercial course. No answer. Line busy. But I know what's going on over here."

Then he'd look at my mother a long time and finally he'd say, "Thomna, you shouldn't go against me these things. You will learn one day—too late!"

My mother, of course, had long, long ago perfected her tactic. Silence. She wouldn't answer, merely smile, as I was smiling, and put the food down in front of him. She knew that would distract

223

him, and we'd all again somehow make it till the time came for his card game.

But my father had one more blast for me. He'd serve himself and my mother, he'd serve my younger brother, Michael, and then me. As he gave me my plate, he'd look at me with such disappointment, such profound disillusionment—oh God, it hurt! Then he'd say, "Don't worry, my boy, I expect nothing from you, Shakespeare! Putter, putter! Chop, chop! I expect nothing. I need nothing." Then there came his final comment, addressed to himself, to his ancestors, to his tradition, and to his gods, to all who would bear witness to the misfortune he'd suffered in his eldest son, to them all he'd announce this verdict: "No hope on him!" Then he'd turn to his dinner.

Maybe you couldn't fairly expect the old man to be different. After all, I was not what he'd been taught to expect in the way of an eldest son.

How had I managed not to follow my father's path? Where had I found the strength or the slyness, the courage or the cunning, whatever it was? All I knew was that now, more than three decades later, it was time to give myself credit. Perhaps I'd managed it only by the tactics of evasion. But under the circumstances I was recalling now on the train to Stamford, it was a remarkable thing for a kid to do. Even to avoid taking the commercial course in high school, how had I managed that with the daily pressure and shaming I suffered? How had I lived from day to day, avoiding the issue, side-stepping any decisive confrontation, managing to keep going my way under his daily surveillance, until I was finally on a course completely opposite to the one he had in mind for me?

I left the train at Stamford, walked down the steps at the side of the station, turned, and crossed the big thoroughfare. There it happened again. I crossed the street as if I were doing a dare, without looking left or right. A car almost hit me. My neck muscles were as taut as those of a wrestler when he bridges. On the curb opposite, my heart pounded like it needed a valve job. I was perspiring so hard I could smell it.

And standing there, I said out loud, "Somebody's still trying to kill you."

I entered the hospital and went straight for the men's room. When I get badly frightened, I have to pee. I flew ATS in the war, landing and taking off on those out-of-nowhere fields with a hump of jungle

224

at one end and a bulldozer working the other, pushing off the wrecked planes or trying to flatten a few more saving yards; many a time I peed my britches.

I leaned over the basin and looked at my face a long time. "The face of my enemy," I said to myself. Recently I had had a lot of trouble looking in the mirror. My face was o.k. when composed— the eyes a little anxious, yes, the whole drawn, but somber, even dignified, rather tragic. But when it became animated, it frightened me. It was breaking into bits. I understood the cubists for the first time.

On the sixth floor I turned a corner, and there they were. The tribe had assembled to witness whatever was happening to my father. I pulled back and then peeked like a thief to see exactly who was there, and what I'd have to face. My brother Michael was talking to my mother. He seemed to be consoling her. Gloria was not in sight. But sitting in a row of hospital wicker were four men in their sixties, my baby uncles, my father's younger brothers. The old man must be pretty bad off, I thought, if they're here.

The great disaster of 1929 not only broke my father's back; it had by some corollary malignancy broken his family of brothers. There had never been any incident, nothing you might call a break, but in the thirty-odd years since, these four men and my father had hardly talked. That's why I thought only death could have brought the four of them to the Stamford General.

It had not been that way before 1929. The brothers saw each other regularly, sported together, roasted the spitted baby lamb, had pastry-eating contests, drank and danced, and gambled at cards and dice. They all had money in their pockets in those fat days; I'd heard it jingle many a time as they hopped out their dance steps. Their businesses were prospering. And for this they were, every one, beholden to my father. He had started them.

My father's own business was so good it ran itself. The out-of-town buyers would come to Sam Arness, Oriental Rugs and Carpets, like on a beam. And they had plenty to spend. My father would take different ones to lunch every day, to the Pavillon d'Orient, or the Bosporus, and he'd feed them silly. After which they'd drop by his store, as if the visit there was incidental, and make their buys: 9 by 12 Sarouks by the pile, a few large silk Keshans for the new millionaires in Sacramento and Kansas City and Omaha. They'd buy mat-size throw rugs in bundles, not bothering to look at the individual pieces, because there was no time before the train left for the track. At Belmont, since everything else was going well, they'd beat the bangtails. And while a runner cashed in their chits, they'd eat those fat chicken sandwiches, all white meat, sitting in the clubhouse and drinking Perrier water (only) with their Scotch. Those were the days! *Inshallah!*

But after the shame, after the National City Bank, which had held and used my father's life's savings, spilled its phony guts and did the circus slide from six hundred-odd to twenty-one or two or three, my father's life changed.

He would spend his days in his store as if under a spell, lying on top of piles of rugs which dwindled each day under him. I remember he used to say to me ("whine" was how I described it to myself; I had no pity then, the college boy, a visitor from a superior intellectual environment), "We're eating our capital, Evangeleh!" He'd lie there, week after week, his stock melting under him, lying on his side, his face in the palm of his hand, waiting for the buyers to come in. But they had disappeared, no one knew where. They just weren't coming to my father's store by then, those birds of passage. They chose not to come back the next year, or the next. Those years you had to make expenses by selling your stock to Syrians and Armenians in the New York wholesale market at a loss, at half—oh yes, at anything!

Before the crash, my father had been the rock of the family. He had helped everyone. Early on, he had to help his older brother Stavros, the one who brought the family to this country from Turkey. Stavros, once many times a millionaire, had gone bankrupt not from any market catastrophe, but from baccarat and pussy.

Above all, my father had helped his four younger brothers, the "boys" now sitting here waiting in the hospital wicker. He had urged them to start their own businesses. They were reluctant entrepreneurs, but my father used to give them twenty, thirty, forty thousand dollars worth of goods on consignment, so they could trade for themselves and make a dollar.

But after the crash, after his own disaster, he couldn't do these boys any good. He had no money to lend, no surplus of goods to consign. So they stopped coming to see him. Perhaps you couldn't entirely blame them; the sight of my father's life blood all over the concrete floor of his store wasn't cheering. But they didn't even drop in to say a human word.

I remember pointing out to my father—I was always teaching him lessons, the man who didn't need lessons, only help and sympathy— I remember saying to him, "Pop, I notice your brothers don't come to see you any more." And he said, I remember well, "They're waiting, Evangeleh; they'll come to my funeral." And another time he said to me, "People come to money, Evangeleh."

I remember how I turned my back on him and his "nobody knows you when you're down and out" philosophy, though I sure as hell ate it up when Bessie sang "The Weeping Willow Blues." But then she was a saint in the left hagiography, and my father just a miserable little burrower in that part of the system I was sure should be destroyed. He deserved his fate, I thought, because he built his life on the dollar. I had no pity for any of them, not even for my older uncle, Stavros, without whom I'd probably be sitting today in a corner of the Closed Bazaar in Istanbul, praying that those followers of Mohammed, the *hamals,* wouldn't smash in my windows the next time there was an anti-Christian riot.

I thought even those pissmires, the four "boys," deserved their fates. I had no pity for them, even though they walked the streets of the thirties and forties with their backs broken, just where my father's back was broken. They had also held National City—and other paper junk.

Well, now there they were on the sixth floor of the Stamford General Hospital, attendants at some old ritual. For although they sat in the white wicker of that immaculate waiting room where cancers are announced, sympathetically but scientifically, a sort of contemporary holy place, they seemed to me to be squatting in some old hollow in the Anatolian forest, around a ritual campfire, surrounded by the dark impenetrable forest of custom, getting ready to eat my father's bones and so prolong their own lives. Their expressions alternated between those of practiced tribal mourners (they never missed a funeral) and the obscene contemporary look of men who spend their days in hotel lobbies, swapping dirty jokes and looking for ready widows to pick up. One of them, the youngest, was stealing an ash tray as I stepped forward and they all saw me and let loose the Anatolian ceremonial cry, a sort of prolonged "ooooh!" which the four boys executed particularly well.

227

The "boys," I thought. Now at least sixty, happily impotent, and so finally out of all trouble. They lived together in one apartment, the beneficiaries of rent control and social security. Long ago three of them had married. One was even a grandfather, though he didn't see his son and had never seen his grandson. "They want something from me," he'd explain. All three marriages were short; the shortest, the one which had resulted in a pregnancy, lasted a week. The longest a year. No one of the brides had lived up to the exacting Greek standards for women. In particular, no one could cook as well as the boys' mother, my grandmother Vasso. As soon as this had become clear to each of the boys, he would come back home.

"Ooooooh!" they chortled, and then once again on a somewhat higher pitch, "Oooooh!" It is essentially a sound of obeisance, this, reserved for the advent of a savior on the scene, which means anyone in the family whom they believe to have a sizable bank account. A quick move on the part of one of them pulled the ash tray out of his younger brother's hands and returned it to the hospital table top. Then they were all over me, kissing me as is the custom. I believe if I had dropped my pants, they would have kissed what was presented, such is the power of money over them. Of course, they had no late bulletins on the state of my bank balance. All they knew was that I had married the daughter of a big man, a college president, lived near Beverly Hills, and had a swimming pool. I had to be rich.

Why do the indigent always worry about the health of the wealthy? There now flowed from the boys congratulations on my appearance and glowing appraisals of my general health. California received much credit. Then came the most optimistic estimates of my life-span-to-be. I had seen my face in the mirror downstairs, and I looked like hell. But they were absolutely sure that I hadn't looked so well in years, that I was growing younger, how did I do it? And by God, I found myself beginning to believe them. I was playing my expected role, the big man of the family!

My questions to them about my father, however, brought quite different reactions. They all suddenly held up their professional mourners' masks, like one of those scenes from the expressionistic theater. They recited with much doleful indirection, sighs, clucks, and shrugs, the mysteries of his sudden decline and imminent death. They were finally so full of rue that all I could say was, "For chrissake, boys, he can't be that bad." And not waiting for their response, I passed through their clustering and embraced my mother.

She was awfully glad to see me, I'm the eldest, and she is old world. She always feels safer when I'm within reach. The long distance phone doesn't really do it.

"Is the old man that bad off?" I said to my brother Michael, referring with my head to the four boys. He didn't answer. "No one could be that bad off unless he was dead," I said. I looked at my mother as I bent to kiss her. She had aged terribly.

Just then Dr. Furillo turned the corner. With him was a Roman Catholic priest. "The doctor," said one of the boys in a tone that he would generally reserve for the Greek Archbishop. The priest was presented to us by Dr. Furillo. "This," he said, putting his arm around the priest's shoulder, "is Father Draddy. He was here, tending to someone in need, and I told him about your father. He thought it might be a good idea to pay him a visit."

"It will make things a heck of a lot easier later on," said Father Draddy. And without waiting for our response to his suggestion, he turned and, smiling rather boyishly, he entered my father's room.

"He's young, but very good at his job," said Dr. Furillo.

"But we're not Catholic," I said.

"I know," said Dr. Furillo, "you're Greek Orthodox."

"We're hardly anything," I said. "Hardly religious at all."

"People say that up to a point," said Dr. Furillo. "You're Michael's brother, the author, very well-known?"

"Yes."

"It's a privilege to meet you. I'm Dr. Furillo. I've been looking after your father." We shook hands.

"Is he . . . ?" I asked.

"Nothing pressing or immediate," he said. "Are these gentlemen with your party?"

The boys had come up and were looking over Dr. Furillo's shoulder. "We're the dead man's brothers," said one of them. Everyone burst out laughing in spite of themselves. The eldest of the boys whacked his brother across the back of the head. He ducked his head in mock humility and woggled away.

Then we all heard someone shouting. "I know, my wife sent you to see me. You're a priest, so tell me the truth! It was my wife, right?"

It was my father, from room 612. His voice was certainly in full vigor. The whole corridor was now acquainted with his disposition. We heard some sort of low murmur from Father Draddy, discreetly below the level of audibility. Then my father again. "I understand priests very good. The Greek Archie-bishop in my day was a thief. They should have put him in jail. Only his beard saved him. Then he married my brother. What? That's right! He married my brother to his daughter. He thought my brother had money . . . what?" Father Draddy could not be heard, only a gentle murmuring. Then, "Tell my wife if I want priest, I send for priest. Now go ahead, send me my son Evangeleh, I want my son, Evangeleh."

Father Draddy came out smiling. He was a good sport. I started in, but Dr. Furillo pulled me to one side, leading my mother with his other hand. "The only important thing," he said to me, ". . . is this lady your mother?" Then he turned to her, still gripping my forearm hard, and said to her, "Mrs. Arness, you must not be upset by anything your husband says now. He can't help what he thinks any more, or what he says. Remember that."

"He sounds vigorous," I said. "What exactly is wrong with him?"

"At the moment? Pulmonary edema. Fluid in his left lung. That's just about cleared up. Actually he could leave the hospital very soon. But the edema is really a symptom of something else."

"Of what else?" I said. "Would you please be very plain with me?"

"Your father," said Dr. Furillo, "is well advanced in arteriosclerosis. In plain language this means his brain is not getting the nourishment it should. At times, his vigor is full. He even makes sense. At other times—you will see for yourself—he is given to extreme paranoia. Unfortunately his present target is your mother. Next week it could be you. He is hallucinatory. By which I mean he imagines things—no, I don't mean that. I mean he *sees* things. Literally. He actually sees what is not there. The brain is simple chemistry, you know that." Then he hesitated. "Excuse me, Mrs. Arness," he said. He took me aside alone and said to me, "I'm going to be terribly frank with you. Your father's brain is deteriorating at a speed which you may find shocking. Sooner than you would like, some of his vital functions will begin to be impaired, the bladder, for instance. Or the kidneys. Uremia. It's a present danger. He's losing control everywhere. For instance, he can't be relied upon to perform his natural functions in a civilized manner. Do you understand what I mean?"

"Is that the whole story?"

"That's the story. I'm sorry."

I went into 612. I hadn't seen him in over a year, and the first thing that struck me was how much thinner his face was. His eyes looked unnaturally brilliant.

A nurse was freshening his bed. He was murmuring something which made her laugh rather obscenely. I had the impression I was watching a pair of lovers. Then he raised his head and saw me.

Whatever he meant to me, I could see that I meant everything to him. I was the big magic to him, the answer to his prayers. "Big shot!" he said, "Oh, my boy!" He strained to sit up, his eyes glaring and his brows at full tension. "That's enough," he said to the nurse, "get out!"

"Now Mr. Arness, I'm not quite done. But if you'll lie still, like a good boy, it won't be much longer."

"You see what happens when you lose your money? Even this one, she talks back." He stared at me, his eyes strangely fixed in a way I hadn't seen before. "Big shot," he murmured. "Come here, for God's sake. Miss Costello, this is the famous man. His *sec*etary gets one hundred twenty-five dollars a week. Imagine!"

"Well!" said Miss Costello, "so you're the one! You're all he talks about."

"He looks like me, doesn't he? This is the big shot I showed you from those magazines, remember? He has three cars!"

"Oh yes," said Miss Costello, "congratulations . . . feel better now?" she said, referring to the reordered bed.

"Oh, yes, everything is going to be all right now. You're just in time, my boy."

"Don't stay too long," said Miss Costello, as she went out. "He should rest."

When I leaned over and kissed my father, he had the tang of the bedridden. "How are you, Pop?" I said.

"How am I? I have no money, that's how I am. And she running wild like an animal. Did you see him out there?"

"Who, Pop?"

"Her boy friend."

"No."

"Sure, when you come he hides in the back, sure. Oh, my boy, smart, smart, my only hope is on you."

"All right, Pop, I'm here now."

"Now you see when I tell you all your life, be careful your money, because when you have no money, they lose respect, did I say that?"

"Yes, Pop. Many times."

"You see now, sending priest in here! They can't wait for me to die, so they can eat my money."

"But, Pop, you said you have no money."

"Yes, but they don't know that."

"But you just said she lost respect for you because you have no money in the bank."

"Yes. Now you understand what I been telling you, right? From California you saw everything. That's what I said to her, from California he see what you're doing to me, I said, and he will come right away. Then you better tell that Irish bum to run. You are a brilliant man, Evangeleh, but why is your hair getting gray, my boy?"

"I'm getting old, Pop."

"You're boy yet, just beginning. You will be millionaire many times, many times. This that happened to me, now, will never happen to you. Tell me how much you made last year? Eh?"

"Oh, last year I paid taxes on about sixty-five thousand dollars."

He chuckled. "Smart!" he said, "smart!" Then he imitated my phrasing. "I pay taxes on about sixty-five thousand. Smart! Oh my God! But how much you make, eh? eh? son of a gun! Tell the truth, ha-ha-hah! eh?"

"That's about what I made, Pop, that's about it."

"Smart! Don't even tell your father. Good! You're right! Your money is your business. Don't tell me. You know what she does?"

"No, Pop."

"She takes that son of a bitch downstairs and shows him my books. Thousand times I tell her, I don't want anybody know my business. She takes him down cellar, show him everything."

In the cellar of the old house, the one we'd all lived in from 1926, my father had boxed all the records of his long-defunct business. A year before my mother just couldn't manage that house alone any longer. So against his protest she had moved herself and him to a small and comfortable apartment, near the home of my brother Michael. But my father had never, in that year, admitted to living there. He'd tell anyone who'd listen that it was temporary; certain things were being done to the old place. Michael, to humor him, kept the electricity and telephone on, and occasionally drove the old boy out for the day. He'd sit on the porch and look at the Sound, muttering by the hour, or he'd sit at the phone and make certain calls; no one ever found out what they were because he talked only in conspiratorial whispers.

"How do you know she takes him down in the cellar, Pop?"

"Evangeleh, don't be fresh! I know my business, what you think! When I go down look my books—you think I don't know my books?" His eyes were bulging, his brows tensed.

"Of course, Pop, of course you do . . ."

"I know what's going on over there. I'm old, but I'm not damn fool, Evangeleh. Tell me, you made hundred thousand last year?"

"No, Pop."

"Smart, smart, don't tell your father, don't tell anybody. You never know who's listening; it's not like old days, no respect now, no respect. Is he out there?"

"Who?"

"What's the matter with you, Evangeleh? I'm your father for God's sake. She bring him into my house. At night I sit one end living room, he sit on the other, waiting till I fall asleep. When I close my eyes, she gets up and he gets up and they go out. Together, you understand, like dogs . . . running together. For some time I have trouble getting up out the chair, some little passing weakness in my legs, it's nothing. I can't move. She won't lift me. She want me stuck in that goddam chair. When she go in kitchen, he go in there with her. Upstairs? He go upstairs. They know I can't get up from that chair. Too weak why? Because she wouldn't give me the medicine doctor order. She want me weak. You know sometimes I don't have strength to take from my mouth the cigarette. Once it fell in my lap burning; go look in the closet my pants, you will see big hole there. I call Thomna, Thomna, I catch fire. No answer. Upstairs with him. I could hear them laughing and talking. They put the radio. News program, talk, talk, talk. So what they say gets mixed up with what this fellow the Columbia was saying. That's what the radio is for, you know. You ever go by room where they're playing radio inside, don't open that door! Because they go at each other like dogs in there, I guarantee, at her age, seventy-two, like dogs. How she can forget what I did for her? I brought her to this country. She was damage goods but I marry her. How can she forget? Like dogs!"

My father was crying. I took his hand and pressed it.

He said, "Thank you, Evangeleh, I'm so glad you here. I say to her thousand time, bring Evangeleh, that's all I ask, he will see what you do to me. But she don't send for you."

"Michael called me, Pop."

"Yes, but not your mother, right? I said you seventy-two, you should be shame bring that Irish here, my own house, sitting end of the parlor looking at me like gangster. And then she say smiling, 'Oh, Seraphim, Seraphim.' Smiling! She always smiling now, you notice?"

"No, Pop."

"You will see. Be careful when they smile too much. But you don't have to worry. You have plenty money. When you have money, they respect. How's Frances?"

"Florence, Pop."

"Sure, fine woman. 'Oh, Seraphim, Seraphim,' smiling. I paid thousand dollar teeth for her. Evening dresses, two fur coats. How many Irish do that? And this is how she pays me. 'Oh Seraphim,' she says, smiling, 'there's no one there, Seraphim. Look! Where is he?' So I say, you show me where he is. I don't know where you hide him. That's how fresh she become. Once I hold her hand and I say, 'Thomna dear, how can you do this to me?' Last time, never again I call her dear!"

He was watering at the eyes again. I noticed that around his eyeballs now there was a band of white, and the pupils were milky.

"I didn't see anyone out there with her, Pop!"

"You know him?"

"No."

"You wouldn't recognize him if you saw him, right?"

"Right."

"So?! Evangeleh, you're my eldest. My only hope is on you. Don't turn against me. So. Change subject! Let's be happy, right? Funny part, one thing. I stay with that woman many years. I had many chances go with other woman. In 1921 I made crossing on Berengaria and there was woman there, Evangeleh, high class, right under her husband's nose, she want chop, chop, monkey business! But I thought, Thomna, poor thing, I wouldn't do such a thing against her. Besides I was, in those days, religious. But when the Archie-bishop stole the church thousand dollars, I understood what that was too.

Fakers! So now she sends priest to say hurry up die. You see when you have no money what happens?"

I tried to change the subject. "Pop, tell me, you must have lots of friends come here to see you."

"Bullshit friends! Armenians! Syrians! When you lose your money, nobody come see you." He laughed. "But they will all come to the funeral. You will see them there, everyone. Tomajian will be there, and Garageuz, and my no-good brothers, cheap stuff, and my sister who doesn't talk to me, she talk to me when I'm dead. And Vartan Kessabian who owes me money, he'll be there, too, to thank me for dying."

"Oh, Pop."

"Oh, Pop, what? I give you good advice, when you were boy, right?" His eyes glared.

I couldn't deny him. "Yes, Pop, you did."

"You take advice, now look. Big shot! Right?"

"Right, Pop."

"How's your wife, how's Frances?"

"Florence, Pop."

"Florence, sure, fine woman, very high class. College president's daughter. Putter, putter. Chop, chop. I wouldn't think it of you, honestly God! I knew you had brain. But it was on wrong things. I didn't think you were going to be big like you are. I used to beg you, remember, learn the goods, Evangeleh, don't go Shakespeare college. Learn something usey-ful. I told you commercial course?"

"Yes, Pop."

"You finally listen your father, right?"

"Right, Pop."

"You have many bad friends at that time. Like that high school teacher, Miss Somebody, she say you have beautiful eyes so you must go college. Bullshit! Waste of time, right?"

"Well, Pop," I said, trying a joke, "after all, that's how I met Florence."

"Sure, sure. She save you. She say listen your father, right?"

"Well, I guess so, Pop. But you have to admit it was a good thing I didn't go into the rug business, when you wanted me to. Where would I be today?"

I had made a mistake. His face filled with blood!

"Don't talk like that to your father. I could start again right now.

I get up from this bed if I had you with me. We go to bank. Father, son! We get loan. Mr. Meyer there, Jewish, but fine man, he know me thirty-five years. We bring goods from Persia, they have beautiful goods there now, Tabriz, Teheran, Keshan. You and me together, we make fortune. Those goddam Armenians, they don't know the business like I know. Ochch, ochch, achch, achch, achch. Evangeleh, Evangeleh!"

"Yes, Pop."

"Come here."

I did.

"I've got to get out of here, Evangeleh. They're trying to kill me. Poison. I eat only from outside of plate here. White bread from package, I eat Tip Top. But nothing they cook. Call nurse to bring some food, you taste. I think they put something in there, you understand, so my brain don't work. You know sometimes I feel very funny. You taste food?"

"Sure, Pop."

"Good boy, Evangeleh. You know once they bring you here, finish! I see everything. At night, they take dead out. In the morning, *tak!* New customers in! System! Go lock the door, Evangeleh."

"Oh now, Pop."

And then a strange thing happened. Something of the terrible fury he had to have when he had his *gissum,* that rage that used to terrorize me when I was a kid, came up. And he yelled, his voice trembling, "Evangeleh, LOCK THE DOOR!" And he held his trembling face fixed upon me till I turned and went to the door and put a chair under the knob; my heart was pounding. I was now forty-four and he eighty, sick, just about finished; still, when his face filled with blood like a sponge and his whole being trembled that way, I felt the old terror; something in me was still obedient.

The door now "locked," I went back to his bed. He was on his side now, reaching under the mattress. It was an effort; you could see what it cost him. He came up clutching something in his hand.

"Come here, close."

"What's that, Pop?"

"Come close."

"Yes, Pop."

He suddenly took my hand in his free one and squeezed it hard. His own hand was moist and it trembled.

"Evangeleh, you love your father?"

"Yes, Pop."

Then he held me even harder and shook me as hard as his strength allowed him to. And he said, "Get me out of here!"

Now he opened his closed hand.

"See!" he said. It contained a little black wallet. "First we go home. I get dressed up nice. Then we take taxi New York. I have money for that. We go Empire State Building, my bank is there, don't tell anyone. In Safe Deposit I have papers, insurances, stocks, everything there. Here is key, see." He opened the little black wallet and I saw a single small key there. "I show you everything I have. Then we sit down nice, and talk to Mr. Meyer about loan, you understand . . ."

I didn't know what to say.

"But, Pop, the doctor thinks you better stay here for a while at least."

"That's her doctor, Evangeleh."

"But Michael says . . ."

"Michael is going to tell me my business? A man forty years old he listens to woman, he still doesn't own his house. And Dr. Furillo? I play pinochle with his father, I put that spaghetti down thousand time. Damn fool can't read cards. How he make son doctor, explain me that?"

"O.K., Pop," I said. I'd given in.

He squeezed my hand with all his might.

"Thank you, Evangeleh, thank you. So tomorrow, eh? Early in the morning, we go. Right? You come with taxi. We go home, I make nice bath, put blue suit, beautiful shirt, tie, banker style, shine shoes, nice hair cut. You will see, I'm not finished!"

"Pop, the doctor . . ."

"Evangeleh, answer me one thing. Is anything going to get better if I stay here? I must make money. You see she left my house! She says too big, too much work. It wasn't too much work when I had money."

His eyes filled with tears and anger.

"Now she have this bum with her. She have no interest take care me. Whole last year I eat can goods. Even soup. Can soup! I say to her, 'Thomna, why suddenly can goods every night?' She don't look my face. That how I find out what's going on over there. Tell me, you have some kind trouble with Frances?"

"Florence, Pop. How did you know?"

"I know. I told you thousand times, marry Greek girl. I told you. They satisfy stay home."

"Yes, Pop, that's what you always told me, and that's what you did. So you mustn't say those terrible things about mother, because they're not true."

"You'll see."

"She gave her life for you, Pop."

"One time, one time."

His eyes filled with tears again. He looked to be in terrible pain. For the first time in my life I was full of pity for him. He saw that.

"You're a good boy, Evangeleh, but you don't know anything about women."

"But Pop, Florence is not running around with other men. That is not my problem."

"How do you know? I don't look to make trouble, but did you ever think, where is she now?"

"She's home, I imagine."

"Imagine, go ahead. And with who? Imagine that too. Even your mother, see? See!"

The door was tried. Then there was a knock. I started to go open it, but he gripped me with his free hand, holding the little black wallet with the other, and pulled me closer, and he whispered, "Let them worry a little!" He said to the door, "Worry! Worry!"

Then he opened the folds of his wallet and again revealed the small key, the only key he had left.

"Tomorrow I show you everything I have. You're a good boy." He pulled me to him and kissed me with all his might. That final sourness was coming into his breath.

Another knock at the door.

The nurse's voice on the other side called out, "Mr. Arness. I'm going to give you your alcohol rub!"

My father smiled. "Alcohol rub," he said. He nodded at me, and I took the hospital chair out from under the door knob.

"He loves his alcohol rub," said the nurse as she came into the room. My father smiled like a happy baby. "You bad boy," said the nurse as she turned him over. No one ever turned over with greater anticipation, not the most ardent lover. My father was still a sensual man.

He had forgotten I existed.

I watched for a while. Whatever I am, I thought, came out of that man. Like it or not.

I remembered how many times I'd been distressed when I noticed some of my father's less attractive characteristics in myself. I knew now if I could understand him, I could understand myself. There's where the secret is, in that terrible old man smiling privately as the nurse spread the cool alcohol over his body. His character was my fate. What he himself was. What he had caused me to be.

Why was I so goddam anxious even now for that man's approval? Could it be that though I had always thought I was living my life in revolt against him, I had actually broken my neck and my heart to get what *he* valued? Who had I lived my life for, that man or me?

Once the cement is poured, can the future differ from the past? Perhaps I couldn't change. Perhaps now, at forty-four, I was, as Gwen had said, too far gone. The concrete had hardened, and perhaps the only way to change the configurations of my being was to blast, use powder, leave rubble. Might I wreck the old, but not have the time or the energy or the materials to make something new, something I'd finally like? Was I ready to take that chance?

My mother was in the corridor, looking towards me; a saint she was, a monument to patience. I put my arms around her and kissed her.

13

I TOOK my mother by the hand and led her to a corner of the sun porch, sat down next to her, and held her hand. It was quiet except for the japing of the hospital public address system. We sat there a long time. Finally I spoke. "How long has he been that way?"

"Oh, Eee," she said. So I sat still. She leaned up and kissed the side of my cheek.

Just then the boys came into the doorway, wanting to say goodbye. They also wanted to be reassured that they hadn't done anything wrong, and were forgiven for anything they may have *thought* wrong. They were spluttering in the doorway like four superannuated vaudevillians whose turn had flopped and who were stalling in a downstage exit, hoping for some little reassuring applause.

When my mother is forced into a social contact she doesn't care to make, she has a simple expedient. She turns a little bakelite control somewhere under her clothing and tunes out the world. Always a gracious and scrupulously polite woman, she now looked at the miserable foursome in the doorway and smiled at them as if she was Mrs. Roosevelt. At the same time her hand was fumbling at her chest, and I knew that whatever message they were there to communicate was not going to reach her. Now, having made the rheostat adjustment, she looked up to reassure me that the electronic door she had just slammed was not slammed in my face.

I finally said something nice to the boys, and they realized that I didn't blame them for my father's condition. Very much relieved, they nudged each other and toddled down the corridor in their adult disguises.

My mother turned her sound up. "What did they want?" she asked.

"Forgiveness," I said.

"What did they do?"

"I didn't ask."

She laughed. This broke the ice a bit. But I decided to wait for her to make the first move. After a while she said, "I can't, Eee, I can't any more."

"You don't have to any more, dear."

"I'll come here every day and I'll sit here. But I don't want to go in there."

She was out of gas. So we sat there, allies in a war waged a long time ago, the issue forgotten, the enemy defeated, and we, victors without spoils. I felt without direction; I had never *not* had that enemy to fight. And the very center pole of my mother's life had been pulled up. Reared as she had been in the old world tradition of complete subservience to her husband, she had faithfully done everything expected of her. She had submitted to his embraces, borne his children, cooked his dinners, done his laundry, cleaned his house, entertained his guests, played out her fate as best she knew how, given her whole life. In every particular she had been perfect. Except one. It was my mother who plotted with me not to go into my father's business. She broke the walls of the Greek ghetto for me, encouraged me to reach out into America. When I was fifteen or sixteen, it was she who made me feel that I was separate from my father and that I could do anything I really wanted to do. She made me wake to the unique possibilities of my own life.

In those days she was married to a man who got out of bed every morning to make money. Even his diversions, the horses and the cards, were a continuation in play of the obsession of his life: beating the other guy to the dollar. That was his life, and he was so unself-questioning and single-minded about it that he had the force of an ocean wave.

So, to save her life, she had to learn how water fights water. She soon knew that if she stood up and opposed him head-on, she would be battered to pieces. But if she resisted as water resists—by yielding, waiting for the crusher to pass, then returning to the same place—in that way, persisting, she could, as she in time did, finally gain her objectives.

241

This tactic she passed on to me. It became the way I lived. In fact it became me, since we are nothing other than the way we live. It was from my mother that I learned the art of the devious. It was from her that I learned the efficacy of silence. She gave me my first mask of compliance. It was from her that I learned to put a smoke screen of indifference around the objectives I wanted most, play it cool, escape all attention myself and so not bring attention to the prize I desperately wanted. It was from her that I learned that the only way I could get the thing I wanted was to go after it tenaciously, yes, single-mindedly, yes, but in silence and secrecy. I learned from her how to live in the territory occupied by the enemy, gain my victory while I seemed to be bowing to his hegemony.

I went to school to my mother.

And since I saw my father for only an hour or so a day, and very little more on Sundays, her lessons in how to survive in his house were centered around dinner and the card games which followed.

My father's requirements for his dinner meal were very strict. The first law was "no can goods!" This was absolute. All vegetables and fruit had to be fresh. The second law was that all meat had to be well-done. He couldn't stand the trace of blood.

He ate ravenously and with desperate speed, satisfying hungers other than the ones of his stomach. If he didn't comment, it meant he was satisfied with my mother's efforts.

She herself rarely ate when he was eating. Standing a little behind him and to one side, she watched the food enter his mouth, and put choice added bits on his plate. If everything went well, the whole meal would go down in a matter of minutes. There would be some sounds of satisfaction as he mopped up the gravy with the crust of the bread. But there was no conversation.

His only grace was fruit. The little sweet white grapes he loved reminded him of the grapes which grew on the highlands above the Anatolian village where he was born and where he spent his youth. Apricots grew there, too, and ripened on the trees, not as with us in their boxes on the way to markets. So if he ever saw these particular little grapes or ripe apricots displayed for sale, he'd bring them home.

My mother would also buy fruit wherever she saw it. But he knew what fruit he had brought home and what she had bought in the markets of Mamaroneck and Rye. My mother's selections only proved to him what he didn't need to have confirmed—that no one could select fruit like he could. There was this one artistry in the man. He'd pick up a melon and feel it, turning it around and around in his hands. Then he'd find the soft spot, the belly of the melon, put his nose to it, and draw in what was there. Then he'd press into the melon with his thumbs and so decide if the fruit was up to the standards of Mr. Sam Arness. A watermelon he judged quite differently. It was by weight and by the sound it made when he plopped it in his hands, and something about the way it looked. I never learned what. He died with that secret.

The meal always ended with Turkish coffee. One reason my mother didn't sit at the table or eat at the same time he did was that she had to time the coffee just right. It took only about a minute to make. But he liked it there, frothing, as he swallowed the last bit of fruit. He did like the way my mother fixed Turkish coffee. The only complimentary attention he ever paid her, that I saw, had to do with her coffee, and now and then a *moussaka* which had blended its ingredients perfectly or a *tass kebab,* particularly succulent. I can't imagine he ever gave her the erotic attention he paid his melons.

Once the meal was over, my father showed some evidence of exhaustion. I always felt it was the way he ate that wore him out. But now I think it was as simple and natural for him to sleep after eating as it is for the predators of the plains to do so. The instant he had finished his coffee, he left the dining room table and headed straight for his couch. There he'd stretch out, on his side, his face in the palm of one hand. In thirty seconds, he'd be fast asleep. And soon enough, snoring.

It was then that my mother would eat her meal from the wreckage he'd left on the dining room table. She ate slowly and thoughtfully, in the kind of letdown which follows anxiety, and in the mood of absolute plainness which often follows pretense. She could hear my father snoring on his sofa, satisfied. She'd got through another meal. All was well.

He would wake just as abruptly as he had fallen asleep. If the game was at Wasserman's or Klipstein's or Spiegel's, the first indication would be, "Evangeleh! Call taxi!" If the game was at our house, the first words would be, "Thomna, fix table!" "Fixing" the table consisted of taking off a circular oriental throw rug, folding it and putting it away, then fitting a special brown felt cover over the bare table top. He himself would place the cards, the ash trays, and the score pads. Just as he got through, the guests would arrive. They would all immediately go into the dining room and close the doors. The game started. My mother and I were alone.

If it was winter, since the house was not insulated and would not heat up very well, my father would take the two electric heaters we had, and put them on top of the old-fashioned glass cabinets which stood on either side of the large window which looked out on Long Island Sound. Then as the winter's cold fell over the shore line, the parlor where my mother and I sat would rapidly cool. I remember her reading in a corner of the room, weary, not from any physical activity, but from the strain of getting through that hour and a quarter with her husband. This relief brought sleepiness. But she was determined to salvage something from the evening for herself. I remember her eyelids growing heavy, her head nodding and falling. But she wouldn't stop, she read on. She wasn't going to let him have it all.

Whether it was a way of fighting sleep, or because the big silly Gothic parlor was so cold, she would get up and go stand behind the biggest radiator in the room, a really big one it was, up to her chest. She would put her book on top of the radiator, and put her front up against it, and read. I would go to the other end of the same radiator and pull a chair up as close as I could. There I'd do my solid geometry or American history, or write my English composition. Little Michael was asleep. Every once in a while there'd be a burst of masculine bickering or laughter from the dining room. Someone had lost and was protesting to his partner. Or someone had won and was laughing at the discomfiture of his opponent. My mother and I, hearing these sounds, would look at each other and smile, delighted to be safe in each other's dear company. That's where the conspiracy was born.

I remember many times looking at her and thinking how abandoned she was, though she never gave a sign; in fact, I'm sure she preferred being spared her husband's presence. Although I didn't know anything about sex at twelve, I knew she was neglected. I felt her pain, as she did mine. And so we were joined together.

I remember one night when the card game was in progress in our dining room, my father called for me. My mother knew I was preparing for an exam the next day. She and I looked at each other. I didn't answer immediately. "Evangeleh!" my father called again. His tone, always peremptory, in front of his friends had the gruffness of an order to a jackass. It was just as frightening as it was intended to be. I started to go in and see what he wanted, even though I knew perfectly well that he wanted me to mount my bike and pedal down to the delicatessen across from the railroad station and bring home half a pound of Virginia ham, and half a pound of Swiss cheese. One of the card players had indicated that he could eat.

Just as I started in, my mother, with the slightest and most feminine of gestures, waved me down. She called in, "He's gone to bed, Sam." (She always called him Sam in front of his friends.) Then she herself went into the dining room, and as she passed me pushed my head down and out of sight. I sat on the floor, behind the arm of my father's sofa, and continued my homework. I heard her ask him what he wanted. After all, he couldn't send her down to the delicatessen on a bike! And the man who had previously complained of being hungry now said that he wasn't. She went back to the icebox, and did what she could for them all. Then she came back and sat on the chair alongside of me and smiled.

Now, as I sat with her in the sunroom of the Stamford General, we knew we had won.

"Eee," said my mother, "I don't complain against him. I always had enough to eat, he didn't run with other women, and every night he came home. What else could I ask?"

I said nothing. What else could she have asked?!

"Many women have worse." She sighed as if in relief.

I looked at her face, the eyes closed, the whole head back against the back of the chair, resting, all of her, wanting nothing except to be allowed to rest. "I don't complain," she murmured.

I remembered the other time she had said, "I don't complain." It was in 1936, a month before I entered college, class of 1940. My father had finally found out there had been secret proceedings behind his back, that not only was I enrolled in a college, but in the cream of the small Ivy.

That very year he was making his big effort to start again in business. Adjusting to the new situation in the rug market and to his own new financial condition, he had taken a much smaller store and moved what was left of his stock to this new location. Naturally he expected me to join him there. He had waited for me to get out of high school. In fact, since he didn't have the capital to employ anything like his old staff of porters, repairmen, and shipping clerks, he had counted on me. I was his eldest son. My father expected of me only what he had every right by his tradition to expect, that I would finally straighten out and pick up my load. Furthermore, had I not, as he put it, eaten from the rugs all my life?

"You owe!" he roared when he found out what had been going on. "Goddam fool, you owe me!"

But whatever he yelled at me, he met only silence and a bowed head. I had been well schooled.

Then my mother did the unexpected. She made the only effort I ever knew her to make to explain to him that I had to find and follow my own way and to hint, however gently, that perhaps the business of importing oriental rugs and carpets was past its best days. And more: that a young man at this crucial juncture of his life might find better roads to follow. When she got all this out, her face pale with fear, the mask of the compliant wife off and off for good, he turned from me and put his eye on her. I saw the realization come to him that it was not I who had made the insanely selfish move to go to a liberal arts college. *She* had put the idea in my head. And she had made sure it grew there.

Then, as I watched his face, I saw him race, quicker than speech, to certain conclusions: that she was striking at him this way, that she wanted to hurt him, that she was a traitor to his house. He looked at her a long time, his eyes glaring, his eyebrows stiff as bone, his face full of blood like a sponge. Then he hit her, open palm across the side of her face, and knocked her to the floor. I have always believed that the reason her hearing went later was that blow.

I remember, all through this, the sound of an automobile horn outside. His friends, the ones who drove to the station with him every morning (a taxi for one was an extravagance in those days), were waiting and impatient. As he put on his suit jacket, his last words to me were, "I expect nothing from you. Hopeh-less case!"

He put on his straw hat and walked out of the house. We could hear him greet his friends just as usual. He never referred to the incident again, never recognized, in my hearing at least, that I was going to college, never came to see me there, not till the day I was graduated. Nor did he ever ask me to come to his store again. When I went there, it was on my own, and as a visitor.

I, for my part, never forgave him for hitting my mother. When he left I started to help her up, but it was not necessary. She had stayed prone only because she had learned all her life that safety was on the floor. It was when she got up and we were alone that she said those same words, "I do not complain."

In the years that followed, my future became her future. She lived through me. She knew the names of each of my teachers. She knew the courses I was taking. When I got good marks, she could taste them! When I brought my schoolbooks home, she would turn the pages slowly, looking at them without reading them, fingering the pages delicately. When I wasn't invited to join a fraternity, it gave her much more pain than it did me. When, in my senior year, I finally won a prize and received some sort of recognition (the prize was for a poem of all things!), she had one of the first completely happy moments of her life.

So it was, I became what I became: a split man, compliant to the general view, a rebel beneath.

My father did not contribute to the cost of my education, nor to my general sustenance during those years. By then, I had begun to think of the world as against me. Anything my father could contribute to the feeling that I was a member of a persecuted minority that would one day win over all, gave me perverse comfort.

It was, by then, all of them against a few of us, me and the other campus misfits, Negroes and Jews mostly. My best friend was a plumber's assistant who got mixed up in all this Ivy by some accident he couldn't explain. My other friends were oddballs all. We were a union of the eccentric and the excluded.

Like most of them, 1 "waited on" for my food, and gloried in it. For four years my clothes smelled of the kitchen and of dishwater. I knew it and I didn't mind. It confirmed the picture of the world as I wanted it to be: the wastrel fraternity boys; the honest cooks, kitchen help, and student waiters. I first worked at the Zeta Psi House, the athletic fraternity. The Zetes got loaded one night and threw rolls at the waiters. So I switched to Kappa Alpha, the gentleman's fraternity. But I scorned the boys in both places. Not that they ever knew it. To them I was that warm little foreign-type kid who was always smiling.

I sent my laundry home each week for my mother to do. I took it to the post office each Monday in my laundry case. I went back Saturday and there it was. Mixed in with the clean shirts and socks and underwear, there would always be extras. First of all, a dollar or two spending money, whatever my mother could steal or save from the household money. He would have exploded if he had found out this final evidence of her disloyalty. Besides the money, there'd be some food—things she knew I particularly liked—brownies, little cinnamon-spiced meat balls, artichokes in olive oil, a jar of Greek olives, some of that old sour cheese I loved. And occasionally *baklava*. Always something that spoke to me of her, telling me that she was living my life with me and that I was living her life for her.

I gathered that things were not going too well for my father in his business. Her letters said nothing, but by the time I got out of college, there was no doubt what was happening. His comeback had not been successful. He was on the skids and going down. And he was confirmed now in his position that I had betrayed him and that he couldn't look to me for anything ever. So he turned to Michael. But in time even Michael—kind, considerate, gentle Michael —had to recognize that there was no longer an oriental rug business. And he too had to begin looking around for something different.

But my father kept going through the motions, even when everyone knew there was no business, when he was eating his capital, when he couldn't find a customer, not one, not for what he had left to sell and not at his prices.

But he just could not get the trade out of his blood. How could he forget the taste of those trips to Persia, the market there, the weaving factories, the hospitality offered buyers from the States? Then when the rugs arrived in New York, many months later, there was the big adventure of opening the bales—you could smell the dust of the old country in the burlap—and the first look at the raw goods, unwashed, coarse in the wool, still smelling of the sheep. Then there was the preparation of the carpets for the American market—that's where the skill came in—the washing, the painting, the touching up, the trimming of the borders, all that, till the nap was silky and luminous with the colors of precious stones.

Even when he was no longer able to buy any goods from Persia, when he didn't have the capital and was barely making expenses by trading in the New York market, a few bucks here and a few there, scrounging desperately—even then he would not give up on the hope that the big days would come back again. It was in this hope, I suppose, that he still got up every morning at the same time, even when there really wasn't anything for him to do in New York, no reason to go there at all. Even when he couldn't afford the taxi to the railroad station, and had to take a bus in the morning and make that long bus ride home at night, even then he was Sam Arness, Oriental Rugs and Carpets.

I didn't witness those years. I was in the army for four of them, and then in California learning to lie like an advertising man. I missed fifteen years at home that way. But my mother lived through every one of them. She saw him being bled and humbled and shamed and humiliated, saw him pretending he had goods when he didn't, pretending he had buyers when he didn't, pretending he had a business when he didn't.

From California I began to send my mother money every month to help out. She was able to keep this from him for a long time. But he finally found out and had another of his fits of fury, though some of the steam was out of him by this time and he had no choice except to close his eyes and let his wife take the monthly checks from me and a contribution from Michael, too.

He wouldn't move out of the eighteen-room Gothic monstrosity on Long Island Sound, though it made absolutely no sense since there was no one there now except his wife and himself. To conserve heat they closed off the third floor and the attic. Michael used to tell him all those rooms were just too much for my mother to take care of, that the work was wearing her out. But he wouldn't even discuss moving.

"I don't hear her complaining," he said. And of course, she didn't.

By the mid-fifties, my mother was being visibly worn down. Michael and I made a strong and determined effort to move them out of the "mansion" on the Sound, and into a small apartment that my mother could take care of without killing herself. This produced the last of his great rages. He cursed us all, stormed and shook for an entire day. He said that his goddam traitor sons, who hadn't come to his aid when he needed them, were not going to tell him how he was going to live and where. There was nothing wrong with that house!

He pointed a shaking finger at my mother and demanded to know, "Did you put them to do this?"

She said, "No, Seraphim, I said nothing."

"Did you make complaints?"

"No, Seraphim, I don't complain."

"Put them out!" he said. Then he picked up a deck of cards and began to play solitaire. My mother came up to us—she had just heard her jail sentence extended to life—and suggested that we go. We did.

Months later, when he had cooled, we tried a different way of getting help to her; we tried to get him to allow a servant in the house. He refused this, too, on the grounds that he didn't want strangers in the house, and he reminded us that his "books" were in the cellar. The real reason was money-pride again. While he could not question where she got money for groceries and staples, he knew that if they had a servant, the money had to come from us. And everybody else would know that, too.

Even at the end, he had a "small office with Armenian"—his description. What he had was desk space, and maybe two, three, four piles of small rugs in a corner. The store belonged to an Armenian who used to work for my father as a repairman in the big days and who had now taken pity on him and allowed him to operate from his store. The man never got much thanks for his generosity. In fact my father was scornful of the Armenian and treated him badly. Very haughtily he would point out to anybody who would listen that the Armenian imported nothing, that he only "scrooged the market, like garbage man," and sold "domestics."

Anyone who dealt in domestics, that is, machine-woven carpets, was a traitor in my father's eyes. They had ruined his business, those goddam domestics; in his mind, he even linked them to the spread of homosexuality, since most decorators were beginning to ask for wall-to-wall carpeting and most decorators who were male were also homosexual.

My father began to miss paying rent, and phone bills, too. The Armenian, after carrying him for several months, finally told us, and we paid the old man's phone bill. The Armenian didn't even insist on the rent. My father must really have been nice to him long ago, because he took abuse from my father, was patronized by him, took his telephone messages down, even forwarded his mail to

Mamaroneck when my father called in his grandest manner and instructed him to "send letters" (what letters?) "to Westchester," because he didn't feel like coming in that day. "Yes, Mr. Arness," is all the Armenian would say. He still called my father Mister.

When the arteriosclerosis started, my father became unbearable. He accused the Armenian of concealing his mail, stealing his customers (he didn't have one, by then, not one!), and of not giving him his phone messages. The Armenian would just smile and do what my mother had learned to do, wait him out. The poor man would simply not say anything against Mr. Arness. He knew, I suppose, that what was killing his old boss might also one day kill him.

My father couldn't afford to play cards any more, at least not to lose. But he wouldn't stop this either. At first his friends noticed that his bidding was not quite as sharp. Well, it's an old rule: when you *have* to win, you lose. My father began to, in large amounts. But he couldn't give up the only diversion in his life. So for years he held on, even when he was no longer going to the office. He kept calling Charlie Klipstein and Artie Wasserman and Joe Spiegel, and when they couldn't play or demurred or even, as they often did later on, said they were engaged when they weren't, he would still manage to get a game together. He'd call up what he called the "second line."

But the "crowd" soon realized they couldn't take money from this man. An unspoken program was launched to stop involving him in their games. It was pretty hard to shake him. Several times Michael had to pay the old man's debts. Other times one or another of his old friends would "tear up" his losses. My father's memory was beginning to be shaky enough so that this was possible.

There had to be a blowup, and finally there was. One day he discovered the conspiracy. The next time he got them together, when they offered to lower the stakes to something nominal—all lying, rather ineptly, that it was for the good of everybody, since everybody's business was lousy—he shouted that he didn't need charity from them, had as much money as any of them—this from a man who no longer tipped shoeshine boys. He accused them—correctly—of having played many times without him. He had one of his famous rages and called them all kinds of lying Jewbastards and kike sons of bitches—this to men with whom he had played cards for thirty years. Finally he threw them out of his house and slammed the door. That was the end of the bridge games.

It wasn't long after that he got Parkinson's. It just came on him one day. Only death made his hands quiet. He used to sit in his armchair—the deep one, next to the big radiator in winter and on the front porch looking out at Long Island Sound in the summer's heat —and just shake the whole day through.

Diversions? Well, I had pieces coming out in the magazines, and he used to read these over and over. Word by word. He'd show them to whomever would come within reach: the boy who cut the grass, the man who came to fix the furnace, the roofer before they gave up calling him because they couldn't afford his services. He would ask them had they seen such and such an issue of *Partisan Review*. Of course, they didn't have the vaguest idea what *PR* was. Not the vaguest. Well, he did. "Very high class," he used to say.

Since habits don't change, he had to play cards. And since there was no one else, he played with my mother. Of course he was scornful of this competition. So he said he was teaching her the game. She picked up gin rummy pretty fast. Despite her bad eyes, impaired hearing, and hesitant manner of playing, and despite his scorn, she began to beat him. He would play swiftly, impulsively, impatiently. She would play slowly, fumbling at the cards in her hand.

"For God's sake," he'd shout, "play a card!"

"Yes, Seraphim," she'd say, "I play." And she would, and usually the right card.

There they'd be alone in the mansion on the Sound, playing gin rummy hour after hour, day after day, the pupil beating the master regularly.

Finally this got too much for him, so he taught her bridge. They began to play at the old dining room table, fixed for the game just as it had been in the old days, the brown felt cover on, the ash trays, the matches ready, the score pad at his side with its pencil. The brown felt, of course, was threadbare. But still. They played, each taking two hands. And bridge was better because it went slower, and so killed more time. My father kept score, so she beat him far less often.

Books were never resorted to. My father never learned how to find pleasure that way. He read only the racing form, the dope sheets, and the stock market quotations. My mother, though, read books. I began to send her those I had enjoyed. In time, she found a whole new life for herself.

Now, sitting in the Stamford General's sixth floor sun porch, she knew she was less tied to him than I was. I'd still fight "him" to the day of my own death. But she had lived it through, not with any ghost, but with the thing itself, the force, the terror, the man! She had earned her freedom, paid for it. She knew the day of her liberation was coming.

We drove home with Michael. The old man had fallen asleep after his alcohol rub, and there was no reason for any of us to be in the hospital till morning.

We had dinner at Michael's house. Gloria had lima beans, baked in a Pyrex dish, and a cucumber salad. Thin fare, I thought.

Gloria was a Greek girl, but third generation. Her name at baptism had been Eleutheria, which means Freedom. You couldn't call a girl that, so they settled for a free translation. It was said of her that she was the survivor of an unhappy love affair with a big blond Californian, and that considering the total nature of her involvement with this person, she was lucky, later, to get a nice "clean" boy like Michael. While there was always about her the smell of the shrew, I had to admit that she was a good mate for Michael, being as hardheaded and on guard as he was openhearted and gullible. She did her cooking and her rearing, built her family's savings by regular deposits, did it all perfectly, and I couldn't stand her.

Now Gloria wanted to know if any one of us had bothered to inquire what the rates were at the Stamford General. None of us had. That's all the opening she needed. She scolded through the whole goddam meal. When she went into the kitchen to get the dessert, I whispered, "Mom," and I did the little turn-off-the-sound-system gesture at my own chest.

My mother laughed. Even Michael laughed.

"What are you all laughing at?" said Gloria, hurrying back through the door, a lemon jello quivering in her hands. "I go out of the room and everybody starts laughing. Why don't you laugh when I'm here? I like a little fun, too, once in a while. What was it?"

"We were just laughing at how deaf I've become," said my mother.

"And how lucky she is to be deaf, sometimes," I added.

"I get it," said Gloria.

My mother leaned over and kissed her on the side of her face, where there were downy black sideburns. She treated Gloria as perfectly as she did everyone else.

"Well, somebody's got to worry about money," said Gloria.

"Of course. And I'm glad you do, Gloria," said my mother. "Now, children, I go to bed, or I'll fall asleep right here."

"I'll walk you to your door," I said, and stood up.

"Jello is not good enough for you people. I can see that much," said Gloria. "Well, we like it, don't we, Michael?"

We weren't around for Michael's response.

"Where are you going now, Eee?" said my mother as we went down the hall.

"I have a date in the city. I was supposed to be at this person's house at six, the latest. It's almost eight-thirty now. By the time I get a train and get there . . ."

We stopped at her door. "One thing I always wanted to tell you," said my mother, "and that is I thank God you have Florence. Michael married nice, and everything like that. But you married someone who gave class to the family. Florence made you something. I had such a beautiful letter from her yesterday. She says take care of Evans. He is a good man. Written so beautiful. She writes letters like they're something to keep. You brought the best thing into this family when you brought her in, Eee. I hope you realize."

"I know Florence is a fine girl."

"Only one time I worried, the day you came to see me and said, like a joke, you were thinking of leaving Florence. I guess you wanted to see how I take it. I took it serious. I said, don't do it, Eee. I said be patient, all fine people are difficult. The easy girls are easy. And I looked out the window when you left—I didn't tell you this—and I saw the girl in your car, waiting for you with her cheap hair. I prayed God you would think what you do. So. Eh? Eee? Will you?"

That was my cue to tell her. But I had learned my lesson from her too well. I didn't say anything but "Sure, Mom, sure."

My mother reached up and kissed me on the cheek. "I know you will think what you do. You always a good boy, Eee." She said good night to me and closed her door.

"You don't want jello, what do you want?" said Gloria as I came back.

254

"Gloria," I said, "do you think I could have a drink?"

"Of course, what do you think we are, haven't even a drink in the house? We had to lock it back here," she added. "Someone was drinking our bottles. I fired one of those mavro cleaning girls, but it still kept disappearing."

"Probably Michael," I said.

"Now you lay off Michael. Is this enough?"

"Gloria, for chrissake, that is one half of one drink."

"Look, Eddie, if you're going to get drunk . . ."

"That's better." She had poured a drinkable amount. "Hey, don't put that stuff away."

She came back, put the bottle on the table and her ass on a chair.

"Gloria," I said, "I have a theory . . ."

"Don't make trouble, Eddie."

". . . that absolutely everybody I know, including that old woman in there, gets by in the world because they are able to wear a disguise of some kind and conceal what they really are and feel. What do you think?"

"I think you're nuts. I've never understood most of what you've ever said to me."

"I know you can't be as mean as you pretend and—"

"I know you're going to get drunk, and I wish you'd go do it somewhere else."

I put down my second drink, kissed Gloria—though the taste was bitter—shook Michael's hand, and left.

14

My skid into a mental institution was by way of a series of discoveries. All the way down I kept having that wonderful sensation: at last, I've found it, the key to everything. But each day the insight that explained it all was not the insight which had explained it all the day before. And the more I learned about myself, the further out of line my thinking became; and the stranger my thinking, the stranger my behavior.

For instance, that day I had made a shattering discovery. I wasn't content to say to myself, "Kid, you learned the art of disguising your truest feelings with your mother's milk, and from that day you have lived your life in one disguise or another." I went on to think of everyone as living in a disguise, the particular disguise necessary to get them what they wanted. I began to think of all appearances, including that of things—of clothes, cars, food packages, public buildings, in fact just about everything that hit my eyes—as false fronts, as techniques of advertising. I began to think of our entire civilization as poses and attitudes, masks and simulacra.

Well, it's harmless enough to think of things that way. The trouble starts when you begin, as I did, to let these perceptions influence your behavior. They say a man is nuts when he begins to live in a world which doesn't correspond to the world everyone else is inhabiting. Such a person behaves from one set of premises and by one set of rules, while everyone else is behaving according to a totally different set of rules and premises. That is when you have to begin to think about society's right to restrain.

I had to walk to the railroad station. I didn't mind. It was one of those damp cool nights I like. Besides, the brown grocer's bag I was carrying, though it looked bulky, was in fact quite light. A word as to how I had suddenly acquired a brown grocer's bag.

Michael and Gloria and their two sons live in one of those long, low apartment houses presently being put up in the suburbs. They are called efficiencies. And they certainly are efficient. The front yard consists entirely of a parking lot for the residents of the building. The apartments run from one side through to the other. The prospect from the back windows is the parking lot of the efficiency apartment building next down the road. You can tell, however, that you are in Westchester and not in Queens or the Bronx, because there are some trees coming through the edge of the macadam of the parking lot. And because traffic gets quiet around nine-fifteen at night. The stores close. You can't get a taxi.

The tenants in an efficiency apartment are required to do certain tasks which janitors do in non-efficiency apartments. For instance, each tenant is expected to carry his garbage out to a shed at one end of the parking lot. This shed, built low so it won't be an eyesore, is made up of a row of numbered bins, each just high enough to house a large garbage can. You have your own bin and can, which is very good, because you never find yourself with no place to put your garbage.

On this particular evening, Gloria had given me, as I left, a brown grocer's bag containing their garbage for that day, and asked me to put it in their bin. But when I found their numbered alcove, the can was full. Since the bin was built just high enough for the can, I couldn't jam Gloria's brown paper bag on top of the rest of the stuff and still close the lid.

For a moment, I considered putting the paper bag in someone else's bin. But there were a rather authoritative-looking group of people on the stoop of the end apartment. The men looked like cops off duty. They pretended to be sitting there innocently, listening to the Met game on a very small transistor. I was convinced they knew what I had in mind, and didn't want to take a chance that I might put my bag in their bin and face a fuss of some kind.

So I turned into the street, still holding the grocer's bag full of garbage, and headed toward the station.

I have never gotten over my fear of policemen. There are days and particularly nights when I become obsessively aware of how many of them there are. Most people say there aren't enough around.

But on certain nights I see them everywhere. I guess since I spent a year on a newspaper, I recognize plain-clothes men where most people can't. I even see them where they aren't. It's not because I feel guilty or anything like that. I have never committed a crime. I never even committed a misdemeanor till later that very night. But I have often felt like a spy in a foreign country.

This feeling was not eased by my four years in that Ivy college. I felt like a white nigger there, disorientated and separate from everyone else. Well, it wasn't just a feeling. I was.

But this is the odd part of it. When it came time for me to buy my clothes, I bought them at the same place where the fraternity boys bought theirs, J. Press, or A. M. Rosenberg's. Later, when I came back from the war and went to work for Williams and Mac-Elroy, I went to Brooks Brothers, which is the same. The fact is that then and at college I wore a disguise. I didn't want to look outside like I felt inside. I wanted to be indistinguishable from "them."

I have long felt that the ordinary male attire, what is called a business suit, is a garment conceived and tailored to deceive people. It's like the facade of the modern bank building. This neo-neoclassic architecture is the way it is for one reason only, and that is to inspire confidence in the honesty and durability of the institution housed therein. That is also the purpose of the business suit; it is an advertisement for the man, and sometimes, as in the case of many ads, it is misleading. It says, "You can trust this man in a business deal." The clothing of the contemporary male is not designed for comfort or protection or adaptability to various kinds of weather. It certainly isn't for beauty. It's made to suggest the opposite of deviousness. It is a do-business suit.

The funny thing is—I was thinking about all this as I walked to the railroad station—that even when I joined the Communist Party in the days of the Popular Front, I still wore the honest three-button Brooks Brothers. This wasn't accidental either, because it was important, in those days, for the Commie to represent himself to be just like everyone else, a little ahead, maybe, but not too much, and never as a person dedicated and determined to bring down this body politic. So the disguise was the business suit. On June 23, 1941, the day after Hitler invaded Stalinland, the comrades rushed out and bought themselves honest cloth in a respectable cut. It was a great day for tailors.

Another policeman passed me. I had the feeling that all the cops were out tonight. Even when I finally got on the train, there was one walking up and down the aisle. You could see the bulge of his concealed pistol, for chrissake. Some plain-clothes man! Why was he riding that train? Did he look at me strangely as he passed? Did I have too much to drink at Gloria's? I was still carrying the brown grocer's bag. Perhaps he was concerned about that. I better put that bag on the floor, out of sight. I had forgotten I was still carrying it. But now suppose someone questioned me, how could I explain it?

In the seat behind me two men were discussing the A.T. and T. stock split.

Actually, about my own clothes, I had a model. His name is Brooks Atkinson, the famous man who used to pass judgment on the season's plays for the New York *Times*. I used to study his photographs. He wore these little suits; whether they were gray or not I don't know because I have never seen the man in the flesh, but they gave off gray. Then he wore those button-down shirts like they wear at Harvard and Williams and Amherst and even Yale. He preferred little flat bow ties, the ones without flare. The whole effect was one of fantastic honesty and superlative modesty. I had the research department at Williams and MacElroy get me some pictures of this man, and I studied his secret. How confidence-inspiring, I used to think, how trustworthy-seeming. Still, I knew from reading the man's reviews that he was as human as the next fellow. His teeth were as sharp, and he liked the salty taste of blood just as any other animal does. He even had his human share of venom and vanity. He enjoyed power to the point of publicly stating he wished he didn't have so much. In other words, he was a descendant of the hunter-ape, as we all are.

Since he was about my size and weight, I took on his image. Of course I'm olive-complexioned, and at first I thought that would be a problem. But once you get the rest of the junk on—the glasses, the bow tie, the vest and all—there isn't much olive to show. About the glasses, I remember well, I had all my glasses changed one week to the little steel-rimmed kind that Mr. Atkinson wears. What the hell, why fiddle around with what's perfect? Everyone else at the agency wore those tortoise temple grippers, but I went in for the old-fashioned kind that Mr. Atkinson wore, the kind that curl behind your ears. I remember I also changed my hair-part that same week, moving it much closer to the middle of my head, where it was less dashing, true, but much much more trustworthy-seeming.

I guess I wanted people not to see the turbulence inside me. I wanted them to think of me as they did of him, decent, selfless, civilized. None of which—so I was fast finding out—was I. In other words, I disguised myself, quite consciously.

I never felt more grateful to Mr. Atkinson than when I walked through those motel lobbies in downtown Los Angeles to my assignations with Gwen Hunt. The desk clerks used to nod their heads as if I was in fact Brooks Atkinson. Then we'd lock the door, and there'd be chaos for a couple of hours. But, after, on would go the button-down shirt, the trim little bow tie, the three-button suit with the modest lapels, and the part in the center of my head. And out I'd prance, modest, even mouselike, but prance I did through the lobby, home free, with the clerks again nodding respectfully, as well they might.

That goddam plain-clothes man came back from the smoking car. He was carrying a briefcase now, but that didn't fool me. They all look like junior executives today. The F.B.I. started that. But I'm on to them. I barely restrained myself from slapping him where his gun bulged. I gave him a real cool little smile and a nod, as if to say, "I know who you really are." And he gave me the same back, as if to say, "I know who you are, too."

The train was slowing down for the stop at 125th Street, which is not where I had intended to get off. But I had an impulse to go look at the neighborhood where my parents lived when they first came to America and where I was born. Gwen would just have to wait a little longer, that is if she was still waiting at all. For the moment, I didn't care.

I knew that neighborhood was part of Harlem now, but forty years ago it was a district for up-and-coming whites. I had always wanted to go back there, walk the streets where I had played, and look at the changes. But year after year, coming to New York for business, I had not had the time. I always scheduled myself for everything except the things that really concerned me. If *I* was interested in it, it had to be less important.

So I started to leave the train and got just to the end of the car, when there was a call from behind me. "Hey, fella, you forgot your package." The conductor was holding up the brown paper grocer's bag. "Oh, thanks," I said, laughing nervously, and hurried back to get it.

On 125th Street, I decided to walk a bit. I also decided to carry the brown bag for a while. I had begun to have an affection for the thing. I held it in the crook of my arm like a big football.

Gloria's drink was wearing off and I didn't want that to happen, so I went into the first bar, Black and Tan. I had a jumbo beer for fifteen cents. Then a shot of rye, then a foot-long hot dog, then another shot, then another beer. That brought me back.

There was a commotion at one end of the bar. Someone had come in off the street and quick-sold a vacuum cleaner to one of the bartenders for fifteen dollars. Inspection showed it to have a prominent brand name, and no motor. The seller had disappeared.

I sized the place up. What the hell was I doing here, a stranger within a stranger, a disguise over a disguise?

I remembered when I came back from the war in '45, how unrelated to me everything seemed. Were these my people? Was this my fatherland? Why did I have so little sense of loyalty or patriotism, I, a twice-decorated soldier? I had fought for this place, seen men die for it. But now, looking at it, I wondered, why did they die for this? I'm not talking about the idea. I'm talking about the place, the way it actually is.

"But," I said out loud, "the whole thing doesn't have to be this way."

The fellow next to me, without turning his head, commented, "No. It doesn't."

"I mean the whole damned thing." I didn't turn to look at him either.

The bar has taken the place of the church. It is the only place in America where men examine their souls.

The fellow next to me said, "I know what you mean." I still didn't turn to look at him, nor he at me.

I had another boiler-maker. I remember I thought then, "This society is insane." I meant all of it—the customs, the clothes, the work, the hours devoted to work, the way people spoke to each other without looking, the homes they lived in, the streets they walked, the air, the noise, the filth, the bread—all the basics. But the real thing that bothered me was that this country, despite all the talk about happiness—was in some pervasive way anti-pleasure.

Oh, I know we're always stuffing something into our mouths—a drink, a cigar, a piece of nickel candy. And we're forever riding here and there. There's music everywhere, even in the elevators, and you can see old movies day and night on TV. "But," I said, "where do you go to really have a good time in this city?"

"What kind of a girl you looking for?" said my elbowmate.

I took a quick look. He was a plain-clothes man, no doubt, offering to pimp for me. A trap. I had a double shot and got out, clutching my grocer's bag tight.

Christ, was I seeing straight? I didn't used to see the world around me this way!

"Of course not. You were part of it, then, so how could you see it?" I said out loud.

Once I did. At college. I felt everyone there was my enemy, and that I had to conceal my true feelings. I behaved as if I was a spy in a foreign country.

I started to run in and out of the crowd like a broken-field runner, holding the brown paper bag in the crook of my arm.

I was spoiling for a fight. About anything. With anybody.

At Lex, I turned downtown. Yes, I thought, this is how I felt in '45 when the atom bomb had cleared Hiroshima off the face of the plain, and then, since twice is better than once, Nagasaki. I remembered then that I felt as I did tonight. Once home, I got me a job at Williams and MacElroy, put on my nice-guy disguise, and twenty years passed like one of those time-passing bits in the movies, the leaves flying off the calendar in the studio-made wind.

I went into a bar on 116th Street, full of Puerto Riquenos far from the clear sea water and the rain forest. And Negroes with no home to be far from. This can't ever be their home, and that other too far back. The whole bar looked like one of those rooms under the concrete risers of a stadium where fighters wait before they go into a ring. It was full of fear and murder. I felt at any minute we'd all drop our disguises and slug our neighbors without turning to see whom we were hitting.

"The whole thing doesn't have to be this way," I said sternly.

My elbowmate at the bar said, "Go and fuck yourself, mister."

I looked at him. He was a Negro. He'd decided not to wear his disguise that night. He was himself.

"It doesn't have to be this way, any of it," I said again. "We just got off on the wrong foot, at the very beginning. So we can't see that any other way is possible."

"Will you move away from me," said my neighbor. He had a bad lump over one eye, and a long welt where someone had tried to cut his throat. He wasn't a cop, I could see that.

But I felt trusting, not threatened. He wasn't a cop, I could see that.

"You see we're not wrong," I said, "it's all the rest of them out there."

"You're full of shit, mister."

"No, I'm not. You know what I'm talking about."

"If you don't like it here, why don't you haul ass out?"

"Where could I go?"

"I don't care where you go. Stop bugging me. What are you, a cop or something? You're a cop, aren't you?"

"Did you know that A.T. and T. split its stock today?"

He took a transistor radio out of his pocket, and turning on a comic real loud, held it flat up to his ear. Then he moved down the bar away from me.

I followed him.

"Will you stay away, you got nothing on me."

The bartender came over. "What's the matter?" he asked.

"This cop is bugging me. I didn't do nothing."

"I was just trying to talk to him," I said.

"What for?" said the bartender.

That wasn't easy to explain. The bartender staring at me didn't make it any easier.

"Everybody's getting along good in here," he said. "You see anybody bothering anybody?" His tone was most respectful.

"I don't even see anybody talking to anybody."

"So we're A-1, what do you want?"

That was hard to explain too.

He continued, "Would you mind doing your drinking somewhere else? If a cop drinks in a place, it keeps customers out. No offense. Would you mind?"

"O.K.," I said. "Give me another belt and I'll go." He did, on the house, and I left.

It had begun to drizzle. I felt loaded for trouble. It struck me as strange, because I'd spent so much of my life in a disguise for the purpose of staying out of trouble.

I was now at 112th Street, where we lived forty years ago. There was nothing there now. Six, seven, eight big co-op apartment buildings. Uniform. Disguises all. Incognito architecture.

A cop walked by. In uniform for a change.

"Where's everybody?" I asked.

"What?" He looked friendly, which was a sure-as-hell disguise. I said, "Where's everything?"

"Where's what?" he said.

"Everything, everybody." I was pretty annoyed and sounded so.

"Inside," he said. "You better get in, too, before you get into trouble."

Then he walked off and up to another man, a plain-clothes man by the look of him, and said something. They both turned and looked at me.

"Well all right," I thought and I walked up to the cop and the plain-clothes man. I'd never done anything like this before.

"What do you mean by telling me I better get in before I get into trouble?" I demanded.

The cop and the plain-clothes man looked at each other and began to laugh.

"What's so funny?" I said belligerently.

"Just move along, will you, mister," the cop said.

"You move along. Go about your business, and stop following me."

By God, they walked away!

A third man, another plain-clothes man obviously, came and stood in front of me. This guy was really disguised. The son of a bitch spoke French.

"Parlez vous français?" he said.

"Oui," I said, "so don't give me that."

"Comment?"

"Speak English," I ordered. "Just cut it out . . . the three of you." I looked around. The other two had disappeared. But I knew they were in a doorway, around a corner, somewhere, watching me. But this last one, the son of a bitch, just stood there.

I walked away, or rather turned away and towards a wall of planks and old wooden doors around a co-op that had just been completed, and I walked smack into a poster for Zephyr cigarettes.

The poster showed a medical type, very WASP, could be a doctor with that white coat, and behind him one of those skinny models with built-up tits watching him with polite lust and—now I remembered. That's my poster! I'd written the copy: SMOKE ZEPHYR. THE MEN YOU TRUST DO. THEY'RE CLEAN AS A BREEZE. Our answer to the cancer scare.

"Pure shit!" I said.

"Comment?" the plain-clothes man, whoever he was, said. He seemed nicer now.

I decided to trust him. I smiled at him, first tentatively, then without caution. He smiled back. Whatever and whoever he was, he had a nice smile.

I bowed and said, "What can I do for you?"

Then he said, "Thank you very much. Can you please tell me where I can urinate myself in this city?"

I didn't have an answer. Big question. The housing development was all around me. Suddenly I had to go, too. Christ, I thought, the honor of America as a civilization is hanging on this very simple question. A proper culture should certainly provide a place where a man could pleasantly relieve himself every so often.

I turned to the Frenchman. I was pretty sure by now he wasn't a plain-clothes man. He was just a fellow, like me, in a foreign country. "It's like Paris here," I said. "You look for the advertisements, and when you see one, like this one *ici,* that's the place! Except here we do it right *on* the advertisements. *Regardez!"*

I took the thing out and pissed all over where it said, "The men you trust do."

He watched. Men are interested on a comparative basis in each other's roots. I was waiting for him to take his out. I'd never seen a French one. I pointed to where it showed this semi-coed type with the "D" cups having her polite sex fit over the doctor type in the white coat. I said, "This is your part. Let her go!"

The Zephyr people, I remembered, had decided to try this campaign in limited areas to get a testing.

Well, that was when the real plain-clothes man and the cop moved in and we had our little fracas.

I enjoyed the ride in the police car. In fact, I was so relaxed I fell asleep on the way downtown. When I woke, it was all pretty hazy.

I remember someone roughed up the Frenchman just outside night court, and I didn't like it. In fact, believe it or not, I dumped somebody who sure as hell was a plain-clothes man because all the loyal plain-clothes men hopped me and muscled me a bit. They couldn't, however, do the job they'd like to have done, because we were in the night court building by then. Besides, I gave them what Godoy gave Joe Louis, the top of the turtle to hit at.

Next thing I remember we were in front of a judge I couldn't see clearly. I put the brown paper bag gently down on the court stenographer's table, and I said to this judge I thought there were too many plain-clothes men around the city. I had a grand moment when I said, "Do you, your honor, know where a visiting Frenchman who is not familiar with our city and customs can urinate on 112th Street and Lexington Avenue, in the middle of the night?"

This stumped the judge, I guess, because he turned and whispered something to the plain-clothes man behind him. "He doesn't know, your honor," I said, "I asked him."

At which the judge pointed to me and said to the plain-clothes man on my right, "Bring him to my chambers."

Then I spoke out again, "I don't go to anybody's chambers unless you let this Frenchman go." The plain-clothes man who was holding my arm twisted it a bit.

"Ouch!" I yelled. "Has this man the right to twist my arm?"

The judge ducked my question, as well he might. He turned and said to the Frenchman, "You can go."

"I think we owe this man an apology," I said.

"Don't push your luck," said the dick.

"I think you owe him an apology," I said. "Suppose you were in Paris and this happened to you. You'd be screaming for the one hundred and first airborne."

The judge rapped his gavel. The cops took the Frenchman away. I never saw him again.

The next thing I remember I was in a dingy little room in the back somewhere, and this judge was taking off his robes. He lit a cigarette, turned and looked right at me, and said, "Don't you remember me?"

I looked at him, and as I did, something of authority and disguise fell off, and there was Beetle Weinstein, or as he came to be known, Ben Winston. "Beetle," I said. "For chrissake, it's the Beetle!"

266

"Yes," he said. "Me."

"You had your teeth fixed," I said.

He acquired the name Beetle because of the hang and the weight of his lateral incisors.

"Yes," he said, "and that's the least of it."

"What the hell are you doing here?" I asked.

"What the hell are *you* doing here?" he said. "And let's have a drink." He reached into the space behind some law books and pulled out that fine square bottle.

A drink put me right back on top. "I've been wanting to do that for years," I said.

"What?" he said, lifting his glass. "To the day!"

"Piss on my ads!" I said. "Tell me, Beetle, how do you take it?"

"How do *you* take it?"

"Stop answering my question with a question, you Hebe bastard, now answer my goddam question, how do you sit up there and represent it?"

"What?" he said.

"You know goddam well what. IT! All of it. The general fraud."

"Patience, my friend, we wait."

"Bullshit, Judge. It all doesn't have to be this way."

"All of what?"

"All of any of this, all of IT!"

"Are you all right?" he said.

"Yes. But I'm nearing a crisis. I'm not just drunk, you know. This is a hell of a lot more than that."

"I can see that," he said, "a hell of a lot more."

"And there's no end to it, Beetle."

"What happened to you?"

"When?"

"Since I last saw you."

"IT happened to me."

"What's IT?"

"Were you in the war?"

"I enlisted the day after Hitler sent Runstedt across the Polish border. Didn't you?"

"Well, you remember when you came back from the war and everything looked insane? I mean literally, the whole civilization, didn't it? Judge?"

"Yes, it did."

"Well, that moment is when you were thinking straight. Then they got around you with the promotions and the money and that robe you just took off. But you had a week or two of sanity back in the summer of '45. Do you remember it? Give me another drink."

"Help yourself."

I did. We sat there for a moment. I was breathing extra hard.

"Are you sure you're all right?" he asked me.

"I've never felt truer. I want to send two telegrams tonight. You will have to help me."

"Sure. What are they?"

"I've got two professions, and I'm going to formally and finally quit both."

"Why don't you do it in the morning?"

"I won't be thinking as clearly in the morning."

There was a knock on the door, and he muttered something that gave one of those plain-clothes men the right to come in. He was, now that I saw him in a different light, just a big Irish kid. He was holding my brown grocer's bag.

"I thought you might want to see this, Judge Winston," he said.

"What is it?" said the Beetle.

"Take a look inside, sir."

I said nothing.

The judge looked inside. "I still don't get it," he said. "What is it, Officer?"

"Just a mess of garbage," the plain-clothes man said. "But when Detective Shepley tried to take it away from him, the prisoner knocked him down."

"He knocked a police officer down?" asked Judge Winston.

"Yes, sir."

"Tst, tst, tst," I said.

The big Irish kid glared at me, then continued. "Just thought you might want to see what he thought was so precious, you know what I mean, Judge? I think it's significant."

"Thank you, Officer, you're right, it is significant."

The plain-clothes man nodded and walked out.

The judge looked at me. He looked more like a judge again.

"Eddie," he said, "what are you carrying this around for?"

"Is it against the law?"

"Stop being so belligerent! I just wondered why you were carrying it around with you."

I thought for a long time about that one. With my new devotion to the truth, I made an effort to clear my mind and answer truthfully. I thought, should I go through the whole goddam story? If I did, would that explain it? Finally I said, "I can't explain, your honor, why I'm carrying that brown paper bag full of garbage around with me."

There was a pause. Then he put his arm around my shoulders and said, "Never mind that 'your honor' poetry. Listen, maybe you ought to not do anything decisive about anything, including your jobs, till you take a long rest."

I got up.

"Beetle," I said, "thanks. But I never felt truer in my life. There isn't a damned thing wrong with me. Everyone else is wrong. And now, speaking as offender to judge, are you going to hold me?"

He looked at me very sad and very concerned. "No," he said, "I'm not going to hold you. You're free."

"How do I get out of here?"

"I'll walk you to the back door," he said. Then he reached for his robe. "I'm afraid if I don't have this on, they won't let me back in." He laughed and I laughed. But he meant it.

"One for the road?" he asked.

"Don't need it," I said. "I feel fine."

"Then one for old time's sake."

"For the old days, yes, that, yes," I said.

He poured.

I was in the Communist Party for a fast ten months. When I went to their Twelfth Street H.Q. to report for my unit (a group of newspaper men doing "united front" speeches and articles for the Party), the man with whom I'd make contact on the 9th floor was Bennie Weinstein. He had a soft spot in him, you could tell even then, so it didn't surprise me that I never heard of his rising higher in his cadre. He was o.k. for the Popular Front days when everyone was friendly. After the war, when things got cold and hard again, he wasn't the right casting.

When I got back from the war, the C.P. meant nothing to me. I wanted to make up for lost time, and make a life for myself. Which I did. From the looks of it, he had too.

"To the old days," he said again, "the real days!"

We drank to that. He put the bottle back behind the law books and showed me out the door. We walked through some corridors, past various attendants. The black cloth received its tribute. The judge nodded and grunted, didn't give much back. He had the authority game down cold.

The passages through the cellar could have been painted by Hopper. The bulbs were unshielded forties. The inhabitants, all in some way connected with administering justice, seemed drugged. They were standing at intervals that didn't relate to function or intention. Perhaps because the building's source of heat was just below us, these nether regions were overheated. The accommodations for the jailors were no better or different than those for the jailed.

Judge Winston (Weinstein) opened the back door. It was still drizzling.

"Nasty night," he said. Then he looked at me anxiously and said, "Everything in the family, right? About the old days and all that? You know?" He was not telling me, he was pleading with me. How rickety was his security, I thought. "You know," he continued, "there aren't many of us left."

"Us what?" I asked.

"Us old rebels," he said.

We stood there for a bit looking at the drizzle. I suppose he was wondering what I thought of him. But when I dared look at him, he smiled and said, "Where you heading for now, old buddy?"

"Guess I'll go get laid," I said, "if I can."

"Gets harder every year, doesn't it?" He laughed, and added, "I wish I could go along with you—oh, not just for that, though I'd like to break out, haven't in a long time. What I meant was that being together has brought back so many memories."

I remembered his wife. She had been the pistol of that family, had gone to Cuba twice, the first time with Clifford Odets, whose girl friend she was that month, and the second time on her own. That time she had stayed there and become a *soldadera* to one of the men who fought in the hills—this long, long before Castro. When this man had been trapped and shot by Batista . . . or was that what had happened? I didn't remember clearly any more.

"Where's Elizabeth?" I asked.

"Oh," he said, "remember her?"

"When did she die?" I said.

"She's not dead," he said. "We're still together. We've been together damn near thirty years now." He dropped his voice. "Did you know that she was once the mistress of Clifford Odets?" Was he boasting? "Then, after that, she lived with one of those real hill *campesinos,* the real thing, buddy my boy, shot by Batista! An American-made bullet right between the eyes. Shame on us. Bastards! But they didn't get her. How she ever got back into this country, don't ask, it's thirty years ago. You'd never, never guess what she's doing now."

"What and where?"

"A stock market analyst on Wall Street. Works for an investment banking firm. Of course, with nearly every hot tip on the street crossing her desk, and with the kind of market we've had for ten years, and never forgetting her thorough knowledge of Marx—that sure comes in handy—she's made us a small fortune. I could quit any time."

"Why don't you?"

"And do what?"

"There's a lot still to fight for, isn't there?"

"You can't do anything today, buddy my boy, you know that, because baby, these are what that fellow called the Years of the Toad. Where are they all today? Mexico. Underground just like you and me. We're all underground in this country. No one knows who's where. Like you. Advertising. A whore's trade. When you're drunk, you feel like quitting; when you're sober, you don't—that's it, isn't it? Because, hell, you're sitting there waiting just like I'm sitting here waiting. Maybe once in a while we do a little something. Like tonight. I bet you were glad it was me at the other end of that gavel."

I didn't answer.

The drizzle showered jewels through the funnel of the street lights. "Well," I said, "guess I've kept you long enough."

"Don't say that," he said. "It's not every day that I meet one of the old ones." He tightened his belt. "You put on weight sitting on that goddam bench every day, looking at the refuse of this filthy society, the sellers and the sold. Man, I could write a book. And I will, some day, I will; I promise you that, Eddie. Hold me to that. Will you hold me to that, Eddie?"

Then he did the last thing I would have expected of him. He reached out and gently touched my cheek in as near to a caress as he was prepared to give another man. "You're going to get laid now, are you? You son of a bitch."

"Well, I'm going to see about it."

"You've kept alive some way. Maybe it's the fucking. Goddam you, you still look as—" he hesitated, "as unreliable and crazy, as hungry and wild and mean as you did twenty years ago. And that's a compliment."

Then he spoke some lines with a pounding rhythm.

> " 'Love which is lust is the lamp in the tomb.
> Love which is lust is the call from the gloom.'

"Remember that? Henley?"

"Did Henley write that?" I asked. "*That* Henley?"

"Yes, buddy my boy, that old Invictus fellow. See, you never know. Remember what Marc Laurence told the Un-American Activities. . . . They asked him why he had joined the Communist Party, and Marc says, 'Because you meet so many pretty girls at their functions.'" He burst out laughing; then he looked over his shoulder again. "You could, too. That's where I met Elizabeth. At a function. They were raising money for the Scottsboro boys, I remember. She was beautiful then. Oh, yes, Elizabeth! You should see her now! A market analyst! Odets told me in 1937 that she had the prettiest pair of cup cakes he had ever seen . . . Were you ever with her? Back then? I know you knew her. Tell me. I don't mind."

"Yes I was. You know, just once . . ."

"I don't mind," he said.

"Well," I said, starting to go.

"I imagine it must still be going on, all that kind of life, somewhere."

"Oh, sure, same game, different players."

"You ought to get yourself a pair of rubbers. I mean your feet. You'll catch cold."

"Well," I said, "so long."

"You know you gave me a lift, you did. I sit in there day after day, I begin to feel like a bug in a box. And . . . well . . . she was good, wasn't she, Elizabeth, in bed?"

272

"Wonderful," I said, "but she would never see me again. It was just one of those accidents, you know, just once."

"Oh, sure, sure, don't worry. I understand . . . but she was . . ."

"Wonderful," I said. I started to go again.

"Well, take it easy," he said, "and be careful."

"Of what?"

"I'm in a precarious position here. Nobody has the least idea who I am! You know?"

"I know."

"So everything in the family? Right?"

I reassured him, waved, and walked away. When I looked back, after a few steps, he was still in the doorway. He stood there alone, no longer thinking of me. Then he entered the heavy building with its barred windows. The door was metal and heavy, and you could hear that when he shut it.

I walked into the cool night.

"AAAAAAAAAaaaaaaaah!!" I said, out loud, clearing something within me. "Aaaaaachch ahhhhh!" blowing out the congestion of hopelessness Beetle Weinstein had left in me. Everybody around me was in disguise and dying, dying in disguise. But tonight, with the warm drink and the bright cool pins of drizzle, I was exhilarated. I had lived through it, I was the sole survivor of a gigantic shipwreck. I had escaped. At least I had postponed extinction. I was fed up with death, fed up with the silent slow surrendering all around me. I had left that behind me. I could see from Beetle Weinstein just how far behind.

"I was that way once!" I shouted. And then, "It doesn't have to be this way!" Out loud, all this, because I was also fed up and for good with my own secrets and my own front, my disguises and my pretenses. I was fed up with "Brooks Atkinson." The drizzle had fogged my glasses, and I took them off and looked less like him. And suddenly, for no reason, I was suddenly fed up with the New York *Times,* too, fed up with the "best" of our civilization as well as the worst. I felt like a foreigner in the whole life around me.

"I'm not part of this," I said. "I'm out of it."

Then I thought, where can I go? What can I do?

Start with a negative. At least I know what I don't like, what not to do. Because what I had been doing had just about killed me. I'd barely escaped with my life.

Love which is lust is the lamp in the tomb!

Well, I don't know about that, probably true, "tomb," yes, that part is true. I was in and now I'm out, and most everyone else is still in. Is "all that" still going on somewhere, Beetle had asked. Is it? Has to be, if it's going on in me.

And lust? Yes. The only thing that had kept me alive through all the years of my success were my indecencies, my infidelities, my "bad" side, my outrages. My decent and faithful, fair, orderly, and considerate side was a mask, and that mask, like the one in the old fairy story, had tightened around my face and my mouth till it just about choked me to death. Where I had lied and sneaked and cheated, it had been to escape the regimen, the terrible *order* that had been killing me. And damned near did.

Walking down Broadway, which was just as crowded with the sellers and the sold as Judge Winston (Weinstein) had said, I took a damned oath that I would suit myself from then on, no matter what the consequences, even if it brought me face to face with my own worthlessness and the scorn of the rest of the world. Perhaps it would bring me some whiff of my own identity. I would not disguise myself from myself again. I would not be law-abiding in respect to conventions and covenants which I had not made or agreed to.

I had a premonition, right there in front of the Astor Hotel, that I was about to pull out of the wall every hook from which I had hung my life. I was returning to the morality of the nipple and the mouth. It would bring down on me disapproval and reprehension. Still it was the next move. That was for sure.

Self-disgust is saving my life, I thought.

My only dignity, I thought, is my self-disgust.

Then I remembered a line, or a paraphrase, perhaps that's all it was, from the Bible. You have to lose your life to save your life. Whoever said that had it right. You have to die before you can live again.

The Paramount Building tower is the ugliest building I have ever seen. Its clock said ten of one. I hopped a cab.

It's totally illogical, I know, but I did expect that Gwen would be there waiting for me. Because, I thought, she is the same as I am. We're different in every way except the essential way; she's also

274

an undigested stranger lost in the streets of this nation of identical streets. She'll be there, and she'll be waiting for me.

And, of course, when I got to her apartment building, the buzzer from above opened the front door immediately. The door to her apartment was ajar waiting for me. Gwen was sitting in a chair knitting. And lying on a sofa reading *Sports Illustrated* was a man she introduced to me as Charles.

15

I WAS trained as an engineer," Charles was saying, "and that sure comes in handy. Like right now, I'm setting up a string of dry-cleaning establishments, sort of you-do-its.

"I think these enterprises are going to go, don't you, Gwen?" Gwen didn't give a sign of having heard, so he turned to me. "I'd like to show you one of them, if you have time."

I was sitting there, a piece of African sculpture, wooden, enigmatic. "I'm not in town for long," I said.

"Well, they're definitely the next step in that field. Definitely. No? Don't you think so?" He turned to Gwen. "You think so, Gwen? No?"

Gwen's concentration on her knitting was enough to make anyone nervous.

"No answer," said Charles. He laughed. "I'm awfully glad to meet you, finally. Gwen would never talk about you. But I like things in the open. I knew you'd been close once . . ." He trailed off.

"We were once," I said, waiting for him to go.

"But you know how Gwen is. See, no comment. Gwen!"

Those dry bones clicked.

Charles turned back to me. "Sometimes you think she's not listening," he said, "but later it turns out she's heard every word, and some you forgot you said."

I examined Gwen. There were new, intent lines on her face. Her eyes were like those of a child who wants something desperately, knows it's forbidden, and is determined to get it. She looked at me for a split second, then dropped her eyes.

"Hey, Gwen," said Charles, "we haven't offered the man a drink."

Gwen got up without a word.

I looked at Charles closely. He was well set up, six-foot-something, bulky through the middle, with those heavy muscles athletes get when they stop training. He looked like the fellow—he could have been the brother of the man—who was Eisenhower's P.R., Haggerty was his name. He had his jacket off but had retained his tie. In his shirt pocket was a case with several colored pencils and a miniature slide rule. A loop of fine chain clasped his tie.

Gwen hadn't forgotten how I took my bourbon. She gave me the glass without looking at me, and went back to her knitting. Close up, I had seen that the line from the nostril to the corner of her mouth, and that from the mouth to below the chin, were becoming one. She wasn't as pretty as I remembered her.

"But I was off on my timing." Charles had launched into something, and I hadn't heard the first part. "Timing is everything. As a successful person, you know that better than I do. Well, then Gwen came to the rescue with this idea for dry-cleaning you-do-its and—well—remember, Gwen?"

Silence. We sat there, three cars in a snowdrift.

"As a matter of fact," said Charles, cranking up again, "I thought, if I was ever lucky enough to meet you, I'd try to get some free advice. I need a trademark and a slogan, you know, for my dry-cleaning chain, at least I hope it will be a chain. I don't seem to be able to settle on anything."

"What ideas have you had?"

"Several. But Gwen didn't think—I'm embarrassed to mention them."

"Oh, come on, take a chance."

"What do you want, Eddie?" Gwen said.

There was another silence, this one for real.

I didn't answer.

"Eddie, what the hell do you want?"

"I want to see you."

"Well, I don't want to see you. In fact, I wish you'd both get the hell out of here."

First I thought the sound came from someone else's apartment. Then Gwen got up and went into a door I hadn't noticed, and closed it after her. There was the sound of an infant crying from that room.

Was that the surprise Chet had meant?

I looked at Charles. He smiled and shrugged.

The door opened, and Gwen stood there holding a kid. "How about it?" she said.

Charles stood up. "Guess we'd better," he said.

I sat there with my drink, stunned. Whose kid was that?

"I'm not going," I said.

"Charles?"

"Yes, dear."

"Will you get him out of here?"

"Yes, I will."

She closed the door. Charles stood up. He was a very big man. "Guess we'd better," he said gently.

"I'd like to finish my drink."

Gwen came out of the door again, crossed over to a bulky package wrapped in dark blue paper, ripped it open, and jerked a diaper out of the bundle.

"Charles," she said, "I'd like to be by myself tonight. Don't come back." Then she turned to me. "Sorry if I was rude, Eddie, but that's the way I feel. Goodbye." She closed the bedroom door behind her.

That last "Don't come back, Charles" once might have been her way of telling me to come back after I had "lost" him. I doubted she meant that tonight.

Charles had his jacket and hat on. "Big freight's pulling out," he said. He came over to me, eased the drink out of my hand, and set it carefully on the table. He was bigger than his brother Chet.

"There's a nice quiet bar across the street," he said. "I'll buy you a drink. I'd enjoy a talk with you."

"I don't know why she's so rude to you," he said to me in the bar after we'd ordered. "Except she is an extremely sensitive girl. I mean that's a basket case up there every twenty-eighth day, you know."

"She must be hot as a pistol then, too."

"Well," he said, "you ought to know." He looked embarrassed.

Could it be this guy's?

The waiter came with the order. Charles was drinking Alexanders.

"Cheers," he said, "and all luck."

"You mean all bad," I said. We both laughed.

"No," he said, "I didn't mean that." He looked me over. "Excuse me for looking at you this way. But I've thought a lot about you. Whenever I meet a successful man, I try to figure out how he did it. You're in the upper tax brackets, I know that, and you did it in your chosen field, that's what's remarkable. I've always admired writers, particularly song writers."

He was making me uncomfortable now. "You a discus thrower?" I asked.

"You see! Now how did you know that? Actually it was shot put. But still. Intuition. Exceptional sensitivity. Gwen told me you were psychic."

"She meant psycho."

"No, she didn't. Oh, you're kidding."

"Why are you looking at me that way?"

"Well, my instinct is to like you. Isn't that strange, everything considered? I admire you."

"Better get yourself someone else to admire."

"Right again. I've had a lot of trouble that way. I'm susceptible to friendship. People keep taking me. Do you know that for the longest time I thought if a person smiled at me and shook my hand, it meant he was my friend. But I'm not the all-American fall guy any more. That's what Chet used to call me. I trained myself to be suspicious. It's not my nature, but I had to do it. Still, if you're too suspicious too early—well, I think the whole problem in life is to stay sensitive on the inside, and be tough outside to hold your own."

"Whose is the kid?"

"Hers."

"Yeah, but whose?"

"I don't know."

"Didn't you ever ask her?"

"If she wanted me to know, she would have told me."

"Aren't you curious, for chrissake?"

"Gwen doesn't like to be crowded."

"Maybe it's yours."

"You wouldn't believe it, I guess, but I haven't had sexual relations, what they call, with Gwen as yet."

"But you stay up there with her."

"She doesn't like to be alone at night."

"You sleep in the same room."

"Some nights, correct, she lets me. I sleep on that cot, you saw it, in the corner. Come to think of it, how did you know that?"

"I'm psychic."

"You sure are. Oh, you're kidding again."

"You mind my asking you about all this?"

"Not so far."

"Well, how can you do that without also . . . ?"

"Do what without what? You've lost me. Oh, I understand what you mean. Well, she's a very unusual person. And, in my way, I am too. Anyway, that's how we want it."

"You mean to tell me that—?"

"You've asked enough now."

"O.K."

"I'm hoping one day it will be for keeps, and the rest is—well, it's complicated. But she's the girl for me."

"Good luck."

"I don't believe in luck. I believe in patience."

"I see."

"And understanding people and—well, I know I'm a little dull compared to someone like my brother, for instance. I haven't too much to give. But there is one thing I have. I've made up my mind to take care of Gwen. She needs someone like me. And as for me— well, I was married before, so I'm in no rush. She has things to work out. And she's doing that. You notice how she's changed?"

"Yeah, I guess so."

"She's come a long way. Of course there are still days when she's dangerous, to herself I mean. I watch those windows and knives. But nothing like when I met her. I've made it my purpose in life to straighten her out."

"You took on a job."

"But I believe in that. The power of patience. Have faith in a person, and a miracle will happen. There's something very fine in that girl. For one thing, she's got a brilliant mind; you found that out. But—well, I'll be plain with you; you hurt her a lot, and after you my brother Chet didn't do her a bit of good. I came in there one day, and he was angry with her, and getting sort of rough, so I had to beat up on him a bit—"

"You beat—"

"Had to. I didn't want him to ever come back."

"And?"

"He didn't."

"Maybe Chet was right to be angry; maybe she did something to him that—"

"I don't care what she did. Or does. No one is ever going to hurt her again." He smiled at me gently.

"Whose kid is that?"

"I told you, I don't know."

"Don't you care?"

"Not particularly. Is it yours?"

"I don't know."

"All that matters to me is that it's hers."

"Maybe she doesn't know either," I laughed.

Suddenly he became very severe. "You see, you laugh," he said, "but that's the sort of thing that cuts a girl to pieces inside. Please don't see her any more."

I looked at him. He meant it. "I really wish you wouldn't," he said.

"I can't promise that."

He finished his Alexander, looked intently at the table top, and frowned. "O.K.," he finally said.

"What does that mean, o.k.?"

"I mean, if that's the way it's going to be."

He studied me for quite a while, then turned and caught the waiter's eye and asked for the check.

"Did anyone ever tell you," I said to him as he was putting on his jacket, "that you look like Eisenhower's P.R., Haggerty?"

"I look like Oscar Hammerstein. You know who he was?"

"*Oklahoma.*"

"Correct. And lots of others." He looked at me again, and said, "I don't think Gwen could ever have loved you if you were as big a bastard as you pretend to be. You mind my saying that?"

The waiter came up.

"Can I talk to you for just another minute?" When I nodded, instead of paying the check he ordered another round.

"Oscar Hammerstein," he said, "is my ideal."

"I didn't even realize you knew him."

"I was the second assistant electrician in the first production of *The King and I.*"

"Oh, really! I didn't know that."

"Don't make fun of me, Mr. Arness. I'm not that stupid." He quickly controlled himself, but he had let slip a bit of the violence he was determined to deny. When he spoke again, his manner was gentle. "Until I met Mr. Hammerstein, I always thought song writers were flibberty gibbets who tooled around with a bag of Mexican beans between their legs. But I watched Mr. Hammerstein carefully through that entire tryout, and at all times he and Mr. Richard Rodgers were the most hardheaded men in that theater. Still they're the Keats and Shelley of our day, you understand?"

"No, actually."

"I mean they've written about love like no one has in our time. But they're also great businessmen, in the altitudinous tax percentiles. And no one's tougher. Now you understand?"

"Getting warm."

"The danger with a guy like me is that a guy like you may get the idea you can take advantage."

"I'm following you now."

"Just because I sound a certain way, and tell you flat out I like you, it doesn't signify. That's why I studied Mr. Hammerstein. He loves his fellow man, right, but can you imagine him letting any person near his wife? Can you imagine what would have happened to any person who tried that?"

"In other words you're threatening me."

"I'm telling you about Mr. Hammerstein."

"I'm getting sleepy."

"I love Gwen, Mr. Arness. She's not going to be hurt any more. I elected myself a committee of one, and that is my total agenda."

"I got it."

"Good. I have my car here. Would it be all right if I drove you home?"

He wanted to make sure where I went. He dropped me off in front of the hotel and performed the ceremony of leave-taking with all courtesies intact. I could see it still confused him that he liked me.

Just before he drove off, I said, "Would it make you feel any better if I told you I was stone broke?"

"In a way it would," he answered.

He must sense, I thought as I walked to the elevator, that he's in way beyond his depth. Parochial-school pink was still on his cheek. Nothing he had ever experienced prepared him for someone like Gwen.

Ellen was out. There was a note from her on my bed. "Dear Daddy," it said, "are we losing touch? Love. Ellen. P.S. Be careful. I am." Across the bottom I wrote, "Tomorrow. Definite."

I went to the bathroom, scrubbed my teeth, swished some mouth wash. Then I went downstairs.

There was an opening-night party in the lobby.

In front of the hotel, on the far side of the street, Charles was sitting in his parked car. I saw him before he saw me, and went back into the hotel. I knew where the service door was. I had used it before.

When I rang Gwen's doorbell, the release buzzer sounded almost immediately. When she opened the apartment door, her absolute matter-of-factness could be taken two ways: that she'd been waiting for me, or that it was a matter of complete indifference to her whether I came or not.

"Were you expecting me?" I asked.

"No, why?" she said.

That "No, why?" was her standard comeback. It was the tactic: fall back, let the enemy give away his battle plan, then so direct your defenses.

"No, why what?"

"No, why do you ask?" she said.

"Because I want to know."

So far no one had given anything away.

"I did think you might try to see me again," she said.

"What the hell does that mean?"

"It means I made the mistake of letting you know that Charles wasn't going to be here tonight."

"And you didn't want to see me."

She turned off the overhead light.

"Of course not. What made you believe I might?"

I didn't think she was telling the truth.

"Does Charles always do everything you tell him?"

"Not always. Generally. Fix yourself a drink. You don't look too good." She walked into the baby's room.

I heard the sounds a child makes after he's been fed. I fixed

283

myself a drink, and tried to figure out how in the world I could weasel out of our heroine whose kid that was. I walked into the bedroom.

"Whose kid is that?" I asked.

"Mine."

"What does that mean?"

"It means I don't want anything from its father."

"Who is . . . ?"

"He doesn't have to acknowledge it; he doesn't have to support it. In fact, except biologically, he's not its father. And the biological part of it is a thing of the past."

I thought the child looked like me.

She turned the radio on to an all-night music station. Were we settling in for an evening?

There was one way to find out not only the answer to that question, but to everything else she was concealing.

I came up behind her where she was leaning over the child. She seemed a little smaller in the breasts. But her waist and hips were as before. Her buttocks, I remembered them. And her legs. I have a gangster's taste in legs. I like them perfect. Hers were. Each leg was made of many curves, yet each leg was perfectly straight.

Now I craved her. My hunger was not that of a young man. I hadn't been with a woman in a long time, yet I had never felt deprived, or starved. But now, my whole body wanted this girl.

Without turning she said, "How do you like him?"

She was changing his diaper. His little pink bird was now revealed. The tiny purse beneath was full of something, not very big yet, but present. The mouth of the urethra was a little darker than the rest. The color of the whole was a familiar one. That's my kid, I thought.

I was very close behind her. She straightened up and said, "Excuse me." Her voice seemed softer. She picked the baby off the bathinette top and moved with him to the bed. She laid him down, and he waved his arms and gurgled. She pointed to the boy as if to say, "There he is, make his acquaintance." She moved to the foot of the bed, and leaned over the metal end to watch our meeting.

"He has a noble brow," I said.

"Didn't have when he was born. First time I saw him, he looked

284

like one of those greeting card jokes, awfully pointy above the ears."

Just then the child got into one of those terrible tangles with his body and began to cry, more in anger than in pain. He glared at me, but I didn't know what the hell to do. She came over to straighten him out, and did it without a word of endearment. She treated him with respect, a woman to a man who was having his difficulties. She put him on his stomach, and he raised his head and glared around him like an angry turtle.

"He doesn't like it when he can't do something," she said. "He's very arrogant."

"Is that good for him, holding his head up like that, the neck is so small?"

"I figure anything he can do, he can do. In a little while, you'll see, he'll get tired, and then he'll lay his head down and fall asleep. Look. See? See there?"

There was something personal and separate about her way with the kid. "We don't need anything from any of you," she seemed to be saying.

I stood directly behind her, put my hand on the small of her back, and slowly moved it down and under . . .

"Don't do that," she said instantly, but didn't move.

I put my hands on the sides of her body where her waist came in.

Now, I thought, we're going to find out what's really what around here.

"You kept your figure," I said.

"You begin to lose it after the second one."

She didn't move. I slipped my hand under her back and held the weight of her abdomen in my palm. Something about the way it felt told me what she would not.

But I didn't come on fast.

The baby made a sound. He was looking around at us.

She moved away from my tightening grip. Her body swayed a little. She sat down on the bed close to the infant, caressed the top of his forehead where he was all frown lines from the strain of holding up that enormous dome. He was falling asleep.

"You'll see how arrogant he is when I feed him, later."

I heard that. I sat down on the bed next to her.

"Gwen?" I said.

"Don't say anything."

"Why not?"

"Because anything you say will be wrong. And you don't have to say a word."

She'd been longing for me, it was soon clear, ever since I'd called her last night. She'd known from the moment she'd heard my voice —as a woman does, no matter what she says—that all that would have to happen was for us to be in a room with a door that would close.

She was ready for me when I entered her.

Now we're going to get the true story, I thought.

I did it slowly. I didn't want to hurry a moment of it, the transformation or the sex. I realized that, as with me, there had been something in her, waiting under cover, something she finally couldn't reason away, that had kept her mine, at least in part, through the many months and was still strong enough to overcome the hostility she felt.

But she'd been right when she told me not to speak, because the act of sexual union was the only thing that could overcome the distrust and the distance between us.

Even now she was holding something back. She was determined not to give me all of it.

Usually if I hadn't been with anyone for that long, I'd have come early on. But I was doing something other than making love to her. I was dealing with her concealment.

I slid a hand under her and lifted her. She still hadn't spoken, but I felt her body arch towards me. Her eyes were softening, her complexion gentled. The harshness I'd noticed was going. And I saw the beginning of that look, the one I remembered.

In spite of herself, she was on her way.

But she still hadn't made a sound.

Suddenly I let up. I stopped.

This made her frantic. "Don't stop," she pleaded in spite of herself, "Don't stop!"

I fed it to her slower and slower and slower.

Then I heard her whisper, "Oh God, I'm in heaven."

But she wasn't talking to me. There was no antagonism in her voice now, or in her eyes, but she still wasn't looking at me.

You could see it coming though.

Suddenly she began to go after me. She had to have it. She seemed needy without end, and began to pull at me with that strength they get, that strength that always surprises me. She held me as she used to hold me, shutting out the rest of it, not hearing, not seeing, leaving that time and that place, reaching to where pain and pleasure meet, and finding relief in spending. I saw that I was the world for her, and that is what I wanted to be. Just that.

She was in heaven.

And I kept her there. I didn't stop.

Then she cried, "What are you trying to do to me?"

And later she said, "Don't make me love you."

Then she gave in to it. She laid her head back and closed her eyes. And when she opened them she was looking at me, and she was unmasked.

I thought, no matter what antagonisms and resentments she has towards me, and no matter what antagonisms and resentments I have towards her, we had no choice. We had to be together.

And maybe the resentments spice it.

Then I forgot everything, because it was all back now the way it had been. I don't remember what we did except couple like we were dying and she was holding me as if I was going to leave her again and this time forever. And as well as I can remember when I burst she was crying and saying something I couldn't understand. And afterwards I was still there, wanting her as much as I had before.

We stayed that way, fastened and still for a time. Finally we drew apart, just enough so she could turn and look at the child. We saw that he slept.

Now she was the aggressor. And for that time there, the best time of anyone's life, we forgot any and all differences. There was nothing in the world but us. It was perfect.

Afterwards, when we were spent, I pulled a pillow down and slipped it under her head and put my head on the other half. We lay face to face, I still inside her.

We had slept that way for an hour—no it was more—when the phone rang. We woke with no panic, because nothing really bad could happen now. She was still half asleep when she said, "Thank you, Charles," saying this gently and lovingly to Charles, who had called to remind her that it was six o'clock and that she should feed the baby. We turned and looked at the infant, who was still happily asleep. "He can wait awhile," she said.

This time we did it in simple mutuality, symphonized as the Greeks say.

What had happened to all the antagonisms?

All the new harshness I had noticed in her face, the lines of disappointment, had lifted and disappeared. She was fourteen years old. Her eyes were soft as silk, soft as all the loving things in nature, the things that get soft when their time comes.

I started to tell her how much I'd missed her, the events that led to my being in New York, everything. But she said, "Shshsh!" And I thought, later, I'll tell her later.

So we listened to morning come into the city. The new set of sounds, different cars at different speeds, different trucks on different missions. Finally we heard the first bus going up the avenue. We went to the window and looked out. The sky to the east was a grimy pink.

The baby stirred now. When he saw her, he waved his arms wildly. Then, as I watched, she cleaned him and rediapered him, and as she did, she sang that oldie:

> I'm a beanbag, a beanbag
> A flippety, floppity beanbag
> Flip, flop, a skip and a hop
> I'm happy as can be
> I worry in a hurry
> It doesn't take me long . . .

The baby rejoiced at being with her. And I didn't care whose he was . . .

Then she nursed him. He was very arrogant, as she'd said, took it so hard Gwen said, "Ouch, you son of a bitch!" He glared at me all the time he was pulling at it.

When he was through, I followed, tasted the milk; sweeter than cow's milk it was, a sort of vanilla flavor.

Then Gwen and I got into bed, at peace for the first time, not needing to do it again. We lay there, I on my back, her leg over mine, her hand across my chest, her head on my shoulder. And there, in that embrace, with the clock, I remember, at ten minutes before seven, she announced her engagement.

"I haven't told him yet," she said, "but I've made up my mind. I'm going to marry Charles."

I didn't say anything. We just lay there, our bodies pressed together, breathing in and out.

"He's the best person I've ever known. And the only one I've ever known who didn't love me if."

"You mean he doesn't care what you do?"

"He's for me no matter what I do."

"Yeah, I think maybe he is."

When I seemed to be agreeing, she tightened her hold on me. "I love him," she said, "in a way I never loved anybody before."

"What way is that?"

"He saved my life. He cares about that. You want to hear, I'll tell you."

"Yeah, I want to hear."

"When you left me and went back to California, I—"

"I didn't leave you; you left me."

"You want to hear this, or don't you?"

"O.K., I'll say nothing."

"I wanted to get back at you, and right away. I took a cab from the airport all the way out to Chet's place. For nearly three months I hardly left that house."

"Whose kid is this?"

"None of your business. Well, you could have driven a hearse through the hole you left in me, and Chet made it worse. One day I said what the hell, this is the same deal all over again, a one-way street. And I left him. But I'm not going to talk about that. Or how I lived after that. I got a place in the Bronx and lived off my savings, plus a fellow I used to be with in Washington got me some work I could do at home. And the time passed."

She looked at the infant. "Then came a day I remember. Andy was due in about a month, and the hospital said I had to get a deposit down right away. I didn't have it, so I had to ask myself who do I go to, which is to say, who's really my friend. That day I measured the people I know. Then I wrote Charles a letter and asked him to send me five hundred dollars. No explanation. I hardly knew the man. I'd met him three or four times at his brother's place, and all I was to him was a girl his brother had been through. But two days later there was this postal money order in the mail, no questions asked."

"Why the hell didn't you ask *me?*"

"I've just been telling you. So then I moved downtown again. I had Andy with me now, and I fell into luck, a good job, the same kind of work, but with decent people. And I felt—well, look at Andy."

I did.

"Can you see how he made me feel? Because there we were with nothing. I should have had somebody for him. So I had to figure that I hadn't found it yet, how to be. And now that I had a chance at a fresh start, I should, for instance, hold off till I found someone I really liked, not just rush here and there like before. I even wondered if I could do without the whole thing; I never had much luck with it, anyway. I did a lot of thinking, what I was and what I needed different from other people. I tried to find the right way for me, do you understand?"

I understood.

"Then one thing happened just naturally. I wasn't going out much —only if I thought maybe this one might turn out. But you know how I hate to stay alone at night. One night I called Charles up, just to pass the time. It ended with his coming over here. He stayed, but he didn't come on with me, which surprised me because you can see that he likes me and all, but he never made a move. If he had, I'd have had to tell him that I didn't like him that way."

"Does he know that?"

"Well, sure, because pretty soon it became a regular thing. Three or four times a week maybe, he stays here, sleeps right on that cot over there—"

"And he never—?"

"That's right. I said it to myself one day—I've got half of it, I said. I've got half of something that works . . ."

"He knew you were going out with other men?"

"Sure. I used to tell him who and when . . . and . . ."

"The details?"

"Everything, just like I might to a girl roommate, you understand?"

"What's the matter with him?"

"There's nothing the matter with him."

"What happens when you have a date?"

"He stays and minds the kid. He's crazy about Andy."

"When you stay out all night—?"

"He knows what to do, the feeding and all."

"And when you want to have someone here, what—"

"I tell Charles not to come by, like you heard, last night."

"And he?"

"He figures he'll end up with me. I can tell you what I figure. I need someone like Charles. Then I need someone else from time to time, and that's not the same. The thing that makes Charles so I would trust him with my life also makes him—well, truthfully, isn't there something about sex which makes the bastard the one who turns you on? Or novelty. A girl isn't supposed to think that way, but I'm talking about how I really am. I mean I'd like to find everything in one person, but is there any such thing? So I figured two people is what I needed, and I began to look around for the other half. Well, did you know that the hardest thing to find in this city is a good man who'll just love you up in a decent friendly way? I mean you have a date, and it looks kosher, starts o.k., maybe the first time fine; then come the tricks. Forget the liquor. Everybody's drunk at night. It's with the marijuana for a start, then pills of all sizes and colors, goof balls like candy, worse. After all that, you get down to sex, if anybody's still interested. But everybody's bored with that already, so then right away quick, it's two to one, then two to two, then all kinds of that's-the-way-I-get-my-kicks routines, and you're in a circus!"

She took a deep breath.

"For instance, there was this guy I'd begun to like, writes foreign news for one of those magazines, speaks the languages, been everywhere, real in, you know, interesting to talk to, you couldn't guess what he might do or say, which I liked, jumped here and there all over the world, part of his job, which was all right with me, too, because I had Charles. So I'd been with him two, three times, and I had begun to think maybe I'd found something. Then one night he shows up here for a date, and he has this Negro girl with him, and his idea is the three of us. But he wants to watch us first. Well, I like Negroes all right, but girls is still girls by me; I'm old-fashioned that way. It turns out she didn't know what she was getting into either. So when this character comes out of the head with Charles's bathrobe on, I sort of went wild, and we both jumped him, and there was a hell of a go; he had to fly down to Pig Island, Nassau, for two weeks of sun, to let the mess heal so he could go back to his office.

"Well, then the dam broke, and I was just going with the tide again, this way and that, didn't make any difference, and if it hadn't been for Andy I would have washed it up right there. In fact one night I could have done one of two things, cut my wrists or call up Charles.

"He came right over, and I don't know if he noticed that I was on the edge of Niagara; he sat there like always, jabbering away. Your silences used to terrify me. Charles is always saying something; you don't have to listen to all of it, but you know he's not having any bad thoughts, because whatever he's thinking, he's saying it.

"That was the night I knew I must not lose that man. So I took a big chance. I told him the truth. I told him my true feelings about him, that I loved him, truly loved him, I did and I do, but, I said, I didn't think I could ever get to like him that way. I told him the way I was, everything I'd done and been through, the complete box score. It means something when you can tell somebody that and leave nothing out. He just sat in his chair, doodling on one of those little graph pads he carried. I told him I didn't want to be that way, that I'd once done without it altogether, and maybe I could again. But I didn't know. I told him that I wasn't sure, for instance, if you came around, if I could stay away from you. Still you saw how he was last night, so sweet and good, admiring even, trying to be friends with you. And you with that snotty smile on your face.

"Anyway, that night, when I got all through, he showed me what he'd doodled on his pad. It said, 'Charles to Gwen. O.K. on all counts.' Something like that. He was in the Navy, went through a lot of battles in the wireless room, and I guess that's where he learned to live in danger and just keep sending out messages of comfort."

"Just for instance," I said, "are you going to tell him what happened here tonight?"

"As far as I'm concerned I would. But he might get upset at you, and you wouldn't want that."

"Gwen, I'm going to make a prediction. That man is going to put an axe through your head one day."

"You would think that."

"You think he can keep on taking it, the way you are?"

"He wants to marry me. It's his idea."

"The way you are?"

"He says I won't always be this way. And I don't want to be. I don't want to be at the mercy of that gun between your legs. It doesn't mean that much to me—any of it, from anybody."

"I don't believe it," I said.

Just then I heard the apartment door opened with a key from the outside, and there was the sound of some heavy soft footsteps. And then a sound of hesitation. Charles spoke softly, "Gwen?"

"I'm here, Charles," she said, "but Charles," and Charles, who had started in, stopped. "I'm with someone, and I wish you wouldn't come in now."

There was a long pause.

After some instants, Gwen said, "Charles?"

"All right," he said, "I'm going."

"Thank you, Charles."

"I'll call you later," he said.

"Please," she said.

The front door closed firmly. Then it was locked, from the outside.

A little later when I went to kiss her, she wouldn't let me. "Guess I'll get some sleep," she said.

I went into the other room and dressed.

16

I DIDN'T go to the hotel. I called
Ellen from the station and gave her the name of a doctor Gwen had
written down for me just before I left. I boarded the train for Stamford twenty minutes early, covered as much of my face as I could
with my coat lapels, and fell asleep.

I thought the conductor was too rough when he woke me for
my ticket. A man is not a public nuisance simply because he protests
rudeness. Some of those passengers looked at me strangely all the
way to Stamford. Their staring kept me awake. And, looking back,
it was the beginning of the feeling which was to obsess me that
whole week, the feeling that people were closing in on me.

For instance, I was walking from the station to the hospital when
a Rolls-Royce pulled up to the curb just ahead of me. Danny
O'Connor, known as Danny the Donkey, jumped out, blocked my
path, and waved me into Mr. Finnegan's car like he was Military
Police.

I had not sent my telegram the night before, so Mr. Finnegan
was technically still my boss. He was sitting in the back of the
Rolls, dictating to Kurtz, but I noticed his eyes on me. I didn't know
if I wanted to get into the car with him. I merely hesitated. That's
not insane, is it? Or "very eccentric" behavior, as he was to say
later?

The Donkey acted as if I had no choice. There was something of
the hoodlum about Danny O'Connor, and everybody at Williams
and MacElroy felt it.

"What do you want?" I said.

"Get in the car."

"What is this, an arrest?"

The Donkey laughed. "Did you hear that?" he called back towards Mr. Finnegan. "Are you nuts?" he said to me. *"Pischer."*

So it *had* gotten around. There must have been a reporter in night court. Of course.

"Eddie!" Mr. Finnegan was leaning out of the car. "Don't mind that idiot. Get in."

"I'm going to the hospital," I said.

"So am I. Get in."

"Be with you in a minute," said Mr. Finnegan, as I sat down next to him. "Want to get these thoughts down before I forget them."

Danny the Donkey closed the door behind me and got in next to the chauffeur. We were off.

I said hello to Mr. Finnegan's secretary, the woman known as Kurtz. She smiled at me, then recomposed her face.

Mr. Finnegan held my forearm. He seemed friendly, and put one of his claro cigars into my breast pocket. "Continuing, Kurtz," he said.

He was preparing a confidential report, to be spoken by him to a group of cigarette manufacturers who had paid him the supreme tribute of asking for his advice on an industry-wide basis. He had, as everyone in the trade soon enough knew, agreed to give them one day of his time without fee if they would make a contribution of five thousand dollars to his wife's favorite charity. The cigarette people were obviously in serious trouble. They had agreed.

Mr. Finnegan was dictating both to machine and to Kurtz. He double-checked everything, mechanical as well as human.

He dictated with the vigor of a political orator, holding my forearm throughout. Occasionally he would make emphatic gestures with his free fist.

"So, gentlemen," he dictated, "I cannot help you. The facts I have just presented are incontrovertible. They show a demonstrable tie-up between our products and the rising rate of lung cancer. We are in trouble. What do we do?"

He looked at me as if I might have the answer.

Then, answering himself, "The first thing is to keep the lights in our laboratories burning night and day until we produce a safe cigarette which is nevertheless a cigarette. In time we shall do this. Never, never doubt that.

"Kurtz," he said to her, "there may be applause there, so put in pause marks for me." He continued, "But obviously we cannot stop marketing our product while our scientists work. Can we?" He turned to me.

"No," I said.

"My old and very good friend, Jack Dempsey, has a saying which he has proved time and again in the ring. The best defense is a good offense. Jack, I might add, is himself unmarked. Comparatively speaking, of course!" Mr. Finnegan pressed down the tip of his nose, making quite a funny face. I laughed.

"Kurtz," he said, "there may be laughter at that point. Pause marks. Continuing: What am I proposing? Let us launch an offensive in our defense. Let us shift the burden of the blame. Pause marks there, Kurtz, not for applause, but just so that will really sink in."

He drew a good breath. "Now get this, Eddie," he said to me. "I now propose, gentlemen, that as a public service, the cigarette industry set up a committee of great scientists. Let this panel be publicly chosen, set up and paid for by our industry, still responsible only to the people of these United States. This committee of great scientists will come up with a report. And this report . . . listening, Eddie?"

"No," I said.

"I wish you would. This is the meat of it."

"Continue."

"This report will say simply that the cause of lung cancer is the industrial waste that chokes the air over our great industrial and urban complexes, the air that we all live in and breathe. Should be applause there, Kurtz, don't you think?"

"Yes, Mr. Finnegan."

"So, pause marks. What's the matter, Eddie?"

"How do you know the scientists will turn in that report?"

"I've talked to some of them. Continuing, Kurtz. I am saying, let us involve in our common problem our brothers in the automobile industry. Pause marks. Let us share the responsibility for this situation with the manufacturers of synthetic chemicals. Pause marks. Our brother industrialists have been getting away with murder. Pause marks."

I applauded.

Mr. Finnegan nodded. "Hell-for-leather," he boasted. "Continuing, Kurtz. It is not cigarette smoke, my friends, that covers the great city of Los Angeles with its lethal blanket. Pause marks."

I applauded with vigor.

"It is not cigarette smoke that sickens the membranes of our nasal passages when we drive over the Jersey meadows."

"Pause marks," I said.

"Right," he said. "What do you think of it, Eddie?"

"Don't ask me," I said, "because I'll tell you."

This threw Finnegan. His ego, nurtured on pause marks, suddenly collapsed. "I see what you mean," he said, soberly. "Too flamboyant."

I hadn't said that.

"You may be right," he said. He sat there very still. Nobody said a word. Mr. Finnegan has the kind of concentration that enforces itself on other people. Moments passed. You could actually hear the electric clock in his Rolls.

It was then that I suddenly realized Mr. Finnegan was going to the hospital to which I was going. Could it be that he was going there to see my father? Mr. Finnegan was a public man with a public code, and part of that code was not to abandon friends in difficulty. Had he come all the way to Stamford, accompanied by his secretary, his dictating machine, and his bodyguard, clown, or whatever, keeping a telephone link to his office open for the entire fifty-minute ride, all because he wished to assure me that despite anything and everything that had happened, Williams and MacElroy was on my side?

He was not a small man, whatever else. He was capable of great ruthlessness, but also of impulsive generosity. I admired that, always had. And he had from the beginning sensed my admiration and felt reciprocal affection for me. That's really the reason why he was here now, to help a friend.

I used to say of him that he alone of any man I'd met lived his life. It didn't live him. So I had given him and his ways detailed study. When I came back from the war in '45, I was determined to arrange the rest of my life so I'd get the most out of it. I have to catch up, I used to say; I've lost four and a half years. I couldn't see why I couldn't arrange my life in my own behalf as efficiently as Mr. Finnegan had arranged his on his behalf. He ordered every minute, my study revealed, so as to give himself the most of what he wanted and the least of what was irrelevant to him.

I don't know what his relations with his wife were. He was so friendly with her that I imagine little if anything went on of a physical nature. The only place you could go to find out what went on between them was to the pages of *Harper's Bazaar*. From time to time their private happiness was spread in this magazine, most recently with her prize-winning Sealyham, another time in their new bubble-top swimming pool, snow outside clearly visible. They were always photographed in such a way as to dramatize the caption which heralded their union as one of the most successful marriages in our civilization. And they looked happy, even to the cynical eye. There was obviously a relationship of acceptance here; they had accepted what had come to be their arrangement.

Whatever they did or did not do at night, she always ended up sleeping in one wing of the house with her prize-winning dogs.

Mr. Finnegan, on the other hand, slept alone in his unheated tower, with all the windows open wide, summer and winter. In effect, he slept out-of-doors. That's all he did in this tower, sleep. There was a photograph of it in *House Beautiful*. On the facing page there was a photo of his almost identical set-up in the West Hollywood hills. The caption said Mr. Finnegan was thus able to enjoy his preferred sleeping arrangement whether he was on a trip to his west coast offices or working out of corporate headquarters in New York. I suppose more of us would sleep Mr. Finnegan's way if we could afford it.

Each morning at seven Mr. Finnegan's manservant went in to wake him. But at that time in the morning Mr. Finnegan had already been awake half an hour. That half-hour, he had publicly said, was when he did his creative thinking, lying there under his Bavarian quilts, with his room so cold in winter that his breath plumed, and cool enough in summer for him to sleep comfortably through any crisis of heat.

By the time his man came in with the vicuña wrap, Finnegan had already done his work for the day. That was his boast! It was in that first half-hour that he earned his pay and pre-eminence. The rest of the day was easy.

Mr. Finnegan was born in Japan, spent his first years there, and so had a great nostalgia for that country's customs. Each morning

298

he went from his cold tower room into an elevator which took him to the cellar, where he found his Japanese-style bath full of steaming fragrant water. Waiting for him there was a glass of lemon juice. It was here that Mr. Finnegan listened to the news, and was given a sheet on which Kurtz had typed the headlines in his world of finance and industry. He scanned these as he lay in the scalding water. Five minutes of this, and he was bundled into an orange (orange for Buddha) terry-cloth robe and taken to a little room looking out on a Japanese garden. It was there that he had his breakfast: two soft-boiled eggs, rye toast, unbuttered, and hot green tea imported from Japan.

After breakfast, Finnegan dressed in sports clothes for his drive to the office. He did not shave. The first thing he did when he got to his office was to take off all his sports clothes and enjoy a massage and a shave. It was then, too, that the roots of his hair were touched up. After these attentions, he dressed in a business suit which was uniform with him, dark blue double-breasted, over a white shirt with semi-stiff collar and French cuffs, initialed links, and a club-stripe tie in blue and black. He bought all these items in lots, so that there was always an identical fresh suit, shirt, and tie ready for him in his office dressing room. Finnegan-at-work never varied in his appearance. No one could ever read his disposition from what he wore.

But I'm getting ahead of myself. At seven his secretary, Kurtz, and the man he called the Donkey arrived at Mt. Kisco in Finnegan's Rolls. This car, chauffeur-driven and equipped with telephone and dictaphone, picked Kurtz and O'Connor up every morning at six in front of the New York office. They drove out each morning to drive in with Mr. Finnegan. On the way in, he dictated his program for the day, the plans he had dreamed up in the tower bed and firmed up in the Japanese tub. He concentrated completely till he reached his office, and no one was expected to break silence unless he did. Danny the Donkey sat in front alongside the chauffeur and didn't say a word. No one ever knew why Mr. Finnegan insisted on having the Donkey with him every morning, but he was always there, his wry Irish face looking straight ahead, a sort of front-seat gargoyle. They had been schoolmates in Fall River, Mass., and the Donkey, at 59, still had the acne of their high school years. His main function was that of a discreet social secretary—or, to be plainer about it, pimp. Another of his functions was to make sure that Finnegan's lunch was on time and according to Mr. Finnegan's requirements. These two functions the Donkey performed perfectly. Most leaders of industry with Finnegan's problem of a split operation would have had a west coast secretary and an east coast secretary. But Finnegan had perfection in Kurtz and the Donkey, so he took them everywhere he went.

The first order of work each morning was to confer one at a time with his executives, assigning them to what needed execution. This usually took till twelve-thirty, when the Donkey entered, followed by a waiter with Mr. Finnegan's lunch.

While the morning had been given to creative programing, the afternoon was concerned with organizational matters. Finnegan himself rarely saw a client. He was fond of saying that he didn't undercut his account executives. By this he meant simply that no one could look good to a client after they had once had contact with Mr. Finnegan himself. He was right. Besides, the way he managed things, there was always an unplayed trump card. If there were some persisting difficulties, the client could comfort himself with, "If this gets any worse, Mr. Finnegan will move in." And Finnegan himself would say in the direct emergencies, "Don't worry; if this keeps up, I'll step in myself."

Finnegan had another practice which made him a legend. He rarely answered any mail. He'd take a quick look at it in the morning when he came in, but he would always assign someone to answer every piece except the most personal. People who wrote Finnegan would get letters from one of his executives or from Kurtz or one of her underlings, all depending on the correspondent's class. These replies would read: "Mr. Finnegan has asked me to tell you, etc." There were few industries whose presidents could boast of a letter from him, so that when Finnegan did answer a letter himself it meant something. He did answer the very personal letters even if they were trivial, especially those from classmates at Fall River High School or from his daughters. Never, under any conditions, did he or anyone on his staff answer a letter from a young female acquaintance.

At five came Finnegan's first period of relaxation. This designation, however, was deceptive. It was really an hour, five to six, for conducting top-level business under the guise of relaxation. For instance, he might play gin rummy with the head of a company whose account he was soliciting. Or he might go shopping for paintings or *objets d'art* and invite the advertising head of a company to go along. In the course of the visit to Rosenberg's or Parke-Bernet, he'd buy some trinket or perhaps a small painting for his guest and at the same time say a few firm words about the difficulties they were experiencing and what, in his opinion, was the solution. Under those circumstances, few could deny him.

At six the second period of relaxation would ensue, either in company with the same man or alone. It was the hour to see what goodies the Donkey had for him that day. Finnegan maintained a small harem, and usually the Donkey would call upon one of his regulars. Mr. Finnegan, of course, had no time for courtship. His present harem was made up of three delightful girls, one a Malaysian, one a model from the Bible belt of Tennessee who still believed, and the third just a jolly old pro. He maintained these girls, paying their rent and their keep. All he ever demanded was that they be always available to him. "And to his close friends," the Donkey sometimes added.

Finnegan kept his feelings uninvolved. These relationships were conducted essentially as part of his health program, not as anything to do with sentiment or affection. Pleasure, yes. But he also liked venison.

Sometime around seven (while he ate a carefully chosen supper), Finnegan called his wife and had a cozy talk with her. He'd inquire if everything was all right at home. It always was. He saw to that. Occasionally, at this time, there would be a call from one of his three daughters. They were married, but they often called him at this appointed time for advice, counsel, and words of love. They were, all three, what Finnegan called "in good shape." The husband of one worked for Williams and MacElroy; the husband of the second was in the regular army and worked under a general, a close friend of Finnegan's with whom he went to Alaska every year to kill a kodiak bear. And the husband of the third didn't really work at all. He was a "sportsman" who sailed out of Bimini and docked in a marina that Finnegan owned. Finnegan was thus able to keep an eye on all three of these carefully chosen husbands. If they strayed, he'd make damned sure the reins were pulled up with a jerk. He didn't approve of "cheating" in his sons-in-law. They had, all three, at one time or another felt the bit.

The only trouble spot in an otherwise idyllic prospect was Finnegan's son. He was a falling-down drunk, determined, so it would appear, to do everything possible to blemish his father's public image. In this perfectly arranged paradise, he was the single discordant note. At one point Finnegan had disowned him, settling on him a sum of money which was to be the last ever. The boy used the money to have an exposé of his father privately printed, one which no reputable publishing house would put out for fear of a lawsuit, but which the son gave away free to anyone and everyone who might find some pleasure in its contents.

So except for Sean (he had so named his son), Finnegan was in perfect control of every aspect of his life. Unlike his competitors and rivals, he found himself in the evening not tuckered out, but revived. For after his sojourn in the saddle and his half-hour of supper, served couchant, he would fall into a natural sleep. His female companion had been given to clearly understand that she was positively not to fall off herself, only to wait in position until he was asleep, and then get out quickly and quietly. She must under no circumstances be there when he woke. Mr. Finnegan woke to a clean slate. And to face Dr. Kruskal. Dr. Kruskal was a shot doctor, and he came to see Mr. Finnegan five evenings a week. On three of these visits he would give Finnegan shots of B_{16} and/or whatever sex hormones were at that moment in favor. Other days he would come in just to see if the boss was all right. On these occasions he might massage his prostate, or look down his throat, or weigh him, or change the bulb in the heat lamp, or something else calculated to make Finnegan feel well-cared-for.

After that there was the needle shower. And then back into the blue suit, a fresh one. People seeing Finnegan dressed the same way late at night as he was early in the morning marveled. How did he work so hard for so many hours and stay so fresh?

Finnegan planned his big client confrontations and his program presentations for the evening. Fresh from his nap and shower, he faced adversaries whose wits had been dulled by long, unrelieved business days. At those meetings, he would have each person present his side of the problem, Finnegan sitting pressed, coiffed, and perfect—and listening with a patience that was legendary (the patience itself a weapon). Then he'd make a decision, and that decision was final. By the time it had gotten to be eleven-fifteen and the people present had sat through so many divergent and bitterly stated points of view, they were longing for someone to make order of the mess. They were relieved when Mr. Finnegan did. They could still catch the last train to Greenwich or Montclair. Mr. Finnegan took that into account, too. He knew when the last trains left.

After which he was driven to his home in Mount Kisco. By that time he was ready for sleep. But he always went into his wife's room to give her a good-night kiss. He was, after all, a good Catholic and a good husband. (Sundays, he always said, belong to my wife. She also played golf, but not in the same foursome. However, they did have the same charities, and they did attend mass together.) What went on in those midnight meetings with his wife no one except Mr. and Mrs. Finnegan knew. Come dawn, he was always asleep in his unheated tower.

Had he broken this perfect routine, I asked myself, to come to the hospital to be at my side?

"Do you have someone at the hospital?" I asked.

"Shshsh!" said Danny the Donkey.

"Oh, that's all right, Danny," said Mr. Finnegan. He turned to me. "Maybe you're right. About the speech. That's the thing, simplicity, the hardest thing to come by. Oh me, oh my. Stop the car. Let's walk a bit, Eddie. No, I came here to see you."

The car stopped. Danny opened the door.

"Come on, boy, stretch your legs, do you good. Are you putting on weight?"

We walked along, the Rolls following forty, fifty feet behind. Mr. Finnegan did the talking.

"First of all, I want to tell you that I'm with you, kid, and that means the company is with you for the duration. I also want to tell you that you're in real trouble, serious enough for me to have taken the liberty, yesterday, of calling your wife . . ."

He hesitated for a split second and looked back over his shoulder reflexively. He had forgotten Florence's name and was looking towards Kurtz, who ordinarily would have gotten the name to him somehow. But the Rolls was too far behind for Finnegan to get any help from her.

"What did you say to *Florence?*" I said, stressing her name.

He picked it right up. "I told Florence that I thought it might be very helpful if she came East."

"And has she?"

"I imagine so. I asked her to come right away. Do you mind?"

Normally, I would have said, "Why, of course not," or something equally graceful and false. But now I said, "Why don't you mind your own bleeding business!"

Mr. Finnegan had absolutely no experience in dealing with remarks of that kind. We walked along in silence for a minute.

"I want to repeat," Mr. Finnegan finally said, "and I say this as calmly as the circumstances permit. You are in genuine trouble. We at Williams and MacElroy are 100% behind you, but . . . well . . . are you aware of what you did?"

"Was it in the papers?"

"One of those newspaper bastards was in night court, yes, questioning the arresting officer and so on. In fact, I had to spend the better part of last evening keeping it out of the papers. But there isn't a man living who could keep it out of the mouths of the petty men and women who unfortunately make up the largest part of the professionals in our business. You committed the urinal joke of the year."

I had to smile.

"What amuses you?" he asked.

"I don't know," I said, "it's just funny."

"Zephyr doesn't think so. And there are no companies of any size who haven't heard about it or who wouldn't soon enough hear about it from our competitors if I tried to assign you to their accounts."

"I see," I said.

"I hope you do. I hope you see how serious it is."

"Final, I'd say!"

"Well, frankly, if you were with any other company . . . but Williams and MacElroy has always operated on the human side. We're people-oriented. I hear your father is nearing his end."

"Who told you?"

"Florence."

"He's sick, but not near his end."

"Is that part of the reason for all this extremely erratic behavior?"

I didn't say anything.

"Don't you think you're behaving erratically?"

"I'm enjoying the hell out of it," I said.

He looked at me, and I looked at him, and then he said, "Let's get into the car." He turned and gave a signal that I couldn't see, but which registered smashingly with his chauffeur. The car slammed up with a Bogart lurch.

"Say something funny," said Mr. Finnegan to the Donkey, as he got into the Rolls.

Florence was waiting for us at the hospital. She rushed past me and into Mr. Finnegan's arms. Florence has always had the greatest respect for authority. My mother was standing close behind them all, and I went up to her. She didn't know who Mr. Finnegan was, so didn't know enough to be impressed. "They're making a lot of fuss about me now," she said.

"And about time too!" Gloria, my brother Michael's wife, was on us.

"I'm all right," said my mother.

"And you're going to stay that way, dear," Gloria said.

I still didn't know what they were talking about, and I didn't find out then because Florence had come up.

"What did you tell him to come here for?" I asked, indicating Mr. Finnegan, who was talking to Michael and a man who looked like a very expensive doctor.

"I didn't tell him anything, darling. *He* called *me*. And he's here because he's your friend." Then she kissed me on the cheek. "And, monster, you need your friends now, you really do." She did have a soft, beautiful voice.

I felt very cornered. "I'm all right," I said.

"You don't look it," said Florence. "You look like hell. Where did you leave your necktie?"

"You don't look well, Eee," said my mother.

"You look like you've been up all night," said Gloria.

"You hit it on the damned head," I said.

Just then Michael and Mr. Finnegan walked up, and with them was this other man.

"This is my personal doctor, Eddie; meet Dr. Clifford Taylor," said Mr. Finnegan. "This is the patient's eldest son, Cliff, our Mr. Edward Anderson."

Dr. Taylor offered his hand.

"I asked Dr. Taylor," Mr. Finnegan said to me, "if he'd be generous enough to lose just a little more sleep and get over here to take a look at your father."

Dr. Taylor said, "I suggest, sir, that we all sit down together."

He looked in the direction of the visitors' lounge. There were four people there, sitting separately, each waiting, as I imagined, for bad news. Clearly there wasn't room there for all of us to sit and hear Dr. Taylor's verdict. Dr. Taylor said, "Wait here a minute, all of you," and hurried off.

I went down the hall to my father's room and looked in. He was sitting up in bed, and the truth was he didn't look well. He seemed awfully relieved to see me.

The nurse was there, the stern one. She saw me and snapped, "Not now, please!"

"Shut up, goddam fool!" said my father. "Come here, you boy."

"I am not responsible," said the nurse to me and left the room.

"Cunt!" said my father, then some choice Turkish.

From outside we heard the nurse saying, "I am not responsible," and more which we did not hear because I closed the door and put a chair under its handle. Then I turned to the old man.

"Who's doctor big shot?" my father asked.

"Mr. Finnegan's doctor, my boss, you know. He's here, too."

"I must be dying sure, so many big men come."

"How do you feel?" I asked.

"I have to get out of here, Evangeleh," he said. "Not much time left."

Suddenly I felt I should take him out of there, even though it made no medical sense of any kind. For the good of his soul. Just for that.

"What's the nurse so excited about?" I asked.

"I did something," he said.

Outside someone knocked pleasantly on the door. I knew it was Florence even before I heard her "Evans?"

"What did you do?" I asked my father.

"I shit the bed," he said.

"Darling," said Florence outside the door, still pleasantly.

"That's Florence," said my father. He remembered her name for a change. "I thought she was California."

"She was," I said. "Mr. Finnegan, my boss, sent for her."

"They think I'm dying, huh?"

"Ev," said Florence, "come on now, this isn't fun any more. Or a bit nice." There was a hairline crack in her composure.

"Evangeleh," whispered my father.

"Yes, Pop."

"Get me out of here. Look, I have money for the taxi." He began to reach under the mattress for his little black wallet.

"I know you have, Pop."

"Get taxi. Wait till they all go, get taxi, get me out."

"Now Evans," said Florence from the doorway, "Dr. Taylor is waiting for us. It's just not polite."

"Got to be polite, Pop," I said to the old man.

He looked at me reproachfully. "Evangeleh," he said, "don't leave me."

"I'll be back, Pop, I promise, soon as I hear what the doctor says."

"I did it on purpose. Ask Dr. Levine."

"Did what on purpose?"

"Shit the bed."

"Why?"

"I want them to put me out. I hear them carry those dead customers out last night again. They think I don't know what's going on here. And that big shot, he's not a doctor. That man is undertaker. Ask Dr. Levine!"

"I'll be back, Pop." I went to the door.

Who's Dr. Levine, I wondered.

Florence was really furious, but smiled at me patiently and said sweetly, "Dr. Taylor has arranged a private consultation room for all of us. Come on, now, please."

In the private consultation room they were all waiting, including the four boys, who had shown up and were presently sitting quietly in a corner and smiling. Gloria was speaking and with some heat.

"I want you all to give some thought to her," she said with all the vehemence of the self-righteous, pointing at my mother. "She's the one to worry about now. Am I right, Florence?"

"Yes, dear," said Florence, just as patient with her as she was with me, just as controlled, "we're going to talk about that now."

Then Florence and I sat down.

"I'll be very brief," said Dr. Taylor, though no one had asked him to be brief. "Your father is suffering from a disease endemic to everyone who is born on this earth, and that is old age."

"What exactly's the matter with him?" I said.

"He's well advanced in arteriosclerosis," said Dr. Taylor.

"He's nuts," murmured one of the boys.

"Will you shut up?" said Gloria.

Dr. Taylor continued as if he had merely paused on his own for a breath. But I did catch him quickly looking at his wrist watch, something all doctors learn to do without anyone noticing.

But Mr. Finnegan noticed, too, and this caused him to say with considerable calm, "I think everybody here ought to listen to what Dr. Taylor has to say without interrupting. He did us all a great favor to come here."

"I was able to arrange my time," said Dr. Taylor modestly.

"It was very nice of you indeed," said Florence.

"I'm aware," said Dr. Taylor, "that the members of the family will have to presently discuss his disposition. But perhaps you can excuse me from that. I happen to agree with . . ." he nodded at Gloria, "that the main object for concern now is the man's wife. This lady here. What happened last night, for instance, is going to happen again, and soon. Increasingly, he won't be able to control his essential bodily functions."

"He did it on purpose," I said.

Everyone burst out laughing.

"He did!" I persisted, desperately. "He goddam well did." I didn't know what the hell I was getting so bowed up about.

"Now, Evans," said Florence, and gave her pleasant little laugh to cover the awkwardness.

"Well, he did!" I said once more.

Mr. Finnegan gave me a sharp look. He was making, I could see, an appraisal that had to do with my future usefulness to "our" company.

Dr. Taylor stood up. I guess he had had it. Florence said, "Now Dr. Taylor, everyone here wants you to tell us everything you know. Please."

"No one," said Dr. Taylor, buttoning his coat, "knows too much about circulatory failures except that they are progressive, and often speedily progressive. One function after another stops. Well, can I be frank . . . ?"

"Oh, please do," said Florence and Gloria in the very same instant, and they both leaned forward to catch what was coming.

Dr. Taylor smiled. His little pantomimed threat of leaving had brought order to the gathering. He undid one button. "I want you all to know exactly—" He stopped. "Is this gentleman one of us?"

We all turned and looked at old Joe Arness standing in the doorway, the picture of terminal corruption, wearing his black box coat and striped trousers, and holding his battered Tammany derby. His front was dusted with cigarette droppings and stained with the sauces of the Automat on 57th Street, where he ate most of his meals, at least those he had to pay for.

"This," said Gloria, "is the patient's older brother, Joe Arness." Gloria had a spectacular detestation of old Joe.

"How are you, sir," said Dr. Taylor, once again buttoning his coat. "I was just going."

Joe Arness bowed low. "Good morning, all!" he said. "Is he dead?" Then he laughed. His teeth were yellowing chaos. Joe had long ago stopped going to the dentist. His reward was a golden smile. "I know," he said, "he be all right with all of you psychologists and geniuses here." He bowed low again.

"Shut up," said Gloria, then, "Dr. Taylor, please."

"All I was going to add," said Dr. Taylor, "was in reference to the little event of last night." He laughed. "They used to call it second childhood. The old gentleman will insist, as most do, that he knew what he was doing, did it on purpose, and so on. It's a sort of desperate effort to recall the act, rather gallant actually. They want to reassure themselves that they are still in control of their faculties. My friends, it's going to happen to all of us if we are lucky enough to live as long as this man has lived. For death, my friends, there is no specific."

I looked at my mother.

Dr. Taylor pressed on. "He will continue to have hallucinations. He will go back and forth in time. He will not know where he is, so he cannot be responsible for what he does. The nurses told me for instance, Mrs. . . ." he nodded at my mother, "that he has been attacking you in a rather personal way. You must not, madam, be distressed. Your husband is no longer himself. He is another man. For example, has he accused you of indiscretions and infidelities?"

My mother didn't answer.

"Well, what's the big secret? Yes! Yes, Doctor!" said Gloria.

"Don't let those things disturb you. But I do urge you now to be selfish. Look out for yourself. You will not—I say this without fear of challenge—you will not be able to take care of him yourself. He should be put into some kind of nursing home. They will look after him in ways you no longer should have to. Get him into a nice homey institution as quickly as possible. You can then visit him as often as you care to without the burden of watching from hour to hour the terrible disintegration that is coming. Have I spoken too sharply?"

"Not at all," said Gloria. "You have said the truth."

"I hope you will take it in the spirit in which it was intended. Mrs. . . ." he nodded at my mother, "save yourself."

I looked at my mother. She had been married to my father for forty-seven years. That was a tall order Dr. Taylor was asking for. I went and sat next to her.

Dr. Taylor swept to the door. Finnegan met him there and shook his hand as if he were congratulating an actor of great reputation who had just made an exit for which he was famous. Now to cap it, Dr. Taylor waved to us all, and departed with the greatest possible good cheer.

Old Joe Arness came over to where I was sitting with my mother, leaned over and whispered in my ear, "What's so new? Sam was always that way!"

He put his arm through mine with the grace of a *boulevardier,* and we walked together to room 612.

"What's the verdict?" asked Pop. Then he saw his brother and said, "What the hell you want? If it's money, go away."

"I'm going," said Joe. "I just want to take one more look at you before you cash your chips!"

"That's going to be after you!"

They began to talk in Greek, very fast. I understood only part, though I did catch "shit my rags," "rags" being colloquial Greek for underdrawers. They were both laughing and cutting up in an obscene way when the strict nurse came in, this time with an orderly, who told us to get out and began unceremoniously to prepare my father for his bed bath.

Outside, Finnegan was looking for me. As soon as I came out of the room, he took my arm and said, "Walk me to my car," and pushing me by the elbow, he started out. As we passed the women, Florence said, "Thanks, Mr. F., many thanks."

And we went out, Finnegan propelling me, the Donkey following.

"Thank you for bringing Dr. Taylor here," I said. "It was nice of you."

"Nothing," he said. "You need help, and if I can provide it—" he sighted his Rolls and headed for it as fast as he could get me to walk, "besides, it's not your father I'm worried about. There isn't much any one of us can do for him. I'm worried about you."

"That's what I want to talk to you about," I said. "I think I'm at the end of the road."

"Nonsense! You've got thirty years yet, thirty productive years!"

"I don't mean that road. I believe my usefulness to your company is over. And I'd like to . . ."

"You're just going through a phase," he said. "I've seen it, even went through it myself, although with me it was just a matter of a few days. Some people call it the male menopause, hot flashes, and all the rest of it; we have them, just like the girls—behave eccentrically, doubt everything, not able to get it up, all soft-on and self-doubt— I know all about it. Besides, you don't live right; you don't have any kind of program of health for yourself; you don't respect your body. I've been in your insanely overheated house; how can you sleep? And what exercise do you ever get? No wonder you can't get it up."

"I want to say," I replied, "that I can get it up. That is not where my trouble is."

"That's where it first shows," he said. "I know."

"I don't have that trouble," I insisted.

"Well, wait," he said ominously, "the day will come. I've seen it with the champions of the ring."

"It's not my body," I said. "I just can't take myself or the world any more."

"Oh that," he said.

"It all seems phony to me."

"What does?"

"Our profession, for one thing."

"Well, sure it's phony, so what?"

"Well, I can't take it any more."

"You're taking it every single day of your life. You're surrounded with it."

"Everyone seems like a liar to me, you do and I do and, everybody."

"Well, of course. How long do you think this world of ours would last if anyone told the truth? We live by the grace of an unspoken agreement not to speak the truth to each other. If anyone in business spoke the truth, who'd buy goods, for one thing? It's our lies—well-intentioned always, that keep this world of ours together. You don't tell me what you really think of me, and I don't tell you what I really think of you."

"But after you do that for a certain number of years, you begin not to have an opinion of your own."

"That's what makes life possible, isn't it? You think your wife tells you what she really thinks of you?"

"I suppose not."

"You're goddam right, not."

"I want to be serious with you for a minute."

"Don't. You're playing with something very dangerous. When this kind of thinking starts, I have noticed, someone usually pays for it with his life."

The Donkey, who had come close enough to listen, burst out laughing.

"Please, can I be serious, just for a . . ."

"Don't be. That's why I have the Donkey with me at all times. He keeps things in proportion."

"What do you mean?" I said.

"Did you ever look at him closely?"

I did then.

Danny had two faces. One half was glinting with hostility, the other with all the humor of the donkey, of the grave, the humor of the man who has learned to endure a society where he is a joke—despised, in fact, but despised by people who are no better than he is himself.

"Do you think," said Finnegan, "that Danny ever tells me what he thinks of me? Danny," he said, "what do you think of me?"

"If I told you," said Donkey, "you'd fire me."

"Right," said Finnegan. "You know," he continued, "you wouldn't believe it to look at that mass of cynicism, but Danny was an idealist in his youth. He was the real thing. An officer of the National Textile Workers Union, Fall River, Massachusetts, local—a believer! But today, what is there to believe in? I ask you. What do you believe in? Solitude and pleasure. They are real. Yes! But anything else? You're telling me about our business! Where would advertising be if we told the truth? Ogilvy, for instance, makes a big deal out of telling facts. But do you really think the loudest sound in my Rolls-Royce is the sound of the electric clock?"

"The loudest sound in your Rolls," said Danny the Donkey, "is the sound of your voice dictating to that bitch Kurtz." And he burst out laughing. But Finnegan did not. "Watch out," he said to Danny, "one day you'll go too far." The Donkey was silent.

Finnegan took me aside. "Just give it a while," he said, "I can't use you now anyway. I can't put you on any account. You see that. I'm going to have to tell people that you've gone away for a long rest, so you might as well go away for a long rest. I can't pay your full salary, but I'm going to keep you on half."

"I don't want it," I said.

Finnegan turned to the Donkey. "Did you hear what he said, Danny? He doesn't want it."

"You better put him somewhere where they have bars in the windows."

They both laughed.

We had reached the car.

The Donkey opened the rear door.

Finnegan took me aside for one last bit. "I understand," he said, "that you still see Gwen Hunt."

"No, I don't."

"I'm sorry you lied to me. You were with her last night."

"How do you know?"

"I pay a large staff to keep me informed on the people who are important to me, and all I can say, kiddo, is beware. I had to get rid of her. I think what's wrong with you right now is that dame. She's got you so you don't know what's important and what's not. She's a destructive person. She doesn't respect the achievements of this civilization or the law of God."

"Neither do I."

For the only time I've ever witnessed, Mr. Finnegan's famous patience thinned.

"I meant to ask Florence," he snapped, "for the doctor's final report on you. She said she'd show it to me."

"What did you want to know?"

"What were his conclusions with respect to your crash? As your friend, I'd like to know. Was there any . . . ?"

"Brain damage?"

"Yes. Do you mind my asking?"

"Not at all," I said. "The doctor said I was o.k."

"But you're not. You're not the boy I've worked with and known so well. For example, this morning you behaved eccentrically from the moment we offered you a ride to the hospital. I mean, Eddie, I'm concerned!"

He stepped into the Rolls. The Donkey held the door.

"And you did something, just an hour ago, that was out of the identical mentality that the young lady I mentioned has. Do you know what I'm referring to?"

"No."

"About my speech. You destroyed it with one little sentence aimed target center, at my most vulnerable spot. But I've thought over what you said. And you're wrong. That's a goddam good speech."

The Donkey slammed the door and they were off.

17

IT was about this time I began
to realize that all the conversation in our circle was not about my
father—they thought him finished—but about me. The question of
the moment was not what to do about old Sam Arness, but what to
do about his son, Eddie Evangeleh.

I noticed something new in people's voices when they spoke to
me. In most conversation, even the most ordinary, there is an under-
lying hysteria which comes from the fact that things are, by the nature of life, perilous. But the tone of the talk around me was one
of compulsive calm and calculated sweetness. I've seen adults handle
children this way. And I have always thought the children realized
they were being conned, resented it, and in their recess planned an
ultimate revenge against the adults who were patronizing them.

I did, too. It seemed to me that I was being shouldered all over
the place. Strangers were looking at me disapprovingly. So I got on
guard and became generally suspicious and quarrelsome.

Michael followed to where Mr. Finnegan had left me on the sidewalk, bringing a message from headquarters: "The girls want to
see you."

"What about?"

"They want to have a family lunch and talk about mother."

I made the gesture.

"Don't be that way, Eddie."

"Why not?"

"What's the matter with you, Eddie?"

"What's the matter with me how?"

"You're not yourself."

"Oh, this is me, all right. Let's get a drink."

Michael wouldn't, but he did go to the bar with me, to see that I didn't have too much, I suppose. Was it paranoid to think that? I had a couple of Gibsons fast and felt worse.

Florence and Gloria were waiting at the elevator door on the sixth floor. They were in earnest conversation which broke abruptly into smiles, or so I imagined, when the elevator doors slid open and revealed me.

"Gloria thinks," said Florence, "that we should have a family lunch."

Gloria smiled at me. I *was* being handled. "There's a wonderful Italian restaurant near here," she said.

"Evans loves Italian food," said Florence. "Maybe they'll have lasagna, Ev."

"Why can't we just go in the sun lounge and talk?"

"Your mother could use a good lunch," declared Gloria.

My mother, standing apart and at a little distance, looked bewildered, but not undernourished.

I stood there in a stubborn stupor. Sometimes children retreat into a daze when they have no other recourse against the firepower of the adults in charge.

"Ev, Gloria is your friend and I'm your wife, but I'm also your friend, so be nice."

"You ought to clean up a bit," said Gloria.

"What's the matter with me?"

"Well, wherever you were last night," said Gloria, answering my question, "you were not at the hotel."

"Oh, Gloria!" said Florence.

I walked over to my mother, and didn't hear the rest of that conversation, except I did notice they kept talking and looking at me.

"They want us all to go out and eat together," I said to my mother, as if it were a very farfetched plan.

"Gloria's not a bad woman," said my mother. "She made Michael good wife, brought him children, don't be bad to her . . ."

I have no way of refusing my mother anything. "All right," I said. I turned to the others. "I'll go clean up." I walked down the hall till I found a phone booth.

Gwen picked up as if she had been waiting for my call.

I told her about my father. "I have this feeling they're plotting how to sweep him under the carpet. He keeps begging me to get him out of here."

"Where does he want to go?"

"His home."

"Take him home."

"If you saw the old place, you'd see that's impossible. Besides, he needs supervision."

"Why don't you take him back to California with you?"

I sat there holding the phone as if it weren't connected to anything.

"Eddie?" said Gwen.

"Yeah."

"Clean up and go to lunch with them. Your wife might have an idea."

"O.K."

"And if you want to get him out of there and have no place to take him, bring him here till you figure out what to do."

"O.K. I mean, thanks."

"Call me what happens."

There was a wise guy in the men's room, one of those little bench jockeys who used to sit behind the posts in the bleachers at Ebbets Field. I was looking at the wreckage in the mirror, and he was at the next sink. I caught him a couple of times looking at me and smiling as if I was a joke. All of a sudden, I was on the verge of hitting him. I controlled myself, but my hands began to tremble, and he noticed it.

"You musta tied on a beaut last night," he commented.

I ripped off my shirt. Two buttons flew and fell. He burst out laughing. I threw cold water in my face. I was in enough trouble without starting a fight in the washroom of a hospital.

"You're the son of 612, aren't you?" he asked. "I'm Dr. Levine. I've been looking after your father."

My God, I thought, I *am* getting paranoid! I remembered how often my father had mentioned Dr. Levine. I dried my hands on my shirt and offered to shake hands. He dried his hands on my shirt and we shook.

"How is he really?" I said.

"He's finished. Otherwise he's fine."

"What the hell does that mean?"

"It means some doctors will BS you, put him on a drug calendar, and slip you a hefty bill. But there's no way back with this thing."

"So what do I do?"

"Make him as happy as you can, for as long as you can. But don't look for the marines. They ain't coming. Would you like to borrow a shirt?"

His shirt was tight for me, but it looked better than what I had. And his razor cut. And while I worked on myself, he told me about my father.

"He calls your mother a lot of names I won't repeat, because she is a fine gentle person. Your father, he's a fine man, too. But that's the way life ends sometimes. You see, all the hostilities and suspicions we feel every day about other people but hold down, they're coming out now in that poor man. It's got to mean that he was that way underneath all along. Now he hasn't got any time left to be false. Actually he's acting more honestly than ever before in his life."

I finished fixing myself up. "Nothing more I can do. I just don't look good today."

"That's how it ends sometimes," said Dr. Levine.

"Let me ask you something, just for the hell of it. Am I getting that way, too?"

"You?" He seemed surprised, but he looked at me differently, too.

"I've begun to notice people talking about me, whispering, you know, as if they have to handle me. I've gotten very suspicious of everybody. When I first saw you, for instance, I thought you were laughing at me, and I wanted to take a poke at you real bad. What do you think?"

"Who am I to say about you?" said Levine. "Besides, there is always the chance you're right. Everybody hollers paranoia, you know, but people also plot against each other. The human animal has a very low tolerance for anyone who gets out of line. All the prisons and institutions are chock full of nuts, but some of them, well, they're right."

"Yeah."

"I guess that's one of the enjoyable things about life. How thin the line is."

"Between what and what?"

"Between fact and fancy, sane and insane. The territory between is very narrow."

It was three in the afternoon by the time we got to the Vesuvio. As Gloria sat down, she said, "I know you think I'm a hard person. But it really is time to face the facts, and no one seems to be doing it. So I've elected myself chief villain, and I don't like that role any better than you like me in it."

"I'm as concerned about my mother as anyone," I said and picked up the menu.

"That's all gone," said the waiter, and he took it away from me and began to cross things out.

Florence came at me from the other side, trying to smooth things over. "When I couldn't find you last night, I called Gloria, and she came into town. We had a nice dinner and went to the theater."

Gloria picked up the hint to approach me more circuitously. "We saw a play by Arthur Miller," she said and looked towards Florence.

Florence said, *Incident at Vichy*. A wonderful play."

"I am as concerned about my mother as anyone here," I said.

Gloria said in a ringing tone, "I don't want your guilt; I want your responsibility!"

"That's a line from Mr. Miller's play," said Florence.

I began to be suspicious about Arthur Miller.

"I don't feel guilty," I said.

"Well, you should," said Gloria.

"Now, Gloria," Florence said, "we are going to order lunch." Florence is the one person in the world Gloria is afraid of.

The waiter gave back the menus with just about everything crossed out. "It's late for lunch and early for dinner."

"Have you clam sauce?" asked Florence.

"Hundred can!" said the waiter.

"Well," laughed Florence, "don't make it sound so romantic." She turned to my mother. "Mother," she said, "would you like some spaghetti with white clam sauce?"

"We have red," said the waiter.

"Anything," said my mother.

Florence went on with the waiter about white and red, but I didn't hear it, because Gloria was hissing in my ear.

"Please, Eddie," she said. "Someone has got to look out for her now."

"We all are."

"You all are not. You've let him use her like a servant, all his life. Oh . . . I'd like a martini . . . I feel so tense talking to you, I feel your hostility and I can't . . . a martini, please, waiter, you have that, I hope?" Then she leaned into my ear again. "Why are you letting him kill her? For the last two years, when he's been cursing her, yelling, hitting her, too, where were you? Sitting in your swimming pool?"

My mother spoke. "Gloria, stop it."

"All right," said Gloria.

Michael said, "Just be silent, dear."

"I will not," said Gloria, starting up again.

Michael said, "Shshsh!"

"I am not one of your shshshable Greek women!" Then she pointed at me. "I can't talk to him. I can't deal with such hostility. How do you stand him?"

Florence leaned forward and kissed my cheek.

We sat in small talk and silence till the linguine came. Sometime during the meal, Florence said to me, "Your mother would like to go out to the old house this afternoon."

Before I knew what I was saying, I had turned to my mother and asked, "Did you say that?"

My mother nodded, then looked at Florence.

Florence was flushed. "Darling," she said, "what's happening to you? You don't believe anybody any more."

The old house was the only family home I'd known. I was five when we moved into it. The legend in my family was that my father had won it (all eighteen rooms) in a poker game. I doubt if that was true. But it was a fact that the first two cars we had in our family were acquired by my father in the course of men's games. The first was an Elgin Six, a red touring car he acquired by covering a track obligation for a friend. The second car was a Pierce-Arrow chauffeur-driven limousine (my mother drove it, with Pop in the back), which he won in the course of settling a weekend-long poker game. The Elgin had long since gone. But the Pierce-Arrow was flat on its tires at one side of the garage. There was also the remains of a motorboat rotting in the remains of a boat house.

I remember on holidays our father used to take Michael and me, in our proud little sailor suits, for a ride in that motorboat. We went across the bay in our part of Long Island Sound to visit other well-off Greeks.

I remember the Greek Easters with the colored eggs! The Fourth of July and the spitted baby lambs! I remember my father's name day when my mother danced with a handkerchief!

After the crash—when "National City" became a curse word in our house, and my father was given to addressing long Shakespearean soliloquies, richly vituperative, to its president, Mr. Charles Mitchell —the money my father had available to keep the old place up became very tight indeed. The real estate tax doubled, then trebled. As the house deteriorated, the heat bill swelled. Those were the days before insulation; all four winds found easy ingress. Essential repairs were not made. One end of the porch collapsed, but it was around the corner, at the side of the house, so my father was able to overlook this, too.

My mother, without telling him, of course, closed the two top stories, turned off those radiators and pulled down those shades, anything to conserve the least bit of heat. But despite anything she could do, the house got more and more unlivable. My father refused to consider the possibility that he might sell the place. And after two decades without care, the house was so old-fashioned and so dilapidated that no sale was possible. The land, yes, but not the house. I learned after my father's death that he had had it priced several times, secretly, and that the amount offered had been so low —after all, the house was worse than valueless; it had to be wrecked and carted away—that he laughed at the offers. He also derived comfort from the fact that he had something other people wanted that he would not give them. Of course, there was something deeper that made him hold on, too. It was his home.

When we drove up to the house that day, it looked drabber than I remembered it. The vines had grown over more of the porch and covered the ground floor bays. The paint was peeling, and the windowpanes, broken at Halloween four years ago, had not been replaced. The front door was locked, and a real estate man had the key. But the pantry window I used to climb through as a kid was still open.

The house, as I walked through it, still showed my mother's hand. It was dusty, but orderly. And awfully bare!

There had never been a book in the main room of this house, not at its liveliest. In our school days, my brother and I brought books in, of course, but we kept them upstairs in our bedrooms. My mother's few precious books, the Bible in Greek and some poetry from her own school days, were kept in her bedroom. But downstairs? Not a magazine.

The one room that had been used a lot was the large, old-fashioned kitchen. In winter it had been the only warm room. The gas stove used to burn there all day with the oven doors open. Here my father had caused my mother to bring in his deep armchair. It was still there, and there also was the TV which Florence and I had given them for Christmas five years ago. My father used to sit for hours watching the westerns.

I stopped a moment in the kitchen, the room where my mother had spent forty years of her life. The wooden drain board at the sink was washed down to a terrible bleached smoothness. The pots and pans were so familiar! Every dent. The whole place was a monument to my mother's endurance. Gloria and Florence were right; it *had* just about killed her.

When I opened the front door to let them in, I said to Gloria, "You're right."

"About what?" said Gloria. "Listen, Florence, he says I'm right about something."

"About my mother," I said. I went over and kissed the old girl, walked her out to the end of the porch. There was an old box there, kind of dirty, that I covered with my coat. I sat her down in the soft light the vines admitted. I crouched at her side and didn't say anything for a moment, paying her some of the respect she had earned; no one could pay it all.

Finally I said, "Tell me what you want to do?"

"I don't know."

"The girls are right. You must look after yourself now."

"If he let me, I look after him. But when I come into a room now, he don't talk. I don't mind that, but he hits me; he's still strong, you know. It's terrible, because I know it's not him, but I'm afraid. And you can't blame him. He worked like a horse all his life and has nothing to show for it!"

I've never been able to stand it when my mother cried.

"I'll take care of him," I said.

"You must," she said, "because I can't any more. We could have an old age, if he knew how to enjoy it. But he knows only to enjoy business and like that. He still talks his old deals, the mistakes he made, and National City, National City, and Mr. Charles Mitchell, the president—I say to him, Seraphim, Mr. Charles Mitchell is dead! He looks at me like his enemy. Then there's the other thing, about me. I ask him, Seraphim, show me where he is? There's nobody, Seraphim, show me where. He says, *you* tell me where, I didn't hide him, you hide him. When he gets quiet and pretends to look at TV, I say to him, Seraphim, let's talk. He says I don't talk to my enemies."

Florence and Gloria came out on the porch. They had evidently made a tour of the house. Florence was wiping the dust off her hands. Gloria glared at me.

"What's eating you?" I said.

"Whenever I look at this house, I could kill you and I could kill Michael."

"Oh, Gloria," said Michael.

"Do you realize she spent forty years in there slaving for that monster . . . ?"

I went up to her. "I don't want to hear another word out of you," I said. I was about to hit her with my fist. I turned to Michael. "She's your wife. Now keep her quiet."

I walked away. Florence came after me. We walked down to the water, to the edge of the pebble beach.

"Darling," she said, "really!"

"She had it coming."

"But it's like shooting a gnat with a howitzer. You're a big person and she's just a—"

"Ball breaker."

Florence laughed. "Why are all you great big males so damned afraid of a little girl like that, even if she does have a pair of tiny scissors in her apron pocket?"

Florence looked remarkably composed, remarkably in order.

"Florence," I said, "what do you want?"

"Darling, I want to take you back home. I want to leave by the next plane."

"I'm not going back."

"You need a deep rest, darling."

"That's the last thing I need."

"All right, Evans," she said cheerily, "all right . . ."

"All right, what?"

"All right."

"All right what . . . what? What?"

Then suddenly she broke.

"Don't, goddam it, don't! I'm trying my best, Ev. Help me, don't make it harder for me."

For a moment she sat there trembling.

"I'm sorry . . . I'm sorry . . . Oh, God . . . I'm sorry!" she said. She just could not stand being seen anything less than perfectly controlled. She walked to the end of the path. There was a row of flower boxes there that hadn't been tended for over a year. They were full of weeds. She began to pull them out.

I went up to her.

"I'm sorry," I said.

She didn't look around. "Give me another chance, Ev, I am trying. I finally figured out what I was doing wrong. I think I can help you."

The cost of it all, our years and our conflicts, the bill for it was all there on her face.

"I'm sorry," I said again, and turned to go.

"Don't go," she said, "talk to me."

"Let's not, now."

"Please, Evans, tell me, whatever it is; don't be afraid, tell me."

So I tried. "Gloria and you have been planning some scheme all morning, and I wish you'd tell me what it is."

"We've only been trying to figure out what to do with your father."

"And?"

"But why get so suspicious, so hostile, Ev, dear? What's the matter, what is it?"

"What's what?"

"You've been that way to everyone, so short-tempered and violent. Why? And why at *me?*"

"O.K., I'm going nuts."

324

"I really think so."

"All right, I am, but answer my question."

"We have no plots; we're only trying to find a solution to a very difficult problem. What do you think we should do? Surely you can see now that you can't put your mother and your father in the same house together? And surely not in this house."

"I can see that."

"It's like those terrible tribes in New Guinea or the Hebrides or whatever. The husband makes a pact with his children that when he dies, they're to kill his wife and throw her into the grave with him."

"You're saying that we are trying to kill her?"

"Yes."

"How come you have so much sympathy for her and none at all for him?"

"I'd rather not answer that question."

"Why not?"

"Because it's loaded."

"With what?"

"With your hatred of me. Ev, dear, what did I ever do to deserve that?"

"So what's your plan?"

"We have no plan."

"I don't believe you."

"Goddammit, Evans, we're looking for a solution to a . . ."

"And what's your solution?"

"What is yours?"

"Mine?"

"Yes, do you have one?"

"Yes, I do."

"And what is it?"

"I want to take him out of that hospital, and I want to take him back to California and I want him to live with us."

I could have better struck her across the face.

She stood there and looked up and away. I realized she felt she should be able to answer that proposal calmly and in good order, but she found that she couldn't; you could see the girl trying to control herself, and not able to.

I suddenly felt so sorry for her, for everybody in the world caught in this web of torturing each other, that I tried to put my arms around her and tried to hug her, but she stood there in my arms like a stack of boards. It was unbelievable, the violence of her reaction to what, perhaps in another society, perhaps with other people, might have been the simplest and most natural of proposals.

Finally she eased herself out of my arms. I think she knew that we had reached some sort of crisis and that she had to make a simple, true answer to my suggestion.

She said, "It just wouldn't work, darling."

"Why not?"

"It just wouldn't. You should be able to see that."

"I'm unable to."

"Well, for one thing we'd have to . . . well, he needs constant care and . . ."

"I want to give it to him."

"Well, it would be just so, so . . ."

"So . . . what?"

"Well, I don't mean it the way it sounds, but it would just be so messy, and I want things to be right for us so we can—"

"He's my father," I said.

"I know that, darling."

"He's near the end, he's dying."

"I know. It won't be long."

"I'm not saying that. I'm not promising you that it won't last long. But it's my house as well as yours, Florence, and I want to take care of him there."

"He'll just be disorientated there."

"What's that mean?"

"It's not his home."

Neither of us said anything for a moment.

"I think you ought to ask yourself one question," I said. "Why are you so violent about this?"

"Violent?"

"Yes. Violent. Very! Admit it! Admit at least that."

"All right," she said, "because I love you. Because maybe we're done, but if we do have a chance at all, it wouldn't be with your father in the same house with us."

"Why not?"

"Because we have a reconstruction job to do."

326

"Why not?"

"Because we have a vast reconstruction job to do!"

"Why not?"

"Because . . . because where were you last night, where were you, all night last night?" She screamed that, but you could hardly hear it as it broke through her controls.

"I was with Gwen last night, on and off all night last night."

She walked into the house without saying another word.

I stayed down by the water and threw pebbles into the Sound, and then through the broken windows of the boat house.

When I walked into the house, Florence was, or seemed, composed again. She was with Gloria and my mother.

"Evans," she said, "we've talked it over, and the only possible solution, it seems to all of us, is to put your father in a home for the aged, where he could get the constant attention and care that he needs. Obviously your mother can't take care of him any more without endangering her own life. And further, as you heard Mr. Finnegan's personal doctor say, he can no longer control any of his bodily functions, and surely you can't wish to submit your mother to that."

"I do," I said. "I think she ought to wipe his ass every day, as the final act of their marriage."

"So," she said, ignoring my last, "we have all agreed that he should be placed in an old age—"

"No go," I said.

"No go what?"

"He's not going to be swept under the carpet."

"Your reasons?"

"Old folks' homes are for old folks without anyone."

"Not necessarily, not at all; you're mistaken."

"And he has me."

"You're quite mistaken about that," said Gloria parroting Florence.

"And I'm not going to have my father's fate decided by two cunts who—"

"Two people, dear . . ."

"—who hate him!"

"Well," said Florence, "the son who loves him seems to prefer to see his mother dead rather than do anything at all about it."

"That's how it seems to people who would rather see *him* dead, am I right, Gloria? Come on, little Gloria, you'd like to see the dirty old son of a bitch dead! Right? Now, right?"

I'll give Gloria credit. She said, "Right."

Then Florence really took charge. "He is going to die soon whether we wish it or not. But I will not sit by and watch him take your mother down with him. We have to look after the living. Furthermore, I don't think you're responsible for your thoughts now, any more than you are responsible for your feelings."

"Nevertheless, in this case what I say goes!"

"Not at all," said Florence. "In this case your mother has the decisive word. Her wishes are the ones that have to be finally respected. And she agrees with us."

"Do you, Mom?"

"Evangeleh, what else can we do? I can't help him now. I can't ask anyone else, can I, the way he is? Gloria and Florence tell me that these homes for old people, they're very nice and very comfortable, some of them."

Gloria said, "Florence and I have a list—"

"How long have you had that list?" I asked.

Gloria did not answer that question. "We're going to look at them this afternoon," she said.

Two hours later, I was in the hospital, and I received a phone call from Gloria saying that she and Florence had found a place that they and mother liked very much. Her priest had recommended it, too; would I come out to see it? I said I would not.

Florence then got on, and told me that the place was surprisingly nice, and that there had been a sudden opening, someone had died last night, right, and we had to move immediately if we wanted the bed because there was a rush on, and we really wouldn't find any place as good as this, because the other person in the room with my father was a very agreeable, quiet, and dignified old man. She was sure they'd get along.

I listened and said nothing.

She insisted that I come out. I refused.

She said then they'd go ahead without my consent and move my father out in the morning. She said Michael had agreed, too. Goodbye.

When I stepped out of the phone booth, there was my old uncle,

Joe Arness, the very model of disbelief. I burst out laughing when I saw him. He had the most cynical smile. He had long, long since given up expecting any good of anyone. I stepped back into the phone booth and called Gwen. I asked if she could get hold of a car. She said Charles could; what for? I told her not to ask any questions, just to have the car in the parking lot at the side of the Stamford General Hospital at ten o'clock that night and wait. I went out of the phone booth, returned Joe's smile, took him by the arm, and we went into my father's room together.

18

MY father was hallucinating. There was short-circuiting throughout the disarrayed coils and links that were his mind.

He started by announcing to me that "she" was getting married.

"Who's she, Pop?"

"Who's she? Your mother. Don't you listen what I been telling you?"

Old Joe tapped his parchment temple. "Finish," he whispered.

My father paid no attention. His mind had switched over to another subject.

"You have ticket?" he demanded of me.

"What ticket, Pop?"

"What ticket? My ticket."

"I don't know anything about that."

"Honestly God!" he exclaimed.

"Tell me, what ticket?"

He didn't answer.

"Pop?" I said.

"Never mind! I do myself!" He seemed stricken with disappointment. I didn't know what to say or do. He looked at me, shaking his head. "I don't understand how you became big shot, honestly God!" he said. "Your memory is gazook."

Uncle Joe was smiling his lupine smile.

My father, shaking his head, reproached me. "Evangeleh," he said, "I have no one to trust here. Only you." He shook his head in amazement at the indifference the whole world, including his eldest son, was showing to his fate.

"I'm sorry, Pop." I was, too. I didn't know exactly what about, but I certainly was sorry. I began to wonder, had he indeed said something about a ticket? A ticket to where? "I'm sorry I forgot about that ticket, Pop," I said. "Tell me again what you want me to do, and I'll do it."

"Never mind," he said, "I'll get myself."

"You can trust me, Pop."

"So far, nothing," he said. "There isn't much time, Evangeleh. You must use your brain to get me out of here."

I couldn't understand how this daft old man still had the power to make me apologetic, even doubt my reason and my memory.

"You see sign they put out there?" he said suddenly.

"No, Pop."

"What's the matter with your eyes?"

"I just didn't notice it, I guess."

"Look out the window, you see sign."

I didn't dare not to. To my surprise there was indeed a large sign to be seen a block or so away. It advertised a brake lining, I think, or a battery. The only thing discernible at that distance was the trade mark, the initials S.P. These had been rendered in large electric letters that flashed on and off, S.P., S.P.

"You see now?" my father asked.

"Yes," I said.

"Now, you understand, right?"

"Right," I lied.

"What you understand?"

"It's something about a brake lining. Is that it?"

"Why you lie, my boy? Why you do that?"

"Well . . ." I didn't know what to say.

"How you become big shot success? Explain me that?"

"I told you, Pop, I don't know."

"You see there S.P., S.P.?"

"Yes, Pop."

"It means something, right?"

"Right."

"What it means?"

"I don't know."

"Seraphim Pay!" he said. "It means Seraphim Pay!"

"Ah ha!" I said.

"So when I tell you they try to poison me here, don't laugh."

"Who's trying to poison you, Pop?"

"In the food. I told you thousand times."

"Why are they trying to poison you?"

"For my money, my boy. What people want, eh? Say!"

"You told me you have no money."

"Then why are they trying to poison me, tell me that?"

"I don't know."

"You don't know! There must be reason, right?"

"But you have no money, right?"

"But they don't know that, right?"

"I see."

"You see nothing. That's why I say to you, get taxi, get me out from here. They have plan I'm going to die here, Evangeleh."

"I know, Pop."

Fortunately his mind sparked onto something else.

"That no good bum," he muttered.

"Who, Pop?"

"Who she's marrying, who! That Irish! She'll find out. He has nothing. No business, no money, no office, not even a desk, nothing, runs with those whores, she'll find out."

"Who is he, Pop?"

"Evangeleh, you must speak to him today. Breaking my home after forty-seven years, it's a sin!" There were tears in his eyes.

"I'll speak to him, Pop. Tell me who he is."

"That's the trouble. I don't know."

He retreated to some recess within himself, trying to figure something out. We all three sat there without speaking. Joe winked at me; then he turned and looked out the window towards the flashing sign.

We kept the silence.

My father lay on his back, breathing with difficulty. The bottom of his face collapsed when he took out his bridge. Both jaws were soaking, now, in a cup at the side of his bed. A few years ago his face had begun to freeze into a mask of anxiety. Fear of death had overcome whatever kindlier aspects his face had once had. He lay there, a soft fish, panting to get what he needed out of the unyielding air. His eyes looked this way and that, on guard against the next and final threat. Where would the finisher come from and when?

He was trying to mutter something. I leaned forward and caught, "I want some grapes. Get me some grapes, Evangeleh." I remembered his taste for those small seedless white ones. I started to go for the nurse when he pulled me down and kissed me with surprising passion.

I rang for the nurse.

When I looked back, he was trying to struggle up in his bed. I went over to help him. He smiled at me, then remembering he had no teeth in his face, he covered his mouth.

"Remember," he said, "once I told you it's just as easy to fall in love with rich girl as with poor girl? Right? Remember that, my boy?"

He laughed and covered his mouth.

"Yes," I said, laughing with him.

"Thank God you did what I tol' you and made success. You listen me, and see what happen?"

"I see, Pop."

"Good boy! Good boy!" He still held my hand. Now he closed his eyes, and his face looked as happy as it possibly could. "You see?" he said softly. "You see?"

Miss Smythe came in. Pop opened his eyes and looked at her. His lips framed the word "cunt!" Miss Smythe was too busy to catch this compliment. She had brought reinforcements with her, Nurse Bentley, a butch type.

"He wants some grapes," I said.

"I don't believe there are grapes on the dinner tonight," she said crisply. "He's going to have his bath now. Would you both leave, please?"

Old Joe had Near Eastern gallantry. He treated all women as sex objects, no matter how undesirable they were. "Goodbye for now, beautiful ladies," he said. Miss Smythe smothered him with silence. But you couldn't insult old Joe. "One more beautiful than the other," he said and bowed to the nurses with his derby over his heart.

Outside Joe engaged the head nurse in earnest conversation. I could hear him explaining that his poor sick brother had insisted he remain at his side. Despite an important business appointment he had in the city that evening, he might be persuaded to remain if the hospital would provide him with one of their wonderful dinners. Joe was very short of cash!

I got Ellen on the telephone. She was in a rush, she said; her boy friend was waiting downstairs in his car. She said that everything had gone well with the doctor, and she was now equipped. I told her to check out of the Algonquin for me, too, and put my luggage in the check room. Also to notify the hotel cashier that I would come by and take care of the bill. Today, I still owe the Algonquin $278.48.

I walked out on a balcony overlooking the parking lot. In the distance "Seraphim Pay!" flashed on and off. As far as I knew, the old man didn't have a friend in the world. One after another he had alienated them. Here at the end, it was I who was left with the old man, and he with me.

What would the old man, at this moment, have a right to expect from his last and only friend? He had been pleading for one thing, for me to get him out of the hospital. I had to do it, not because it was the sensible or medically correct thing, but simply because, *in extremis,* that is what he wanted. It was the last thing he would ever ask me to do for him. Who else could he turn to, to make this final event of his life his own?

Then, suddenly, it seemed absurd, just not possible. I had to stop encouraging him in that idea. I'd just bring on the old man's death that way.

Miss Smythe came running down the hall. "Will you please come in?" she said. "Your father wouldn't let us turn him over, and when Miss Bentley tried, he struck her."

I rushed in. The bed was in total disarray. The pan of water was all over the floor, also the washrag and the bar of soap. The alcohol bottle had broken when it fell. When my father saw me, he burst out, "I don't want her touching me, that wrestler." He pointed at Nurse Bentley. She was crying. My father's rage, especially the first time anyone saw it, was an awesome phenomenon. Butch Bentley was just a little girl after all.

When I went over to the bed, he pulled me down and whispered in my ear, "Where's the taxi?" And before I knew it, I had again said what he wanted to hear: "It's coming, Pop, it's coming."

I must stop that, I thought; I must stop encouraging that idea.

Old Flat Tire Joe was in the doorway, laughing. "She sent for the policemans, Seraphim!" he said. "They're going to lock you up at last, Seraphim!"

"Go home," said my father, "I don't want see you."

"Who you see if you don't see me?" said Joe. "You got no friends left, you son of a bitch!"

They went on insulting each other, half in Greek, with some English and odd bits of Turkish for emphasis. Finally I made out, "Not one cent!" from my father. "You ate all my money, and now you want more?"

"What the hell are you going to do with it? You're finished! Lying there like broken egg. At least my carfare to come here," Joe said. Suddenly he ran to the closet, threw open the door, and frantically began to go through the pockets of his brother's clothing.

My father winked at me and laughed his gummy laugh. "You think I'm stupid?" he shouted to Joe. "Not till I'm dead I leave money loose in my clothes. Wait till I'm dead, goddam fool!"

"You son of a bitch," said Flat Tire Joe, "give me my carfare."

My father winked at me, and laughed and coughed and laughed.

Miss Smythe came back. With her were Butch and the marines, Dr. Levine and Father Draddy, the young priest who had tried to talk to my father earlier and hadn't been able to.

Dr. Levine seemed to relish the struggle. Signs of life, I suppose. The young Father held back. After one rejection, he knew that he had to approach this particular quarry with care. Dr. Levine was talking to my father, and they were laughing. Dr. Levine leaned back over his shoulder and indicated to Smythe that she should move in. Even Butch Bentley seemed reassured. She made a playful gesture to hit the old man, and he made a playful gesture to hit her. They began to give him his bed bath. I think the old man enjoyed the respect his violence had gained him.

Father Draddy, the young priest, eased over to me.

"How old is your father?" he asked.

"How old are you now, Pop?"

"I'm idle," said Pop.

The young priest laughed appreciatively, and then he asked, "What did he say?"

"He said he was idle."

The priest laughed again.

I noticed that Father Draddy was a little tipsy. To my surprise, I found I liked him.

"What are you building with those socks, Father?" I asked. The young Father was wearing his reversed collar and black suit, but at his ankles were a pair of brilliantly colored argyles.

"Oh," he said, pulling his black pants down, "those?"

"That's no answer," I said.

"Ouch," said my father, "what the hell are you doing, you wrestler!"

"Dr. Levine!" yelled Butch Bentley.

Dr. Levine hurried to the old man's side.

"Are those the latest effort to humanize the priesthood?" I said to the young Father.

"No," he said, "I was playing golf, and I forgot I had to show up at Danny Roach's wake. So I dressed as fast as I could, and I forgot."

"That's enough," yelled my father. "Go way."

Miss Smythe and Miss Bentley looked at Dr. Levine. He motioned them to go, which they were glad to do. Dr. Levine stuffed two pillows under my father's head, which enabled him to see the priest for the first time.

He glared at him.

I was ready for anything.

But my father was in a better mood now. That glare was not what he felt. It was the way his face had frozen.

"I'm Father Draddy."

"Very nice, very nice," my father said. "Sit down."

He smiled at the young priest, reached over, and taking his plates out of their receptacle, put them in his face. He was ready for company.

"Evangeleh," he said, now in better voice, "get the Father a ginger ale, Coca-Cola, something what you like, Father? Evangeleh!"

I leaped to attention.

"Oh, nothing, thank you very much," said Father Draddy.

"You must have something," he said to the young priest, then, "Evangeleh!" in his most peremptory tone.

"You must have something," I said, doing my best.

"Well, some juice, perhaps. Some grapefruit juice."

"Good!" said my father.

That was the last that was said or done about that.

"Just thought I'd pay you a visit," said Father Draddy.

"Wonderful," said my father, "sit down. Evangeleh, the Father is standing."

I got Flat Tire Joe up out of the only chair in the room and put it bedside.

"You know," said my father to the priest, "I'm going to surprise you."

"How's that, sir?"

"I'm not going to die."

"I firmly believe you won't."

"I'm going to surprise everybody."

"I'm going to pray for your continuing health."

"You know," said my father, "I was altar boy once?"

I had never heard that before, but it turned out to be true.

"Ah, you're a Catholic," said Father Draddy.

"Orthodox!" said my father. "I could sing the scripture. I had a beautiful voice. Stavros," he said to his brother, "you remember my voice?"

"I remember," said Flat Tire Joe sourly.

"You son a bitch, don't talk that way in front of priest, what's the matter with you?"

"I say nothing," said Flat Tire Joe.

"You sing?" my father asked the priest.

"No, I'm afraid not."

"Then how you give holy book?"

"We speak the scripture, in a sort of rhythm, intone it, sort of . . ."

"Let me hear."

"What?"

"Let me hear whatever is good for me now, you understand? Come on," he said. He smiled at the priest. "He's shy," he added, "very nice, very nice."

The priest didn't know whether he was being put on or not. I tried to reassure him he wasn't, that my father did expect some help from his ministrations.

There was a silence, broken only by Flat Tire Joe, who was cracking his jaw and clicking his teeth.

"Pssst!" said my father to his brother, sternly.

Flat Tire Joe was silent. We all were.

The priest saw that it was up to him to fill the silence.

"Oh God," he intoned, doing his best to give it some rhythm, body, and melody (although these things were quite foreign to him personally, if not to his tradition), "oh, Jesus, who washes clean the sins of the world, grant this man peace. Forgive him his sins, oh Lord."

My father interrupted.

"No sins," he said. "No sins. I did everything right, that's what I did wrong! National City Bank. That was the right thing. In 1926 I bought thousand share—"

"Oh, Pop," I said, "the Father doesn't want to hear about that—"

"Just a second," he said, the fury beginning to come back to his face. "Evangeleh!" he rumbled, warning me. Then he resumed, "I put all my money, one thousand shares, two hundred fourteen thousand dollar," he said. "Was that a sin?"

"I didn't mean that," said the young priest.

"It went to six hundred eighty. Then one day—"

"Not one day," said Flat Tire Joe. "You had time to get out."

"What the hell time to get out," screamed my father, his lips trembling, the spittle reappearing, and his eyebrows stiff as bone.

"Lots of people got out," said Flat Tire Joe.

"Yes, but I had faith in American system. I'm patriot, but when it goes to twenty-three? The whole thousand shares? What do I say?"

I made the mistake of saying, "Oh, Pop, that's ancient history."

"And we must forgive," the priest added.

"Forgive?!" exploded my father. "Forgive who? President Mitchell of National City Bank is dead, but I don't forgive his soul. I'm not religious, you know."

"Oh, yes, you are," said Father Draddy.

"Oh, no, I'm not, but I believe in the soul, and I do not forgive the soul of Mister Charles Mitchell of National City Bank stocks!"

"May he rest in peace," said the priest.

"May he not rest in peace, the son of a bitch," said my father.

"Tsststtt, tsst, tsst," said Father Draddy.

That was his finish.

"Don't make that tsst, tsst, tsst to me. Did you ever lose two hundred fourteen thousand dollar in one week when dollar was dollar?"

"But those are not the important things, now."

"Not important? When you have no money, they don't come in the door. You see any buyers in this room?"

"No, I can't say that I do," said poor Father Draddy, looking around nervously. "But your true friends, certainly . . ."

"I have no true friends! Only this boy here, Evangeleh. He follow my ideas and he made success."

"But your wife—"

"My wife," he yelled, "is fucking other man, excuse me, priest, but I don't know the nice American word for that. Did your wife ever fuck another man, tell me that?"

"I'm sure you're mistaken. I met Mrs. Arness."

"Never mind you met Mrs. Arness! She sent you here, right? Tell truth, priest, she send you?"

The old man was trying to get out of the bed.

Father Draddy backed away.

Dr. Levine moved in, and I don't know what it was he said to my father, but the old man turned heavily on his stomach and hid his face in the pillow like a child.

Father Draddy came to me. He seemed disturbed, even a little beat.

"I'm sorry I wasn't able to help him," he said.

"I'll take care of him."

"He's got a long way to go," he said.

Old Uncle Flat Tire Joe was humming a Turkish dance and swaying.

"You mean in regard to cleaning his soul of sin before he dies, preparing for the last judgment and all?"

"I know you don't accept that concept," said Father Draddy, "but you see the result?"

"What result are you talking about?" I asked.

He pointed to the bed.

"That man," I said, "spent his entire life doing exactly what this society told him to do. He never broke a law. Is it any wonder he's bewildered now?"

My father heard that, and he turned heavily around in the bed.

"I had many chances, the Berengaria, the Aquitania, the old Mauretania, the greyhound of the seas, full of beautiful women.

I was a handsome man, not this what you see. Damn fool, goddam fool!"

Dr. Levine quieted him again.

Father Draddy and I went to the farthest corner of the room. Dr. Levine joined us.

"I want to take him out of here," I whispered.

"When?" he said.

"Now, tonight."

"You'll have to get a release from the doctors attending."

"I'm not going through all that," I said. "It's very complicated. There are differing opinions in the family."

Dr. Levine's eyes quivered in the direction of the young Father. He was warning me to be careful what I said.

"What would you say," I asked him, "if I kidnapped him tonight?"

"What's the hurry?" said Dr. Levine.

"Is it doing him any good here?"

"I don't think it's doing him any harm." Dr. Levine was hedging.

Father Draddy was listening with the keenest interest. I wondered if he knew Gloria. I knew she took communion. From Father Draddy?

"Can anything really help him now?" I asked Dr. Levine.

"You mean lengthen his life? No. But a lot of things, like accidents and so on, could shorten it. He's got to be watched, every single minute."

"But essentially . . ."

"I told you. He's had it."

"Could anything make him feel better?"

"Physically or spiritually?"

"Physically."

"Nothing."

"Spiritually?"

"Ask Father Draddy."

"I'm asking you."

He ducked. "Well . . . I don't know."

"I think he might feel a hell of a lot better out of here," I said. "And when it comes to supervision, it depends by whom, doesn't it, whether it makes him feel better?"

"I think I'd agree with that."

"The problem is that nobody wants him. They plan to put him in a home."

"One thing occurred to me," said Dr. Levine. "Why don't you and your wife take him home? You seem to be well off. You could afford a nurse. Your mother might even come and visit."

"There are personal reasons why I can't do that."

"Like what?" said Father Draddy.

"Like none of your business," I said. "I'm sorry, Father."

"Forget it," said the Father. "Only you were just talking about kidnapping and . . ."

"I was thinking about taking him to Florida," I said, "to Tarpon Springs, and sitting him in the sun."

"Does he like the sun?" asked Dr. Levine.

"What he likes is a store full of buyers."

"Then what's the point?" asked Father Draddy.

"The point, Father, is that Tarpon Springs is full of beat old Greeks who were brought to this country a long time ago to dive for sponges. But now we've developed a synthetic sponge that is cheaper to make and to market. So these fellows down there sit around all day in the coffee houses, play backgammon, and bitch. I think my father would find a lot of congenial company down there, fellows who feel just like he feels—and in Greek, too."

I went on, fabricating as I went along, laying down this false lead in the hope that Father Draddy would pick it up and, when the time came, pass it on.

"All this, Father," I said, "is strictly between us."

"Of course," he lied.

"So what would you say? If I could steal him out of here, without a medical release."

Dr. Levine looked at Father Draddy. "Well," he said, "seems to be a fog coming up. You think planes will be taking off to Florida tonight?"

"I just made a reservation for two," I lied. "They said operations were normal. They go right up through that stuff."

"Wouldn't mind a week in Florida myself," said Father Draddy, laughing nervously.

"Well," I said to Dr. Levine, "what would you say?"

"Whatever I felt about it as a human being," answered Dr. Levine, "I couldn't possibly condone it as a doctor."

"Neither could I," said Father Draddy, who wasn't one.

"Well, if you two fellows feel that way," I said, "I'd better give it up. I guess it's just not a good idea."

"I'm awfully glad you feel that," said Father Draddy. "I'm only a priest trying to be of service here, so forgive me if I say that it would be so much better if you could find a solution that everybody—doctors, relatives, and his wife, of course—all would agree upon."

"And him?" I said.

"I don't think he's responsible," whispered Father Draddy. "And perhaps," he whispered, even more cautiously, "perhaps you shouldn't be so bearish on a home. Some of them are very nice, you know. I was saying to Gloria, that is, she was good enough to ask me, and I said . . ."

There it was.

When he was through, I said, "Thank you, Father, for the good advice. I certainly will follow it. And please, about my crazy idea, you know, just between us, eh?"

"Of course, of course," said Father Draddy sincerely. "And listen," he continued, "you better take care of yourself."

"What?"

"Well, you seem . . . I mean, relax, kid, relax. Give him a pill, Doc. I think he's the real patient here, haha." He smiled and shook my hand. He was a nice guy and wouldn't say anything, at least not till after I had succeeded in kidnapping the old man.

My father was glassy-eyed again and didn't respond when Father Draddy came over to say good night and left.

Dr. Levine thought it best to follow immediately.

As he went out, he turned at the door and quickly said, "At midnight I'll be giving the nurses on this floor some detailed instructions that will require their full attention. If anyone were going to try the foolish thing you described, that would be the best time."

At midnight, exactly, I opened the door from my father's room to the corridor. We walked, my father and I, slowly but without challenge, to the elevators. Dr. Levine, as he promised, was giving an extremely detailed briefing to the nurses who had just come on. I could see out of the corner of my eye, as we passed, that he had arranged the girls so that their backs were to the corridor. Sometimes a plan works because it is so downright simple.

Gwen and Charles were waiting for us in his station wagon. We drove not to Kennedy, but to 31 Shore Road. That's where he wanted to go; I didn't have to ask. We stopped and picked up some stuff for breakfast.

I heard later what happened at the hospital. On the far-out chance that we might benefit from a little confusion in the ranks of the enemy, we had done up old Flat Tire Joe in his brother's hospital nightgown and left him in the bed, face down. Joe told me later that no one came to look at him the whole night through. I suppose they were contented to leave well enough alone. It was only after the floor waitress had brought him breakfast, and he had consumed most of it, that Nurse Smythe came in and found out what had been done.

I carried my father into the old house. He weighed like a bag of old clothes. He was in pretty good spirits, however, despite the fact that by the time we got him there his pallor was scary. I undressed him while Gwen made his bed. Then we got him into it. Gwen sat alongside. He liked her immediately.

After a minute—apropos of what, I don't know—he said to me, "Next time, big shot, listen what I tell you." Then he looked at Gwen, and they smiled at each other. "You stay here," he ordered. "He can go!"

Of course I wanted Gwen to stay, but I knew she had a sitter at home. And Charles waiting.

My father was getting sleepy. He opened his eyes, looked at Gwen and mumbled, "Very nice, very nice."

Gwen got up. "I'll be right back," she said. Charles was sitting by the front door waiting. I could see her talking to him earnestly. He nodded. Then he nodded again. Then she kissed him on the side of his face. He smiled at her, and she saw him to the car.

I went back to my father's bed. "She's going to stay," I told him. But he was asleep, and didn't hear Charles's car drive away.

19

WHAT did Charles say?" I asked her when she finally got into bed. She'd been stalling her undressing.

"Nothing, why?" she said.

"He said nothing a long time. Come on, what did he say?"

"It was o.k. with him."

"That's all?"

"That's all."

"Some conversation."

"So don't push it. Good night," she said and fell asleep.

We came together in the middle of the night without really wakening. The fact is we didn't allow ourselves to fully wake, because awake our problems were insoluble; asleep or near asleep we were lovers.

But she did say one thing, with complete conviction.

"I'm never going to do this to him again."

We lay there a long time without talking, her leg over mine.

"You won't have to," I said.

I made up my mind to marry her.

I couldn't sleep. She was exhausted and fell off, but I lay there watching her.

With all she had been and done, with all she was going through now, she still looked innocent and childlike. What the appeal of that—that "childlike"—is to me, I don't know. But it seems to mean something to me.

I lay there for hours. It was the room I had occupied when I was in my first teens. In this room I had had the Spanish influenza and the clock nightmare. The shades were down as they had been then.

Light, so they believed at that time, encouraged the malignancy of the disease. In a corner stood a clothes tree. I remember when I was sick and delirious, it used to frighten me. Covered with clothing and robes, it was an enemy waiting in the night for me to fall asleep. It seemed a friend now, returning me to the days before I gave my life away.

I suddenly realized that, for no reason I could name, I was on an upturn. I guess it was because I had taken some sort of action, no matter how eccentric or unreasonable. I had made up my mind to take the step, to marry this woman lying next to me, whom I distrusted, couldn't really understand, but nevertheless loved.

Towards dawn she turned over spoon style. Just as she made herself comfortable, she became aware that I wasn't asleep. She turned and looked at me.

"What's the matter?" she said.

"What did he say?" I asked.

"He said he'd wait."

"For what?"

"For me."

"And this?"

"He said it didn't make any difference to him."

"I don't believe that, do you?"

"That's what he said."

"So what are you crying about?"

"So I can't do this to him any more. He's too sweet . . ."

"I guess that's what he figures."

"I don't think he figures anything except . . ."

"Except?"

"Except he said he won't be able to take you. Nobody can take you except me, he said."

"You believe that?"

"Could you do what he's doing now, sitting in my apartment, taking care of someone else's kid? And me here? Could you?"

"No."

"That's what I mean. Sometimes, Eddie, sometimes I think the strongest people are those who just hang on. Especially with people like you and me, who don't know from one day to the next what they really want and don't account today for what they did yesterday . . . Don't . . . Eddie . . . don't. . . . I don't want to, Eddie, so don't, please, Eddie, don't. . . ."

Afterwards she said, "Eddie, why do you think you can solve anything and everything that way?"

We lay there for a time. Then I said to her that I wanted to marry her.

She separated herself from me.

"You're just no damned good, Eddie," she said.

"Why?"

"You're such a liar. You don't take responsibility for anything you say."

"I'm not that way any more."

"You lie, Eddie. The first time you said that to me, I thought it meant something. But I know better now, Eddie."

"You don't know better now."

"I woke one morning a week after you'd gone back to California and felt like a chicken a butcher has stuck his hand into and pulled out the guts. I was cold dead and hung, Eddie. And it was your lies that killed me. Not only the lies you spoke to me, but the ones you *did* to me. Those were the ones I really believed, the way you did me like we were one—that's a laugh, yeah—when you held on like we could never be apart again, that was a yock, wasn't it, kiddie? Yeah! Like we could never get along without each other; you can't top that for comedy, can you? I really believed those lies you did me, goddam you, Eddie! And now you show a year and God knows how much later, come on with the marriage shit, that rank shit, and you think I'm going to believe it? What do you think I am, you son of a bitch, I'll kill you, you son of a bitch!"

She was hitting me with her fists on my chest, the way a girl does who loves you.

She got out of the bed, walked to the window. "Don't play games with me, Eddie," she was saying, "goddammit, don't play games with me any more."

The trees, which had been pruned regularly in my father's good days, had grown out. They were lying all over the pitched roof. In the wind they scratched against the sides of the old structure and made one hell of a racket.

"Come back to bed," I said.

346

She did. "Eddie," she said, quite calm now, "all it is, is this. I don't believe you."

"You will," I said.

"If you had just given up one thing that is comfortable and convenient to you."

"I quit my jobs."

"What difference do you think that makes to me? Oh Eddie," she said and sighed deeply, "it's way too late."

"It's not," I said, "you'll see."

She turned and lay up against me, but she was silent. She had the slim body of a waif.

"I'm going to marry you," I said.

"It's too late, Eddie."

I used to be frightened by the tears of women, but it seems to be the most natural expression they have. I lay there now and she cried and it was all right.

After a while she said, "Charles is such a sweet guy."

"I don't believe him," I said.

"You couldn't do what he does."

"He can't either, baby. He's frying now just as I would be. Expect him to put an axe through your head one day. Or mine."

"I trust him."

"Trust him to do that. He's calm when he shouldn't be. He looks like a maniac to me."

"You just can't believe that anyone can be tolerant or kind or understanding, can you?" she said.

"Not of what *you* do to *him*. He's got to be insane to be patient with that."

"Well, he's taken it a long time, not just with you but before you, with others."

"Who?"

"Oh, others."

"Who?"

"Are you asking who?"

"Yes."

"His brother for one."

"I know about him. Who else?"

"You can't take it. He can. You can't face the way things are."

"Try me. Who else?"

"With someone I met at a party whose name I've forgotten is who else. He brought me home. I woke next morning and he'd gone and hadn't even left a note."

"Who else?"

"With a Negro boy I used to know in high school who was in love with me then."

"And you did it to him in high school?"

"No. But three months ago I did."

"Who else?"

"With his best friend."

"Also a Negro?"

"You got something against Negroes?"

"Yes, I don't want them fucking my girl. Nor ofays, neither, nor chinks, nor spics, nor frogs, nor wogs, neither!"

"I'm not your girl. I'm telling you this so you'll see it's too damned late. You let too much go by. I'm not where you left me waiting for you. I'm not luggage to check."

"Who else?"

"You think you can walk away without a word, lock me up, disappear, keep me on ice?"

"Who else?"

"A fat old man who's a movie producer, an Italian who is a Communist and a faggot, pig-rich and arrogant, who made me feel like nothing because he said boys were better. I liked him a lot."

Suddenly she turned on me.

"I don't like you," she said. "I don't want to be hooked on you!"

"Who else?"

"A fellow I saw at Sardi's having lunch with an actress. When she left to go to rehearsal, he suggested he might move to my table. I said nothing doing, but on the way out, he was still waiting for me, so I sat down with him. 'You're in luck today,' I said."

"Where did you do him?"

"In my apartment. The place where we were, the same bed."

"How did he get up there?"

"I asked him to come up. I had to see how the kid was, didn't I?"

"You've seen him since?"

"Only once."

I didn't say anything.

"Had enough?"

"Who else?"

"How do you like those tomatoes so far?"

"I don't. Who else?"

"You think you can leave me and have nothing happen, don't you? I'm not your mother, always there, always forgiving."

"Who else?"

"You thought I'd stay on ice for you? Didn't you? Say!"

"Who else?"

"Jack Schnee, the poster man . . . who else? What's the difference who else? You get the idea?"

"Jack Schnee! That creep?"

"Yes."

"What was his attraction?"

"That you didn't like him. I remembered that. So you see the account is dead. Close the books."

"Who else?"

"I can't begin to remember."

"Try."

"But so far, am I reaching you?"

"You are."

"You thought you could take it, didn't you?"

"I can."

"Who else?"

"That's enough, I get the idea."

"Still want to marry me?"

"I'm going to marry you."

"You want to know who was the best of the bunch? And why?"

"No."

"The old Italian. He was fantastic. He had the ability to lie back on the bed with two pillows under his head and—"

"O.K. I get it—"

"No, I want you to hear this. He'd lie there, and no matter what I'd do for how long, take a trip around the world on it, he'd stay hard. And he's an old man, with a nothing body, lying on his back there with two pillows under his head; he had a pot, too, no beauty, you know, altogether. But he'd look up at me and smile that soft Italian smile, look at me with such affection, like admire me when I sat up there on it. He'd hold my belly in his two hands, those soft

Italian hands with those big liver spots all over them, like the hands of one of those old saints."

"O.K., O.K.," I said.

"No malarkey about love and all that, but such affection, the purest and most believable and the most honest thing, that. Affection! I'd have married him for affection. But not for love. They say love in the heat, and the next day they're gone and there isn't even a note. Love is the word they say before they pull your chicken guts out."

"O.K."

"You say love, but what you feel is God knows, hate maybe, that's why you're turned on by a bitch like me. You make me even a worse bitch, like just before with your goddam 'Who else?' so you can get turned on."

"That's not true."

She got out of bed and walked into the bathroom, where she had left her clothes the night before. In the silence I became aware that my father had been calling me. To judge by the "Evangeleh!" he was normal and "sane." I got up and put on my shorts.

Gwen called me from the bathroom. She was just throwing her dress over her head. As she buttoned it, she said to me, "I'll fix him his breakfast."

Then she came up to me and said, "You see, it's hopeless—what you were talking about."

"No, it's not."

We had fixed the old man's bed in the parlor for fear if he was up where we were, he might start walking around daft in the middle of the night and fall down the stairs. We had also put a lot of furniture across where the stairs started, like you do with a kid, so he couldn't climb them. From there the old man called again, very commanding he was, "Evangeleh!"

I called down, "O.K., Pop, right away, Pop . . ."

He grumbled and rumbled down below.

The nice thing about girls is they look so good after the storm. Fighting exhilarates them. Why not? They're the prize that's being fought over. Gwen was blooming in pink, and peach, and other delicate colors. Her eyes were washed with her tears, and glistening.

"Eddie," she said, "I'm going to tell you the chance we got. Will you listen?"

350

I nodded. She was full of some conviction.

"I'm going to marry him, Eddie, just like I told you."

"No, you're not."

"I am. That's for sure. I'll turn him on you if you try anything. I'm going to tell him this afternoon when he comes out here that if he wants to marry me, we better go down to wherever it is and do the trick. But . . . well, here's what I think is the only solution, Eddie, afterwards . . . afterwards we could see each other."

"How?"

"Like we used to."

"You're kidding."

"No, I'm not."

"But you said before—"

"This would be different. I'd be married. We'd have a regular thing, you understand?"

"And you'd tell him?"

"Yeah . . . I mean, yeah . . . since it's the situation."

"And?"

"We'd keep house. I mean we'd get a regular place and fix it up, and I'd take care of you there."

"I don't believe you mean it."

"I do. That way I'd feel safe because I had him and all, understand? And that way I could trust you. I would take good care of you some part of each day. That's all you want of me anyway; you don't want the mess and the dishes, and you don't want the kid; you want the night stuff. Like all was perfect. It all can't be, but as much as can be perfect would be, and let's not look at the rest. We'd have our ordinary lives like other people. You could even go back to your wife, if she could understand it this way. Maybe she'd like it. It's the way things really are, isn't it, everywhere? Nearly everybody I know—"

"Evangeleh!" from downstairs.

I went and leaned over the stair railing.

"Yes, Pop," I said, "we're coming down."

"Have you inquire what young lady wants for breakfast?" he said. "We must take good care of her."

"No, I haven't yet, Pop."

"Evangeleh," he said, reproachfully, "your mother is not here, is she?"

"I don't think so, Pop."

"So it's up to you. Fix her some nice pancakes."

"Would you like some nice pancakes?" I said, turning to Gwen.

"No," she said, then, "Think it over, what I said. You'd really like it."

"Evangeleh! What did she say?"

"She doesn't want pancakes, Pop."

"Well then, fix her nice scramble eggs. Listen what I tell you! I know what's good. Come down here, two of you. We have to hurry. We're going down to the vault today . . ."

"Where, Pop?"

"To the bank. In New York."

"Where?"

"I told you last night. What happened your memory, my boy?"

"Do you remember his telling anything about going to the bank today?" I said to Gwen.

"If he says so," she said, then continued, "Let's face it, we're two unusual people, maybe freaks. We got to find our own way, not like any other two people. I have to have someone I can count on no matter what. I can't count on a man like you who has fits, and is liable to move out, and is different every day!"

"Evangeleh!" the old man roared. "Come down immediately."

"Think it over, Eddie," she said as she ran down the stairs. "It could work."

I took a shower.

Evidently Gwen and Pop got along, because when I got downstairs it was like lovers. He was taking advantage of the fact that he had a fresh ear and was telling her his life story, all about National City, and cussing out poor old Mitchell again, going into details of the man's life after the crash, how he broke everybody in 1929, but he himself came right back and built an even bigger fortune by 1935! How they tried him in court, but when they're that big, he said, you can't get them. Nobody with plenty money was ever in jail. And how he saw him once in the lobby of the Waldorf, Peacock Alley, and how good he looked, how handsome, better than ever, better than ever, a man who should have shot himself, he said, for the sake of justice.

Gwen was shoveling the eggs into his face as he was talking, waiting for him to get through each sentence and then, when he opened his mouth and held still, filling it again, as you do a kid, even wiping under his chin with a bib. She seemed to be enjoying it all. She evidently liked old men. I recalled the old Italian with the liver spots on his hands.

He saw me and took a sudden new tack.

"She was a fine woman," he said.

"Who was, Mr. Arness?" and she filled his mouth with the eggs.

"His mother used to keep this place beautiful. Then I lost my money and . . ." He started to go on about that so I headed into the kitchen.

"Evangeleh!" I suddenly heard. "Where are you going?"

"To get a cup of coffee."

"Do you mind waiting till I finish my sentence?" he said. "You see, miss, when you lose your money they don't wait till you finish your sentence, even my own son."

"I listen, Pop."

"Is a cup of coffee more important than what your father is saying?"

"No, Pop."

"So sit down. I'm talking."

I sat down.

Then he forgot what he was saying. He went blank. We all just sat there. Finally Gwen came to the rescue. "You wanted to tell Evangeleh to call a taxi," she said.

"Yes, Evangeleh, call taxi immediately, we're going to New York, downtown."

"Where?"

"I told you just now, Evangeleh. How you become big shot success, some day tell me that." He turned to Gwen. "He lost my memory!" he said and laughed, shaking his head in absolute amazement. "We are going down to the Cornuh Exchange Bank, the safe deposit there; I have some business, Mr. Meyer, their vault department. Jewish fellow, but very fine man, I'll introduce you," he said to Gwen.

"Thank you," she said.

"I'm sorry my wife not here. But perhaps," and he winked meaningfully, "just as well, she is not very broadminded these subjects." He smiled. "I personally have no objections. But . . ." He saw me standing looking at him. "Did you call the taxi, Evangeleh?"

"No, Pop."

"What are you waiting?"

"I'm going to do it right now."

"You see," he said to Gwen, "now I have to remind him everything. My business is not important to him any more." Then he looked at her coyly and said, "Is there a little more?" He was referring to the eggs.

"Yes, Mr. Arness," she said, "right away."

As she passed me, going to the kitchen, I said, "What do I do?"

"Call a taxi," she said.

The three of us rode down to the Empire State Building, in the subbasement of which my father had his safe deposit box. I think it was one of the happiest days of his life. He was in love with Gwen by this time. And she was at her most obliging, giving each thing he said the same evaluation he gave it, encouraging him to go on and on with his personal reminiscences, the battles he had fought, the victories, the tragedies, the deals, the betrayals, the old, old jokes. On this trip he told her the whole story of his life, how his brother had brought him to this country, their early hard times in New York, their quarrels, the day he decided to go on his own, how he made a success of it. And how before the crash he had seen Mitchell at the old Belmont track with a woman who wore a big hat and a veil, and he noticed that Mitchell was not introducing her to anyone. He had a hunch that day, he said, to take his money out of National City. But he didn't. He remembered when Mitchell's female companion crossed her legs, he saw her ankle. He liked nice legs, he told her, and patted Gwen's knee and winked at me, and said I had inherited from him an appreciation of women's legs. Then he began to go over the catalogue of my girl friends' legs: some too skinny, some too thick in the calf and thigh. Finally he got to Florence. He said it was a wonderful thing for me when I married Florence, because she was very high class, very respectable, college president's daughter, he said. She had taught me to save my money. I was a very smart boy to take her, he said. But he was also cavalier about occasional lapses (he patted Gwen's knee again) so long as a girl was clean. He smiled at her. Then, getting even friendlier, he advised her to give up the life she was leading and get married. I got the idea, about this time, that he thought Gwen was a prostitute.

When we got to the Empire State Building, he told the taxi to wait. I don't know where he figured the money was coming from. I was beginning to run short myself. But he behaved the way he wanted Gwen to see him. Big shot! He confided in us that he was seriously considering moving his safe deposit holdings to the Colonial Trust, where there was a Mr. Manning, an Irish, but very fine man. He couldn't make up his mind which of the two was safest.

Downstairs, just as he had said, there was Mr. Meyer. He was a dignified old person, with a soft, indoor face. The moment he saw my father enter, he came across the foyer and took him off my arm, greeting him warmly. My father had been coming there since 1932, when the branch opened, and Mr. Meyer had been there all that time, too, in one capacity or another, gradually mounting the ladder of success till now he was in charge, a sort of Charon, who presently conveyed my father across the marble floor and through a gate which Gwen and I couldn't penetrate, because we had no safe deposit box there. Mr. Meyer held the gate open for my father to go through ahead of him. The old fellow looked back at Gwen and me to see if we were impressed by the courtesies that were being shown him.

We withdrew to a respectful distance. Mr. Meyer, an expert in handling old people, as he had to be, slowly took my father to a private room. He was still very feeble, but enspirited by the occasion and the elaborate courtesies. The little room where he was now being seated was the biggest and the best, and shed its glow of security, however temporary, on all who entered. I could see why the trip meant so much to my father. There was now a little ceremony, my old man taking out his black wallet, the one he had hidden under the mattress of the hospital bed. It contained the key he now passed over to Mr. Meyer. Mr. Meyer bowed and thanked him for the trust, as it were, and then proceeded out of the room, at his own slow pace, through an enormous mock-up of a safe door and into corridors lined with safe deposit boxes. When he disappeared from sight, my father got up and went to the door of his private room so he could watch Mr. Meyer in the recesses of the vault and check on whatever was going on there in the way of unlocking and withdrawal.

Satisfied that everything was kosher, he went back to his chair. By the time Mr. Meyer returned with the flat metal box, my father was seated again in the armchair, looking directly ahead, his back very straight.

Mr. Meyer put the metal box on the table in front of my father. Then he gave him a pad, a pen that was attached by a little chain to a stand, a box of paper clips, and a small scissors. He moved the table lamp a little closer. He asked my father if there was anything else he wanted, was he perfectly comfortable? The old boy, not making the least move towards the box, nodded, his back stiff and erect. Then Mr. Meyer withdrew, and closed the door after him, and my father was lost to sight.

As Mr. Meyer went back to his desk he smiled that soft indoor smile. "He's been coming here for thirty-two years," he said.

"What's he got in there?" I asked.

"Oh, we wouldn't know that."

Gwen and I were alone.

"You won't face the facts, will you?" she said.

I didn't answer.

"That's the only way you and I can be together."

I didn't answer.

"It's impossible," she said, "for a person to get all he or she needs from another single person. It's the thing nobody faces."

"I don't believe that," I said.

She shrugged.

"And I'm not going to allow it."

"Once I say go to him, how the hell are you going to stop it?"

I didn't have an answer for that.

The door of the cubicle opened. My father saw us and nodded.

Two months later, as executor of my father's estate, I had to open this same box in front of a representative of the United States Department of Internal Revenue. There were many, many insurance policies, all lapsed. There were twenty-odd sheets of paper with long lists of figures in my father's small, crabbed hand. These sometimes ran the length of the sheet, and were totaled at the bottom. But neither Michael nor Mr. Meyer could say what things of value the figures stood for. There was a piece of paper which declared my father to be the owner of ten shares of National City Bank stock. Either he had never entirely lost faith in this company, or more likely, it seemed to me, he didn't want to be caught looking foolish if it came back strong. There were some pieces of oriental jewelry, mostly trinkets, nothing of value—except one piece. This was a locket and chain, both of heavy gold. It had belonged to my father's mother's mother, and it had been brought to this country by my grandmother when she came over from the other side in 1905. This piece, a jeweler's appraisal told us, was of considerable worth.

Mr. Meyer had sent a clerk upstairs to Walgreen's Drug Store to buy a gilt model of the Empire State Building, perhaps four inches high, the kind of thing that tourists take home. As we left, he made a presentation of this to my father. "Very nice, very nice," my father said, and accepted it. Then he said with some gravity, "I have decided not to move to another bank."

Mr. Meyer said, "Thank you, Mr. Arness. Thank you very much." They shook hands. Mr. Meyer was never to see my father again. He himself died shortly after my father did.

All the way home my father slept, his head on Gwen's shoulder, holding the little model of the Empire State Building.

Gwen and I looked at each other. She did have an enchanting smile. Finally, when we were out of the thick traffic and had turned onto Pelham Parkway, she said to me, "I would have run away anywhere with you once. All you had to do was say, 'Let's go.'"

It was evident she was tapping a terrible hurt in her memory.

Later Gwen said, "I should have left you where I found you—asleep in the dell."

"What dell?"

"The dell of respectability, that's what dell."

"Now you're being superior."

"Because I am superior to you," she said. "I'm more honest. You can't face the facts of what you are and what you feel. I was o.k. with you so long as I was the ghost who walked the corridors of that crummy-elegant motel on Wilshire Boulevard, the girl who took off her clothing and didn't say a word, and who you never saw close up by the light of day. But as soon as I started to be somebody, a person, you couldn't take me. Now it's too late!"

We drove to the house. I paid off the cab.

"You're sad," she said.

"You're not reading me right," I answered. But she was.

"You can't really blame me if I didn't believe you; you're just an old disappearer, aren't you, baby?"

"I was," I said. "I *was.*"

She leaned over and kissed me. "I'm sorry," she said. "I'll tell Charles not to come tonight. I'll tell him tomorrow. And then that will be it! O.K.?"

"O.K.," I said.

We put the old man to bed.

Later, we heard a car drive up. It was Charles. Gwen went down to talk to him. She came back in about ten minutes, carrying Andy. Charles had to go out on business in the morning, she said, and couldn't look after him again.

"He says he'll come for me after work tomorrow and for me to be ready to go."

"And what did you say?"

"I promised him."

We heard the car drive away.

· 20 ·

A LAST night together passes minute by minute. We lay on our backs, side by side, not touching, our bodies cool and without configuration. When we talked, we talked in the past tense.

"There was one thing I always wanted to do with you, Eddie; I wanted to get a car and drive you down and show you what I came out of."

"I'd like to have done that."

"You lived on the cream, Eddie; this house must have been a mansion when you were a kid."

"Actually some people called it that. Maybe it was."

Later, I noticed her smiling and asked her what about.

"There was this Jewish guy I used to go with long ago. I was remembering something he used to say to me."

"What was that?"

"What for are you laying there like a lox?"

"Well, why are you lying there like a lox?"

"I didn't know what a lox was in those days. They don't have any where I come from. But he was right. I was like that then."

We didn't talk for a bit. We'd never been like that before, enjoying the talking and listening and then the quiet. On the last night you discover the things you might have enjoyed.

"You know, Eddie, you should have been proud of me—and maybe if you had seen what I came out of—"

"I was proud of you."

"Yeah, sure. Did you notice what your father thought I was yesterday?"

"Yeah, that was funny."

"Wasn't it?"

"Oh, come on."

"But I'll never understand why you weren't proud of me, what I made of myself. You had to duck and dodge a bit when you were a kid, but you lived in clover."

"Sure."

"I mean it. Even like your father, what the hell was so wrong about him? He's not a bad old guy."

"Why are you lying there like a lox?"

"You were always feeling sorry for yourself and complaining about your father. You should have met mine."

"What was so terrible about him?"

"Nothing, to look at him. He's the town grocer, but he believes it's his mission on earth to keep that town for the white man. And he does. He'll go for weeks and you'd never suspect anything, the way he is in that long white apron. Then all of a sudden he busts loose. You think your father has a temper? When mine has one of his white mule fits, every black man in that town stays indoors. He's a small man but—well, you've seen how I get when I go. Mind you, he's got no legal position down there; he's head of some sort of white council, and he had his brother made sheriff, but he himself is just the town grocer.

"I didn't have a mother who could help me like yours did. Mine was like a piece of white soap that's been in the water too long, with those limp hands. She used to boast she'd never learned to light a stove. Sure, she had colored to do everything for her all her life. She was deadly afraid of—well, she wouldn't go out of the house after dark, and she was right, too, because my father had murdered five or six of their men, and everybody expected that sooner or later he'd get a bullet or a knife."

"By now, maybe he has."

"I'm talking about the hill country, Eddie, back on the Alabama-Georgia border. No, he's still down there walking around with the bottoms of his pants inside his boots. I don't know how they ever made me. I slept in the same bed with her till I was fourteen, and I can't remember one single night when he came to her. He used to get what he needed from the white trash and the colored girls. Whenever he sighted one he favored, he got his brother to jail her on some pretext. The pair of them had this room in the back of the jailhouse, their riding academy, with this well-sprung leather couch.

"Well, if my father never got into my mother's bed, my uncle did. Except my mother wasn't in it. I was. She'd gone over to Rosedale, Mississippi, to visit her sister. My father was up to Stuttgart to meet the ducks which were just then coming down to the rice fields. Five weeks later, when the deer season opened, my uncle decided not to go with my father and some of their bunk buddies to the cabin they have in the hills. He came calling on me again, chasing my mother out of the house—she was so scared she didn't make a squeak like any mouse would have. Afterwards, she pretended nothing had happened.

"I was fourteen years old. I knew I had to do something for myself, since no one else would. And that's when I ran away. There was a traveling commercial show came to town. They had these girls in pink dresses standing there holding up their tits and the product, Rose Petal Shortening it was, while this man made a spiel. They took me on, and that's how I got to Nashville.

"There the spieler got sick of the rose petal he was doing it to, and began to come into my room at night. He'd get the passkey from the hotel clerk. So I got me a job in the five-and-dime, lying about my age and my schooling. Man, I couldn't make change! I worked there awhile, but that wasn't going anywhere either.

"So then a man offered to take me up north, to Washington. This man was honest with me, I mean he was exact. I knew the score by then. I thought what the hell does it mean anyway, I just lie there—yeah, like a lox, right.

"So I made a deal. I know you think that's terrible, but don't you see how it could happen? No? Well, it's not something I like to remember myself. But what else did I have that anyone wanted? It's a world where no one remembers your name after they shoot their load.

"O.K., so I saw I was getting laid a lot but wasn't getting anything out of it, certainly wasn't having any fun. So I met this assistant to a congressman—the Jewish fellow I mentioned—and I took up with him. Then I met his boss, the congressman; a young man he was, not like what congressman sounds like. He liked me, I don't know why except I was becoming real pretty about then. He found me a room, gave me my rent and some regular money for food and stockings and so on. He insisted I had to be only for him. He didn't know what a relief that was—to be like that.

"That gave me my chance. I had time to look around. I fixed up my room real pretty. I went to high school. Nobody could figure me out there. I was three, four years older than the others and very studious. I didn't date. Nobody knew where I lived. I never accepted invitations to girls' houses, because I had no way of inviting them back. All I did for the longest time was read. A book a day. And talk to my congressman. He was the first person who had any respect for me. He taught me how to understand people and how to live with myself. He used to come to my place sometimes just to study his reports and work on his papers. I'd fix him something to eat and all. I learned to talk from him.

"But after a while, less and less happened in bed. Like I said, I'd started wrong, and I didn't like sex, I really didn't. I couldn't figure what was supposed to be so wonderful about it; I never came, so no wonder. Well, then one day he said that I really didn't like him physically, and he'd found this girl who did. Only thing, I knew this other girl. It didn't mean anything to her either. You know a lot of girls pretend. 'Are you coming?' the man says, because they read these books, and they know they're not supposed to let go till you have. So then the girl makes all the moves and sounds, and they call it love.

"Well, most men, you're gone, you're gone. But the last thing my congressman did for me was he got me a job, interviewing for this research outfit. He even told me how to do it. There's quite a technique to it, you know. I found I was naturally good at it. Most people will talk to a pretty girl. Then I found out something else, that I could hold a job. When I found that out, I didn't need a man any more. So I stopped doing it altogether, believe it or not, for nearly two years. I kept trying to look good, sure, a girl dresses sexy, that's professional. But the fact was that I was happy not to bother with it. At all!

"From an interviewer, I became a researcher. I was good at that, too. I found I could write a report—nothing fancy, but like you write a telegram, the facts. Mr. Finnegan told me when I started to work for him that most people see what they want to see, but I saw what I saw. That's why he gave me the job I had with him. He

362

had something else in mind, too. He was a terrible man, 'I'll-send-the-Rolls-for-you-dear' and all that.

"I never enjoyed the other business till I got with you. I don't know why with you; you were no different or better. Maybe I was just ready then. Maybe it's because when I met you, you were so needy. When I saw you at that Christmas party and you had that needy look in your eyes, I figured it finally might happen.

"You thought I was so experienced and all, didn't you? But you see it had never really happened to me. That's why I took so much guff from you later. That's why I kept coming back to you even though—well, I'll tell you now, there is something in you I do respect, despite what I always say. I guess I respect that you're up the creek without a clue and you admit it. That way you're honest. And let me tell you, the further up I got and I got to the damned top, the more it was the same. Girls see a lot from the bottom of this life that they don't photograph for *Life* magazine."

She sat up, the cover falling off her front. She looked like a youngster, and she said, "Do you think you can judge me the way you can other girls who had regular fathers and mothers and families? Tell me, come on. No, forget it! I don't want to cop a plea either. But someday you'll see what I mean. I think you should have been proud of me instead of the way you were. I made something of myself."

We lay there, and the minutes passed.

"I could have done a lot for you," she said.

Then after another while, she said, "I don't expect you to like the way I was. But I don't want to be judged by you, either. Or by anybody. Or put down. That's why I say, let's forget it. I have Charles."

The baby began to whimper. She got up and brought him into the bed and put him between us. It was funny, the way he was so happy being in bed with her. She had some natural animalism that immediately affected the kid, and he fell asleep. I held her hand—a gesture of admiration, I suppose—and I wanted to make love to her. But with the kid there and all, I didn't. After a time we fell half-asleep, the three of us. I was thinking that it must have taken a lot of courage to tell me all she had, without tipping it in her favor. I would have left out some things.

Then she opened her eyes and looked at me. There was an absolute freshness about her face, her lips just parted, her gray-green eyes barely open, the lashes, the delicate pallor of her cheeks. I mean there was color, but it was so delicate.

There was nothing to do except gently lift myself over the infant and settle over her. But I didn't touch her anywhere. I waited, not moving, not helping. Slowly she began to reach for me. And to provide herself, bit by bit. It was a magical way of doing it, because there was such holding back of desire, still knowing what was coming, that it was all going to happen.

There was a sound from downstairs. I heard my father's voice. "The old man's in good shape this morning," I whispered.

She kissed me in a particular way, so telling me to tend to business.

I reached under and pulled her up to me. Each time I moved now, I drove some voice out of her. Her thin white fingers were holding on. Her breathing came harder and harder. She raised her legs farther, kicking off the covers, wrapping her legs around my waist.

Then she stopped abruptly. She was looking over my shoulder.

I turned and looked around and there was Florence.

Behind her, at the door which they had just entered, was Gloria.

Later I found out that Michael had indeed gone down to Florida. After a night's search, checking the motels and so on, he had called up to say that as far as anyone in Tarpon Springs seemed to know, Pop and I had not come into town.

That's when Gloria, who was quite properly suspicious of me, had her hunch. That hunch had brought them to the house on the Sound.

Florence was looking at the bedful. She stood there, squinting her eyes, as though measuring the bed for a coverlet.

Gloria wasn't looking at us. I guess she had had a good look.

Well, it all hung there for a moment, like one of those dishes placed on exhibition across the entrance of very expensive restaurants, or a fish or a bird in jelly, where the former living matter is suspended in a thickened kind of space, fixed in an attitude.

Come to think of it, there was nothing really to say or do if you were civilized. I don't know what an uncivilized woman would have done.

Poor Florence.

364

Since she was what she was, she turned and left. Gloria followed, closing the door.

I was aware of a vast feeling of relief, even of elation. There was such happiness in having it over with. It was like the moment at the end of those old mystery plays where, five minutes before the final curtain, everyone who has been dodging everyone else all evening comes out on the stage, and you know it's over; there's no possible plot left. And as the curtain drops and the lights go on, you wonder how in the world it could have taken so long to get to that point.

I felt disencumbered. I felt literally lighter.

And the kid laughed. Maybe it wasn't the first time he had laughed out loud, but it was the first time I heard him. It must have been a novelty for Gwen, too, because she began to laugh.

"Who was that with her?" she asked.

"Who'd she look like?"

"Like a short policewoman," she said, "or maybe a researcher for *Playboy* . . ."

"She's my sister-in-law," I said.

That's not a funny remark. But it broke us up. We got into one of those jags of laughter!

Later at my hearing there was testimony in writing from Gloria that as they left, they could hear "peals of obscene laughter" and a baby crying. The baby was not crying, and we weren't aware that we were being obscene. But we did get up out of the bed, and didn't dress. There was nothing to hide any more, so we pulled the window shades all the way down and let them fly.

Gloria's estate wagon was driving off.

Without realizing it, we had been talking in whispers ever since we'd been there, the shades down, as few lights as possible, and whispers. Now everything seemed to be returning to something we had long forgotten: the normal.

I had done what I had unconsciously wished. I had burned the bridge back to the mainland.

Poor Florence.

But what a relief!

I called the grocer. I ordered everything I like: sausages, the little Jones Boys kind, thick-sliced bacon, eggs, a turkey for that night, and Pepperidge Farm ready-mix stuffing, and some sage and chestnuts and sherry to spice it with, and oregano to add to everything, and May wine to drink, and, to drink before that, some Daiquiri mix and brown rum, and those little smoked oysters—the works. I figured since my father and mother still had these charge accounts, I might as well use them till my credit collapsed.

I suppose the old man was puzzled by all the laughing and racket. He shouted from below, "What's going on up there?"

So we went down. We wouldn't have minded that morning how nutty he was. He seemed not only sane and normal, but inspired.

It seemed he had had a dream.

"Evangeleh," he said, "come here."

"I'm going to make you some breakfast, Pop," I said.

"Let the womans do that!" he said; very peremptory, he was, very much like his old self, the one I didn't like.

"There's only one woman here, and she doesn't know her way around this kitchen," I said.

"She'll find. Come here next to me."

"I'll make the breakfast," said Gwen. "What would you like, Mr. Arness?"

"A few olives and a piece of cheese," he said.

Gwen whispered to me, "Where in the hell am I going to find a few olives and a piece of cheese?"

"Don't pay any attention to him," I said.

"How about some scrambled eggs, Pop?" I said.

"Too much trouble," he said, "I don't want to give trouble."

"He wants eggs," I said to Gwen.

I sat next to the old man. He'd apparently been up for a couple of hours; his eyes were shining with all kinds of energy. He seemed like himself again, that is, absolute, demanding, competitive, and just a little malignant. Where the new energy had come from, I don't know.

"How did you sleep?" I said.

"I didn't sleep all night," he said. "I had a dream. Very important."

In my family, dreams are as real as the events of the waking hours, and far more important.

"There was a couple of womans here," he said. "One looked like your wife, Frances, you know . . ."

"That wasn't a dream, Pop. She was here."

366

"But my father," he said, "my father, was he here?"

"Pop, your father died in 1913 on the boat *Kaiser Wilhelm* in passage from Turkey to the United States of America."

"He was here last night."

I gave up. "What did he say?"

"He said to me, 'Seraphim, you're not finished!' Then in manner of Greek Orthodox priest he intoned, 'Seraphim, you're not finished yet. Start again, Seraphim.' "

Gwen had come in from the kitchen and was listening.

"How was he dressed?" I asked.

"How he usually dresses. He has only one suit. The other he gave to Stavros, your uncle Joe, when he left for America the first time. But let me tell you! He came on a white horse, and he held a *boozookie*."

"Where did he get the white horse?"

"How should I know?"

"And he held a . . . what?"

He made a gesture from which I understood that the old man riding the white horse had held an oriental guitar.

"Oh," I said, "a *boozookie*."

"Isn't that what I said?"

"Yes."

"So? What's the matter with you?"

"I didn't know he could play one."

"He couldn't."

"So that *is* kind of strange."

"He must have learned," said my father.

I looked at Gwen. She smiled and went back into the kitchen. The coffee had begun to perk. I had no choice except to go on with the conversation.

"How was he feeling?"

"He was angry with me," my father said. "He has a bad temper, your grandfather. He sat there and looked like a storm, and he said to me, 'Seraphim, what are you doing?' I had no answer. Then he said, 'Seraphim, you're not finished yet.' "

"What did he mean by that?"

"He meant I'm not finished. It's very simple. What is confusing you this morning?"

"I'm sorry," I said, "but he meant what?"

"He meant I should start in business again."

"Oh."

I suddenly felt very nervous. If this maniac, I thought, gets it into his head that—

"'You know the market, Seraphim,' he said, 'you know it better than those Armenians and Syrians. They know cheap goods and domestic. You know fine goods. I taught you how to look back of rug and tell quality. You know weave and you know the dyes and you know the market.'"

"It's true, Pop, you did." I was trying to be subtle, but it didn't work.

"What did? I do. I can today look at the back piece of goods and tell you where it was bought, how much it cost, who knows market better than I do?"

"I can't imagine," I said.

"So what are you arguing?" he asked. He was flaring at me, his eyebrows tensed in their raised position, stiff as bone. His left eye was bloodshot.

"No one," he said, "no Armenian, Syrian, Jew, or I don't know what, Egyptians, none of those thieves now in business . . ."

He got up. He was on some wave of aggression and optimism. It was wonderful to see. He was waving his arms and shouting, "They don't know market, they don't know goods."

"You're right, Pop," I said.

"I don't need you to tell me I'm right."

"I'm sorry, Pop, I didn't mean—"

"There's nothing the matter with me."

"Good."

"Everybody's acting like there's something the matter with me!"

"Well, Pop, you have been a little . . ."

"Everybody trying to bury me."

"Now, Pop . . ."

"You, too, sometimes you look at me funny."

"Well, Pop, you've been a little sick."

"Because you found me in hospital doesn't mean I'm sick. They make there like I can't walk. I walk. I just don't want to walk where they want me to walk. Walk to ambulance, they say. Why should I walk to ambulance? I don't call ambulance, Gloria and Michael call ambulance. Your mother I don't mention her name. Walk to bed, they say. I don't want to go to bed. I'm not finished!"

I thought, how can I stop this man?

"Pop, you look much better this morning."

"You can't bury me yet."

"Why do you think I want to bury you, Pop?"

"We soon find out." He was glaring at me in fury. I suppose his fury was at death. But I seemed to be included in the scattershot. He was shaking with rage.

"I can still do anything I could use to do!"

There was nothing I could do but placate him.

"I know, Pop."

"And I'm still known in the market. 'Where's Sam?' they all ask. 'Where's Sam Arness?' All I have to do is open my door."

"I know that, Pop."

"I feel fine . . . see . . . see . . ."

He was doing some grotesque gymnastics.

"I'm glad, Pop."

"I hope you mean that."

"I do, Pop."

"We soon find that out," he said.

"Find what out?"

"How glad and so forth!"

"Why do you keep doubting me, Pop?"

"Because I want you to give me some money."

"Oh," I said.

"I want to start my business again."

"Oh."

He was glaring at me, looking for the least crack in my loyalty.

"Well . . ." I said fighting for time, "well . . ."

"This morning I walk down to the water like I used to every morning in my big years."

"Good, Pop." What the hell else could I say?

"Those trees, you know, they are the same trees we had behind the house in Asia Minor. The house where I was born and Stavros, your uncle Joe, was born. You never saw them."

"I remember you telling me about those trees."

"You should have gone to Anatolia and seen them in the spring. You are stupid, my son."

"I know."

"Those trees 1 have near the water here, did you go down to see them?"

"I didn't have time yet."

"What have you been doing so important you don't have time yet? Monkey business, right?"

"I will go later."

He started to get up. "I'll take you now. Come."

"She's bringing your breakfast, Pop."

"Well, then, after breakfast . . ."

"Good."

"Good." Was he mocking me? "Why the hell do you think I'm telling you about these trees?"

"I guess they are pretty trees."

"They're not so pretty, you damn fool."

"Well, I always thought—"

"Now in the spring they put out flowers, you understand, and the whole neighborhood smells beautiful from them. You smell?"

"No."

"So, now, smell."

By God, he was right. He was not imagining this. I could smell them.

"Oh, yes, yes," I said.

"And that is the same way they smell in Kayseri, Turkey."

"It's a beautiful smell, like gardenias."

"No, not like gardenia, like what they are, acacia. The whole neighborhood. Why do you think I tell you about this?"

"Well, because you want me to smell how beautiful—"

"Evangeleh, for smart boy maybe genius, you damn fool."

"Well, then—"

"How you make all that money? Explain me that!"

"Well, then tell me, what—"

"Some things you stupid."

"Well, Pop, you just said . . ."

"I walked down to water and those trees, I told you."

"Yes, I know."

"You know nothing."

It was the way he used to bully me when I was a kid, and I was beginning to resent him and still I was frightened of him, just as when I was a kid.

"Well, Pop . . ."

"Well, Pop, well, Pop! You see any nurses here?"

I didn't know what to say.

"You see nurses, yes or no?"

"No."

"Right for change."

I was relieved to see Gwen coming through the door with the eggs and some coffee on a tray.

"Did you hear that cunt nurse tell me in the hospital you can't walk, Mr. Arness?"

"Pop, there are ladies present."

"I'm sure she heard the word before, right, Miss?"

He still thought Gwen was a hooker.

"I heard it before," said Gwen.

"When they trying kill you, you can't always be polite, right, Miss?"

"That's what I think too, kid," said Gwen.

"What do you think?" he said to me.

"Well . . . well . . ." I sputtered.

"Wellwellwellwell?!?!" he said, mocking me.

I was really burning up by now. At the same time I had to admit that my father had become himself again.

"What you thinking now?" he said.

"Why, nothing."

"Lies, lies, when you don't speak, you think plenty! What you think, Evangeleh?"

"That you've become yourself again."

"Son of bitch, eh?"

"Right," I said, "but . . ."

"But you don't see no nurses here, and those trees, where are they?"

"Down near the water."

"Right!" he shouted. "Far away! So figure it out!"

Now he looked at the tray which Gwen had placed in front of him. "I don't want these eggs," he said. "I ask for eggs?"

"Pop, don't talk that way to her."

"Now you're going to tell me how to talk?"

Gwen interceded. "What would you like, Mr. Arness?"

"Anything," he said. "I don't want to make trouble."

Then he looked at her and smiled charmingly, and he reached out and took her hand.

"You very lovely little lady. I wish I was young man, I take you away from my son. You know when I was young man, I could go all night. Of course I only had his mother. But even when I was sick and tired of her, I could go all night. Poor woman had no peace. She look at me and say, 'Seraphim! Again?' " He laughed and squeezed her hand. Then he sang, "All day, all night! Seraphim. Poor woman!"

I felt very uncomfortable whenever my father talked of his sex life with my mother, and he knew it.

"He don't like it when I squeeze his mother here and there when he was little boy. He used to pull my hand away. Remember?" he said to me, "remember? He called this thing here," he put his hand on Gwen's breast, "he called it his dinner, and when I put my hand there, he pull it away. Look, he wants to do it again . . ." and he laughed uproariously. "All day, all night, Seraphim," he sang.

Gwen liked him. "Bet you could still, Mr. Arness."

"Don't make fun of me, Miss. Not in love business any more, that finished when I was forty-five. Finished."

"Well, you never know," said Gwen.

"Don't tell me what I know," he said. "In that department, finished. But not in rug business. I walk to the water today. Alone. No nurse. No help. What you think of that?"

"That is wonderful, Mr. Arness," said Gwen.

"Yes, it is wonderful! Did he tell you," he said, "my father he came to me in a dream?" He looked at me rather slyly and said, "He thinks, damn fool son, that I don't know difference true and dream. But dreams tell everything, you believe that, Miss?"

"Yes," said Gwen.

For chrissake, she was yessing him now.

"Good," he said. "After dream I think maybe I see someone around here who doesn't wish me dead."

"Pop," I remonstrated, "I don't wish you dead."

"We see," he said ominously, "we see." He fixed his eye on me. "How much money you have?" he asked.

I certainly was slow. Only then did I realize what he was up to. "I don't know," I ducked.

He was silent for a moment, then turned to Gwen and asked, "Miss, you ever hear grown man doesn't know how much money he has?"

"No," said Gwen, the bitch.

"Peh, peh, peh!" said my father. This "peh, peh, peh" of his was a sound he used to make when I was a kid. A most scornful sound it was, and one that still had the power, thirty-odd years later, to infuriate me. "Peh, peh, peh."

"How much money you have?" he said, "you and Florence?" He turned to Gwen. "Florence, Mrs. Arness Junior, very high class woman, father big shot, also has money."

"I really don't know, Pop."

He didn't look at me but went right on talking to Gwen. "I find in my life, all conversation change when you talk money. You find that, Miss? When you ask for money next morning, different story, right? Before, honey, darling, sweetheart, lollipop, so forth. After, 'I don't know how much money I have?' Big lie!"

I had to control myself.

"Before, all kisses, I love you and so forth, squeezes here, there, you know, you know . . . eh?"

"I know, all right," she said, playing the part. "But that's life."

"But from your son, you expect maybe something different."

"Your son is a good man, Mr. Arness," said Gwen.

"We see," he said. He turned to me now. "I don't ask favors," he said. "I speak business, I want to do business with you."

Suddenly he looked down at the eggs and said, "This is cold!"

"Well . . ." said Gwen. Then she looked at me. Neither of us knew what the hell to say to that but he helped us out.

"That's all right," he said. "No harm done. I don't want make trouble. Dear Miss, give me your hand, your hand warm, eggs cold. I squeeze hand lillie bit, then I feel warm, too." Then he forgot all that and began to eat the eggs. "Very nice," he said, "scrambley eggs," as though he had just noticed them for the first time. "Very nice!"

Then he noticed me again.

"I need no favors my life. Strictly business!" He was devouring the eggs now. "Very nice!" he said.

I stood there trembling. I was ashamed of the power this old bastard still had over me. I couldn't look at Gwen. I suppose she could feel my embarrassment, because she came over and put her arm through mine. We watched him taste the coffee.

"No cream," he said. "I like lillie hot milk."

"He doesn't like cream," I said to Gwen. "Just heat up a little—"

"We have no milk," she said.

"Then what is this?" he asked. He picked up the little pitcher and looked at it very critically. Then he lifted it up to his nose and smelled its contents. "What's this?"

"Condensed," said Gwen.

"Take it away," he ordered, thrusting the pitcher at Gwen, "no can goods here!"

He glared at me. Then he softened. "I drink without milk, that's all right, don't want to make trouble."

He smiled at me. "Evangeleh," he said, "come here, Evangeleh."

I approached him cautiously.

"See," he said to Gwen, "he knows what is coming and he's afraid of me. My own son. Once you mention money, even my own son."

He pulled me down and kissed me on the cheek. "Don't worry," he said, "money isn't everything." Then he burst into obscene and anxious laughter. "Money isn't everything!"

I laughed, too, but I was ready to hit him.

"Peh, peh, peh," said the old man scornfully. "It's a good thing I don't want to borrow money from my eldest son, eh, young lady?"

I felt I would lose control any minute. Again I was cautioning myself not to, to wait this out. It couldn't go on much longer.

"Look," he said to Gwen, "see how scared he is. He thought I was finished, he thought he wouldn't have trouble from me any more, eh? Tst! tst! tst! tst! tst!!"

"Pop," I said, "really, really, I'm glad you're better."

"But the other subject. No discussion, right?"

I didn't say anything.

"O.K., I don't want to borrow money from you, forget it. I don't want your money!"

"I don't have any money, Pop, but I do have a little property."

"You damn right you have a little, more than a little. You have money, too."

"No, I don't, I truly don't."

"You ever see anything like that, Miss, lying to father?"

"I guess he means he doesn't know exactly," said Gwen.

374

"He my son, and he know exactly. He just scared shit."

Suddenly I was not going to take it any more. "What am I afraid of, Pop?" I said.

"You afraid I take your money."

"Why would I be afraid of that? You can't take it, because I don't have any. But if I did, I wouldn't give it to you."

"You have, and I can take it."

"No, you can't. You're not in Turkey, Pop."

"I can take it. But I don't want—"

"Yes, you want, Pop, you want money from me."

"No, I want business basis," he said. "Six per cent, but you think I'm finished like everyone else. You laugh," he said, waving his arms. "But my son, cunt nurse, same thing. He wish me finish."

"I don't wish you finished, Pop."

"He think my brain sick, too, right? You think my brain no work, eh?"

"Pop," I said, "I don't!"

"Then why don't you give me money? Your papa is asking. Why you make me ask you so many time in front of stranger like this young miss here? Evangeleh, this is my only chance. Everybody laughing at me and say I'm finished. No brains. You want me to die like this, with nothing?"

"You have plenty brains, Pop."

"If you have no money, you have no brains. That's why people laugh at me. That's why I ask my son, give me chance now. I know the market, I know goods . . ."

"That's not the point, Pop."

"I know the point. Money means more to you than your blood."

"In that respect, I'm just like my father," I said. It was out before I knew it. Gwen looked at me sharply. But the old man went right on as if he'd always known the antagonism was there and didn't expect any better or any different.

"You hear, you hear," he said to Gwen. "You hear my eldest son. I should beat him with stick, what he say to his father."

"Pop, I'm sorry. I love you, Pop."

"Then why don't you give me money to start business again?"

"Pop, I don't have any, just some property with Florence. In the second place, to start in business today is a big deal."

"I don't start big deal. I buy maybe twenty, thirty thousand dollars worth goods Persia, what they call it now?"

"Iran."

"Iran, yes! And maybe I buy another twenty Istanbul market, and maybe some goods here, present New York market, memorandum, I get half a floor space, that's all!"

I just stood there.

"Evangeleh," my father's voice trembled with anxiety. He was doing the thing he didn't want to ever do; he was finally begging his son. "It's my last chance, Evangeleh. You say no to me, I'm finished, and they right to laugh at me, no brain! I'm joke. You have the money, Evangeleh . . ."

There was no way to convince him that I didn't. Since he thought of me as he did.

"He doesn't talk. Mr. Silent. He should go on TV, my eldest son. New program. Mr. Silent, Say Nothing."

"Pop, listen . . ."

"I don't need listen. I understand, very well. After everything I do for you, you forget everything."

There was no use pointing out the facts of this. I just gave up.

"Silent!" he said to Gwen. "Now the time speak for his father, not with words, I love you and so forth, but real thing. But Mr. Moto, Wang Choo, chop, chop, say nothing!" He turned to me. "After everything I do! You think those goddam Armenians and kikes send their boys through college, what you think?"

"I think I worked my way through college, Pop."

"And who told you to go?"

"Mother told me to go."

"Don't mention that woman name here!" my father roared.

"And you did everything you could to stop me."

Gwen pulled at my arm.

He turned to her. "I gave that woman permission! He want to go, I said, let him go. You think she let you go if I say No! Eh? I ask only one thing, tell boy take usey-full course, not waste time like American boys, with that Shakespeare foolishness and so forth, those books his mother give him, love and so forth foolishness!"

"Mother had nothing to do—"

"You take her side, I see that."

"Sure I take her side."

"Get out!" he roared. "Get out this house."

"Shshsh," said Gwen.

"Don't shshsh, young Miss, if you please, this my house . . ."

"You wouldn't even buy me a suit to go to college with," I said.

"Who bought you suit?"

"Mother bought it, that's who."

"And where you think she get money, she have a business, get money, eh? She steal from my pocket, she steal from grocery bills, she think I don't know what she do. I lose my whole life's business, and she steal money grocery bills to send my good-for-nothing son, Shakespeare and so forth, not coming to store to help his father when he need help or die. Remember when President Mitchell was killing your father with National City Bank and I say to you one day, 'Leave that college and come help your father in bad trouble.' And what you say . . . eh? Remember?"

"I remember. I said no."

"You remember right. No! But you follow my way, not her, you smart boy. You sell your goods good price, like your father, and you marry like your father say, smart girl, you have merchant blood in there, you get your brains from me!"

He was inarticulate with rage, his face flushed, his left eye completely bloodshot. But I only remembered that afterwards. At the time I had lost control.

"I'm not like you," I was saying, "I wouldn't be like you. I became someone in spite of you, in spite of you . . ."

Gwen was shaking my arm and trying to pull me away.

"And don't give me that Shakespeare shit any more, ever again, you corrupt and selfish old man; I'm not like you, you corrupt and hateful and vicious . . ."

Gwen was dragging me out of the room.

We walked down to the shore.

Long Island Sound is a lifeless body of water. It lapped at the pebbles like a dog licking his master's shoes.

I was shaking.

"Oh, God, what did I do?" I said. "I'm sorry, I'm sorry."

"Let's go for a row," Gwen suggested.

We got into the rowboat that was pulled up on the beach. It hadn't been in the water for a while, and it began to leak, the boards having dried out. There was an old Chock Full O' Nuts coffee can on the dock, and Gwen bailed as I paddled.

We went beyond the point, way out to the rocks and around to the other side, where I used to go when I was a kid. I stopped, out of sight of the old house, and I leaned forward to take the can and spell Gwen with the bailing. She then gave me the warmest kiss I think I've ever had from a woman, soft and so loyal. I suppose she felt I was in awful pain, which I was. I had done a damned fool thing, which could not be understood, only forgiven.

"What the hell got into me?" I said. "I thought I got over all that. Oh, my God, what a thing to do. What did I call him?"

"Corrupt or something, selfish, forget it," she said.

"Oh, my God, I'd forgotten I felt that way."

"You'd better bail a little faster," she said, "or we'll have to swim."

"Let's go back," I said.

"I wouldn't worry," she said.

"I'll go back and tell him I'm sorry."

I gave her the can, and I picked up the paddle and bent to it. "Well," I said, "I let the son of a bitch down again."

"Oh, come on, what else could you do? He was dishing it out pretty good," said Gwen.

I paddled.

"He must have been a bastard for a kid to deal with," she said.

"But that's the way they're brought up to be," I said. "He doesn't know different."

"Don't be so Christlike," said Gwen.

"That's the tradition he's brought up in. What else could he expect, except for his son to follow in his footsteps. And to come to his aid when he was in trouble." I paddled harder.

When we rounded the point, we saw the scene far away, like something in a silent movie.

Gloria's estate wagon was drawn up in front of the house. Standing by the car was an attendant in a white coat and pants. Gloria and Florence were leading my father down the porch stairs, towards the car.

The old man was remonstrating and protesting and resisting.

And then it happened.

He jerked his arm out of Florence's grip. And then with both his hands he pushed Gloria away with all his strength. As he pushed her away, he pushed himself back. And as well as I could tell at that distance—we were about a quarter of a mile away—he turned over on one foot and fell hard on his side.

Now the orderly, who had been standing quietly in the background, rushed in and picked the old man up and carried him to the waiting car.

My father did not resist the orderly. He seemed to be holding on to him.

We were too far away to realize that when the old man fell, he had broken his hip.

But we did hear, just before the orderly got the old man into the back of the estate wagon, we did hear him call out, "Evangeleh! Evangeleh!" It was pretty faint, that cry at that distance, but there was no mistaking it.

They got in, the orderly in the back with him, Gloria and Florence in front. And off they drove.

I started to paddle back.

It was too late to do anything, so I didn't hurry.

"Look," said Gwen, "there's Charles."

As Gloria's car drove off, Charles's station wagon drove in.

I think Gwen hated to leave me that day.

She changed the kid's diaper, and as she was pulling on his little rubber pants, she said to me, without looking up, "Chet thinks Andy is yours. But it's his. I'm never going to tell him. But I thought if I told you, you'd understand why it's better all around this way."

I didn't walk her to where Charles was waiting. I sort of nodded, when she left, and that was it.

I sat on the front porch. It was quiet. I could smell the acacia trees.

In the afternoon, a delivery boy came with the grocery order.

I spent the night alone in the old house.

21

THE only sound was the one made by the branches riding the breeze off the Sound. They scratched the sides of the house and the porch roof. No, there were other sounds: the water licking the pebbles, some dead leaves rustling up the breeze, a neighbor's dog barking, a distant outboard.

I hadn't done that since I was a kid, lie in bed in the morning without feeling the compulsion, "I've got to get up, I've got to get going."

The breeze was a cool wash, as light as a tune on a whistle. I threw the covers off, lay there naked, and let it play over me.

The phone rang. I didn't answer. My whole approach to the telephone had changed. I was not thinking, who wants to talk to me. I was thinking, who do I want to talk to. It rang again. I didn't answer.

From then on through the morning it rang at intervals of fifteen minutes.

I found the long Havana claro Mr. Finnegan had thrust into my breast pocket when I first got into his Rolls—when was it? Yesterday? I lit it. Then I went and urinated.

On one wall of the big old-fashioned bathroom hung an ornate mirror. If I remember correctly, my uncle Joe had had it in his suite at the St. Moritz. It didn't fit into the decor when Joe, enjoying his prime, had moved to the Ritz Towers. So my father had brought it home in the back of the Pierce-Arrow. I remember he sat in the back with this baroque mirror, and my mother sat in the chauffeur's compartment. The frame might have been pressed by a pastry chef out of a whipped cream bellows. It must have looked wonderful framing a naked Follies Girl.

I, though, wasn't up to it.

I stood, looking at my naked self.

I don't remember being so aware of my body since the day I first noticed the pubic hairs.

I had a pot. It was sizable. Not small, sizable! My head protruded from my shoulders. I was not sure that the angle was the one intended by nature. I looked as if I were about to do something confidential.

Clearly, clothes were important for me. I didn't look right without them.

My ass was dewlapped. I looked in the buttocks like a figure out of Cranach. My biceps, when relaxed, hung like those of an old woman, the kind Weegee used to photograph on the strand at Coney Island. My tits looked all right—till I bent over. Then I saw that the crepe had started there.

I got a chair, placed it in front of the mirror and placed myself on it. My pot, sitting, was bigger. My penis disappeared between my legs. The cigar was the most impressive thing about me.

I realized that for years I had been avoiding looking into the mirror. It had made life easier.

I turned the chair so I was confronting my image directly. All that trouble, I thought, all those hysterics, near suicides, cries in the nights, fits and accusations of betrayal, all those declarations of passion, all that thunder and lightning—for that?! For what I was looking at in the mirror?!

I sat well forward and let my balls hang over the edge of the chair. One testicle moved mysteriously, mounted and fell. But Junior himself was resting. Consider him, I thought, as a piece of gristle, muscle, and gland, all connected and fed by blood vessels; then consider all the emotions that had been whipped up around this little member. Disproportionate, I thought, very disproportionate.

I could see why clothes are necessary. Not to protect the body from the weather, but from the scrutiny of other humans. I made a much more forceful and convincing impression clothed. At one time, I remembered, I could quiet a roomful of panicky sponsors simply by entering. I certainly couldn't have quieted a roomful of panicky sponsors by walking in naked, even with Mr. Finnegan's long cigar in my mouth.

In the first place, they'd see at a glance that I didn't have a cent on me. I started to reach into my pocket to see how much money I had left. Then it was too much trouble to go into the bedroom and find my pants and look. Besides, what I'd find would be depressing. Better not look. The facts would catch up with me soon enough. And I didn't want to move. I was fascinated with myself.

When the moment comes for me to dress, I wondered, how should I dress?

If all clothing is an advertisement for what's inside, what should I declare myself publicly to be? Who was I now?

Reliable? I wasn't. An intellectual? I wasn't. A lover? I doubt if I ever really loved anybody. Trustworthy? I doubted if anyone could trust me any more to do anything except the things I wanted to do. A friend of the race? The fact was that I was hostile to just about everyone. Indispensable Eddie? Don't make me laugh. Honest Eddie? Sort of. In need of others? I was uninterested and selfish. Should I wear clothes that said, come be with me, I need company? No, the opposite! I preferred to be alone. How did I dress to show that?

The plain fact was that I didn't want to put on any clothes. I didn't want to impress anyone or be with anyone. I was back at the starting line, naked and alone, just as I had come into the world. I was disconnected and unobligated. At that moment I didn't have the vaguest idea what day of the week it was, or what hour of the day. Or who was where.

Somebody must be up somewhere, because the phone kept ringing at regular intervals.

I had pulled down the entire edifice of my old life. Now the question was, what did I have to take its place? I wasn't any longer doing anything I didn't want to do. Now, what did I want to do?

It occurred to me that I didn't have to *do* anything. I could just live. For as long as it lasted.

How long could it?

I had a little money and my father's roof over my head, and maybe another roof in Los Angeles, and no bank account but some insurance, though that was in Ellen's name. I wasn't going to be rained on tomorrow or the day after.

A friend of mine always sneered at the problems of the middle-class sensitive soul. He said he couldn't feel concern or compassion for the problems of any man who could go out and get himself a job. The only people worthy of concern were those in the submerged and impoverished areas—say India—who lived in the weather and couldn't feed their bellies.

But it seemed to me there were other ways of starving to death. Thousands of people were beginning to know it, and millions would. There were other sicknesses than those caused by physical under-nourishment. You couldn't walk the streets of our cities, look at the faces, and say those people had no problems.

They had been kept secret, those problems, disallowed. People were embarrassed to admit them. But they were there.

Still, in another way what my friend said was true. I could "afford" this problem. It was a problem of affluence, no matter how tenuous. After all, while I had no cash, I did have a roof, some credit, a little insurance, and—

I'd better fill the icebox, I thought, while I still have credit. Then just stay here. Admit the grocery boy bringing me supplies, then lock myself in.

As for the question of clothes, I could postpone that problem. I didn't need clothes to call the grocer. The phone was ringing again. I waited for it to stop. Then I picked up and dialed the grocer.

The grocery was one my mother and father had been dealing with for three decades, Bristols'. Actually the man's name was Embrostelis. He was a Greek from the Island of Mytilene. He had, a few years before, returned to that island, and was living there now on social security and regular allowances from his son who presently ran the business.

My father and Mr. Embrostelis had been great friends.

Young Tom Embrostelis (Tom? Thodoros!) had no heart. He informed me, in the jocular manner of an energetic and successful second-generation American, that he had just had instructions that the account was closed, and that the family was no longer responsible for any bills I might run up.

He thought it some kind of joke.

"Who the hell did that, Tom?"

"Your wife," he said. "She was calling for your mother."

"Did my mother get on the phone?"

"No. Your wife was speaking for her."

"Well, Tom, what the hell . . ."

"Well, I'll tell you what the hell. It never occurred to me before, but I looked up your bill, and it's over a hundred dollars. Ordinarily I wouldn't mind, but you know, we're in business too . . . and . . . well, hell, Eddie, tell me what you want and I'll send it out. But I wish you'd take care of that bill."

"Well, Tom, we've always . . . hell, Tom!"

"Tell me what you want," he said.

So I placed my order. But it was much smaller than I had planned. It didn't fill the icebox or cover the shelves. I had enough for maybe three days. That was Tom's way of closing the account.

I left the phone and walked around the house.

It was a museum to my father's way of life. If it could have been enclosed in a time capsule, it would have perfectly illustrated to future generations the life of people like my father.

The living room was especially apt. The only signs of living were some family pictures. The most interesting was the picture taken in 1927, the year of my father's greatest prosperity. It conformed to every tradition of that unquestioning era. My father sat. My mother stood. I stood on his other side, my hand on his shoulder. The gesture said, "Don't worry, Pop, you bet when you get old, I'll take care of you. Meantime, many thanks for everything you've done for me, your loving son, Evangeleh." Michael, being the second son, was well to the rear. The background scene was a nonexistent park. The print was tinted rose.

This photograph rested on an enormous grand piano. Neither my father nor my mother could play a note. I don't believe the piano was opened more than once a year. That occasion usually was my uncle Joe's yearly visit. His mistress could play "On the Banks of the Wabash," which, unaccountably, was my uncle's favorite air.

After I left home, I learned to enjoy doodling on the piano. There had been one in the Commons Club at college, and afternoons when everyone was out somewhere being athletic, I used to sit and improvise on a single blue phrase of Near Eastern music, playing it over and over, wandering, returning, getting louder and louder each time, till there was a complaint from the other non-fraternity outcasts who lived in the dorm above.

There had also been a piano in the social room of the summer camp where I worked as public relations man the summer after graduation. Nights, when the guests were screwing other guests or had passed out from the punishing meals, I used to sit at the keyboard and improvise. I had two phrases by then and could go on for hours.

Florence, who had taken piano lessons but didn't enjoy any music except that of intellectual conversation, had seen to it that we had a grand in our California home. I used to improvise on that, too. Florence resented my music. It sounded full of regret and unfulfilled longing, she said. She told me I had several talents, but none of them was for musical composition. I tried to play when she wasn't there. Several times I remember her storming into the garden or out in her Continental to escape the aggressive misery (her phrase) of my self-hypnotic musical narcissism (her phrase). I have to admit that other times, when I was angry with her, I would play just to break down her goddam composure.

I lifted the lid of the grand. It was horribly out of tune. But so was I. I sat and played my two goatish melodies, over and over, louder and louder and louder. The phone rang.

Who did I want to talk to, I asked myself. That took care of that.

I did want to see my father, and soften what had happened between us. I played some music for him, then. He would have thought it insane of me, sitting there naked with that cigar, and playing that wild stuff. But he would have understood the Near Eastern musical vocabulary.

I played for my mother, entirely alone as she was, without even the relief of a quarrel.

I played for Ellen, and all the discoveries she was going to make, and how painful they were going to be.

I played for Florence, bound in the coils of her shoulds, seeing things only one possible way.

For Michael, hopefully still in Tarpon Springs eating pompano, among people who would understand what I was playing.

"You simply have no ear, Ev dear, let's face it." That's what Florence had said.

She was right. I hit it harder and louder.

Modulate, baby, modulate. Louis Armstrong and Velma. Oh, Louie, Louie.

I modulated.

I played for the whole goddam staff of Williams and MacElroy, still back there among the hush-a-phones.

I played for Gwen, now married. No, not yet, it took three days, I thought. Anyway, Gwen.

That Near Eastern stuff was full of cynicism and pity.

I played for little Andy.

But not for his father.

I played for Charles.

I was real loud now.

Somebody was pounding at the door.

Probably a neighbor complaining.

I should have a gun.

Let him pound!

When I got all through, I'd burn the house down; that would really give them something to complain about. Say, that was a good idea! I didn't have the nerve to do it, but that's exactly what I should do next, I thought. This relic did not deserve commemoration. A museum in flames, an era forgotten.

I played to the Near Eastern fire that would consume this Near Eastern museum misplaced in WASPland. Actually the place was a fire trap. There were newspapers and toys, bushel baskets and old radios, including the crystal set that had first brought in KDKA. And all my father's ledgers and business papers, they were all there. The boat house adjacent was filled with boats that wouldn't float, but could burn. I played to them, the boats that belonged to this once seafaring race and that could no longer breast even tired, old, chemical-loaded, refuse-polluted Long Island Sound. What would float them again? I played to that.

I took a deep breath, threw my head back to release some unmeasurable tension, and fell on that discordant and disharmonious piano again. I pounded my life through it.

At the same time I was aware of someone looking at me through the window.

Some complaining neighbor? The hell with him!

Then I became aware that it was not some complaining neighbor. It was Arthur Houghton. He was looking at me as if I were an exotic new arrival in the bird cage of the zoo.

"What the hell are you doing, Edward?" he said through the window.

His inflection suggested, as it always did, a tolerant amusement. He was most practiced in patronizing.

Arthur Houghton, our family lawyer, always called me Edward. He was, in fact, the only one who addressed me as Edward. He was also the only man who, when he introduced me to a stranger, sooner or later dropped in the bit of information that he and I had gone to the same college. I always felt it was a sort of apology for me. Arthur Houghton was a senior when I was a freshman. He had been a member of Everything. And for once the boys were right when they selected him "Most Likely to Succeed." In fact it was hardly a prediction. Everyone knew that Arthur was going to go directly from college into the law firm of Florence's uncle, the brother of our college president. The seal of success was on Arthur from the beginning. The poor son of a bitch never had a chance.

For many complicated reasons we were friends. I suppose the main reason on my side was that Arthur, more than anyone else, made me feel "in"—in, that is, with the WASPS. I, therefore, valued him, and if I could have been glad to see anyone that day, it might have been Arthur.

But I really didn't want to see anyone. I knew that what I decided this day and what I did the next would decide my fate. I had certain desperate ventures in mind. Having tasted a bit of the hog, I wanted all of it. So I had looked forward to a day alone, absolutely alone. And I was determined to have it.

Arthur was still at the window, staring at me.

"A little original composition of your own?" he asked.

"Just an Anatolian war song," I said, "to meet the present emergency."

God, I didn't want to be interrupted!

Then I thought, why should I be; I didn't ask him to come out here.

I walked to the screen door and latched it.

Then I wished I hadn't. I wished I could have sent Arthur away without an act so obviously hostile. But I didn't know how, and this was better than nothing.

Arthur walked along the porch, came to the screen door, and looked at me.

"Edward," he said, "your fly's open."

"What do you want?" I said.

"Aren't you going to invite me in?"

"I don't think so."

"I'd like to visit with you for a few minutes."

"You'll have to make an appointment."

"Oh, come on, Edward, get off it."

"One thing I have always liked about your Yankee tradition, Arthur, is that it disapproves of the unannounced visit."

"Didn't my secretary speak to you?"

"No, your secretary did not."

"I told her to call you at fifteen-minute intervals till she got you."

"I have not been answering the telephone."

One power Arthur had was to get me talking like him.

"Oh, Edward, put on some clothes and come out here. It's a beautiful day."

"What do you want?"

"Great Scott, Edward, I want to talk with you."

"Arthur, look, I simply must have some time to myself today."

"Now, Edward, come off it. This whole affair is taking on most serious propositions. After all, I am not only your friend; I am also your lawyer. And as your lawyer I must now tell you that you are in dire need of counsel."

I didn't answer.

"Edward, I'm your friend; I am here to help you."

"I believe you are my friend, Arthur, so do something generous and understanding and most friendly."

"What's that, my boy?"

"Leave me alone. I'll be ready to see you in a few days."

"That won't do."

"That will have to do."

"A few days will be too late. Things have gone too far. Now please behave like a civilized man and open this door."

I didn't answer.

"May I give you an example?"

"Yes," I said.

"Well, then, let me in. And do put some clothes on. I can't talk seriously to you when you're naked as a jay bird."

"Would you please excuse me?" I said.

I started to close the door.

"No, I won't excuse you," he said. He pulled the screen door, not expecting it to be latched. "Edward, I cancelled a very heavy calendar to come out here to see you. In the name of our friendship, twenty-odd years of it, how can you receive my solicitude with such rudeness?"

"I'm sorry, Arthur," I said, "I'm just not in the mood."

"Oh, bosh! Pure bosh! All right, we'll talk through the screen." He went and pulled an old white chair over to the screen door. I didn't move on my side.

"Are you aware," he said, "of the consequences, of the most serious consequences, of your recent behavior?"

"For example?"

"For example, and I assure you that this is a very minor example, have you tried to cash a check today?"

"No."

"Well, try it."

"Meaning what?"

"Meaning that Florence has acted in respect to your joint account. You will find yourself without the benefit of funds."

"Well, then, as my lawyer," I said, "I instruct you to enjoin her, or in some other legal fashion summarily prevent her, from such course of action."

"Now," said Arthur, "now, may I come in?"

"Kindly go and do what I told you to do."

"Edward, in about another five seconds I'm going to put my foot through that screen door and come in and give you a good thrashing."

"I suggest you don't try that."

"Edward," he said, "that was a joke. What's the matter with you? You're not yourself—Oh—" he interrupted himself. "Oh, I understand!"

"You understand what?"

"You have a guest. Is she here?"

"That is none of your business."

"I have no objection to speaking in front of her."

"I gather you'd prefer it. But, Arthur, I do have a private life, and it is my private life, and you're my lawyer, in my employ."

"Is the child here, too?"

"What child?" I wanted to see how much he knew.

"Your child. Your child with her."

Who the hell could have told him that?

"That was a shock, wasn't it, Edward?" he said.

I didn't answer.

"Now may I come in?"

"No," I said.

"And, for your information, I know a great many other things about this relationship."

"How?"

"How does anyone find out anything today, Edward? Florence engaged a person to look into the young lady and her relationships."

"A spy?"

"An investigator."

"Well, that is an . . . an . . ."

"It's an absolute outrage," he provided, "and at the same time it is Florence's perfect right."

"And you so advised her?"

"It wasn't my idea," he said, "but when she asked me some weeks ago what I thought of the suggestion I must confess I didn't talk her out of it."

"Are you my lawyer, or hers, Arthur?"

"I am the lawyer to your family."

"Does that give you the right to nuzzle your nuzzle down between my sheets?"

"It's not the most appetizing duty I have performed in my life, but it is one that I here consider absolutely necessary. Tell me, would you challenge Florence's absolute right to find out everything about a relationship that is endangering her life?"

I didn't answer.

"I must judge your silence with respect to that question as an affirmative answer. She, of course, does have the right."

"So she engaged a spy."

"An investigator. And now she has a complete dossier. On you and on Miss Hunt. One which I had occasion to study thoroughly."

"Oh."

"One amazing thing about this phenomenon, the prevalence of investigators—that kind of practice which, I must say, in theory I totally disapprove of—one amazing thing is the co-operation they receive. People seem to *want* to tell. Our investigator had no trouble finding people who wanted to tell all." He gave a little chuckle. "I

390

met the man, and he's not an attractive sort. Still, there wasn't a single person whom he saw who wasn't completely—what's the word for it? It was used opprobriously in relation to Communists and former Communists?"

"Co-operative."

"Of course, co-operative."

"Still," I said, "I am surprised that Florence and . . ."

"Yes," he said, "so was I. But the world has moved very fast towards what seems to me to be a sort of civilized barbarism. It has rather left me behind, but I . . ."

"But you approved of this investigation, this spying on me?"

"I absolutely abhor it, but in this particular circumstance, knowing the cost to Florence—"

"Arthur," I said sharply, "talk straight to me."

"All right," he said, "all right, old boy. Straight talk. Did you know for example that Miss Hunt was the constant companion—paid, I believe—of an old Italian Communist who was last week invited to leave this country by our Department of State? And did you know that this same Miss Hunt, before that, was the mistress of a Mr. Collier, whose personal history is extremely varied in this area? And that episodes like these, the old Italian and the other man, were nothing but straight lines by contrast to the sexual doodling she previously indulged in? In Washington, for instance, she was an available woman, kept by any number of men. Edward, answer me; is this the kind of woman for whom you'd throw over a fine home?"

"Arthur," I was furious, "this is not a criminal court."

"Nevertheless, I must ask you to answer. Please let me hear, are you ready now to give up your home, which means Florence—as fine and decent and as *clean* a woman as you could find anywhere, an immaculate person—for a female that has been handed back and forth, been reamed in and out, sprung and plumbed every which way, bought and sold, for God's sake, Edward? Are you?"

Unable to restrain himself, Arthur pulled with all his strength at the screen door, sprang the latch and burst into the room, and, without losing a breath, continued. "I said a piece of common tripe that two black men passed back and forth and whom they most co-operatively referred to when they spoke to our investigator as Poor White Gash."

I hit him with all my might.

He was down on his back. He was a big man, but I had hit him just right. Blood oozed from his mouth.

He got up slowly.

"You know," he said, "I'm in excellent shape, much better than you, and I could take you apart."

"Don't try it," I said.

"But I intend to continue whether you like it or not."

"Whose goddam lawyer are you?" I shouted. "Mine or hers?"

"Don't make me choose, because if I had to choose right now, I certainly wouldn't choose you."

"Well, then, if you are her lawyer, get the hell out of here."

"I said I am not her lawyer. I am yours and hers."

"I pay you, you son of a bitch, and I don't pay you to put spies on my ass."

"I don't think that son of a bitch was at all necessary, Edward." He had found the blood. "Could you lend me a handkerchief?"

"I haven't one on me," I said.

He laughed. "Then some paper toweling?"

The blood was filling his mouth. He tried his teeth.

"They o.k.?" I asked.

"I think so."

"I'll get you a towel."

"The things a lawyer has to do in line of duty," he said.

I hurried to the kitchen, and wet a corner of the towel at the sink. I was thinking of Arthur with some respect. It must have taken courage, and considerable concern, for him to have talked to me as he did. He must really care. As I went back with the towel, I said to myself, come on, be nice to him, listen to the man.

He sat down and mopped his mouth and jaw with the kitchen towel. Then, as I watched, I again felt what I've always felt about him in a crisis, that I may not entirely like him, but that the man has class. No wonder, I said to myself, he is as successful as he is. He cleared his throat now and looked at me, till he had my full attention.

"Edward," he said, preparing the air for what he was about to say, "there are times when the best service an attorney at law can provide a client is to protect him from himself."

"Arthur," I answered, "I'm awfully sorry about this, and I hope you will be able to forgive me. I'm not quite myself . . ."

"You are definitely not yourself, Edward." He composed himself in a chair, the large armchair my father used to sit in. And there he was, perfectly poised, like it was his courtroom and he presiding over the judgment that was to be passed on me.

"You don't need to say anything further about all this," he pointed to his jaw. "It is forgiven."

"I did want to suggest that you don't know the young lady, and perhaps you are not in a position to . . . to . . . well . . . insult her . . ."

"I was merely citing what is detailed in a report that Florence has on her dresser at this moment. The young lady's sex habits and her personal morals don't interest me in the least. I am concerned about Florence and, above all at this moment, you. And," he said, making a joke, "I really wouldn't go into the matter of any compensation I may have received from you. The plain fact is that there hasn't been any, not since well before your accident. If I may be crude for a moment, our firm has been carrying you."

"I'm sorry," I said. Every time I apologized I got angrier.

"I have been working without compensation for your family because of the long duration of our association, and because of our intimate connection with Florence's father, but above all because I believe you will become yourself again."

"Well," I said, "I wish you'd send me a bill—"

"I will when you have the means."

I was ready to hit him again.

"Now I wonder if I could have a glass of cold water before I continue."

"How about some coffee?"

"That would be wonderful," he said.

I rushed to the kitchen, grateful for the chance to get control of myself. I put the coffee on. I filled a glass with water.

When I got back, he was jotting some notes on a library card.

He drank the water, smiled his thanks at me, and cleared his throat. I sat down as if I had been so ordered.

"Edward," he announced, "this marriage can be saved. That is what I consider my duty as a family lawyer to be." He paused. There was now no question of my interrupting him.

"My great problem is not you. We have to find how to deal with the hurt that has been done to Florence."

393

"I don't want to hurt Florence," I said like a goddam ninny.

"Of course not," he approved. "But I must tell you that something awful happened last night."

"To Florence?"

"Yes. Among other things that confounded investigator turned up was the fact that Ellen had not gone back to Radcliffe, as Florence supposed, but was living in a rather sleazy hotel. With her is a young man, also of college age, a Negro; did you know he was a Negro?"

"Have you something against Negroes?"

"Edward, may I remind you that I am on the board of the American Civil Liberties Union!"

"Well, twice, this is the second time, you have mentioned color with what seemed to me to be a clear intimation that no white girl could do anything worse than have a personal association with a Negro."

"Well answer me truthfully, wouldn't you prefer if it had been a white boy?"

I had to answer, "Yes, I would."

"So then? Ellen is a child, Edward. When Florence and you asked me to be her godfather, and when after considerable self-questioning I accepted, I assumed certain responsibilities. I swore to look after her. Well, once Florence had made this discovery and phoned me, I was able to arrange to have Florence admitted to the room they were using. There in the bathroom, Florence found a contraceptive, the kind women wear. Then, can you just see her, poor dear, she sat alone in the room and waited for them to come home, till four in the morning it was, very late indeed. Ellen finally came in and with her this young man. Florence asked the young man to excuse them, which he made the mistake of refusing to do. Ellen had to tell him to leave. Florence questioned the girl and found out everything, including the fact that it was you who had given the permission and made the arrangement for this nineteen-year-old to have herself fitted. Well, this came as near to finally and completely alienating Florence from you as anything could."

Suddenly I found myself going out of control again.

"Arthur," I heard myself saying, "I really don't want to lose my temper with you again. But I ask you to relate to me as my lawyer, not as my judge. I am not in the least obliged to make explanations to you."

"That is your guilt speaking, my boy!"

"Your whole tone—"

"My tone, my dear boy, is my tone. No one has ever been able to do anything about that. Besides, I'm quite satisfied with it."

"I insist you act as my lawyer, if that's what you are. If you're not, I'll get me another one. You are not *the law,* you know!"

"Whoever said I was?"

"Well, the way you sit there . . ."

"The way I sit!"

"Yes," I practically shouted. "You are not the law. You are merely someone who is paid to advise me about the law."

"Edward, may I suggest again that you not go into the question of compensation. That opens a chasm which I don't think we should look down into. Now try to act like a member of civilized society and sit down, will you?"

I sat down.

"Don't you think Florence has been a saint of patience with you? She has taken fantastic abuse, unceasing provocation, and deprivation the nature of which you will recall without my reminding you."

"No, you'd better remind me." I craved a fight with this man.

"She has told me everything, Edward."

"Good."

"Let's pass the sarcasm. She has every right to tell me anything she considers pertinent, as I am your family lawyer, and as such it is essential that I know the key facts of our situation."

"And what are the key facts of our—"

"Well, it does seem to me that one of them is that you have not been her husband in deed for three years. And further, that you pretended impotence while you were having countless affairs."

"I'm sure Florence would have preferred me impotent."

"Countless affairs, all of which we know about in detail. Thanks again to our investigator. How many women of your acquaintance would have endured that?"

"Maybe Florence should not have."

"She did because she thinks, as I do, that this marriage can be saved."

The coffee boiled over in the kitchen in the nick of time. I rushed out and took as long as I could laying out a tray. I fixed it with meticulous care. When I came back and laid it before him, he gave me a little smile.

"Thank you, Edward," he said. "That's the remarkable thing about what we call civilization. You just hit me very hard. Yet here we are, in control of animalistic feelings, working together to see what can be done about our situation."

He settled himself in the big chair and prepared his coffee exactly to his taste.

"Now, if you don't mind," he said, "I will say what I have to say. In the first place, I am not your friend, or Florence's; I am the friend of your marriage. I can remember not so long ago when, in our circle of civilized people, it was considered the perfect marriage; you were the golden couple. This phrase did not refer to your bank account, although that was golden healthy, too."

He took out a cigar, a Dunhill Number 23, long, thin, and deliciously mild, a cigar so expensive that it didn't even have a paper ribbon around it, and so special that he could confidently give it at Christmas to his most select clients.

"Will you have one?" he asked. "Go on," he added when I hesitated, "I don't expect anything in return." He laughed. I took his cigar.

"Now," he said, "you're practically fully dressed." He carefully lit my cigar and then his own. He sat back, completely at ease, and said, "Edward, we live in a civilized society. You have been doing everything you can to smash its laws. All right. Let us say it's a sign of your vitality. I even know something of how you feel. Believe me, I have some sympathy for you; it does seem to me you're doing all this much too late in life, but still."

He smiled at me affectionately. "Now the challenge to you, Edward," he went on, "is how much are you ready to give up for your new course? To get the kind of irresponsible freedom you seem to desire, the cost may be higher than you can afford to pay. Society, Edward, has its rights. It will fight you back. People are being hurt, Edward. They'll fight you back. Your actions have already had consequences you may not like. May I illustrate?"

"Go ahead."

"For instance, did you know that your father fell yesterday and broke his hip?"

Silence.

"Right on this front lawn."

"When they were dragging him to his car?"

"That's not accurate. I'm certain they were not dragging him."

"Broke his hip?"

"Splintered his pelvic bone."

"Goddam them!"

"Why *them?*"

"The old man didn't want to go."

"Are you sure?"

"He kept calling for me. They were forcing him against his will."

"Edward, one does not leave an old man of his age and in his condition alone in a house which—"

"Where is he now?"

"In the hospital."

"I've got to get over there."

"You won't be able to see him."

"Why the hell not?"

"Because," he looked at his watch, "in about an hour he will be in the operating room—"

"Operating?"

"—where they will put a pin in his hip, and wire the bits together, depending upon what they find. The X rays were not good."

"Well, I want to be there."

"The hospital, I'm sorry to have to tell you, Edward, has received orders not to allow you to see Mr. Arness."

"He's not Florence's goddam father," I said, "he's mine."

"I don't think excessive emotionalism will help in this circumstance. You should certainly not have done what you did. You kidnapped a man who doesn't know which end is up any more, and you left him in an emotionally upset condition alone in this house while you were out on the Sound in a pleasure boat with your doxy. They tell me that when they came here to get him, he didn't even know where he was. And he was calling for you, not to obtain your help as you seem to think, but to continue a quarrel which you obviously had had with him. Didn't you have a quarrel?"

"I am not guilty for what happened to my father."

"You are, and you know it. You feel guilty as hell. And now to speak of further consequences. Do you imagine Mr. Finnegan can ever again employ you? Do you think that any company will employ you? Change your name, Edward; go back to Turkey or wherever."

He burst into what was for him uncontrolled laughter. Then he continued. "I must now admit to you that it is with my advice that Florence has taken legal steps to make your bank accounts unavailable to you. I'm sure, if you were yourself, you would want your lawyer to protect your funds. And those of your wife."

"Oh, that was your idea?"

"Yes, I simply could no longer tolerate your irresponsibility and your cruelty towards her."

"Sounds like you're preparing a divorce action."

"That is not going to be necessary, if you follow our advice."

"Which is what?"

"Florence wants you to go to a place where you will get professional care and sympathetic attention, and take a long rest."

"I don't want to go anywhere, and I don't need a long rest."

"The first, of course, is your decision. The second statement is simply erroneous. On the face of it, you certainly do need a long, long rest."

"In other words, you have tied me up so I can't move."

"Exactly. Because this isn't you, Eddie, it isn't you."

"You instigated these restrictions and pressures and . . ."

"I did."

"I don't have to ask you any longer where you stand."

"I told you where I stand. I stand for the marriage. I'm going to save it."

"Are you in love with my wife?"

"Edward—"

"Have you slept with her?"

"Edward, that's disgusting . . . what do you think I am?"

"I don't know. I suddenly had an intuition that some such emotion might explain what you've been doing. Well, what do you think? You can't speak? Try! Try! Try to answer this simple question. Are you in love with Florence?"

"If this is a game, Edward, it's a very ugly one . . ."

"It's not a game. I mean it. Are you?"

He measured me. Then he did his best.

"I think Florence is an extraordinary woman who is being slaughtered on the altar of an ego that's run wild. I've watched you lash this poor girl with your selfishness and your willfulness, the like of which I've never seen in thirty-five years of dealing with egomaniacs."

"Now we're talking," I said.

"Only a true and profoundly devoted woman could have borne up under it. When I behold her now and—"

"Forgetting the courtroom lettuce for a moment, tell me, I did hit on something, didn't I?"

"Of course not. That is the only way that you, in your present state, can experience what I've been trying to do. You can't imagine anyone ever doing what I'm doing for any reason except lust or—"

"And that, of course, is why you want to put me away into an institution, isn't it?"

He'd begun to recover.

"No, my dear Edward, not at all. It is for your sake. It is the essence of my advice to you. I've taken the liberty—since I'm so sure it's the right thing—of making a reservation for you."

"Suppose I don't take your advice?"

"You will have to take the consequences."

"Where is the reservation for?"

"Now you're beginning to think reasonably! It's at a place—we happen to be their legal representation—called the Armstrong-Roberts Sanitarium in Lenox, Massachusetts. You will live there for a few months."

"Yes . . ."

"You will daily consult a psychiatrist on the grounds."

"And . . ."

"You will receive treatment in other ways too, occupational therapy, certain baths, group discussions, as well as private consultations . . ."

"And . . ."

"It's a beautiful place; the grounds are exquisitely landscaped."

"Will I be confined there?"

"Confined? In what sense?"

"In the usual sense. Can I leave whenever I want to? Come to New York, say?"

"Well, no, the institution would not be what it is if you could do that. The essence of it is unremitting treatment, freedom from tension, isolation from the—"

"And I pay you, you son of a bitch!"

"That's why I'm taking all this abuse at your hands, because you pay me, you son of a bitch; that's why I'm doing all this, it's for the sake of your money!"

"No, it's for the reason I said."

"This much of that is true. I am not going to allow you to hurt Florence further. Later, when you are back with her, you will bless me for it. Florence is the most patient and the most courageous woman I have ever seen. She is really your Rock of Ages. You would be nowhere without her. And let me tell you something more. You *will* be nowhere again."

His face twisted into savage vehemence.

"NOWHERE! If you don't have her at your side."

"And I pay you, you son of a bitch."

"Will you stop saying that—particularly since you don't, and haven't, and soon won't have the price of a square meal unless you come to your senses fast and follow my instructions."

He stopped. He must have realized that he wasn't behaving like the man he liked to think of himself as being. He again became moderate and spoke in a modulated tone.

"I'm really sorry to be this rough with you. It is painful to me. But one day you will bless Arthur Houghton. I will save your marriage. And the physical accouterments of your marriage. But in order to do this I have to be drastic now. That is why I put the stop on your moneys. And that is why I have seen to it that Finnegan stops carrying you."

"You prevailed on Finnegan to—"

"I've had to do that. The moment I feel you have become yourself again, I will see that your semi-monthly payments are resumed."

"And meantime?"

"Meantime, Florence is protected."

"Sorry, I wasn't thinking about Florence; I was thinking selfishly again. I have a contract with Williams and MacElroy?"

"That contract, if you will remember, has the standard morals clause. I told Mr. Finnegan that because of certain unmistakable . . . let's call them eccentricities in your behavior, he has an incontestable out."

"You did that before this meeting?"

"Of course! At the same time Mr. Finnegan gave me his word that the moment I can accredit that you are yourself again—"

"You would intercede in my behalf?"

"I overlook the sarcasm. Yes. Quite. We are in a crisis. It's now or never. You have reached the limit!"

"Do you set the limit?"

"Since you don't, I've had to. Florence is too good to be firm with you. Somebody's got to."

Just then an automobile drove up outside.

Arthur Houghton moved with surprising speed to the window, and looked out. There was something anxious and uncomposed about this quick move.

"It's Ellen," he said. "I instructed her not to come out here."

"You instructed her?"

"Yes," he said, "on behalf of Florence."

He turned full on me, and spoke with the most direct force he had employed all morning.

"Now I must ask you, and most seriously, in the name of my client—"

"Slips!"

"—not to see Ellen. Florence can forgive you anything except your further corruption of Ellen."

"Arthur, get up out of that chair and get out of this house!"

"You are not to see Ellen," he said, "until you have permission from Florence. You have garbled this girl's moral machinery sufficiently."

I turned and ran upstairs. As quickly as I could, I put on a pair of pants and a shirt, and as I zipped up, I moved to the window and saw Houghton running across the lawn to where Ellen's boy friend, the Negro boy, had stopped the car. Houghton leaned into the car, which was a trick, considering he is so tall and the vehicle an old Chevy with small windows. And he was talking to her.

I threw open the window. It let out on the sloping, shingle roof of the porch. I stepped out and called, "Ellen! Ellen!"

Ellen saw me, and pushed the door open, pushing Arthur out of the way to do so. She ran towards me, waving. "Daddy," she said. She sounded both frightened and exhilarated.

Houghton said something very pointed to her.

She made a gesture of rejection, so sharp that it was almost a sound.

Arthur, at this, stood still for a moment, and very erect. Then he looked up at me, smiled rather sadly, and as if with some regret, waved goodbye. I'm sure he had promised Florence better results than he had obtained. I waved back. He crossed to his car and drove off.

I went downstairs to meet Ellen.

22

STEREOTYPES change. The stereotyped notion I had prepared for Ellen's boy friend was that he'd be resentful and militant. He turned out to be a soft-spoken boy with a delicately wrought face, and eyes that were unbelievably lambent. When he sensed I was in trouble, he instinctively did what he could to make me happier.

Ralph Scott's Chevy had cost him seventy-five dollars. While he had done some fussing with it, it was essentially what he had bought from the junkyard near his home in Riverhead, Long Island. I asked him why he bothered to drive it around through the city traffic. He told me he didn't want to explode—and would—the next time a white cab driver passed him by.

Ralph had about him an elegance which he wore as defiance, as if the last thing the foe would expect of him was elegance in his clothes and his deportment. Or kindness—the last thing a white person might expect from him was kindness.

In his dress he was an aristocrat. He wore soft doeskin pants, and those soft natural-leather shoes which come up over the ankles and have been called desert shoes. His shirt was made of cotton velvet, a fawn color. The effect was comforting and confident. This young man had won a great victory somewhere, sometime. Perhaps it was only that he had decided to try not to hate. I kept wondering how a Negro boy of twenty years could be that way.

He liked Ellen. But with her, too, there was some profound pride in his deportment. He was giving rather than taking. While you didn't feel resentment from him, you also didn't feel its opposite: a frantic need to be loved. He seemed to like me moderately well—

not in the compulsive way contemporary people either like or dislike someone they meet.

Ellen adored him.

He gave me the sense that he was pleased enough to be in my company, content to drive me to the hospital, and, once we got there, perfectly ready to wait for me. But, nothing more; that was it.

I walked away from the car, from Ellen and Ralph, feeling better than I had in a long time. I progressed through the hospital cellar, up the elevator to the sixth floor, and then down the corridor to my father's room. It was empty and the windows were up. I remembered when my father told me about the people who died at night and disappeared by morning, he had particularly noted the airing a room got after the body had been taken away.

I asked the floor nurse where Mr. Arness was. She said he was in the operating room. She asked who I was. When I told her, her manner changed. I asked her where the operating room was. Her answer was that I couldn't go up there. I walked to the elevator, and the operator not only told me where it was; he took me there.

On the ninth floor, I was told by the doctor in charge that my father had come through the operation all right. He also told me to go away and not come back.

"Those are the instructions we have received," he said.

"From whom?"

"From the family."

"But I am the family!"

"Those are my orders," said the doctor. "Please don't make difficulties."

"I am not making you difficulties," I said. "You are making me difficulties. I want to see my father. I am anxious about his health."

"His health is o.k.," said the doctor. "We've put a pin through his hip bone and into the top of his femur. He's now in the recovery room, out to the world, and will be kept under sedation for the next day or two. You can call the hospital any time you wish to know how he is, and you will be told. Meantime we have orders—"

"I don't give a damn what your orders are."

"Bernie," said the doctor.

An orderly hustled me towards the elevator.

"Take your hands off me!" I warned.

"Let's go, mister," said Bernie.

I pulled my left arm free of Bernie's grip, and crossed my right over. As he went down, I remembered Ellen's boy friend. Ralph Scott, I thought, has taken much more provocation all his life and not resorted to his fists.

Another orderly ran up and helped Bernie to his feet.

I determined to be like Ralph Scott.

I bowed and murmured something soft and, I thought, conciliatory. (All this was part of the testimony at the hearing later. Item: I had knocked an orderly down, then smiled and bowed.)

The two fellows in white coats picked me up and rushed me into a back elevator. They were not to be conciliated by my smile, and despite my bows, they threw me out of the building and instructed the guard at the door not to allow me in again.

It was all kind of funny to me because of my sudden resolve not to hate my enemies, to behave like Ralph Scott. The only time I got to be like Ralph Scott was with Ralph Scott.

"What were those fellows doing to you?" he asked.

"Their duty as they saw it," I said. "I raised a bit of a rumpus on the ninth floor."

"How's Grandpa?" asked Ellen.

"He's in the recovery room," I said. "They put a pin in his hip. Ellen, who gave orders that I shouldn't be allowed in there?"

"Mummy and Gloria."

"What did they think I'd do to the old man?"

"Oh, Daddy," said Ellen, as if I was embarrassing her, "you know what you did."

I realized that Ellen, too, thought I had been behaving peculiarly.

"Do you think I've been behaving strangely, Ellen?"

"Well, Daddy," she said, "do you want me to talk in front of Ralph?"

"Can I bring either of you some coffee?" said Ralph.

"You would be doing me a kindness," I said.

"How do you prefer it?"

"Almost black and perhaps . . ."

"I'll bring sugar and cream on the side."

"I want to tell you, young man," I said, "that I admire you."

"Thank you," he said, coolly, perhaps mildly grateful, but basically unimpressed. He had a gentle, patient smile. Perhaps in time I can get to be like that, I thought.

"Daddy," said Ellen as Ralph walked away, "I've got to tell you. Mummy thinks that . . ." Tears filled her eyes, suddenly.

"I'm sorry," she said. "Mummy," she started again, "thinks that you're not responsible any more. And she feels—you know how Mummy is—she must do something about it."

"Do what?"

"Well, she thinks that . . ."

I decided to relieve the girl.

"Arthur thinks I should be put away somewhere and made to take a long rest. Perhaps he's right."

"Oh, I wish you would, Daddy," she said.

I had reached for a denial from her. I was shocked to find her agreeing with Arthur. Was I that far gone?

"Am I that far gone?" I said.

"Daddy, dear, you've been doing some strange things lately, and maybe rest *would* do you good. Only thing, I don't like Arthur; it's just instinct. Ralph says instinct is usually prejudice, but I don't care. Every time I come into Mummy's room, he's talking to her in this confidential tone. Mummy says he's thinking only of your good but . . ."

"But what?"

"I really don't know." She looked frightened.

"I think I'll go over and see her," I said.

"I wish you would. I wish you'd go over there, like Odysseus, and kill all of them with your bow and arrow, right through the heart, goddam that smooth son of a bitch. And that psychoanalyst arrived this morning. I think he sort of likes her, too. And there is another man hanging around. Oh, Daddy, I wish you'd go over and . . ."

"All right, darling, I will, right through the heart."

As we walked through the lobby of the Gotham, where Florence was staying, I thought, my God, it must be at least fifty dollars a day here. That's the level I used to live on!

Ellen knew Florence's room number, so we knocked on the door unannounced.

We could hear a low murmuring inside, which stopped at our knock. Arthur Houghton opened the door cautiously.

"Well, Edward," he said good and loud, not saying hello to me, but telling the other people in the room that I had arrived and that they should shut up.

406

"Come in, Edward, glad to see you, come in!"

He may have been glad to see me, which I doubt, but Florence and the others were not.

I had eyes only for Florence. This was the first time she had seen me since she had seen me in bed with Gwen. How should a woman behave who has just seen her husband two-backing it with another woman? For a long moment, I stood there and thought about that social problem. Later, at the hearing, Arthur testified that when I walked into the room I seemed stunned. I stood and stared into space, he said, and was definitely not myself.

"What are you thinking about?" said Arthur.

"I was thinking," I explained, "that I am not myself any more."

"I'm glad you have realized that," said Arthur briskly. "You know these other folks," he said, real folksy.

I stood there like a stupe, staring straight ahead, dazed, as if a dozen flash bulbs had been set off in my face. Perhaps it was the hot wave of distrust that came at me from all of them. It was as if I was what Florence had once called me: a wild animal suddenly turned loose in their midst, and they had to figure out how to cage me. I resolved to smile and I did; I smiled and I bowed as I imagined Ralph Scott might have.

Then Charles broke the silence.

"I've got to go," he said.

That was the first time I realized Charles was in the room. What the hell was he doing there? Oh yes, I remembered, Arthur had told me that he and Florence had gotten together. How apt, I thought, two people who really had a goal in common: that I should never see Gwen again. I bowed to him again like I imagined Ralph Scott might have. Take a leaf from that boy's elegant book, I said to myself —still not talking, still, as far as they could see, stunned—take a leaf from that sweet boy's book. Play it cool but friendly. Give your enemies more courtesy than they deserve, hit back at them by being nicer than they are, more elegant and "civilized." Meet intolerance with tolerance, scorn with pride, hatred with gentleness.

"Charles," I announced, "I'm glad to see you."

Well, there's no use lying, I said to myself, tell the truth.

"Well," I said, "I'm not really glad to see you; what the hell are you doing here?"

They all burst out laughing at this, looking at each other and then mostly at Dr. Leibman. I remembered the spaces between his front teeth, but I couldn't remember his name. So now, again, I stood there looking at him, without moving, staring at him longer than is considered natural. I noticed there was something dead about his eyes. Then he smiled at me, and that seemed even worse. "I," he said, "am Dr. Leibman."

"Oh," I said, "oh!"

"I'm glad to see you," said Dr. Leibman. "Are you glad to see me?"

"I don't know."

"Are you surprised to see me?"

"Yes. That's it. I'm surprised to see you."

"Why quite so surprised?"

"Well, what the hell are you doing here?"

"We may have occasion to go into that later," he said.

Florence explained, "I asked Dr. Leibman to come and spend a few hours with me."

"All the way from California?"

"I've got to go," said Charles to no one in particular.

"Go ahead," I said.

"Yes," said Florence, "all the way from California. Isn't that kind of him?"

Everybody here wants to put me away, I thought. Except Ralph Scott. He doesn't care, one way or the other. I continued to stare at them all.

No wonder they thought I was nuts.

"Sit down," said Arthur.

"Where?" I said.

Actually I was right. There was no place to sit.

Charles got up. "I've got to go," he said. "But I'd like to speak to you a minute first."

I seemed to be two or three remarks behind in the conversation. "I imagine," I said to Florence, referring to Dr. Leibman, "we're paying him."

Nobody seemed to know what I was talking about.

"Him," I said, pointing to Dr. Leibman. "He's not here out of the kindness of his heart, is he?"

There was an embarrassed silence. Everybody, I thought, is always embarrassed whenever the subject of paying psychoanalysts comes up.

"Everybody is always embarrassed," I said, "whenever the subject of paying psychoanalysts comes up."

"Dr. Leibman had to disrupt a very busy schedule," said Florence.

"Oh, I'm so sorry," I said.

Ellen burst out laughing.

"Ellen," said Florence with what was immense control, "I wonder if you and the young man could take a stroll, do some shopping."

"No," said Ellen. "I want to hear."

"Of course we will," said Ralph Scott. "When shall we come back?"

It took me about twenty seconds to realize that Ralph was addressing me. My reflexes had slowed to a crawl. I kept thinking, all these people want to put me away. Then I thought, I don't believe Florence would do that. Not Florence; the others yes, not her.

Ralph said, "Mr. Arness!"

Arthur said, "He's talking to you, Edward," and Dr. Leibman followed with, "Who did you think he was talking to?"

"Oh," I said, "I don't know. Who did *you* think he was talking to?"

"I'd rather not say, for the moment," said Dr. Leibman.

"Well, perhaps we'll have occasion to go into that later," I said. And I gave him that Ralph Scott smile. I'd found a way of dealing with them. I began to feel pretty good. I noticed it was they, not I, who felt edgy.

"Mr. Arness," said Ralph, "we'll come back in an hour, and if that's too early, we'll go and have another lunch."

"Why don't you stay for the fun?" I said.

"Through the heart!" said Ellen, as she turned to go.

"Good luck," said Ralph, taking Ellen by the arm and disappearing from sight.

I turned around from seeing them disappear and there stood Charles, smack in front of me.

"I'd like to say a few things to you," he said.

"Go ahead," I said, smiling my Ralph Scott smile.

"Maybe you'd step out in the hall with me?" he said, indicating the door.

There was something ominous about his tone.

"There is something ominous in your tone," I said, "but I'll be glad to go with you." I noticed I was saying just what I felt, no matter what it was. And this made me feel fine.

"I'm saying just what I feel," I said to them all. "It's a new way of living for me. It seems to make me feel real good."

"I don't think you're saying quite all you think," said Dr. Leibman. "For instance, I wish you'd tell us why you feel so threatened by Charles?"

"I won't tell everybody," I said, "but I'll whisper it to *you*."

At this time they all looked ominously at each other.

"Why are you looking so ominously at each other?"

"What makes you think our expressions are ominous?" asked Dr. Leibman.

Well, I thought to myself, this can go on forever.

"Well," I said, "this can go on forever. Incidentally, who gave orders that I wasn't to be admitted to see my father?"

I stared gently at them all, one after the other. They all looked rather embarrassed.

"You all look rather embarrassed," I said, "but nevertheless, I'd like my question answered, please. Which one of you had the temerity to leave instructions with the hospital police that they were to eject me forcibly if I came to the hospital to see my daddy?"

I started to walk towards Arthur.

"Was it you, Arthur?"

"No," he lied.

"You're lying," I said. "It was you."

"It was I," said Florence.

"I don't believe it was you, Florence; I believe it was Arthur, and now he's got to face the consequences of that act. There are consequences for every act, right, Arthur?"

"I've got to go," said Charles.

"O.K.," I said. Then I turned and faced them all. They looked damned uncomfortable. "I know you have things to talk over," I said, "unfinished business. Well, finish it. I'll be back. I don't imagine Charles has too much to say to me, have you, Charles?"

"Just want to ask you one thing," he said.

I walked over to Florence. "The others, yes," I said, "but I don't believe it of you." Then I bowed and left the room. Charles followed.

Out in the hall I walked to a window that looked out over the inside of the 55th-54th Street block.

"This o.k.?" I asked Charles.

"Any place is o.k."

"Shoot," I said.

"I want your word of honor that you will never see Gwen again."

Well, I thought, that's fair enough.

"Well, that's fair enough," I said. "You're getting married?"

"Yes," he said.

"When?"

"Day after tomorrow."

"Where?"

"It's none of your business."

"That's fair enough. Not the tone, but the content. Fair enough."

"So I want your word. It's not worth a great deal but—"

"What makes you believe my word is not worth a great deal?"

"Because you've been behaving in a completely unreliable fashion."

"Says who?"

"Says everybody."

"Everybody where?"

"Everybody in that room. And say I. I think you're nuts and should be put away!"

"Put away?"

"Certainly! You're a menace to decent people."

"Is that what they're arranging in there?"

"They'll tell you what they're arranging in there. Meantime I want you to give me your word. How about it?"

"No."

"What?"

"I won't give you my word when you ask that way."

"O.K."

"O.K."

I turned and started away.

"Mr. Arness!"

I turned around.

He walked up to me. "If you ever bother Gwen again, or go near her, or . . ." He was breathing hard, at a loss how to finish the sentence he'd started.

"Take your time," I said.

"If you go near her, you know how I mean, I'll have to kill you. I've taken all I'm going to take."

Threats and violence were not natural to this man. I wondered if his brother Chet had been pumping him up. I looked at him and felt rather friendly. But Charles, perhaps feeling that he might soften and again become tolerant of me, turned and walked away.

I walked back into Florence's room without knocking. They all looked up at me from where they'd been bundling over a couple of pieces of legal-size paper. Arthur turned one sheet face down on the American Colonial table. The other he put in his pocket.

"Shall I stay out a little longer?" I asked.

"No," said Arthur. "Come in."

"What's that legal paper? And the one you put in your pocket?"

"Oh," said Arthur, "it's nothing that concerns you presently."

"I doubt that," I said. These people don't deserve the Ralph Scott treatment, I thought. It's too good for them. I'll try something else.

"I smell money," I said.

"What does that mean?" said Dr. Leibman.

I was looking straight at him.

"Whenever I see a psychoanalyst, I smell money," I said, sniffing the air, "but this time I smell it all around me."

Dr. Leibman stood up. Apparently I had reached him. "May I ask you to explain that remark?" he said.

"Dr. Leibman, please," Arthur intervened, "I have an appointment—" Arthur looked at his wrist "—five minutes ago."

"I must catch the noon plane," said Dr. Leibman.

"And I've got a date with the manicure girl downstairs," I said. To hell with them I thought. They don't deserve to be treated well. I postponed my effort to be like Ralph Scott.

"You have what?" said Dr. Leibman.

"We're going to do it during her lunch hour," I said. I could always get a rise out of Dr. Leibman.

"Do what?" he said.

"The well-known business," I said. "We're going to do it in the barbershop supply room on top of the pile of dirty towels."

Arthur took over. "Let's all sit down," he said.

I sat down next to Leibman. "You're my very special doll," I said to him. "I'd like to spend a whole week just playing with you."

412

He gave me the freeze, looking straight down his long distinguished nose. "Will you hold my hand?" I said, "I'm frightened."

"Do you mind?" said Arthur very sternly.

"Of course I mind," I said. "I came here to see my wife, Florence, my estranged wife. I didn't come here to talk to you jokers or to be threatened by Charles—I think I better buy me a pistol, don't you?" No one answered. "Dr. Leibman?" I said. "I'm talking to you."

Dr. Leibman sat there looking like a piece of Mount Rushmore.

"Will you stop being frivolous?" said Arthur.

"Well," I said, "I'm in a frivolous mood." Then I leaned over close to Dr. Leibman and whispered, "I can fix it up for you with that manicurist! She's a bit of a pot roast, but what the hell, you're in a strange city and this is short notice. I'll give you the first ten minutes of her lunch hour. What do you say? Should I carry a pistol?"

Dr. Leibman got up and crossed to the other side of Florence, and sat looking straight ahead. Florence lit a cigarette and looked obliquely up at the ceiling. Arthur looked at his wrist watch.

"Well," I said, "my time is worth nothing. I hope I'm not paying for the time of you bums. I'll bet you, Florence, I can outwait them all!"

Florence didn't answer me.

"Arthur," she said.

"He can't do anything with me," I said. "I'm not in the mood today for a serious talk with a lawyer, even my own. You are still my lawyer, Arthur?"

"Arthur," said Florence, "what do you suggest we do?"

"I have a suggestion," I said. "I suggest that Mount Rushmore go down and tend to the manicurist. Then I suggest that Arthur go to 54th Street and 7th Avenue and bring me back a hot pastrami sandwich from the Stage Delicatessen, also some garlic pickles! What do you all think of that proposal?"

"Arthur," said Florence.

"I don't know what to do," said Arthur.

"Then why don't you take my suggestion?" I said.

Florence screamed. It was a hell of a scream!

Dr. Leibman jumped over to her, and she buried her head in his stomach.

"Now look what you did," said Arthur.

"Leave her alone," I said to Dr. Leibman. "Let her cry. It's the only way. I know from years of experience."

"Dr. Leibman," said Arthur, "can I see you over here a moment?" He walked over to the window. Dr. Leibman didn't know what to do. But Florence made some sort of sign, and he walked over to where Arthur was.

Florence began to dab at her eyes, then went into the bedroom, to get a tissue, I suppose.

"I guess I'll go," I said. Then I got up, moved quickly to the door of her bedroom, opened it, and went in.

Arthur was hard on me.

Florence jumped when she saw me and called, "Arthur."

"All right, dear," said Arthur, "I'm here."

"Dear!" I said. "Dear!"

Dr. Leibman stood in the doorway like a statue of Dr. Leibman.

"I have to go pretty soon," I said, "and I'd like to bring this meeting to some semblance of order. Now I want to talk to my wife. But I'm not going to do it in front of a lawyer, even my own. And Dr. Leibman just makes me jumpy. I want to be at ease for what may be my last interview with my wife. I'm not going to do her any harm."

"Wonderful," said Arthur.

"Wonderful what?" I asked.

"You're behaving like a reasonable, civilized man."

"Well, I wouldn't go that far, would you, Dr. Leibman?"

"Dr. Leibman and I will just sit here, at the side," said Arthur.

"This is not acceptable," I said.

"What do you want?"

"I want you to get the hell out of here."

"I'm not going to be alone with him," said Florence.

"Well, then," I said, "I have one final suggestion, and that is that you fellows go into the other room and leave Florence and myself in here. Sit with your ears to the door so in case I go berserk, you can rush in and two-to-one me. How would that be, Florence?"

"I think that would be fine," said Arthur, not sounding too confident about it. He shifted his eyes around, like Dick Nixon making one of his stronger statements and not being quite sure he means it.

"Is that all right with you, Dr. Leibman?" I asked.

Dr. Leibman didn't answer me.

"Dr. Leibman," I said, "seems not to be talking to me."

Dr. Leibman leaned over to Florence and began saying something to her that I couldn't hear.

"Now I know this is a tough decision for you all to reach, considering my condition," I said, "so I'm going to go into the other room and let you all talk it over."

I walked out into the other room.

Arthur followed me. "All of us have only one purpose here," he said, "to protect Florence until you become yourself again."

"Wonderful," I said.

"I'm sure," he continued, "that somewhere deep inside you, you must be concerned about Florence, too."

"I must be," I said.

Dr. Leibman opened the door.

"Arthur," he said. He was smiling again. Arthur rushed into the other room and closed the door.

I still smelled money, and I wondered if the piece of paper which Arthur had turned face down on the table would throw any light on the reason for that strong money smell all through the room.

So I read it.

It was a declaration to be signed by me and witnessed by Arthur and Dr. Leibman. This declaration, which I read in the modern all-at-one-glance method, said that I was signing away all the equity I had in our community property to Florence; the land, the houses, the effects, all were to be hers until I was again, in Florence's judgment, a responsible person.

I looked up, and there were Arthur and Dr. Leibman watching me read. I finished it in my own time. Then I said something that surprised even me.

"I have no objection to signing this," I said.

They were astonished!

"It's perfectly o.k. with me."

Arthur came over and shook my hand.

"I knew it would be," he lied.

"Is this what this is all about?" I asked.

"Yes," said Arthur in what seemed like a burst of candor. But in fact he was lying again, as I soon found out.

"May I use your pen?" I asked.

Arthur didn't waste a moment.

Neither did I. I took his pen, and I signed his name to it with a flourish. And, as I guessed, he was so glad to have it that he didn't look at the signature, but quickly folded the paper and put it into his inside pocket.

"Now you must be sure I'm nuts," I said.

Arthur laughed. Suddenly he was friendly.

"Arthur," said Dr. Leibman, "there is no need for me to remain here further, if you could stay here till they have their interview?"

"I'm ten minutes late to a very important meeting," said Arthur.

"Now, boys," I said, "why don't you both go? You have your paper all signed."

They went into the bedroom again, and I could hear them talking in there. Then Arthur came out.

"Dr. Leibman's going to catch the two o'clock plane," he said. "I have to go." He reached for my hand.

"Arthur," I said, "could you lend me fifty dollars? I have no money now. I don't know when I'll be able to pay you."

"Of course," he said, "of course!" Out came his billfold. "Would forty do?" he asked. "I only have fifty-odd, and I'll be using taxis all day."

"Well, maybe you could send me the other ten later," I said querulously.

"Of course," he said. "Congratulations, this is all going to work out."

"Of course it will," I said.

"I always said your heart was in the right place."

"And now you're sure," I said.

"Time heals," he said.

"And, Arthur," I said, "you fellows have no other dastardly plots against me, have you?"

"What are you talking about, Edward?" he said. "After all, I'm your lawyer."

"That's what worries me."

He laughed nervously, in a way I didn't at all like. Then he took his homburg, waved it at me and left.

Dr. Leibman came out of Florence's bedroom just then. He began to look around absent-mindedly, as if unaware that I was in the room.

416

I watched him for a while. He was an odd little animal, and suddenly seemed friendless and without cheer.

"Anything the matter?" I asked.

"I have a headache," he said.

"Why don't you lie down and close your eyes? You've been under a strain."

"I think I'll do that," he said, "thank you." He lay down on the sofa, and closed his eyes.

I went into the bedroom.

Florence was lighting a cigarette.

"Florence," I said, "I have an important announcement."

"Yes?" she said apprehensively.

"And that is: I am not nuts."

This seemed to make her more nervous.

"In fact," I said, "I feel rather better than I have in years. I signed that paper because I thought it would make you feel more secure."

She didn't answer.

"I hope it has," I said.

She didn't answer.

"But I see it has not."

"Money," she cleared her throat, "doesn't mean anything to me."

"What does?"

"I want it back the way it was."

"What back the way what was?"

"I want you back the way you were."

"But, Florence, dear. I wasn't really with you for years and years, was I?"

"I don't expect perfection," she said, "but I want a chance to . . . to make a life, to make a good life."

"Well, now you have a chance, and I have a chance."

"I can even forget what I saw the other morning," she said. "Charles, who is a very decent man, tells me he's going to marry that girl. Why he wants to marry a tramp is his business. But I'm glad it's him and not you . . . and . . . Ev . . . oh, Ev . . ."

She began to weep a little.

"Don't mind my crying," she said.

"I don't," I said.

"You son of a bitch, you son of a bitch . . . but I can get over that, I really can, if you just give me time. I can erase what I saw that day. After all, I'm a civilized person, and you are a civilized person."

About this time I realized for a fact that Florence wanted me back.

"You want me back?" I said. I must have sounded very surprised.

"Of course," she said, "that's all I ever wanted. Just give me time to forget that dreadful thing I saw. But it's over, isn't it?" she said. "You kicked her out?"

"No, *she* left *me*," I said.

"I don't think so."

"Why not?"

"I don't think any woman would leave you."

I burst out laughing.

"You son of a bitch!" she said, looking at me very intently, "you look very well, you know, very well. You have absolutely no business looking so well, but you do."

My cue to take her in my arms. But I didn't.

She apparently didn't need much time to erase that dreadful memory, because her eyes were coming on strong.

"I can't go that fast," I said.

"Of course not, neither can I. Time is what we need." She came over and sat close to me. The fact that I'd signed that paper, I thought, certainly worked miracles. But I decided not to say that.

"I may never work again," I said.

"What are you going to do?"

"I may do nothing."

"Nothing?"

"Nothing anyone can see. I may just walk and think. I may just start out and walk places and sit down and think."

"Like Tolstoi?"

"Did he do that?"

"Yes, he did . . . he just walked out one day, cut himself a walking stick and headed out."

"No, not like that, like myself."

"But Tolstoi," she said, "was a rich man."

"Well, we have some property we can sell and get some money."

"I don't know about that."

"About what?" I said, now talking to the boss.

"Whether we have enough to be really secure. I mean I wish you could see the new bills that have come in out of the blue."

"Well, I'd like you to pay them all, and then sell the house, sell the place in Indio, sell the cars, sell all the records and paintings and books, sell all our possessions, in fact, sell everything and . . ."

"Evans, be sensible; where would we go?"

"We just need two rooms. We can get a little inexpensive apartment here in New York."

"I'm too old and too nice to be that uncomfortable, Evans."

"There's a better way to live . . ." I started to say.

"It sounds rather dirty and terribly uncomfortable. I'm just too old to be that uncomfortable, really I am."

"But we were not really comfortable out there, at least I wasn't, I was miserable, I wanted to kill myself, in fact, I tried to kill myself, can you remember? Twice!"

I was getting out of control, and I stopped and walked away from her. I knew it was now or never. I went over and took her hands and held them hard and sort of shook her.

"Florence, Florence," I said, "I know I've done bad things to you and to other people. But nothing like I've done to myself. My sin is against myself. I betrayed myself. I became everything I set out in life *not* to be. I despised myself, Florence, the way I was."

"I loved you the way you were."

"I'm not that man any more."

"I don't mean you were perfect, but you had some consideration for other people—oh, Ev darling, be a decent man, be yourself again! Think of someone besides yourself!"

"All I ever did was think of someone besides myself. That's what was wrong. I lost myself. I became—goddammit, Florence—everything I despised. I'm not going to be that way any more!"

"Well, one good thing you did, you got rid of her."

"It has nothing to do with her, or with you. It has to do with me. I lost myself. I am not that man now, I am not that man."

"Ev, calm down. Try to tell me who you are then?"

"I don't know yet. But that doesn't make me insane. Maybe the rest of the world is insane. I am not."

"Ev—"

"No, let me finish! None of it has to be this way, none of it!

There can be a good life on this earth, but the way it is here and now makes no sense; it's insane. I'm not insane, *it's* insane!"

I could hear my voice rising up and out of control.

"I'm not going back to that or anything like that. Never! Never!"

"Then what are you going to do?"

"The minutes! My minutes! I'm not giving them to anyone any more."

"Evans, calm down."

"I don't feel calm; why should I calm down? I'm not calm!"

"What are you going to do—ouch, you're hurting my hand!"

I let her goddam hands go. Then I took them again.

"Right now, I want to do nothing."

"Well, I can't say I admire that."

"I want not ever again to work at jobs I despise. I want never to lie to people again, or beat them down, or get the better of them, or . . ."

I gathered some breath. Florence looked scared stiff.

"I want to do one small good thing before I die, one small thing that I really admire myself for doing, that is my own, that is myself . . . can you understand that?"

"Of course, Ev—"

"That's what I want."

"Of course."

"I despise the life we had, Florence. I'm sorry, I despise you and me together. I'm going to find a way to live that I respect . . ."

"Such as fucking that tramp!"

"Don't call her a tramp," I said quietly.

"Why shouldn't I call her what she is?"

"She's a human being like you, and she is less a tramp than most of our friends, and—"

"She's a filthy tramp!"

"How would you know?"

"Because I have an instinct! I can tell a tramp when I see one. So when you tell me about your great new steps to freedom, I know what they mean!"

"What do you know about her?"

"Everything!"

"You don't know a damned thing."

"I had her investigated. I found out whom she was with and how many times . . . and what she was paid for it. Do you hear that, paid! Paid!"

"So what?"

"Paid!"

"I like her better than I do you."

"Evans."

"She is more human than you are and more trustworthy! She wouldn't prepare commitment petitions behind her husband's back."

"I didn't do that."

"She wouldn't plot to put me in a mental institution."

"I didn't agree to that."

"Don't you think I know what's really going on in here? There's a paper in your lawyer's inside pocket this minute that would put me in a mental institution, on a writ signed—"

"I refused to sign that."

"I said signed by that phony" (and I raised my voice till it really filled the suite) "Dr. Leibman! And the truth is that you *are*, at this very instant, considering whether you should sign it."

She screamed again. "Dr. Leibman!" she screamed. "Dr. Leibman!" I'd been shaking her hard.

Dr. Leibman must have jumped six feet, because it didn't take him more than a smart second to get in there.

Or for me to get out. I didn't know where I was going, but I was going.

The elevator doors opened, and coming out and past me so fast and so furious that he went by without seeing me was Arthur Houghton. He was heading towards Florence's suite, and he was fit to be tied.

23

D OWNSTAIRS I ran into super-
goy. Mr. Finnegan often lunched at the Gotham. I found out later
that he had made the reservation there for Florence and was signing
her bills.

I stood with him as he waited for his Rolls. The traffic was heavy,
the car had to be late, Finnegan could see this, but it didn't make
him any the less impatient with his driver. The whole entry was
aware of his displeasure.

I noticed my reflected image in the glass door. To my surprise, I
seemed to be watching Finnegan with admiration. That was not how
I felt. Looking at my smiling self in the glass, I wondered was that
me?

Then I understood clearly what it was I'd been feeling for the
several days just passed. Simply, that I was two people. One was
Eddie, the fellow now giving Mr. Finnegan such perfect attention,
the fellow Florence had just said she wanted back, Eddie who behaved in predictable ways, concealed his animosities beneath a smile,
and snuffed out his resentments before they got too hot.

Then there was another man. He had no name yet, nor a face.
But he was aborning as sure as Eddie was dying. These two people
were locked in a deadly struggle, one slowly conquering the other.
When the time came, Eddie would die and whoever was replacing
him would be me.

As soon as that death happened, the franchise would go to the new
incumbent. A person, no less than a business, has a right to go
bankrupt, pay some debts or perhaps a small percentage on all, and
then start again. The emergent should not have to carry through the

rest of his life the full weight of obligation to the mistakes and mis-steps Eddie had made.

I began to watch Eddie as if he were another man.

Finnegan had decided to give me some advice, "Well, Eddie, did you make it up?"

"Make what up?" said Eddie.

"With Florence, you idiot. Are you listening?"

"Of course," said Eddie, smiling.

"Well, I dunno. Are you?" Finnegan looked at Eddie critically. "You really are going nuts; what the hell is the matter with you?" He didn't wait for the answer to this question, walked over to the doorman and gave him a dollar.

"Get me a cab," he said, then back to me, "No kidding, kid, how long do you figure this will go on? I mean it's quite a luxury."

"A luxury?" said Eddie to Finnegan, smiling.

"Yes. Do you really think you can afford all this?"

Again he didn't wait for an answer, but turned and looked up to the head of the street. Fifty-fifth at Fifth was glutted.

"I hope the mayor is having a good time on Sea Island, the son of a bitch," he growled out loud for the benefit of everyone nearby. "Every time the situation gets impossible and he is forced to do some-thing, he fires one traffic commissioner, hires another, and this act leaves him with such a sense of accomplishment that he picks up and goes on a vacation for a month, the son of a bitch."

A number of people laughed.

So did Eddie.

"What would you do about the city?" said Eddie, as if he gave a damn.

"Abandon it," said Finnegan. "Frank Lloyd Wright had it right. Hit it with the bomb and start over."

Eddie laughed. "No kidding," he persisted, as if he cared. "The traffic, I mean?"

"Fire the present traffic commissioner, hire another, and go on a vacation for a month."

Eddie laughed.

"Come on," said Finnegan.

They started down Fifty-fifth Street at a lope.

"Where are you going?" Finnegan shouted over his shoulder.

"With you," said Eddie, "natch!"

"I mean after that?"

"Haven't the foggiest."

"That's what I mean," Finnegan said and spurted. "You have no sense of purpose or direction now," he shouted over his shoulder, "and notice how you're panting. You're dangerously out of shape, kid."

Finnegan saw an empty halfway down the block. "Come on!" he said and charged.

In the cab he leaned forward and gave the driver a dollar bill. "There's another one coming to you if you get me to the Astor in five minutes," he said. The cab driver, one Silverman by his license, took the bill and shrugged. "What's that shrug?" demanded Finnegan.

"I get no ulcers," said Silverman. He wasn't an Eddie.

"The amazing thing is that you look awfully well," said Finnegan. "I've noticed that about people right after they die. They look just wonderful, like the cares of the world had suddenly been lifted off their aching backs. Which is true, right?"

Eddie nodded, smiled, even laughed.

Finnegan was still appraising him. "You're not crazy, are you?" he asked.

"I hope so. I mean" (Eddie had slipped) "I hope not."

"There's no time for all that, so snap out of it, kid. Now! I'm going to tell you what to do. You want to hear?"

"Absolutely."

"When you drop me at the Astor, go back to the Gotham. If anybody is with her, throw them out. Then give her a bang. She'll stop thinking you're crazy, but quick."

Silverman had been trying to slip through a traffic lane. We heard the scrape. Silverman pulled up on his brake and, after one long look of accusation at Finnegan, slowly opened the front door and waddled to the point of contact. The ritual of the exchange of cards and numbers was about to be played out.

"Come on," said super-goy, as he leaped out of the door. Eddie followed as best he could.

"Order some drinks and lunch, room service," Finnegan said as he ran for another empty. They were at Sixth Avenue, and this one was heading north. As Eddie got in, Finnegan was still talking. "They have delicious Crab Dewey there. I just had some. Then if you can do it, bang her again. You'll find there's nothing further to talk about except the vacation you're going to take together, for which I'm going to lend you my house in Eleuthera, fully staffed." Eddie must have looked grateful, because Finnegan said, "You're welcome. You can go right down from here for a week."

The cab had crossed Fifty-sixth Street by then, and the driver was still waiting for his orders.

"Oh, yes, Hotel Astor, driver," said Finnegan. "What's worrying Florence," he resumed, "is not your mental health, but your continuing indifference to her. So have a couple of Gibsons, turn off the lights, and do your duty. Otherwise, my friend," (Eddie smiled) "you're going to have some real trouble, by which I mean the only real kind, money trouble. But after that week on Eleuthera, you can go back to L.A. and do anything you want to anybody you can get." (Eddie laughed appreciatively.)

Suddenly Finnegan noticed the cab was going east!

"Where the hell are you going?" he yelled at the driver.

"No left turn on Fifty-seventh," the driver said. "I got to go east on Fifty-eighth to Fifth and around the block."

"Chhrrrissttt!" yelled super-goy as he hit the ceiling. "I'm worse off than when I started." He leaped out and, giving the driver a dollar bill, said, "Take this man to the Gotham Hotel." Then he put his head in the window and smiled. "So! Everything is all right again? Right?"

"Right!" said Eddie, smiling. "Thanks."

"You made the mistake of admitting something to Florence. Never admit anything! Deny, deny, deny, that's been my motto with women all my life. Now I've got to walk to the Astor. Give her a bang or two. Then call me on the telephone. I'll put you back on full salary as of now! How's that?"

"Just wonderful!" said dear old Eddie.

"But no tickee, no washee, get the point?" He laughed and disappeared.

In front of the Gotham sat an unbecoming vehicle with Ralph Scott in the driver's seat. Ellen was in the back, lying down. She had a headache.

Ralph didn't say a word all the way to the Sound. In front of the old house, I stepped out of the car, kissed Ellen goodbye, shook Ralph's hand and that was it. I don't remember being more grateful to anyone in my life than to Ralph Scott that day for his silence.

When they left, all I wanted to do was sit on the front porch. I understood how animals are often content to just sit. The silence was profoundly comforting. I felt the breeze on my cheeks. I smelled my father's acacia trees. I watched the sails on the Sound; there must have been shouting and talking and laughing on those boats, but I was grateful I couldn't hear. Everything seemed to be happening elsewhere to people who did not concern me.

From a distant barrier, I could hear huge concussions. At regular intervals now, there came those booms—not quite sounds—the vibrations of the membrane air.

Had the war started? I didn't care.

I was on the verge. I knew something irrevocable was going to take place that afternoon. Or at the latest, that night.

Boom. Boom. Boom.

It wasn't thunder, though rain did seem imminent. The surface of Long Island Sound looked like poured lead. There were sudden gusts of wind, like flights of birds, passing over the surface of the water. Then again the concussions or distant thunder. Concussions, likely. Too regular to be thunder.

Something dreadful was going to happen that day. Something final.

I got up and walked slowly down to the old tennis court.

There was a pressure inside my head, like that which must precede a stroke. Was it from the concussions?

The tennis court had long overgrown, two rusted posts in a stand of field grass and vine, surrounded by rusted iron fencing. I remembered the last time, a generation ago, that court had been cared for. A big buyer from a Cleveland department store was coming out for the weekend. My father had heard that he liked to play tennis. Of course Pop didn't play, and he didn't have any interest in keeping the court up for us kids. But for this occasion experts were brought in. When the buyer woke that Sunday midmorning, the court was ready for him. But as it happened, there had been a poker game the night before, and the man woke with a hangover. He didn't even go down to see the court. He sat on the porch, looked out on the Sound, said it reminded him of Lake Erie, and announced that he was going to leave early.

Michael and I used the court that summer. But by the next spring the clay had collapsed in places, and the frost had pushed up some surprisingly large boulders (where had they come from?).

Now, a full generation later, the court stood there, a rectangle of weeds, another of the unvalued things that marked my father's life, like the piano, the motor boat—the things that he had acquired but never enjoyed. Count among these, I thought, my mother.

The concussions were now heavier over the darkening continent. I was in an enormous drum, it seemed, and my ears felt the booming, more as pressure than sound.

The rain began to fall, soundlessly, in great fat drops. I remembered the rain described in Hersey's book on Hiroshima.

I stood in the middle of the tennis court and wondered, among all the neglected things, what things my father had cared for, had kept up. Where were they? What was left, I wondered, of the effort and passion, the sheer energy of his life?

The tennis court offered no resistance to the fall of the heavy drops. The rain disappeared silently into the heavy grasses. Like time, without a mark.

My past, I was thinking—may it disappear without a trace!

I walked slowly towards the house. On the porch I sat and watched the rain fall equally on everything, an agent of time, obliterating the past. Fire and flood, the old book said; pure ablution, someone else said. Keats. He had died young. I haven't much time, I thought. It's late, I thought. But at least I've started. I've pushed everybody off the cliff, and I've almost pushed Eddie off, and I will him, too, soon. Then I'll be the single inhabitant of my own world.

I sat and sang some old songs, my favorites: *Me and My Shadow; It's All Right with Me; Bye, Bye, Blackbird.* And the number-one song on my personal hit parade: (Everybody's worried about Eddie, but) "Eddie Doesn't Live Here Any More."

It's disgusting, all this self-pity in the rain, I thought. So what, I thought.

It occurred to me that all that was left of Eddie was the evidence of this house. I had cleaned out the rest, but I still needed to deal with this house. I hit the wall of the porch. The paint showered off in flakes. This is all that's left of him, I thought, the last trace.

I began to feel a need for some violence to celebrate the death and rebirth, to wash or burn away the old, to celebrate the new. All change is accomplished by bloodletting of some kind, even the

427

first change, birth. Flood and fire seem to be necessary from time to time. Jehovah wasn't cruel. He was true.

It seemed to me that the human race, at certain intervals in its legend, had felt what I was feeling that day: the need to pronounce something bad, to obliterate it, and so make space for the new to grow.

It has always amazed me how quickly the new grows in. I remembered a time when, in an effort to make life on the west coast bearable, I bought a ranch in the Ojai; a hundred-odd acres, it was, of mesquite, sage, thorn bush, and rattlesnakes. I spent a couple of years cleaning that land, without really making much of a dent, and, in the course of that effort, I burned a great deal of brush. I used to put a couple of old auto tires under the brush piles, soak them in kerosene, and let 'em go. I don't know what chemicals they put into tires, but they're potent. That blaze devoured everything, no matter how wet or green. The next day nothing would be left of those enormous piles of brush except some rings of wire that had been in the rubber body of the tire. And ash, inches deep. That ash had hardly cooled before little green shoots were coming through it. The roots had survived in the ground.

I got up and hit the side of the porch again. The flaking paint fell, exposing the wood. A firetrap, I thought.

Inside I stopped and listened. From above, louder than the rain, came the sound of many, many drops of water falling onto metal pans. For the first time I went up the stairs to the part of the house which my mother had cut off from heat and water and care. The stairs on the top floor ended in a little square hall, lit only by a skylight. There were four doors leading to three servants' bedrooms and an enormous attic, which I now entered. When I opened the door, I found under the many large leaks in the roof the assorted pots and pans of the household. When Gwen and I were cooking, we had noticed there were very few cooking utensils in the kitchen. Here they all were, on tables, on chairs, on the floor, rapidly filling with water. In some places the leaks were so bad you could see the sky.

In the attic I found my father's luggage, the veterans of his forty-nine ocean crossings. The soft brown leather had crumbled like dead skin, the buckles and straps broken. But you could see where my father had had his good days, the stickers of the great hotels of that time: Claridge's London, the Ritz in Paris, the Grand in Venice, the Grande Bretagne in Athens, Shepheard's in Cairo, and Tokatlian's in Constantinople.

There, too, was my mother's trunk. I took a saucepan almost half-filled with water off it, pulled the trunk to a dry place, and opened it. My mother had accompanied my father only rarely, but she did have this trunk, London made, heavy canvas stretched on a bent-wood frame. Inside, put away against the day when she might wear them, were her gaily colored clothes, her courtship clothes, her holiday clothes, her happiness clothes. I had never seen my mother in any of them. She had always worn the somber garments of her tradition. I could hardly imagine her wearing anything else.

But she had. Because also in the trunk were photographs of her and my father when I was a small boy, put there, I imagine, to be forgotten, because it would be painful to remember them. But now, revealed to me, there was my mother in the gay dresses of the second decade of this century, in a spreading hat on top of a pompadour of hair. Underneath was her face, the same face, but so full of innocence and hope. She had been a beautiful girl. There was one photograph of her and my father when they had that look of sharing a secret which sexed people have. Where had that look gone? How long had it taken to snuff it out?

There was a photograph of my father and me under the acacia trees, the summer when his fortunes were at their zenith. He sat, and I stood at his side, my hand on his knee, my face turned towards him in an expression of worship. Where had that look of adoration gone? What had killed it?

There were other testimonials to the dearest and the most human parts of our lives, the parts that had not been lived. There were my mother's books, some of her schoolbooks and books of poetry in Greek. Were they, too, waiting for the day when life would become more human so they might be enjoyed again? Or had she locked them away here so they would not remind her of what she had missed?

Also in her trunk was the gift I had brought her when I came home from the war, a piece of fine sari cloth from New Delhi. The gold threads running through it had not lost their luster. I recognized the sea-green of the cross threads. I had given it to her with the suggestion that it would make a lovely dress-up dress; "party

429

dress" is what I had said. She kissed me, I remember, and smiled at me, and her expression had said clearly, what parties? What she had actually said was, yes it was beautiful and she would get a seamstress and a pattern and make a dress of it, and yes, it would be lovely. And she had put it in the trunk.

My mother had done this with all the good things, as if her life was a disgrace and she condemned to live out a certain number of years, and perhaps if she did, a day would come when it would be right for her to wear pretty clothes, read poetry, and be photographed again. In my memory, my mother had not let herself be photographed, but, to judge from the pack of pictures in the trunk, there had been a day when she had enjoyed it.

I put the sari cloth under my arm and closed the lid of the bentwood trunk. Let its contents be forgotten, put away for shame, and unused like the tennis court. Like the gaiety that had been in my mother once. Neglected like her sexuality. Unused like her humanity.

All this had been put aside in the name of what? Where were the evidences of the life that had been lived? Where were the footprints of the victor?

I walked down the stairs to the floor below. There were four bedrooms. In my father's room (they slept in separate bedrooms from the time of my earliest memory), there was a small tray with some medicine on it and nothing else. It was a neat room, no sign of human disorder. Where had he lived his life? Where were the traces of the things he *had* valued?

Then I saw the photograph.

It was a poor example of that art, in coloring dun, in delineation soft. But it was the only picture on his walls. None of his sons, no picture of his wife. There were no photographs of his store, of his stocks, of the National City Bank, or his collection of Oriental Rugs and Carpets. Or of his card-playing cronies. None of them, none of us, meant that much to him. But this photograph did.

The subject was Mount Aergius, the great symmetrical snow-capped mountain which stands over my father's town in Anatolia, the place of his birth. Aergius, the lofty, clean, perfect mountain. My grandmother, when she was alive, never stopped telling me about it: the way the water from the snow top ran down the mountainside all summer long, the orchards of fruit, the picnic places, the summer villas on the slopes. Here it was, now, the magnet of whatever longing my father still had aching within him, the one image of love on the old man's wall.

The mountain represented in that photograph seemed to be demanding some judgment of me, some verdict. What do you think, it seemed to say, what do you really think? And if I had been forced to answer and give a verdict at that moment, I would have had to say that I thought the whole passage of my family to this country had been a failure, not the country's fault perhaps, but the inevitable result of the time and the spirit in the air in those days. The symbols of affluence gained had been empty even by the standards of the market place. The money they had acquired wasn't worth much; they had found that out in 1929. As for the other acquisitions—the homes, the furniture, the cars, the pianos, the decorations, the clothes, the land—they had meant nothing. These men who had cried America, America! as the century died had come here looking for freedom and the other human things, and all they had found for themselves was the freedom to make as much money as possible.

I looked at Aergius again. My grandmother had always claimed that this, not Ararat, was the mountain where Noah had landed his ark. He and his people and his animals had walked off onto those sloping sides. It was beautiful, fitting that legend.

Why had my family left such a beautiful place? There were reasons, true, but the question must have remained in my father's heart: what had he acquired here to make that migration worthwhile? He must have wondered. Or else the photograph could not have been the only thing on his wall. Something that that picture made him feel would not rest and die. They had left that country with its running water, and its orchards of fruit, and all, all that my grandmother never stopped talking about; they had left that to find a better place to live, and all they had found was a better place to make money.

Fire and flood! I wondered if my father had ever hoped for another flood, one that would force him back there, to land like Noah on the sides of Mount Aergius, in a fruit orchard, perhaps, by a rush of mountain water.

When I left my father's bedroom, I took the framed photograph with me, the only thing in the house I wanted.

Coming down the stairs into the living room I noticed the rugs on the floor. I remembered well that these rugs had been in my father's store for years and years, until he had given up hope of selling them and had put them in his own home. I remembered about the furniture, too. We had acquired most of it when a furniture store in Toledo had gone out of business while owing my father a great deal of money. He had been paid off in these monstrosities.

That's how we had acquired the piano, an ornamented grand, edged with rococo wood trim and corner pieces, and borne on the legs and feet of heraldic animals. It looked like a bookie's millions, but it was an old friend.

As I played, I remembered one hot Sunday afternoon in New Delhi, when, with nothing to do, I set out from where I was billeted and walked through the old part of town into the countryside. There, along a low ridge, I saw a great crowd of people. I went towards them, because they seemed to be engaged in something that made them happy. When I got close, I saw that they were all piling sticks, twigs, and boughs of trees around the body of a dead person. The body had been placed in a chair, sitting up, the head bowed over a bit, but sitting there—an old woman it was—in what must have been her favorite chair. I asked who she was, and the people told me easily and readily that she was a holy person—by which they only meant a good person—a woman who had done a lot for many of them, and that she was their friend. She had died just two hours before, they said, of the "eating" disease, cancer. They told all this without bitterness or sadness or even regret. They took the end of life as a matter of course. Why shouldn't her friends be happy, one of them said to me; the old lady had lived a good life, and it was time to celebrate that. It was also time to celebrate, the man said, the fact that we were all still alive, and that we had good years to live. Although their lives would be different, not as good, without this fine old person, still she would want them, now, to have a party (that was my word; it did seem like a party) to celebrate the fact that they were still living. He gave me the piece of wood he was holding and suggested that I put it on the bier. Which I did, thinking here is acceptance and here is celebration, and the acceptance and the celebration are one. The acceptance was that what was past was past and no regrets. The celebration was that we were alive.

It was then that I remembered another place I hadn't been for twenty years, longer, since before I left for the war. The cellar!

There I got the answer to the question I'd been asking myself: where were the traces of the life my father had led?

Covering most of that broad floor were crates of all different sizes, crates which had originally held oriental rugs and carpets coming from Persia and Turkey, and now held my father's business records. Some of the crates were open and covered only with newspapers; others were partly covered with boards; the oldest ones, from the affluent days, were securely nailed. I took the newspapers off the top of one crate, and there they were: the ledgers, the daybooks, the memorandum books, the debtors' books, the stock books. There were all the bankbooks and the cancelled checks. And files upon files of business correspondence: the orders, the bills, the accountings, the letters demanding payment and the letters lying that money was on the way. Here were recorded the facts of my father's life: what he had paid, what he had owed, what was owed him, what he had bought, what he had sold, the salaries paid, the bonuses declared, the interest collected. Everything dealt with the flow of money, the quarrels over money, the negotiations over money, the thirst for money. That was it, and that was all.

There were some nests, too; rats had used the business letters to keep warm.

I sat and read some of the correspondence. How passionate the letters were! I had thought of business letters as cold and formal. And these did have their formalities. But many of them were violent, full of reproaches, pleas, threats, abuse, disappointment, disgust, and the most hysterical anger. There were happy ones, too, announcing profits, anticipating big sales. This was really living! I had only to listen to hear my father and my uncle and the Messrs. Nassib, Boyajian, Tokatlian, Khouri, and all the out-of-town buyers, yelling at each other in anger, joy, reproach, wheedling, threatening, the full catalogue of their emotions.

Here is where my father's life had been lived. Here was his passion, now distilled and dried, his life's blood. Here is what I had grown up in.

Could I have been different than I was?

Nonsense, I thought! I had become what I'd chosen to become.

The world where time was rigidly partitioned into hours was far away. I sat in that cellar and read hundreds of those letters.

Then, to my surprise, I found, buried in the business correspondence, two letters to my father from myself, written during the winter of my second year at college.

Dear Pop: (went the first)

Thank you for your present. I have to admit I was surprised. But it made me awfully happy to get it. I'm sure glad you had that good day at the races. I can use those five dollars. And I promise to buy, like you say, something useful.

Please don't worry any more about my appendix. In the first place, it's out. They showed it to me. In the second place, that operation doesn't amount to anything these days. And the nurses were real good to me. I only wish they were prettier, ha-ha.

I do understand why you couldn't come. Business first, right? Anyway there was nothing you could have done if you'd been here.

I've always wanted to say something to you, and maybe this is a good chance. I know you're disappointed in me. Don't say you're not, because I know you are. The reason I don't mind is that I know you'll be proud of me some day. You have the right to expect your eldest son to pay you back for everything you did for him, and support you in your old age. It's just that I didn't ever get so I understood the rug business. I tried, but I don't understand figures. Although the funny part of it is that the only subject I get "A" in here is math. But I don't seem to be a salesman type. All I can think of are the reasons why people *shouldn't* buy things. Ha-ha!

But don't worry, I don't want to be a teacher or anything like that! I've just got to find my own way. Give me time and I will. You've been very patient about money. Now I got this job at the Zete house waiting on, and I got a room there in the cellar, so from now on all I got to scratch up is tuition. I know it's tough for you to have to shell out dough for a son who doesn't even know what he

434

wants to be, or why he's studying what he's studying. But I'll work this summer and maybe get most of it myself. It's just two more years. And some day I'll make it up to you, you'll see. Some day you'll be proud of me. I'll find something I want to do and at the same time make a lot of dough. That's the secret of life, as I see it, to make your living at what you want to do. I know a man has to be practical and all, and like you say, somebody's got to pay the bills right now, and I know that's not me. But it will be. Believe me! I'm sorry for everything.

Your loving son,
Shakespeare, ha-ha.

When I got through my face was burning at the way I used to be. But I did go the one more.

Dear Pop: Well after I got your letter, I did just what you said. I went and looked in the mirror. And I have to admit the scenery was terrible. I mean the pimples, for instance, I wish they'd go away. Like your friend Mr. Klipstein says, it's time already! I did try that medicine you sent me. Three nights in a row I slept with it all over my face, like one of those women. But the pimples keep popping. And I'm losing my hair, there's no doubt about that any more. I tried everything, but every time I use a comb about half of what I still got comes out.

You do have one thing all wrong. I'm not planning to be an actor or anything like that. For chrissake! I'm not that dumb. So there's no need, like you suggested, for me to go look in the mirror to warn myself away from that. I sort of got lured into that play. I wasn't even going to tell you about it, but here's the thing. There's this girl, see, acting in the play, and I like her. At the same time she's the sweetheart of my best friend, Archie—you met him—so that makes it tough. Not that I'd ever try to do anything to her, especially under the circumstances, Archie, I mean. But still I've been having some difficulty getting this girl off my mind. I guess I'm at that age. It goes with the pimples. Right? Ha-ha! Well, anyway, she said, why don't I, and it's only a small part, and every time I come out the audience laughs. It's sort of fun. Anyway, don't worry, I don't take this acting business seriously. What do you think I am, Shakespeare? Ha-ha!!

Seriously, I know I'm a disappointment to you so far. But like I've been telling you, I'm not as dumb as I look. And some day you'll be proud of me, I promise.

> Your loving son,
> Evangelos
> ex-Shakespeare, ha-ha!

Across the bottom of the letter was written in my father's handwriting *HOPELESS CASE!*

I don't know why I felt so violently about those two letters. Or about the business records. I can't explain why I did what I did, throwing the ledgers everywhere, ripping up the files, scattering the letters to all sides. I actually was off my rocker for a while, there is no doubt of that. In fact when I got through reading them I was crying hysterically, like a kid, or like someone had died.

There was one other thing I found in a corner of the cellar, a little toy bank, one that my father had given me when I was a kid. It was a cash register, a game; you'd put a dime or a nickel or a quarter in the appropriate slot and press a lever, and the total would come up. I guess that was what really got me bawling the way I did. I'd forgotten that damned bank.

That was when I chopped the oil line from the supply tank with the old axe. The cellar floor was soon awash with fuel oil.

In answer to the booming concussions of the world preparing to destroy itself, I made my counter demonstration. I had a need for that fire. I had been planning it all day.

As I lay in the deep grass of the tennis court and watched the futile efforts of the orderly organizations of man to put out the burning testimony of my having forever left one life and, now in good health and with all possible zest, starting another, I felt so unburdened and so happy. The flames satisfied something essential in me. I was celebrating the death of someone; the fellow I had been thinking about, worrying about all my life, no longer existed. Eddie was going up in that glorious fire, riding with the sparks up through the dusk and into the night sky.

I got up, no longer hiding, and walked among the crowd watching the fire. I noticed how exhilarated they were by what was consuming the old monster house. They seemed to have the same need I had for something big and destructive that would flush out the self-disgust that loaded their bellies. Their faces were grave, but grateful, intent, satisfied. None of them paid any attention to me.

I walked away, still holding the framed picture of Mount Aergius. I wanted to give it to my father. Perhaps it would bring him comfort.

Someone had wanted to see the fire so badly that they had taken a local cab to get to it. I told the driver to take me to the Stamford General Hospital. As we drove away, he said, "It's about time that old eyesore went down."

24

I FELT as light as a boy; I felt as I had at college. How effortlessly I used to run then. How I used to leap over the privet hedges which were in front of Fraternity Row. In the spring, when the brooks were breaking out of winter's ice, I would bound from rock to rock and be part of the season. I'd make friends with the dogs that guarded the farmhouses, and we'd run across the fields together. I felt the same exuberance now. I let myself knock around the back of the cab as we hit the ruts and the winter holes, bounding from side to side like a handball, till the cab driver looked back in wonder. Then he smiled at me, and I felt he understood. Oh, I thought, oh, those solitary drunks I used to go on when spring freed the New England countryside. I remembered I used to run in the rain. I remembered moonlit nights when I walked alone in the woods.

I was again in love with the simple sensation of living. It was wonderful to feel one hundred and thirty-five pounds again, and bounce from side to side in that cab like a piece of balsam wood, thoroughly dried.

"I feel no ill will to anyone!" I said out loud.

The cab driver didn't hear.

I could not imagine that I was the object of any ill will.

Even Charles! Even Chet! I felt that if I could just say to each of them that I was sorry for any pain I'd caused them, they would be convinced. They couldn't continue to hate or resent me now.

I felt brotherly towards everyone.

How easy it would be, for instance, to make friends with Charles now. I didn't want Gwen any more. I felt without desire of that kind, disburdened of that, too.

I wanted to go out and clasp everyone I had harmed and ask them to forgive me. I wanted people to know, not in so many words—they couldn't understand the words—but by how I was, that Eddie was dead, and, therefore, wouldn't bother them any more.

I would pay Eddie's debts, too.

I determined to see everyone in my little circle of friends, sparring partners, roommates, former victims, antagonists, lovers, and clients, whoever and whatever, and give them anything they wanted that I could give them that would make them happier. But above all, I would make them understand that there was nothing further that I wanted of them, and so disencumber them and at the same time disencumber myself. I wanted to settle all my scores and leave nothing behind but friendship and brotherliness.

I wanted Charles to feel he was relieved of me as a threat.

I wanted Chet to know that I was sorry I'd done him harm and that I'd make it up to him if he could show me a way.

Above all else, I wanted Florence to know that I wasn't any longer the man she had married, that I would do everything I could to make up for the hurt Eddie had given her, but Eddie himself wasn't around any more.

I vowed to spend the next week or so going around and, avoiding no pain, denying no debt, do the best I could to pay them all.

Then I would disappear, physically, totally.

But I would pay the debts first. I didn't want to leave hatred behind me.

I knew I could do it, because I had no hatred in me. I didn't have anything anyone wanted. I was in competition with no one. I didn't want to get the better of anyone. I had nothing to hide.

I felt like a kid at play, potent with large friendly gestures, ready with the extravagant games of friendship.

So goodbye, all! Goodbye, goodbye forever. May you be happy. I'm sorry I did you harm. But it's all over now!

"Oh, my God," I said out loud, "I feel wonderful."

"What did you say?" said the cab driver.

"I said I feel wonderful."

"I enjoy a fire myself," he said.

I noticed the clock said three dollars and twenty cents. I'd have to start to watch my money. But that was simple, too. What did I really need? I couldn't think of a single damned thing. I had a pair of shoes I liked, and that was it.

Where would I sleep tonight?

What's the difference? There was nowhere I had to be. I could go anywhere.

For all my old show of being in revolt, I suddenly realized how circumscribed my actual physical limits had been. Like the watchman in a big building at night, I had had to pass through a series of checkpoints every hour of every day, and fulfill my function in each, do my bit, sign my name, write my piece, say my speech, calm somebody, sell somebody, pay somebody, correct somebody, fire somebody, straighten out somebody, threaten somebody, kill somebody, adjust, temper, modify. I had to be at a fixed place, at a fixed time, leave my pug mark, then pass on to the next checkpoint. I had often said that the use of money was the liberty it bought. But money had only made it necessary for me to be in certain places at certain times with certain people, and most often with people I didn't really want to be with. And in places I really loathed. What possible excuse was there for any man to live in New York City? Or Los Angeles?

They were not fit habitations for men.

Now I had undivided the world again.

Now I could live where the world was most beautiful and most natural and most for humans.

I began to think of the Wolfgangsee and the Serengeti, the Costa Brava and Virgin Gorda, of Barcelona and Salzburg and the Cyclades of Greece. Not alternatives. Not either-or! There was no reason to stay in one place. Now I could live in them all.

We had arrived at the hospital.

I walked around the grounds a number of times, carrying the large photograph of Mount Aergius. I wasn't quite ready to go in yet. I wanted a few more minutes. I had to make some plans! What I felt as euphoric, the rest of the world might think of as erratic, even dangerous.

The authorities would be after me.

But I was ready for that. I'd explain; I'd be patient. I would return good for evil, gentleness for fury. I would befriend the world. I would lose all the wars. I would ask nothing but my skin.

I would try to promote a few hundred dollars from someone so I could make my first move. If I failed, it might be fun to deliver telegrams for a while. In time I could write pieces for travel magazines from wherever I was.

The only thing I had to do in a practical way before I left was to make sure my father was taken care of.

I approached the guard at the emergency entrance. He seemed to be expecting me, because he went straight for the telephone. I had the strongest feeling that I was in trouble, but I was determined not to run. I was going to pay Eddie's debts. If my new way had value, it would now prove itself in action. I was ready for the police.

Who came was Dr. Levine. He took me out in the parking lot.

"How much money have you got?" he asked.

"Very little," I said. "How much do you need?"

"Have you enough to go to another city and stay there awhile?" He indicated with a gesture of his bug-eyes an ambulance parked near us. It was lit in intermittent flashes of red from a police car parked on the other side of us. "You're the door prize tonight. Everybody who goes in hopes to come out with you."

On the side of the ambulance I read "Greenmeadow."

"What's that?" I asked Dr. Levine.

"Our regional mental hospital," he said. "Behind that ambulance are the local police."

"How'd they know I'd be here?"

"They figured the next move you'd make was come see your father, who's got a pin in his hip and doing as you could expect an old man to do who's lost blood in a two-hour operation. Now's a good time. Go, before they come out."

"I don't want to go," I said. "I want to explain—"

"They're not going to let you explain; they're going to take you for a ride in that ambulance and lock you up! Now go on . . . hurry!"

I did.

Before I took the train, I called Gwen and told her that I had news for her, didn't mean to bother her, just wanted to see her once more. She said come ahead. I asked if she was alone. She said she was. So I planned to go there and make my final settlement with her first.

But I think, the way I felt that day, if she had told me that Chet and Charles were there, I would still have made the visit. I wanted to talk to them, too.

I got my wish.

A sort of intense family conference seemed to be going on when I arrived. Something serious was interrupted by my entrance, and no one knew where to pick up.

I sat down, putting Mount Aergius behind my chair. No one spoke.

I could see that Chet and Charles didn't expect me, and that while Chet, for his own reasons, was glad I had dropped in, Charles wanted me to turn around and go.

"Charles," I said, "you have nothing to fear from me any more. I'm going away for a long time. I have come here to say goodbye, and I want to wish you and Gwen well in your life together."

I stopped. I had expected him to be overjoyed, or at least to receive my announcement with some show of satisfaction. But he didn't seem to believe what I was saying.

Some people, when they are troubled, their thinking processes slow up. Everyone waited for Charles to respond to what I had said. But he sat there looking straight ahead. In his own time, he turned to Gwen and asked, "Were you expecting him?"

"No," Gwen lied.

Charles sat another while, staring straight ahead. His concentration was so intense that no one else spoke either.

Finally he said, "I wish I could believe you."

Chet burst out laughing.

"Well, I don't," said Charles to his brother.

"Neither do I," said Chet.

"Then what the hell are you laughing at?" demanded Charles.

"At the subtlety of women and the naïveté of men."

Charles let that remark sink in. It took time. Charles seemed dazed. I felt sorry for him, this huge man without the equipment or the experience to deal with the situation he was in.

"Charles," I said, "please, Charles, believe me, I don't want anything from Gwen any more. I'm sorry I have caused you grief—" I was pleading with him; I hoped he knew that—"I really am, and I don't bear you any ill will."

"Tell him," said Chet, "tell him, Charles, that you don't bear him any ill will either."

"Why should I do that?"

"Because it's a lie, and that's how people get along."

"Chet," I said to him, "I know how you feel about me. I know you have reason to bear me ill will."

"I love that ill will," he said. "Where did you pick up that ill will?"

"Well, however you'd describe it, I want you to know that if you will tell me how I can make it up to you, I . . ."

"You want to make it up to me?"

"Yes. So tell me, if you know, how I can straighten things out."

"How much time have you got?" said Chet.

"Well, I hope to leave town and this part of the world sometime in the next week or two."

"That doesn't give us much time, does it?"

"I have no ticket anywhere."

"Well, I'm glad to hear that."

I knew he was mocking me, but I believed that if I took a certain amount of punishment, the time would come when my sincere desire to make amends would be felt.

"Well," said Chet, "here's the first thing you do."

Charles was staring at me in the most peculiar way.

"What is it, Charles?" I said.

"Never mind him," said Chet. "Take care of me first. Isn't that what you said?"

"I want to do everything I can."

"Then let's get going. You go straight to the people who put out that magazine and ask them for equal time, that is, space! Then you write a piece of confession and say to all their readers and yours that you knew what you were going to write before you ever saw me, that you wrote out of pique because I had your girl friend, or was about to, and that you lied factually and misrepresented me totally! In short, that you're corrupt, prejudiced, and venal."

Gwen said, "Cut it out, Chet."

"Well, he asked me what he could do."

Then he turned to me, getting up out of his chair, and standing over me, he said, "You go to that magazine, putting off whatever you came here to do with her, and say it's a matter of life and death that they give you equal space. I'll warrant that. Then come up to

443

my place and we'll write your piece together, and you'll tell the world, or at least the part of it which reads that filthy—eh? What? How does that strike you?" He was standing right over me.

"Well," I said, "well . . ."

"Rise when you speak to me," said Chet.

"Chet, cut it out," said Gwen.

"It's o.k.," I said to Gwen, "I'll rise. I don't mind if it's necessary for him to punish me; there is a certain amount of it that I can take."

"How much can you take?" said Chet.

"I don't want to leave here with you hating me."

"You know that magazine is not going to give you an inch of space."

"You'd better go, Eddie," said Gwen.

"I don't want to go," I said.

"Why do you keep lying to me?" asked Chet.

"I'm not lying to you."

"Then why did you pretend to me that you'd ask the magazine to . . . ?"

"I didn't pretend that . . ."

"What did you come here for? Can you answer that one question truthfully?"

"For just what I said."

Chet turned, walked into the hall, and from there into the bathroom.

I turned to Gwen. "Don't take him seriously," she said. "He's only trying to give you a bad time."

"Not him," said Chet from the bathroom. "You."

"What happened?" I said. "Has something happened?"

Charles didn't say anything. He just kept staring at me.

"Why are you looking at me that way, Charles? I don't mean you any harm. I don't want anything from anybody."

"Then why did you come here?" said Chet from the bathroom.

"I told you why," I said.

"Just forget it now, Eddie," said Gwen.

"Yes, now is not a good time, Eddie, later!" Chet called from the bathroom. He slammed the medicine cabinet door.

"Charles," I said, "why are you looking at me?"

"I told you," said Charles, slowly and heavily, as though he was pronouncing the most solemn obligation, "that if you ever saw Gwen again, I'd kill you."

"He knows you were only kidding," called Chet.

"I remember that, Charles," I said, "and that is why I came here, to tell Gwen that I was not going to see her again, not because you threatened me, Charles, but because . . ."

"Didn't you believe me?" asked Charles.

"Well, I knew you felt strongly."

"But still, you're here. Didn't you believe what I said to you?"

"He meant," said Chet, walking back into the room, "literally, that he would kill you—not the way you intellectuals kill people, by lying in print, but physically, by firing a bullet of lead at high velocity into your lamb's heart, or through your chicken's brain. He wants to know if you believed that."

"Are you asking me," I said, "if I believed that literally?"

"Isn't that what I just said, Gwen?" Chet asked.

Then, with her attention directed towards him, he put down on the coffee table in front of her what he had gone into the bathroom to get, a circular plastic receptable about four inches across and perhaps three-quarters of an inch through. "I haven't opened this," he said. "I wanted to open it in front of you all."

"Now you just get out of here, Chet," said Gwen. "Just get the hell out of here!"

"What have you to fear if you are telling the truth and weren't preparing to entertain—that's the word, isn't it—entertain him?"

Gwen has guts. She hauled off and smacked Chet across the face with all her might, which was considerable right then. She was as furious as I'd ever seen her.

"Do you want to open it, or do you want me to?" said Chet.

"Chet," said Charles, "what are you doing?"

"I think she expected him, and I think she's lying. I know *he's* lying. It's his total conversation."

He handed the plastic container to me. "I think you should open it," he said. "Come on! Let's see your class. Open it."

"Charles," said Gwen, "if you don't take your brother out of here right now, I will never talk to you again. You know I mean that."

"I haven't peeked into it," continued Chet. "I'll bet you what I have in my pocket, Eddie, against what you have in your pocket, that it's empty. So if it's empty, what was in it is somewhere, and that means she was expecting you, and that means not only that you're a liar, which is natural, but that she is a liar. She wasn't getting ready for Charles, that's for sure!"

Suddenly he snatched the plastic container from my hand—I don't know what the hell I was doing holding it—and he flung it on the table. The impact opened it. And it was, as he had said, empty.

Then Chet said to Charles, "And she wasn't getting ready for me."

That is when Gwen had her fit.

She took the poker from the fireplace set and began to hit Chet about the face. Chet backed behind a chair where she couldn't reach him, so she took out after Charles, who shielded his face with his arms and kept saying, "Gwen, don't! Gwen!" to all of which she paid no mind; all she would say was, "Get out of here right now, you two bastards, right now, out of here, now."

Then she suddenly seemed to lose all control, and threw the poker at Chet and went after him, leaping or climbing (it was so fast I couldn't tell which) over the armchair and onto his neck, biting his face and scratching at his eyes, one of which began to bleed. She tore his ear lobe with her teeth, and I think she got a piece, because it began to bleed there, too. At the same time she was kicking at his groin with her knee. She meant to exterminate him, there was no doubt of that. It wasn't a matter of Chet's restraining himself from fighting back on equal terms with equal weapons. He was no match. He wasn't up to it. All Gwen's gutter guts were up, the backroom brawler, complete and admirable. You could only hope that such a woman would be around if you were in trouble, and that if she were, she'd be on your side. She'd always played it so cool, but this was pure bloody beautiful murder!

Suddenly, beyond reason, she ran into the kitchen, came back with the meat knife, and took out after Chet, going straight for his vitals. But he had had a chance to recover and picked up a straight chair from the dining room set, which proved that he knew something about brawling, too, and poked it into her, all the time shouting at Charles to get out. Which Charles was only too glad to do. Her ferocity and her deadliness were awesome. She was inspired with murder. Poor Charles was saying, "Gwen, Gwen, don't be like that! Gwen, Gwen, don't be that way," and other such totally inadequate remarks.

I was lost in admiration.

Charles was out the door now, and Chet followed, and no sooner were they out than Gwen locked the door.

We could now hear the child crying.

She went into the other room and quieted him. It was very quiet everywhere for a couple of minutes.

Then I heard Chet calling from the street. "Eddie! . . . Eddie!"

I opened the window for a quick look and then leaned back out of sight.

I had had a glimpse of the two brothers in the middle of the street, standing like beasts in the field. There was a small crowd circling. Chet's front was bloody.

"Eddie . . ." he yelled.

I leaned forward, this time so he could sight me.

They were surrounded by a small crowd looking at Chet. I was right; there was blood on his shirt and coat, and he was still bleeding, but he was too full of adrenalin to know or care. "Eddie!" he yelled, "we're waiting for you. Come on down."

Gwen came back into the room. "I think they mean to kill you," she said.

"Come on, Eddie," yelled Chet. "Don't keep us waiting!"

A policeman was walking up to see what the disturbance was all about.

"Eddie," yelled Chet, "we'll wait for you in Clancy's." He pointed to the bar across the street, the place where Charles and I had had our long talk some nights before.

As the cop got near, the brothers turned and crossed the street. The crowd wouldn't answer the policeman's inquiries.

I closed the window.

"Charles has a gun," said Gwen. "I told him last night that I'd changed my mind, so naturally they expected I'd be with you. That's the way those men think. 'It's either me,' they think, 'or someone else.' What do they think I am?"

I didn't answer that one.

"I'm going to call the police," said Gwen.

She went for the phone.

"Don't do that," I said.

"They're liable to shoot you—not Chet, he's too cagey; he'd do it some other night with his fists and a bottle end, but Charles is pure,

447

and he'd shoot you, that sin-sick choirboy. Chet's got him thinking that I'm a demon of evil and you're even worse, and that if he wiped you out, he could expect a medallion from the Madonna and a seat at Christ's right hand."

"I'm going down and talk to them."

She saw that I meant it, and then she said, "Bring me some milk for the kid when you come back, or better, stop by the grocer's before you go into Clancy's and ask them to send up a couple of quarts and a box of Pablum. You might not be able to later."

Then she came over to me.

"Did you hear what I told you before?" she asked.

"I guess so. What was it?" It turned out I hadn't.

"I told Charles I'd changed my mind. I got thinking about taking instruction and all, I promised him I'd do that, but then I realized that I wasn't ever going to stand for those sisters filling Andy full of catechism water. So that started me thinking a lot of things. I told him let's be friends and he could come up and live with me, but no go on Andy's education, or anything like that! But Charles wouldn't go for it. He wanted all or nothing, and suddenly I said the hell with it all, and called it off. Well, those boys think in a straight line, and the arrow points to the villain, and that's you. The pair of them paid me an unexpected call, thinking you'd be here. You weren't, but you didn't keep them waiting long."

"So . . ."

"So now they want you—understand?"

"I want to see them, too."

And I left.

"I've been telling this short-cocked, mush-hearted, waggle-tailed spaniel," Chet was saying, "to forget about her. I told him he was overmatched, and to start looking in the libraries for a school-teacher; don't you think I'm right, Eddie, say?"

I had sat so that Charles was between us. I could see that they had both had troubles, but the drink, instead of inflaming Charles, had—well, all I could think of was a bomb which had been dropped but had not exploded, and I had the job of removing the fuse. I had to work carefully.

Chet was going on, "I told him, dear little pigeon-hearted Charles, you were misled by that sincere look in her eye. All that is, my boy, is a congenital cast, right, Eddie? She's slightly cockeyed, and has no slight eye for cock, and Eddie's got the one she wants. We have to face that, Charles boy."

"Charles," I said, "I want you to listen to me, please, will you, please, give me a chance?"

"I mean she needs someone a lot tougher than you are, kid," Chet said to his brother. "You're too good for her, Charles, too gentle. Show this girl kindness and she'll call it weakness. Drop your guard and she's on you like a cat, goes right for your filet mignon with a knife like she did me. I mean it takes a man like Eddie to handle her; you've got to learn to live with that, Charles boy."

Charles turned and directed his gaze at me, without blinking, like a lion will when you stand in front of his cage.

"Charles, please, I want you to know that I had absolutely nothing to do with what happened between you and Gwen."

"You don't have to lie any more, Eddie," said Chet. "I told our boy you couldn't be expected to tell the truth—especially under these circumstances."

"Charles, I haven't even talked to her, not in days, you have to believe me—"

"And forgive him, too, Charles; after all he was only doing what comes natural to him. And to her. Come on Charles, the man wants your forgiveness. Give it to him!"

Charles didn't say a word. He seemed to be deciding something.

Chet lifted his right arm, drew it back slowly and deliberately, and clouted Charles across the face. Charles didn't make a move.

"There, you see," said Chet, "the triumph of religious training. The sisters taught him patience. Turn the other cheek of your ass, Charles, and let our friend here give you the business again!" He turned to me. "By the way, Eddie, did you get into her after we left? She'll move very quick, I know from experience, up, in and out. No answer? Well, if you didn't, I'm sure Charles will go up with you and tuck you in. It's a shame to waste that good jelly. What do you say, Charles, there's true beauty in suffering; even an ex like me knows that. Come on, true believer. Christ suffered for you, you son of a bitch; He bled for you, so you can't do too much. Go tuck 'em in!"

"I want you to know," I said to Charles, who still gave no sign of what he might do, "that I'm going away sometime within the next two weeks. I'll be gone for a long time, and I won't see Gwen again—"

449

"Do you mean that?" said Charles suddenly.

"I do, Charles, I do."

"How can I believe you?"

"You can," I said, "you will see."

"But tell me, why did she do that?"

"I'll tell you why," said Chet. "It's because no woman wants a pig in a poke, and she kept waiting for you to make your move, and you didn't, and meantime our little friend here and God knows what salty-blooded niggers and what circumcised Jew-dogs off the Broadway beat, what sailors off the fleets of the world—!"

"Charles," I said, "could you come over and sit down at that table in the corner? I want to talk to you, and I can't here."

"Oh, sure, you can," said Chet. "I'll shut up. See, I'm silent. Talk. Let's see you comfort him."

"Charles," I begged.

Charles stood up. "Go over to the bar," he said to his brother. "I want to talk to him alone."

"Comfort him, Eddie, go on, he'll believe anything you tell him." Then, in a quick move, Chet was over at the bar, hacking it up with the flies there. But he watched every move we made.

Charles sat down again.

"Charles," I said in the silence, "I've always believed you were a good man. I've always felt your goodness. Charles, are you listening?"

"I'm a little drunk, but I'm doing my best."

"Did you hear what I just said?"

"Say it again."

"I said that I have always believed you were a good man. I knew it the first time I saw you."

"Don't lie to me," he said. "Let's tell the truth now."

"Yes, and the truth is I always knew you were a good man."

"All right. Now I want to say something to you."

"Go ahead."

"When I first saw you, I thought, this is not the kind of fellow I'm used to, or understand easily, but still he's someone who wants to be decent—you do, don't you? You're not common dirt like the rest of the wise guys and café society phonies, are you?"

"No," I said, "I'm not, especially now I'm not."

"Then why did you talk against me to Gwen?"

"I didn't," I said, "I swear—what can I swear on . . . ?"

"On your mother's grave!"

"What?"

"Swear on your mother's grave!"

"But she's not dead yet."

"O.K. But you're not lying to me, are you, like Chet says? I wish you were religious. People who aren't religious don't believe in anything, so there's nothing for them to swear on!"

"I never said one bad word against you."

"I want to believe you."

"You can."

"If I catch you lying about this now, I will kill you; you know I will, don't you? I'm not one of these in-and-out, any-bed-will-do guys. I had plans, you know. Chet says that you—"

"I'm going to tell you something about him which will be hard for you to take."

"We're going to try to tell the truth, aren't we?"

He was way back there. I went back with him.

"Now, about your brother . . ."

"You don't like him."

"I'm sorry to say I don't."

"Neither do I."

"I'm sorry because I want to like everybody now. But I can't really say I like your brother. Even now when I'm determined to at least understand—"

"I don't like him either. I never did. But that doesn't make what he says less true, does it?"

"Yes, it does. Even when he gets the facts right, his intent is hateful, and his inference is . . ."

"True! True! But let's deal in facts." He gripped my arm again. (Chet was watching every move from the bar.) "Tell me the truth!" Now he put his other arm around my shoulder and shook me. Undeniably, he was much stronger than his brother. But his grip, which hurt a little, did not frighten me, because I felt he wanted to be friendly.

"Tell me one thing, will you, did you talk against me to Gwen?" There was something terrifying, but touching, about his slow, simple-minded effort to understand what had happened to him so suddenly. "Now think back, did you say anything to Gwen?"

"I swear, not a word."

"Then how come she called me last night? I did everything she wanted, everything, just like she asked."

"She said something about a disagreement about the education of the boy."

"But there I was only doing what was right! It's for the boy's own good. Even you must realize that!"

He tightened his grip on my shoulder. "Were you with her when she called me last night?"

"No," I said, pleading for his belief, "I wasn't—"

"That's what Chet's been telling me. He says that when she called him to break off, she was in bed with someone else. That's the way she is, he says. I hope you're not lying."

"I'm truly not."

"You see I've been imagining that scene, you and her. I can't get that scene out of my mind. That's why I don't talk much, you know; I keep thinking of that."

"But there's no truth to it, Charles."

"Where were you last night?"

"I've forgotten," I said, and then realized with a jolt that this would seem like an evasion to him.

"You're lying," he said, with such sadness. "You're lying to me, you see?"

"No. I really did forget."

"How can a man forget where he was last night? Last night! You see?"

Tears were in his eyes. "Oh, Jesus, help me," he murmured.

"You must believe me," I pleaded, "that's the way I am. I'm in trouble. Many times lately I haven't known from hour to hour what lay ahead of me. Or what I had just done. But now I remember where I was last night. I was burning down a house."

"Oh, my God," he said and laughed a little. "Can't you make up anything better than that?"

"It's true, on my mother's grave!"

"All right, all right. It's farfetched, but I'm going to believe you." Then he looked at me strangely, and he said, "Are you partly insane, please tell me?"

"I may be, yes."

"Poor soul."

"I certainly think I have been. I was."

"Poor soul!" he murmured.

"But I don't think I am any more. Just a little, maybe. For instance, you can believe me absolutely that I did forget and that is where I truly was last night. I do forget like that; my mind is not in order."

"I see that."

"But I was not with her."

"Then who was she expecting?"

"I've been wondering that, too."

"It's an awful question. Who was she expecting? Will you tell me the truth?"

"Yes."

"What I mean to say is, if it had been you, would you now tell me, me being the way I am?"

"Yes. I believe I would. I have achieved something, Charles, not where anyone can see it, but inside myself where I can feel it. You understand me, I see that. I don't have anything to lose any more, nothing to protect. I'm going to give all my possessions and all my money away, for instance."

"You are?"

"Yes. I don't want anything. I don't want anybody. I don't want Gwen any more. I did once. When I came to New York a few days ago, I thought being with her would solve all my problems. But now I know that no one else is going to solve my problems. It's between me and me. So you can have her. I'm going to disappear."

"Where are you going?" he asked.

"Into myself. I'm saying goodbye to everyone."

"You better see a doctor or something, don't you think?"

"No, I tried that!"

"A priest? See a priest!"

"All I need is to be alone. She's yours, I won't even be here; I didn't talk to her last night, and she wasn't waiting for me; you do believe me, don't you?"

"I do," he said. "Now I really do."

"O.K. That's all I want," I said. "I wish you happiness. I think of you as my friend."

"You may," he said.

"Thank you," I said.

He pulled open his coat, and I saw a pistol. "Ever since she told me on the phone that it was off, I've had this with me. I was going to kill you. I can't believe it as I hear myself say it. Even a few minutes ago, right here, I said to myself, if he's lying to me now—but now I see you're in worse trouble than I am, so it's wishing you luck. Goodbye. I'm sorry about this." He meant the pistol.

"As long as we're friends," I said.

He stood up. And I did. It was a formal parting. He put his arms around me. "I want to ask you one more question," he whispered in my ear as he held me. "Tell me the God's truth! Do you think I'm sexually unattractive to a woman?"

"I don't see why," I said.

"Thank you," he said, "thank you."

I turned to go. Chet was watching us.

Charles said, "Don't worry about him. I'll walk you to the door."

Chet didn't make a move as I walked out.

I couldn't wait to tell Gwen that my new way had worked. I intended to pick up my photograph of Aergius and go.

As I waited for her to open the door, I could smell bath salts.

She told me later that she had been frantic, kept watching the bar front from her window. After some minutes of this, she decided that whatever was going to happen would happen, ran a very hot bath, loaded it with salts, had a triple slug of bourbon, and got into the water.

What with the fight, the scalding soak, the alcohol, and not knowing who might be ringing her bell, she could hardly get the door opened. The first glimpse I had of her over the police chain told me how frightened she'd been, this girl who doesn't scare.

When she got the door open all the way, she pulled me in and held me like I'd made it back from the dead. I hadn't known she felt so much for me. Or could.

She wouldn't let go of my arm. She pulled me back to the sofa, and lay down with my hand under her gripped in both of hers. She buried her face in a pillow, only her eyes visible and upon me. They seemed overbright.

I tried to tell her what had happened in the bar, but she didn't seem to care, now that I was safe. She wasn't listening to anything I was saying.

"Have you taken something?" I finally asked.

"Taken what?"

"You look drugged."

"You think I use drugs?"

"I mean like three or four Miltown."

"It's the bourbon. I was so frightened, Eddie. My nerves are shot."

"Feel all right now?"

"I feel sort of sleepy. I don't want to move, like. I want everything brought to me. And I want to be taken care of. You know?"

"I'm sure Charles will be calling soon."

"I don't want to see Charles."

"You were wonderful when you went after Chet—the way you did."

"They were right, though. You knew that, didn't you?"

"Right?"

"I *was* waiting for you."

It had crossed my mind.

So then . . . well . . . truly I didn't see how else I could say good-bye to her, after what we had been to each other. What could I do, shake her hand? And I did admire her so much, the way she had gone after Chet, and loved her because she had been so frightened for me.

So it really was the most natural thing in the world!

At any rate, when Charles, who had a key to the apartment, came in, we were in bed together.

He shot me in the side of the buttock, I turning away just in time. That wasn't where he aimed his shot.

Then he shot at me again, trying this time to kill me. But I was falling, and he missed my head. That's the last I remembered.

When I came to, I knew I was in some kind of hospital. But I was so weak that I didn't much care where. I wanted to think. But all I could do was fall asleep again. Immediately. And that was it.

25

S TRANGE kind of hospital I thought, bars across the windows.

I was aware of someone else in the room, a man in his sixties. His thin legs, skinned in parchment, dangled over the side of his bed. Was he grinning at me?

"Where am I?" I asked.

"You are in a building of the Greenmeadow Mental Hospital."

"How did I get in here?"

"A person close to you signed a petition that you be confined here. Have you a wife?"

"Yes. What are you smiling at?"

"I've been waiting a long time to see you come to."

"Why?"

"I wanted to see the expression on your face when you realized where you were."

He had a very amusing face, chipper with intelligence. You could see the thoughts hopping here and there, never still.

"My name is Teitelbaum," he said. "Arnold Teitelbaum. May you live to be a hundred."

I laughed. But when I did, my chest hurt. The second bullet Charles had fired missed my head and entered the shoulder muscle on the left side. He had just missed killing me. Then I remembered the first shot and quickly reached down to see if I was intact.

I was vastly relieved.

"Where did you say I was?" I asked.

"Greenmeadow Mental Hospital."

So Florence had signed the paper after all.

"What am I in here for?"

"That's everyone's secret and your problem."

"What's my problem?"

"How to get out of here."

"I'm not sure I want to."

"In a few days you may want to very much. Then remember I am a lawyer. I will tell you something they won't."

"What is that?"

"You have already been deprived of some of your basic rights."

"I have?"

"Try to make a phone call."

I didn't speak. He was making me weary. He had a conversational drive which I, at the moment, could not stand up to. And he kept at me.

"What do you intend to do?"

"When?"

"Now."

"Enjoy the silence."

"I might be able to help you."

"Mr. Teitelbaum," I said, "I have my own problems."

"Naturally," he said, "or else you wouldn't be in here."

"I have to figure out what my situation is."

"Go ahead. You're thinking well."

"And in order to do that I really need silence."

"No one knows the value of concentration better than I do."

"I mean I wonder if *right now* you could . . ."

"Well," he said, "it's difficult for me to keep silent now, because we have just met, and I am understandably curious."

I tried to turn over on my stomach.

"You can't turn over, my friend. And that won't be necessary. Don't worry. I have long periods when I am absolutely silent. In fact, there will be times when you will wish I'd say something."

"I doubt that."

"You will see. Now why don't you just close your eyes and try to relax. You will soon need every bit of your strength."

I grunted.

"And I will be of help to you. I will arrange many, many . . ."

"Would you please, please, arrange for some silence in here, now!"

457

"Don't treat me as a fool or as an insane person," said Arnold Teitelbaum, showing a strength and dignity I had not expected. "I am neither. I once ran the most successful chain of grocery stores in the state of Connecticut. I won't mention the name, but you have heard it. I committed the error of retiring. I thought I would enjoy the rest of my life better if I didn't work. I made a foolish mistake. But this does not give you the privilege of making fun of me. I will have you know, furthermore, that I am an accredited member of the bar in two states. I am not incompetent in a court of law. I will correct wrongs done me that have already been forgotten by the wrongdoers. I will humble my enemies; I have forgotten nothing! Blood will run in the streets of Bridgeport; there will be sudden justice and general carnage." His voice was very loud now. "The cries of my enemies will be heard in public places!"

A man in a white coat hurried into the room. Arnold Teitelbaum sat panting on his bed like a pocket Lear. He looked at the attendant with regal scorn. Then he fell back on his bed, and put his forearm over his eyes.

The attendant purposely ignored him. "How are you?" he said to me.

"I don't know," I said. "When is the doctor coming to tell me?"

"Won't be too long now." Then he walked over to Teitelbaum's bed. "Mr. Teitelbaum," he said, "I think you should leave this gentleman in peace. He needs to rest."

"He started the conversation," said Teitelbaum, uncovering his face, and covering it immediately.

"Then I had no right to blame you," said the attendant and walked out of the room.

"That was Dr. Lloyd," Teitelbaum said, "and that's the last damned advice you're going to get out of me. He's the psychiatrist on this floor. Now, suffer in silence."

I fell asleep, and what woke me was an intern ripping off the tape that held my bandages. He seemed to be satisfied with what he saw, because the next thing I knew he was gone and a nurse was re-bandaging me. I kept falling asleep all through that day. Teitelbaum was out on the grounds, so all was quiet. When he did come back, it was supper time, and I was glad to see him. I told him that I kept falling asleep, and he told me what I should have guessed, that I was doped to the eyeballs.

I felt much better the next day, and a young nurse helped me into a wheel chair and took me out into the sun. For the next few days, as I sat at the side of one of the big brick buildings, a succession of patients visited with me, coming up, as a dog might, to sniff and see what I was. They were friendly and had one thing in common. They would come on as if they were full of secrets they would never divulge. But let the attendant nurse walk away for a moment, and out would come tales of persecution and betrayal or plain villainy that scorched my ears. To my considerable surprise, I believed what they told me. They sounded so convincing. These people, it seemed to me, were often at most reasonable odds with the society and people around them.

I had expected that everyone would be obsessed with how to get out. Most of the inmates, however, were concerned with how long they could manage to stay in. Some of them had never had it so good.

For instance, there was one young wife, maybe twenty-six, and already with five children. Her husband disapproved of birth control, and so her prognosis was, in one word, more! What had she to go back to? Some dark rooms, kids three in a bed, a litter of unpaid bills, laundry piled high in one corner, a sink always full of dirty dishes, the whole place never really clean, the demands on her time and attention unceasing and insatiable, her poor tits pulled limp long before their time, and all of her chronically tired and hopelessly demoralized. Greenmeadow was her Riviera. She was presently enjoying the only young-womanhood she had ever known, talking freely to other young women like herself, swapping clothes and laughing it up on the lawn, lounging around the coffee shop, having flirtations which didn't threaten to end in another armful of responsibilities. Why should she hurry back?

I soon felt the same way. I didn't even want a phone call. I thought I might talk to Gwen to see if she was o.k. But for no reason except my perfect lassitude, I didn't.

I finally did obtain permission to speak to my brother. The nurse got the number for me, and I asked Michael how my father was.

"Coming along," said Michael cautiously. I could hear Gloria breathing in his ear. He didn't ask me how I was. I volunteered that I didn't need anything.

Finally I had my meeting with Dr. Lloyd. He was a young man with a Sunday school hair-do and a most earnest manner. He asked me how I felt. I said, o.k. He said did I need anything. I said I didn't. Was I happy? Perfectly! He smiled and walked away.

Then he turned around and looked at me. Something about my answers apparently disturbed him, because he came back.

"You're not going to put me out, are you?" I asked.

"Well, we do like to move people as quickly as we can."

I felt, suddenly, that I had given this man the wrong answers, that I was in danger. "Why send them out," I said, "into the situation which put them in here to begin with?" He studied me. "I'm crazy enough to like it here," I said. "In fact this is the only place I've seen where there is time for self-contemplation. It's our equivalent of the Buddhist retreat, wouldn't you say?"

"No, I wouldn't say that."

He smiled and left me.

As soon as he was gone, some of the patients came up and asked me what he had said. "He's not going to let me stay here," I said, putting on a sad face. They all laughed, and that irreverent sound came to the ears of Dr. Lloyd as he stood at some distance making his notes on our conversation.

Then they all sat around asking questions and giving advice.

The general drift related to my hearing. The law said that I couldn't be kept there longer than ten days except under a formal order of commitment. It turned out that these hearings were conducted right on the hospital grounds. A probate judge, having heard both sides, decides whether the person should be committed formally and for how long.

My hearing took place in a little replica of a courtroom. There was a raised section at one end of the room for the judge's desk. Flanking him was the American flag and the state flag of Connecticut. Facing the judge's desk was a long table, behind which could be seated five or six people. I was brought in by an attendant. With me, ready to answer questions, was Dr. Lloyd.

Seated behind the long table and waiting for us were Florence, Arthur Houghton, and Dr. Ochs. Dr. Ochs, it turned out, was with Florence, and new.

Florence gave me a kindly smile. The mood of all three was one of commiseration.

The judge was a thickset man, past middle age. He looked like a gentleman farmer. The first impression I had of him was that he was in a hurry. He quickly read through the petition for commitment and the physicians' report.

"I see," he said, "that this is duly signed by the wife in the case, and two physicians, who have given the patient a thorough examination. Is that right?" He looked up. No one answered.

"Well?" said the judge.

"Yes, sir," said Arthur Houghton.

"Yes, sir, what?" said the judge.

"The examinations were thorough, your honor."

"Which of the doctors are you? You are . . . come on, come on, you are Doctor . . . ?"

"I am not a doctor. I am Arthur Houghton."

"What is that?" said the judge, whom I was beginning to like.

"I am the family lawyer."

"You represent . . ."

"The family."

"Well, you can't represent them both; which one do you represent?"

"Well, your honor, this is a unique situation."

The judge turned to me. "Does he represent you?"

"No," I said.

"Then you represent her—does he?" he asked Florence. She whispered, "Yes." She was very upset.

"I'm a little deaf, so you'll have to talk up," said the judge, not looking at anyone. He began to read the papers on his desk again. I winked at Arthur Houghton.

"I'm wondering," grumbled the judge, his mouth full of gravel, "since you're not one of the examining doctors, how you know the examinations were so all-fired thorough?"

Arthur was not going to take any more guff from this small-town judge. "Because I know the two doctors who made the examinations. I know them very well!" he said with some asperity in his voice.

The judged looked up at him and smiled.

Then he turned to Dr. Ochs. "You are Dr. Taylor?" he said.

"No, your honor," said Dr. Ochs.

"Then by a simple process of deduction, you must be Dr. Leibman?"

"No, your honor," said Dr. Ochs.

"Well then, who the dickens are you, and where are the two signatories? This is a mess, clerk; I'll have to remand this case a month. I can't proceed with this."

He threw the papers down on his table and grumbled something about having a pile of papers at home that he had to read, and so forth, the clerk all the time quieting him.

Arthur spoke up. "They are on the way, your honor."

"Who's on the way?"

"Doctors Leibman and Taylor. They're driving up from New York."

"Why aren't they here? I'm here."

"We had a call, just before entering this chamber, that they're on the way, in fact ten miles from here."

The judge turned to me. "Do you want this case postponed?"

I didn't have a chance to answer. Arthur said, "Please, no, sir, my client has to be back in California tomorrow."

"Well, you should have had these doctors here. This may not be New York City, but we have due process here, too. I am not sitting to condemn this patient, but to protect him. I am here to look after his rights."

"And those of society, your honor."

The judge smiled. "I see you're a lawyer, all right." He looked at his watch again. "Well," he said, "what do you want to do?"

Arthur said, "It will only be a very few minutes. Perhaps—till then —we can chat informally."

"All right," said the judge. "Chat!" He wheeled his chair around so he was at least half turned away from Houghton but waiting to listen.

Arthur was well enough prepared to be absolutely chatty. He leaned back, lit his pipe, and said, "I want you to know first of all, your honor, and I know you will accept this in the spirit in which I offer it, that I am this man's lawyer. That is not a matter of opinion. One-half of one large file storage room in my firm's Beverly Hills headquarters is given over to his personal and business papers and contracts. I think he would be the first to acknowledge the many services I have rendered him." And at this Arthur rose and stood on his feet, and we were no longer in an informal hearing room but in a court. "It is, therefore, extremely painful for me to appear here, and I do so, I assure you, only because his wife in my opinion needs more help at this moment, more relief, more understanding" (Florence was crying) "than he does. In fact, your honor, she said she would appear here only if I came with her."

Arthur paused, I suppose, so that everyone could hear the sound of Florence's muffled sobs.

Then he continued. "The most painful thing of all, your honor, is the realization which I fully faced before I came here, that what I must detail before you will cost me this man's friendship forever. Still, I must."

Then he went down the list of my misdeeds, the nuisance on the Zephyr ad, my flying the plane around the Los Angeles skyscraper, which he said had endangered the lives of thousands and for which the Civil Aeronautics people had grounded me in perpetuity.

"Well," interrupted the judge, "not that I condone that kind of thing, but many of us, with a few drinks, have done—well, I mean, aren't they in the category of pranks? Remember you are asking society to detain this man in an institution, and that is extremely serious."

"I do remember that, your honor," continued Arthur. "I would not be three thousand miles away from my office if all I had to present before you was a series of pranks, no matter how serious."

Then he went on with some of the more erratic behavior. I stopped listening. It was all true. He even had the police report on the bag of garbage I had carried around. I don't know who got this list together for him, but whoever it was had done a workmanlike job. Arthur presented it without flourish, rather underplaying it to harmonize with the general mood of commiseration.

Still, it was obvious from the behavior of the judge that he was not impressed with the reasons presented thus far for committing me.

But Arthur was a skillful man, and he knew how to husband his ammunition. His voice then became even simpler, which is the way of most successful histrionics. He told the story of Ellen and the diaphragm, and how her mother had found the device, waited in the hotel room, and how finally Ellen had come home with a Negro boy. Her father, he said, for some unfathomable reason, arranged and stage-managed that whole affair.

Then Arthur said there had followed something even worse. "The greatest damage a person can do to another person is inside that person's heart and soul." With this introduction he described the occasion when Florence and Gloria had arrived unannounced at 31

Sound Drive and found Gwen and me *in flagrante delicto* (on certain occasions Arthur Houghton has reminded me of Senator Everett Dirksen). "And there in bed with the fornicating couple was a child, no one knows whose. This sight, your honor," said Arthur, "induced a shock which, as you can see for yourself, my client has still to get over. That corrosive image is always with her . . .

"I'm certain this man deeply regrets what he has done to his wife. At any rate, whether he does or not, she will finally endure through everything I've told you. What she is most concerned about, and the reason she thinks that perhaps your honor's judgment might be that this man should be allowed to benefit from psychopathological treatment, the best obtainable, has to do with damage he has done not to others, but to himself. Perhaps your honor read about the fire."

Then he described the fire I had set, except he presented it as though I had locked myself in the house and intended the fire to be a gigantic pyre for myself. Which, of course, it had been, but he didn't know it. At any rate, he drew the picture very well and held my full attention.

"That fire was only a variation of what is perhaps the key episode of this whole sad story. Mr. Anderson narrowly, only very narrowly, survived an accident on one of our freeways. The accident consisted of a near head-on collision between his Triumph racing car—he has always had a penchant for fast foreign cars, your honor—and a trailer truck. The fact that he survived was a miracle. When Mr. Anderson was asked how the crash had occurred, his answer was that a hand from outer space, your honor—outer space, please, not *his* hand, mind you—had taken hold of the wheel of his car and turned it into that trailer truck."

Arthur paused again.

For the first time the judge turned and took a good look at me. I smiled at him, which must have made an eerie impression.

"We thought, your honor, that his was a temporary aberration. But now, seven months later, he tries to burn himself alive in the house of his father and mother, the house in which he was brought up, filled to overflowing with countless family possessions and priceless mementos. Also containing, your honor, the commercial records, the files, every one, of his father's business life. The old gentleman, when he heard about it, broke down and wept."

At this moment Doctors Leibman and Taylor sidled in, with many apologies. The judge barely noticed their entrance.

"Well . . ." said the judge. He sighed. "Let's see," he said, "let's see."

He looked at me and then at Florence.

"Mrs. Anderson, have you anything to say?"

Florence could not talk.

"Would you like a cigarette first?"

She nodded.

"Clerk," said the judge, "we'll adjourn for five minutes."

Florence turned to me. "Will you come with me? I just have to have a cigarette."

Outside the light was strong, and when she felt me looking at her, she turned her back to the sun. "I didn't sleep too well last night," she said. "I have trouble sleeping in that awful city."

"What are you going to do?"

"Oh, it depends on . . ." She stopped. "I was going to say it depends on you. I'm going back on the eleven o'clock."

"And Ellen?"

"She's coming back with me."

"She is?"

"Yes. It turned out that Ralph is not the best balanced person in the world. Well, how could you expect him to be?! He suddenly turned on her one night—without any conceivable provocation—and called her a spoiled bourgeois bitch. That's a quote. I simply told Ellen that she didn't have to take that sort of rudeness from anybody. And you know, now, for the first time, we're genuinely friendly, Ellen and I? And she's not pregnant. I'm grateful to you for that."

"I liked Ralph."

"So did I. But aren't you glad she's not pregnant?"

"Yes, I am."

"I want to say . . . oh, it's so hard here, because the way it is and everything, I mean I did sign that paper, you realize that?"

"Yes, I don't think you could have done anything else—the way I was going."

"Oh, thank you—I've been feeling ashamed. Because it does seem like I'm prosecuting you. You don't feel that, do you?"

"No, I don't."

"I sent for Dr. Ochs, too. I know it's all terribly expensive, but how many crises do you have in your life like this one?" She laughed uneasily. "Anyway, I got him here. He has helped me a lot in the last week or so. You know what he does, don't you?"

"I'm not quite clear."

"He's a hypnotist. No one else has ever succeeded in hypnotizing me, but he has, several times. He did last night. While I was under his control, he made me say something over and over again; he made me say, 'It would be nice to have him, but I don't need him. It would be nice if we got together, but I can get along without him. Want, yes; need, no. Want, not need; want, not need . . .'"

"Did it work?"

"I don't know. It's a *process*. He's going to do it again to me tonight. Just before I get on the plane. You see I've got to prepare myself; I don't know where I stand or what you feel. What do you feel?"

"That you're only doing what you must."

"And you, what you must?"

"That's right . . ."

"That's not saying too much, is it?"

"What else is there to say?"

"Well, I'll try anyway. How can I do this without being vulgar? What I want to say is . . . oh, Ev, why don't we forget the whole damned thing and just go home and make a fresh start?"

"It's pretty late for that, isn't it?"

"May I ask you one simple pointed question? Is all this, is all this about another woman? Is it about her?"

"No, not at all. It is not."

"What is it about then?"

"It's about my lost self-respect."

"That's all?"

"All?"

"I thought it was *something* . . . well . . . something . . ."

"Serious?"

"No. I didn't say that. That's unfair!"

She was flushed and breathing hard, her lip trembling. "I should slap you right across the face for that. How dare you?" Her eyes were again filled with tears.

"I'm sorry," I said, "you're right to be so angry."

"I was only going to say I thought it was something I couldn't help you with."

466

The little clerk came out and said, "The judge is ready to resume."
Florence held my arm urgently.

I felt so sorry for her, because I knew what she wanted to say and
couldn't quite. What she did say was, "No, please don't go in, please!
Just stay another moment. Listen, this can be over in a minute. All I
have to do is go in there and say a few words to Arthur. I feel so relieved; I thought it was about that filthy little bitch, but it isn't, you
said, and if it's really about yourself, if that's all—I don't mean 'all'
the way it sounds—*that* I can help you with, because I know there is
nothing really the matter with you. You've behaved like an absolute
son of a bitch, but I know that when it's all out of your system, you'll
be yourself again. I'll wait for that day. I can help you, you understand? I will stick by you . . . all I have to do is go and say a word to
Arthur, and he'll speak to the judge. All right? Evans? All right?"

Arthur Houghton was in the doorway. "Florence," he said, "the
judge is waiting."

Florence made a violent and heartfelt gesture to Arthur. She wanted
him quiet. Then she turned to me, and she was almost irresistible;
desire is irresistible when it is that strong.

"Will you . . ." she said, "will you give me another chance?"

"I don't know," I said. But I knew. I wouldn't. Because it was my
life as well as hers, and I wasn't only escaping Florence, but the
whole thing, the whole way that she could not escape ever, but I
now knew I could. How could I tell her, with her looking at me that
way.

"I'll think about it . . ." I said.

"But let me stop this awful farce. You and I know there is nothing
the matter with you. Let me stop this shameful farce."

"No," I said, "I'm enjoying it."

"You son of a bitch!" she said. I could swear she smiled at me with
some kind of admiration.

Arthur was walking towards us in a way that showed that this
time he wasn't to be denied.

"But you will think about it?" she said.

I was relieved from answering. Arthur had her arm, and they were
walking back into the little courtroom, and I was following.

"Did you settle anything out there?" asked the judge as we walked
in and sat down.

"What did you say, your honor?" said Arthur.

"It's been my experience that most lawsuits are settled amicably in the intermissions—not that this is a lawsuit, is it, Mr. Houghton?"

"No, sir."

"But still . . . was anything settled?"

"No, sir," said Arthur.

"Mrs. Anderson," observed the judge quite accurately, "looks hopeful . . ."

No one said anything.

"So let us resume," said the judge.

"Absolutely nothing has been settled, your honor," said Arthur again, needlessly, I thought.

Then I looked at Arthur and I looked at the judge, and I remembered that as I walked Florence out of the room so she could have her smoke, I had seen Arthur moving towards the judge, accompanied by the three doctors—the whole intermission had been planned and— oh, stop it, I thought, you really are becoming paranoid.

It was the turn of Dr. Taylor. He described my behavior at the hospital; overwrought, he called it, and paranoid. He was right. Then Dr. Leibman had his say, and it was more detailed and psychoanalytical. He referred to our three sessions in Beverly Hills, and to our meeting in the Gotham. I was surprised how much he'd gotten out of those encounters. He summed it up: "In my professional opinion, he is, I am sorry to say, a dangerous person."

The judge was looking at me. What would I say? I felt my heart pounding.

"Mr. Anderson, is there anything you'd like to say?"

I surprised myself. "I think there is," I said.

"You can just sit there if you like."

"I'll stand like the others."

I stood up and faced the judge.

"I'm guilty!" I said. "I deny nothing."

"But we're not trying you," said Arthur.

"Don't turn me out of here. If you do I will be destructive beyond anything you have seen and beyond anything you'd guess me capable of."

Florence said something. I heard but apperceived nothing.

"Let me tell you the worst of it. I had a reason for everything I did. Each act on Mr. Houghton's list seemed reasonable at the time. I am not ashamed. I have no regret. I don't guarantee what I'll do in the future. I look at the world as a new deal. You are free of me and I am free of you. Florence, I am sorry. If it's any comfort to you, and I think it may be, you can have everything we own: that is, the houses, the paintings, the Picasso drawings and the Gwathmey included, the cars, the stocks, the bonds, the insurance, my stock in Williams and MacElroy, all of it—I've forgotten what else, but everything."

About in here the judge stopped me. He said that he wanted to speak to me alone. I imagine they were all glad to leave. Florence did a nice thing as she went out. She stopped where I sat, and kissed the top of my head.

I heard the judge ordering the clerk and the stenographer to go out. Then I looked up and saw the old man coming down to where I was. He had an odd little face, and he was taking off his robe, revealing a funny little sports coat, not too clean really. His hands were heavy and calloused. He put them on the table as if to rest them. Then he decided to have a pipe, so he filled it slowly and lit it. He sensed that I was all stirred up and that I'd appreciate the rest. An attendant opened the door, and poked his head in to convey a message from Arthur Houghton that if it was all right with the judge, they'd start the drive back to New York. The judge said for them to go ahead but to call him that evening at a number that he scribbled on a piece of paper. Then all was quiet.

"Well," he said, "I tell you, Mr. Anderson, I have a problem. I don't know what the hell to do with you. I think you are a menace to society and to other people. And maybe to yourself, although I've always believed that a person has every right to terminate this whole thing when he finds it intolerable or even unpleasant going, every right. But—well—what would you like me to do?"

"Would you believe it, I don't care?"

"I do believe it. But that's not particularly helpful. I'm not supposed to waste the taxpayer's dollar."

"May I make a suggestion?"

"Wish you would."

"Why don't you keep me here for a few weeks?"

"I'm not sure what point would be served."

"Nothing with relation to me. It's for the others. They'll think justice has been done, and they'll have clean consciences. I really think it will help them."

"O.K., we'll try it for a few weeks. But after that I have a more serious and more practical problem that I've got to do something about. You probably got the idea that during the intermission your wife's staff came over and talked to me? Well, you were right! I listened, and said I'd think about it. But I'd rather tell you about it and let you take your choice. Because it gets right down to something pretty simple. Maybe I'm over-simplifying, but as I see it you have one of two choices. That is to say, I have one of two choices that I'm consulting with you on. One: that I remand you in your wife's custody, that you go back and live as you used to with her. I think your wife wants you very much. By the way, she doesn't seem to have much give in her, does she? On the other hand I'd have to say this for her: it is difficult to accept change in a person you've been close to for so many years, especially when that change threatens your—I'm talking about your wife's—security. Anyway, I could put her in charge of you; you would be legally in her custody for a certain period—one that I would fix at, say, eighteen months.

"Then you have the other choice, which is for me to declare you . . . er . . . er . . . unmanageable—I guess that's as good a word as any—and not salvageable in relation to your marriage. In that case your wife would divorce you. She would do so in the State of California, and she has enough on you and on the record here today, and in the combined strength of her chiefs of staff, to leave you nothing but birdseed."

"Judge, may I say just a word. It will save you a lot of time and worry. I appreciate your concern. I certainly don't want to be her ward or whatever you call it. I meant what I said before. I don't want any of my property."

"I thought you meant it, but I understand there's quite a figure involved, over a hundred thousand dollars, real property and all."

"Almost two hundred thousand dollars, I'd guess, mostly real property."

"Well, you must have worked hard all your life to get it."

"I did work hard. I sold out my damned life day by day, all the years of it. I'm begrieved about it. And ashamed. I'm sorry I did what I did to Florence, and others, too. But now I'm going to start a second life, and I don't want any of the possessions that cost me so dear. That is my way of saying that all is not over for me, that I'm not giving up anything except that which almost killed me."

"Now, now," said the judge.

"I know that's hard to understand."

"I just want to make sure you mean it. Let me put it to you once more and in the simplest terms. No one can live completely as he'd wish. We all pay something in time and in disgust for rent and for groceries. It's an arrangement you make with society, which is itself an arrangement, you understand? To be old-fashioned about it, it goes like this: I give up a piece of my soul; you give me bread. We all, to one degree or another, pretend we like what we abhor. Usually we do it for so long that we forget we abhor it. But, despite all this, it is a civilization of sorts, isn't it? No? Say!"

"You say."

"I say it is. It's the best we have. So, hell, I wish you'd just tell me and get this over with, are you no longer ready to make this deal?"

"That's right."

"And you say this, knowing full well that in a week or whatever, you won't have coffee money?"

"Oh, come on, I'll get a job. It isn't so important to me where I work any more. Or at what."

"Goddam it, I'm not trying to convince you one way or the other. Just give me your answer and let's finish this. Are you sure that in a month or a year you will still feel all right about it? You realize you will have to sign a binding legal document."

"Lead me to it!"

He sat thinking quite a while. Then . . .

"I'm convinced you are nuts."

"Well, you're wrong, I knew what the consequences would be; you have no right to pronounce me nuts. And damn it, you know better!"

"Kindly eliminate the profanity."

"Put your robe back on and I will."

"I think you are nuts! And since I'm here not to punish you, but to protect your rights, I don't think you're in a state of mind to decide your whole future. I think you may very well feel differently with the passage of time. I'm going to allow for that."

"Is that your decision?"

"What the hell is your rush? I'll tell you when I've made my decision! I've watched a lot of you goddam neurotics, and the reason you're all in such a hurry is that in your hearts you are uncertain. Eh? I notice you don't say anything."

"What is there to say?"

"You're giving up too much money and security and standing, and too much of your own past and sweat. Maybe you'll finally decide that is what you want, but this case is now postponed. Or put off. I put it off."

"O.K."

"I see you're relieved a little."

And the truth is that I was, just a little, and it embarrassed me.

The judge got up. "I commit you to this mental institution formally and legally. Any agreements you come to while you're here are not legal and so not binding. I will inform your wife that you have not accepted her offer to be responsible for you. I will tell her that in my opinion you are not presently fit to make any decisions. That is my decision. Goodbye."

He pumped my hand and left.

Outside the other patients were standing around, mostly under trees, watching a storm move in. I watched it, too, joining them now as one of them. Finally, after much roaring, the storm broke and drove us all to cover.

It seemed safe and quiet inside. Even when the lights went out. The electrical plant—Greenmeadow had its own—broke down. But it didn't make any difference. I remembered I was in New York when the 59th Street plant which fed electric power to the great office buildings broke down and the heart of the metropolis was paralyzed. There had been the most subtle but complete panic. There was none here. Teitelbaum and I lay on our beds, brought closer together by the inconvenience. In the dark I told him what had happened and what I had done.

"You're really sick," he said. "Take a lesson from me. Only when I gave it up did I realize that all I was was a greengrocer—on a big scale, maybe, but still Arnold the Grocer. That's what I was good at and that's what I was happy at. I retired into nothing. Notice how many people die on vacations or after they retire. Millions! Take it from me, in a month or two you won't know who you are."

"I'm that way already."

"A man is what he does and does well. That's one thing I learned in my life."

472

"Why do I have to do anything?"

"Because if you don't, you are nobody."

"Not at all. I'll be the man who does nothing."

"I tried all that, golf, cruises, afternoon bridge, and I went nuts. Well . . . you've got to go through it, I guess. I'm sorry for you. But I like you. You know what I'm going to do?" And he said this with such a sense that he was conferring a great honor. "I'm going to let you read my case."

"Thank you," I said, "I consider it an honor."

Just then the lights came on.

"Would you like to start right now?"

"Why not? I have nothing else to do."

He went over to the bureau and took out three packed manila envelopes. He brought them to me and said, "This is my life, as they say on the TV. It is my experience. May you read and learn and not make the same *meshugeneh* mistakes I made."

26

T

HE CASE FOR ARNOLD TEI-
TELBAUM was a magnificent document, not in its language—its
language was legal pastrami—but in the degree of human pain it
contained and in the awful sense of "too late" which had soaked
every page. I stayed up all night reading it.

It told how Arnold the Grocer had founded his "mother" store,
and proceeded to build his business from this single place into the
Tuttle chain. It told how proud he was of his stores, and how
proud he was of his own abilities, his cunning, his courage, and particularly his power to seduce.

The chain grocery business, as he saw it, was a mass seduction
of women. He noted that if the shoppers who came into one of the
Tuttle Stores had only bought what was on their lists, he would have
gone broke long ago. His job was to seduce these women into buying
what they had not planned to buy and even didn't want to buy,
luxury items on which the mark-up was sizable. Teitelbaum had
been successful in this because he understood the women, and he
understood them because he had started by running a single store
and had run it himself, face-to-face with his customers. He knew
where to put what and how to display it, what to hide, what to
feature. He knew women's needs, what their problems with their
husbands were. He was one of them, both the men and the women.

So the Tuttle Stores had proliferated, and finally became so
numerous and so successful that Arnold Teitelbaum reached the
pinnacle. This, in our society, in our time, is the capital gains sellout.
He was offered an awesome sum of dollars for his business. The
offer came from his wife's nephews, Stuart and Irwin Goldman. The

negotiations were a family affair, but strictly legal! The deal was reported triumphantly in the Bridgeport paper, and Teitelbaum was, for a few days, alone on the peak.

Suddenly he was a very rich man, with absolutely nothing to do. And this—his doing nothing—he described in petit point. He told about taking up golf: the special clothes, the Arnold Palmer clubs, the snotty caddies. He told about installing a swimming pool, and his troubles with its circulating system. He described his experiences with a flower garden and with the diseases roses suffer. He told about putting a TV in every room, so that he could watch the ball games wherever he happened to be.

He had always felt romantic about the sea. He and his wife first wintered at a resort on a Florida key, where everyone ate five meals a day and the sun blistered his skin. Then they tried California, Nassau, Acapulco. There he rented a boat to go big game fishing, ended up playing gin rummy with his wife in the galley while the crew boys fished. This boat was small, and he got seasick. He vowed no more small boats. So there were cruises: North Africa, the Isles of Greece, South America. These boats were very big, but he still got seasick. He had to face it, at last; he hated the sea. In Rio, he met another retired grocer, and they spent the week talking the grocery business. It was there that he realized the colossal nature of his mistake.

He began to talk to himself. "What the hell did I think I was going to do the rest of my life, watch other people swim in my pool? Put up with caddies laughing at my strokes when they think I'm not watching? Or puking over the rail of some dirty Mediterranean cruise boat, they put olive oil on their meat those Greeks! And every steward looking at me as if I was a tip machine. I don't like fishing, I don't like boats, I don't like gardening! I don't like roses, they won't grow for me! I don't like to play cards in the middle of the afternoon. I don't like golf ever. I don't like sports clothes. I like business suits, and I like being a grocer. That is what I enjoy: finding a new product, figuring out how to market it, making the girls buy it in quantities. Even when it comes to people, I like shoppers and I like other grocers, they're my people."

So he moved back into his house in Bridgeport, and that summer he didn't have his pool summerized.

In the capital gains deal there was a provision that his nephews would pay him a salary for ten years. This had been intended as nothing more than a tax dodge, a way to "spread" the money. The legal excuse was that he would over this period give the new owners the "benefit of his years of experience and vast knowledge of the retail grocery business."

Teitelbaum began to take this literally. He hung around the stores he used to run, now in the capacity of kibitzer. Nothing was going the way he thought it should. Goods were not properly cleaned, displayed, or freshened. He quickly realized his nephews were making a fortune by cutting quality. He found employees stealing and exposed them to the nephews. But the unspoken fact was that the nephews had allowed for a little gentle pilfering by their more trusted employees. It gave them a weapon in case of a union struggle. He detested the "stamps," something he had, in his time, refused to go for. But a stamp company had offered the nephews a large sum under the table if the Tuttle Stores would issue their stamps with purchases. You couldn't expect the nephews to walk away from something in six figures. Now Teitelbaum urged them to cut the stamps out and give the customers what was saved through lowering prices. His proposal wasn't even considered. The name Tuttle Stores, which had once stood for the best, had come to mean something that embarrassed its founder: the most gimmicky.

Inevitably, the nephews, Stuart and Irwin, began to resent his presence in the stores. He would turn up unexpectedly at a different one each day and badger the manager into a frenzy. Then he would come to the main office and demand to see his nephews. They would be out, at least to him. He took to following Stuart to the golf course and Irwin to his marina. And, cornering them, he would scold by the hour.

The climax came one day when they asked him to leave a store where he was raising a fuss. When he refused to go or keep silent, the police were called, and he was forcibly ejected. Everyone in town heard about it, and the experience was so humiliating to Teitelbaum that he never went back. He stayed in his den—never going out, never talking, hardly eating—just sitting in his leather recliner and stewing.

Then one day he went to see his old lawyer and asked him to look for loopholes in the deal. But the lawyer had written the deal and said there were no loopholes. The fact also was that this lawyer had so impressed the nephews that he was now their lawyer. And their account was alive, while Teitelbaum's was dead. So Arnold had to find himself a young lawyer, one just starting, give him a large retainer, and begin from scratch.

But at last he had a reason for living. He worked feverishly, going over records and figures, meeting with his lawyer, dictating to his dictaphone machine at night and to a new secretary by day. He wanted that deal broken.

It was at this time that everyone, including himself, began to see signs that he was cracking up. He began to hear things. He began to have nightmares. He began to suspect his wife of talking behind his back to the nephews, and of being on their side. When she left the house, he had her followed by an old pinochle crony. He began to lift the phone extension, as if by mistake, when she was talking, to see who she was talking to and what they were saying. His suspicions proved to be false, although his wife occasionally did speak to Stuart and Irwin, and he couldn't have liked what they said about him.

His paranoia became general. He suspected everyone. He felt he was being followed. He was sure "certain people" were trying to "get things" on him. He had a new lock put on his den. He got an unlisted telephone, had it checked for tapping.

The worst of his delusions had to do with his only grandchild, a little boy of five, Mendel (Michael, in school) Teitelbaum. He would wake in the middle of the night, leap out of bed, and run to see if the little boy had fallen into the swimming pool. Finally, he had the pool filled with topsoil and landscaped. He began to suspect that his enemies, unspecified, were out to kill this child in order to get back at him.

He frequently telephoned his son, a doctor, late in the evening on some pretext, but really only to see if the boy was safe in his bed asleep. He would follow the child to the park and, staying at a distance, watch the nurse, whom he suspected. He made lists of who came up to talk to her. He gave these to his doctor son and urged that he fire the nurse. When he wouldn't do this, Arnold begged him to have a private detective follow the boy at all times. He would pay. The doctor, of course, would not do this.

Finally an awful thing happened. The little boy went for a walk with his grandmother, Mrs. Arnold Teitelbaum. Mendel, for an instant, let go of his grandmother's hand and was struck by a truck. Teitelbaum, in a fury of grief, insisted on a thorough investigation. But it revealed nothing except that for an instant the old lady had been careless and the little boy impulsive. The boy was dead. Mrs. Teitelbaum was untouched. Arnold Teitelbaum cracked.

He never talked to his wife again, except in rage.

He moved out of their house and lived for a time in the Stratford Hotel. He was finally asked to leave because he fought with the entire staff. He moved from motel to motel. No one could say where he lived. But he'd make certain unexpected appearances. He took to breaking into his wife's bedroom in the middle of the night to storm at her. Finally she had the locks of the house, his own house, changed.

One memorable day he cornered his son's wife and begged her to tell him where the little boy was really buried, because he wanted to move the body to another city where it would be safe. The woman went into hysterics.

Now Teitelbaum, his paranoia vindicated as he saw it, began to put the most fantastic efforts into the case that he was preparing with the young lawyer. All he wanted was his name back, Tuttle, that is. He wanted to start the Tuttle Stores again, first one store, then rebuild the chain and, this time, not sell out. He went to see the bankers and came away with the impression that if he did get his name back, he could have from them the financing necessary to start again. The bankers, on the other hand, took away the impression that he was seriously deranged.

That word began to get around. The young lawyer, aware that the case was becoming a laughingstock, suddenly withdrew. After all, he told Arnold Teitelbaum, he didn't want to be thought of as a crank lawyer. He had his career to think of. He advised Teitelbaum to give up. His story then was that Teitelbaum tried to kill him. A shout brought the police, who had been asked by the young lawyer to be ready in his anteroom. They found a pistol in Arnold Teitelbaum's clothing. A newspaperman who had smelled something cooking was there for the arrest. He heard Teitelbaum accuse the young lawyer of having taken money from the nephews, Stuart and Irwin, to withdraw from the case. This was true, so when it came out in the papers, it was a genuine embarrassment to the family. With this, they decided; it was no problem to have Arnold Teitelbaum committed.

All this was shamelessly set down in what I read, sometimes in excruciating detail, sometimes between the lines, all written in the man's blood. He had more human pain in that highly ungrammatical THE CASE FOR ARNOLD TEITELBAUM than I had in everything I had ever written.

And I had patronized that man!

I could hardly speak to him the next morning for shame. I did say that I had liked it. He wasn't interested. He regretted having let me read it, made me swear, again and again, that I would not reveal its contents. I swore, again and again.

This episode affected me profoundly. I began to spend long hours, every day, talking to other people on the campus. For the first time in my life I found I was able to have genuine relations with people not of my kind. I didn't feel superior to any of them. I could talk directly and honestly, listen simply and without prejudice, even to the most ridiculous of them.

For instance, every Sunday an old woman of eighty-odd, still chipper and in good health, came out to visit her son, a "boy" in his early sixties. She brought a home-prepared picnic lunch. She would take her boy out onto the lawn if the weather was good, lead him by the hand to the shade of a tree, sit him down, bib a napkin around his neck, and feed him by spoon. People would pass by, and she'd smile at them. When she left, she would bob and grin and ask the officials to take good care of her little boy. Of course Freud and I knew all about her; she had castrated her son, wanted him helpless. But I got talking to her one Sunday, and she said, "He was almost nine before I realized he was always going to be that way." After that, I saw things from her point of view.

For the first time in my life I was able to feel close to people, because for the first time I didn't make those judgments-in-advance, and pigeon-holings-out-of-hand, that had made it impossible for me in the past to get to really know anyone. Our conversations were truly person-to-person, not, as on Ed Murrow's old show, a matter of showing the face you wanted the world to see.

I got to know the criminally insane, too. Their recreation area was confined. But I used to sit up against the fence and talk to them. That was when I began to think, there but for the grace of God, because the acts which had been the cause of their legal confinement were nearly always things I had been on the verge of doing, or had done and gotten away with, or dreamed of doing and might still do.

I remember with affection one realistic-minded colored kid who had been restricted behind that fence for raping another patient. He explained, quite reasonably it seemed to me, "Man, I thought I was doing that chick a favor! Did you see her?"

I had no letters from the outside, except a cryptic note from Gwen which said she would see me soon and all was o.k. But nothing else. Did anyone care? Why should they? Did I? Surprisingly little! I realized I did not have and never had had any friends. My relationships—those I did have—were either professional or functional. I had a boss and an editor or two or three, several servants, a wife, many former mistresses, now elsewhere with other men, a literary agent, several secretaries, past and present, several professional collaborators, and three hundred people to whom I sent cards every Christmas. I knew some fellows in my office who either feared me or flattered me, but whom I did not meet outside of our functional relationship. I had sponsors, and clients, PR men, account executives and district managers.

I knew an even bigger host of service people, the men who fixed the hi-fi, the TV, the icebox, the Disposall, the electric stove, the air-conditioner, the pool-circulator, the three cars. There were the people who sold me books and records, the tailor who cut my suits, and the haberdasher who made my shirts, initialed at the side of the French cuffs.

But you couldn't call these friendships. I hadn't talked or related to any of these people, except for some use or function. I hadn't touched any of them humanly. They were things to me.

As for people like my mother and father and Michael, with whom I had old relationships, I had kept them, as I had tried to keep Gwen, at arm's length, personal symbols, the stuff of dreams.

These discoveries disturbed and depressed me, and my melancholia did not go unnoticed. One morning I was told that I was going to be given shock treatment, that this treatment would do me a lot of good, in fact was "specific" for "involutionary melancholia." I had no objection to taking this treatment; in fact, I was curious what might evolve if there was some electric jiggling of my brain cells.

It was simpler than it sounded. Some wires were attached to my skull and a current fed through. Afterwards I slept, and when I woke the same noises were everywhere, but I heard them less. All day long sounded like early Sunday morning.

It was somewhere in here that I began to feel friendly towards myself, for the first time. That was a new experience. I first realized that I wanted myself to succeed in whatever it was that I was attempting. I could look back at my life now from some sort of eminence, as, when you're lost after hiking a long time through thick country and you finally arrive at a cleared place on top of a hill, you look back to where you have just been and realize how far you've come and that you are never going back there. You may still be lost but not in the same place.

I was my friend now, and while I knew I was in a genuine crisis, indeed at a turning point, I liked myself for having made it thus far. I encouraged myself to use this pause and this eminence, to size things up before going back down into the thick. I admired Arnold Teitelbaum. He had gone through hell and come out with the knowledge of who he was. I had gone through a lot, too, but so far I knew only who I was not. "Eddie" was dead, but the nameless one was not yet in command. I knew what I didn't want. What did I want? I knew what I hated. What did I love?

One problem was that for the first time in my life, I wasn't doing something. I had always relied on accomplishing something every day that proved my worth to others and so to myself. This had kept me going. Work had been a drug for me, and now that I was kicking that habit, naturally I felt the withdrawal pains.

I understood now why so much of the energy of the professionals in advertising, communications, and the performing arts is spent in making new contracts. It isn't the increase in money payments. It is the new arrangement as symbolic evidence of the person's worth. Each contract had to say, someone above wants you more than he used to. Result: your self-esteem is raised; your self-doubts quieted.

The reassurance could also come from someone in sudden need of you: a frantic phone call, a pleading memo, an invitation to sit in on some hopelessly stalled conference, an urgent call to placate a client about to cancel. But in the end, the reaffirmation of worth had to be expressed in the legal poetry of a new contract.

Now all these reassurances which had at one time kept me going weren't there any more. What would take their place?

"What has kept the human soul going through the wilderness of universal confusion? One thing and one thing only, the fear of God!"

It was Father Burns, one of the campus characters, talking to his followers. "Man," the defrocked minister, a Negro, was saying, "needs something to believe so he can believe in himself. He needs something bigger than himself. Without that polestar we are all adrift. We need to be told what is right and wrong. We need to fear!"

I had been walking along, talking to myself, and I was now at the edge of the campus in a place under some large elm trees, a favorite gathering place for Father Burns and his disciples.

"God has been pushed off his throne in the middle of our universe. So now, man, without authority over him except the authority of other men, acts like himself. The son of a bitch gets fresh! There is no divine magnet of right and wrong in the center of our universe to hold him in orbit. And when man loses fear, my friends, he becomes a beast. I can testify to that from personal experience."

Then Father Burns, for what must have been the fifth time in my hearing, regaled the group around him with his own case, how he had fallen out of the orbit of terror, lost his fear of the Lord, and found himself suddenly directionless. Then, in this condition of un-fearing, he had in fact become an animal and raped a twelve-year-old girl in his parish. He described this act in the most lurid detail. The eyes of the women around him were popping as I walked away.

Dr. Lloyd was looking for me. He said I had an important phone call, and hurried me to the administration building. I was surprised to notice he was tagging along after me.

It was Michael. My father, he said, had pneumonia, and I'd better come. The old man was asking for me. Dr. Lloyd quickly arranged my leave.

I was furious with Michael. The last I had heard from him was that the old man was doing "as well as could be expected."

The first person I encountered in the hospital was Gloria. She was at the newsstand just off the main lobby reading the week's crop of magazines for free. A cigarette smoked in her face. Her pixie, green-tinted hornrims sat incongruously on the bridge of her large practical nose. She saw me as soon as I came through the revolving door and came at me like Carrie Nation, holding a magazine for an axe.

The small hairs at the back of my neck were making like a dog's. I had to warn myself to try to see Gloria, too, from her own viewpoint, give her at least as much understanding as I had the young rapist. When she said, in a very huffy tone, "Isn't anyone with you?" (an attendant she meant) I had to hold on hard. I didn't want to muck up my new era of Christian-Understanding-for-Everyone. So I darted into the up elevator and saved myself the necessity of answering her.

Michael looked so guilty and stricken that I couldn't be angry. I put my arms around him, and kissed him.

Then I noticed that he was with Dr. Beattie, the man who had put the pin in my father's hip and had me thrown out of the hospital. Dr. Beattie, when he saw me, reached out and detained his attending orderly, who had been about to leave him.

I surprised Dr. Beattie; I extended my hand and we shook. I greeted him with respect. Even when he came out with, "Your father is doing as well as can be expected," I nodded as if he had said something. And when I said in a subdued voice, "Thank you, Doctor, but in view of the circumstances I wonder if you could give me just a little more information?" he nodded to the orderly, dismissing him. Then he turned to me, all his professional arrogance restored, and said, "He has pneumonia, and at his age, when a man is bedridden, and can't sit up, let alone walk, the threat of pneumonia is always present, and its incidence frequent. Your father is full of antibiotics and—"

"Dr. Beattie is doing everything possible," said Gloria. How had she arrived on the sixth floor so quickly, I asked myself. I had a very unchristian answer. She must have flown up the air-conditioner conduit. But I didn't say anything like that.

I noticed Gloria looking at the doctor, and unless I read her eyes wrong, she was indicating to him that he might better just go on about his other business.

"Wait a minute, Dr. Beattie," I said, "tell me—"

Gloria interrupted. "I don't think the old man should have visitors in his present condition, do you, Doctor?"

And then I did it. Before I knew what I was doing, I did it. I have seen Greeks do it, and Italians, too. I have seen Turks, Serbs,

Arabs, the common Wog, and the Philippine Huk do it. But after all, they're next to savages. I have seen the Japanese do it, and lower-caste Indians, and those poor Chinese who live on the mainland opposite the British Crown Colony of Hong Kong. But they have a different religious and cultural background. I saw a Cuban do it when he was dead drunk. But I have never seen a decent white American do it in public. But I did it. I slapped Gloria, hard, right across her face. That silenced her. Order was restored. Michael didn't protest. Maybe, in his heart, he applauded.

Your Christian era, dear boy, I said to myself, is going to be postponed a bit. I took a firm hold of Dr. Beattie's arm and said, "Now, Dr. Beattie, I don't want any more of that as-well-as-can-be-expected shit from you," and I marched him into my father's room.

As I opened the door, I heard the breathing. The labored pumping of pneumonia had begun.

I didn't really have to wait for a bulletin from Dr. Beattie. I immediately got one from another source. My uncle Joe, silhouetted against the window, was the first person I saw. He saw me, too, and, after a quick look to make sure my father wasn't watching, he dangled his hand from the wrist and wagged it a few times eloquently. That was his medical report.

My father's eyes stared at the ceiling. But they were still active, the eyes of a man who was planning his escape from prison and knew there was no time to waste.

My mother sat at the head of his bed, as irrelevant to his purposes now as she had been all her life. As Dr. Beattie went through the ritual of checkpoints—the pulse, the breathing, the blood pressure —I kissed the top of her head. She looked up and smiled weakly.

Despite the moribund mood of the room, my father was better than I had expected he would be. For one thing he had certainly not given up, even if Dr. Beattie had. When he saw me, he winked as if I was an accomplice long delayed, now arrived with the jail-break tools.

There was still mischief in the old man. "Doctor," he said, "where are my white grapes?"

"We'll see if we can't get you some with your lunch," said Dr. Beattie.

My father was being fed intravenously.

Dr. Beattie said to me, "He seems a little better."

I walked him to the door. "But that doesn't mean anything, does it?"

"His heart is still strong. Amazing, the tenacity of that muscle!"

"But still, you don't have any hope, do you?"

"We are waiting," he said, in the most scientific statement I had ever heard him make, "for a miracle."

"What about his white grapes?" I asked.

"Yesterday it was peaches," said Michael. "He's got fruit on the brain. Nothing he says makes any sense."

"Out of the question," said Dr. Beattie. "I'll be back in the late afternoon. I would keep it as quiet in here as possible till then. I really do think you should go. He should sleep as much as he can."

"Does it actually make any difference," I asked, "if he sleeps or not? I mean if I were in his situation, it seems to me I'd be making every effort to stay awake, to *not* go under. I wonder if this desire to live and the energy it arouses isn't of greater value than sleep."

"I suggest, Mr. Arness," answered Dr. Beattie, "that you engage another doctor. You don't seem to have any faith in me."

"I don't," I said.

"Oh, Eddie," said Michael. And he turned and followed Dr. Beattie out of the room, remonstrating as he gave chase.

I went over to Joe. I took five dollars from the thirty-odd I had left and said, "Go get him some white grapes. I don't care if you have to go all the way to New York."

"If I have to go to New York, a few more of these may be necessary," said Joe, holding up the five-spot, "unless you want the grapes slow freight."

I gave him another deuce, and he picked up his derby and left.

I went over to my father. He was nodding his head as if he had heard everything, and everything he had heard only confirmed the dim view he took of the world and its inhabitants. "Thomna!" he said to my mother, "go keep everybody out!"

She left without answering. She was really bushed.

We both heard the door shut.

"Evangeleh," said the old man with a surprising show of energy, "lock door!"

"No key there, Pop."

"Put chair like before, you still damn fool, Evangeleh!"

I wedged the upright of the chair under the door. I knew I was about to catch hell.

"You forget your father, Evangeleh, eh?"

"I came to see you, Pop, but they wouldn't let me in." That son of a bitch still had me apologizing. "Then I called on the telephone, and they told me you were all right."

"Yeah, yeah, come to my funeral, you'll see all my friends there. Where's Joe?"

"He went to get your grapes."

"What grapes?"

"You asked for grapes."

"White grapes I want. Seedless. Come here, big shot. You forget your father, right?"

"Then I had some trouble, see." I showed him my shoulder bandage. "They put me in a hospital."

"What kind trouble?"

"Something about a woman. I was shot. See?"

"When your father has trouble, you go to woman, is that right thing? Honestly God! Come here. I get tired whisper, come, come, I'm not going to hit you." He lay back exhausted for the moment, waiting for some strength.

I put my hand on his head. He had a fever. But not nearly as bad as I expected it to be.

"I have no fever," he said. He was looking around the room anxiously.

"There's nobody here, Pop."

"Sure?"

"Sure!"

He lifted his heavy chest and propped his body up on one elbow. Then he reached under the mattress, fishing and fumbling till he brought up the little black wallet which held the key to his safe deposit box. He held it in his fist and fell back, exhausted by his effort. But he winked at me. I could hear his lungs pumping.

I waited silently while he gathered strength again. Now he made a sign for me to come closer.

I did. He smelled bad.

"Evangeleh," he said, "I'm going to tell you something, don't tell me no."

"I won't tell you no, Pop."

486

"We see. I want you do something."

"You can have anything you want, Pop."

"We see that, too."

"I'm listening, Pop. Lie back."

"Never mind lie back business. I want you now to do what I tell you. I ask you this one thing and finish! Don't tell anybody, not Michael, not anyone. I have many enemies here, you understand?"

"I understand."

"I hope so. Now, say you will do."

"Do what?"

"Do what I am telling you."

"I will, Pop."

"You swear!"

"I swear!"

"I don't want to die this goddam hospital. I don't want to lie dead in their hands and they bury me and so forth. I depend on you, Evangeleh."

"All right, Pop, all right."

"I want—even for five minutes . . . !"

"You want what, Pop, even for five minutes?"

"I still have strength left. I don't show other people. I show you!" He took my hand and squeezed it so hard his whole body shook. His face strained and filled with blood. Then he fell back, his head on the pillow, his eyes looking up, his mouth open. "You see?" he whispered. "You see?"

"Yes, Pop, I see."

"I want for even five minutes."

"What, Pop, what do you want for even five minutes?"

"This not a prison here. They can't keep me here if I don't o.k., right?"

"Right, Pop. This is not a prison."

"Then why do I have to lock door and whisper like Syrian pimp? It eats my strength to whisper. Come, come close, big shot, Shakespeare, come so I don't have to whisper, you're good boy, don't mind what I say."

I came very close.

"I want to see Anatolia again," he whispered.

I didn't answer.

"You hear me, Evangeleh? Even for five minutes."

"Yes, Pop."

"I have arrange everything. You understand?"

"Yes, Pop."

"The ticket is ready. I went myself to airplane ticket office last night, I arrange everything, perfect reservation! You must go airplane ticket office and give money for ticket. Put inside your coat pocket, right away, and bring here to me, your inside pocket, you hear?"

"Yes, Pop."

"Tomorrow night, we go, like before, we walk out, taxi waiting . . ."

"But Pop—"

"But nothing. They're waiting for me."

"Who?"

"My friends in Anatolia. In the garden there, on top of the cliff, he's waiting for me, near my old house . . ."

"Who?"

"Never mind who. Are you F.B.I. here?"

"I only mean, how do you know they're waiting for you, Pop?"

"I talked to them."

"How?"

"What's the difference how? How should I know how? F.B.I.! I'm tired now, but here," he reached out the little black wallet, "take this," he said.

I took it.

"Take it, Evangeleh."

"I have it, Pop."

"Good boy."

"I have insurance there. You go, give it back, get cash money. Then go airplane ticket office, get ticket."

"What line, Pop?"

"What?"

"What airplane line?"

"I went there last night and made all arrangements perfect. Wait! I will remember! I will remember! Don't worry."

He was getting panicky at the thought that he might now not be able to remember the name of the airline.

"Evangeleh," he said, his eyes bugging, "I have written down, look pants pocket, piece of paper, Evangeleh!"

"Was it TWA, Pop?"

"Yes," he said, "TA tomorrow night. Go to office, they have ticket ready."

Then he lay back and again waited for some drops of energy to flow back into the reservoir of his strength. There was now a flush in his cheeks, and his eyes gleamed.

"I don't want to hear NO from nobody around here, Evangeleh! I don't want anybody get fresh with me now, you hear? I want you to put me on airplane tonight. Finish!"

This embattled moment seemed to exhilarate him. His cheeks burned. I thought, God, God, he might beat this thing, he just might. He wouldn't have long in any case, maybe like he said just five minutes, maybe a day, maybe a week, but if it were only five minutes!

"Evangeleh, it's June now, right? The month of June?"

"Yes, Pop, just turned."

"Paradise! In June the cleanest snow from the top of the mountain melts. The waters come together and run down the sides of the mountain. You can hear them running at night, mountain water, you don't know what that is! You think we have water in this city? Here you can't take a drink of cold water with pleasure, it tastes from medicine."

He made a series of sounds like he was spitting. This exhausted him again, and he lay back while he filled up.

"This man has a garden," he resumed. "A Turk, but fine man. Old friend. He has every kind fruit tree. In the winter he lives in stone house on the side of the hill so he can look after these trees and take good care. In summer these trees give fruit, each one, different time. There is no week in the summer when there isn't some kind of fruit there ready. Now, June, he has apricots. I want to sit under the tree and slowly pull the branch down and—*Tak!* I pull the little soft fruit off, so easy, because it is ready, not like here, looks good, no taste! I will sit with this Turk, this old man, and I'm an old man, and we will eat the fruit together and be in peace. That's the last thing I ask."

He lay down, and his imaginings colored his face. He didn't seem sick, only tired and at ease. He smiled at me softly.

Then I had it, the sensation. For the first time in my life I looked at him, crazed as he was, not as a problem to deal with, not as an authority to evade and handle, but as a human whose being was opened and revealed to me so I could see that his troubles were like my troubles. He was one human and I was another. He was my brother.

489

"I know you are busy man, Evangeleh, you big shot, thank God, and have no time to go with me. I don't ask that. Put me on airplane. From there, don't worry. People look after me. All my life I make friends quick. And the Turks, never mind what you hear, they are fine people, like neighbors. They will take me to this man's garden. That is all I ask from the world. Five minutes!"

He shut his eyes now and waited for me to speak.

I had heard of the wounded in war being carried great distances in airplanes, sometimes in oxygen tents, too. An oxygen tent, I thought, he would need that. His breathing seemed heavier again. A man with pneumonia drowns; his lungs fill with his own fluids and he drowns.

He suddenly stirred, as if he had dropped off into a kind of sleep and had just quivered out of it.

"Evangeleh," he said, "say. Don't be afraid of your father. I'm not brought up in this world to expect good, even from my sons, Evangeleh!"

It was not a time to placate this man. I either had to say yes, and mean, yes I would, or tell him no, and why and, in effect, leave him there to die.

"Evangeleh!" he rumbled.

"Yes, Pop, I will do it!"

"You're a good boy."

He kissed my hand, the first time in our lives he had ever done this, and almost immediately fell asleep.

And there he lay.

Five minutes of a June day! A single piece of fruit.

I'd have to hurry, I realized, if I was really going to . . . if . . . was I really going to? I'd said I would. Yes. And it wasn't impossible; it could be done.

If I cashed his insurance, if indeed there was any insurance, then my mother would be left with nothing. So I must not disturb that.

Meantime, my own money, if it any longer was my own, was no longer available to me.

I'd get an airplane ticket somewhere; I had to. But what about the oxygen tent and the rest . . . ?

Was it possible?

If you had money, anything was.

He slept now in the firm belief that I would.

He trusted in me.

In fact, this man I had feared and resented and rebelled against all my life long, was now at my mercy.

He had asked me to do the single thing that would give his life meaning at the end. And I was so glad that at the end he had turned to me, that I had said yes!

He had trusted my word enough to fall asleep.

I saw him now again as a human in trouble, not my father, not that figure of legend, just another person no less in trouble than anyone in Greenmeadow, no more in trouble than me.

"I'm going to try, Pop," I said.

I don't know if he heard.

I'd have to hurry, I thought. At his age pneumonia gallops.

The door of the room slowly opened, and there stood a little boy of five and another of three. They were Michael's children. And behind them were Michael and Gloria.

27

GLORIA and Michael were very proud of their two boys. To be more accurate, Gloria was very proud, Michael a little bewildered. Something was happening he had not anticipated: they were turning out to be Greek children. And while this made him officially proud, it made him privately uncomfortable.

For example now. Gloria had brought the boys to see their grandfather for what she obviously believed was to be their final meeting. She had taught the kids that when they saw their grandfather after any considerable interval, they should kiss his hand. This was the correct courtesy to show a Greek patriarch. But since nothing in their environment reinforced this custom, Aleko and Teddy kept forgetting it. So now, the first thing I heard was Gloria's voice, importunate to the point of being frantic, saying, "Run and kiss your grandfather's hand, Aleko!" and then, "Run, Teddy, what's the matter with you? Run and kiss Papoo's hand."

I think, perhaps, these two kids might have even liked their grandfather without her gun in their back. But they never had a chance. Here they were now, dressed in identical blue suits, a stampede of two bugs to kiss the old man's hands.

The fact is he liked it. He smiled like crazy, and Gloria and Michael beamed at the little boys' good Greek manners. The greeting was so successful, in fact, that they did it all over again. "Say, I love you, Papoo," said Gloria. And the two kids did their duty. "I love you, Papoo," said Aleko, and "I love you, Papoo," said little Teddy. And the old man broke up, it made him so goddam happy! The kids would always remember that moment, and the old man would die happier because of it, but it was more than I could take.

Gloria and I hadn't looked at each other. Heading for the elevator I remembered Gloria's admission following the family lunch, that she wished the old man dead.

Still, why not preserve the forms of love, as Gloria had done with her two children? If we didn't have the forms, would we have anything at all? That's why that big, soft word was used so frequently and in the most casual contexts. Because if people didn't say it as frequently as they did, they would have to face the fact that they had no emotion that could go by that name.

I entered the bar across the street.

The person I liked most at the moment was Mr. Arnold Teitelbaum. Forget love, as Gwen had once said; I did have affection for him, and that was genuine.

I wondered how long the authorities in charge of Greenmeadow would allow me to stay there. I couldn't wait to get back.

I finished my double Dewars, paid for it, ordered another. Arthur's forty was going fast. Well, I didn't need money at Greenmeadow.

While the barkeep was getting the drink, I went to a phone booth and looked up the number of TWA. They had a plane to Istanbul, I knew that from the ads. I found it and took out my pencil to make a note of the number. Then I put the pencil back and flopped over the telephone book on its rack so that I lost the place.

What the hell, was I crazy? He wouldn't survive the cab ride to the airport. Why hadn't I immediately told the sick old man, "There is no way to get you into the middle of Asia Minor alive. So stay here, die in comfort, surrounded by Aleko and Teddy; die to the well-rehearsed murmurs of 'Papoo,' 'Papoo' from their treble voices!"

All that shit about the apricot trees and the mountain water! "Drink the chlorinated stuff with the rest of us," I should have said. "I hope you like the grapes, but you're not going to see a tree again with apricot fruit on it, or the snow top of Aergius, either."

Why had I kidded him along?

I had done it in a rash of love, but I had not made things easier for him. I had made things tougher for myself.

Now I had to go back in there and tell him the truth, that there was no way to do what I had promised him I would do.

Perhaps I'd merely say that an oxygen tent on a plane was not possible.

No, that would be a lie, too. It was sure as hell possible. The

Kennedy boys would do it for their daddy if he asked them. Of course they had the means and all, but they also loved their father that much; you could see it from the photographs.

I didn't care that much.

Now what was I going to tell him?

I ordered another Dewars.

It was then that I saw Uncle Joe at the far end of the bar. He had seen me, apparently, well before, and was hoping I wouldn't notice him. Now he waved to me, and brought his drink down and set it next to mine.

"One drink," he said, "that's all. Then I go in. See I got the grapes!" He opened the little brown paper bag he was carrying and held it up so I could look down into its contents.

They were indeed the little white seedless grapes my father liked.

"One drink," he repeated, his eyes phlegmed like those of an old dog.

"I'm having one, too," I said.

Joe didn't look too good.

"I'm glad to see you, Joe," I said, and suddenly, in a burst of affection or love or whatever, I put my arm around him and squeezed him.

"Ouch," he said, but he smiled.

I'd never liked that man, but now. . . . I think it was all because of Teitelbaum. I understood some people differently since Teitelbaum, more in terms of the total effort of their lives, or as they saw themselves; perhaps that was it.

Here he is, I thought, the man who started everything, the one who brought our family here. Were it not for him, I'd be living in Turkey, a member of a terrified Greek minority. Here he was, at the end of the road, living his own last months. His brother's going must panic him. It was a token. He knew it and I knew it.

I looked at him as I had never looked at him before. His face, corroded with living, was the consistency of goat's cheese, white and reeky; in the darkened bar, it glowed like a white night worm. Only his eyes were dark with the courage of the last stand, the courage that has no choice.

I stood in the bar, holding him around the shoulder, not letting go. He was the first one, I thought. He had left his own home, the place to which my father now meant to return. The rest was family

494

legend: how his father had sent him on his way on the back of a single donkey; how he had worked night and day, literally, holding two jobs and sometimes three, until he had made his way to America; how he had worked there scratching and saving till he could send enough money home to bring to the United States his five brothers and his two sisters, his mother and his father; how he went to the boat to meet them and found that his father had died in passage and had been buried at sea; and finally how he had worked here, skillfully and fiercely, established the family business, done so well that he had, in time, become fabulously rich, in the millions, at a time when millions were millions; and how he had acquired all the real wealth that went with the money, the great store, the two Rolls-Royces, one in New York, one in Paris, the chauffeurs and the showgirls, the apartment in the Ritz Towers when that building was first put up in 1926, an apartment which contained—I remember it with wonder still—a small personal gym and a ticker tape in the bedroom.

The rest of his biography was written on his face. The collapse of his business following the crash of the stock market had broken his back with one quick snap and left him scorned and impotent, Flat Tire Joe, hoping for the favor of anybody and everybody, foolish, hounded, improvident, often without money for food except what he could sponge up from old friends who had managed to survive the storm which had sunk him. Now he was sewage in a social system which he could no longer understand, this man who in November, 1918, when the armistice was celebrated by a march of soldiers through a triumphal arch, had selected the most expensive silk Keshan he had in his stock and caused it to be placed under that arch to be torn to waste by the hobnails of the boys in khaki.

I ordered us both another round, and I said to him, "Uncle Joe, I want to ask you, do you think I fucked my life away?"

"I hope so," he said, laughing his abashed and guilty laugh. "I hope so." He wriggled and giggled.

"No, really," I said. "What do you think of me?"

"You're a big man," he said, his eyes glowing with hypocrisy.

"But lately," I said, "lately I've thought . . ."

"You thought you could have made much more money. That, I agree. You can never have too much. Hold on to your money, my boy!"

"I'm thinking of giving it away, Uncle Joe."

The bartender put the drinks in front of us, and Joe took his right away to fortify himself for the response he had to give me.

"Then you damn fool," he said. "You genius, but wrong philosophy of life. You will end up like me broke, everybody laughing at you, and begging please give me two dollars, I give you good horse today, please buy me lunch, I tell you new joke, very funny, buy me drink! Damn fool genius, look your uncle! Before it's too late, learn. Money is everything."

"Well, Uncle Joe," I said, "I didn't tell you the truth before. The fact is that I have already given my money away; I gave it to my wife, because I am leaving her and—"

"Oh, my God," he said. "Fact?"

"Yes," I said.

He took off his derby hat and gave me a mock bow and said, "Welcome stranger."

"Thank you," I said.

"You gave your money?"

"Yes."

"To woman?"

"My wife is a woman."

"I'm sorry to hear it. You sure?"

"Yes."

"Oh, my God!"

"Now I have, total capital," I reached into my pocket, "twenty-three dollars."

It was Uncle Joe's turn to put his arm around my shoulder and embrace me. "Welcome stranger!" he said. And he burst into obscene laughter.

Then, after some of this, he said, "Why you do that, damn fool?"

"Because I was not happy with my life."

"Now you think you be happy? You should be in bug house."

"That's what I think, too."

"You go bug house, take Flat Tire Joe with you," he laughed. "Welcome stranger!" he roared, and spluttered, and coughed, and spat.

"I won't take you," I said, "because I think you're sane."

"Man broke without penny, not sane."

"You have the right philosophy for this world. What I want to ask

you, Uncle Joe, is you came all the way here from Anatolia, you
brought your whole family, you worked hard all your life—"

"Now look!"

"You're broke. You went through millions, and now you're a
floater."

"Complete disaster! Titantic!"

"Maybe the *whole thing* is wrong. That man in there, your brother,
he wants only one thing, to go back to Anatolia to die. You think
possibly you made a mistake in the first place, that you should not
have brought them all here? What do you say?"

He was at a loss for words.

"Damn fool!" was all he could say, "damn fool!"

"I know I'm a damn fool, but still I wish you'd answer my
question."

"I answer you."

"Yes, please. Think."

"I make big mistake. Yes."

"What was that mistake, Uncle Joe?"

"I make big, big mistake."

"Tell me what it was."

"I play wrong horses."

He laughed, his yellow teeth flashing. Then suddenly he got serious. "But now," he said, "now I have correct system."

He reached into his pocket and brought out some folded letter paper that he had stolen from the writing desk in the lobby of a hotel.
It was covered with tiny figures. He began to explain to me the work-
ings of his new system; he had been trying it out without venturing
his capital, he said (his capital!), and it could make us not a fortune,
but a decent, steady living, one you could count on, since it de-
pended upon playing favorites, one-to-three, one-to-four shots.

So I ordered another round and listened.

When we left there, my uncle Joe and I were brother mortals.
We re-entered the hospital, warmed by drink and by each other. I
liked him even more than I liked Arnold Teitelbaum.

We tiptoed into my father's room. He was asleep. His breathing
now was frightening, like he was pumping air through a tank of water. Perhaps, I thought, I'll be able to duck the whole issue about the
air trip to Anatolia!

My mother was again sitting at the head of the bed. Joe went to the window and watched the S.P. sign flash on and off. We were waiting for the old man to go.

I remembered that I was supposed to call Dr. Lloyd. He was glad to hear my voice. And I his—like calling home, I thought.

"How are you getting along?" he said.

"I find I'm eager to come back."

We both laughed, and he asked me about my father. I told him about his breathing.

"Can he sit up?"

"I don't know."

"Does he?"

"No."

"I better get your leave extended," he said.

On the way back from the phone booth I ran into Father Draddy. I can't say he offered me any false comfort.

"I was with your father about an hour ago," he said. "He's failing. I'm sorry. But I think he's ready for what's coming."

"As ready as he'll ever be," I said.

I sat with the nurses at the head of the corridor for a while. It was all the same to them.

Then they got a call that he was awake and needed a bed pan, and one of them went in. I followed after a little.

I passed the nurse coming out of the room. She had the bed pan, and a towel was over it.

"How is he?" I asked.

"The same," she said.

He didn't seem the same to me. His breathing was noticeably heavier. My mother smiled at me weakly. She had also noticed the deterioration in his breathing. The sound now filled the room.

We didn't talk. There wasn't anything to say.

Towards seven that evening he woke and looked around. He was looking for me.

I was terribly frightened.

"Evangeleh?" he said hoarsely. "Evangeleh?"

I went over to his bed and held his hand. It was much cooler than it had been. But his forehead was burning.

His eyes stared at me.

"Joe got the grapes, Pop." And I signaled Joe to come to the bed-side with the bag of grapes.

The old man smiled when he saw them. Joe held up the cluster, and the old man reached for it. I pulled one off its stem and put it into his mouth. His teeth were in their cup at the side of the bed. He masticated as best he could with his gums. Then he nodded and asked for another. Then he asked for a third. He seemed absorbed in the taste of the grapes.

Then he made a sign to my mother. He glared at her, waved his eyes, and she left the room. Joe went back to the window. He was out of sight there.

"Evangeleh," he said.

"Yes, Pop." This was it.

"What happened?"

"No go, Pop," I said.

"What happened?"

"Nothing."

"Did you go to the bank?"

"No, Pop."

"Nothing, eh . . . nothing . . . ?"

"It's better if you wait till you get a little stronger."

"I'm not going to get stronger, Evangeleh."

"Just a little stronger. Right now it wouldn't be good."

"I'm finished, Evangeleh."

"No, you're not, Pop."

"Don't wait for anything, Evangeleh."

"You have a little fever, Pop, and—"

"I don't care about that. I want you to do what I told you. Go, Evangeleh, go to the bank now and . . ."

He was exhausted. He lay back. The breath gurgled through his respiratory tract.

"It's better to wait a little, Pop."

He stared at me, his eyes fixed.

"You liar, Evangeleh," he said, and closed his eyes. He tried to turn away from me in the bed, but didn't have the strength. He breathed through his open mouth. His eyes were open to the ceiling. I could see the thought sink home that I was going to do nothing for him. Then his eyes turned and stared at me. They were now filled with disappointment and hatred. "Liar," he said and kept staring at me. After a time he fell into a sort of sleep. I was grateful for that.

In the middle of the night he had a little diarrhea. My mother, by then, had gone to Michael's house, and Joe was asleep in a wicker armchair in the sun parlor. I was sitting, almost asleep, in a corner of the room when I noticed the odor. There was no mistaking what it was. I called the night nurse, and she did the dirty work. She turned the old body one way and then the other, and she remade the bed. The old man was now never entirely conscious.

It was the grapes, I thought, but no regrets.

I went over close to look at him, but he had fallen into a coma, and what he saw he didn't recognize. He didn't know me; he simply stared at me.

For a day and a night and another day he breathed through the fluid that was filling his lungs. I appreciated what Dr. Beattie had said about the muscles of the heart. How it kept going with that weight of fluid in his lungs!

Just before dawn on the second day of the coma, Father Draddy looked in. He recognized what was happening.

"Well," he said, "there's nothing for it now."

"Father," I said, "I've been wondering how you measure it all at this point?"

"I don't have to and you don't have to," he said. "It's done later, in the next world."

"Father," I said, "tell me this one thing truthfully; do you really believe that?"

"If I didn't believe that, I wouldn't know what to believe. There would be no explanation, or reason, or excuse for all this. I'd be lost."

"That's where I am."

"Well, you have time. It's not too late."

"I don't like lies," I said, "though I've told my share."

"We're all sinners," he said, "but we can't go on blaming ourselves, and we can't go on living despising ourselves. We can't carry that load of self-scorn all our lives. That's why Jesus Christ and His Church speak of redemption."

"Redemption?"

"Yes. That's why He's called the Redeemer. He gives us, by His grace, what we all most need."

"And what is that?"

"A second chance."

I blew some air through my mouth.

"It's easy to be scornful," said Father Draddy.

"I wasn't then, I really wasn't."

"Of course you were. But the Holy Words have not endured through the centuries just because He spoke them. They have endured because man needs them. They make life on this earth possible."

"Not for me," I said.

"This man, your father, would be much happier now, if he believed. But he put his faith in something else . . . well, you know what."

"Say it."

"Himself."

"I thought you were going to say money."

"No. Himself. And that's not enough. No man is big enough in himself to give life a meaning. Man needs God!"

"I don't believe that."

"May I ask you a question?" he said. "You've been openly scornful of me . . ."

"Have I?"

"Of course. Every time I've met you. I'm used to that; we're all used to that, and we don't mind—oh, some, perhaps, but we know that we have to live and work in that, because we know Christ lived and worked in that. But now, may I ask you a question?"

"What is that?"

"Are you yourself enough for yourself? Are you reason enough for living? Are you and your concerns worth this awful struggle? Your ambitions, your desires, and your appetites—are they enough to justify the pain and the cost and all the rest of it?"

"How can you talk to me that way?"

"Because I know you," said Father Draddy.

"But you don't."

"I see your face, friend; I see many faces, and many faces I see are like yours."

"And what do you see on my face?"

"Do you want me to tell you?"

"Yes."

"Self-doubt, and . . . are you sure you want to hear?"

"Yes."

"Well, I'm sorry . . ."

"Tell me."

"Self-disgust."

"Yes."

"You're not sure of anything or of any value."

"That's true."

"In a way I admire the courage of men like you. I do."

"What is that? Men like me?"

"I mean men who live by human values alone. Tell me, what gives you the strength to draw one breath after another?"

"I'm going to tell you the truth; I don't know."

"And you can live in that doubt?"

"I live *by* that doubt."

"Then answer me, is it any wonder you don't have respect for yourself?"

"But I do," I said, and I was surprised to hear myself say that. I didn't know I felt that! "I do respect myself," I said.

"Then tell me, please do tell me, since every man has to have, somewhere, somehow, a reason to respect himself, what is yours? Why do you respect yourself?"

"It's hard to put . . ."

"You see, it's easy to sneer at me, and to be superior to me, but when I ask you that question, my friend, do you have an answer?"

"Yes, I do." And I was surprised to hear myself say that, too.

"Tell me what it is. I'd like to hear."

"I'll tell you. It's *because* I doubt. It's because I think it takes courage not to take the answers of other men. It takes courage to look back in scorn at myself and say NO to myself, and to look at this world and to say NO to this world."

It was the first feeling I had ever had of loyalty to myself. My God, I thought, I'm defending myself, what do you know!

"And," I continued, "once having said NO, to then change it all, or try to, to then start again, not because someone BIG has given me a second chance, but because I gave it to myself."

Father Draddy didn't answer.

"And about what you see on my face—self-disgust, you said. Well, that . . . that, I think, is man's hope, his dignity."

There was some stirring from the bed.

We both went over and looked down at my father.

He was having a dream. His lips were moving, and he was trying to say something. I couldn't make it out. But his face was rather happy as he remembered what he was remembering.

"He seems to be having a dream," I said to Father Draddy.

"They often do at the end. They often relive things, have fantasies and . . ."

My father opened his eyes.

They were lambent again, in a feverish way; something was lighting them from within. He smiled now, with a kind of love I had never seen on his face.

Father Draddy leaned forward and put his ear almost up against the moving lips. I was silent. We both listened. When my father's lips moved again, Father Draddy heard his last words.

"What did he say?" I asked.

"What does 'Papoo' mean?" he said.

I didn't answer. How could I explain it?

"He said it twice," said Father Draddy. "Is the Greek priest called Papoo?"

"Yes. But I don't think that's it here."

"He wants a priest of his own faith," said Father Draddy. He seemed very excited.

"I don't think that's it," I said.

"But suppose he does!"

"I doubt it."

"But suppose, suppose!"

Father Draddy was genuinely aroused.

"I'm going to get hold of Father Anastasis in Norwalk," he said. "Excuse me."

And was gone.

I was surprised how concerned he was. It impressed me very much.

My father died just before six o'clock that morning.

The last time I looked at his face, the grimace of anxiety had eased. You could see what he might have been.

· 28 ·

AFTER the doctors covered my father's face with the sheet, I taxied over to Michael's house.

A tension was out of the world. It all seemed a lot simpler.

My mother was sleeping like a girl. She had let her hair down, and it was all over the pillow. Her face was innocent and relaxed. It was, I thought, as if she had had the news, and for her, too, there had been an immediate lifting of the tension in the world.

I had to shake her shoulder to wake her.

She knew immediately what it was. She sat up.

"Oh, Seraphim, Seraphim!" she said.

I went into the living room to wait for her to dress. When she came out, I noticed she had not cried. I kissed her and held her hand as we went to the car for the trip to the hospital.

She walked right into the room where my father was.

The bedside curtain had been pulled closed.

There was another bed in the room, and there was a man in it. He was about my father's age, fidgety and cranky. He knew that there was a dead man in the room with him and he didn't like the idea.

My mother went to the body of the man to whom she had been married for forty-seven years, and she kissed him on the forehead. Then again. She sat there, for a few minutes, as she had when he was alive. She had no prayers to tell.

After a while they came for the body, and they took it away. No one asked where they were going to take it, or what they were going to do with it.

It was time now to make the funeral arrangements and to find a grave.

504

As we left the hospital, the boys arrived. They were late to see my father alive and early for the funeral. They were in uniformly good spirits, chattering like monkeys among themselves. Michael told them what had happened. They crossed themselves. As we left, we saw them standing there wondering what to do next.

I heard later that Father Draddy had finally tracked Father Anastasis to his bed, where he was in a heavy sleep. The night before there had been the weekly bingo game at the Greek Orthodox Church. But Father Anastasis gamely got into his clothes, climbed into Father Draddy's car, and came to give the corpse his blessings.

We went to Michael's house. We were surprised to find we were hungry. Gloria put on some coffee, and my mother made some bacon and eggs. Michael and I were alone.

"You better start taking care of yourself now," he said.

"You worried about me, Michael?"

"Sure, you nut, what do you think? I'm your brother."

"You worry about me, Michael, do you?"

"Sure, when I see that look coming back."

"What look?"

"The look you had in your eyes when you came back from the war. I recognize it. And you've stopped talking."

"I got nothing to say to anyone, Mike."

"Well, you really ought to say one thing to one person. Do it for me, will you? You don't know it, but every time Mother was in real trouble, it was Gloria, not me and not you, who went over there and stayed with her, helped her."

"I'm sorry about what I did to Gloria."

"How's she supposed to know that? Say something to her."

"I will." I kissed my brother on the cheek.

Later I got Gloria alone in the kitchen and apologized. She just nodded. I guess I was too late with it.

After breakfast we had a family meeting. Gloria felt strongly that we should patronize the Taunton Funeral Home. She knew Mrs. Taunton through the country club. No one had a better idea, or even a different suggestion.

At the funeral home we selected a coffin. Mr. Taunton himself waited on us. He recommended a concrete vault inside of which the coffin would be put. It was guaranteed waterproof; there would be no seepage, he promised. When we hesitated, he said if we didn't have one of these concrete vaults, we'd have to be prepared for a collapse of earth after a couple of seasons of rain and frost.

The whole deal was awfully expensive. I didn't know where I was going to get the money for my share.

We decided not to get the vault.

While Gloria and Michael made the detailed arrangements with Mr. Taunton, Mother and I went to look for a cemetery site.

It was soon evident to me that she knew she was looking for a final place for herself as well.

The Catholic cemetery was full. They said they might make a place, however.

I remembered hearing that the Jewish cemetery in Prague has bodies piled six and seven deep, one on top of the other. The ghetto, there, followed the dead.

The Catholic cemetery near Rye, New York, is a suburb. The dead rub shoulders.

We went elsewhere. It was a long day.

We finally found a plot at a neglected corner of a nonsectarian cemetery. This corner was not popular, we were told, because a new superhighway was being put through along that edge of the cemetery. We asked to see it.

There it was, six lanes, three already being used, not twenty feet away from where my father now lies. The earth-movers, gigantic machines on giant wheels, were at work.

But we could see that when the highway was completed that corner would be quiet. Except, of course, for the whizzing of the cars. There was a certain fitness in this. My father had spent over thirty years of his life commuting to and from New York City. In the morning most of the traffic would be going in as he had gone in every morning. In the evening most of the traffic would be coming home, as he used to in my memory. My mother, in time, would lie there with all this, just as she had endured it all her life.

She looked at the plot for a while. It was clearly not what she had imagined or hoped for, but she shrugged, said all right, and we left. I called Michael from the office and told him he should come over and see it.

"He'd better hurry," said the man in charge. "There's another party interested."

Michael said he'd hurry. He told us the body had been moved to the funeral parlor.

When we arrived there, the boys were sitting in one of the parlors like a row of crows. The body was still being worked on somewhere in the building. Mr. Taunton asked if he could talk to me alone. I prepared for a question of delicacy.

"Your father's shoes," he whispered, "are not in good shape; in fact, there is a hole in one sole and—well, they're pretty old. Of course it won't matter, because the mourners will see him only from the waist up . . . just depends how much you care. Thought I'd mention it."

"Where's he going to walk?" said my mother when I told her what the drama was about. My father had another pair, she said, dress shoes, but they had burned up in the fire. It was the first time my mother had mentioned the fire.

For some reason I wanted him properly shod. I walked my mother slowly down the main street looking for a shoe store.

For several hours now I'd had the impression that my mother had something to say to me. I took her into a restaurant. "You must eat something," I said.

She did. She ate rather well.

She asked for a second cup of tea.

People have signals they don't know they're sending. When my mother asks for a second cup of tea, it means that she has something to say and she is arranging for more time so she can say it.

Out it came. "Eee," she said, "I don't think you're crazy."

I had to laugh. "I've just come to the conclusion that I am," I said.

"Why do you think that, Eee?" she said and took my hand.

"Well, I don't think like other people any more."

"Are you sure that's bad?"

"I don't love anybody any more—you, but no one else."

"What happened to Florence?"

"I tried to get her on the phone; the maid said she was away on a trip, a vacation, she said—oh, you mean in relation to me?"

"Florence is a fine woman."

"I didn't like my life with her."

"She was a fine woman, and she helped you."

"She is a fine woman, and she was killing me. And I her."

"Well, that's your affair; you would know what is best there, but still that doesn't make you crazy."

"Well, crazy is not the word. But I am dangerous to other people and to the way other people live."

"For instance?"

"Well, the fire . . . for instance."

My mother chewed that one a minute, and then she said, "I wished many times over the years, many, many times, that I had the courage to do what you did. When I heard you done it, I said, thank you."

"Well, I'm glad."

"That house had too many rooms!"

"It did."

She leaned forward and kissed me. "I don't care about the insurance and all that. I hated that house. I lived in it for thirty years, and I hated it for thirty years."

"All right, dear," I said. "All right, darling."

But she wasn't to be stopped.

"That house ate my life," she said.

I knew who had eaten her life. But she was too well brought up to say his name now except in respect.

Then she did say it.

"Your father," she said, "didn't know how to enjoy his old age. He would sit there, go over his mistakes, all the bad deals he had made, who still owed him money after forty years, people long dead. I'd say, Seraphim, forget that now, read a book, read a magazine. Then finally he would say, 'Bring the cards.' He used to say, 'Look what God left me with at the end of my life. An idiot!' But I beat him at gin rummy, and I beat him at pinochle, and I beat him at bridge. He thought I was cheating. He hit me and yelled on me. 'Don't cheat again here!' The house shook. But I didn't care."

"What are you going to do now, Mom?"

"Poor Seraphim," she said, "poor Seraphim!"

"Are you going to live at Michael's house now?"

"I'm going to get a room with nobody in it. I will cook each day just enough for myself, and it will be very quiet, and I will never see cards again. Every day or so I will walk to the public library and take out a book, and when I have finished that book, I will get another. I will watch the news on television, Chet Huntley, very fine man, and compare what he says with the papers. I will live, that's all."

Her chest was going up and down; she was breathing hard. "God forgive me, I'm going to live," she said.

She was seventy-two.

There was no escaping it. She was rejoicing that her husband was dead. She was heartened by his passing.

She had her second tea. And an eclair.

I watched her enjoy it.

She finished the eclair, wiped her lips, and smiled at me.

We got the old man a hell of a pair of shoes, and in that way told our memory of him that we could love him now, that it wasn't his fault either, that that was the way he had been brought up, and the best he knew.

It was very hot and very muggy, the day we buried him. The smog lay over the parkway. Everyone's eyes smarted.

People he hadn't seen for years came to his funeral and wept.

My mother did not weep.

She accepted the sympathy of the mourners gravely, nodding to them, saying nothing.

29

IF the right people sign the right paper, it's easy to get into Greenmeadow. But unless the right person signs another paper, it's not easy to get out.

One day I saw Dr. Lloyd hustling between two buildings, ran and caught him. I held on to him, because he's a shifty listener, and I put it to him.

"Dr. Lloyd, I'm ready to leave here now."

"No problem, Eddie. Next time Judge Morris holds court on the grounds, we'll stand up together, and as soon as he signs your release, you'll be free. Now, tell me, have you got a place to live and have you got a job waiting?"

"A home and a job's not what I need, Dr. Lloyd."

"Well, the judge's going to ask how you propose to eat and pay the rent."

"There's no trick to that, Dr. Lloyd, if you have no money. It only gets complicated when you're doing well."

"Very amusing, Eddie," he laughed, and looked around, "but Judge Morris doesn't make our regulations; he administrates them."

"That's why I want you to convince him for me. Tell him I'm planning not to go to work."

"For how long?"

"Forever. I've retired."

He laughed and looked over his shoulder. "Now, Eddie, be sensible for a minute. I happen to know you have a very nice home and—"

"And a very nice wife, much too nice to have me inflicted on her again. Dr. Lloyd, all I need now is silence and isolation, not a lot of people—"

510

"But Eddie, there happen to be a lot of people in that big world out there and—"

"I'm not going to bother them. They can go their way and I'll—what's the matter?"

"Why?"

"You keep looking around."

"I'm wondering if there isn't some other person who might take you in for a while and—"

"I did have a girl friend, but I think she ought to have a chance to find someone who needs her."

"And you don't?"

"I don't need anyone. I'm returning to selfishness."

"Eddie," he laughed, "lack of selfishness was never your problem."

"That was it exactly. That's why I'm putting this wall around myself. I don't want to be part of this civilization."

"You are part of it. And what's so wrong with it?"

"Let's not go into that, because if we did, you'd never let me out."

"Oh, Eddie, it's so cheap to pop off that way, blame everything on everybody except yourself. Suppose it was all in your hands and you—"

"I'd burn it down."

"Burn what down?"

"The whole thing."

"You mean you don't like this country, is that it?"

"It's a beautiful country."

"But nevertheless you think it should be burned down, all of it?"

"No, just all the cities."

"You mean the ghettos, Harlem and—"

"No, I don't mean only the ghettos. Harlem, sure, we know we can't fix that, so level it like Tokyo, then start from scratch. But the rest of New York, too. The whole city's no good. We've got to start from the bare earth again. And we can afford it—"

"Easy on the arm, kid, I've got a tennis elbow." He looked around. "Eddie, if you go around talking this way, people will think you're a monster."

"When they said they liked me, I was killing myself."

"Seriously, Eddie, you don't know the impression you make. There's already been lots of comment. People have noticed you don't answer when they talk to you."

"Oh, yes, I've stopped talking to anyone, and it's been great. It's not necessary to make contact all the time. Disconnect! Connect with yourself."

"Eddie, I disagree with you. I think we need more dialogue between people, and between nations, too."

"Oh, there's much too much of that now. All this friendliness on every side. It's bad to pretend that. You can't understand, because you've got to be friendly to everybody, and by now you probably don't know any more who you're really friendly to."

"But that's not true, Eddie."

"You don't know much about yourself, Dr. Lloyd. There's nothing wrong with not liking people. I'm not saying hate them. Just good old Yankee distance! All this talk about our Christian civilization. We have a business civilization. The idea is not to love your brother but to get the better of him, and do it so there won't be any blood to wash off your hands in public. Everybody knows that's the way it is. But we live in pretense. The pretense end the facts, and the gulf between is getting bigger every year. Well, I've stopped pretending, and you'd be amazed how much that eliminates of what a person usually does all day."

Suddenly I felt so exuberant, I shouted.

"What's the matter?" asked Dr. Lloyd.

"I feel great," I said. "Come on, let's walk. Don't go to work this morning."

"The arm, kid, the arm," he said. I released him. "Eddie, the judge may believe that for your own good it would be advisable for you to stay with us just a little longer."

"No, it's you who believe that because of what I've been saying. But don't worry about me. I'm just a solitary nut, sort of a harmless prick. It certainly wouldn't do me any good to stay here. I don't think you do anybody much good here, do you? Don't answer that if you don't want to, but I haven't noticed anyone improve here. I hope you don't mind my saying that."

"No, I want you to say what you believe."

"Well, you really don't, do you? That's what's causing the strain, saying you do when you don't. And also you've been trying to evade my questions. So now I'm going to have to ask you again. Will you recommend to Judge Morris that he just let me walk over the hill?"

512

"Eddie, sooner or later, you're going to have to find a way to get along with people."

"I've found it. I don't talk to them."

"Now, Eddie, I know you're overwrought and—"

"O.K., forget it."

"I don't really feel, Eddie, that I can go to Judge—"

"O.K., don't worry about it."

"I think you need to be with someone who will assume responsibility for your behavior just a little longer. I read your entire folder this morning . . ."

I walked away. "We'll talk some more," he called after me.

I walked to the shady side of the O.T. building. Here was the territory of the quietest group on the campus, all there, now, sitting or lying on the ground, the lost souls. No one ever came to visit them, and there was no prospect anyone would. I liked to sit among these gentle disconnected people, perhaps because they didn't want anything except what I wanted, to sit still while time flew past. An official booklet described part of the hospital's function as "a human dumping ground."

One day Gwen appeared on the grounds. It was a strange encounter, a meeting without agenda of a two-man chapter of a veteran's organization, the sole survivors of what was once a goodly company. I wondered why she'd come, waited for her to say. She seemed to be inspecting me, but if she had any reaction, she didn't express it.

I noticed she had her hair cut close to her head. The effect was to make her features larger, her eyes, her mouth, her nose all heavier. She wasn't as pretty, but she was more what the Greeks call *anthropos,* that is, human. Most girls are candy, wrapped in semi-transparent stuff, and living in the hope that some man soon will want to unwrap it. Gwen had none of this aspect now.

I led her to the edge of the hospital property. We lay there on the field grass, our faces to the sun. She told me she had moved out of New York to a small community in western Connecticut where an uncle of hers owned the liquor store in a rural shopping center. I recalled the general area. The shopping center seemed to be out in the open country, but hidden behind the hills, along the dirt back roads and in the wooded country just off the numbered highways, there were enough people to make that package store a profitable enterprise. And the old man had a good clientele. They liked his transplanted hillbilly humor and stories. But as a businessman, he was too easygoing, in fact had so much outstanding, he couldn't pay his bills for new stock. He didn't care enough to do much about collecting. What he cared about was rabbits. On the side of a wooded hill behind the shopping center, he had a little city of hutches, and there he spent most of his time. This old man had finally found what he liked to do.

Since he couldn't as yet rely on his rabbits for total income, he had to keep the liquor store going. Hearing by accident that Gwen was "moving around," he asked her if she wanted to bring the kid and spend the summer. He had an empty top floor. Once there, he became reacquainted with Gwen and liked her. And he was crazy about the boy. Andy, of course, liked the rabbits. After a week it would have been difficult to separate them. The uncle solved this by offering Gwen his top floor, rent free, and a third of the take from the liquor store if she'd run it for him. To his great surprise, she accepted.

"So if you want to move in?" she said to me.

"No, thanks."

"O.K. That's all I want to know."

"I don't want to hook up with anybody now."

"Who the hell would want to marry you? I was just offering you a place to go. You're not going to stay here the rest of your life, are you?"

"I'm going to go traveling as soon as I get a couple of thousand dollars together."

"Where?"

"Everywhere."

"Well, till then. What? Look if you want to, o.k.; if you don't, o.k. Actually it's a nice place, nothing extra for looks, but at night, when the shopping center closes down, it's real quiet. And it's a living."

"What would you get out of it?"

"That's my problem."

"I don't have anything for anybody."

"I'm not asking anything."

"You sure?"

She lay back on the grass. "I was just trying to help you," she said. I knew what an effort it had been for this girl to take the chance she might be turned down. Out of everybody, I thought, she's the one who cares enough to offer help. Come in out of the storm, she was saying, stay till it's over, go when you feel like it.

"I don't expect anything, Eddie," she said again.

"What happened to Charles?"

"That wasn't a good idea. And I have no other ideas. None. You want it or don't you?"

I accepted Gwen's offer precisely as she had presented it, a temporary shelter. She said I could help her with the accounts and tend counter. I'd have food and keep. I said I wanted nothing more. "That's good," she said, "because I have nothing more to offer." There were no hints, no unspecific references. She made no suggestions. I made no guesses. We vowed no commitments, pledged no guarantees.

Now I could wait for the probate court hearing with confidence. I had somewhere to go.

A couple of days later I was told I had visitors, and to proceed to the administration building. There, waiting for me, were Arthur and Florence.

It was a very hot day. August had singed the grass so it had lost its hold on the crumbling soil and looked as if it would never come back. The shade was almost black. On the campus the patients huddled under the trees and in the corners of the buildings, the homeless, almost invisible to the eye lensed down for the hot sun.

Arthur was perspiring heavily, as much from nerves, I soon saw, as from the heat. The best I could offer for our conversation was a black splotch under a tree. Arthur spread his jacket of Italian silk on the ground for Florence. I got the idea.

Florence told their story as if it were a humorous anecdote about a friend, one not too close to her, towards whom she felt a certain amusement.

"I think what I wanted most," she said, "was attention. I took about a dozen pills, is that right, dear?" She turned to Arthur.

"That," said Arthur, "is the usual number people take who want to attract attention but don't want to die."

They laughed together.

"I immediately called Arthur to make arrangements for the funeral and for Ellen's future. Of course Arthur got there with the ambulance and that much-used Beverly Hills stomach pump, and a few hours later I was comfortably asleep. The next noon, when Arthur called by to see how I was, I was still asleep, but when he came that night I was awake and looking pretty good, I must say, all fixed up in that pretty bed jacket you gave me for Christmas two years ago, remember, Ev, the one with the little lace cuffs?"

I didn't really remember it, but I nodded.

"Well, you know, dear" (this time the "dear" referred to me) "even as I took those pills, I realized that there was a significance to the fact that it was Arthur I called and not you. Even the fact that Arthur was in the same city seemed meaningful. You were simply not where I needed you.

"And as the pills worked, even as they took effect and I was thinking what a cowardly thing to do, I also realized that it was my only way of flirting with Arthur. At my age and in my psychological condition and in our culture, perhaps it truly was the only way for me to make a sexual advance. Is that right, dear (Arthur)?"

"Nonsense!" said Arthur, smiling at me a little lamely.

"Well, the point is that Arthur got there, and the next day we had a nice talk and, well—at our age!—one thing led to another, and before we knew it we were in a drawing room on the train to British Columbia. Imagine! Of course, we both needed the vacation very much! And you'd be surprised, dear (me), how little getting used to each other and all that was necessary. Is that right, dear (Arthur)?"

"Oh, Florence," Arthur protested.

"And our very first thought was for you. We were both immediately concerned that we do nothing that would aggravate your upset. Arthur even more than me! He was the one who insisted that we come here on the first flight east. I've hardly any clothes with me, one ridiculous bag, but here we are."

I smiled at them both, but still didn't say what she was waiting for, so she filled the conversational gap as she always did.

"I must tell you that Arthur—and I hope this doesn't embarrass you, dear (Arthur)—takes brilliant care of me. Every morning when he comes for breakfast, he brings a little typed list on a piece of that pink memo paper you gave me, remember, dear (me)? Those are my orders for the day: what I must remember to do, where we are going for dinner and what to wear, or who is coming to dinner and what I should ask cook to prepare. Arthur simply moved his cook into our house, and she is divine! And then what errands I should tend to, priority one, and what errands, priority two, and where to meet him for lunch—we nearly always have lunch together, and what a change that is: it anchors the whole middle of my day, and it was positively not my idea, was it, Arthur?"

"Actually it was," said Arthur. He seemed very ill at ease. Florence told him he could be excused.

We watched him walk away. He was peering at the lost souls in the shade of the O.T. building. He was very myopic, Arthur, and this made him protrude his head in an attitude of deep concern.

"He's really a dear," said Florence, "and so good with Ellen. You know I gave her Dr. Leibman, and she's so much better. She had some very serious problems—about you, believe it or not. But they're under control now, so don't worry about her; she's going to be fine."

Oh, Ellen! I thought, but didn't speak.

Florence leaned forward and touched my hand lightly with hers. She was waiting for some word from me. Was it for my permission to leave me?

"Of course," she said, "it's nothing like what we had. I don't expect anything like we had ever again in my life." She lifted her gentle, elegant hand. "But you see what a dear he really is, don't you? I mean he makes me feel cared for, you know, Ev? And I never felt anything but temporary with you, like you might leave me at any moment. But Arthur's for me and only for me. And don't you think, Ev dear, don't you really think I've earned that? Well, I have, I really have. You see, I just want regularity now. I mean you're a wonderful man, but you're deeply neurotic. Every analyst I ever had told me that. Dr. Weisbart, he's new and just wonderful, I told him all about this with Arthur and all about you, and he says that I'm doing absolutely the only thing I could do, that you're an emotional cripple and need deep therapy. I told him you wouldn't. But he said you might now. Well, now it's not my business any more —I mean I'm concerned, I'll always be con—don't look so hurt, dear, you really don't want me any more; you really haven't for a long time, you know you haven't. I used to think I could help you, that I wouldn't be a good person or a successful person unless I did. But there comes a time when you have to face the facts and, if you've failed, to admit it. And I have with you, dear, I've failed; I'm sorry, Ev, I'm very, very sorry—"

I leaned forward and kissed her. "Bless you," I said, "bless you both."

"Oh, thank you, dear," she said. "That is so damned generous of you." Then she laughed and said, "I guess I always should have had a lawyer for a husband." Then she called, "Arthur!"

He wasn't far away.

"Arthur!" Reassured that he was coming, she turned to me. "I'm sure we can make a settlement that is equitable. I have really given you the best years of my life, and you are still an attractive and energetic man, whose earning powers are simply enormous."

Arthur walked up. "If you like," he suggested, "I could still represent you. Might save money all around."

"I'll get another lawyer," I said quickly. Then suddenly I thought, what the hell, make her happy.

"I've changed my mind, Arthur," I said. "I'd like you to continue as my lawyer—if you will still have me. There is only one thing I ask—"

"And that is what?" said Arthur, frowning sympathetically.

"That you give Florence first priority in every respect. Her needs come first."

Florence embraced me. Arthur goddam near embraced me.

"I'll draw up a letter agreement," he said, "which will be—in my mind—fair to both of you, and I'll come up again in a few days."

"Do it tomorrow," said Florence quickly.

"Well, perhaps I can if I move some appointments around. I think quite possibly I can." (He did. I gave Florence everything in exchange for total future irresponsibility.)

He rose. And Florence rose. He shook out his coat. Florence took my arm, and we began the walk back to their car.

"Arthur and I thought we'd go to Mexico City—it's the season now—sort of a honeymoon combined with a divorce combined with business. Arthur has some clients there who have a large hacienda." She laughed and looked at Arthur with considerable affection.

"How long will you be here, Edward?" he asked.

"Oh yes," said Florence, "how long and can we help? Oh, it's just too absurd; imagine, Arthur, a man tries to kill him and they put *him* away. Imagine!"

We all had a good laugh, and that seemed as good a time as any for them to leave.

518

"What do you intend to go into now?" asked Florence, as she and Arthur fastened the safety belts on their Hertz.

"I'm thinking of going into the liquor business," I said.

"Oh, that's very interesting," she said. "Goodbye." And off they drove.

At the probate court hearing, I told Judge Morris I was going to work for a man who raised rabbits commercially. "And there he is." I pointed to Gwen and her uncle, who had come down to vouch for me.

"Oh, that's very interesting," said the judge, and released me immediately. Dr. Lloyd didn't say a word. The judge signed his name on the order, and that was it.

"I want you to report to me at regular intervals," he said later as we walked to his car.

"Like when?"

"About once a year. Incidentally, tell me, what really did happen to you?"

"I wanted to experience resurrection," I said, "so I had to kill myself."

"Whatever the hell that means, don't do it again. I'm letting you go against good psychiatric advice. Don't louse me up."

We lived together, Gwen, Andy, and I, on the top floor of the old man's house. I had my own room, but sometimes I'd bunk in with her. Other nights we didn't want to and didn't. We had a wary truce. Each morning when we woke, we looked at each other to see if it was still "on." We were like two jungle cats, for those first months, two tigers who had crossed each other's paths and fallen into cohabitation, hunting together, eating together, sleeping in the same thicket. But there was some final distrust, not only of the other, but of the jungle in ourselves.

Over the counter of the liquor store I got to know a whole graveyard candidates' class. Despite the fact that I hardly spoke, people sensed something sympathetic in me. Many of them must have had no one else to talk to, because in no time at all they were making the most trusting revelations, as if they wanted me to vouch for them, be their partisan in this gigantic unequal contest.

I soon became that shopping center's free spiritual counselor. In a small way I became famous. My customers brought me gifts, the surplus of their gardens and henhouses. The rumor got around that I liked raspberries. I don't particularly, but if I'd had a mania for them, I would have had enough. I got jars of homemade jam and chili sauce and all sorts of winter apples and Seckel pears. An old woman, a helpless drunk as you might have seen her, knit me a beautiful Galway sweater. Readers brought me their books when they got through with them, and their magazines a few days late. I was, before I knew it, the beneficiary of a community subsidy.

But I lived for my mornings. Gwen opened the store; the old man tended to the noon rush, so I didn't come on till two. That gave me a big piece of time, which I made bigger by falling on my typewriter at first light.

I started anywhere, a letter to my father, written not as the start of a book or story, but for my own sake. (I had to deal with him first.) From there it took off. A memoir? A confession? It was my experience with myself, a way of living simultaneously on several planes of time.

After a few weeks I was writing a story which had to do with my father and me (Mount Aergius hung on the wall over my writing table) and particularly that moment when I recognized him as a brother, not a father, and when I saw that, given the way it had been for him, he couldn't have been otherwise.

Then I put these pages away, without a sense of failure, since I hadn't been writing to interest anyone. I began to work on a story about a college boy, obsessed with hatred of one person, who transfers that hatred to everyone else he meets, revenging himself against them all, and never taking the pleasure of loving anyone. In time a young girl came into the narration, and she was understanding and patient and finally loving, the first person he allowed to be that way to him.

And that all took I don't know how many months. I didn't care. I was in no hurry. It was the first time in my life that I didn't want anything more. I even forgot about my plans to travel. I just did the same old thing every day (as Gwen said to a friend) seven days a week. And Sundays, when the store was closed, was the best day of all, because it was all mine.

I'd never before had the experience I had on certain of those mornings, like I'd been rescued from suffocation, could breathe freely for the first time.

I was surprised, too, at how much I'd been through in my life, and how much of it I could bring back. I was the man who once couldn't remember what he had had for dinner, and now I was remembering things said thirty-five years before, the very words. I could hear the voices.

But most of all I was surprised that I felt a friendliness towards everyone and particularly towards Florence. I wrote a sort of celebration of her, paying overdue tribute to the girl's goodness and her patience with an impossible boy. I remembered how I had loved Florence way back then; the feeling itself returned.

I slept like a man who has to get off a train in the middle of the night and doesn't dare permit himself to fall off completely. I couldn't wait for each new day.

A year passed this way. And most of another. It was the first completely happy time of my life.

That's why it took me so long to notice that Gwen was feeling neglected.

There had been signs that should have told me what was developing. For instance, there was a decompression process I had to go through every day when I quit work. It took time for me to travel the distance, ever increasing, from me back to us. Gwen said amen to the fact that I was working so happily, but goddammit when I quit work couldn't I quit work? Because, she said, I kept cooking on the back burner for hours afterwards. She noticed I was everlastingly scribbling on little pieces of paper—not that there was anything wrong with that, but when she'd be talking to me and I'd start scribbling something down that obviously had nothing to do with what she was saying—well, what was she supposed to think about that?

Even at night, she said, I didn't stop. I'd be going through the most vivid dreams, all about other people and other days, in the course of which I'd talk to myself out loud and perspire. Or I'd wake up in the middle of the night, put on the bedlight, and make one of my goddam notes—and half an hour later, on would go that little bedside light again, and she'd look up to see me sitting on the edge of the bed scribbling something else down. I explained that if I didn't, I'd forget, and that I'd already lost some good things that way.

There were nights when I'd devour her sexually. But she soon realized these bursts were generally when I'd had a bad day, and what I was doing was squeezing out of her the satisfaction I wished I'd been able to get elsewhere (from Miss Underwood, Gwen said). This wasn't a function she particularly enjoyed performing; in fact, there was something about my violent and unpredictable bursts of desire, and their equally sudden voiding, that left her on edge and totally unsatisfied.

There were an increasing number of nights when I didn't go into her room at all. Since I was getting up with the first light, I was often simply too tired. In fact, it was becoming my habit to fall asleep as soon as I lay down. This was usually as she was giving Andy his bath. By the time she had put him to bed and came looking for me, I'd be snoring. (I'd begun to snore for the first time since she'd known me; she particularly noted that.)

She wondered how long this was going to go on. She asked me (it was more like a suggestion) whether, when I finished whatever it was I was writing, the whole thing would ease up? I said I didn't think so. What I didn't add was that I hoped it would never ease up.

Another thing that must have disturbed her was that I didn't talk about what I was doing. I inhabited a world I wouldn't let her into. It was obviously more important to me than anything else, including, she had to admit, herself.

Gwen gave the problem a lot of thought. She began to leave Andy in the care of his uncle when the old man took his turn at the counter, and she'd come up to see me in the empty house, bringing me my lunch. I was usually over my first burst by then and susceptible to a beer and a sandwich—and other interruptions. She'd lie down deep in the old blue sofa, watching me as I ate, and waiting. As often as not, when I'd finished the refreshments, I'd move from the desk to where she was waiting for me.

I kept the shades of my room completely drawn, so that the light at my desk would be the brightest in the room. When this light was off, the room was left in a spooky twilight, very like the way we'd kept the motel rooms where we used to meet in the old days. Gwen was trying to revive the fervor of that time.

It was clear that this wasn't going to work either. One day she went too far. She must have noticed some wavering of resolution in my eye as I finished my sandwich, because she lifted her foot and flicked off the wall switch that controlled the central fixture from which I drew my desk light. Well, in the first place, it is nowhere in the Greek sexual catechism that the woman should aggress. But more than that, what she did made me aware that I had begun to resent her visits, and what I resented was that she thought she could interrupt me whenever she wished.

I told her to turn on the light, and I resumed working. But after that distraction, I didn't return to work with much appetite, just as I had found on occasions when we had made love that I wasn't able to resume in good style. A man has just so much energy.

A few days later I was having one hell of a morning when I heard her come in downstairs. Goddam if I wanted to be diverted, but finally she came on with me and on with me, till the event took place. But, as some saving reservation, I suppose, instead of going to bed with her, I bent her over the table where I was working. Later she pulled me into the other room. But I couldn't get with her. After some devout waiting for the member to rise to action again, I went downstairs and walked from room to room, trying to get back onto what I'd been doing before she'd come in.

I heard her getting ready to leave. When she came down, I told her I would skip lunch from then on, work right through, and have something to eat later at the liquor counter.

She nodded, said nothing, left. What the hell, I thought, as I heard the front door slam, I'd told her when we made our vows on the back lawn of Greenmeadow that I didn't have anything for anyone else, and she'd said o.k. Now if she felt neglected—well, she could take care of herself.

"You're not a very nice guy," I thought. "So what," I thought.

As some further declaration of independence, I didn't go to the store that day. When Gwen got home, I was still over the typewriter. I told her I'd gotten onto something and didn't want to break off. She shrugged.

The day had to come when it was clear to us both that I had stopped making love to Gwen. That doesn't mean that we didn't make love. But now, whenever anything happened, she'd have to start it and keep after me until, almost in spite of my preoccupations, my body responded, and she "took it away from me." More often than not, I did it in perfect silence, like sleepwalking, or automatic writing.

And sometimes even her best efforts didn't work.

"I guess I just don't want to," I said one day when it wouldn't. She didn't pick up the topic for discussion.

"I guess I've turned the corner," I said in the middle of another night. No answer. "I'm past that forty-five mark now," I said.

She nodded and didn't speak. Later she said, "It's temporary."

But she must have remembered those days long ago when I'd walk out of any meeting of any group of executives conferring on any subject just to get into bed with her for an hour.

Most women would have found some way to get along with all this, most women, at some time or other, have to. But Gwen wasn't a girl to shovel her feelings under for very long.

One night, when I walked into the house after locking up the store, she wasn't there. I was hungry, and I called her name. No answer. Then I went into the kitchen; there was nothing on the stove. I turned to see what was in the icebox, and there she was in a corner, crying. For some reason this annoyed me, as if she had broken her word to me. When I asked her what the matter was, she just looked at me for a long time and didn't say.

It was weeks later that she told me she had been to the doctor that afternoon, and that he had confirmed what she had guessed. She was pregnant. Ironic that, after all the wild go's we had, she got pregnant then. She had stopped paying the respect of precaution.

I didn't ask her later why she hadn't told me immediately. It was obvious—especially when I thought back on the circumstances—that Gwen wouldn't have.

I scratched around in the icebox. When she wants to talk, she'll talk, I thought.

And after a while she said, "Eddie, what do you need me for?"

"Occasional companionship," is what I said. It just popped into my head, and I said it. She didn't react, but I knew it hit her. I remembered Dr. Lloyd had said people would think I was a monster.

It took quite a while before she went on. "Eddie," she said, "you're treating me just like you used to treat your wife."

I answered that if she meant I was banging a lot of girls, I wasn't. "In fact," I added (I guess I thought this would clinch it), "I'm not interested in sex any more."

Well, if I was trying to avoid a crisis, that wasn't the way to do it. I saw that and softened what I'd said. I assured her I was perfectly contented with the way we were living.

"Well, I'm not," she snapped back.

I cut myself a piece of store cheese, pulled the tab off a Bud, and went into the other room. I picked up a movie magazine, began to read about the sex lives of the stars and to wonder about my own. Maybe I didn't need the whole damned thing. Animals, big, violent, physical monsters, get along for months and even years without giving copulation a thought. Why had it become so obsessive for man? Was it worth the trouble?

I was still thinking about this in bed when she made what I realized later was her last reach. It didn't work.

"What are you turning over on your stomach for?" she asked.

"I don't feel like it," I said.

Something woke me at dawn. There hadn't been a sound or a stir. But when I opened my eyes, there she was, up on one elbow, looking at me. Her face bleeds out in a crisis, and her eyes suck back into their sockets. She looked awful.

"Gwen," I said, "what's the matter?"

"I'm giving up, Eddie."

She said it regretfully, even tenderly, with a sense of time misspent. Then she got out of bed, dressed herself and Andy, and went down to the store to do her morning's tour.

For the next few days, all was surprisingly calm. But it was in those next few days that I first took notice of Keith Robinson.

Gwen had taken to killing time at the liquor store talking with a fellow who worked in TV. My first impression of him was that he bought a lot of vodka. Gossips told me that this was mostly for his wife, who was, they said, a lush.

I first became aware of Keith's existence, as a factor I mean, when he gave Andy some presents. That is always a sign.

Then one day a TV set appeared on our top floor, in fact in Gwen's bedroom. It was a very big set, color and all, and it was a present from this guy. It turned out Keith was sort of a celebrity, a "top creator," who wrote his dramatic shows in the country, then would go in for a few days to attend to their production in New York. Gwen said he wanted her to watch his efforts and tell him what she thought.

I knew if I asked about him, her jealousy game, if that's what it was, would be working successfully. I didn't have the stomach for that kind of caper now.

But I did take a good look at the guy. He was about my size, maybe ten years younger, with troubled eyes and that abstracted look many talented people have. All things even, I would have liked him. He didn't showboat or come on too strong; in fact, he behaved as if he was a failure, which never fails to please. But on the TV bigtime there was his name featured at the end of a prime time, fifty-two-minute original. He was self-effacing, sure, but he was big!

One nice thing about him, he played the horses and really knew form. He gave me a few tips, especially a couple at fifteen to one that breezed and brought me a bundle, which I salted away. And a whopping daily double. Keith seemed awfully anxious to do well by me in respect to money.

"I can see why you like this guy," I said to Gwen, intending to make a joke about the inside he was throwing me on the horses.

But she played it straight, said there was nothing between them, and added that he wasn't her type. Which, if you've been around, you will recognize as a sign, too, when they insist on telling you that. I hadn't asked if he was her type.

But then came the real tip-off. She told me how much better Keith was than the work he was doing. "He despises those shows of his," she said, "as much as we do!"

"Are you fucking him?" I asked.

"What are you talking about?" she demanded, absolutely delighted. Having received this bit of encouragement, she went on and on about him, and about his wife, who it turned out was, besides an absolute lush, a suicide candidate. The point was, Gwen insisted, his wife didn't have a clue to what Keith could accomplish if he ever began to do his own work. His talent was much too good for the garbage he had to write for the idiot box.

I realized she was spinning the same trap around this guy—and herself, too—which had caught me.

We spent some evenings, Gwen and I, watching the man's shows. No sooner were the final credits rolling on than there'd be a phone call from New York, and it would be Keith asking what she thought.

"Why doesn't he ever ask me what I think?"

"He knows you don't give a damn about anything except your-self."

After a while she began to take his calls downstairs, because she said she didn't want their frivolous chatter to disturb all that heavy thinking I did every night in bed.

Sometimes these phone calls went on for an hour. But whenever I picked up accidentally and heard a bit, they actually were talking about the writing and the casting and the direction and the timing, and all that inside stuff. It was amazing how much they could find to say about one lousy TV show. Gwen was talking sense, too. And he really cared what she thought.

After a while it seemed the man couldn't go to sleep unless he had his little telephone conference call with Gwen. And I soon gave up waiting for her to finish on the phone. I went to sleep.

The whole thing was some bizarre playback on certain events of the past with the cast of characters juggled.

I wondered what his wife thought of it all. "They're coming to dinner Friday," Gwen said one day. So I'd find that out pretty quick, what she thought. And pretty quick, too, my cue to do or not to do something about it was coming up. How much did I really care?

I looked back to that afternoon on the back lawn of Green-meadow when we had made our pledges of noncommitment.

That night the store stayed open till nine. When I got home, the house was reeking of bath salts, and Gwen was in the tub.

I looked at her breasts. Since Andy they had deflated a little. I suddenly felt very tenderly towards her.

She had noticed where I was looking. "You don't like them any more, do you?" she said.

"What makes you think that?"

"You never fondle them. You don't unbutton my blouse when we're driving like you used to and put your hand in—"

"But all that's kid stuff. We live together, for chrissake."

"You don't know I'm alive. Is that kid stuff?"

When she came out of the bathroom, she was crying.

"What's the matter now?" I said.

"Don't give me that what's the matter now! I'm not your goddam wife. And if you want to know what's the matter now, you're the matter now!" She screamed all that, and then she said, "You're insane, you know, they're right; you're really insane."

After I had taken my shower, I found her much calmer. She was watching Andy put himself to bed—he was quite a little boy now—and I stood in the doorway. That kid, I thought, is another one, up and down, sometimes all in an uproar, other times like now, quiet and extraordinarily sensitive.

"What's the matter, Mummy?" he said.

"I'm lonely," she said. "I'm lonely for a boy I used to know long ago." She didn't look at me.

After she'd put Andy to bed, I tried to explain to her that the boy for whom she was lonely didn't exist any more. "I'm a different person now, and you're right, a lot more selfish—"

The phone rang.

"I'm getting jealous of this guy," I said.

"You're not jealous of him, you son of a bitch. You should be, but you're not. You're a complete bastard."

The phone rang again.

"Before you talk to your boy friend," I said, "there is one thing I want to tell you that you should bear in mind when you do whatever you're going to do. Don't look for that needy little vice-president to come back, because he ain't about to. This is the new model, and I like it a hell of a lot better."

"Well, I don't," she said, putting on her robe. "That other man, he was interested in things. All you do is sit inside your skin and watch like everything's happening miles and miles away and you can barely hear the sounds of life in the distance."

The phone was still ringing.

"O.K. You're going to get your wish," she said. "You've won the contest, you've shut out the opposition, you're the champ, the most selfish man in the world. All alone by yourself!"

I smiled at her.

"And that smile! I'm so sick of that soft smile. Who the hell are you, Christ, or Buddha, or who? You used to be for or against things. Now you just understand everybody out of existence with that goddam smile."

She picked up the phone. "Keith," she said, "hold on, will you? I'm going downstairs." Then she turned to me. "Hang up after I pick up downstairs, will you?" She stood there and looked at me, seemed to be waiting for something.

"What do you want me to do, pretend I'm concerned about you and this guy?"

"No," she said, "pretend you're human."

"Well, I am jealous."

She made a scoffing sound.

"What do you want me to do, beat him up?"

"That would be something."

"You're the one who started the thing; why should I beat him up?"

"Then beat me up."

"You'd like that, wouldn't you?"

"I'd like some sign that you're human," she said.

"In the second place, if I don't give you what you need, you'll get it somewhere else, is that it?"

"I only do what everybody else does, all those respectable dames. How long did your wife wait, tell me that?"

And she left the room.

I thought I'd try. I picked up the phone. "Keith?"

"Oh, hello. Yes."

"I don't want you to call Gwen any more."

"I think," said Keith, after a moment of surprise, "I think she ought to be the one to tell me that, don't you?"

Gwen got on the phone and said, "Hang up, will you, Eddie?"

I hung up. "Your heart just wasn't in that, kid," I said to myself.

The odd part of it was that I wasn't angry with Gwen. She was doing what she had to do, waiting to see how much I'd let her get away with, which was her way of measuring what my true feelings were. And if it showed up that I didn't give a damn, why shouldn't she go to someone else?

Still, as she was doing what she had to do, I was doing what I had to do. Which seemed to be to let it go—her, everything, the last of it.

Well, this was the moment to stop it if I was going to.

A person finds out what he wants by what he does, and what I did that finally told me was not with Keith, but with the boy, Andy.

30

I T's an embarrassing incident; I'm not proud of my part in it.

Andy was suddenly in a phase. Nothing pleased him, nothing was as he thought it should be. He had made Gwen's uncle his slave; that old man gave him anything he asked for. When Gwen denied him anything, he'd throw fits of anger that were frightening in their intensity. All we have in us of animal ferocity was suddenly released in that boy.

Gwen, who had read the books, informed me that Dr. Spock describes the way Andy was behaving precisely, so this phase was perfectly normal.

But as I saw it, she loved the kid so frantically that it was difficult for her to discipline him. And the boy, taking advantage of her feeling, was constantly testing her to see how much he could get away with. I told Gwen that he was begging to be told off, needed a quick rap across the tail. Her answer was that I must be just as old-world as my father and not to interfere. But it became more and more difficult for me to stand by and take the boy's behavior.

It happened at breakfast on the day the Robinsons were coming to dinner. Andy didn't like what Gwen put before him and threw it on the floor. Gwen's reprimand triggered a storm of anger. Then I saw Gwen give up. Grown men, who had wanted to, had not beaten her down, but this kid, that morning, had her licked. And without meaning to—we hadn't spoken for two days—she looked to me for help. The boy was screaming and beating at her, and Gwen suddenly looked towards me, then covered her face with her hands and just took it.

My intercession came in a form that shocked me. I picked up the raging boy as you might a loose-skinned kitten, by a handful of his clothing, took him back to my room, and closed us in. Now he turned on me, screaming, "Go away! I don't like you! Go away!" I'd never seen such violence in so small a creature. "I don't want you," he screamed, "I don't want you."

When the first slap didn't quiet him, I hit him again. And again even harder.

Then he was quiet, except for a whimper. An outline of my hand was flushing on his cheek, red as an infection.

I had wanted to kill that boy, I, who had never paid him the least attention, barely talked to him, never talked about him; I, who had in effect refused to admit his existence except to glower at him and tell Gwen she ought to be tougher, had finally put a hand on him, and it was the hand of murder.

Was that the way I felt about him?

There was the evidence, a whimpering little animal, trembling, beaten, with the print of my hand on the side of his face.

I didn't know what to do.

I tried to talk to him, tell him what his mother expected of him, what she would stand for, what she could not stand for, when she would punish him and why, what the rules were. But it all sounded so arrogant when I looked at him and saw my hand on his face.

What I needed from him now was not discipline or obedience, but a gesture of forgiveness.

I tried again, telling him how much his mother cared for him (more than for me, I said), and how much she'd done for him. I spoke up for Gwen, but again I felt my superior posture was shameful when I considered the circumstance into which we adults had dumped this child.

So I was silent again.

He stood there looking at me and waiting, and it was my imagination, I know, but I thought he was waiting for me to say something about him and me. What could I say? That I had resented him because he was Chet's kid?

"Are you my daddy?" he said.

"No."

"Why aren't you?"

I'd never figured out what to say if he asked me that. Gwen had never told the boy anything.

That kid was coming up against a tough deal.

I did my best. "Don't worry," I said, "I'll always look after you."

He looked at me, and, for the time, let it go at that.

Then at last I told him what I truly felt, that I was sorry I'd hit him that way, and would never do it again. I put the soft inside of my hand over the red on his face and asked him to forgive me. I meant forgive everything, the way I'd always been to him, and what we'd all done to him.

He didn't say anything for a minute. Then he suddenly hugged me and kissed me. Whether it was simply relief from terror, or, as I guessed in time, an instinctive recognition that my striking him was friendlier than my distance, I didn't know and I didn't care. He had his arms around me.

We stayed in that room talking a long time. When we came out, he was mine.

I expected Gwen to be furious when she saw his face. But all she said was, "You could be arrested for that." She said that quizzically, in a way that puzzled me. Then she put the boy before his food, and he ate it. A few minutes later, they left for the liquor store.

That particular afternoon was to have been my private holiday. I had stayed up late the night before and finished revising my first complete story. My plan had been to read it fresh in the morning, fuss with it a bit more, mail it off, then celebrate. But all I could think of, as I sat at my table, was what had happened between Andy and me. I had to see if the mark of my hand was still on his face. It must have begun to fade by now, I thought, it must have.

I couldn't do anything with the story, couldn't even read it, so I walked down to the post office and mailed it off as it was. Then I hurried over to the store.

As I came up, Gwen's uncle drove by in his old pickup. Sitting in the cab with him was Andy. I couldn't see his face clearly.

In front of the store was Howie, the town drunk. He was standing, as he always stood, staring straight ahead of him, oblivious of everything and everybody in the world. I didn't want to go into the store and face Gwen, so I stood in front, alongside of Howie (he did not acknowledge my presence), and waited for the boy to come back.

Howie was a man of dignity. He bought a fifth every day of his life, not muscatel or sixty-nine-cent blackberry brandy, but a decent blend. He was a World War II veteran, and the United States government provided him with enough money for this. Apparently he needed nothing else.

The consumption of this whiskey did not change Howie's behavior. You couldn't say he was ever sober, but no matter how much he drank, you could not say his deportment was drunken. He simply stood and stared into space. He generally arrived at the shopping center (no one knew exactly from where) in the middle of the morning. He took up his position and stood there, not speaking, not acknowledging greetings, not—as far as anyone could see —taking note of any event in his environment. But he knew when Gwen's uncle came on, because a few moments after that change of guard, Howie went into the store and bought his fifth. He would not buy from Gwen or from me.

I looked at him, and it struck me that this was the man I had described to Dr. Lloyd as the perfectly disconnected man. Someday, I've got to find out his secrets, I thought.

Andy was friendly to me when he came back with his uncle, but the mark was still there. I don't know what the old man thought. I couldn't face him. Andy soon went off with Gwen, and he smiled at me. How can he be so generous, I wondered.

Now that I had seen things from the boy's view, I couldn't stop thinking about him. He was having the simplest human trouble: I should have been sympathetic to that. When at last I had gotten down off my adult horse and spoken to him person-to-person, he had been so eager to meet me on the common flat ground.

I remembered the years I had waited for my father to say some simple kind words to me. How I would have hugged him if he had. The impulse to do that was still alive inside me; I could feel it. And yet when it came my turn, I had left a mark on Andy's cheek.

All that afternoon I had a stream of customers, my regulars coming in and out, and they too seemed consanguineous with me now, not eccentric or different. Even when they were far gone, when they had sunk deep and out of reach like Howie, pickled within the containers of their bodies, what was covered down there was the toll of a human problem like my own. It must be; after all, that's where I had been headed.

Step down to the flat ground, Evangeleh.

Perhaps if I had learned anything from my long voyage departing Williams and MacElroy, yet could not write any truth about myself, I could to some extent speak for others. I might even, one day, get to speak for Howie, since I had been him, too.

I imagined that when Gwen came to me long ago, that hot August day on the grounds of Greenmeadow, I must have seemed to her as Howie had seemed to me this morning, a person who was self-enclosed, sealed away, giving nothing back, on guard against everything offered. It had taken great courage, I saw, for her to offer me shelter that day, and even some sympathy, and to keep offering these human gifts despite my abruptness, despite my suspicions, and to offer them again and again, to come to my hearing with her uncle and to stand up for me there as Dr. Lloyd had said he would and did not. Then to take me home, Howie, give me a place, a job, a living, for which I returned arrogance to her warmth, indifference to her patience, the 27th degree of aloofness to her food, drink, and shelter, and—most cutting of all—coldness to her sexual warmth. Gwen had courage.

Towards the end of that afternoon, I realized that whatever I thought of myself, one good thing had happened: I had finished and mailed a story, and that story was in praise of a person, of Florence—not full of hatred and detoured revenge—the first one, I hoped, of many like that. And since I had some cause, I decided to celebrate. So I bought a bottle of the same fifth of blended whiskey that Howie liked, and opened it. And when certain of my favorite customers came in, I took them into the back room, told them I had a reason to celebrate, and I'd like it if they would have a drink with me.

By this process—I had many friends there—I became rather drunk by the time I was ready to close up. When I arrived at the party Gwen was throwing for the Robinsons, I was perfectly in tune; they'd been drinking, too.

In fact, everything was boiling up pretty good. Keith, in my absence, had become the man of the house, fixing the drinks, and enjoying hell out of being between two women.

The man's wife, I discovered, was a desperate alcoholic. She had very large breasts and, like many heavy-drinking women, very thin legs. Apparently she had been drinking steadily from the moment they entered. Her husband kept up, drink for drink, but in much smaller quantities. I maintained my own pace. Gwen didn't drink —not at first.

I can't remember anything about the dinner, except that Keith was extraordinarily kind to his wife, very gentle, very considerate. At one point, when he thought she wasn't looking, he tried to hide her glass. But he did it rather clumsily (she caught him at it), and I began to suspect that under all his solicitude, he was carefully getting his wife drunk—drunk enough so she wouldn't see what was happening between him and Gwen, but not such a mess that he'd have to take her home. If that was his idea, he succeeded brilliantly, because an hour after the last dirty dish had been stacked in the sink, Mrs. Robinson had passed out on our sofa, fast asleep, and quite comfortable.

Apparently my ineffectual effort to make Keith discontinue his nightly telephone intercourse with Gwen had convinced him that I was no problem. The more he drank, the more he behaved as if I wasn't there. Very soon, Gwen and he were gabbing away, and I was sitting silently in a corner, audience, not participant.

First of all there was conversation about Keith's life in art, in the course of which Gwen tore his career down to the ground and, I must say, did it with unassailable accuracy. The man must have been a psychopathic masochist to take it. He couldn't get enough, it seemed, of her fouling all over him and his shows. He kept adding illustrations to her points. And I kept seeing myself in him, myself and Gwen three years before. Just as she had with me, she was telling him that he was much too sensitive and much too honest to be working on TV, that he had much more to him than that. Keith's expression suddenly opened into the most boyish hunger to believe. I had to admit he was attractive. Gwen was saying that his real talent would be revealed once he began to please himself and not the merchants who ran the networks. All a playback; I could cue her line for line! And how charming she was (then and now) as she explained to him (as she had to me) how he was selling himself out.

Was she reminding me how much she had done for me?

"I don't know," I suddenly said from the side lines. "I think Keith may be better off right where he is, in TV."

They took this to be a hostile remark.

"You don't know what you're letting yourself in for, Keith," I said with utter sympathy.

Keith acted as if I hadn't spoken. But Gwen looked at me. I'd had a lot to drink.

"Perhaps Keith has nothing of his own he really cares to write about," I said. "You know, Gwen, you have to be careful when you upset a man that way."

Keith looked at me for the first time.

Gwen, I suppose, was trying to figure out what my angle was, just as I was still in the dark about her intentions.

"What the hell do you know about Keith, Eddie?"

Then she looked at the bottle. Gwen hardly drinks. I filled her glass.

"I'm not too far off, am I, Keith?"

"Shut up, will you, Eddie?" Gwen said.

I poured myself another drink. I had cause to celebrate, I thought. I felt proud of what I had done with myself. I felt good remembering those old days, and the distance I'd traveled since.

In the middle of all that self-praise (a new mood for me, certainly), I heard Gwen saying, "Don't pay any attention to that bastard. He's just getting drunk."

"Right," I said. "Don't pay any attention to that bastard, and I am drunk. O.K. I don't want to be a spoilsport. Maybe I should take a walk; how would you two like it if I—"

"Why don't you?" Gwen said. "It's a nice night."

I smiled affectionately at her.

"You know," I said, "I was really only trying to help Keith with a little advice."

"Yeah, I'm sure. Go on out now, like you said."

I guess most people would have said, that bitch, coming on that naked way with another fellow right in front of her supposed-to-be steady boy friend. But I admired her. What could be more desperate than what she was doing?

They were sitting side by side now, and close, and talking in voices I couldn't hear. But I could feel her talent for destruction. That word, destruction, I thought, is a very fine word, sometimes a very necessary word. It was I, after all, who had said to Dr. Lloyd I'd like to burn it all down, all of it, down to the bare earth, total like Tokyo: not just Harlem, but all of it, I'd said, start from scratch.

"Burn it down, Gwen, baby, burn it all down, kid."

"I thought you were going for a walk."

"I am." I got up, and crossed to where the drinks were. "But I'm going to have another drink first. I'm celebrating tonight."

"What the hell are you celebrating?"

"Oh, a lot of different things, all the same thing."

"You're drunk, Eddie."

"I am," I said, "I am very happy."

"Well, spare us the reasons."

"She's sore at me, Keith," I said in my gentlest tone, "because I stopped making love to her."

"Shut up, Eddie."

"Would you like me to fill your glass, too, Keith?"

"No, I'm all right, fella."

"Did you happen to be in Tokyo at the end of the war, Keith?"

"No."

"Eddie!" said Gwen.

"Yes, Gwen, what is it, baby, tear it down, baby."

"You're drunk, Eddie."

"Right. See, Keith, there's a time for that, for total destruction. But then you have to start from the bare earth. Like Tokyo. I saw it. They built it up. But can you do that? I was just trying to say . . ."

Then I stopped, and thought a moment. I was pretty drunk all right, but that was the least of it. "You didn't tell me, fella," I said, "were you in Tokyo at the end of the war? I was. I visited Hiroshima, too. What we did there was a kind of genius. But what did we put in its place, that's the test, kid. The same thing? The trick is to put something better in its place. Understand what I mean?"

"Yes," Keith lied.

"What do I mean? Tell me."

There was quite a silence. And we noticed that Mrs. Robinson, who was lying opposite, was snoring.

Gwen went over and covered her with a light blanket. Then she turned off the floor lamp which had been shining in the woman's face. Now the room was lit only by the light which hung in the entrance hall.

"Ah!" I said, "lover's light."

Gwen sat on the sofa, right next to Keith. She composed herself at his side again, and then she looked at me. And I at her. I smiled at her lovingly, I think, because she sensed this Keith wasn't up to her. She must be desperate, I thought, to reach for him. But reach she did. She put her hand in his lap.

"Now what are you going to do, Keith?" I said.

The man looked at me. He had just crossed the line from "God, I'd like to lay this liquor dealer's woman right here on his own sofa," and had reached the more dangerous ground of, "God, I'll never be able to get along without this girl. She was made for me."

"I think you better take Mrs. Robinson home now, Keith."

That, I thought, is his cue to take charge if he's capable of it.

They both looked at me, and then at each other.

"I wonder," he finally said, "if you'd take her home, fella. There's really an awful lot I've got to talk to Gwen about, and we've barely begun."

"Don't wonder about it, fella," I said, "I won't." I had to admire him; he had more nerve than I thought. "Go on, Keith, take your wife home and put her to bed."

They sat there trying to figure out what to do.

I had another drink.

"Let's take her home, Keith," said Gwen. She got up and began to tend to the woman. I watched, with the distant but penetrating sight of the absolute drunk. I saw all sides of all sides of everything. For instance, I saw Gwen had a new problem, one she hadn't anticipated and didn't relish, the burden and the care of Mrs. Keith Robinson. Keith was wishing his wife dead. I saw that clearly, too.

"You made her drink too much, Keith," I said. "I think you want her dead, don't you?"

I poured myself another drink, and this one did it. For the rest of that evening, everything was blurred. I remember I went into the kitchen for more ice, and when I came out, I wasn't in the room, but somewhere in the yard, and they were jamming the drunken woman into Keith's car. I believe I followed them to Keith's house in Gwen's uncle's pickup. I must have driven that distance, though I don't know how I managed, since I literally couldn't see straight. Then I was in their master bedroom, and they had Mrs. Robinson undressed, and I noticed that her body was very dehydrated, and Gwen was doing a merciful act, I thought, when she covered that

538

body with a nightdress. I think it was soon after this that I took Gwen's arm and said something firm about our going home. I remember she said, "I gave up on you three weeks ago, Eddie." And I kept saying, "Three weeks, what's that, three weeks?" Then I was half carrying, half pushing Gwen down the stairs, saying, "I love you, baby, I do love you, and you're going home with me." But this didn't please her. I guess she had had quite a lot to drink, too, because she said a lot that was irrational, but what I remember is, "You're trying to kill me, Eddie; I'm not going to let you kill me."

I don't remember how the fight started, but I remember at first it was not between Keith and me—in fact, it was never between Keith and me—it was between Gwen and me. She was all over me. But my cause was good, and I had strength. I got her downstairs, and we were bouncing off the walls, and shelves full of old American folk art objects were coming down. But I stuck to business and was getting her out of that house, when she burst loose, and saying, "I'm not going back into that, I'm not," she rushed into the kitchen, and came back in a minute with a knife. I guess the knife looked bigger because I was so drunk; it looked like a scythe to me, that knife.

When Keith saw her and this long businesslike blade and the very businesslike look on her face, and heard her screaming for my blood, he rose to the occasion. I must give him credit, he had guts, because he grabbed her. By that time, she didn't know wrong from right, foe from friend. So she turned on him. He dove for a corner, but had a terrible cut across the heels of his left hand. And Gwen still after him, still wanting blood—his, mine, anybody's.

"What the hell is the matter with her?" Keith yelled at me, blood all over him. He'd never seen that Gwen before.

"She's a monster," I said.

"Get her out of here," he yelled. "Get her the hell out of here."

So I did.

Some months later, Keith and I became good friends, played tennis together many a Sunday morning.

That night, there was no long telephone call during which the esthetics of television were discussed.

Anyway, we couldn't have lifted the phone off its cradle, we were that far gone. We just got into bed and, holding each other, we blacked out.

In the middle of the night, she was awake and looking at me.

"You never said it before," she said.

"Never said what?"

"You said I love you; you never did say that before."

"Sure I did."

"When?"

"Many times. When did I say it last night?"

"Just before I cut poor Keith's hand."

At the memory of this we began to laugh, and we lay there liking each other. And after a while we were together, and it hadn't been that good since the last night in the house on the Sound, the night before the morning Florence and Gloria walked in on us.

Then we were quiet. We were both old hands, and we both knew that what had happened didn't really change anything, except it did tell us that it was still there somewhere and could still be good when we could get it back.

What we had said in the heat didn't change anything, we knew that.

I told her, "I can see why you like him. He makes you mean something. I can see where you would feel necessary with him."

"Oh, Eddie, I think he's scared off. For good."

"Well, he'd never seen that particular side of you. It takes getting used to."

"God, the thought just came to me, maybe we're stuck with each other; maybe there's no one else that can take me, and I know I'm the only one who can take you. Geezuz! Oh, Geezuz!"

Then she fell asleep, like she used to, with her head on my shoulder. This is a pretty damned good girl for me, I thought, as I felt her body fill and empty with the breath of sleep.

I praised her in my heart for everything she had done for me. Now if I want her, I thought, I'll have to do something about it. I may have to insist; I may have to hold on hard. Because she was going to wake up, if not tomorrow, the next morning or the next, and see that what had come so close to smashing us up for good was still there.

And just as I had once said that there was a limit to how much I'd accommodate myself to other people, I had seen that there was a limit to how much she'd accommodate herself to me. Perhaps finally she might be happier with Keith, or someone like him. Someone who needed her desperately, if only to shoot down the balloons of pretense and respectability from which he hung. Maybe that's what she could do for a man, and she had already done that for me.

From my own past, I'd found the only way I could retain my life was to let it go and see what would happen. Perhaps connections between living people have to change every once in a while, like a skin that has to be shed because what is developing beneath is different and maybe bigger. Perhaps if we are going to keep a relationship alive, we have to throw it away every once in a while and see if it will come back on its own, because if it doesn't, maybe it shouldn't.

I went in to look at Andy. The side of his face still carried my mark. I sat and looked at the sleeping boy. I didn't want to leave him now.

"I'm going away for a while," I said to Gwen after she'd had her breakfast.

"You don't have to do that."

"I'll let you know where I put down. After that you won't hear from me for a while. It's up to you then. You know how I am. I do love you, but we talked about that word; it's not everything, is it? I'm finally going to do what's best for me, and I know you'll finally do what's best for you. That way it's got a chance, whatever it is, and whoever it's with."

I had to go down to the liquor store, because the money I'd saved was in an envelope in the back of the till. The three of us walked down together.

There was a small crowd in front.

On the ground in the middle of the circle, lying on his back, was Howie. He was dead, but even now his eyes were open and staring straight ahead.

We sat around the store till the ambulance took him away. His secrets went with him.

We walked towards the bus stop. "I haven't the energy to start looking for someone else," Gwen was saying. "I can't go through all that again. Anyway I don't want anybody else, when it gets right down to it. I just want you to be a certain way."

"Am I?"

"No."

"So?"

"So then I have to take a chance; maybe I'll get to straighten you out."

"And I have to take a chance. If you do straighten me out, it may kill me."

The bus drove up and I kneeled to say goodbye to Andy.

"You come back tomorrow," he ordered.

"No. Not for a while. But I'll be seeing you."

I touched his cheek.

"When I do something bad," he said, "kiss me and I won't do it."

Gwen walked me to the bus. "That mark on his cheek," I said, "I'm worried about it. It's still there."

"It's going away," she said. "You just can't see that it is."

"What the hell kind of a mother are you anyway? I thought you'd murder me when you saw that."

"It's the first attention you ever paid the kid; why should I get sore at that?"

I could see she had something else to say to me.

"You know I read it, Eddie, you left it lying around and yesterday—"

"How did you like it?"

"I really didn't. You know how to tell a story, sure—"

"But?"

"Some day, Eddie, take a chance, love somebody."

I'd thought for the first time in my life I had.

Andy was pointing to the bus, which was ready to leave. Gwen and I kissed each other, and meant it. But whether we meant goodbye or see you soon, neither of us knew.

"I'll let you know where I am," I said through the window.

I visited my mother. She cooked me a Greek dinner, and we watched Huntley-Brinkley. After which I told her that Florence had divorced me. She was sad at this; she'd always liked Florence. All she said was, "Well . . . well . . ." And then she said, "Don't worry, Eee, you'll come back." She patted my cheek.

"Sure, sure," I said. There wasn't a sound for a few minutes except the driving rain. I realized that my mother thought I was a failure. I wanted to say something to reassure the old lady, but I couldn't think of a damned thing.

"It's raining pretty hard, you better sleep here tonight," she said. She made me a bed on her sofa. She went to bed, and I lay there and listened to the rain. I thought about Gwen and how much she'd done for me. She was a monster and I was a monster, but who else would still be there and now waiting for me again, who else but a damned fool?

When I opened my eyes the next morning, my mother was sitting by the window, sewing a loose button on my jacket. The way she patted the coat when she got through told me she thought it a little threadbare and not what she had become accustomed to seeing on the back of her eldest son.

She kissed me goodbye. Then she looked at my hair, which I hadn't combed, and said, "You know what your father would say if he was still alive. He'd say, 'Evangeleh, here's dollar, go get hair cut.'" Then she kissed me again and said, "You're still a nice-looking fellow. Don't let yourself go."

I took the ferry at Bridgeport and crossed the Sound to Port Jefferson. I walked right through that town, south towards the sea. It had rained hard all night. Without my making a sign, a fellow in a potato truck stopped and gave me a ride. He was going to the very end of the island. On the ocean side of Montauk Village, I got a room. It was long out of season, and the rate was cheap.

After supper, I wrote Gwen and told her where I was.

It rained all that night. And I could hear the sea, the same ocean it was that my uncle and my father had crossed long ago. Now at the moment when I was staring out again, I had come back to where they had started. They had made a run at a false prize. Now I had paid some of their debts—it had cost me many years of my life—and was ready to make my own run.

By morning the rain had stopped, and after breakfast I walked to the beach. The wind was from the east, and it brought the sea up so that its wet and chill filled the air.

There wasn't a soul in sight, not a footprint on the sand. As I walked along, between the dunes and the surf, I felt a sensation I'd never had. I guess I didn't recognize it because I'd never experienced it before. At first I thought it was only that I had survived. But it was more. I felt some power of my own, some capability I'd never had before. Yes, as I walked the shore which the rain had washed clean, and felt the sting of the cold damp air in my nostrils, I had my first experience with the thing, hope. It was an exhilaration new to me. And I knew that everything that was possible for me at the beginning was now possible for me again. And that the only thing that was not possible was the way I'd been before.

I also knew that whatever was going to happen or not happen to me was going to happen or not happen on account of me. In a way it didn't make any difference where I was or who I was with. I was not dependent on other people for my worth, nor did I need to look to them for my peace of heart. I was finally on my own.

A few days later, sitting on the beach, I saw them coming. Gwen sat down next to me casually and without explanation. What the hell was there to explain? The marriage of the monsters was performed by the mayor of Patchogue, who was staying at the same place I was staying. He'd come out to the end of the island for stripers and had done so well that he performed the ceremony with the greatest gusto. When the landlady saw my family, she gave us better quarters at the same rate. It was way out of season.

It was later that night that Gwen told me she was pregnant. I kissed her and thanked her. It was to be my first child.

We own the liquor store now. I finally sold the Cessna, the thirty-odd per cent of it I owned, and I got back just enough to make a first payment to Gwen's uncle. We also own a small house. I got that for next to nothing; I signed some papers at the bank and that was it. To my surprise I found that my credit was exceedingly good. In fact, without meaning to, I'd become a solid citizen. There was even a move to put me up for selectman. I ducked that.

All in all it's not an adventurous life, and that worries me a little —for instance, that people think I'm so reliable. I'm not sure that's good. I still think I'm a rebel. But even Gwen thinks I'm—well, steady. We have our scraps, sure, but they're nothing like they used to be. It's sort of late for any fundamental changes.

Have I satisfied my ambition? What was it? I have trouble remembering. I hope that's because I've satisfied it. I do write every morning. But I wonder, for instance, what happened to my resolve to leave the country? I felt that so strongly once. But why in the hell should I leave? We take trips, yes; when something comes in from a story, we put it aside for that. But I don't feel estranged here any more. It's my place. And the third generation is moving in.

But I do worry sometimes. Is this what all that drama, that great overthrow was for—this simple living and working, this day to day confluence?